EDGAR ALLAN POE

THIRTY-TWO STORIES

EDGAR ALLAN POE

THIRTY-TWO STORIES

Edited, with Introductions and Notes, by

STUART LEVINE AND SUSAN F. LEVINE

Hackett Publishing Company, Inc.
Indianapolis/Cambridge

Copyright © 2000 by Hackett Publishing Company, Inc.

All rights reserved

Printed in the United States of America

06 05 04 03 02 01 00   1 2 3 4 5 6 7 8

For further information, please address
Hackett Publishing Company, Inc.
P. O. Box 44937
Indianapolis, Indiana 46244-0937

www.hackettpublishing.com

Cover design by Brian Rak and John Pershing

Interior design by Meera Dash and Abigail Coyle

Composition by Agnew's, Inc.

Library of Congress Cataloging-in-Publication Data

Poe, Edgar Allan, 1809–1849.
Thirty-two stories / Edgar Allan Poe ; edited, with introductions and notes by Stuart Levine and Susan F. Levine.
p. cm.
Includes bibliographical references (p.).
ISBN 0-87220-498-7 (pbk. : alk. paper) — ISBN 0-87220-499-5 (cloth : alk. paper)
1. Detective and mystery stories, American. 2. Fantasy fiction, American. 3. Horror tales, American. I. Title: 32 stories. II. Levine, Stuart. III. Levine, Susan. IV. Title.
PS2612 .A3 2000
813′.3—dc21   99-048766

The paper used in this publication meets the minimum standard requirements of American National Standard for Information Sciences—Permanence of Paper for Printed Library Materials, ANSI Z39.48–1984.

∞

Contents

Introduction

The creepy image of Poe purveyed by the popular press and by late-night TV has been very slow to die, but Poe scholars no longer believe in it. It was in large part the creation of the Reverend Rufus Griswold, a talented editor and anthologist with whom Poe had once quarreled. Saying that she was acting on Poe's instruction, his mother-in-law had, on Poe's death in 1849, taken his literary remains to Griswold, entrusting him with the task of bringing out an edition. But Griswold was an insecure person whose grudge against Poe survived Poe's death, and he included in the edition a biography of Poe which seemed credible, yet which in fact slandered him. A trustworthy biography which revealed the extent of Griswold's forging, tampering, and lying did not appear until nearly a century later, in 1941.

The truth is that scholars know relatively little of the texture of Poe's day-to-day life. We do not know that he was an alcoholic or a drug addict; it is not clear what his assorted "affairs" and "flirtations" really amounted to; we have no idea of the nature of his relationship with his very young wife. It is plain that he could behave very foolishly at times, that he apparently could not hold liquor, that he was in several ways impractical, that he tried to sponge money from friends and acquaintances, and that almost alone among our major writers he was a social and racial bigot. Opposed to this negative evidence is the record of his skill and diligence as a magazine editor, reviewer, essayist, poet, and author of fiction. He was a contentious literary adversary, but if we except a few foolish and unjust battles, by and large he fought on the side of the angels against genuine abuses in the literary world of his day. Diligence and ethics seem incompatible with the seamy picture painted by Griswold and writers who followed his lead.

The most important hard facts about Poe's life may be outlined:

Poe's Early Years

1809 Born, January 19 (date not certain) in Boston. Mother and father, Elizabeth and David Poe, are actors. Nine months later family moves to New York. Mrs. Poe later leaves New York and appears in numerous plays in southern cities. Seems to have separated from David.

1811 December 18: Elizabeth Arnold Poe dies at age twenty-four. Edgar placed with Mr. and Mrs. John Allan of Richmond, Virginia. Recent studies show John Allan as more agreeable and generous than had been thought.

1815 Family moves to England. Allan's business not going well. Edgar enrolled in Manor House School under the Reverend John Bransby (see "William Wilson") who says (perhaps inaccurately) that the Allans tend to spoil Edgar.

1820–25 Family back in Richmond. Tension in the household; Poe probably aware of John Allan's infidelity. Hazy accounts of Poe's early romantic attachments. Attends private Richmond school.

1826 Enters University of Virginia during period when students are out of control: frequent riots, heavy drinking, violence, gaming, and whoring. Poe does well in his studies. Allan refuses to continue financing Poe's education and, perhaps, to pay Poe's gambling debts. Poe leaves university in December.

Poe's Professional Years

1827 **Personal:** Poe is in Richmond after leaving the University of Virginia. His engagement to Sarah Elmira Royster is broken. Goes to Boston; enlists in Army. **Publication:** *Tamerlane and Other Poems.*

1828 **Personal:** In Army.

1829 **Personal:** Frances (Mrs. John) Allan dies. Poe leaves Army. **Publication:** *Al Aaraaf, Tamerlane and Minor Poems.*

1830 **Personal:** John Allan marries again. Poe enters West Point.

1831 **Personal:** Poe departs from West Point, lives in New York, and then lives with the Clemms in Baltimore. Maria ("Muddy") Clemm is his aunt; her daughter, Virginia Clemm, is 8. Poe tries to get teaching job. His brother Henry Poe dies. Poe enters a contest sponsored by the *Saturday Courier* of Philadelphia. **Publication:** *Poems* ("Second Edition").

1832 **Publications:** *Courier* tales: "Metzengerstein," "The Duc De L'Omelette," "A Tale of Jerusalem," "A Decided Loss" ("Loss of Breath"), "The Bargain Lost" ("Bon-Bon").

1833 **Personal:** Poe wins a $50 prize sponsored by the *Saturday Visiter.* He tries to sell "Epimanes" ("Four Beasts in One") and other "Tales of the Arabesque." His friendship with John Pendleton Kennedy begins. **Publication:** "MS. Found in a Bottle."

1834 **Personal:** John Allan dies. **Publication:** "The Visionary" ("The Assignation").

1835 **Personal:** Poe makes another attempt to obtain a teaching job. He writes a desperate letter to Muddy and Virginia Clemm. He brings them to Richmond. **Editorial:** With Kennedy's help, Poe gets *Southern Literary Messenger* (SLM) editorial job in Richmond. **Publications:** Portions of *Politian* (a poetic drama set in Italy but based on a famous incident in Kentucky), "Berenice," "Morella," "Hans Pfaall" ("Hans Pfaal"), "Shadow," "King Pest."

1836 **Personal:** Poe marries Virginia Clemm. Harper & Brothers rejects a book of tales. **Editorial:** Poe has troubles with Thomas White, the owner of SLM. He publishes extensive criticism in SLM. **Publication:** "Epimanes" ("Four Beasts in One/The Homo-Cameleopard").

1837 **Personal:** Poe leaves SLM and moves to New York, completes *The Narrative of A. Gordon Pym,* but is unable to find good work. **Publications:** First chapter of *Pym,* "Von Jung" ("Mystification").

1838 **Personal:** Poe moves to Philadelphia. **Publications:** "Ligeia," "The Psyche Zenobia" ("How to Write a Blackwood Article"), the complete *Pym.*

1839 **Editorial:** Poe joins *Burton's Gentleman's Magazine* in July. **Publications:** "The Man That Was Used Up," "The Fall of the House of Usher," "William Wilson," "The Conversation of Eiros and Charmion," *The Conchologist's First Book.*

1840 **Editorial:** Poe leaves *Burton's* in May and begins a long series of attempts to found his own magazine. Burton sells out to George R. Graham, who combines *Burton's* with *The Casket.* **Publications:** "The Journal of Julius Rodman," "The Philosophy of Furniture," "The Man of the Crowd," *Tales of the Grotesque and Arabesque.*

1841 **Editorial:** In January, Poe joins the staff of *Graham's Magazine* at $800 per year. **Publications:** "The Murders in the Rue Morgue," "A Descent into the Maelström," "The Island of the Fay," "The Colloquy of Monos and Una," "Eleonora."

1842 **Personal:** Virginia is ill. **Editorial:** Poe leaves *Graham's* in May. **Publications:** Review of Nathaniel Hawthorne's *Twice-Told Tales,* "The Masque of the Red Death," "The Landscape Garden" ("The Domain of Arnheim"), "The Pit and the Pendulum," "The Mystery of Marie Rogêt" (November and December 1842, February 1843).

1843 **Personal:** Poe's "The Gold-Bug" wins the *Dollar Newspaper* contest. **Editorial:** Poe negotiates for a position with *The Saturday Museum* but apparently fails to agree to terms. **Publications:** "The Tell-Tale Heart," "The Gold-Bug," "The Black Cat," "Raising the Wind" ("Diddling"), *The Prose Romances of EAP.*

1844 **Personal:** Poe's family moves to New York. **Editorial:** Poe joins the staff of *The New York Mirror* in September. **Publications:** "The Balloon-Hoax," "A Tale of the Ragged Mountains," "The Premature Burial," "Mesmeric Revelation," "The Oblong Box," "The Purloined Letter," "Thou Art the Man," "The Literary Life of Thingum Bob, Esq."

1845 **Personal:** Poe gains great fame from "The Raven," first published in the *Evening Mirror,* January 29. In March, he meets Mrs. Frances Osgood and begins a literary flirtation which is made into a scandal by Mrs. E. F. Ellet. **Editorial:** Poe leaves the *Mirror* in February to join the editorial staff of *The Broadway Journal,* where he continues a literary war with Longfellow that began at the *Mirror.* In July, Poe becomes the sole editor, and in October, the proprietor of *The Broadway Journal.* He is listed on the staff of the *Aristidean.* **Publications:** "The Raven," "The Power of Words,"

"The Imp of the Perverse," "The Facts in the Case of M. Valdemar," *Tales,* and *The Raven and Other Poems.*

1846 **Personal:** Poe moves to a cottage in Fordham. Personal indiscretions and his sharp comments on contemporary authors in "The Literati" ruin his reputation. He receives a sweet and flattering letter from Elizabeth Barrett Browning about his fame in England, and a flattering and friendly letter from Hawthorne. He initiates a civil suit for libel (*Poe* v. *Fuller and Clason*), and he gives his famous Boston Lyceum lecture. **Editorial:** *The Broadway Journal* folds on January 3. Poe's reviews and criticism appear in *Graham's.* **Publications:** "The Literati of New York City," "The Philosophy of Composition," "The Cask of Amontillado."

1847 **Personal:** Virginia Poe dies. Poe wins his lawsuit and $225 in damages. He is at work on *Eureka.* **Publication:** "Ulalume." Poe is represented in Griswold's *The Prose Writers of America.*

1848 **Personal:** Poe allegedly enters into affairs with Mrs. Shew, Mrs. Richmond, and Mrs. Whitman. **Publications:** "The Rationale of Verse," *Eureka.*

1849 **Personal:** Poe dies in Baltimore on October 7, while on a trip to arrange his wedding with Sarah Elmira Royster Shelton. **Publications:** "Hop-Frog," "Von Kempelen and His Discovery," "X-ing a Paragrab," "Landor's Cottage."

1850 **Personal:** Griswold's forgeries are published in *The Works of the Late Edgar Allan Poe.* **Publication:** "The Poetic Principle" (published posthumously).

Quality, polish, and discipline have a lot to do with Poe's continued remarkable popularity. The magazines in which his stories appeared contained some very bad writing, but they also contained a surprising amount of interesting, original, and unusual fiction. Much of it is by authors one has never heard of, in part simply because they did not produce a body of published fiction substantial enough to establish their names in literary history. Poe did, in spite of the onerous press of other duties. Much of the weaker fiction in these magazines is poor because its authors seem to lose patience with good ideas and fail to work them out thoroughly. Poe always gives good value for money; the jobs he starts, he finishes. These are, perhaps, not very dramatic or romantic reasons for his continued success, but they are very important.

Hundreds of literary studies show that Poe took his ideas from published sources, using them systematically and "commercially" because he knew which ideas were marketable and attractive to readers. It is therefore perilous to psychoanalyze Poe on the basis of the subjects of his stories. There is no evidence to suggest that he wrote "compulsively," and a great deal to demonstrate detachment from his more morbid subjects: he repeatedly satirized the gothic fiction industry.

Poe's great popularity in the United States in the 20th century is, of course, based in large part on the continuing appeal of his most frequently anthologized gothic tales. Other aspects of his popularity are perhaps less well known. He has been enormously important for Continental writers. French Symbolism, with its strong flavor of occultism, responded to that aspect of Poe, as Patrick Quinn explains. Similar characteristics gave him his great status among the *modernistas* in Spain and Latin America. His current very high standing among contemporary fiction writers, especially in Latin America, is in part because of what many lay readers have always known in Poe, that he is very good at what he does, but in large part also because knowledgeable readers have come to appreciate the extent to which Poe anticipates 20th-century fictional techniques and attitudes. Throughout his fiction, but especially in his satirical stories, Poe plays with ideas, associations, and language in ways which seem strikingly akin to those of modern authors as different as James Joyce and Julio Cortázar. He is also very much a "metafictional" author, one, that is, who plays with the act of writing, who keeps his readers aware that there is an author back there, playing with materials which he might just choose to arrange in a different way for the reader's eyes. This side of Poe suggests a tie to modern metafictionists such as Carlos Fuentes, a connection that Fuentes acknowledges. Literary historians have known for a long time that Poe is an important 19th-century precursor of detective stories, of science fiction, and of the modern cult of the macabre; we now see him as a precursor of more sophisticated forms, as well.

The creative playfulness comes as a surprise to some readers, but it seems to be present in even Poe's most "serious" prose. As scholars have come to understand "Romantic irony," they have added yet another dimension to our image of Poe.

A few decades ago it was possible for a major critic to assume that every reader would agree with him when he said that Poe's work revealed no trace of contact with the environment in which he worked. We now know how thoroughly Poe's work springs from his environment. There are the obvious literary connections; Poe is a representative Romantic, who reminds readers that in the past and in other cultures artistic inspiration was understood as a source of knowledge, truth, and power. The "message" of his "The Domain of Arnheim" or "The Purloined Letter" is precisely the same as the message of Percy Bysshe Shelley's "A Defense of Poetry." Such works are the response of artists to the threat posed to the artist's status by modernization; Poe, like Shelley, writes to remind us that artists are not merely specialists who produce pretties. In other ages they have been regarded as seers, prophets, and truth-givers as well. Thus Poe seems a characteristic literary figure of his era.

On a more everyday level, Poe's prose turns out to grow very much from the texture of his life. It is filled with allusions to new inventions, new economic situations, contemporary American society, politics and political debate, the newly developed mass media, the railroad, the telegraph. The narrator in "The Man of the Crowd" has been sitting in a coffee shop browsing through the advertisements. The tie there to a place and a time is sufficiently obvious. But even the lonely man on the desert rock in "Silence" has ties to the world around Poe, for we know that Poe constructed his story from materials he took from a popular contemporary novel.

If we know less about Poe's personal life in 2000 than we thought we did in

1940, well and good. His eating and drinking habits and his sex life, after all, are none of our business. It probably can be said of the work of generations of Poe scholars and critics that they have led a sensible tactical retreat in matters biographical, while pressing forward to a better understanding of his literary place and his literary worth. His work has never seemed so important as it does today.

A Note on the Texts There is, alas, no authoritative scholarly text of Poe's short stories. We make no special claim for our text: we did not go to the manuscript sources which the editors of a Center for the Editions of American Authors (CEAA) text would have used. We did, however, do extensive comparative checking of printed sources, comparing the text of our 1976 *The Short Fiction of Edgar Allan Poe* to Thomas Ollive Mabbott's 1978 Belknap/Harvard text, and when there were still ambiguities, to the magazines in which Poe published, especially *The Broadway Journal,* and to the Griswold edition of 1850 and 1856. (The 1976 text had been based on comparison between the 1902 James A. Harrison edition [the "Virginia" and "New York" edition] and the same magazines.) Although their limitations are undeniable, we cannot think of examples of errors or ambiguities in earlier editions which importantly affect meaning for the general reader.

Our commission as editors both in 1976 and in the present volume was to explicate, not to establish a scholarly text. We agree with Joseph Moldenhauer that "Scholars and critics who are seriously concerned about the validity of the text they analyze will still be forced to consult and cite the manuscripts, specific lifetime printings, and unique copies of printed works bearing Poe's autograph revisions" if they are concerned with the completely dependable paper trail which a full critical edition should contain. We have tried only to provide a good text of Poe's stories, explicated to enhance enjoyment and understanding.

Acknowledgments Our most important debts are to Poe scholars. What we owe to whom is explained in the Bibliography. The debt to Burton Pollin is especially heavy, for reasons outlined in our 1976 edition. To the many people thanked in the "Acknowledgments" in that volume we would add Michael Shaw, who helped us with classical allusions and whose name was inadvertently omitted in 1976; the directors of the Harvard University Press, who graciously invited us to make use of anything in the 1978 Harvard/T. O. Mabbott Poe which we found useful; and Sandee Kennedy, who remained cheerful and supportive throughout the onerous task of steering Poe through a word-processor.

Publishing this volume with Hackett delights us because our editing of Poe began with an invitation in the 1960s from John Henry Raleigh on behalf of the Library of Literature, whose excellent director was William Hackett, founder of the present firm. Knowing that connection, we thought to give the firm "first refusal" on *Thirty-Two Stories.* We could not be happier with the treatment we have received: Frances Hackett, who received our first inquiry, was unfailingly gracious and positive; Brian Rak's judgment and advice are excellent; Meera Dash, our Managing Editor, manages splendidly and expeditiously. Beth Alvarez is a wonder of sharp-eyed and erudite copyediting. But we expected as much, for our good friend Stan Lombardo, whose brilliant English rendition of the *Iliad* Hackett brought out in 1997, had told us how very good the Hackett crew was to work with.

Metzengerstein

In his first published story, Poe shows us both his interest in gothic material and his detachment from it. "Metzengerstein" was going to be part of a collection of satirical tales, each allegedly the work of a different member of the Folio Club, an imaginary group of "Dunderheads" who assembled periodically to hear and criticize one another's fiction. "Metzengerstein" was probably told by "Mr. Horribile Dictu" (Thompson 2, 4). We do not know all of Poe's plan for the Folio Club—he never found a publisher for his project—but we do know that Poe was not serious about the gothicism in "Metzengerstein"; indeed, A. H. Quinn, Thompson, and others see it as a satire on the gothic mode. Certainly the story spends a good deal of its space telling us of its own absurdity, and Thompson (2, 4) catalogues ironic and contradictory elements within it: everything is so complicated and cockeyed that Poe must be joking. Incongruities abound, too, as when Poe tells us that "near neighbors are seldom friends," and places castle and palace so close together that the families can look into one another's windows, a modern urban phenomenon comically cozy for such rural and aristocratic protagonists. Readers who are unfamiliar with gothic literature or who have trouble understanding Poe's joke are urged to read Thompson's good essay, which spells out Poe's hoax in detail. The essay and an expanded discussion of its ideas appear in Thompson (4).

We suggest comparing this tale first with "Mystification" (see Levine 4), to see how Poe handles "meaninglessness," and second with some of his more serious gothic efforts, such as "The Fall of the House of Usher" or "The Pit and the Pendulum." Poe never ceases to "put us on," of course; there are hoaxes and little jokes hidden in all types of stories. But "Usher" and "The Pit" lack the peculiar itchy quality of this tale; it seems clear that here Poe's primary intention is humor.

***A note of explanation:** The gothic wonders which Poe introduces into "Metzengerstein" were all readily available in literature which Poe knew. In a poem of 1827 by Richard Henry Dana, for instance, there is a horse which an evil pirate is compelled to ride to his destruction; in Horace Walpole's* Castle of Otranto *(1764) are both a prophecy parallel to Poe's and an "ancestral picture" which comes to life; in Benjamin Disraeli's* Vivian Grey *(1826) are a comparable picture of a horse and bitter rivalry between neighboring aristocrats (Mabbott 9, II).*

In Poe's favorite book of comparative mythology, Jacob Bryant's Ancient Mythology *(1774–76), red horses were connected through etymology to palm trees, death in fire, and phoenixlike rebirth (Levine 6). The connections between "Metzengerstein" and Bryant are too intimate to be coincidental. So Poe's spoof also has mythological resonance.*

PUBLICATIONS IN POE'S TIME

The Philadelphia Saturday Courier, January 14, 1832
The Southern Literary Messenger, January 1836 (with a subtitle: "A Tale in Imitation of the German")
Tales of the Grotesque and Arabesque, 1840 (Poe thought of changing the title again, to "The Horse-Shade," when he tried to publish another collection of his stories in 1842.)

METZENGERSTEIN

Pestis eram vivus—moriens tua mors ero.
Martin Luther[1]

Horror and fatality have been stalking abroad in all ages. Why then give a date to the story I have to tell? Let it suffice to say, that at the period of which I speak, there existed, in the interior of Hungary, a settled although hidden belief in the doctrines of the Metempsychosis.[2] Of the doctrines themselves—that is, of their falsity, or of their probability—I say nothing. I assert, however, that much of our incredulity (as La Bruyêre says of all our unhappiness) "*vient de ne pouvoir être seuls.*"[3]

But there were some points in the Hungarian superstition which were fast verging to absurdity. They—the Hungarians—differed very essentially from their

[1]"I was your plague, living; dying, I will be your death" (Carlson 2). Martin Luther (1483–1546) spoke these words when Pope Clement VII summoned the Council of Trent in 1526: "O Pope, if I live I shall be a pestilence to thee, and if I die I shall be thy death."
[2]Belief in the transmigration of the human soul.
[3]Mercier, in *L'an deux mille quatre cent quarante* seriously maintains the doctrines of the Metempsychosis, and I. D'Israeli says that "no system is so simple and so little repugnant to the understanding." Colonel Ethan Allen, the "Green Mountain Boy," is also said to have been a serious metempsychosist [Poe's Note]. The information about Mercier and D'Israeli (Disraeli) is from an article entitled "Metempsychosis" in Disraeli's *Curiosities of Literature,* a book Poe leaned on heavily throughout his career as a short-story writer. Disraeli's book did not appear in its modern forms until 1839 and later, but the portions Poe uses here were in print at least as early as 1817. **Mercier:** Louis Sebastien Mercier (1740–1814), French writer and politician. His *L'an 2440* is "a work of prophetic imagination." Ethan Allen, the Revolutionary War hero (1737–89), caused considerable theological excitement through his vocal Deism and his authorship of "Ethan Allen's Bible" (*Reason the Only Oracle of Man,* 1789), a Deist tract, but he did not, so far as we know, believe in Metempsychosis. His Deism was of the usual rationalistic sort. ***"vient de ne pouvoir être seuls"*:** "Comes from not being able to be alone." See "The Man of the Crowd," note 1.

Eastern authorities. For example. "*The soul,*" said the former—I give the words of an acute and intelligent Parisian—"*ne demeure qu'une seule fois dans un corps sensible: au reste—un cheval, un chien, un homme même, n'est que la ressemblance peu tangible de ces animaux.*"[4]

The families of Berlifitzing and Metzengerstein had been at variance for centuries. Never before were two houses so illustrious, mutually embittered by hostility so deadly. The origin of this enmity seems to be found in the words of an ancient prophecy—"A lofty name shall have a fearful fall when, as the rider over his horse, the mortality of Metzengerstein shall triumph over the immortality of Berlifitzing."[5]

To be sure the words themselves had little or no meaning. But more trivial causes have given rise—and that no long while ago—to consequences equally eventful. Besides, the estates, which were contiguous, had long exercised a rival influence in the affairs of a busy government. Moreover, near neighbors are seldom friends; and the inhabitants of the Castle Berlifitzing might look, from their lofty buttresses, into the very windows of the Palace Metzengerstein.[6] Least of all had the more than feudal magnificence thus discovered a tendency to allay the irritable feelings of the less ancient and less wealthy Berlifitzings. What wonder, then, that the words, however silly, of that prediction, should have succeeded in setting and keeping at variance two families already predisposed to quarrel by every instigation of hereditary jealousy? The prophecy seemed to imply—if it implied anything—a final triumph on the part of the already more powerful house; and was of course remembered with the more bitter animosity by the weaker and less influential.

Wilhelm, Count Berlifitzing, although loftily descended, was, at the epoch of this narrative, an infirm and doting old man, remarkable for nothing but an inordinate and inveterate personal antipathy to the family of his rival, and so passionate a love of horses, and of hunting, that neither bodily infirmity, great age, nor mental incapacity, prevented his daily participation in the dangers of the chase.

Frederick, Baron Metzengerstein, was, on the other hand, not yet of age. His father, the Minister G——, died young. His mother, the Lady Mary, followed him quickly. Frederick was, at that time, in his eighteenth year. In a city, eighteen years are no long period: but in a wilderness—in so magnificent a wilderness as that old principality, the pendulum vibrates with a deeper meaning.

From some peculiar circumstances attending the administration of his father, the young Baron, at the decease of the former, entered immediately upon his vast possessions. Such estates were seldom held before by a nobleman of Hungary. His castles were without number. The chief in point of splendor and extent was the

---

[4]Poe apparently wrote this "quotation" himself, for the French is faulty in grammar and vague in reference: "[the soul] resides only once in a sensate body: besides, a horse, a dog, even a man is [are] nothing more than a faint resemblance of such animals."

[5]One of many places where Poe hints that the tale itself is not serious. Note his comments on absurdity in the paragraph above; see our headnote.

[6]See our headnote.

"Palace Metzengerstein." The boundary line of his dominions was never clearly defined; but his principal park embraced a circuit of fifty miles.

Upon the succession of a proprietor so young, with a character so well known, to a fortune so unparalleled, little speculation was afloat in regard to his probable course of conduct. And, indeed, for the space of three days, the behavior of the heir out-heroded Herod,[7] and fairly surpassed the expectations of his most enthusiastic admirers. Shameful debaucheries—flagrant treacheries—unheard-of atrocities—gave his trembling vassals quickly to understand that no servile submission on their part—no punctilios of conscience on his own—were thenceforward to prove any security against the remorseless fangs of a petty Caligula.[8] On the night of the fourth day, the stables of the Castle Berlifitzing were discovered to be on fire; and the unanimous opinion of the neighborhood added the crime of the incendiary to the already hideous list of the Baron's misdemeanors and enormities.

But during the tumult occasioned by this occurrence, the young nobleman himself sat, apparently buried in meditation, in a vast and desolate upper apartment of the family palace of Metzengerstein. The rich although faded tapestry hangings which swung gloomily upon the walls, represented the shadowy and majestic forms of a thousand illustrious ancestors. *Here,* rich-ermined priests, and pontifical dignitaries, familiarly seated with the autocrat and the sovereign, put a veto on the wishes of a temporal king, or restrained with the fiat of papal supremacy the rebellious sceptre of the Arch-enemy. *There,* the dark, tall statures of the Princes Metzengerstein—their muscular war-coursers plunging over the carcasses of fallen foes—startled the steadiest nerves with their vigorous expression: and *here,* again, the voluptuous and swan-like figures of the dames of days gone by, floated away in the mazes of an unreal dance to the strains of imaginary melody.

But as the Baron listened, or affected to listen, to the gradually increasing uproar in the stables of Berlifitzing—or perhaps pondered upon some more novel, some more decided act of audacity—his eyes were turned unwittingly to the figure of an enormous, and unnaturally colored horse, represented in the tapestry as belonging to a Saracen ancestor of the family of his rival. The horse itself, in the foreground of the design, stood motionless and statue-like—while, farther back, its discomfited rider perished by the dagger of a Metzengerstein.

On Frederick's lip arose a fiendish expression, as he became aware of the direction which his glance had, without his consciousness, assumed. Yet he did not remove it. On the contrary, he could by no means account for the overwhelming anxiety which appeared falling like a pall upon his senses. It was with difficulty that he reconciled his dreamy and incoherent feelings with the certainty of being awake. The longer he gazed, the more absorbing became the spell—the more impossible did it appear that he could ever withdraw his glance from the fascination of that tapestry. But the tumult without becoming suddenly more

[7]A phrase Poe used repeatedly. See "William Wilson," note 10.

[8]Caligula (12–41), famously cruel Roman emperor (37–41), "wanted to make his *horse* a consul" (Thompson 2; Mabbott 2).

violent, with a compulsory exertion he diverted his attention to the glare of ruddy light thrown full by the flaming stables upon the windows of the apartment.

The action, however, was but momentary; his gaze returned mechanically to the wall. To his extreme horror and astonishment, the head of the gigantic steed had, in the meantime, altered its position. The neck of the animal, before arched, as if in compassion, over the prostrate body of its lord, was now extended, at full length, in the direction of the Baron. The eyes, before invisible, now wore an energetic and human expression, while they gleamed with a fiery and unusual red; and the distended lips of the apparently enraged horse left in full view his sepulchral and disgusting teeth.

Stupefied with terror, the young nobleman tottered to the door. As he threw it open, a flash of red light, streaming far into the chamber, flung his shadow with a clear outline against the quivering tapestry; and he shuddered to perceive that shadow—as he staggered awhile upon the threshold—assuming the exact position, and precisely filling up the contour, of the relentless and triumphant murderer of the Saracen Berlifitzing.

To lighten the depression of his spirits, the Baron hurried into the open air. At the principal gate of the palace he encountered three equerries. With much difficulty, and at the imminent peril of their lives, they were restraining the convulsive plunges of a gigantic and fiery-colored horse.

"Whose horse? Where did you get him?" demanded the youth, in a querulous and husky tone, as he became instantly aware that the mysterious steed in the tapestried chamber was the very counterpart of the furious animal before his eyes.

"He is your own property, sir," replied one of the equerries, "at least he is claimed by no other owner. We caught him flying, all smoking and foaming with rage, from the burning stables of the Castle Berlifitzing. Supposing him to have belonged to the old Count's stud of foreign horses, we led him back as an estray. But the grooms there disclaim any title to the creature; which is strange, since he bears evident marks of having made a narrow escape from the flames."

"The letters W. V. B. are also branded very distinctly on his forehead," interrupted a second equerry; "I supposed them, of course, to be the initials of Wilhelm Von Berlifitzing—but all at the castle are positive in denying any knowledge of the horse."

"Extremely singular!" said the young Baron, with a musing air, and apparently unconscious of the meaning of his words. "He is, as you say, a remarkable horse—a prodigious horse! although, as you very justly observe, of a suspicious and untractable character; let him be mine, however," he added, after a pause, "perhaps a rider like Frederick of Metzengerstein, may tame even the devil from the stables of Berlifitzing."

"You are mistaken, my lord; the horse, as I think we mentioned, is *not* from the stables of the Count. If such had been the case, we know our duty better than to bring him into the presence of a noble of your family."

"True!" observed the Baron, drily; and at that instant a page of the bed-chamber came from the palace with a heightened color, and a precipitate step. He whispered into his master's ear an account of the sudden disappearance of a small portion of the tapestry, in an apartment which he designated; entering, at the same time, into particulars of a minute and circumstantial character; but from the low tone of voice in which these latter were communicated, nothing escaped to gratify the excited curiosity of the equerries.

The young Frederick, during the conference, seemed agitated by a variety of emotions. He soon, however, recovered his composure, and an expression of determined malignancy settled upon his countenance, as he gave peremptory orders that the apartment in question should be immediately locked up, and the key placed in his own possession.

"Have you heard of the unhappy death of the old hunter Berlifitzing?" said one of his vassals to the Baron, as, after the departure of the page, the huge steed which that nobleman had adopted as his own, plunged and curveted, with redoubled fury, down the long avenue which extended from the palace to the stables of Metzengerstein.

"No!" said the Baron, turning abruptly towards the speaker, "dead! say you?"

"It is indeed true, my lord; and, to the noble of your name, will be, I imagine, no unwelcome intelligence."

A rapid smile shot over the countenance of the listener. "How died he?"

"In his rash exertions to rescue a favorite portion of his hunting stud, he has himself perished miserably in the flames."

"I—n—d—e—e—d!" ejaculated the Baron, as if slowly and deliberately impressed with the truth of some exciting idea.

"Indeed;" repeated the vassal.

"Shocking!" said the youth, calmly, and turned quietly into the palace.

From this date a marked alteration took place in the outward demeanor of the dissolute young Baron Frederick Von Metzengerstein. Indeed, his behavior disappointed every expectation, and proved little in accordance with the views of many a manœuvring mamma; while his habits and manners, still less than formerly, offered anything congenial with those of the neighboring aristocracy. He was never to be seen beyond the limits of his own domain, and, in this wide and social world, was utterly companionless—unless, indeed, that unnatural, impetuous, and fiery-colored horse, which he henceforward continually bestrode, had any mysterious right to the title of his friend.

Numerous invitations on the part of the neighborhood for a long time, however, periodically came in. "Will the Baron honor our festivals with his presence?" "Will the Baron join us in a hunting of the boar?"—"Metzengerstein does not hunt"; "Metzengerstein will not attend," were the haughty and laconic answers.

These repeated insults were not to be endured by an imperious nobility. Such invitations became less cordial—less frequent—in time they ceased altogether. The widow of the unfortunate Count Berlifitzing was even heard to express a hope "that the Baron might be at home when he did not wish to be at home, since he disdained the company of his equals; and ride when he did not wish to ride, since he preferred the society of a horse." This to be sure was a very silly explosion of hereditary pique; and, merely proved how singularly unmeaning our sayings are apt to become, when we desire to be unusually energetic.

The charitable, nevertheless, attributed the alteration in the conduct of the young nobleman to the natural sorrow of a son for the untimely loss of his parent;—forgetting, however, his atrocious and reckless behavior during the short period immediately succeeding that bereavement. Some there were, indeed, who suggested a too haughty idea of self-consequence and dignity. Others again (among whom may be mentioned the family physician) did not hesitate in speaking of morbid melancholy, and hereditary ill-health; while dark hints, of a more equivocal nature, were current among the multitude.

Indeed, the Baron's perverse attachment to his lately-acquired charger—an attachment which seemed to attain new strength from every fresh example of the animal's ferocious and demonlike propensities—at length became, in the eyes of all reasonable men, a hideous and unnatural fervor. In the glare of noon—at the dead hour of night—in sickness or in health[9]—in calm or in tempest—the young Metzengerstein seemed riveted to the saddle of that colossal horse, whose intractable audacities so well accorded with his own spirit.

There were circumstances, moreover, which, coupled with late events, gave an unearthly and portentous character to the mania of the rider, and to the capabilities of the steed. The space passed over in a single leap had been accurately measured, and was found to exceed by an astounding difference, the wildest expectations of the most imaginative. The Baron, besides, had no particular *name* for the animal, although all the rest in his collection were distinguished by characteristic appellations. His stable, too, was appointed at a distance from the rest; and with regard to grooming and other necessary offices, none but the owner in person had ventured to officiate, or even to enter the enclosure of that horse's particular stall. It was also to be observed, that although the three grooms, who had caught the steed as he fled from the conflagration at Berlifitzing, had succeeded in arresting his course, by means of a chain-bridle and noose—yet no one of the three could with any certainty affirm that he had, during that dangerous struggle, or at any period thereafter, actually placed his hand upon the body of the beast. Instances of peculiar intelligence in the demeanor of a noble and high-spirited horse are not to be supposed capable of exciting unreasonable attention, but there were certain circumstances which intruded themselves per force upon the most skeptical and phlegmatic; and it is said there were times when the animal caused the gaping crowd who stood around to recoil in horror from the deep and impressive meaning of his terrible stamp—times when the young Metzengerstein turned pale and shrunk away from the rapid and searching expression of his earnest and human-looking eye.

Among the retinue of the Baron, however, none were found to doubt the ardor of that extraordinary affection which existed on the part of the young nobleman for the fiery qualities of his horse; at least, none but an insignificant and mishapen little page, whose deformities were in everybody's way, and whose opinions were of the least possible importance. He (if his ideas are worth mentioning at all,) had the effrontery to assert that his master never vaulted into the saddle, without an

---

[9]To point out all of Poe's sly gags in this tale would be to fill the page with footnotes. This one, however, is easy to miss and especially funny: as Thompson noticed, "in sickness or in health" comes from the Prayer Book Marriage Ceremony.

unaccountable and almost imperceptible shudder; and that, upon his return from every long-continued and habitual ride, an expression of triumphant malignity distorted every muscle in his countenance.

One tempestuous night, Metzengerstein, awaking from heavy slumber, descended like a maniac from his chamber, and, mounting in hot haste, bounded away into the mazes of the forest. An occurrence so common attracted no particular attention, but his return was looked for with intense anxiety on the part of his domestics, when, after some hours' absence, the stupendous and magnificent battlements of the Palace Metzengerstein, were discovered crackling and rocking to their very foundation, under the influence of a dense and livid mass of ungovernable fire.

As the flames, when first seen, had already made so terrible a progress that all efforts to save any portion of the building were evidently futile, the astonished neighborhood stood idly around in silent, if not apathetic wonder. But a new and fearful object soon riveted the attention of the multitude, and proved how much more intense is the excitement wrought in the feelings of a crowd by the contemplation of human agony, than that brought about by the most appalling spectacles of inanimate matter.

Up the long avenue of aged oaks which led from the forest to the main entrance of the Palace Metzengerstein,[10] a steed, bearing an unbonneted and disordered rider, was seen leaping with an impetuosity which outstripped the very Demon of the Tempest.

The career of the horseman was indisputably, on his own part, uncontrollable. The agony of his countenance, the convulsive struggle of his frame, gave evidence of superhuman exertion; but no sound, save a solitary shriek, escaped from his lacerated lips, which were bitten through and through in the intensity of terror. One instant, and the clattering of hoofs resounded sharply and shrilly above the roaring of the flames and the shrieking of the winds—another, and, clearing at a single plunge the gateway and the moat, the steed bounded far up the tottering staircase of the palace, and, with its rider, disappeared amid the whirlwind of chaotic fire.

The fury of the tempest immediately died away, and a dead calm sullenly succeeded. A white flame still enveloped the building like a shroud, and, streaming far away into the quiet atmosphere, shot forth a glare of preternatural light; while a cloud of smoke settled heavily over the battlements in the distinct colossal figure of—*a horse.*

---

[10]A. H. Quinn believes this passage is based on Poe's memory of a real place, the approach to the estate "Oakland," Christ Church Parish, South Carolina.

The Duc De L'Omelette

When one serves a fattened, sizzling ortolan cooked over an open flame, one is supposed to wrap the bird's legs in paper so that diners won't get their fingers greasy. If you didn't know that, welcome to the club—neither did Poe until he read about it in a review of a novel (we don't think he had read the novel). But one has to know a few such things to understand this very funny story. It is probably the best example in this volume of a Poe story which is impenetrable without some explanation, and which "comes clear" with the explanation.

Daughrity has figured out what "The Duc De L'Omelette" is about: N. P. Willis at the time was editor of The American Monthly Magazine *and wrote for it a column called the "Editor's Table" in which he invited the reader to share the pleasures of his office: two dogs, a pet "South American trulian" (a bird of his own invention, apparently), perfume for the quill of his pen, crimson curtains, all manner of exotic lounges, ottomans and divans, olives, japonica flowers, and a bottle of Rudesheimer.*

Willis was attacked and teased for these affectations; they were well enough known so that James Paulding, in explaining that a group of Poe's tales was rejected because the targets of Poe's satires would be missed by most readers, also said that this story was one of the exceptions—everyone would understand it. Twentieth-century scholars caught on first to a second joke buried in the tale: the Duc's affectations come from The Young Duke *by Benjamin Disraeli. Hirsch informed us of another quite private joke: Poe probably never even read the Disraeli novel. Our explication (see note 2 and "A note of explanation," below) adds still another: Poe hadn't read all of his other "sources," either.*

A note of explanation: *Poe plays with stories of people so precious that they expire from slight offenses to their aesthetic sensibilities. His footnote is meant to be another funny illustration. But it was puzzling in some ways, and unraveling what Poe had done to come up with it gives an unusually good sense of how Poe worked—where his ideas came from, how he tinkered with them, how clever, playful, and even downnright sneaky he could be.*

Poe slightly misquotes Gabriel Guéret's Le Parnasse Réformé *(1668), in which Montfleury (Zacharie Jacob Montfleury, 1600–67) is made to say,*

> Qui voudra donc savoir de quoy je suis mort, qu'il ne demande point si c'est de la fièvre, de l'hydropisie, ou de la goutte, mais qu'il sache que c'est d'Andromaque.

In English,

> *The man then who would know of what I died, let him not ask if it were of the fever, the dropsy, or the gout; but let him know that it was of* the Andromache! *(Disraeli's translation)*

Poe's version translates,

> *The man then who would know of what I died, let him not ask if it were of fever or of gout (in the feet) or of something else, but let him understand that it was of* The Andromache.

The translation given in the Southern Literary Messenger *version, however, is identical to Disraeli's translation. Poe probably got the idea for this reference and note from Isaac Disraeli's article "Tragic Actors" in his* Curiosities of Literature, *in which his translation appears. We guess that Poe began with Disraeli's English, and translated it into French, without ever having seen the French original. Hence his* L'homme donc, *etc., instead of* Qui voudra donc, *etc. Probably he skipped "dropsy" because he didn't know the word; hence also the use of another word for "gout."*

PUBLICATIONS IN POE'S TIME

The Philadelphia Saturday Courier, March 3, 1832
The Southern Literary Messenger, February 1836
Tales of the Grotesque and Arabesque, 1840
Bentley's Miscellany (London), 1840, a shorter version
Bentley's Miscellany (New York), 1840, a shorter version
The Broadway Journal, October 11, 1845

THE DUC DE L'OMELETTE

And stepped at once into a cooler clime.
Cowper[1]

Keats fell by a criticism. Who was it died of "*The Andromache?*" Ignoble souls!—De L'Omelette perished of an ortolan. *L'histoire en est brève.* Assist me, Spirit of Apicius![2]

---

[1]Poe's motto is from William Cowper (1731–1800). Book One of *The Task* is called "The Sofa"; Poe quotes line 337, changing "stepp'd" to "stepped." This section deals with a walk in an estate; the preceding lines give the context:

> *Refreshing change! where now the blazing sun?*
> *By short transition we have lost his glare,*
> *And stepp'd at once into a cooler clime.*

[2]**Keats:** John Keats (1795–1821). In point of fact, Keats died of tuberculosis, but the poet did feel that critics had destroyed his chance of making a living through poetry, and Byron's

A golden cage bore the little winged wanderer, enamored, melting, indolent, to the *Chaussée D'Antin,* from its home in far Peru. From its queenly possessor La Bellissima,[3] to the Duc De L'Omelette, six peers of the empire conveyed the happy bird.

That night the Duc was to sup alone. In the privacy of his bureau he reclined languidly on that ottoman for which he sacrificed his loyalty in outbidding his king,—the notorious ottoman of Cadêt.[4]

He buries his face in the pillow. The clock strikes! Unable to restrain his feelings, his Grace swallows an olive. At this moment the door gently opens to the sound of soft music, and lo! the most delicate of birds is before the most enamored of men! But what inexpressible dismay now overshadows the countenance of the Duc?—"*Horreur!—chien!—Baptiste!—l'oiseau! ah, bon Dieu! cet oiseau modeste que tu as déshabillé de ses plumes, et que tu as servi sans papier!*"[5] It is superfluous to say more:—the Duc expired in a paroxysm of disgust.

* * *

"Ha! ha! ha!" said his Grace on the third day after his decease.

"He! he! he!" replied the Devil faintly, drawing himself up with an air of *hauteur.*[6]

---

scornful line about how he had let himself "be snuffed out by an article" perpetuated the idea which Poe borrows. Poe used a paragraph very similar to this one in "Marginalia" (*Godey's Lady's Book,* September 1845) in which he says, a little more accurately, "Keats did (or did not) die of a criticism. . . . " **Who was it . . . "*The Andromache?*":** Montfleury. The author of the *Parnasse Réformé* makes him speak in Hades:—"*L'homme donc qui voudrait savoir ce dont je suis mort, qu'il ne demande pas s'il fut de fièvre ou de podagre ou d'autre chose, mais qu'il entende que ce fut de 'L'Andromaque'*" [Poe's note]. See "A note of explanation," p. 9, for translation and explanation. ***The Andromache:*** A tragedy (1667) by Jean Racine. **ortolan:** Literally, a kind of European bunting and gourmet delicacy. But Poe is less interested in birds than in Nathaniel Parker Willis. Poe got the precious details about naked ortolans, soft music, etc., from a review of Benjamin Disraeli's *The Young Duke* (Hirsch). See our headnote. ***L'histoire en est brève:*** The story of it is short. **Apicius:** Marcus Flavius Apicius (fl. C.E. 14–37), a Roman epicure who wrote a book on the ways of tempting an appetite; " . . . his own name is still proverbial in all matters of gastronomy."

[3]***Chaussée D'Antin:*** A street in Paris noted as the residence of "*gens à la mode*"—people of fashion. See Map of Poe's Paris in "The Murders in the Rue Morgue," pp. 136–7, for its location. **far Peru:** See our headnote. A Peruvian ortolan = a South American trulian. **La Bellissima:** The most beautiful.

[4]**ottoman:** Willis supposedly had a "copy of the ottoman in the Governor General's mansion in Quebec" (Daughrity). See our headnote. **Cadêt:** Pollin (3) says it might be Antoine Cadet de Vaux.

[5]**olive:** See our headnote. **"Horreur . . . papier":** "Horror(s)! Dog! Baptiste! [Willis pretended that he had a servant named Alphonse.] the bird! oh, good God! this simple bird whose feathers you have removed and which you have served without paper frills." Willis's "Editor's Table" was filled with French, hence Poe's frequent use of it here.

[6]Haughtiness.

"Why, surely you are not serious," retorted De L'Omelette. "I have sinned—*c'est vrai*[7]—but, my good sir, consider!—you have no actual intention of putting such—such—barbarous threats into execution."

"No *what?*" said his majesty—"come, sir, strip!"

"Strip, indeed!—very pretty i' faith!—no, sir, I shall *not* strip. Who are you, pray, that I, Duc De L'Omelette, Prince de Foie-Gras, just come of age, author of 'Mazurkiad,' and Member of the Academy, should divest myself at your bidding of the sweetest pantaloons ever made by Bourdon, the daintiest *robe-de-chambre* ever put together by Rombêrt[8]—to say nothing of the taking my hair out of paper—not to mention the trouble I should have in drawing off my gloves?"

"Who am I?—ah, true! I am Baal-Zebub, Prince of the Fly. I took thee, just now, from a rose-wood coffin inlaid with ivory. Thou wast curiously scented, and labelled as per invoice. Belial[9] sent thee,—my Inspector of Cemeteries. The pantaloons, which thou sayest were made by Bourdon, are an excellent pair of linen drawers, and thy *robe-de-chambre* is a shroud of no scanty dimensions."

"Sir!" replied the Duc, "I am not to be insulted with impunity![10]—Sir! I shall take the earliest opportunity of avenging this insult!—Sir! you shall hear from me! In the meantime *au revoir!*"—and the Duc was bowing himself out of the Satanic presence, when he was interrupted and brought back by a gentleman in waiting. Hereupon his Grace rubbed his eyes, yawned, shrugged his shoulders, reflected. Having become satisfied of his identity, he took a bird's eye view of his whereabouts.

The apartment was superb. Even De L'Omelette pronounced it *bien comme il faut.* It was not its length nor its breadth,—but its height—ah, that was appalling!—There was no ceiling—certainly none—but a dense whirling mass of fiery-colored clouds. His Grace's brain reeled as he glanced upwards. From above, hung a chain of an unknown blood-red metal—its upper end lost, like the

---

[7]It is true.

[8]**Foie-Gras:** *Pâté de foie gras* is a famous French gourmet food, a paste made of the liver of geese. As one of the Duc's titles, it suggests Willis's luxurious affectations. See our headnote. **"Mazurkiad":** Apparently a made-up title. A "mazurka" is a Polish dance, and the suffix "iad" suggests an epic. **Academy:** Daughrity thinks Poe may mean a famous Boston supper club which had as members two men from each of a number of professions; Willis was one of the two author-members. **Bourdon:** Pollin (3) says this is the name of a bona fide tailor. ***robe-de-chambre:*** See "The Murders in the Rue Morgue," note 15. **Rombêrt:** Pollin (3) says this name Poe made up.

[9]**Baal-Zebub:** Beelzebub, Prince of demons, the devil, associated with the ancient Philistine deity who was worshiped as Lord of the Flies. **rose-wood . . . ivory:** Willis said his office had a rosewood desk. See our headnote. **curiously scented:** Another dig at Willis, this time for his bottle of "perfumed Hungary water." See our headnote. **Belial:** In Milton's *Paradise Lost,* Beelzebub is the Prince of the Fallen Angels and Belial is another of the fallen angels.

[10]Another favorite phrase of Poe's. See "The Cask of Amontillado," note 8.

city of Boston, *parmi les nues.* From its nether extremity swung a large cresset. The Duc knew it to be a ruby; but from it there poured a light so intense, so still, so terrible, Persia never worshipped such—Gheber[11] never imagined such—Mussulman never dreamed of such when, drugged with opium, he has tottered to a bed of poppies, his back to the flowers, and his face to the God Apollo. The Duc muttered a slight oath, decidedly approbatory.

The corners of the room were rounded into niches.—Three of these were filled with statues of gigantic proportions. Their beauty was Grecian, their deformity Egyptian, their *tout ensemble*[12] French. In the fourth niche the statue was veiled; it was *not* colossal. But then there was a taper ankle, a sandalled foot. De L'Omelette pressed his hand upon his heart, closed his eyes, raised them, and caught his Satanic Majesty—in a blush.

But the paintings!—Kupris! Astarte! Astoreth!—a thousand and the same! And Rafaelle has beheld them! Yes, Rafaelle has been here; for did he not paint the——?[13] and was he not consequently damned? The paintings!—the paintings! O luxury! O love!—who, gazing on those forbidden beauties, shall have eyes for the dainty devices of the golden frames that besprinkle, like stars, the hyacinth and the porphyry walls?

But the Duc's heart is fainting within him. He is not, however, as you suppose, dizzy with magnificence, nor drunk with the ecstatic breath of those innumerable censers. *C'est vrai que de toutes ces choses il a pensé beaucoup—mais!*[14] The Duc De L'Omelette is terror-stricken; for, through the lurid vista which a single uncurtained window is affording, lo! gleams the most ghastly of all fires!

Le pauvre Duc! He could not help imagining that the glorious, the voluptuous, the never-dying melodies which pervaded that hall, as they passed filtered and transmuted through the alchemy of the enchanted window-panes, were the wailings and the howlings of the hopeless and the damned! And there, too!—there!—upon that ottoman!—who could *he* be?—he, the *petit-maitre*—no, the Deity—

---

[11]***bien comme il faut:*** The way it should be. ***parmi les nues:*** Among the clouds. The dig at Boston is for its reputation as the capital of American arts, and particularly at the mystically tinged Transcendentalist writers. See Mabbott (9, II) for Poe's targets in earlier versions. **cresset:** A metal holder for a light. Apparently, Poe means that the ruby is inside. **Gheber:** A fire-worshiper or Parsee.

[12]Total effect.

[13]**Kupris:** Cyprus, traditionally the birthplace of Aphrodite, whose worship there in ancient times is synonymous with licentiousness. **Astarte:** In Phoenician mythology, Astarte is the goddess of love. She is associated with Aphrodite. **Astoreth:** The same goddess as Astarte and Aphrodite. **Rafaelle:** Raphael (1483–1520), the great Italian painter. The only "scandal" which seems strong enough to explain Poe's reference to damnation involves Raphael's use of his lovely mistress "La Fornarina" (the baker's daughter), whose real name was probably Margarita Luti, as his model for a number of paintings, among them two Madonnas—the face of the Sistine Madonna and the Madonna of Francis I in the Louvre, as well as in the Saint Cecilia in Bologna.

[14]"It is true that he thought a good deal about these things—but!"

who sat as if carved in marble, *et qui sourit,* with his pale countenance, *si amèrement?*[15]

Mais il faut agir,—that is to say, a Frenchman never faints outright. Besides, his Grace hated a scene—De L'Omelette is himself again. There were some foils upon a table—some points also. The Duc had studied under B——; *il avait tué ses six hommes.* Now, then, *il peut s'échapper.*[16] He measures two points, and, with a grace inimitable, offers his Majesty the choice. *Horreur!* his Majesty does not fence!

Mais il joue!—how happy a thought!—but his Grace had always an excellent memory. He had dipped in the "*Diable*" of the Abbé Gualtier. Therein it is said "*que le Diable n'ose pas refuser un jeu d'écarté.*"[17]

But the chances—chances! True—desperate; but scarcely more desperate than the Duc. Besides, was he not in the secret?—had he not skimmed over Père Le Brun?—was he not a member of the Club Vingt-un? "*Si je perds,*" said he, "*je serai deux fois perdue*—I shall be double *damned—violà tout!* (Here his Grace shrugged his shoulders.) *Si je gagne, je reviendrai à mes ortolans—que les cartes soient préparées!*"[18]

His Grace was all care, all attention—his Majesty all confidence. A spectator would have thought of Francis and Charles.[19] His Grace thought of his game. His Majesty did not think; he shuffled. The Duc cut.

---

[15]***Le pauvre Duc!:*** The poor Duke! ***petit-maître:*** Fop. ***et qui sourit:*** And who smiled. ***si amèrement:*** So bitterly.

[16]***Mais il faut agir:*** But one must act. **B——:** Daughrity thinks this is probably Joseph T. Buckingham, with whose *Courier* Willis had carried on a half-serious battle over Willis's affectations. See our headnote. This story was written too early to refer to Willis's experience with a duel. ***il avait tué ses six hommes:*** He had killed his six men. ***il peut s'échapper:*** He can escape.

[17]***Mais il joue!:*** But he gambles! **the "*Diable*" of the Abbé Gualtier:** This allusion has eluded us (S.G.L.). Mabbott (9, II) concludes that Poe invented it. ***que le diable n'ose pas refuser un jeu d'écarté:*** That the Devil doesn't dare refuse a game of *écarté* (a card game).

[18]**Père Le Brun:** Possibly Le P. Laurent le Brun (1608–63), a French Jesuit, author of *Virgilius Christianus* (1661). He was a classical theoretician, apparently well-known in his time. Another possibility is that Poe remembered the name "Le Brun" from Disraeli's article "Tragic Actors," mentioned in "A note of explanation," pp. 9–10. Two other possibilities: Pierre Antoine Lebrun (1785–1873), a lyric and dramatic poet, author of *Mary Stuart* (1820) and *Voyage en Grèce* (1827); Ponce Denis Ecouchard-Lebrun (1729–1807), a lyric and epigramatic poet, author of *A Buffon* and *Le Vengeur.* We lean to the first Le Brun because of an item about him in *The Southern Literary Messenger,* in the December 1835 issue, early in Poe's association with that magazine. ***Si je perds:*** If I lose. ***je serai deux fois perdu:*** I shall be doubly damned. ***voilà tout!:*** That's all! ***Si je gagne . . . soient preparées!:*** If I win, I shall return to my ortolans—let the cards be made ready!

[19]Francis I of France (1494–1547) reigned 1515–47; Charles V (1500–58), Holy Roman Emperor (1519–56) and King of Spain (1516–56). The two monarchs clashed repeatedly during a lengthy and complex series of confrontations. Mabbott (9, II) relates a story about how Francis's jester, who kept a "calendar of fools," put first Charles and then Francis on his list for trusting one another despite their strong emnity.

The cards are dealt. The trump is turned—it is—it is—the king! No—it was the queen. His Majesty cursed her masculine habiliments. De L'Omelette placed his hand upon his heart.

They play. The Duc counts. The hand is out. His Majesty counts heavily, smiles, and is taking wine. The Duc slips a card.

"*C'est à vous à faire,*" said his Majesty, cutting. His Grace bowed, dealt, and arose from the table *en présentant le Roi.*[20]

His Majesty looked chagrined.

Had Alexander not been Alexander, he would have been Diogenes; and the Duc assured his antagonist in taking leave, "*que s'il n'eût pas été De L'Omelette il n'aurait point d'objection d'être le Diable.*"[21]

---

[20]***C'est à vous à faire:*** It's your turn. ***en présentant le Roi:*** While presenting the King.
[21]**Had Alexander . . . Diogenes:** Poe contrasts the great conqueror (356–23 B.C.E.) with the Cynic philosopher (c.412–323 B.C.E.) who is supposed to have used a lantern to search for an honest man at noon. Alexander is supposed to meet Diogenes and ask him what he (Alexander) can do for him. Diogenes says, "Stand out of my light." Alexander is delighted, and says, "If I were not Alexander . . . etc." **"*que . . . Diable*":** That if he hadn't been De L'Omelette he wouldn't have had any objection to being the Devil.

MS. Found in a Bottle

Adventure on the ocean was probably the single most popular genre of fiction in Poe's day. Continental writers had been fishing these waters for years; Poe, in "A Descent into the Maelström," his novel, The Narrative of Arthur Gordon Pym, *and other fiction, tried his hand at it, too; Melville's most commercially successful novels of sea adventure would be published while Poe was alive. Poe, as usual, responded to current interests and trends in fiction.*

The tale is told by a somewhat nervous and moody isolated aristocrat whose weird adventure is made at least partially credible by his psychological instability. The narrator of "MS. Found in a Bottle" has been reading works of "eloquent madness"; perhaps the wild experience is simply a vision.

It is interesting to see how soon in his career Poe developed his basic patterns; this is a very early tale (see note 1). Yet we recognize devices Poe was to use in almost all his fiction. Though the narrator takes pains to tell us how rational he is, how prone to explain everything in physical and scientific terms, he has been reading that "eloquent" German "madness," is temperamentally restless and nervous, cut off from family and country, and ill-used: enough like the usual Poe narrator to lead us to conclude that Poe's most frequent formula for keeping a fantasy at least reasonably credible occurred to him very early in his career.

Poe combined folklore, current pseudoscientific speculation, and material from a well-known contemporary book. The folklore is the "Flying Dutchman" story, which has to do with a fated ship which is supposed to appear as a terrifying omen to mariners whose own ships are about to sink. Any number of authors of Poe's time made fiction of the old superstition; the best-known use of it today is probably Wagner's opera "The Flying Dutchman" (1843).

The pseudoscience is the belief that the earth is open at the poles. This was taken seriously enough for an American Congress to appropriate funds for an expedition to find out; the notion was propagated in John Cleves Symmes's fiction and in his book Symmes' Theory of Concentric Spheres *(1826) (Mabbott 9, II). Poe liked the idea—it is used in his story "Hans Pfaal" (see Levine 4); Poe's episodic novel* The Narrative of Arthur Gordon Pym *also ends with the hero plunging to an unknown fate at the South Pole.*

Publications in Poe's Time

The Baltimore Sunday Visiter, October 19, 1833
The People's Advocate (Newburyport, Mass.), October 26, 1833
The Southern Literary Messenger, December 1835
The Gift, 1836
Tales of the Grotesque and Arabesque, 1840

The Broadway Journal, October 11, 1845
The Richmond Semi-Weekly Examiner, October 10, 1849 (three days after Poe's death)

MS. Found in a Bottle[1]

Qui n'a plus qu'un moment à vivre
N'a plus rien à dissimuler.
—Quinault—Atys[2]

Of my country and of my family I have little to say. Ill usage and length of years have driven me from the one, and estranged me from the other. Hereditary wealth afforded me an education of no common order, and a contemplative turn of mind enabled me to methodize the stores which early study very diligently garnered up.—Beyond all things, the study of the German moralists gave me great delight; not from any ill-advised admiration of their eloquent madness, but from the ease with which my habits of rigid thought enabled me to detect their falsities. I have often been reproached with the aridity of my genius; a deficiency of imagination has been imputed to me as a crime; and the Pyrrhonism of my opinions has at all times rendered me notorious. Indeed, a strong relish for physical philosophy has, I fear, tinctured my mind with a very common error of this age—I mean the habit of referring occurrences, even the least susceptible of such reference, to the principles of that science. Upon the whole, no person could be less liable than myself to be led away from the severe precincts of truth by the *ignes fatui*[3] of superstition. I have thought proper to premise thus much, lest the incredible tale I have to tell should be considered rather the raving of a crude imagination, than the positive experience of a mind to which the reveries of fancy have been a dead letter and a nullity.

After many years spent in foreign travel, I sailed in the year 18—, from the port of Batavia, in the rich and populous island of Java, on a voyage to the Archipelago

---

[1]This early tale had a long publication history in Poe's lifetime. He entered it in a contest, won, and saw it in print in 1833. That prize was Poe's first pay as an author, and most writers feel it was instrumental in making him decide to pursue writing as a profession.
[2]Carlson (2) translates the motto:

He who has only a moment longer to live
Has no longer anything to conceal.

Philippe Quinault: French dramatist (1635–88). ***Atys:*** An opera libretto which Quinault wrote for Lully.
[3]**Pyrrhonism:** Skepticism. ***ignes fatui:*** Tantalizing but misleading attractions.

of the Sunda islands.[4] I went as passenger—having no other inducement than a kind of nervous restlessness which haunted me as a fiend.

Our vessel was a beautiful ship of about four hundred tons, copper-fastened, and built at Bombay of Malabar teak. She was freighted with cotton-wool and oil, from the Lachadive islands. We had also on board coir, jaggeree, ghee, cocoa-nuts, and a few cases of opium. The stowage was clumsily done, and the vessel consequently crank.[5]

We got under way with a mere breath of wind, and for many days stood along the eastern coast of Java, without any other incident to beguile the monotony of our course than the occasional meeting with some of the small grabs[6] of the Archipelago to which we were bound.

One evening, leaning over the taffrail, I observed a very singular, isolated cloud, to the N.W. It was remarkable, as well for its color, as from its being the first we had seen since our departure from Batavia. I watched it attentively until sunset, when it spread all at once to the eastward and westward, girting in the horizon with a narrow strip of vapor, and looking like a long line of low beach. My notice was soon afterwards attracted by the dusky-red appearance of the moon, and the peculiar character of the sea. The latter was undergoing a rapid change, and the water seemed more than usually transparent. Although I could distinctly see the bottom, yet, heaving the lead, I found the ship in fifteen fathoms. The air now became intolerably hot, and was loaded with spiral exhalations similar to those arising from heated iron. As night came on, every breath of wind died away, and a more entire calm it is impossible to conceive. The flame of a candle burned upon the poop without the least perceptible motion, and a long hair, held between the finger and thumb, hung without the possibility of detecting a vibration. However, as the captain said he could perceive no indication of danger, and as we were drifting in bodily to shore, he ordered the sails to be furled, and the anchor let go. No watch was set, and the crew, consisting principally of Malays, stretched themselves deliberately upon deck. I went below—not without a full presentiment of evil. Indeed, every appearance warranted me in apprehending a Simoom.[7] I told the captain my fears; but he paid no attention to what I said, and left me without deigning to give a reply. My uneasiness, however, prevented me from sleeping, and about midnight I went upon deck.—As I placed my foot upon the upper step of the companion-ladder, I was startled by a loud, humming noise, like that occasioned by the rapid revolution of a mill-wheel, and before I could ascertain its

---

[4]The old name for Borneo, Celebes, Java, Sumatra, the Molucca Islands, and Nusa Tenggara.

[5]**Lachadive islands:** Now spelled "Laccadive," these islands are located in the Indian Ocean off the southwest coast of India. **coir:** Fiber from coconut husk. **jaggeree:** Jaggery, a kind of coarse sugar made from the sap of a variety of palm tree. **ghee:** A foodstuff made by processing the butterfat of buffalo milk. **crank:** A nautical term meaning "liable to heel or capsize" (Carlson 2).

[6]East Indian coasting vessels (Carlson 2).

[7]A meteorological term usually used to refer to a hot, dry desert wind. Poe means a big storm.

meaning, I found the ship quivering to its centre. In the next instant, a wilderness of foam hurled us upon our beam-ends, and, rushing over us fore and aft, swept the entire decks from stem to stern.

The extreme fury of the blast proved, in a great measure, the salvation of the ship. Although completely water-logged, yet, as her masts had gone by the board, she rose, after a minute, heavily from the sea, and, staggering awhile beneath the immense pressure of the tempest, finally righted.

By what miracle I escaped destruction, it is impossible to say. Stunned by the shock of the water, I found myself, upon recovery, jammed in between the stern-post and rudder. With great difficulty I gained my feet, and looking dizzily around, was, at first, struck with the idea of our being among breakers; so terrific, beyond the wildest imagination, was the whirlpool of mountainous and foaming ocean within which we were engulfed. After a while, I heard the voice of an old Swede, who had shipped with us at the moment of our leaving port. I hallooed to him with all my strength, and presently he came reeling aft. We soon discovered that we were the sole survivors of the accident. All on deck, with the exception of ourselves, had been swept overboard;—the captain and mates must have perished as they slept, for the cabins were deluged with water. Without assistance, we could expect to do little for the security of the ship, and our exertions were at first paralyzed by the momentary expectation of going down. Our cable had, of course, parted like pack-thread, at the first breath of the hurricane, or we should have been instantaneously overwhelmed. We scudded with frightful velocity before the sea, and the water made clear breaches over us. The frame-work of our stern was shattered excessively, and, in almost every respect, we had received considerable injury; but to our extreme joy we found the pumps unchoked, and that we had made no great shifting of our ballast. The main fury of the blast had already blown over, and we apprehended little danger from the violence of the wind; but we looked forward to its total cessation with dismay; well believing, that, in our shattered condition, we should inevitably perish in the tremendous swell which would ensue. But this very just apprehension seemed by no means likely to be soon verified. For five entire days and nights—during which our only subsistence was a small quantity of jaggeree, procured with great difficulty from the forecastle—the hulk flew at a rate defying computation, before rapidly succeeding flaws of wind, which, without equalling the first violence of the Simoom, were still more terrific than any tempest I had before encountered. Our course for the first four days was, with trifling variations, S. E. and by S.; and we must have run down the coast of New Holland.[8]—On the fifth day the cold became extreme, although the wind had hauled round a point more to the northward.—The sun arose with a sickly yellow lustre, and clambered a very few degrees above the horizon—emitting no decisive light.—There were no clouds apparent, yet the wind was upon the increase, and blew with a fitful and unsteady fury. About noon, as nearly as we could guess, our attention was again arrested by the appearance of

---

[8]**Our cable:** Poe refers to the anchor cable. Seeing that the ship was drifting toward shore, the captain had anchored it. **New Holland:** The old name for Australia (Carlson 2).

the sun. It gave out no light, properly so called, but a dull and sullen glow without reflection, as if all its rays were polarized. Just before sinking within the turgid sea, its central fires suddenly went out, as if hurriedly extinguished by some unaccountable power. It was a dim, silver-like rim, alone, as it rushed down the unfathomable ocean.

We waited in vain for the arrival of the sixth day—that day to me has not arrived—to the Swede, never did arrive. Thenceforward we were enshrouded in pitchy darkness, so that we could not have seen an object at twenty paces from the ship. Eternal night continued to envelop us, all unrelieved by the phosphoric sea-brilliancy to which we had been accustomed in the tropics. We observed too, that, although the tempest continued to rage with unabated violence, there was no longer to be discovered the usual appearance of surf, or foam, which had hitherto attended us. All around were horror, and thick gloom, and a black sweltering desert of ebony.—Superstitious terror crept by degrees into the spirit of the old Swede, and my own soul was wrapped up in silent wonder. We neglected all care of the ship, as worse than useless, and securing ourselves, as well as possible, to the stump of the mizen-mast, looked out bitterly into the world of ocean. We had no means of calculating time, nor could we form any guess of our situation. We were, however, well aware of having made farther to the southward than any previous navigators, and felt great amazement at not meeting the usual impediments of ice. In the meantime every moment threatened to be our last—every mountainous billow hurried to overwhelm us. The swell surpassed anything I had imagined possible, and that we were not instantly buried is a miracle. My companion spoke of the lightness of our cargo, and reminded me of the excellent qualities of our ship; but I could not help feeling the utter hopelessness of hope itself, and prepared myself gloomily for that death which I thought nothing could defer beyond an hour, as, with every knot of way the ship made, the swelling of the black stupendous seas became more dismally appalling. At times we gasped for breath at an elevation beyond the albatross—at times became dizzy with the velocity of our descent into some watery hell, where the air grew stagnant, and no sound disturbed the slumbers of the kraken.[9]

We were at the bottom of one of these abysses, when a quick scream from my companion broke fearfully upon the night. "See! see!" cried he, shrieking in my ears, "Almighty God! see! see!" As he spoke, I became aware of a dull, sullen glare of red light which streamed down the sides of the vast chasm where we lay, and threw a fitful brilliancy upon our deck. Casting my eyes upwards, I beheld a spectacle which froze the current of my blood. At a terrific height directly above us, and upon the very verge of the precipitous descent, hovered a gigantic ship of, perhaps, four thousand tons. Although up-reared upon the summit of a wave more than a hundred times her own altitude, her apparent size still exceeded that of any ship of the line or East Indiaman in existence. Her huge hull was of a deep dingy black, unrelieved by any of the customary carvings of a ship. A single row of brass cannon protruded from her open ports, and dashed from their polished surfaces the

[9]A legendary Norse sea monster.

fires of innumerable battle-lanterns, which swung to and fro about her rigging. But what mainly inspired us with horror and astonishment, was that she bore up under a press of sail[10] in the very teeth of that supernatural sea, and of that ungovernable hurricane. When we first discovered her, her bows were alone to be seen, as she rose slowly from the dim and horrible gulf beyond her. For a moment of intense terror she paused upon the giddy pinnacle, as if in contemplation of her own sublimity, then trembled and tottered, and—came down.

At this instant, I know not what sudden self-possession came over my spirit. Staggering as far aft as I could, I awaited fearlessly the ruin that was to overwhelm. Our own vessel was at length ceasing from her struggles, and sinking with her head to the sea. The shock of the descending mass struck her, consequently, in that portion of her frame which was already under water, and the inevitable result was to hurl me, with irresistible violence, upon the rigging of the stranger.

As I fell, the ship hove in stays, and went about; and to the confusion ensuing I attributed my escape from the notice of the crew. With little difficulty I made my way unperceived to the main hatchway, which was partially open, and soon found an opportunity of secreting myself in the hold. Why I did so I can hardly tell. An indefinite sense of awe, which at first sight of the navigators of the ship had taken hold of my mind, was perhaps the principle of my concealment. I was unwilling to trust myself with a race of people who had offered, to the cursory glance I had taken, so many points of vague novelty, doubt, and apprehension. I therefore throught proper to contrive a hiding-place in the hold. This I did by removing a small portion of the shifting-boards,[11] in such a manner as to afford me a convenient retreat between the huge timbers of the ship.

I had scarcely completed my work, when a footstep in the hold forced me to make use of it. A man passed by my place of concealment with a feeble and unsteady gait. I could not see his face, but had an opportunity of observing his general appearance. There was about it an evidence of great age and infirmity. His knees tottered beneath a load of years, and his entire frame quivered under the burthen. He muttered to himself, in a low broken tone, some words of a language which I could not understand, and groped in a corner among a pile of singular-looking instruments, and decayed charts of navigation. His manner was a wild mixture of the peevishness of second childhood, and the solemn dignity of a God. He at length went on deck, and I saw him no more.

* *

---

[10]**gigantic ship:** In the legend of the Flying Dutchman, the ghost ship is supposed to appear when a ship is going down. Poe's ghost ship is right on schedule, as the ensuing paragraphs reveal. **ship of the line:** A large warship. **East Indiaman:** "A ship of large tonnage engaged in East Indian trade" (OED). **press of sail:** Sailing ships in storms normally run under light storm sails, designed to provide some control in the high winds and to minimize the dangers of capsizing, or damage to sails, masts, and rigging.

[11]**hove in stays:** "A vessel in the act of tacking is said to be . . . hove in stays" (OED). **went about:** Headed into the wind. **shifting-boards:** Partitions in a ship's hold to keep cargo from shifting.

A feeling, for which I have no name, has taken possession of my soul—a sensation which will admit no analysis, to which the lessons of by-gone times are inadequate, and for which I fear futurity itself will offer me no key. To a mind constituted like my own, the latter consideration is an evil. I shall never—I know that I shall never—be satisfied with regard to the nature of my conceptions. Yet it is not wonderful that these conceptions are indefinite, since they have their origin in sources so utterly novel. A new sense—a new entity is added to my soul. *

It is long since I first trod the deck of this terrible ship, and the rays of my destiny are, I think, gathering to a focus. Incomprehensible men! Wrapped up in meditations of a kind which I cannot divine, they pass me by unnoticed. Concealment is utter folly on my part, for the people *will not* see. It was but just now that I passed directly before the eyes of the mate—it was no long while ago that I ventured into the captain's own private cabin, and took thence the materials with which I write, and have written. I shall from time to time continue this journal. It is true that I may not find an opportunity of transmitting it to the world, but I will not fail to make the endeavor. At the last moment I will enclose the MS. in a bottle, and cast it within the sea. *

An incident has occurred which has given me new room for meditation. Are such things the operation of ungoverned Chance? I had ventured upon deck and thrown myself down, without attracting any notice, among a pile of ratlin-stuff and old sails, in the bottom of the yawl. While musing upon the singularity of my fate, I unwittingly daubed with a tarbrush the edges of a neatly-folded studding-sail which lay near me on a barrel. The studding-sail is now bent[12] upon the ship, and the thoughtless touches of the brush are spread out into the word DISCOVERY. * * * * * * * * * * * * * * * * * *

I have made many observations lately upon the structure of the vessel. Although well armed, she is not, I think, a ship of war. Her rigging, build, and general equipment, all negative a supposition of this kind. What she *is not,* I can easily perceive—what she *is* I fear it is impossible to say. I know not how it is, but in scrutinizing her strange model and singular cast of spars, her huge size and overgrown suits of canvass, her severely simple bow and antiquated stern, there will occasionally flash across my mind a sensation of familiar things, and there is always mixed up with such indistinct shadows of recollection, an unaccountable memory of old foreign chronicles and ages long ago. * * * * * * *

I have been looking at the timbers of the ship. She is built of a material to which I am a stranger. There is a peculiar character about the wood which strikes me as rendering it unfit for the purpose to which it has been applied. I mean its extreme *porousness,* considered independently of the worm-eaten condition which is a consequence of navigation in these seas, and apart from the rottenness attendant upon age. It will appear perhaps an observation somewhat over-curious, but this

---

[12]**yawl:** A small boat. **studding-sail:** A sail set beyond the leeches of any of the principal sails during a fair wind (OED). **bent:** In use.

wood would have every characteristic of Spanish oak, if Spanish oak were distended by any unnatural means.

In reading the above sentence a curious apothegm of an old weather-beaten Dutch navigator comes full upon my recollection. "It is as sure," he was wont to say, when any doubt was entertained of his veracity, "as sure as there is a sea where the ship itself will grow in bulk like the living body of the seaman." * * * * * * * * * * * * * * * * * * *

About an hour ago, I made bold to thrust myself among a group of the crew. They paid no manner of attention, and, although I stood in the very midst of them all, seemed utterly unconscious of my presence. Like the one I had at first seen in the hold, they all bore about them the marks of a hoary old age. Their knees trembled with infirmity; their shoulders were bent double with decrepitude; their shrivelled skins rattled in the wind; their voices were low, tremulous and broken; their eyes glistened with the rheum of years; and their gray hairs streamed terribly in the tempest. Around them, on every part of the deck, lay scattered mathematical instruments of the most quaint and obsolete construction. * * * * * *

I mentioned some time ago the bending of a studding-sail. From that period the ship, being thrown dead off the wind, has continued her terrific course due south, with every rag of canvass packed upon her, from her trucks to her lower studding-sail booms, and rolling every moment her top-gallant yard-arms into the most appalling hell of water which it can enter into the mind of man to imagine. I have just left the deck, where I find it impossible to maintain a footing, although the crew seem to experience little inconvenience. It appears to me a miracle of miracles that our enormous bulk is not swallowed up at once and forever. We are surely doomed to hover continually upon the brink of Eternity, without taking a final plunge into the abyss. From billows a thousand times more stupendous than any I have ever seen, we glide away with the facility of the arrowy sea-gull; and the colossal waters rear their heads above us like demons of the deep, but like demons confined to simple threats and forbidden to destroy. I am led to attribute these frequent escapes to the only natural cause which can account for such effect.—I must suppose the ship to be within the influence of some strong current, or impetuous under-tow. * * * * * * * * * * * * * * * *

I have seen the captain face to face, and in his own cabin—but, as I expected, he paid me no attention. Although in his appearance there is, to a casual observer, nothing which might bespeak him more or less than man—still a feeling of irrepressible reverence and awe mingled with the sensation of wonder with which I regarded him. In stature he is nearly my own height; that is, about five feet eight inches. He is of a well-knit and compact frame of body, neither robust nor remarkably otherwise. But it is the singularity of the expression which reigns upon the face—it is the intense, the wonderful, the thrilling evidence of old age, so utter, so extreme, which excites within my spirit a sense—a sentiment ineffable. His forehead, although little wrinkled, seems to bear upon it the stamp of a myriad of years.—His gray hairs are records of the past, and his grayer eyes are Sybils[13]

[13]**Sybils:** Sibyls.

of the future. The cabin floor was thickly strewn with strange, iron-clasped folios, and mouldering instruments of science, and obsolete long-forgotten charts. His head was bowed down upon his hands, and he pored, with a fiery unquiet eye, over a paper which I took to be a commission, and which, at all events, bore the signature of a monarch. He muttered to himself, as did the first seaman whom I saw in the hold, some low peevish syllables of a foreign tongue, and although the speaker was close at my elbow, his voice seemed to reach my ears from the distance of a mile. * * * * * * * * * * * * * * * *

The ship and all in it are imbued with the spirit of Eld. The crew glide to and fro like the ghosts of buried centuries; their eyes have an eager and uneasy meaning; and when their fingers fall athwart my path in the wild glare of the battle-lanterns, I feel as I have imbibed the shadows of fallen columns at Balbec, and Tadmor, and Persepolis,[14] until my very soul has become a ruin. * * * * * * * *

When I look around me I feel ashamed of my former apprehensions. If I trembled at the blast which has hitherto attended us, shall I not stand aghast at a warring of wind and ocean, to convey any idea of which the words tornado and simoom are trivial and ineffective? All in the immediate vicinity of the ship is the blackness of eternal night, and a chaos of foamless water; but, about a league on either side of us, may be seen, indistinctly and at intervals, stupendous ramparts of ice, towering away into the desolate sky, and looking like the walls of the universe. * * * * * * * * * * * * * * * * * * *

As I imagined, the ship proves to be in a current; if that appellation can properly be given to a tide which, howling and shrieking by the white ice, thunders on to the southward with a velocity like the headlong dashing of a cataract. * * *

To conceive the horror of my sensations is, I presume, utterly impossible; yet a curiosity to penetrate the mysteries of these awful regions, predominates even over my despair, and will reconcile me to the most hideous aspect of death. It is evident that we are hurrying onwards to some exciting knowledge—some never-to-be-imparted secret, whose attainment is destruction. Perhaps this current leads us to the southern pole itself. It must be confessed that a supposition apparently so wild has every probability in its favor. * * * * * * * * * * *

The crew pace the deck with unquiet and tremulous step; but there is upon their countenances an expression more of the eagerness of hope than of the apathy of despair.

In the meantime the wind is still in our poop, and, as we carry a crowd of canvass, the ship is at times lifted bodily from out the sea—Oh, horror upon horror! the ice opens suddenly to the right, and to the left, and we are whirling dizzily, in immense concentric circles, round and round the borders of a gigantic amphitheatre, the summit of whose walls is lost in the darkness and the distance. But little time will be left me to ponder upon my destiny—the circles rapidly grow small—we are plunging madly within the grasp of the whirlpool—and amid a

---

[14]**Eld:** Antiquity. **Balbec, and Tadmor, and Persepolis:** Ruined cities of the Near East (Carlson 2).

roaring, and bellowing, and thundering of ocean and of tempest, the ship is quivering, oh God! and—— going down.[15]

---

[15]NOTE—The "Ms. Found in a Bottle" was originally published in 1831, and it was not until many years afterwards that I became acquainted with the maps of Mercator, in which the ocean is represented as rushing, by four mouths, into the (northern) Polar Gulf, to be absorbed into the bowels of the earth; the Pole itself being represented by a black rock, towering to a prodigious height [Poe's note]. If the tale was printed in 1831, no scholar has yet found it in a periodical for that year.

The Assignation

"The Assignation" is a convincing exercise in Byronic romanticism. It incorporates a poem which Poe wrote in the style of Byron, and which, as Mabbott (9, II) puts it, "is closely related to lines Byron wrote out for Mary Chaworth," Byron's first love. It uses details of Byron's well-known biography—that the poet was a good swimmer, that the "visionary" hero who rescues the baby, like Byron, is (probably) an English poet living in a palazzo in Venice. Like Byron, he is in love with the young wife of a villainous old man (Countess Guiccioli and the Count, who actually threatened Byron). Even the narrator may be identifiable as the Irish poet and friend of Byron, Thomas Moore, though Moore was a good friend, and not just a slight acquaintance. Poe might, in fact, want readers to think that it was Poe *who knew Byron slightly, and fished him out of the canal one night in Venice.*

Noting the connections between "The Assignation" and Byron's life (which periodicals of the time covered the way ours cover the doings of stars or royalty), Benton (1) argues that the tale is a hoax. Yet though the Byron material is present, we are not sure that "hoax" accurately describes Poe's intention: too many elements in the tale suggest serious purpose. Poe was capable of producing stories serious in intent yet filled with satiric or simply "hidden" allusions and referents. He was also a commercial journalist, and the idea of writing a story in which his readers would recognize Byron and his adventures would have been appealing. "Hoax" seems not quite the right word: the Irving-Hughes "autobiography" of 1971 was apparently a hoax, as were the "Hitler memoirs" of 1983; what Poe did in 1834 involves exploitation of a celebrity's notoriety, but is in no way an attempt to defraud or even fool anyone. Besides, the story is in its way very beautiful, and certainly successful for many readers, who are carried along by the romantic setting and the operatic plot.

Publications in Poe's Time

The Lady's Book, January 1834
The Southern Literary Messenger, July 1835
Tales of the Grotesque and Arabesque, 1840
The Broadway Journal, June 7, 1845
See also note 20 for the publication history of the poem.

THE ASSIGNATION[1]

Stay for me there! I will not fail
To meet thee in that hollow vale.
[Exequy on the death of his wife, by Henry King, Bishop of Chichester.][2]

Ill-fated and mysterious man!—bewildered in the brilliancy of thine own imagination, and fallen in the flames of thine own youth! Again in fancy I behold thee! Once more thy form hath risen before me!—not—oh not as thou art—in the cold valley and shadow—but as thou *shouldst be*—squandering away a life of magnificent meditation in that city of dim visions, thine own Venice—which is a star-beloved Elysium of the sea, and the wide windows of whose Palladian[3] palaces look down with a deep and bitter meaning upon the secrets of her silent waters. Yes! I repeat it—as thou *shouldst be.* There are surely other worlds than this—other thoughts than the thoughts of the multitude—other speculations than the speculations of the sophist. Who then shall call thy conduct into question? who blame thee for thy visionary hours, or denounce those occupations as a wasting away of life, which were but the overflowing of thine everlasting energies?

It was at Venice, beneath the covered archway there called the *Ponte di Sospiri,*[4] that I met for the third or fourth time the person of whom I speak. It is with a confused recollection that I bring to mind the circumstances of that meeting. Yet I remember—ah! how should I forget?—the deep midnight, the Bridge of Sighs, the beauty of woman, and the Genius of Romance that stalked up and down the narrow canal.

It was a night of unusual gloom. The great clock of the Piazza had sounded the fifth hour of the Italian evening. The square of the Campanile lay silent and deserted, and the lights in the old Ducal Palace were dying fast away. I was returning home from the Piazetta, by way of the Grand Canal. But as my gondola arrived opposite the mouth of the canal San Marco,[5] a female voice from its recesses broke suddenly upon the night, in one wild, hysterical, and long continued shriek. Startled at the sound, I sprang upon my feet: while the gondolier, letting slip his single oar, lost it in the pitchy darkness beyond a chance of

---

[1]When Poe published this first in 1834, it was called "The Visionary." He changed the name to "The Assignation," referring to the lovers' meeting in death.

[2]See note 23.

[3]**Elysium:** See "Shadow," note 4. **Palladian:** A modified classicism in the style of Italian architect Andrea Palladio (1518–80).

[4]***Ponte di Sospiri:*** The "Bridge of Sighs," which Byron made famous in these lines (Benton 2):

I stood in Venice on the Bridge of Sighs
A palace and a prison on each hand

[5]For the location of places in this tale, see Map of Poe's Venice, p. 28.

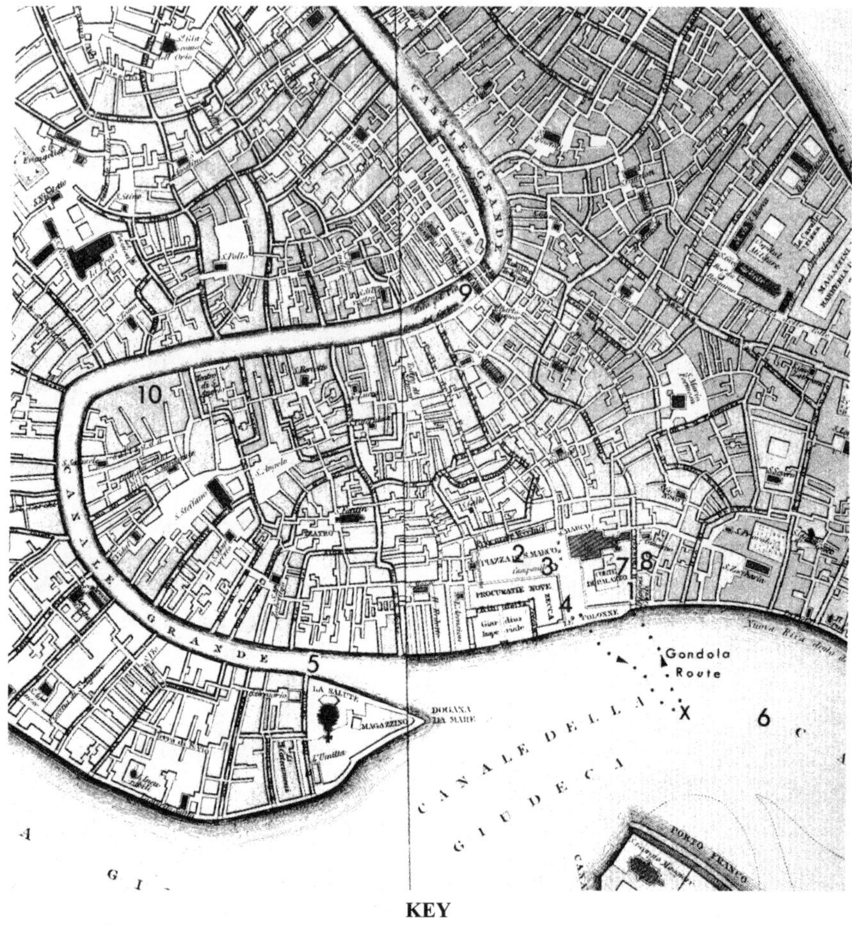

KEY

1. Ponte di Sospiri (Bridge of Sighs)
2. Piazza di San Marco
3. Campanile
4. Piaz[z]etta
5. Canale Grande
6. Canale di San Marco
7. Palazzo Ducale (Ducal Palace)
8. Prigioni (prison)
9. Ponte di Rialto
10. Palazzo Mocenigo (Byron's home. See note 11)

X Approximate spot where narrator hears cry and gondolier loses oar

• • • ➤ • • • ➤ Route of narrator's gondola

Figure 1a. Poe's Venice, from a map roughly contemporary with Poe's tale, published in 1835 by the Society for the Diffusion of Useful Knowledge (see "How to Write a Blackwood Article," note 4).

Figure 1b. The Piazzetta, looking in from the juncture of the Grand Canal and the Canal San Marco toward the Piazza San Marco. The Ducal Palace is on the right and the Campanile is in the left, middle distance. Despite the 1835 caption, St. Mark's Church (San Marco) is hidden by the palace. Figures 1c–1g show other places mentioned in "The Assignation," and come from the same 1835 map used to locate the sites in the story.

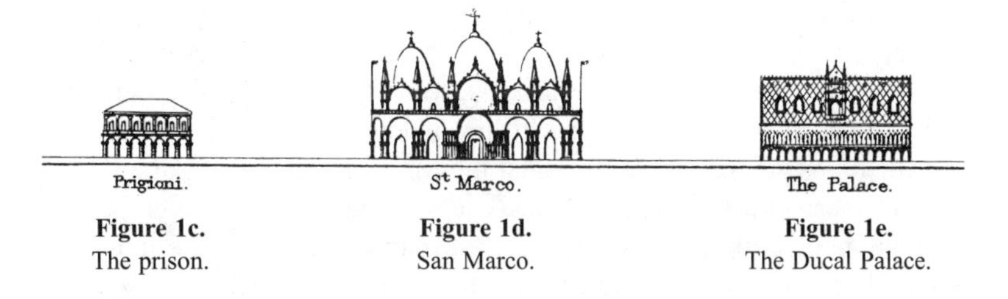

Figure 1c. The prison.

Figure 1d. San Marco.

Figure 1e. The Ducal Palace.

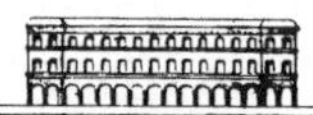

Figure 1f. Ponte di Rialto.

Figure 1g. Building facade, Piazza di Rialto.

recovery, and we were consequently left to the guidance of the current which here sets from the greater into the smaller channel. Like some huge and sable-feathered condor, we were slowly drifting down towards the Bridge of Sighs, when a thousand flambeaux flashing from the windows, and down the staircases of the Ducal Palace, turned all at once that deep gloom into a livid and preternatural day.

A child, slipping from the arms of its own mother, had fallen from an upper window of the lofty structure into the deep and dim canal. The quiet waters had closed placidly over their victim; and, although my own gondola was the only one in sight, many a stout swimmer, already in the stream, was seeking in vain upon the surface, the treasure which was to be found, alas! only within the abyss. Upon the broad black marble flagstones at the entrance of the palace, and a few steps above the water, stood a figure which none who then saw can have ever since forgotten. It was the Marchesa Aphrodite—the adoration of all Venice—the gayest of the gay—the most lovely where all were beautiful—but still the young wife of the old and intriguing Mentoni, and the mother of that fair child, her first and only one, who now deep beneath the murky water, was thinking in bitterness of heart upon her sweet caresses, and exhausting its little life in struggles to call upon her name.

She stood alone. Her small, bare, and silvery feet gleamed in the black mirror of marble beneath her. Her hair, not as yet more than half loosened for the night from its ball-room array, clustered, amid a shower of diamonds, round and round her classical head, in curls like those of the young hyacinth. A snowy-white and gauze-like drapery seemed to be nearly the sole covering to her delicate form; but the mid-summer and midnight air was hot, sullen, and still, and no motion in the statue-like form itself, stirred even the folds of that raiment of very vapor which hung around it as the heavy marble hangs around the Niobe. Yet—strange to say!—her large lustrous eyes were not turned downwards upon that grave wherein her brightest hope lay buried—but riveted in a widely different direction! The prison of the Old Republic[6] is, I think, the stateliest building in all Venice—but how could that lady gaze so fixedly upon it, when beneath her lay stifling her only child? Yon dark, gloomy niche, too, yawns right opposite her chamber window—what, then could there be in its shadows—in its architecture—in its ivy-wreathed and solemn cornices—that the Marchesa di Mentoni had not wondered at a thousand times before? Nonsense!—Who does not remember that, at such a time as this, the eye, like a shattered mirror, multiplies the images of its sorrow, and sees in innumerable far off places, the wo which is close at hand?

Many steps above the Marchesa, and within the arch of the water-gate, stood, in full dress, the Satyr-like figure of Mentoni himself. He was occasionally occupied in thrumming a guitar, and seemed *ennuyé*[7] to the very death, as at intervals he gave directions for the recovery of his child. Stupefied and aghast, I had myself no power to move from the upright position I had assumed upon first hearing the

---

[6]**the Niobe:** The mother whom Zeus turned into a stone after her children were killed. Tears flowed from the stone. **prison of the Old Republic:** See Map of Poe's Venice.
[7]Bored.

shriek, and must have presented to the eyes of the agitated group a spectral and ominous appearance, as with pale countenance and rigid limbs, I floated down among them in that funereal gondola.

All efforts proved in vain. Many of the most energetic in the search were relaxing their exertions, and yielding to a gloomy sorrow. There seemed but little hope for the child; (how much less than for the mother!) but now, from the interior of the dark niche which has been already mentioned as forming a part of the Old Republican prison, and as fronting the lattice of the Marchesa, a figure muffled in a cloak, stepped out within reach of the light, and, pausing a moment upon the verge of the giddy descent, plunged headlong into the canal. As, in an instant afterwards, he stood with the still living and breathing child within his grasp, upon the marble flagstones by the side of the Marchesa, his cloak, heavy with the drenching water, became unfastened, and, falling in folds about his feet, discovered to the wonderstricken spectators the graceful person of a very young man, with the sound of whose name the greater part of Europe was then ringing.[8]

No word spoke the deliverer. But the Marchesa! She will now receive her child—she will press it to her heart—she will cling to its little form, and smother it with her caresses. Alas! *another's* arms have taken it from the stranger—*another's* arms have taken it away, and borne it afar off, unnoticed, into the palace! And the Marchesa! Her lip—her beautiful lip trembles: tears are gathering in her eyes—those eyes which, like Pliny's acanthus,[9] are "soft and almost liquid." Yes! tears are gathering in those eyes—and see! the entire woman thrills throughout the soul, and the statue has started into life! The pallor of the marble countenance, the swelling of the marble bosom, the very purity of the marble feet, we behold suddenly flushed over with a tide of ungovernable crimson; and a slight shudder quivers about her delicate frame, as a gentle air at Napoli about the rich silver lilies in the grass.

Why *should* that lady blush! To this demand there is no answer—except that, having left, in the eager haste and terror of a mother's heart, the privacy of her own *boudoir,* she has neglected to enthrall her tiny feet in their slippers, and utterly forgotten to throw over her Venetian shoulders that drapery which is their due. What other possible reason could there have been for her blushing?—for the glance of those wild appealing eyes? for the unusual tumult of that throbbing bosom?—for the convulsive pressure of that trembling hand?—that hand which fell, as Mentoni turned into the palace, accidentally, upon the hand of the stranger. What reason could there have been for the low—the singularly low tone of those unmeaning words which the lady uttered hurriedly in bidding him adieu? "Thou

---

[8]Although the episode of rescuing the baby has no parallels in Byron's career, the poet was known as an excellent swimmer and brags playfully in *Don Juan* of having swum the Hellespont.

[9]Poe got his information from the Horace Smith novel *Zillah: A Tale of Jerusalem* (1828), a bestseller he knew well—he wrote a funny parody of it called "A Tale of Jerusalem" (see Levine 4). Smith speaks of "what Pliny calls the soft and almost liquid Acanthus." Smith's source is Pliny the Younger, *Epistolae,* V, vi, 16 (Mabbott 9, II).

hast conquered—" she said, or the murmurs of the water deceived me—"thou has conquered—one hour after sunrise—we shall meet—so let it be!"

* * *

The tumult had subsided, the lights had died away within the palace, and the stranger, whom I now recognized, stood alone upon the flags. He shook with inconceivable agitation, and his eye glanced around in search of a gondola. I could not do less than offer him the service of my own; and he accepted the civility. Having obtained an oar at the water-gate, we proceeded together to his residence, while he rapidly recovered his self-possession, and spoke of our former slight acquaintance in terms of great apparent cordiality.

There are some subjects upon which I take pleasure in being minute. The person of the stranger—let me call him by this title, who to all the world was still a stranger—the person of the stranger is one of these subjects. In height he might have been below rather than above the medium size: although there were moments of intense passion when his frame actually *expanded* and belied the assertion. The light, almost slender symmetry of his figure, promised more of that ready activity which he evinced at the Bridge of Sighs, than of that Herculean strength which he has been known to wield without an effort upon occasions of more dangerous emergency. With the mouth and chin of a deity—singular, wild, full, liquid eyes, whose shadows varied from pure hazel to intense and brilliant jet—and a profusion of curling, black hair, from which a forehead of unusual breadth gleamed forth at intervals all light and ivory—his were features than which I have seen none more classically regular, except, perhaps, the marble ones of the Emperor Commodus.[10] Yet his countenance was, nevertheless, one of those which all men have seen at some period of their lives, and have never afterwards seen again. It had no peculiar—it had no settled predominant expression to be fastened upon the memory; a countenance seen and instantly forgotten—but forgotten with a vague and never-ceasing desire of recalling it to mind. Not that the spirit of each rapid passion failed, at any time, to throw its own distinct image upon the mirror of that face—but that the mirror, mirror-like, retained no vestige of the passion, when the passion had departed.

Upon leaving him on the night of our adventure, he solicited me, in what I thought an urgent manner, to call upon him *very* early the next morning. Shortly after sunrise, I found myself accordingly at his Palazzo, one of those huge structures of gloomy, yet fantastic pomp, which tower above the waters of the Grand Canal in the vicinity of the Rialto. I was shown up a broad winding staircase of mosaics, into an apartment whose unparalleled splendor burst through the opening door with an actual glare, making me blind and dizzy with luxuriousness.[11]

[10]Lucius Aelius Aurelius Commodus (161–92), emperor from 180 to 192. See Figure 2.
[11]Byron lived in the Palazzo Mocenigo on the Grand Canal below the Rialto Bridge, and in describing it, Thomas Moore used language similar to that of this paragraph (Benton 1). See Map of Poe's Venice.

Figure 2. The "classically regular" features of the Emporor Commodus. *Left:* The emperor as shown in a plate from M. Brunus, *Romanorum imperatorum effigies* (1617). *Right:* As he appears in Jacobus de Strada, *Imperatorum romanorum omnium orientalium et occidentalium verissimae imagines ex antiquis numismatibus* (1559). Both woodcuts are based on Roman coins. From the Summerfield Collection, Spencer Research Library, University of Kansas. Used by permission.

I knew my acquaintance to be wealthy. Report had spoken of his possessions in terms which I had even ventured to call terms of ridiculous exaggeration. But as I gazed about me, I could not bring myself to believe that the wealth of any subject in Europe could have supplied the princely magnificence which burned and blazed around.

Although, as I say, the sun had arisen, yet the room was still brilliantly lighted up. I judge from this circumstance, as well as from an air of exhaustion in the countenance of my friend, that he had not retired to bed during the whole of the preceding night. In the architecture and embellishments of the chamber, the evident design had been to dazzle and astound. Little attention had been paid to the *decora* of what is technically called *keeping,* or to the proprieties of nationality. The eye wandered from object to object, and rested upon none—neither the *grotesques* of the Greek painters, nor the sculptures of the best Italian days, nor the huge carvings of untutored Egypt. Rich draperies in every part of the room trembled to the vibration of low, melancholy music, whose origin was not to be discovered. The senses were oppressed by mingled and conflicting perfumes, reeking up from strange convolute censers, together with multitudinous flaring and flickering tongues of emerald and violet fire. The rays of the newly risen sun poured in upon the whole, through windows formed each of a single pane of crimson-tinted glass. Glancing to and fro, in a thousand reflections, from curtains which rolled from their cornices like cataracts of molten silver, the beams of natural glory mingled at length fitfully with the artificial light, and lay weltering in subdued masses upon a carpet of rich, liquid-looking cloth of Chili gold.[12]

"Ha! ha! ha!—ha! ha! ha!"—laughed the proprietor, motioning me to a seat as I entered the room, and throwing himself back at full length upon an ottoman. "I see," said he, perceiving that I could not immediately reconcile myself to the *bienséance* of so singular a welcome—"I see you are astonished at my apartment—at my statues—my pictures—my originality of conception in architecture and upholstery—absolutely drunk, eh? with my magnificence? But pardon me, my dear sir, (here his tone of voice dropped to the very spirit of cordiality,) pardon me for my uncharitable laughter. You appeared so *utterly* astonished. Besides, some things are so completely ludicrous that a man *must* laugh or die. To die laughing must be the most glorious of all glorious deaths! Sir Thomas More—a very fine man was Sir Thomas More—Sir Thomas More died laughing, you remember. Also in the *Absurdities* of Ravisius Textor, there is a long list of characters who came to the same magnificent end. Do you know, however," continued he musingly, "that at Sparta (which is now Palæochori), at Sparta, I say, to the west of the citadel, among a chaos of scarcely visible ruins, is a kind of *socle,* upon which are still legible the letters ΛΑΣΜ. They are undoubtedly part of ΓΕΛΑΣΜΑ. Now at Sparta were a thousand different divinities. How exceedingly strange that the altar of Laughter should have survived all the others! But in the present instance," he resumed, with a singular alteration of voice and manner, "I have no right to be merry at your expense. You might well have been amazed. Europe cannot produce anything so fine as this, my little regal cabinet. My other apartments are by no means of the same order; mere *ultras*[13] of fashionable

---

[12]***grotesques . . . painters:*** The term "grotesques" refers to a type of decorative wall painting and is Roman, not Greek. **Chili gold:** This could be a trade name for a textile in Poe's day, but we did not find it in catalogs or histories of textiles. Two possible reasons for the name: (1) Chilean gold is found in long tenuous strands in the ore. A fabric made of long strands of imitation gold might have been known as "Chile gold." (2) The province of Chihli (now Hebei), in northern China, was famous for its rugs. Perhaps it produced a characteristic gold rug with the "liquid" texture Poe describes.

[13]***bienséance:*** Propriety, decorum. **Sir Thomas More:** Poe probably has in mind Robert Southey's account of More's death in *The Doctor* as it appeared in 1834: "It is one thing to jest, it is another to be mirthful. Sir Thomas More jested as he ascended the scaffold." Poe reviewed *The Doctor* in 1836. See our headnote to "Shadow." Benton (1) thinks Poe has "Byron" introduce the idea to help the reader identify the narrator; he intends a pun on Sir Thomas More (c.1478–1535, canonized in 1935) and Thomas Moore (the Irish poet, 1779–1852). Moore was Byron's friend. ***Absurdities* of Ravisius Textor:** Jean Tixier, Seigneur de Ravisy, French humanist (1430–1524). We have found many references to Tixier's

insipidity. This is better than fashion—is it not? Yet this has but to be seen to become the rage—that is, with those who could afford it at the cost of their entire patrimony. I have guarded, however, against any such profanation. With one exception you are the only human being besides myself and my *valet,* who has been admitted within the mysteries of these imperial precincts, since they have been bedizened as you see!"

I bowed in acknowledgment; for the overpowering sense of splendor and perfume, and music, together with the unexpected eccentricity of his address and manner, prevented me from expressing, in words, my appreciation of what I might have construed into a compliment.

"Here," he resumed, arising and leaning on my arm as he sauntered around the apartment, "here are paintings from the Greeks to Cimabue, and from Cimabue to the present hour. Many are chosen, as you see, with little deference to the opinions of Virtû. They are all, however, fitting tapestry for a chamber such as this. Here too, are some *chefs d'oeuvre*[14] of the unknown great—and here unfinished designs of men, celebrated in their day, whose very names the perspicacity of the academies has left to silence and to me. What think you," said he, turning abruptly as he spoke—"what think you of this Madonna della Pietà?"

"It is Guido's[15] own!" I said with all the enthusiasm of my nature, for I had been poring intently over its surpassing loveliness. "It is Guido's own!—how *could*

---

work, but no mention of his *Absurdities.* However, in *The Doctor,* Southey presents Textor's works as absurd and retells two of his dialogues which involve men making merry in defiance of Death. **Sparta . . . Palæochori:** Poe is only approximately right: a town called Sparta still stands on the site of ancient Sparta. One portion of it is labeled "Palaiopolis," "the old town," on tourist maps; it contains the area in which Sparta's acropolis stood. The important excavations were not begun until 1906, however, so Poe may not have known these details. His word "Palæochori" means "the old place" and might well refer to the same area. ***socle:*** A base or pedestal. See next item. **ΓΕΛΑΣΜΑ**: Laughter. Poe got this information from Chateaubriand's *Itinéraire de Paris à Jérusalem* (1811) (Engstrom). The passage in the *Itinéraire* also used the word *socle,* and Poe probably italicized it because he figured it was French. It is, but the same word is used in English architectural terminology. ***ultras:*** Poe's intention seems to be "extreme examples." The *Oxford English Dictionary* reports instances of "ultras" used to refer to people (the meaning is "extremists"), but no examples of the word used as Poe employs it here.

[14]**Cimabue:** Giovanni Cimabue (Cenni di Pepo), the great Florentine painter (c.1240–c.1302), and a logical breaking point in art history: for his departure from the Byzantine tradition, he is often called the father of modern European painting. **Virtû:** Connoisseurship. ***chefs d'oeuvre:*** Masterworks.

[15]Poe probably refers to Guido da Siena (active c.1250–c.1275), who produced a large and important Virgin and Child, and is felt to be the founder of a new and important neo-Byzantine school, but about whom little is known. Hence a work by him would be exceedingly rare. There is another late 13th-century "Guido" about whom Poe might have read scholarly speculation: Guido Graziano. Little is known of him, though he is intriguing because he is mentioned in contemporary sources. Mabbott (9, II) votes for a Madonna by Guido Reni (1575–1642).

you have obtained it?—she is undoubtedly in painting what the Venus is in sculpture."

"Ha!"[16] said he thoughtfully, "the Venus—the beautiful Venus?—the Venus of the Medici?—she of the diminutive head and the gilded hair? Part of the left arm (here his voice dropped so as to be heard with difficulty), and all the right are restorations, and in the coquetry of that right arm lies, I think, the quintessence of all affectation. Give *me* the Canova! The Apollo, too!—is a copy—there can be no doubt of it—blind fool that I am, who cannot behold the boasted inspiration of the Apollo! I cannot help—pity me!—I cannot help preferring the Antinous. Was it not Socrates who said that the statuary found his statue in the block of marble? Then Michael Angelo was by no means original in his couplet—

'Non ha l'ottimo artista alcun concetto
Chè un marmo solo in se non circonscriva.'"[17]

It has been, or should be remarked, that, in the manner of the true gentleman, we are always aware of a difference from the bearing of the vulgar, without being at once precisely able to determine in what such difference consists. Allowing the remark to have applied in its full force to the outward demeanor of my acquaintance, I felt it, on that eventful morning, still more fully applicable

---

[16]A letter from Byron to his publisher which Poe probably knew because Moore published it in his 1830 *Letters and Journals of Lord Byron, With Notice of His Life* contains a passage very similar to the following paragraph. Moreover, when Moore visited Byron in his Venice Palazzo (see note 11, above), the two discussed art, and Byron expressed his unconventional views in much this manner (Benton). There is also the familiar couplet from *Don Juan* ii, 118:

I've seen much finer women, ripe and real
Than all the nonsense of their stone ideal.

[17]**Venus of the Medici:** See Figure 3. The statue is now in Florence. **Canova:** Antonio Canova (1757–1822), Italian sculptor of great influence, called by some the key figure in the neoclassical school. His "Venus" was placed on the pedestal of the "Medici Venus" when that work was moved to Paris. **Apollo:** Byron is supposed to have looked much like the Vatican Apollo. To have him dislike it here is, Benton (1) feels, a humorous device on Poe's part. **Antinous:** Antinoüs (fl. c.110–130) was a favorite of the emperor Hadrian. After his death in Egypt in 130, Hadrian honored him through a religious cult, by naming cities after him, commanding that statues be made showing him as an ideal of youthful beauty. ***'Non . . . circonscriva.':*** Poe's attribution of the lines of Michelangelo is correct. Isaac Disraeli translates them,

The sculptor never yet conceived a thought
That yielding marble has refused to aid.

But a more literal translation in Carlson (2) is more to Poe's point: "The best artist has no concept which the marble itself does not contain."

Figure 3. The Venus of the Medici: Our photo shows a version by Massimillano Soldani, a bronze from about 1710. The position of the arms to which Poe's Byronic hero objects is clear enough. Courtesy of the Nelson Gallery-Atkins Museum, Kansas City, Missouri. (Acquired through the Elmer F. Pierson Foundation.)

to his moral temperament and character. Nor can I better define the peculiarity of spirit which seemed to place him so essentially apart from all other human beings, than by calling it a *habit* of intense and continual thought, pervading even his most trivial actions—intruding upon his moments of dalliance—and interweaving itself with his very flashes of merriment—like adders which writhe from out the eyes of the grinning masks in the cornices around the temples of Persepolis.[18]

I could not help, however, repeatedly observing, through the mingled tone of levity and solemnity with which he rapidly descanted upon matters of little importance, a certain air of trepidation—a degree of nervous *unction* in action and in speech—an unquiet excitability of manner which appeared to me at all times unaccountable, and upon some occasions even filled me with alarm. Frequently, too, pausing in the middle of a sentence whose commencement he had apparently forgotten, he seemed to be listening in the deepest attention, as if either in momentary expectation of a visiter, or to sounds which must have had existence in his imagination alone.

It was during one of these reveries or pauses of apparent abstraction, that, in turning over a page of the poet and scholar Politian's beautiful tragedy "The Orfeo," (the first native Italian tragedy,) which lay near me upon an ottoman, I discovered a passage underlined in pencil. It was a passage towards the end of the third act[19]—a passage of the most heart-stirring excitement—a passage which,

[18]Persepolis: The ancient Persian capital.

[19]Angelo Poliziano (Ambrogini, 1454–94), Florentine humanist, dramatist, and poet. Politian's brief play *La Favola d'Orfeo* (1480) is not divided into acts and scenes. It concerns

although tainted with impurity, no man shall read without a thrill of novel emotion—no woman without a sigh. The whole page was blotted with fresh tears, and, upon the opposite interleaf, were the following English lines, written in a hand so very different from the peculiar characters of my acquaintance, that I had some difficulty in recognising it as his own.

Thou wast that all to me, love,
For which my soul did pine—
A green isle in the sea, love,
A fountain and a shrine
All wreathed with fairy fruits and flowers;
And all the flowers were mine.

Ah, dreams too bright to last;
Ah, starry Hope that didst arise
But to be overcast!
A voice from out the Future cries
"Onward!"—but o'er the Past
(Dim gulf!) my spirit hovering lies,
Mute, motionless, aghast!

For alas! alas! with me
The light of life is o'er.
"No more—no more—no more,"
(Such language holds the solemn sea
To the sands upon the shore,)
Shall bloom the thunder-blasted tree,
Or the stricken eagle soar!

Now all my hours are trances;
And all my nightly dreams
Are where the dark eye glances,
And where thy footstep gleams,
In what ethereal dances,
By what Italian streams.

Alas! for that accursed time
They bore thee o'er the billow,
From Love to titled age and crime,
And an unholy pillow—
From me, and from our misty clime,
Where weeps the silver willow!

---

the descent of Orfeo into the underworld to plead for the return of his love. Poe probably refers to Orfeo's pleading at the gates of hell, where his grief is so intense and his poem so beautiful as to halt the various hellish activities. The play *could* be divided into three parts, but the "third part" deals just with the Bacchantes gloating after cruelly killing Orfeo and sacrificing him to Bacchus for pursuing his otherworldly love.

That these lines were written in English—a language with which I had not believed their author acquainted[20]—afforded me little matter for surprise. I was too well aware of the extent of his acquirements, and of the singular pleasure he took in concealing them from observation, to be astonished at any singular discovery; but the place of date, I must confess, occasioned me no little amazement. It had been originally written *London,* and afterwards carefully overscored—not, however, so effectually as to conceal the word from a scrutinizing eye. I say this occasioned me no little amazement; for I well remember that, in a former conversation with my friend, I particularly inquired if he had at any time met in London the Marchesa di Mentoni, (who for some years previous to her marriage had resided in that city,) when his answer, if I mistake not, gave me to understand that he had never visited the metropolis of Great Britain. I might as well here mention, that I have more than once heard, (without of course giving credit to a report involving so many improbabilities,) that the person of whom I speak was not only by birth, but in education, an *Englishman.*

* * *

"There is one painting," said he, without being aware of my notice of the tragedy—"there is still one painting which you have not seen." And throwing aside a drapery, he discovered a full length portrait of the Marchesa Aphrodite.

Human art could have done no more in the delineation of her superhuman beauty. The same ethereal figure which stood before me the preceding night upon the steps of the Ducal Palace, stood before me once again. But in the expression of the countenance, which was beaming all over with smiles, there still lurked (incomprehensible anomaly!) that fitful stain of melancholy which will ever be found inseparable from the perfection of the beautiful. Her right arm lay folded over her bosom. With her left she pointed downward to a curiously fashioned vase. One small, fairy foot, alone visible, barely touched the earth—and, scarcely discernible in the brilliant atmosphere which seemed to encircle and enshrine her loveliness, floated a pair of the most declicately imagined wings. My glance fell from the painting to the figure of my friend, and the vigorous words of Chapman's *Bussy D'Ambois* quivered instinctively upon my lips:

---

[20]Byron, of course, *is* an English poet; Poe is joking. This poem is generally known as "To One in Paradise." Basler feels Poe's poem is inspired by Byron's famous love affair with Mary Chaworth; indeed, he says that that affair may be a source of the story itself. The poem seems to predate the tale: Poe printed it as "To Ianthe in Heaven" in the July 1839 *Gentleman's Magazine,* the 1841 *American Melodies,* the February 25 and March 4, 1843 *Saturday Museum,* the May 10, 1845 *Broadway Journal,* the 1845 *The Raven and Other Poems,* the *New York Daily Tribune* for November 29, 1845, and the 1849 *Poets and Poetry of America.*

> *"He is up*
> *There like a Roman statue! He will stand*
> *Till Death hath made him marble!*"[21]

"Come!" he said at length, turning towards a table of richly enamelled and massive silver, upon which were a few goblets fantastically stained, together with two large Etruscan vases, fashioned in the same extraordinary model as that in the foreground of the portrait, and filled with what I supposed to be Johannisberger.[22] "Come!" he said abruptly, "let us drink! It is early—but let us drink. It is *indeed* early," he continued, musingly, as a cherub with a heavy golden hammer, made the apartment ring with the first hour after sunrise—"It is *indeed* early, but what matters it? let us drink! Let us pour out an offering to yon solemn sun which these gaudy lamps and censers are so eager to subdue!" And, having made me pledge him in a bumper, he swallowed in rapid succession several goblets of the wine.

"To dream," he continued, resuming the tone of his desultory conversation, as he held up to the rich light of a censer one of the magnificent vases—"to dream has been the business of my life. I have therefore framed for myself, as you see, a bower of dreams. In the heart of Venice could I have erected a better? You behold around you, it is true, a medley of architectural embellishments. The chastity of Ionia is offended by antediluvian devices, and the sphynxes of Egypt are outstretched upon carpets of gold. Yet the effect is incongruous to the timid alone. Proprieties of place, and especially of time, are the bug-bears which terrify mankind from the contemplation of the magnificent. Once I was myself a decorist: but that sublimation of folly has palled upon my soul. All this is now the fitter for my purpose. Like these arabesque censers, my spirit is writhing in fire, and the delirium of this scene is fashioning me for the wilder visions of that land of real dreams whither I am now rapidly departing." He here paused abruptly, bent his head to his bosom, and seemed to listen to a sound which I could not hear. At length, erecting his frame, he looked upwards and ejaculated the lines of the Bishop of Chichester:—

---

[21]Chapman's *Bussy D'Ambois: The Tragedie of Busye D'Amboise* (1607). The lines Poe has in mind are in Act V, Scene iv, 95–97, but he altered or misremembered them. Bussy speaks:

> *. . . I am up*
> *Here like a Roman statue! I will stand*
> *Till death hath made me marble. . . .*

Bussy, an ambitious and unscrupulous courtier, has been shot, and determines to prop himself up with his sword, and thus die standing. The passage is appropriate, for Bussy D'Ambois's murder is the result of his illicit affair with Tamyra, the wife of Count Montsurry. See Levine (4), "The System of Dr. Tarr and Prof. Fether," note 1.

[22]Wine from Johannisberg, Hessen, Germany, on the Rhine.

Stay for me there! I will not fail
To meet thee in that hollow vale.[23]

In the next instant, confessing the power of the wine, he threw himself at full length upon an ottoman.

A quick step was now heard upon the staircase, and a loud knock at the door rapidly succeeded. I was hastening to anticipate a second disturbance, when a page of Mentoni's household burst into the room, and faltered out, in a voice choking with emotion, the incoherent words, "My mistress!—my mistress!—poisoned!—poisoned! Oh beautiful—oh beautiful Aphrodite!"

Bewildered, I flew to the ottoman, and endeavored to arouse the sleeper to a sense of the startling intelligence. But his limbs were rigid—his lips were livid—his lately beaming eyes were riveted in *death.* I staggered back towards the table—my hand fell upon a cracked and blackened goblet[24]—and a consciousness of the entire and terrible truth flashed suddenly over my soul.

---

[23]Bishop of Chichester: Henry King (1592–1669). The lines are from his "Exequy on the Death of a Beloved Wife" (1657).

[24]Mabbott (9, II) points out that medieval Venetian glass "was supposed to break if filled with poison."

SHADOW

This powerful story can stand without explanation. But Poe, as he wrote, had very specific meanings in mind, meanings which are not apparent to any reader who has not just read two of Poe's favorite books. So a few paragraphs of explanation should be helpful.

"Shadow" is constructed of material which Poe took from a chapter of Thomas Moore's The Epicurians *(Pollin 12). It is not, however, really a satire on Moore: as Pollin notes, the tale's poetic evocation of the voices of the departed is too "beautifully wrought" not to be compelling even for the reader who knows what game Poe is playing. We think Poe here, as in "Silence," is deliberately writing a virtuoso piece, demonstrating how well he can take another man's materials and make them work for him.*

The other basic source of "Shadow" suggests as much: Jacob Bryant's Mythology. *We are certain that Poe connects Bryant to this story (see note 4 especially); he also praises Bryant elsewhere. Bryant was one of a group of speculative and imaginative mythologists; Poe loved his book. Bryant thought he recognized interrelations among ancient religions, and between them and modern beliefs. Although his* Mythology *is, as Poe knew, terribly unsound, it is still haunting and evocative. Bryant's work presents, in its analysis of ancient myth, the philosophical and mythical framework of Poe's tale; it also contains much of Poe's language and even the proper names Poe uses—including the "foul Charonian canal" which has hitherto puzzled scholars.*

"Zoilus" is likely Poe's rendition of Jacob Bryant's "Coilus," which " . . . in the original acceptation certainly signified heavenly. . . . [Coilus] was . . . a sacred or heavenly person" (Bryant, Vol. I, 140).

Bryant also seems to be the source of the name Oinos. In a complicated explanation, he equates the Dove from the Ark with Ion, Ionah [Jonah], and Oinas of the Greeks, "the interpreter of the will of the Gods to man." Bryant identifies Oinas with Eanus (Janus), whom he consequently equates with other deities—Apollo, Diana, Helius, Dionysus, and Saturn.

Bryant describes Janus as having "two faces"—one pointing toward the past and one toward the future—and as representing "the end and the beginning of all things." He presides, Bryant says, "over everything that could be shut or opened; and . . . [is] the guardian of the doors of Heaven." In rites in honor of both the gods Saturn and Dionysus, originally a sacrifice was made, representing the end of one period and the beginning of another. (Dionysus is, in fact, listed in Greek dictionaries as one of the meanings of οἶνος.*) The name Oinos, its form in Poe, is identical to an archaic Latin form for the modern* unus, *"one." With or without the classical wordplay, clearly*

Poe had in mind the idea in Dionysian rites that life and death lead into each other as one.

If the names Oinos and Zoilus are given meanings based on references in Bryant, "Shadow," like Poe's tales "Eiros and Charmion" and "The Colloquy of Monos and Una," may be read as a myth of rebirth. The reading might go as follows: Zoilus, the heavenly one, is dead. The planets are in a period of Saturnian darkness. Oinos (and possibly the seven men as a whole, if we take into account the magical properties of the number seven) is perhaps equated with Dionysus—the new representation of a God—or with the Dove which reveals God's will. In this dark period the group is passing "through the Valley," the abyss (symbolically represented in the story by the bottomless image reflected in the surface of the ebony table), Hell, "Helusion," the place from whence the Shadow comes and from whence the voices of the dead are heard, and is suffering the rite of purification which must be endured before resurrection. Death leads to life.

There is no question that Poe had such meanings in mind when he wrote "Shadow," for they are in Jacob Bryant, and Poe clearly built his story out of Bryant's book. The motto added to the story in its 1840 version suggests that another beginning is to take place. Death must be experienced but is not to be feared because there is "something" beyond—a continuation.

Another possibility, given Poe's capacity for irony, is that Poe, while he admires Bryant's erudition, also sees the humor in the seemingly unending chain of connections which Bryant is able to make from any given proper name. In "Four Beasts in One," a story first published just six months after the first publication of "Shadow," Poe makes jokes based upon antiquarian etymologies. His narrator remarks, "what great fools are antiquarians!" The time was ripe for making fun of Bryant. In Chapter 176 of The Doctor *by Robert Southey, Doctor Daniel Dove was delighted " . . . when in perusing Jacob Bryant's Analysis of ancient Mythology, he found that so many of the most illustrious personages of antiquity proved to be Doves, when their names were truly interpreted or properly understood!" Southey carries the derivation of the name Dove through Bryant's explanation to its comical extremes. Poe could not have seen the passage: he was probably reading the first two volumes of the novel at about the time he wrote "Shadow," for his review of it appeared soon after, but the version of it Poe read did not contain the Bryant passage. What this proves is the intimacy of Poe's ties to the intellectual world of the British magazines. (Southey was a frequent contributor to* The Quarterly Review.*) References to reflections in "ebony" also suggest British magazines, for "ebony" was the code name which writers for* Blackwood's, *the most famous magazine of the age, used for their boss, William Blackwood, and Poe used "ebony" several times in stories in which he seems to have wanted to indicate an Edinburgh connection.*

PUBLICATIONS IN POE'S TIME

The Southern Literary Messenger, September 1835
Tales of the Grotesque and Arabesque, 1840
The Broadway Journal, May 31, 1845

SHADOW
A Parable

Yea! though I walk through the valley of the Shadow:
Psalm of David[1]

Ye who read are still among the living: but I who write shall have long since gone my way into the region of shadows. For indeed strange things shall happen, and secret things be known, and many centuries shall pass away, ere these memorials be seen of men. And, when seen, there will be some to disbelieve, and some to doubt, and yet a few who will find much to ponder upon in the characters here graven with a stylus of iron.[2]

The year had been a year of terror, and of feelings more intense than terror for which there is no name upon the earth. For many prodigies and signs had taken place, and far and wide, over sea and land, the black wings of the Pestilence were spread abroad. To those, nevertheless, cunning in the stars, it was not unknown

[1]The verse, from Psalm 23, reads, "Yeah, though I walk through the valley of the shadow of death, I will fear no evil: for thou art with me; thy rod and thy staff they comfort me." Poe added the motto when he revised the 1840 *Tales of the Grotesque and Arabesque,* hoping to publish another selection.

[2]A "stylus of iron" has special resonance for students of Poe. Poe dreamed of owning and controlling editorial policies of a literary journal, and even wrote, printed, and mailed prospectuses to potential subscribers in a series of attempts from 1840 through 1848 to generate capital to enable him to begin publication. The first prospectuses called the proposed new periodical "The Penn Magazine"; in the later versions it is called "The Stylus," and a motto appears:

______ unbending that all men
Of thy firm TRUTH may say—"Lo! this is writ
With the antique *iron pen."*
Launcelot Canning.

There is also a drawing showing the stylus of iron in the hand of someone writing with it. "Launcelot Canning" is discussed in note 15 to "The Fall of the House of Usher"; he is Poe's invention.

that the heavens wore an aspect of ill; and to me, the Greek Oinos, among others, it was evident that now had arrived the alternation of that seven hundred and ninety-fourth year when, at the entrance of Aries, the planet Jupiter is conjoined with the red ring of the terrible Saturnus.[3] The peculiar spirit of the skies, if I mistake not greatly, made itself manifest, not only in the physical orb of the earth, but in the souls, imaginations, and meditations of mankind.

Over some flasks of the red Chian wine, within the walls of a noble hall, in a dim city called Ptolemais, we sat, at night, a company of seven. And to our chamber there was no entrance save by a lofty door of brass: and the door was fashioned by the artizan Corinnos, and, being of rare workmanship, was fastened from within. Black draperies, likewise, in the gloomy room, shut out from our view the moon, the lurid stars, and the peopleless streets—but the boding and the memory of Evil, they would not be so excluded. There were things around us and about of which I can render no distinct account—things material and spiritual—heaviness in the atmosphere—a sense of suffocation—anxiety—and, above all, that terrible state of existence which the nervous experience when the senses are keenly living and awake, and meanwhile the powers of thought lie dormant. A dead weight hung upon us. It hung upon our limbs—upon the household furniture—upon the goblets from which we drank; and all things were depressed, and borne down thereby—all things save only the flames of the seven iron lamps which illumined our revel. Uprearing themselves in tall slender lines of light, they thus remained burning all pallid and motionless; and in the mirror which their lustre formed upon the round table of ebony at which we sat, each of us there assembled beheld the pallor of his own countenance, and the unquiet glare in the downcast eyes of his companions. Yet we laughed and were merry in our proper way—which was hysterical; and sang the songs of Anacreon—which are madness; and drank deeply—although the purple wine reminded us of blood. For there was yet another tenant of our chamber in the person of young Zoilus. Dead, and at full length he lay, enshrouded;—the genius and the demon of the scene. Alas! he bore no portion in our mirth, save that his countenance, distorted with the

---

[3]**Oinos:** See our headnote and "The Power of Words," note 1. In Bryant's *Mythology,* one of Poe's sources, see Vol. III, pp. 81–90 and *passim.* The meaning "wine" for Oinos makes some sense in this tale, for Oinos tells us of his drinking. **alternation . . . Saturnus:** An astronomer friend kindly checked out Poe's figures for us, and reports that Poe is correct. Not knowing what values Poe used for the orbital periods of Jupiter and Saturn, he used "P" to represent Poe's values and worked an equation to find "P." "J" represents Jupiter; and "S" Saturn.

794 years = 67PJP = 27PSP

Modern values turn out very close to Poe's: modern Jupiter is 11.8622 years. Modern Saturn is 29.4577 years; Poe's Saturn is 29.4074 years. Either way, Jupiter and Saturn will be in the same position with respect to the sun every 794 years, as Poe says. Poe's "the entrance of Aries" means "Spring." The planets were in this position during Poe's lifetime—spring 1822. Simple subtraction thus gives us possible dates for the setting of the story: 1028, 234, 560 B.C.E., 1354 B.C.E., and so forth. Mabbott (9, II) dates the tale by the first appearance of the plague (542). His date does not work.

plague, and his eyes in which Death had but half extinguished the fire of the pestilence, seemed to take such interest in our merriment as the dead may haply take in the merriment of those who are to die. But although I, Oinos, felt that the eyes of the departed were upon me, still I forced myself not to perceive the bitterness of their expression, and, gazing down steadily into the depths of the ebony mirror, sang with a loud and sonorous voice the songs of the son of Teios. But gradually my songs they ceased, and their echoes, rolling afar off among the sable draperies of the chamber, became weak, and undistinguishable, and so faded away. And lo! from among those sable draperies where the sounds of the song departed, there came forth a dark and undefined shadow—a shadow such as the moon, when low in heaven, might fashion from the figure of a man: but it was the shadow neither of man, nor of God, nor of any familiar thing. And, quivering awhile among the draperies of the room, it at length rested in full view upon the surface of the door of brass. But the shadow was vague, and formless, and indefinite, and was the shadow neither of man, nor of God—neither God of Greece, nor God of Chaldæa, nor any Egyptian God. And the shadow rested upon the brazen doorway, and under the arch of the entablature of the door, and moved not, nor spoke any word, but there became stationary and remained. And the door whereupon the shadow rested was, if I remember aright, over against the feet of the young Zoilus enshrouded. But we, the seven there assembled, having seen the shadow as it came out from among the draperies, dared not steadily behold it, but cast down our eyes, and gazed continually into the depths of the mirror of ebony. And at length I, Oinos, speaking some low words, demanded of the shadow its dwelling and its appellation. And the shadow answered, "I am SHADOW, and my dwelling is near to the Catacombs of Ptolemais, and hard by those dim plains of Helusion which border upon the foul Charonian canal."[4] And then did we, the

---

[4]**Chian wine:** Wine from Chios in the Aegean Sea. Bryant points out, in Vol. V, p. 176, that Chios is famous for its wine. **city called Ptolemais:** Three ancient cities bear this name: one in Cyrenaica, one on the west coast of the Red Sea, and the town now called Acre, in Israel. **the artizan Corinnos:** A made-up name, apparently, intended to suggest an artisan from Corinth, famous for its metalwork in ancient times. **seven iron lamps:** Curious that Poe uses approximately the same lighting fixtures here as in his other tale of plague-terror, "The Masque of the Red Death." Perhaps because both share details based on Moore's *The Epicurean,* Poe associates the two tales in his mind. He also seems to associate iron lamps with the Devil: see Levine (4), "Bon-Bon," note 11. **Anacreon:** Greek poet (c.563–c.478 B.C.E.) associated with celebration of love and wine. See Teios, below. Pollin (12) points out that if Poe is parodying "pseudo-poetic transcendental fictions" as G. R. Thompson (2) says he seems to be, Thomas Moore is a likely butt of the parody. Moore was often referred to as "Anacreon" Moore, and his *The Epicurean* contains a section which Pollin (12) feels is the basis of Poe's tale. **Zoilus:** Poe uses the name of a fourth-century B.C.E. Greek rhetorician famous for his dislike of Homer; the epics he felt too fabulous. In general usage, a "Zoilus" is an over-critical critic. But we feel Poe's source is Bryant's *Mythology.* See headnote. **Teios:** Τέως, town in Ionia where Anacreon was born. It should be spelled Teos. **Catacombs . . . canal:** Poe's source is Bryant's discussion of places of Amonian worship in Vol. I, p. 34 of *Mythology:* "The Elysian plain, near the Catacombs in Egypt, stood upon the foul Charonian canal; which was so noisome, that every fetid ditch

seven, start from our seats of horror, and stand trembling, and shuddering, and aghast: for the tones in the voice of the shadow were not the tones of any one being, but of a multitude of beings, and, varying in their cadences from syllable to syllable, fell duskily upon our ears in the well remembered and familiar accents of many thousand departed friends.

---

and cavern was from it called Charonian." "Helusion" is Poe's spelling of Ἠλύσιον, Elysium, Bryant's Elysian plain. Bryant's word "Charonian" evokes Charon, who in Greek myth ferried the dead to Hades over the River Styx. However, Bryant's use of the word suggests that he might have had a specific place in mind. For more on Poe and Bryant, see Levine (5).

Silence

Poe planned a collection of satirical stories which was to have been called "Tales of the Folio Club." Poe scholars are not positive exactly which stories were to have been included, but they know that "Silence" was one of the group. So we have Poe's own word that "Silence" was supposed to be a satire. Yet its evocative and ritualistic language works so well that we think of it less as a satire than as Poe's demonstration that he could use another author's materials better than the author could. It is in addition an important exercise in the symbolic use of materials from myth.

The Folio Club tales were to have been the work of "Dunderheads." "Silence," like the others, uses material from then-current prose. But Poe does not seem just to be making fun of his sources or using them to tease popular editors or authors. A number of scholars noticed, for example, that Bulwer's "Monos and Daimonos, A Legend" is a source for "Silence." Many elements in "Silence"—even whole sentences—come from Bulwer. The Bulwer story is about a man whose father lived on a rock; it contains a sentence which begins, "As the Lord liveth, that fable which the Demon told you . . . ," while Poe writes, "As Allah liveth, that fable which the Demon told me. . . ." Yet "Silence" is not only a spoof of Bulwer's "Monos and Daimonos"; it is at least partially a lesson in how powerful a tale one could produce from the same materials Bulwer used. Poe's tone seems undeniably serious; we would suggest that his intention is not simple.

Moreover, the Bulwer story is not all that Poe uses; clear echoes of Jacob Bryant's Mythology *(see the headnote to "Shadow") are audible, too. The connections between Bryant and "Silence" do much more than make a scholar's point—they enrich the story by showing what Poe had in mind as he played with myth and ritual. (1) Bryant explains the ancient custom of worshiping on a stone or upon high places: ". . . there is in the history of every oracular temple some legend about a stone; some reference to the word Petra." "Petra," indeed, is, in the "first ages," a name for the Sun Deity, Bryant explains, which was later applied to the Deity's temple, then to the other temples, then to temples erected on a rock, and finally to the rock itself. (2) Bryant says, ". . . the whole religion of the ancients consisted in . . . the worship of Daemons: . . . the souls of men deceased." These demons were supposed to have existed in the time of Cronus and were "guardians of mankind." (3) Poe's hippopotamus and water lilies (the lotus is a water lily) are explained in Bryant: "Hence the crocodile and the hippopotamus, were emblems of the Ark; because during the inundation of the Nile they rose with the waters, and were superior to the flood. The Lotus, that peculiar plant of the Nile, was reverenced upon the same account. . . ." (4) In related Egyptian rites, according to Bryant, there is "a person preserved in the midst of waters." (5) Many other details—"Libya," "Dodona," "Magi," and "Sybils"—as well as those named above are discussed prominently in Bryant. By themselves they would not be convincing, since they might appear in any book on myth and ancient religion. In conjunction with the others, they are. Identifying the sources of Poe's ideas is not tantamount to explaining his intentions, however. Poe elsewhere showed that he thought Bryant's work funny and that he was at the same time moved by it. What moved him were resonances from the deepest chambers of the human imagination: Poe's fiction is powerful in part because he has a sophisticated awareness of the myth beneath the fable.*

A note of explanation: *One must be careful in claiming that one work is the "source" of another. The poetic fragment from which Poe takes his motto seems a sure source of Poe's ideas, but in fact Poe originally used a motto from a poem of his own which also matches the ideas in "Silence." (See note 2 for details.) The Alcman quotation might be the source of both. Poe, when he wrote "Silence," might not have had it handy, and decided for other reasons to use his own equally appropriate lines. Or he might have found the Alcman later, been struck by its appropriateness, or attracted by the chance to show erudition, and replaced his with it.*

We conclude first that the idea was in circulation, and second, that one must be very cautious in interpreting all aspects of "Silence."

Different scholars reach different conclusions about which member of the Folio Club tells this tale. Hammond thinks it was Poe himself, possibly because, among other things, "Siope" (Poe's first title, Greek for "Silence") is an anagram: "is Poe," and because "Silence" uses imagery from Poe's own poetry. We know that this story was written a number of years earlier than its first publication because there is a fragmentary manuscript of material for his Folio Club project.

PUBLICATIONS IN POE'S TIME

The Baltimore Book, 1838 (actually printed in late 1837, as "Siope/In the Manner of the Psychological Autobiographists")
Tales of the Grotesque and Arabesque, 1840, as "Silence/A Fable"
The Broadway Journal, September 6, 1845

SILENCE
A Fable[1]

Εὕδουσιν δ' ὀρέων κορυφαί τε καὶ φάραγγες
Πρῶονές τε καὶ χαράδραι.
The mountain pinnacles slumber; valleys, crags and caves **are silent.**

Alcman.[2]

---

[1]Poe's original name for this tale was "Siope/In the Manner of the Psychological Autobiographists." Bulwer (Edward Lytton Bulwer, 1803–73, a popular British novelist) and De Quincey (see note 5, below, and "How to Write a Blackwood Article," note 7) are among the psychological autobiographists.

[2]The first version of the story used a motto from Poe's "Al Aaraaf":

Ours is a world of words: Quiet we call
"Silence"—which is the merest word of all.

The later motto is from the work of Alcman, a poet believed active in Sparta in the mid-seventh century B.C.E., whose work survives only in a few fragments, saved often because other writers quoted his work. A burst of classical archeological discoveries connected with the Egyptological work in the early 19th century (see the illustration to "The Balloon-Hoax" on p. 276, for instance) had brought several new fragments to light. Poe's lines come from a fragment which survived because Apollonius, a Greek lexicographer of the first century B.C.E., quoted it in his *Homeric Lexicon* and commented on it. Curiously, none of the modern translations we examined uses the idea of silence which Poe emphasizes in his free translation of the first two of the fragment's seven lines. But the idea appears in a translation by the Scottish poet Thomas Campbell (1777–1854) whose work Poe knew. Campbell's translation reads,

The mountain summits sleep: glens, cliffs, and caves
Are silent—. . . .

The entire fragment is relevant to the tale; the remainder of Campbell's version reads,

. . . all the black earth's reptile brood—
The bees—the wild beasts of the mountain wood:
In depths beneath the dark red ocean's waves
Its monsters rest, whilst wrapt in bower and spray
Each bird is hush'd that stretch'd its pinions to the day.

Beyond the concept of busy nature now stilled, Poe might also have responded to Alcman's "monsters" because of his own use of the "behemoth" (see note 6). Indeed, Apollonius' comment on the fragment has to do with what Alcman means by the words "beasts" and "monsters." Poe certainly saw that; he also may well have remembered that Aristotle mentions Alcman as an example of a famous man who died of "this disease [*morbus pediculairis*] when the body contains too much moisture," an idea which ironically echoes the mythological theme from Bryant (see our headnote) of the "person preserved in the midst of waters." Moreover, Campbell's translation speaks of a red ocean (other versions make it purple brine) which suggests the rain of blood in the fourth paragraph of this story. So the lines of ancient poetry were a superb choice, so good that had they been in the tale's first version, scholars would argue that "Silence" is an imaginative expansion of the Alcman fragment. Our Greek follows David Campbell, *Greek Lyric Poetry* (New York, 1967). Poe's is identical but without accents.

"Listen to *me,*" said the Demon, as he placed his hand upon my head. "The region of which I speak is a dreary region in Libya, by the borders of the river Zaïre.[3] And there is no quiet there, nor silence.

"The waters of the river have a saffron and sickly hue; and they flow not onwards to the sea, but palpitate forever and forever beneath the red eye of the sun with a tumultuous and convulsive motion. For many miles on either side of the river's oozy bed is a pale desert of gigantic water-lilies.[4] They sigh one unto the other in that solitude, and stretch towards the heaven their long and ghastly necks, and nod to and fro their everlasting heads. And there is an indistinct murmur which cometh out from among them like the rushing of subterrene water. And they sigh one unto the other.

"But there is a boundary to their realm—the boundary of the dark, horrible, lofty forest. There, like the waves about the Hebrides, the low underwood is agitated continually. But there is no wind throughout the heaven. And the tall primeval trees rock eternally hither and thither with a crashing and mighty sound. And from their high summits, one by one, drop everlasting dews. And at the roots strange poisonous flowers lie writhing in perturbed slumber. And overhead, with a rustling and loud noise, the gray clouds rush westwardly forever, until they roll, a cataract, over the fiery wall of the horizon. And by the shores of the river Zäire there is neither quiet nor silence.

"It was night, and the rain fell; and, falling, it was rain, but, having fallen, it was blood. And I stood in the morass among the tall lilies, and the rain fell upon my head—and the lilies sighed one unto the other in the solemnity of their desolation.

"And, all at once, the moon arose through the thin ghastly mist, and was crimson in color. And mine eyes fell upon a huge gray rock which stood by the shore of the river, and was lighted by the light of the moon. And the rock was gray, and ghastly, and tall,—and the rock was gray. Upon its front were characters engraven in the stone; and I walked through the morass of water-lilies, until I came close unto the shore, that I might read the characters upon the stone. But I could not decypher them. And I was going back into the morass, when the moon shone with a fuller red, and I turned and looked again upon the rock, and upon the characters;—and the characters were DESOLATION.

"And I looked upwards, and there stood a man upon the summit of the rock; and I hid myself among the water-lilies that I might discover the actions of the man. And the man was tall and stately in form, and was wrapped up from his shoulders to his feet in the toga of old Rome. And the outlines of his figure were indistinct—but his features were the features of a deity; for the mantle of the night, and of the mist, and of the moon, and of the dew, had left uncovered the features of his face. And his brow was lofty with thought, and his eye wild with care; and, in the few

---

[3]**Demon:** See our headnote. **Libya:** In old Greek usage, "Libya" meant simply "Africa." See our headnote. **Zaïre:** The old name for the Congo, now in use again.

[4]See our headnote.

furrows upon his cheek I read the fables of sorrow, and weariness, and disgust with mankind, and a longing after solitude.[5]

"And the man sat upon the rock, and leaned his head upon his hand, and looked out upon the desolation. He looked down into the low unquiet shrubbery, and up into the tall primeval trees, and up higher at the rustling heaven, and into the crimson moon. And I lay close within shelter of the lilies, and observed the actions of the man. And the man trembled in the solitude;—but the night waned, and he sat upon the rock.

"And the man turned his attention from the heaven, and looked out upon the dreary river Zäire, and upon the yellow ghastly waters, and upon the pale legions of the water-lilies. And the man listened to the sighs of the water-lilies, and to the murmur that came up from among them. And I lay close within my covert and observed the actions of the man. And the man trembled in the solitude;—but the night waned and he sat upon the rock.

"Then I went down into the recesses of the morass, and waded afar in among the wilderness of the lilies, and called unto the hippopotami which dwelt among the fens in the recesses of the morass. And the hippopotami heard my call, and came, with the behemoth,[6] unto the foot of the rock, and roared loudly and fearfully beneath the moon. And I lay close within my covert and observed the actions of the man. And the man trembled in the solitude;—but the night waned and he sat upon the rock.

"Then I cursed the elements with the curse of tumult; and a frightful tempest gathered in the heaven where, before, there had been no wind. And the heaven became livid with the violence of the tempest—and the rain beat upon the head of the man—and the floods on the river came down—and the river was tormented into foam—and the water-lilies shrieked within their beds—and the forest crumbled before the wind—and the thunder rolled—and the lightning fell—and the rock rocked to its foundation. And I lay close within my covert and observed the actions of the man. And the man trembled in the solitude;—but the night waned and he sat upon the rock.

---

[5]**rock:** See our headnote. **solitude:** Major writers said a great deal about solitude in Poe's day; see Poe's tale "The Lighthouse" (Levine 4) for a character with similar yearnings. Poe knew Isaac Disraeli's essay on solitude in *Curiosities of Literature.* He did not know a passage in De Quincey's *Suspiria de Profundis* because it was published in 1845, but it certainly illustrates how frequently the idea appears, and how close one writer is to another in what he says about it. De Quincey calls solitude "silent as light" and "a secret heiroglyphic from God." His passage forcibly suggests Poe's story "Silence" because it connects supernatural writing with the idea of solitude, and because De Quincey is a psychological autobiographist (see note 1).

[6]**Then:** Poe's use of "and" and "then" to begin so many of his sentences is part of his attempt to create a scriptural tone. Whimsy and a scriptural tone are not incompatible, however. A notable scriptural parody, "The Chaldee Manuscript," made fun of Edinburgh magazinists and used a similar tone. Poe certainly knew it: it was published first in *Blackwood's* in 1817, and its principal author, James Hogg, appears frequently in Poe's writing. Poe probably considered Hogg a psychological autobiographist as well as poet and satirist. See also note 8, lynx. **behemoth:** See Job 40:15–24; see our headnote and note 2.

"Then I grew angry and cursed, with the curse of *silence,* the river, and the lilies, and the wind, and the forest, and the heaven, and the thunder, and the sighs of the water-lilies. And they became accursed, and *were still.* And the moon ceased to totter up its pathway to heaven—and the thunder died away—and the lightning did not flash—and the clouds hung motionless—and the waters sunk to their level and remained—and the trees ceased to rock—and the water-lilies sighed no more—and the murmur was heard no longer from among them, nor any shadow of sound throughout the vast illimitable desert. And I looked upon the characters of the rock, and they were changed;—and the characters were SILENCE.[7]

"And mine eyes fell upon the countenance of the man, and his countenance was wan with terror. And, hurriedly, he raised his head from his hand, and stood forth upon the rock and listened. But there was no voice throughout the vast illimitable desert, and the characters upon the rock were SILENCE. And the man shuddered, and turned his face away, and fled afar off, in haste, so that I beheld him no more."

* *

Now there are fine tales in the volumes of the Magi—in the iron-bound, melancholy volumes of the Magi. Therein, I say, are glorious histories of the Heaven, and of the Earth, and of the mighty sea—and of the Genii that overruled the sea, and the earth, and the lofty heaven. There was much lore too in the sayings which were said by the Sybils; and holy, holy things were heard of old by the dim leaves that trembled around Dodona—but, as Allah liveth, that fable which the Demon told me as he sat by my side in the shadow of the tomb, I hold to be the most wonderful of all! And as the Demon made an end of his story, he fell back within the cavity of the tomb and laughed. And I could not laugh with the Demon, and he cursed me because I could not laugh. And the lynx[8] which dwelleth forever in the tomb, came out therefrom, and lay down at the feet of the Demon, and looked at him steadily in the face.

---

[7]A passage in Thomas Carlyle's *Sartor Resartus/The Life and Opinions of Herr Teufelsdröckh* (1831), which Poe knew well, concludes, "Speech is of time, Silence is of Eternity" (Book III, Chapter 3). The idea of words changing Poe could have taken from William Beckford; as Mabbott points out, this happens to characters inscribed on a cliff in *Vathek,* Beckford's famous, early (1786) gothic novel.

[8]**Magi:** Persian priests. See our headnote. **Genii:** Magical beings in near Eastern lore. **Sybils:** Prophetesses in Greek and Roman belief. See our headnote. **Dodona:** Site of a sacred grove at which a priest and priestess read oracular meanings in the sounds of rustling leaves. See our headnote. **lynx:** One of the symbolic animals representing writers in "The Chaldee Manuscript" (see note 6).

Ligeia

In Poe's long (264-line), unfinished poem "Al Aaraaf" appears Nesace's song to Ligeia, "the soul of beauty," or "the goddess of harmony" (A. H. Quinn; Carlson 2). A contemporary explanation which Poe editorially supervised (and so presumably approved) said that Ligeia was a "personification of music" (Mabbott 9, II; see also Mabbott, Collected Works of EAP, *I, 123–4). Poe's poem is mystical in message: only intuitive creativity can achieve cosmic and supernal beauty. Scientific knowledge is a lesser path; its "Truth is Falsehood."*

Poe's stories of the death of a beautiful woman share several important features. First, the transcendent message implied by the name "Ligeia" is common to all. Some critics use stronger language than "transcendent": magical, or occult. In each story, a visionary sees the underlying truths of the universe. The world he sees is sentient; the human mind, which, to the enlightened, is identical with the universe, also creates the universe; and "equivalences" are real and not merely symbolic. The corpse of Rowena moves each time only after the narrator dreams of Ligeia. One can question Poe's seriousness; at least two tales in this group are also satirical. Mysticism and humor, however, are not incompatible, and Poe's other writings also suggest his commitment to "the perennial philosophy."

Secondly, the psychological connection between death, sexuality, and creativity which would be noted later by Freud is extremely explicit here. The fascination with death so evident in art and popular culture in Poe's day is doubtless unwholesome, and deserves the satire which Poe, Hawthorne, and later Twain directed against it. It is, we should note, no stronger in Poe than in other artists of the time: how many sopranos expire gracefully, belting out da capo *arias, in operas of the period? It is perhaps a sign of health that the artistic credo which Poe enunciated in "The Philosophy of Composition" now seems unsavory to us: "The death of a beautiful woman is, unquestionably, the most poetical topic in the world. . . ."*

And finally, in each tale of this sort, Poe provides an escape valve. We see the action through the eyes of narrators who are wounded, drugged, insane, terrified, or a combination of such states. We can, if we wish, read these tales as psychological studies and assume that what occurs in them is not "real," but rather the vision of a deranged intelligence. Or we can say that they reflect the belief common in folklore and occultism that the insane, drugged, or deranged can see truths inaccessible to most of us.

A note of explanation: *The paragraph located by note 6 seems important in Poe's thought. Romantic artists, reacting against the modern tendency to see artists as at best specialists in producing aesthetic artifacts, repeatedly harkened back to times when artists were also seers, prophets, visionaries, founts of truth and inspiration. So Ligeia pursues knowledge of occult religions, which exemplify such unity. The "circle of analogies" in this* *paragraph is orthodox occultism. In occult religions—the subjects of Ligeia's studies—analogies are not understood as "representing" similarities between two or more objects or ideas; rather, since the universe is one, a whole, all parts of which partake of the holy unity, they are interpreted literally. They don't* "represent," *they* "are." *The narrator is on the verge of transcendent realization. The transformations at the close of the story and the theme of the power of the will are further examples of the "linked analogies" (to use Melville's phrase) which underlie all creation and ideality. See "The Power of Words" for an unusually clear exposition of Poe's use of occult beliefs.*

Mabbott (9, II) suggests two important sources for "Ligeia"—Scott's Ivanhoe, *whose hero has two wives, the first accused of witchcraft, the second, a blond named Rowena; and Dickens's* Pickwick Papers, *which, in Chapter Eleven contains a number of parallels.*

PUBLICATIONS IN POE'S TIME

See note 8.
American Museum, September 1838
Tales of the Grotesque and Arabesque, 1840
New World, February 15, 1845 (with the poem included for the first time [Stovall 2])
The Broadway Journal, September 27, 1845

LIGEIA[1]

> *And the will therein lieth, which dieth not. Who knoweth the mysteries of the will, with its vigor? For God is but a great will pervading all things by nature of its intentness. Man doth not yield himself to the angels, nor unto death utterly, save only through the weakness of his feeble will.*
>
> Joseph Glanvill.[2]

I cannot, for my soul, remember how, when, or even precisely where, I first became acquainted with the lady Ligeia. Long years have since elapsed, and my

[1]For the meaning of the name, see our headnote.

[2]Scholars have failed to find this passage in the writings of Joseph Glanvill (1636–80). Poe's choice of Glanvill is apt, however. Though he is best remembered in the literary histories for his philosophical skepticism and for his contribution to modernizing and simplifying English prose style, Carlson (2) speaks of his "intuitional idealism and cabalism." This is, in fact, an occult story, if we are to take seriously Ligeia's study of mystic texts, the doctrine of the "will," and the final transformation.

memory is feeble through much suffering. Or, perhaps, I cannot *now* bring these points to mind, because, in truth, the character of my beloved, her rare learning, her singular yet placid cast of beauty, and the thrilling and enthralling eloquence of her low musical language, made their way into my heart by paces so steadily and stealthily progressive that they have been unnoticed and unknown. Yet I believe that I met her first and most frequently in some large, old, decaying city near the Rhine. Of her family—I have surely heard her speak. That it is of a remotely ancient date cannot be doubted. Ligeia! Ligeia! Buried in studies of a nature more than all else adapted to deaden impressions of the outward world, it is by the sweet word alone—by Ligeia—that I bring before mine eyes in fancy the image of her who is no more. And now, while I write, a recollection flashes upon me that I have *never known* the paternal name of her who was my friend and my betrothed, and who became the partner of my studies, and finally the wife of my bosom. Was it a playful charge on the part of my Ligeia? or was it a test of my strength of affection, that I should institute no inquires upon this point? or was it rather a caprice of my own—a wildly romantic offering on the shrine of the most passionate devotion? I but indistinctly recall the fact itself—what wonder that I have utterly forgotten the circumstances which originated or attended it? And, indeed, if ever that spirit which is entitled *Romance*—if ever she, the wan and the misty-winged *Ashtophet*[3] of idolatrous Egypt, presided, as they tell, over marriages ill-omened, then most surely she presided over mine.

There is one dear topic, however, on which my memory fails me not. It is the *person* of Ligeia. In stature she was tall, somewhat slender, and, in her latter days, even emaciated. I would in vain attempt to portray the majesty, the quiet ease of her demeanor, or the incomprehensible lightness and elasticity of her foot-fall. She came and departed as a shadow. I was never made aware of her entrance into my closed study save by the dear music of her low sweet voice, as she placed her marble hand upon my shoulder. In beauty of face no maiden ever equalled her. It was the radiance of an opium-dream—an airy and spirit-lifting vision more wildly divine than the phantasies which hovered about the slumbering souls of the daughters of Delos. Yet her features were not of that regular mould which we have been falsely taught to worship in the classicial labors of the heathen. "There is no exquisite beauty," says Bacon, Lord Verulam, speaking truly of all the forms and *genera* of beauty, "without some *strangeness* in the proportion." Yet, although I saw that the features of Ligeia were not of a classic regularity—although I perceived that her loveliness was indeed "exquisite," and felt that there was much of "strangeness" pervading it, yet I have tried in vain to detect the irregularity and to trace home my own perception of "the strange." I examined the contour of the lofty and pale forehead—it was faultless—how cold indeed that word when applied to a majesty so divine!—the skin rivalling the purest ivory, the commanding extent and repose, the gentle prominence of the regions above the temples; and then the raven-black, the glossy, the luxuriant and naturally-curling tresses, setting forth the full force of the Homeric epithet, "Hyacinthine!" I looked at the

[3]Poe knew *Rees's Cyclopaedia,* which identifies Ashtophet as a Sidonian goddess; she is thought to be connected with Ashtoreth, Astarte, Aphrodite, and Venus (Mabbott 9, II).

delicate outlines of the nose—and nowhere but in the graceful medallions of the Hebrews had I beheld a similar perfection. There were the same luxurious smoothness of surface, the same scarcely perceptible tendency to the aquiline, the same harmoniously curved nostrils speaking the free spirit. I regarded the sweet mouth. Here was indeed the triumph of all things heavenly—the magnificent turn of the short upper lip—the soft, voluptuous slumber of the under—the dimples which sported, and the color which spoke—the teeth glancing back, with a brilliancy almost startling, every ray of the holy light which fell upon them in her serene and placid yet most exultingly radiant of all smiles. I scrutinized the formation of the chin—and, here too, I found the gentleness of breadth, the softness and the majesty, the fullness and the spirituality, of the Greek—the contour which the god Apollo revealed but in a dream, to Cleomenes,[4] the son of the Athenian. And then I peered into the large eyes of Ligeia.

For eyes we have no models in the remotely antique. It might have been, too, that in these eyes of my beloved lay the secret to which Lord Verulam alludes. They were, I must believe, far larger than the ordinary eyes of our own race. They were even fuller than the fullest of the gazelle eyes of the tribe of the valley of Nourjahad. Yet it was only at intervals—in moments of intense excitement—that this peculiarity became more than slightly noticeable in Ligeia. And at such moments was her beauty—in my heated fancy thus it appeared perhaps—the beauty of beings either above or apart from the earth—the beauty of the fabulous Houri of the Turk. The hue of the orbs was the most brilliant of black, and, far over them, hung jetty lashes of great length. The brows, slightly irregular in outline, had the same tint. The "strangeness," however, which I found in the eyes, was of a nature distinct from the formation, or the color, or the brilliancy of the features, and must, after all, be referred to the *expression.* Ah, word of no meaning! behind whose vast latitude of mere sound we intrench our ignorance of so much of the spiritual. The expression of the eyes of Ligeia! How for long hours have I pondered upon it! How have I, through the whole of a midsummer night, struggled to fathom it! What was it—that something more profound than the well of Democritus—which lay far within the pupils of my beloved? What *was* it? I was possessed with a passion to discover. Those eyes! those large, those shining, those divine orbs! they became to me twin stars of Leda,[5] and I to them devoutest of astrologers.

---

[4]**Delos:** The Greek island in which Apollo and Artemis were supposed to have been born (Carlson 2). **"There is . . . proportion":** Poe slightly misquotes his source, Francis Bacon (1561–1626), the great English essayist. In Bacon's "Of Beauty," the line reads, "There is no excellent beauty that hath not some strangeness in the proportion." **Cleomenes:** The supposed Greek sculptor of the Venus of Medici. Carlson (2) reports that the dream sent by Apollo is not part of Greek myth; apparently Poe made it up.

[5]**Nourjahad:** "An allusion to Francis Sheridan's *The History of Nourjahad,* an oriental novel" (Carlson 2). Our reading of the novel, however, failed to reveal any "gazelle eyes." Poe might have had the *Arabian Nights* in mind; gazelle eyes are mentioned there. **Houri:** In Muslim belief, those who attain Paradise enjoy the favors of beautiful young virgins called "houri." **the well of Democritus:** Poe's frequent allusions to this well are actually to a proverbial saying attributed to Democritus and current in many renderings by different authors. Democritus actually said, "Of a truth we know nothing, for truth is in an abyss" (ἐν

There is no point, among the many incomprehensible anomalies of the science of mind, more thrillingly exciting than the fact—never, I believe, noticed in the schools—that in our endeavors to recall to memory something long forgotten, we often find ourselves *upon the very verge* of remembrance, without being able, in the end, to remember. And thus how frequently, in my intense scrutiny of Ligeia's eyes, have I felt approaching the full knowledge of their expression—felt it approaching—yet not quite be mine—and so at length entirely depart! And (strange, oh strangest mystery of all!) I found, in the commonest objects of the universe, a circle of analogies to that expression. I mean to say that, subsequently to the period when Ligeia's beauty passed into my spirit, there dwelling as in a shrine, I derived, from many existences in the material world, a sentiment such as I felt always aroused, within me, by her large and luminous orbs. Yet not the more could I define that sentiment, or analyze, or even steadily view it. I recognized it, let me repeat, sometimes in the survey of a rapidly growing vine—in the contemplation of a moth, a butterfly, a chrysalis, a stream of running water. I have felt it in the ocean; in the falling of a meteor. I have felt it in the glances of unusually aged people. And there are one or two stars in heaven—(one especially, a star of the sixth magnitude, double and changeable, to be found near the large star in Lyra) in a telescopic scrutiny of which I have been made aware of the feeling.[6] I have been filled with it by certain sounds from stringed instruments, and not unfrequently by passages from books. Among innumerable other instances, I well remember something in a volume of Joseph Glanvill, which (perhaps from its quaintness—who shall say?) never failed to inspire me with the sentiment;—"And the will therein lieth, which dieth not. Who knoweth the mysteries of the will, with its vigor? For God is but a great will pervading all things by nature of its intentness. Man doth not yield him to the angels, nor unto death utterly, save only through the weakness of his feeble will."

Length of years, and subsequent reflection, have enabled me to trace, indeed, some remote connection between this passage in the English moralist and a portion of the character of Ligeia. An *intensity* in thought, action, or speech, was possibly, in her, a result, or at least an index, of that gigantic volition which, during our long intercourse, failed to give other and more immediate evidence of its existence. Of all the women whom I have ever known, she, the outwardly calm, the ever-placid Ligeia, was the most violently a prey to the tumultuous vultures of stern passion. And of such passion I could form no estimate, save by the miraculous expansion of those eyes which at once so delighted and appalled me—by the almost magical melody, modulation, distinctness, and placidity of her very

---

βύθῳ). Since Poe had Bacon in mind as he wrote this tale (see note 4, above), he was probably reminded of the saying by Bacon's version, "The truth of nature lieth hid in certain deep mines and caves." Regarding Democritus see "A Descent into the Maelström," note 1. **Leda:** In Greek legend, the wife of Tyndareus, King of Sparta, and the mother of Clytemnestra. In one legend, Zeus, in the form of a swan, fathered Helen (in one egg) and Castor and Pollux (in another) by her.

[6]See "A note of explanation" in our headnote. **Lyra:** A constellation, "the Lyre" or "the Harp." "The bright star in Lyra . . . is Vega. The changeable star . . . is Epsilon Lyra" (Mabbott 9, II).

low voice—and by the fierce energy (rendered doubly effective by contrast with her manner of utterance) of the wild words which she habitually uttered.

I have spoken of the learning of Ligeia; it was immense—such as I have never known in woman. In the classical tongues was she deeply proficient, and as far as my own acquaintance extended in regard to the modern dialects of Europe, I have never known her at fault. Indeed upon any theme of the most admired, because simply the most abstruse of the boasted erudition of the academy, have I *ever* found Ligeia at fault? How singularly—how thrillingly, this one point in the nature of my wife has forced itself, at this late period only, upon my attention! I said her knowledge was such as I have never known in woman—but where breathes the man who has traversed, and successfully, *all* the wide areas of moral, physical, and mathematical science? I saw not then what I now clearly perceive, that the acquisitions of Ligeia were gigantic, were astounding; yet I was sufficiently aware of her infinite supremacy to resign myself, with a child-like confidence, to her guidance through the chaotic world of metaphysical investigation at which I was most busily occupied during the earlier years of our marriage. With how vast a triumph—with how vivid a delight—with how much of all that is ethereal in hope—did I *feel,* as she bent over me in studies but little sought—but less known—that delicious vista by slow degrees expanding before me, down whose long, gorgeous, and all untrodden path, I might at length pass onward to the goal of a wisdom too divinely precious not to be forbidden.

How poignant, then, must have been the grief with which, after some years, I beheld my well-grounded expectations take wings to themselves and fly away! Without Ligeia I was but as a child groping benighted. Her presence, her readings alone, rendered vividly luminous the many mysteries of the transcendentalism in which we were immersed. Wanting the radiant lustre of her eyes, letters, lambent and golden, grew duller than Saturnian lead. And now those eyes shone less and less frequently upon the pages over which I pored. Ligeia grew ill. The wild eyes blazed with a too—too glorious effulgence; the pale fingers became of the transparent waxen hue of the grave; and the blue veins upon the lofty forehead swelled and sank impetuously with the tides of the most gentle emotion. I saw that she must die—and I struggled desperately in spirit with the grim Azrael.[7] And the struggles of the passionate wife were, to my astonishment, even more energetic than my own. There had been much in her stern nature to impress me with the belief that, to her, death would have come without its terrors; but not so. Words are impotent to convey any just idea of the fierceness of resistance with which she wrestled with the Shadow. I groaned in anguish at the pitiable spectacle. I would have soothed—I would have reasoned; but, in the intensity of her wild desire for life,—for life—*but* for life—solace and reason were alike the uttermost of folly.

---

[7]Saturnus is the alchemical name for lead. Alchemy, usually described simply as the primitive precursor of modern chemistry, or as a persistently foolish effort to transmute lead into gold, was, in point of fact, an occult discipline in which the "transmutations" were intended to bring the practitioner into transcendent illumination. Mabbott (9, II) adds that "Saturnia" is Virgil's poetic name for Italy, and that Italian lead is graphite, dull stuff indeed. **Azrael:** The angel of death.

Yet not until the last instance, amid the most convulsive writhings of her fierce spirit, was shaken the external placidity of her demeanor. Her voice grew more gentle—grew more low—yet I would not wish to dwell upon the wild meaning of the quietly uttered words. My brain reeled as I hearkened entranced, to a melody more than mortal—to assumptions and aspirations which mortality had never before known.

That she loved me I should not have doubted; and I might have been easily aware that, in a bosom such as hers, love would have reigned no ordinary passion. But in death only was I fully impressed with the strength of her affection. For long hours, detaining my hand, would she pour out before me the overflowing of a heart whose more than passionate devotion amounted to idolatry. How had I deserved to be so blessed by such confessions?—how had I deserved to be so cursed with the removal of my beloved in the hour of her making them? But upon this subject I cannot bear to dilate. Let me say only, that in Ligeia's more than womanly abandonment to a love, alas! all unmerited, all unworthily bestowed, I at length recognized the principle of her longing with so wildly earnest a desire for the life which was now fleeting so rapidly away. It is this wild longing—it is this eager vehemence of desire for life—*but* for life—that I have no power to portray—no utterance capable of expressing.

At high noon of the night in which she departed, beckoning me, peremptorily, to her side, she bade me repeat certain verses composed by herself not many days before. I obeyed her.—They were these:

Lo! 'tis a gala night
Within the lonesome latter years!
An angel throng, bewinged, bedight
In veils, and drowned in tears,
Sit in a theatre, to see
A play of hopes and fears,
While the orchestra breathes fitfully
The music of the spheres.

Mimes, in the form of God on high,
Mutter and mumble low,
And hither and thither fly—
Mere puppets they, who come and go
At bidding of vast formless things
That shift the scenery to and fro,
Flapping from out their Condor wings
Invisible Wo!

That motley drama!—oh, be sure
It shall not be forgot!
With its Phantom chased forever more,
By a crowd that seize it not,
Through a circle that ever returneth in
To the self-same spot,
And much of Madness and more of Sin
And Horror the soul of the plot.

But see, amid the mimic rout,
A crawling shape intrude!
A blood-red thing that writhes from out
The scenic solitude!
It writhes!—it writhes!—with mortal pangs
The mimes become its food,
And the seraphs sob at vermin fangs
In human gore imbued.

Out—out are the lights—out all!
And over each quivering form,
The curtain, a funeral pall,
Comes down with the rush of a storm,
And the angels, all pallid and wan,
Uprising, unveiling, affirm
That the play is the tragedy, "Man,"
And its hero the Conqueror Worm.[8]

"O God!" half shrieked Ligeia, leaping to her feet and extending her arms aloft with a spasmodic movement, as I made an end of these lines—"O God! O Divine Father!—shall these things be undeviatingly so?—shall this Conqueror be not once conquered? Are we not part and parcel in Thee? Who—who knoweth the mysteries of the will with its vigor? Man doth not yield him to the angels, *nor unto death utterly,* save only through the weakness of his feeble will."

And now, as if exhausted with emotion, she suffered her white arms to fall, and returned solemnly to her bed of death. And as she breathed her last sighs, there came mingled with them a low murmur from her lips. I bent to them my ear, and distinguished, again, the concluding words of the passage in Glanvill—"*Man doth not yield him to the angels, nor unto death utterly, save only through the weakness of his feeble will.*"

She died;—and I, crushed into the very dust with sorrow, could no longer endure the lonely desolation of my dwelling in the dim and decaying city by the Rhine. I had no lack of what the world calls wealth. Ligeia had brought me far more, very far more than ordinarily falls to the lot of mortals. After a few months, therefore, of weary and aimless wandering, I purchased, and put in some repair, an abbey, which I shall not name, in one of the wildest and least frequented portions of fair England. The gloomy and dreary grandeur of the building, the almost savage aspect of the domain, the many melancholy and time-honored memories connected with both, had much in unison with the feelings of utter abandonment which had driven me into that remote and unsocial region of the country. Yet although the external abbey, with its verdant decay hanging about it, suffered but little alteration, I gave way, with a child-like perversity, and perchance with a faint hope of alleviating my sorrows, to a display of more than regal magnificence within. For such follies, even in childhood, I had imbibed a taste, and now they came back to me as if in the dotage of grief. Alas, I feel how much even of incipient madness might have been discovered in the gorgeous and fantastic

[8]Poe first published this poem separately in *Graham's Magazine,* January 1843.

draperies, in the solemn carvings of Egypt, in the wild cornices and furniture, in the Bedlam patterns of the carpets of tufted gold! I had become a bounden slave in the trammels of opium, and my labors and orders had taken a coloring from my dreams.[9] But these absurdities I must have pause to detail. Let me speak only of that one chamber, ever accursed, whither, in a moment of mental alienation, I led from the altar as my bride—as the successor of the unforgotten Ligeia—the fair-haired and blue-eyed Lady Rowena Trevanion, of Tremaine.

There is no individual portion of the architecture and decoration of that bridal chamber which is not now visibly before me. Where were the souls of the haughty family of the bride, when, through thirst of gold, they permitted to pass the threshold of an apartment *so* bedecked, a maiden and a daughter so beloved? I have said that I minutely remember the details of the chamber—yet I am sadly forgetful on topics of deep moment—and here there was no system, no keeping, in the fantastic display, to take hold upon the memory. The room lay in a high turret of the castellated abbey, was pentagonal in shape, and of capacious size. Occupying the whole southern face of the pentagon was the sole window—an immense sheet of unbroken glass from Venice—a single pane, and tinted of a leaden hue, so that the rays of either the sun or moon, passing through it, fell with a ghastly lustre on the objects within. Over the upper portion of this huge window, extended the trellis-work of an aged vine, which clambered up the massy walls of the turret. The ceiling, of gloomy-looking oak, was excessively lofty, vaulted, and elaborately fretted with the wildest and most grotesque specimens of a semi-Gothic, semi-Druidical device. From out the most central recess of this melancholy vaulting, depended, by a single chain of gold with long links, a huge censer of the same metal, Saracenic[10] in pattern, and with many perforations so contrived that there writhed in and out of them, as if endued with a serpent vitality, a continual succession of parti-colored fires.

Some few ottomans and golden candelabra, of Eastern figure, were in various stations about—and there was the couch, too—the bridal couch—of an Indian model, and low, and sculptured of solid ebony, with a pall-like canopy above. In each of the angles of the chamber stood on end a gigantic sarcophagus of black granite, from the tombs of the kings over against Luxor, with their aged lids full of immemorial sculpture. But in the draping of the apartment lay, alas! the chief phantasy of all. The lofty walls, gigantic in height—even unproportionably so—were hung from summit to foot, in vast folds, with a heavy and massive-looking

---

[9]Poe frequently provided readers with an alternative "rational" way of accounting for the fantastic. In "Ligeia," the narrator's "incipient madness" and his addiction to opium provide the needed margin of credibility: all that follows may be an illusion. Note, however, that madness and drugs are traditionally believed to be routes to transcendent truth. One chooses one's own interpretation.

[10]**pentagonal:** The pentagon is the five-sided figure contained within the pentagram or pentacle, the "star of five lines" in occultism. It is part of an occult system for "getting through" to the power inherent in transcendent knowledge. See Figure 4. **semi-Gothic, semi-Druidical; Saracenic:** See "The Domain of Arnheim," notes 18 and 19.

tapestry—tapestry of a material which was found alike as a carpet on the floor, as a covering for the ottomans and the ebony bed, as a canopy for the bed and as the gorgeous volutes of the curtains which partially shaded the window. The material was the richest cloth of gold. It was spotted all over, at irregular intervals, with arabesque figures, about a foot in diameter, and wrought upon the cloth in patterns of the most jetty black. But these figures partook of the true character of the arabesque only when regarded from a single point of view. By a contrivance now common, and indeed traceable to a very remote period of antiquity, they were made changeable in aspect. To one entering the room, they bore the appearance of simple monstrosities; but upon a farther advance, this appearance gradually departed; and step by step, as the visitor moved his station in the chamber, he saw himself surrounded by an endless succession of the ghastly forms which belong to the superstition of the Norman, or arise in the guilty slumbers of the monk. The phantasmagoric effect was vastly heightened by the artificial introduction of a strong continual current of wind behind the draperies—giving a hideous and uneasy animation to the whole.[11]

In halls such as these—in a bridal chamber such as this—I passed, with the Lady of Tremaine, the unhallowed hours of the first month of our marriage—passed them with but little disquietude. That my wife dreaded the fierce moodiness of my temper—that she shunned me and loved me but little—I could not help perceiving; but it gave me rather pleasure than otherwise. I loathed her with a hatred belonging more to demon than to man. My memory flew back (oh, with what intensity of regret!) to Ligeia, the beloved, the august, the beautiful, the entombed. I revelled in recollections of her purity, of her wisdom, of her lofty, her ethereal nature, of her passionate, her idolatrous love. Now, then, did my spirit fully and freely burn with more than all the fires of her own. In the excitement of my opium dreams (for I was habitually fettered in the shackles of the drug) I would call aloud upon her name, during the silence of the night, or among the

Figure 4. Pentagon and Pentacle. The shaded area is the pentagon.

[11]The bridal chamber merges the black and dark imagery connected with Ligeia with the gold imagery connected with Rowena (who is purchased from her parents). Griffith argues that Poe's real intention in the tale is satirical, and that his targets are the two schools of romantic transcendentalism, German (Ligeia and the dark imagery) and English (Rowena and the gold). It is also possible that Poe's whimsy is operating. "Ebony" was the insiders' code word for William Blackwood, proprietor of *Blackwood's Edinburgh Magazine.* "Sculptured of solid ebony" might well mean "This story is made of pure *Blackwood's* material." See "A note of explanation" to "The Man of the Crowd." See also "How to Write a Blackwood Article" and "A Predicament" in which Poe satirizes the pet topics of *Blackwood's* fiction writers.

sheltered recesses of the glens by day, as if, through the wild eagerness, the solemn passion, the consuming ardor of my longing for the departed, I could restore her to the pathways she had abandoned—ah, *could* it be forever?—upon the earth.

About the commencement of the second month of the marriage, the Lady Rowena was attacked with sudden illness, from which her recovery was slow. The fever which consumed her rendered her nights uneasy; and in her perturbed state of half-slumber, she spoke of sounds, and of motions, in and above the chamber of the turret, which I concluded had no origin save in the distemper of her fancy, or perhaps in the phantasmagoric influences of the chamber itself. She became at length convalescent—finally well. Yet but a brief period elapsed, ere a second more violent disorder again threw her upon a bed of suffering; and from this attack her frame, at all times feeble, never altogether recovered. Her illnesses were, after this epoch, of alarming character, and of more alarming recurrence, defying alike the knowledge and the great exertions of her physicians. With the increase of the chronic disease which had thus, apparently, taken too sure hold upon her constitution to be eradicated by human means, I could not fail to observe a similar increase in the nervous irritation of her temperament, and in her excitability by trivial causes of fear. She spoke again, and now more frequently and pertinaciously, of the sounds—of the slight sounds—and of the unusual motions among the tapestries, to which she had formerly alluded.

One night, near the closing in of September, she pressed this distressing subject with more than usual emphasis upon my attention. She had just awakened from an unquiet slumber, and I had been watching, with feelings half of anxiety, half of vague terror, the workings of her emaciated countenance. I sat by the side of her ebony bed, upon one of the ottomans of India. She partly arose, and spoke, in an earnest low whisper, of sounds which she *then* heard, but which I could not hear—of motions which she *then* saw, but which I could not perceive. The wind was rushing hurriedly behind the tapestries, and I wished to show her (what, let me confess it, I could not *all* believe) that those almost inarticulate breathings, and those very gentle variations of the figures upon the wall, were but the natural effects of that customary rushing of the wind. But a deadly pallor, overspreading her face, had proved to me that my exertions to reassure her would be fruitless. She appeared to be fainting, and no attendants were within call. I remembered where was deposited a decanter of light wine which had been ordered by her physicians, and hastened across the chamber to procure it. But, as I stepped beneath the light of the censer, two circumstances of a startling nature attracted my attention. I had felt that some palpable although invisible object had passed lightly by my person; and I saw that there lay upon the golden carpet, in the very middle of the rich lustre thrown from the censer, a shadow—a faint, indefinite shadow of angelic aspect—such as might be fancied for the shadow of a shade. But I was wild with the excitement of an immoderate dose of opium, and heeded these things but little, nor spoke of them to Rowena. Having found the wine, I recrossed the chamber, and poured out a goblet-ful, which I held to the lips of the fainting lady. She had now partially recovered, however, and took the vessel herself, while I sank upon an ottoman near me, with my eyes fastened upon her person. It was then that I became distinctly aware of a gentle footfall upon the carpet, and near the couch; and in a second thereafter, as Rowena was in the act of raising the wine to her lips, I saw, or may have dreamed that I saw, fall within the goblet, as if from some invisible spring in the atmosphere of the room, three or four large drops of a brilliant and ruby colored fluid.[12] If this I saw—not so Rowena. She swallowed the wine unhesitatingly, and I forbore to speak to her of a circumstance which must, after all, I considered, have been but the suggestion of a vivid imagination, rendered morbidly active by the terror of the lady, by the opium, and by the hour.

Yet I cannot conceal it from my own perception that, immediately subsequent to the fall of the ruby-drops, a rapid change for the worse took place in the disorder of my wife; so that, on the third subsequent night, the hands of her menials prepared her for the tomb, and on the fourth, I sat alone, with her shrouded body, in that fantastic chamber which had received her as my bride. Wild visions, opium-engendered, flitted, shadowlike, before me. I gazed with unquiet eye upon the sarcophagi in the angles of the room,[13] upon the varying figures of the drapery, and upon the writhing of the parti-colored fires in the censer overhead. My eyes then fell, as I called to mind the circumstances of a former night, to the spot beneath the glare of the censer where I had seen the faint traces of the shadow. It was there, however, no longer; and breathing with greater freedom, I turned my glances to the pallid and rigid figure upon the bed. Then rushed upon me a thousand memories of Ligeia—and then came back upon my heart, with the turbulent violence of a flood, the whole of that unutterable wo with which I had regarded *her* thus enshrouded. The night waned; and still, with a bosom full of bitter thoughts of the one only and supremely beloved, I remained gazing upon the body of Rowena.

It might have been midnight, or perhaps earlier, or later, for I had taken no note of time, when a sob, low, gentle, but very distinct, startled me from my revery. I *felt* that it came from the bed of ebony—the bed of death. I listened in an agony of superstitious terror—but there was no repetition of the sound. I strained my vision to detect any motion in the corpse—but there was not the slightest perceptible. Yet I could not have been deceived. I *had* heard the noise, however faint, and my soul was awakened within me. I resolutely and perseveringly kept my attention riveted upon the body. Many minutes elapsed before any circumstance occurred tending to throw light upon the mystery. At length it became evident that a slight, a very feeble, and barely noticeable tinge of color had flushed up within the cheeks, and along the sunken small veins of the eyelids. Through a species of unutterable horror and awe, for which the language of mortality has no sufficiently energetic

---

[12]One critic suggests that in reality the narrator poisons Rowena's wine, deluding himself, in his drugged state, into believing in spiritual intervention and the transformation which ends the tale.

[13]The association between sexuality and death is a favorite theme for Freudian critics. Their theory, briefly, is that in prudish ages, there takes place an imaginative substitution of death for sex. Hence the female corpses in bridal dress laid out upon their wedding beds, and, in this tale, the deathly bridal chamber.

expression, I felt my heart cease to beat, my limbs grow rigid where I sat. Yet a sense of duty finally operated to restore my self-possession. I could no longer doubt that we had been precipitate in our preparations—that Rowena still lived. It was necessary that some immediate exertion be made; yet the turret was altogether apart from the portion of the abbey tenanted by the servants—there were none within call—I had no means of summoning them to my aid without leaving the room for many minutes—and this I could not venture to do. I therefore struggled alone in my endeavors to call back the spirit still hovering. In a short period it was certain, however, that a relapse had taken place; the color disappeared from both eyelid and cheek, leaving a wanness even more than that of marble; the lips became doubly shrivelled and pinched up in the ghastly expression of death; a repulsive clamminess and coldness overspread rapidly the surface of the body; and all the usual rigorous stiffness immediately supervened. I fell back with a shudder upon the couch from which I had been so startlingly aroused, and again gave myself up to passionate waking visions of Ligeia.

An hour thus elapsed when (could it be possible?) I was a second time aware of some vague sound issuing from the region of the bed. I listened—in extremity of horror. The sound came again—it was a sigh. Rushing to the corpse, I saw—distinctly saw—a tremor upon the lips. In a minute afterward they relaxed, disclosing a bright line of the pearly teeth. Amazement now struggled in my bosom with the profound awe which had hitherto reigned there alone. I felt that my vision grew dim, that my reason wandered; and it was only by a violent effort that I at length succeeded in nerving myself to the task which duty thus once more had pointed out. There as now a partial glow upon the forehead and upon the cheek and throat; a perceptible warmth pervaded the whole frame; there was even a light pulsation at the heart. The lady *lived;* and with redoubled ardor I betook myself to the task of restoration. I chafed and bathed the temples and the hands, and used every exertion which experience, and no little medical reading, could suggest. But in vain. Suddenly, the color fled, the pulsation ceased, the lips resumed the expression of the dead, and, in an instant afterward, the whole body took upon itself the icy chilliness, the livid hue, the intense rigidity, the sunken outline, and all the loathsome peculiarities of that which has been, for many days, a tenant of the tomb.

And again I sunk into visions of Ligeia—and again, (what marvel that I shudder while I write?) *again* there reached my ears a low sob from the region of the ebony bed. But why shall I minutely detail the unspeakable horrors of that night? Why shall I pause to relate how, time after time, until near the period of the gray dawn, this hideous drama of revivification was repeated; how each terrific relapse was only into a sterner and apparently more irredeemable death; how each agony wore the aspect of a struggle with some invisible foe; and how each struggle was succeeded by I know not what of wild change in the personal appearance of the corpse? Let me hurry to a conclusion.

The greater part of the fearful night had worn away, and she who had been dead once against stirred—and now more vigorously than hitherto, although arousing from a dissolution more appalling in its utter hopelessness than any. I had long ceased to struggle or to move, and remained sitting rigidly upon the ottoman, a helpless prey to a whirl of violent emotions, of which extreme awe was perhaps the least terrible, the least consuming. The corpse, I repeat, stirred, and now more vigorously than before. The hues of life flushed up with unwonted energy into the countenance—the limbs relaxed—and, save that the eyelids were yet pressed heavily together, and that the bandages and draperies of the grave still imparted their charnel character to the figure, I might have dreamed that Rowena had indeed shaken off, utterly, the fetters of Death. But if this idea was not, even then, altogether adopted, I could at least doubt no longer, when, arising from the bed, tottering, with feeble steps, with closed eyes, and with the manner of one bewildered in a dream, the thing that was enshrouded advanced boldly and palpably into the middle of the apartment.

I trembled not—I stirred not—for a crowd of unutterable fancies connected with the air, the stature, the demeanor of the figure, rushing hurriedly through my brain, had paralyzed—had chilled me into stone. I stirred not—but gazed upon the apparition. There was a mad disorder in my thoughts—a tumult unappeasable. Could it, indeed, be the *living* Rowena who confronted me? Could it, indeed, be Rowena *at all*—the fair-haired, the blue-eyed Lady Rowena Trevanion of Tremaine? Why, *why* should I doubt it? The bandage lay heavily about the mouth—but then might it not be the mouth of the breathing Lady of Tremaine? And the cheeks—there were the roses as in her noon of life—yes, these might indeed be the fair cheeks of the living Lady of Tremaine. And the chin, with its dimples, as in health, might it not be hers?—but *had she then grown taller since her malady?* What inexpressible madness seized me with that thought? One bound, and I had reached her feet! Shrinking from my touch, she let fall from her head, unloosened, the ghastly cerements which had confined it, and there streamed forth into the rushing atmosphere of the chamber huge masses of long and dishevelled hair; *it was blacker than the raven wings of midnight!* And now slowly opened *the eyes* of the figure which stood before me. "Here then, at least," I shrieked aloud, "can I never—can I never be mistaken—these are the full, and the black, and the wild eyes—of my lost love—of the Lady—of the LADY LIGEIA!"

How to Write a Blackwood Article

Poe writes here in an old form of literary satire which might be called "The How-to-Do-It Piece." A writer in a tight spot turns to someone more knowledgeable for advice about how to succeed in an established literary genre. Poe likely had two "How-to-Do-It" satires in mind when he wrote this burlesque of the standard practices of sensational fiction-writing—the Prologue to Part One of Cervantes's Don Quixote, *in which Cervantes has his "author" beg advice from a friend about how to deck his work out in proper literary finery, and Frederick Marryat's "How to Write a Fashionable Novel," in which a poor student author, who knows nothing of "fashionable" life, is hard pressed for time to produce a "fashionable" novel under contract, and asks* his *friend what to do. The satires are very different, but in each the friend says, in effect, "Don't worry—just remember these simple formulas and start writing."*

Such satire is funny for any reader who knows the formulas and clichés of the genres being satirized. Poe knew Blackwood's Edinburgh Magazine *very well, and greatly admired many aspects of it. But he knew also that the "intensities," the special stories of sensation which it had pioneered, had often fallen into the hands of less gifted writers than* Blackwood's *best, and that the formulas were easy to copy badly. "Mr. Blackwood's" advice to the Signora Psyche Zenobia is filled with errors and misattributions, but it is not impossibly bad advice—Poe, after all, followed it carefully himself in some of his best work. It's just that Poe, unlike Zenobia, had the skill and the erudition to make high art of the formulaic materials of then-popular periodical fiction. So "How to Write a Blackwood Article" is an important document of Poe's professional attitude toward his material. High art often results when genius comes to a commercial field of entertainment, as Shakespeare to Elizabethan popular theater, Keaton to silent film comedy, Verdi to Italian opera, or Poe to magazine fiction.*

A note of explanation: *McNeal, working on circumstantial evidence, identifies Zenobia as a caricature of Margaret Fuller, scholar, literary critic, and "leading female light" among the Transcendentalists of Boston, Cambridge, and Concord, writers at whom Poe sniped whenever the opportunity arose. Specialists are by no means certain that McNeal is right; Poe invented "Zenobia" before Fuller was famous. Our notes point out some of McNeal's evidence.* It *is interesting that when Hawthorne in 1852 wrote a novel about New England Transcendentalists, he named his female lead "Zenobia" and was so certain that readers would take her for Fuller that he inserted a careful disclaimer.*

There is no point in trying to hide Poe's offensive racism. References to blacks in his works are almost universally stereotyped, condescending, or even sneering. The suggestion that Zenobia/Margaret Fuller is in love with a black man could also be a snide—and sexist—allusion to the outspoken liberalism of most of the Transcendentalists.

Publications in Poe's Time

The American Museum of Science, Literature and the Arts, November 1838, as "The Psyche Zenobia"
Tales of the Grotesque and Arabesque, 1840, as "The Signora Zenobia"
The Broadway Journal, July 12, 1845, as "How to Write a Blackwood Article"

How to Write a Blackwood Article[1]

"In the name of the Prophet—figs!!"
Cry of the Turkish fig-peddler[2]

I presume everybody has heard of me. My name is the Signora Psyche Zenobia. This I know to be a fact. Nobody but my enemies ever calls me Suky Snobbs. I have been assured that Suky is but a vulgar corruption of Psyche, which is good Greek, and means "the soul" (That's me, I'm *all* soul) and sometimes "a butterfly," which latter meaning undoubtedly alludes to my appearance in my new crimson satin dress, with the sky-blue Arabian *mantelet,* and the trimmings of green *agraffas,* and the seven flounces of orange-colored *auriculas.* As for Snobbs—any person who should look at me would be instantly aware that my name wasn't Snobbs. Miss Tabitha Turnip propagated that report through sheer envy. Tabitha Turnip indeed! Oh the little wretch! But what can we expect from a turnip? Wonder if she remembers the old adage about "blood out of a turnip," etc.? [Mem: put her in mind of it the first opportunity.] [Mem again—pull her nose.]

[1]Poe tinkered with his title each time he revised his tale. See "Publications in Poe's Time" in our headnote.
[2]Poe took his motto from a parody of Dr. Johnson in James and Horace Smith's *Rejected Addresses:*

> He that is most assured of success will make the fewest appeals to favor, and where nothing is claimed that is undue, nothing that is due will be withheld. A swelling opening is too often succeeded by an insignificant conclusion. Parturient mountains have ere now produced muscipular abortions; and the auditor who compares incipient grandeur with final vulgarity is reminded of the pious hawkers of Constantinople, who solemnly perambulate her streets, exclaiming "In the name of the Prophet—figs." (Pollin 7; Schuster)

Where was I? Ah! I have been assured that Snobbs is a mere corruption of Zenobia, and that Zenobia was a queen—(So am I. Dr. Moneypenny always calls me the Queen of Hearts)—and that Zenobia, as well as Psyche, is a good Greek, and that my father was "a Greek,"[3] and that consequently I have a right to our patronymic, which is Zenobia, and not by any means Snobbs. Nobody but Tabitha Turnip calls me Suky Snobbs. I am the Signora Psyche Zenobia.

As I said before, everybody has heard of me. I am that very Signora Psyche Zenobia, so justly celebrated as corresponding secretary to the "*Philadelphia, Regular, Exchange, Tea, Total, Young, Belles, Lettres, Universal, Experimental, Bibliographical, Association, To, Civilize, Humanity.*" Dr. Moneypenny made the title for us, and says he chose it because it sounded big like an empty rum-puncheon. (A vulgar man that sometimes—but he's deep.) We all sign the initials of the society after our names, in the fashion of the R. S. A., Royal Society of Arts—the S. D. U. K., Society for the Diffusion of Useful Knowledge, etc., etc. Dr. Moneypenny says that S stands for *stale,* and that D. U. K. spells duck, (but it don't,) and that S. D. U. K. stands for Stale Duck, and not for Lord Brougham's society[4]—but then Dr. Moneypenny is such a queer man that I am never sure when he is telling me the truth. At any rate we always add to our names the initials P. R. E. T. T. Y. B. L. U. E. B. A. T. C. H.—that is to say, Philadelphia, Regular,

---

[3]**Zenobia:** Margaret Fuller was noted for her love of finery and for her imperious ways. Poe probably got the name Zenobia from an 1837 novel by William Ware; Queen Zenobia in the novel is not a parody of Miss Fuller, though she is " 'a true New England woman born too soon' " (McNeal quoting Van Wyck Brooks). Hawthorne's Zenobia, in *The Blithedale Romance* (1852), is unquestionably modeled loosely on Miss Fuller, whom he knew well and who, by then, had died tragically. McNeal is sure that Hawthorne knew both Ware's Zenobia and Poe's. **Suky:** Not, as Zenobia says, a corruption of Psyche, but rather a lower class nickname for Susan. Its connations are vulgar. See, for instance, Gay's "The Beggars' Opera." **sky-blue . . . *mantelet:*** A mantelet is a short cloak. Poe dressed many of his absurd characters in sky-blue cloaks. In Levine (4) see "The Devil in the Belfry" and "Bon-Bon." ***agraffas:*** Ornamental clasps. Pollin (12) writes, "One suspects that he really meant colored 'aigrettes' or ornamental tufts of feathers." ***auriculas:*** Flowers of the primrose family ("bear's-ears"). Pollin (12) guesses Poe is referring to sleeves but that he "invents" his own word for the occasion. **Dr. Moneypenny:** Emerson (McNeal). **my father was "a Greek":** Miss Fuller learned Greek from her father, but McNeal thinks this points to Timothy Fuller or more likely to Bronson Alcott. She taught at Alcott's Temple School in 1837. Mabbott (9, II) says that "a Greek" has an old slang meaning of "a hard drinker, a gambler, or an Irishman." In vulgar usage, it also means "homosexual." Poe clearly meant to be insulting.

[4]**R. S. A.:** A British society founded in 1754. **S. D. U. K. and Lord Brougham:** Henry Brougham (1778–1868), political, social, and educational reformer, long connected with *The Edinburgh Review.* His famous defense of J. and J. L. Hunt on a libel charge for an article on military flogging they wrote in 1811 for the *Examiner* (see note 6) probably connected him and the *Examiner* in Poe's mind. In 1825, as part of his large-scale reform and educational activities, Brougham established the Society for the Diffusion of Useful Knowledge to provide cheap and useful publications on useful topics; he wrote the first volume himself in 1827. Also see "The Literary Life of Thingum Bob, Esq.," and "The System of Dr. Tarr and Prof. Fether" in Levine (4).

Exchange, Tea, Total, Young, Belles, Lettres, Universal, Experimental, Bibliographical, Association, To, Civilize, Humanity—one letter for each word, which is a decided improvement upon Lord Brougham. Dr. Moneypenny will have it that our initials give our true character—but for my life I can't see what he means.

Notwithstanding the good offices of the Doctor, and the strenuous exertions of the association to get itself into notice, it met with no very great success until I joined it. The truth is, the members indulged in too flippant a tone of discussion. The papers read every Saturday evening were characterized less by depth than buffoonery. They were all whipped syllabub. There was no investigation of first causes, first principles. There was no investigation of anything at all. There was no attention paid to that great point, the "fitness of things." In short there was no fine writing like this. It was all low—very! No profundity, no reading, no metaphysics—nothing which the learned call spirituality, and which the unlearned choose to stigmatize as cant. [Dr. M. says I ought to spell "cant" with a capital K[5]—but I know better.]

When I joined the society it was my endeavor to introduce a better style of thinking and writing, and all the world knows how well I have succeeded. We get up as good papers now in the P. R. E. T. T. Y. B. L. U. E. B. A. T. C. H. as any to be found even in *Blackwood.* I say, *Blackwood,* because I have been assured that the finest writing, upon every subject, is to be discovered in the pages of that justly celebrated Magazine. We now take it for our model upon all themes, and are getting into rapid notice accordingly. And after all, it's not so very difficult a matter to compose an article of the geniune *Blackwood* stamp, if one only goes properly about it. Of course I don't speak of the political articles. Everybody knows how *they* are managed, since Dr. Moneypenny explained it. Mr. Blackwood has a pair of tailor's-shears, and three apprentices who stand by him for orders. One hands him the *Times,* another the *Examiner* and a third a "Gulley's New Compendium of Slang-Whang."[6] Mr. B. merely cuts out and intersperses. It is soon done—nothing but *Examiner,* "Slang-Whang," and *Times*—then *Times,* "Slang-Whang," and *Examiner*—and then *Times, Examiner,* and "Slang-Whang."

But the chief merit of the Magazine lies in its miscellaneous articles; and the best of these come under the head of what Dr. Moneypenny calls the *bizarreries* (whatever that may mean) and what everybody else calls the *intensities.* This is a

---

[5]**syllabub (or sillabub):** A dish made by mixing milk or cream with wine or cider, and then whipping it into a froth or boiling it until solid. **Dr. M.:** This abbreviation of Moneypenny McNeal takes as a pun on Em-erson. **"cant" . . . K:** See note 10.

[6]**"Mr. Blackwood":** William Blackwood (1776–1834) gave his name to *Blackwood's,* but here Poe uses the name in a more general sense. ***Times:*** The most distinguished London paper of this period. ***Examiner:*** See note 4, above. **Gulley:** John Gully (1783–1863) the remarkable English boxer, legislator (via a pocket borough), race-horse owner, and colliery proprietor. His humble antecedents (at 21 he was in prison for debts) are the basis for Poe's joke. So far as we know, he never wrote a book. Poe misspelled his name. **Slang-Whang:** Poe got the name from a fable in *The New York Mirror;* Slang-Whang is a Chinese editor who hits the brandy bottle, and may, indeed, be Poe himself, since the *Mirror* at the time bore him a grudge (Pollin 14). For more on his feud with the *Mirror,* see the tale "Mystification" in Levine (4).

species of writing which I have long known how to appreciate, although it is only since my late visit to Mr. Blackwood (deputed by the society) that I have been made aware of the exact method of composition. This method is very simple, but not so much so as the politics. Upon my calling at Mr. B.'s, and making known to him the wishes of the society, he received me with great civility, took me into his study, and gave me a clear explanation of the whole process.

"My dear madam," said he, evidently struck with my majestic appearance, for I had on the crimson satin, with the green *agraffas,* and orange-colored *auriculas.* "My *dear* madam," said he, "sit down. The matter stands thus: In the first place your writer of intensities must have very black ink, and a very big pen, with a very blunt nib. And, mark me, Miss Psyche Zenobia!" he continued, after a pause, with the most expressive energy and solemnity of manner, "mark me!—*that pen—must—never be mended!* Herein, madam, lies the secret, the soul, of intensity. I assume upon myself to say, that no individual, of however great genius, ever wrote with a good pen,—understand me,—a good article. You may take it for granted, that when manuscript can be read it is never worth reading. This is a leading principle in our faith, to which if you cannot readily assent, our conference is at an end."

He paused. But, of course, as I had no wish to put an end to the conference, I assented to a proposition so very obvious, and one, too, of whose truth I had all along been sufficiently aware. He seemed pleased, and went on with his instructions.

"It may appear invidious in me, Miss Psyche Zenobia, to refer you to an article, or set of articles, in the way of model or study; yet perhaps I may as well call your attention to a few cases. Let me see. There was '*The Dead Alive,*' a capital thing!—the record of a gentleman's sensations when entombed before the breath was out of his body—full of taste, terror, sentiment, metaphysics, and erudition. You would have sworn that the writer had been born and brought up in a coffin. Then we had the '*Confessions of an Opium-eater*'—fine, very fine!—acute speculation—plenty of fire and fury, and a good spicing of the decidedly unintelligible. That was a nice bit of flummery, and went down the throats of the people delightfully. They would have it that Coleridge wrote the paper—but not so. It was composed by my pet baboon, Juniper, over a rummer of Hollands and water, 'hot, without sugar.'" [This I could scarcely have believed had it been anybody but Mr. Blackwood, who assured me of it.] "Then there was '*The Involuntary Experimentalist,*' all about a gentleman who got baked in an oven, and came out alive and well, although certainly done to a turn. And then there was '*The Diary of a Late Physician,*' where the merit lay in good rant, and indifferent Greek—both of them taking things with the public. And then there was '*The Man in the Bell,*'[7] a

---

[7]**"The Dead Alive":** A tale by this name appeared in *Fraser's Magazine,* IX (1833), 411. "Mr. Blackwood's" outline, however, is of a *Blackwood's* piece called "The Buried Alive," which Mabbott (9, II) located in an 1821 issue. **"Confessions of an Opium-eater":** *The Confessions of an English Opium-Eater* (1822) by Thomas De Quincey (1785–1859), actually published first not in *Blackwood's* (though De Quincey had been connected with that journal), but rather in *The London Magazine* for September and October of 1821.

paper by-the-by, Miss Zenobia, which I cannot sufficiently recommend to your attention. It is the history of a young person who goes to sleep under the clapper of a church bell, and is awakened by its tolling for a funeral. The sound drives him mad, and, accordingly, pulling out his tablets, he gives a record of his sensations. Sensations are the great things after all. Should you ever be drowned or hung, be sure and make a note of your sensations—they will be worth to you ten guineas a sheet. If you wish to write forcibly, Miss Zenobia, pay minute attention to the sensations."

"That I certainly will, Mr. Blackwood," said I.

"Good!" he replied. "I see you are a pupil after my own heart. But I must put you *au fait* to[8] the details necessary in composing what may be denominated a genuine *Blackwood* article of the sensation stamp—the kind which you will understand me to say I consider the best for all purposes.

"The first thing requisite is to get yourself into such a scrape as no one ever got into before. The oven, for instance,—that was a good hit. But if you have no oven, or big bell, at hand, and if you cannot conveniently tumble out of a balloon, or be swallowed up in an earthquake, or get stuck fast in a chimney, you will have to be contented with simply imagining some similar adventure. I should prefer, however, that you have the actual fact to bear you out. Nothing so well assists the fancy, as an experimental knowledge of the matter in hand. 'Truth is strange,' you know, 'stranger than fiction'—besides being more to the purpose."

Here I assured him I had an excellent pair of garters, and would go and hang myself forthwith.

"Good!" he replied, "do so;—although hanging is somewhat hackneyed. Perhaps you might do better. Take a dose of Brandreth's pills,[9] and then give us your sensations. However, my instructions will apply equally well to any variety of misadventure, and on your way home you may easily get knocked in the head, or run over by an omnibus, or bitten by a mad dog, or drowned in a gutter. But to proceed.

"Having determined upon your subject, you must next consider the tone, or manner, of your narration. There is the tone didactic, the tone enthusiastic, the tone natural—all commonplace enough. But then there is the tone laconic, or curt, which has lately come much into use. It consists in short sentences. Somehow

---

Coleridge wrote the paper: De Quincey published *Confessions* anonymously, but the secret was not well kept. **rummer:** A glass or cup, generally a tall glass without a stem; it can also mean what's in the glass. **Hollands:** A variety of gin, made by adding the juniper to the mash instead of to the distilled spirits. **"The Involuntary Experimentalist":** A piece about "a physician who falls into a large cauldron at a burning brewery and describes his sensations as the walls begin to glow" (Pollin 12). **"The Diary of a Late Physician":** Samuel Warren (1807–77) published in *Blackwood's* a number of short stories, later printed in book form as *Passages from the Diary of a Late Physician* (1838). **"The Man in the Bell":** A work by William Maginn, a member of *Blackwood's* team of writers.

[8]**put you *au fait* to:** Inform you of. Poe is probably making a joke on the use of French in the works of American and British authors of his day with this strange construction.

[9]See "Some Words with a Mummy," note 26.

thus: Can't be too brief. Can't be too snappish. Always a full stop. And never a paragraph.

"Then there is the tone elevated, diffusive, and interjectional. Some of our best novelists patronize this tone. The words must be all in a whirl, like a hummingtop, and make a noise very similar, which answers remarkably well instead of meaning. This is the best of all possible styles where the writer is in too great a hurry to think.

"The tone metaphysical is also a good one. If you know any big words this is your chance for them. Talk of the Ionic and Eleatic schools—of Archytas, Gorgias, and Alcmæon. Say something about objectivity and subjectivity. Be sure and abuse a man called Locke. Turn up your nose at things in general, and when you let slip any thing a little *too* absurd, you need not be at the trouble of scratching it out, but just add a foot-note and say that you are indebted for the above profound observation to the '*Kritik der reinen Vernunft,*' or to the '*Metaphysische Anfangsgründe der Naturwissenschaft.*'[10] This will look erudite and—and—and frank.

"There are various other tones of equal celebrity, but I shall mention only two more—the tone transcendental and the tone heterogeneous. In the former the merit consists in seeing into the nature of affairs a very great deal farther than anybody else. This second sight is very efficient when properly managed. A little reading of the *Dial* will carry you a great way. Eschew, in this case, big words; get them as small as possible, and write them upside down. Look over Channing's poems and quote what he says about a 'fat little man with a delusive show of Can.'[11] Put in something about the Supernal Oneness. Don't say a syllable about

---

[10]**Ionic:** Founded by Thales of Miletus in Asiatic Ionia, it was the first of the ancient sects of philosophers. **Eleatic:** The Eleatic philosophers were attractive to romantic authors because of their belief in the universal unity underlying creation. See Mr. Blackwood's comments below about "the Supernal Oneness." **Archytas:** Eminent Greek philosopher of the Pythagorean sect, a mathematician and general who lived about 350 B.C.E. **Gorgias:** Sicilian orator and sophist of the fifth century B.C.E.; a character in one of Plato's dialogues. **Alcmæon:** A natural philosopher, native of Croton, who lived in the sixth century B.C.E. and was a pupil of Pythagoras. **Locke:** John Locke, 1632–1704, the rationalist British philosopher. ***Kritik der reinen Vernunft:*** *Critique of Pure Reason* (1781) by the German philosopher Immanuel Kant (1724–1804). ***Metaphysische Anfangsgründe der Naturwissenschaft:*** *Metaphysical Foundations of Natural Science* (1786), also by Kant. If critics are correct in assuming that Poe knew little German, it is very doubtful that Poe had read this work; an English translation did not appear until long after his death.

[11]***Dial:*** *The Dial* was the journal of the Concord Transcendentalists, and Margaret Fuller became, in 1840, its first editor. This paragraph and the one above are substantially new: Poe added them for the 1845 version of his story. See also "Never Bet the Devil Your Head" in Levine (4). **Channing:** Poe had written for *Graham's Magazine* in August 1843 a wickedly scathing attack on William Ellery Channing (II)'s newly published *Poems.* Channing (1818–1901) was the nephew of William Ellery Channing, the admired essayist of Emerson's group. McNeal points out that to make matters worse, Channing was by the time of Poe's last publication of "How to Write a Blackwood Article" Margaret Fuller's brother-in-law, and Emerson, in an article in the October 1840 *Dial,* had found some encouraging

the Infernal Twoness. Above all, study innuendo. Hint everything—assert nothing. If you feel inclined to say 'bread and butter,' do not by any means say it outright. You may say any thing and every thing *approaching* to 'bread and butter.' You may hint at buck-wheat cake, or you may even go so far as to insinuate oat-meal porridge, but if bread and butter be your real meaning, be cautious, my *dear* Miss Psyche, not on any account to say 'bread and butter'!"

I assured him that I should never say it again as long as I lived. He kissed me and continued:

"As for the tone heterogeneous, it is merely a judicious mixture, in equal proportions, of all the other tones in the world, and is consequently made up of every thing deep, great, odd, piquant, pertinent, and pretty.

"Let us suppose now you have determined upon your incidents and tone. The most important portion—in fact, the soul of the whole business, is yet to be attended to,—I allude to *the filling up.* It is not to be supposed that a lady, or gentleman either, has been leading the life of a book-worm. And yet above all things it is necessary that your article have an air of erudition, or at least afford evidence of extensive general reading. Now I'll put you in the way of accomplishing this point. See here!" (pulling down some three or four ordinary-looking volumes, and opening them at random). "By casting your eye down almost any page of any book in the world, you will be able to perceive at once a host of little scraps of either learning or *bel-esprit-ism,*[12] which are the very thing for the spicing of a *Blackwood* article. You might as well note down a few while I read them to you. I shall make two divisions: first, *Piquant Facts for the Manufacture of Similes;* and second, *Piquant Expressions to be introduced as occasion may require.* Write now!—" and I wrote as he dictated.

"PIQUANT FACTS FOR SIMILES. 'There were originally but three Muses—Melete, Mneme, Aœde—meditation, memory, and singing.' You may make a good deal of that little fact if properly worked. You see it is not generally known, and looks *recherché.* You must be careful and give the thing with a downright improviso air.[13]

---

things to say about young Channing's poetry. Hence Poe, who attacked Transcendentalists every chance he got, includes a gratuitous pot-shot at the unoffending amateur poet. **"fat . . . Can":** Poe misquotes the lines. In his own review, he quoted Channing:

Thou meetest a common man
With a delusive show of can.

Poe intends a pun on the vulgar slang meaning of "can." See also "The Angel of the Odd" in Levine (4).

[12]Poe adds the English ending "ism" to the French words *bel esprit,* meaning "wit" or "genius," and uses his new word in the sense of "witticism."

[13]**Melete, Mneme, Aœde:** In one account, the muses were three daughters of Zeus and Mnemosyne: Aœde (song), Melete (meditation), and Mneme (memory). ***recherché:*** Refined, studied. **improviso:** An obsolete word meaning "unforeseen" or "unexpected."

"Again. 'The river Alpheus[14] passed beneath the sea, and emerged without injury to the purity of its waters.' Rather stale that, to be sure, but, if properly dressed and dished up, will look quite as fresh as ever.

"Here is something better. 'The Persian Iris[15] appears to some persons to possess a sweet and very powerful perfume, while to others it is perfectly scentless.' Fine that, and very delicate! Turn it about a little, and it will do wonders. We'll have something else in the botanical line. There's nothing goes down so well, especially with the help of a little Latin. Write!

"'*The Epidendrum Flos Aeris,*[16] of Java, bears a very beautiful flower, and will live when pulled up by the roots. The natives suspend it by a cord from the ceiling, and enjoy its fragrance for years.' That's capital! That will do for the similes. Now for the Piquant Expressions.

"PIQUANT EXPRESSIONS. '*The Venerable Chinese novel Ju-Kiao-Li.*'[17] God! By introducing these few words with dexterity you will evince your intimate acquaintance with the language and literature of the Chinese. With the aid of this you may possibly get along without either Arabic, or Sanscrit, or Chickasaw. There is no passing muster, however, without Spanish, Italian, German, Latin, and Greek. I must look you out a little specimen of each. Any scrap will answer, because you must depend upon your own ingenuity to make it fit into your article. Now write!

"'*Aussi tendre que Zaïre*'—as tender as Zaïre—French. Alludes to the frequent repetition of the phrase, *la tendre* Zaïre, in the French tragedy of that name.[18] Properly introduced, will show not only your knowledge of the language, but your general reading and wit. You can say, for instance, that the chicken you were

---

[14]A reference to Coleridge, who writes in "Kubla Kahn,"

In Xanadu did Kubla Kahn
A stately pleasure-dome decree:
Where Alph, the sacred river, ran
Through caverns measureless to man
Down to a sunless sea.

[15]A variety of Iris called "Persian Iris" does exist. It has white upper petals and brown speckled lower petals. We have not located a reference to the peculiar qualities which Poe mentions.

[16]Pollin (12) guesses this reference came from the work by Patrick Keith cited in "Scheherazade." Varner refers us to an item in *The Philadelphia Public Ledger* for July 22, 1839, in which the "*Epidendrum* or air plant" is mentioned.

[17]*Yu Chiao Li (The Beautiful Couple),* a late-Ming Dynasty novel (whose author is unknown) which had been translated into French, German, and English in the 1820s, and discussed in a number of places (Benton 5). Pollin (12) writes: "Poe's source of information was a paper by Philip Pendleton Cooke that Poe, as editor, had published in *The Southern Literary Messenger* of April 1836, 'Leaves from My Scrap Book, Part II.' Cooke is commenting on the plagiarism from the 'Chinese novel, *Yu-Kiao-Li,*' in a motto written by E. Irving."

[18]*Zaïre* (1734), a play by François-Marie Arouet (Voltaire).

eating (write an article about being choked to death by a chicken-bone) was not altogether *aussi tendre que Zaire.* Write!

'Ven muerte tan escondida.
Que no te sienta venir,
Porque el plazer del morir,
No me torne a dar la vida.'[19]

"That's Spanish—from Miguel de Cervantes. 'Come quickly, O death! but be sure and don't let me see you coming, lest the pleasure I shall feel at your appearance should unfortunately bring me back again to life.' This you may slip in quite *à propos* when you are struggling in the last agonies with the chicken-bone. Write!

'Il pover' huomo che non sen'era accorto,
Andava combattendo, ed era morto.'[20]

"That's Italian, you perceive—from Ariosto. It means that a great hero, in the heat of combat, not perceiving that he had been fairly killed, continued to fight valiantly, dead as he was. The application of this to your own case is obvious—for I trust, Miss Psyche, that you will not neglect to kick for at least an hour and a half after you have been choked to death by that chicken-bone. Please to write!

'Und sterb'ich doch, so sterb'ich denn
Durch sie—durch sie!'[21]

"That's German—from Schiller. 'And if I die, at least I die—for thee—for thee!' Here it is clear that you are apostrophizing the *cause* of your disaster, the chicken. Indeed what gentleman (or lady either) of sense, *wouldn't* die, I should like to know, for a well fattened capon of the right Molucca breed, stuffed with capers and mushrooms, and served up in a salad-bowl, with orange-jellies *en mosaïques.* Write! (You can get them that way at Tortoni's,)[22]—Write, if you please!

---

[19]This quotation is from, but not by, Miguel de Cervantes (1547–1616): Cervantes was quoting Juan Escriva (Robbins). The lines occur in a poem which appeared in the 1511 edition of the *Cancionero* de Hernando del Castillo. Poe used the epigram elsewhere in his column "Pinakidia."

[20]The lines are from Berni's *Orlando Innamorato LIII,* 60. Poe probably became confused because of the similarity of the title of Berni's work to Ariosto's *Orlando Furioso.* This seems to be an honest mistake. The passage also occurs in Poe's "Pinakidia," where he attributes it correctly.

[21]This time Poe's error is deliberate; the lines are from Goethe (Robbins).

[22]**Molucca:** We find no mention of a variety of capon from Molucca. Pollin (12) says that Poe may have deliberately or accidentally confused Molucca with Minorca. Minorcan chickens were a delicacy. ***en mosaïques:*** In *The French Cook,* Ude includes an article on "Mosaic Jelly" (Pollin 12). **Tortoni's:** A Parisian café which has by now disappeared.

"Here is a nice little Latin phrase, and rare too (one can't be too *recherché* or brief in one's Latin, it's getting so common,)—*ignoratio elenchi.* He has committed an *ignoratio elenchi*—that is to say, he has understood the words of your proposition, but not the idea. The man was *a fool,* you see. Some poor fellow whom you addressed while choking with that chicken-bone, and who therefore didn't precisely understand what you were talking about. Throw the *ignoratio elenchi* in his teeth, and, at once, you have him annihilated. If he dares to reply, you can tell him from Lucan (here it is) that speeches are mere *anemonœ verborum,* anemone words. The anemone, with great brilliancy, has no smell. Or, if he begins to bluster, you may be down upon him with *insomnia Jovis,* reveries of Jupiter—a phrase which Silius Italicus[23] (see here!) applies to thoughts pompous and inflated. This will be sure and cut him to the heart. He can do nothing but roll over and die. Will you be kind enough to write?

"In Greek we must have some thing pretty—from Demosthenes, for example. Ἀνὴρ ὁ φεύγων καὶ πάλιν μαχήσεται. [Aner o pheugon kai palin makesetai.] There is a tolerably good translation of it in Hudibras—

For he that flies may fight again,
Which he can never do that's slain.[24]

---

[23]***ignoratio elenchi:*** Ignornance of the point under discussion. ***anemon(o)ae verborum:*** Not from Marcus Annaeus Lucanus (39–65), a Roman epic poet, but rather from the "Lexiphones" of Lucian (125–200) (Norman). Translated by H. W. and F. C. Fowler as "unsubstantial flowers of speech." Poe's source, as so often, is Isaac Disraeli, who writes, "Lucian happily describes the works of those who abound with the most luxuriant language void of ideas. He calls their unmeaning verbosity 'anemone-words'; for anemonies are flowers, which however brilliant, only please the eye, leaving no frangrance." Poe spelled the word "anemonæ" and "anemonœ" in different reprintings of his story. ***insomnia Jovis:*** "Poe correctly attributes the phrase . . . to Silius Italicus" (Norman). Pollin (12), discussing Poe's knowledge of Longinus, mentions that in the first version of this story, Poe attributed the words to Longinus.

[24]Poe probably copied this information from the footnotes to an edition of Samuel Butler's *Hudibras.* We examined one edition done ten years after Poe's death which is supposed to reprint the best notes of earlier editions. The lines Poe quotes are from Part 3, Canto 3, lines 243–44, and the note explains that Butler did not write

He that fights and runs away
May live to fight another day.

The idea, the note goes on, "appears to be as old as Demosthenes; who, being approached for running away from Philip of Macedonia, at the battle of Chaeronea, replied, Ἀνὴρ ὁ . . . (etc.)." The note goes on to give other examples of the idea in 16th- and 17th-century writers. Poe put in the bracketed transliteration so that readers who didn't know Greek could get the joke when "Zenobia," in "A Predicament," "quotes Demosthenes": "Andrew O'Phlegethon, you really make haste to fly." Pollin (12) points out that A. H. Quinn located the "Demosthenes quotation, with its *Hudibras* translation, in the sixth chapter of the 'Scriblerus' papers."

In a *Blackwood* article nothing makes so fine a show as your Greek. The very letters have an air of profundity about them. Only observe, madam, the astute look of that Epsilon! That Phi ought certainly to be a bishop! Was ever there a smarter fellow than that Omicron? Just twig that Tau! In short, there is nothing like Greek for a genuine sensation-paper. In the present case your application is the most obvious thing in the world. Rap out the sentence, with a huge oath, and by way of ultimatum at the good-for-nothing dunder-headed villain who couldn't understand your plain English in relation to the chicken-bone. He'll take the hint and be off, you may depend upon it."

These were all the instructions Mr. B. could afford me upon the topic in question, but I felt they would be entirely sufficient. I was, at length, able to write a genuine Blackwood article, and determined to do it forthwith. In taking leave of me, Mr. B. made a proposition for the purchase of the paper when written; but as he could offer me only fifty guineas a sheet, I thought it better to let our society have it, than sacrifice it for so paltry a sum. Notwithstanding this niggardly spirit, however, the gentleman showed his consideration for me in all other respects, and indeed treated me with the greatest civility. His parting words made a deep impression upon my heart, and I hope I shall always remember them with gratitude.

"My dear Miss Zenobia," he said, while the tears stood in his eyes, "is there *any* thing else I can do to promote the success of your laudable undertaking? Let me reflect! It is just possible that you may not be able, so soon as convenient, to—to—get yourself drowned, or—choked with a chicken-bone, or—or hung,—or—bitten by a—but stay! Now I think me of it, there are a couple of very excellent bulldogs in the yard—fine fellows, I assure you—savage, and all that—indeed just the thing for your money—they'll have you eaten up, *auriculas* and all, in less than five minutes (here's my watch!)—and then only think of the sensations! Here! I say—Tom!—Peter!—Dick, you villain!—let out those"—but as I was really in a great hurry, and had not another moment to spare, I was reluctantly forced to expedite my departure, and accordingly took leave *at once*—somewhat more abruptly, I admit, than strict courtesy would have otherwise allowed.

It was my primary object, upon quitting Mr. Blackwood, to get into some immediate difficulty, pursuant to his advice, and with this view I spent the great part of the day in wandering about Edinburgh, seeking for desperate adventures—adventures adequate to the intensity of my feelings, and adapted to the vast character of the article I intended to write. In this excursion I was attended by my negro-servant Pompey, and my little lap-dog Diana, whom I had brought with me from Philadelphia. It was not, however, until late in the afternoon that I fully succeeded in my arduous undertaking. An important event then happened, of which the following Blackwood article, in the tone heterogeneous, is the substance and result.

A Predicament[25]

What chance, good lady, hath bereft you thus?
Comus[26]

It was a quiet and still afternoon when I strolled forth in the goodly city of Edina. The confusion and bustle in the streets were terrible. Men were talking. Women were screaming. Children were choking. Pigs were whistling. Carts they rattled. Bulls they bellowed. Cows they lowed. Horses they neighed. Cats they caterwauled. Dogs they danced. *Danced!* Could it then be possible? *Danced!* Alas, thought I, *my* dancing days are over! Thus it is ever. What a host of gloomy recollections will ever and anon be awakened in the mind of genius and imaginative contemplation, especially of a genius doomed to the everlasting, and eternal, and continual, and, as one might say, the—*continued*—yes, the *continued and continuous,* bitter, harassing, disturbing, and, if I may be allowed the expression, the *very* disturbing influence of the serene, and godlike, and heavenly, and exalted, and elevated, and purifying effect of what may be rightly termed the most enviable, the most *truly* enviable—nay! the most benignly beautiful, the most deliciously ethereal, and, as it were, the most *pretty* (if I may use so bold an expression) *thing* (pardon me, gentle reader!) in the world—but I am always led away by my feelings. In *such* a mind, I repeat, what a host of recollections are stirred up by a trifle! The dogs danced! *I*—I *could* not! They frisked—I wept. They capered—I sobbed aloud. Touching circumstances! which cannot fail to bring to the recollection of the classical reader that exquisite passage in relation to the fitness of things, which is to be found in the commencement of the third volume of that admirable and venerable Chinese novel the *Jo-Go-Slow.*

In my solitary walk through the city I had two humble but faithful companions. Diana, my poodle! sweetest of creatures! She had a quantity of hair over her one eye, and a blue ribband tied fashionably around her neck. Diana was not more than five inches in height, but her head was somewhat bigger than her body, and her tail being cut off exceedingly close, gave an air of injured innocence to the interesting animal which rendered her a favorite with all.

And Pompey, my negro!—sweet Pompey! how shall I ever forget thee? I had taken Pompey's arm. He was three feet in height (I like to be particular) and about seventy, or perhaps eighty, years of age. He had bow-legs and was corpulent. His mouth should not be called small, nor his ears short. His teeth, however, were like pearl, and his large full eyes were deliciously white. Nature had endowed him with no neck, and had placed his ankles (as usual with that race) in the middle of

---

[25]Our notes do not explicate the blunders of the heroine/narrator because they are explained in the first part of the story. Poe's first title for "Zenobia's" portion of his spoof was "The Scythe of Time." Poe used the idea again in "The Pit and the Pendulum," in which his narrator, seeing the diabolical apparatus which is intended to cut him in two, says, "It was the painted figure of Time as he is commonly represented, save that, in lieu of a scythe, he held . . . a huge pendulum." See also note 29.

[26]From John Milton's masque "Comus" (1634), line 277. The Lady answers, "Dim darkness and this leavy labyrinth."

the upper portion of the feet. He was clad with a striking simplicity. His sole garments were a stock of nine inches in height, and a nearly-new drab overcoat which had formerly been in the service of the tall, stately, and illustrious Dr. Moneypenny. It was a good overcoat. It was well cut. It was well made. The coat was nearly new. Pompey held it up out of the dirt with both hands.

There were three persons in our party, and two of them have already been the subject of remark. There was a third—that person was myself. I am the Signora Psyche Zenobia. I am *not* Suky Snobbs. My appearance is commanding. On the memorable occasion of which I speak I was habited in a crimson satin dress, with a sky-blue Arabian mantelet. And the dress had trimmings of green agraffas, and seven graceful flounces of the orange-colored auricula. I thus formed the third of the party. There was the poodle. There was Pompey. There was myself. We were *three.* Thus it is said there were originally but three Furies—Melty, Nimmy, and Hetty—Meditation, Memory, and Fiddling.

Leaning upon the arm of the gallant Pompey, and attended at a respectful distance by Diana, I proceeded down one of the populous and very pleasant streets of the now deserted Edina. On a sudden, there presented itself to view a church—a Gothic cathedral—vast, venerable, and with a tall steeple, which towered into the sky. What madness now possessed me? Why did I rush upon my fate? I was seized with an uncontrollable desire to ascend the giddy pinnacle, and then survey the immense extent of the city. The door of the cathedral stood invitingly open. My destiny prevailed. I entered the ominous archway. Where then was my guardian angel?—if indeed such angels there be. *If!* Distressing monosyllable! what a world of mystery,[27] and meaning, and doubt, and uncertainty is there involved in thy two letters! I entered the ominous archway! I entered; and, without injury to my orange-colored auriculas, I passed beneath the portal, and emerged within the vestibule. Thus it is said the immense river Alfred passed, unscathed, and unwetted, beneath the sea.

I thought the staircases would never have an end. *Round!* Yes, they went round and up, and round and up and round and up, until I could not help surmising, with the sagacious Pompey, upon whose supporting arm I leaned in all the confidence of early affection—I *could* not help surmising that the upper end of the continuous spiral ladder had been accidentally, or perhaps designedly, removed. I paused for breath; and, in the meantime, an accident occurred of too momentous a nature in a moral, and also in a metaphysical point of view, to be passed over without notice. It appeared to me—indeed I was quite confident of the fact—I could not be mistaken—no! I had, for some moments, carefully and anxiously observed the motions of my Diana—I say that *I could not be* mistaken—Diana *smelt a rat!* At

[27]***If:*** In his "Fifty Suggestions" (*Graham's Magazine,* May, June 1854), Poe, making a pun on the name of Mirabeau's dwelling, writes, "Mirabeau, I fancy, acquired his wonderful tact at foreseeing and meeting *contingencies,* during his residence in the stronghold of *If.*" **what a world of mystery:** In his poem "The Bells" (1849), which also deals with bells and bell towers, Poe echoes this phrase. He uses several variations of it in the present story and in another literary satire, "The Literary Life of Thingum Bob, Esq." See also note 28 below.

once I called Pompey's attention to the subject, and he—he agreed with me. There was then no longer any reasonable room for doubt. The rat had been smelled—and by Diana. Heavens! shall I ever forget the intense excitement of the moment? Alas! what is the boasted intellect of man? The rat!—it was there—that is to say, it was somewhere. Diana smelled the rat. I—*I could not!* Thus it is said the Prussian Isis has, for some persons, a sweet and very powerful perfume, while to others it is perfectly scentless.

The staircase had been surmounted, and there were now only three or four more upward steps intervening between us and the summit. We still ascended, and now only one step remained. One step! One little, little step! Upon one such little step in the great staircase of human life how vast a sum of human happiness or misery depends![28] I thought of myself, then of Pompey, and then of the mysterious and inexplicable destiny which surrounded us. I thought of Pompey!—alas, I thought of love! I thought of my many false *steps* which have been taken, and may be taken again. I resolved to be more cautious, more reserved. I abandoned the arm of Pompey, and, without his assistance, surmounted the one remaining step, and gained the chamber of the belfry. I was followed immediately afterward by my poodle. Pompey alone remained behind. I stood at the head of the staircase, and encouraged him to ascend. He stretched forth to me his hand, and unfortunately in so doing was forced to abandon his firm hold upon the overcoat. Will the gods never cease their persecution? The overcoat is dropped, and, with one of his feet, Pompey stepped upon the long and trailing skirt of the overcoat. He stumbled and fell—this consequence was inevitable. He fell forward, and, with his accursed head, striking me full in the—in the breast, precipitated me headlong, together with himself, upon the hard, filthy, and detestable floor of the belfry. But my revenge was sure, sudden, and complete. Seizing him furiously by the wool with both hands, I tore out a vast quantity of black, and crisp, and curling material, and tossed it from me with every manifestation of disdain. It fell among the ropes of the belfry and remained. Pompey arose, and said no word. But he regarded me piteously with his large eyes, and—sighed. Ye Gods—that sigh! It sunk into my heart. And the hair—the wool! Could I have reached that wool I would have bathed it with my tears, in testimony of regret. But alas! it was now far beyond my grasp. As it dangled among the cordage of the bell, I fancied it alive. I fancied that it stood on end with indignation. Thus, the *happy-dandy Flos Aeris* of Java bears, it is said, a beautiful flower, which will live when pulled up by the roots. The natives suspend it by a cord from the ceiling and enjoy its fragrance for years.

Our quarrel was now made up, and we looked about the room for an aperture through which to survey the city of Edina. Windows there were none. The sole light admitted into the gloomy chamber proceeded from a square opening, about a foot in diameter, at a height of about seven feet from the floor. Yet what will the energy of true genius not effect? I resolved to clamber up to this hole. A vast quantity of wheels, pinions, and other cabalistic-looking machinery stood op-

---

[28]Poe echoes his humorous writing in his serious. Compare "how vast a sum of human happiness or misery depends!" with such lines in "The Bells" as "What a world of solemn thought their monody compels!"

posite the hole, close to it; and through the hole there passed an iron rod from the machinery. Between the wheels and the wall where the hole lay there was barely room for my body—yet I was desperate, and determined to persevere. I called Pompey to my side.

"You perceive that aperture, Pompey. I wish to look through it. You will stand here just beneath the hole—so. Now, hold out one of your hands, Pompey, and let me step upon it—thus. Now, the other hand, Pompey, and with its aid I will get upon your shoulders."

He did every thing I wished, and I found, upon getting up, that I could easily pass my head and neck through the aperture. The prospect was sublime. Nothing could be more magnificent. I merely paused a moment to bid Diana behave herself, and assure Pompey that I would be considerate and bear as lightly as possible upon his shoulders. I told him I would be tender with his feelings—*ossi tender que beefsteak.* Having done this justice to my faithful friend, I gave myself up with great zest and enthusiasm to the enjoyment of the scene which so obligingly spread itself out before my eyes.

Upon this subject, however, I shall forbear to dilate. I will not describe the city of Edinburgh. Every one has been to the city of Edinburgh. Every one has been to Edinburgh—the classic Edina. I will confine myself to the momentous details of my own lamentable adventure. Having, in some measure, satisfied my curiosity in regard to the extent, situation, and general appearance of the city, I had leisure to survey the church in which I was, and the delicate architecture of the steeple. I observed that the aperture through which I had thrust my head was an opening in the dial-plate of a gigantic clock, and must have appeared, from the street, as a large key-hole, such as we see in the face of the French watches. No doubt the true object was to admit the arm of an attendant, to adjust, when necessary, the hands of the clock from within. I observed also, with surprise, the immense size of these hands, the longest of which could not have been less than ten feet in length, and, where broadest, eight or nine inches in breadth. They were of solid steel apparently, and their edges appeared to be sharp. Having noticed these particulars, and some others, I again turned my eyes upon the glorious prospect below, and soon became absorbed in contemplation.

From this, after some minutes, I was aroused by the voice of Pompey, who declared that he could stand it no longer, and requested that I would be so kind as to come down. This was unreasonable, and I told him so in a speech of some length. He replied, but with an evident misunderstanding of my ideas upon the subject. I accordingly grew angry, and told him in plain words, that he was a fool, that he had committed an *ignoramus e-clench-eye,* that his notions were mere *insommary Bovis,* and his words little better than *an ennemywerrybor'em.* With this he appeared satisfied, and I resumed my contemplations.

It might have been half an hour after this altercation when, as I was deeply absorbed in the heavenly scenery beneath me, I was startled by something very cold which pressed with a gentle pressure on the back of my neck. It is needless to say that I felt inexpressibly alarmed. I knew that Pompey was beneath my feet, and that Diana was sitting, according to my explicit directions, upon her hind legs, in the farthest corner of the room. What could it be? Alas! I but too soon discovered. Turning my head gently to one side, I perceived, to my extreme horror, that the huge, glittering, scimetar-like minute-hand of the clock had, in the course of its hourly revolution, *descended upon my neck.*[29] There was, I knew, not a second to be lost. I pulled back at once—but it was too late. There was no chance of forcing my head through the mouth of that terrible trap in which it was so fairly caught, and which grew narrower and narrower with a rapidity too horrible to be conceived. The agony of that moment is not to be imagined. I threw up my hands and endeavored, with all my strength, to force upward the ponderous iron bar. I might as well have tried to lift the cathedral itself. Down, down, down it came, closer and yet closer. I screamed to Pompey for aid; but he said that I had hurt his feelings by calling him "an ignorant old squint-eye." I yelled to Diana; but she only said "bow-wow-wow," and that "I had told her on no account to stir from the corner." Thus I had no relief to expect from my associates.

Meantime the ponderous and terrific *Scythe of Time* (for I now discovered the literal import of that classical phrase) had not stopped, nor was it likely to stop, in its career. Down and still down, it came. It had already buried its sharp edge a full inch in my flesh, and my sensations grew indistinct and confused. At one time I fancied myself in Philadelphia with the stately Dr. Moneypenny, at another in the back parlor of Mr. Blackwood receiving his invaluable instructions. And then again the sweet recollection of better and earlier times came over me, and I thought of that happy period when the world was not all a desert, and Pompey not altogether cruel.

The ticking of the machinery amused me. *Amused me,* I say, for my sensations now bordered upon perfect happiness, and the most trifling circumstances afforded me pleasure. The eternal *click-clak, click-clak, click-clak* of the clock was the most melodious of music in my ears, and occasionally even put me in mind of the graceful sermonic harangues of Dr. Ollapod.[30] Then there were the great figures upon the dial-plate—how intelligent, how intellectual, they all looked! And presently they took to dancing the Mazurka, and I think it was the figure V who performed the most to my satisfaction. She was evidently a lady of breeding. None of your swaggerers, and nothing at all indelicate in her motions. She did the pirouette to admiration—whirling round upon her apex. I made an endeavor to hand her a chair, for I saw that she appeared fatigued with her exertions—and it was not until then that I fully perceived my lamentable situation. Lamentable indeed! The bar had buried itself two inches in my neck. I was aroused to a sense

---

[29]Pollin (12) notes the similarity of this situation to that in Poe's "The Pit and the Pendulum" (1842).

[30]Dr. Ollapod was a character in George Colman, Jr.'s very popular farce *The Poor Gentleman.* William Burton, for a time Poe's employer (*Burton's Gentleman's Magazine*), had played the part and became popularly identified with it, so Poe, during his association with Burton, changed "Dr. Ollapod" to "Dr. Morphine." Poe and Burton never got on well, and in the 1845 version, Poe changed the name back to "Ollapod." The character in the play is a charlatan who wants to overdose everyone with cathartics (see the allusion to Brandreth's pills in the first part of this story). "Ollapod" is from the Spanish "Olla podrida," hodgepodge (Pollin 6). Willis Clark's pen name in *The Knickerbocker* magazine was "Ollapod" (Whipple 3). See "The Literary Life of Thingum Bob, Esq.," for more details about Clark.

of exquisite pain. I prayed for death, and, in the agony of the moment, could not help repeating those exquisite verses of the poet Miguel De Cervantes:

Vanny Buren, tan escondida
Query no te senty venny
Pork and pleasure, delly morry
Nommy, torny, darry, widdy!

But now a new horror presented itself, and one indeed sufficient to startle the strongest nerves. My eyes, from the cruel pressure of the machine, were absolutely starting from their sockets. While I was thinking how I should possibly manage without them, one actually tumbled out of my head, and, rolling down the steep side of the steeple, lodged in the rain gutter which ran along the eaves of the main building. The loss of the eye was not so much as the insolent air of independence and contempt with which it regarded me after it was out. There it lay in the gutter just under my nose, and the airs it gave itself would have been ridiculous had they not been disgusting. Such a winking and blinking were never before seen. This behavior on the part of my eye in the gutter was not only irritating on account of its manifest insolence and shameful ingratitude, but was also exceedingly inconvenient on account of the sympathy which always exists between two eyes of the same head, however far apart. I was forced, in a manner, to wink and to blink, whether I would or not, in exact concert with the scoundrelly thing that lay just under my nose. I was presently relieved, however, by the dropping out of the other eye. In falling it took the same direction (possibly a concerted plot) as its fellow. Both rolled out of the gutter together, and in truth I was very glad to be rid of them.

The bar was now four inches and a half deep in my neck, and there was only a little bit of skin to cut through. My sensations were those of entire happiness, for I felt that in a few minutes, at farthest, I should be relieved from my disagreeable situation. And in this expectation I was not at all deceived. At twenty-five minutes past five in the afternoon, precisely, the huge minute-hand had proceeded sufficiently far on its terrible revolution to sever the small remainder of my neck. I was not sorry to see the head which had occasioned me so much embarrassment at length make a final separation from my body. It first rolled down the side of the steeple, then lodged, for a few seconds, in the gutter, and then made its way, with a plunge, into the middle of the street.

I will candidly confess that my feelings were now of the most singular—nay, of the most mysterious, the most perplexing and incomprehensible character. My senses were here and there at one and the same moment. With my head I imagined, at one time, that I, the head, was the real Signora Psyche Zenobia—at another I felt convinced that myself, the body, was the proper identity. To clear my ideas on this topic I felt in my pocket for my snuff-box, but, upon getting it, and endeavoring to apply a pinch of its grateful contents in the ordinary manner, I became immediately aware of my peculiar deficiency, and threw the box at once down to my head. It took a pinch with great satisfaction, and smiled me an acknowledgement in return. Shortly afterward it made me a speech, which I could hear but indistinctly without ears. I gathered enough, however, to know that it was astonished at my wishing to remain alive under such circumstances. In the concluding sentences it quoted the noble words of Ariosto—

Il pover hommy che non sera corty
And have a combat tenty erry morty;

thus comparing me to the hero who, in the heat of the combat, not perceiving that he was dead, continued to contest the battle with inextinguishable valor. There was nothing now to prevent my getting down from my elevation, and I did so. What it was that Pompey saw so *very* peculiar in my appearance I have never yet been able to find out. The fellow opened his mouth from ear to ear, and shut his two eyes as if he were endeavoring to crack nuts between the lids. Finally, throwing off his overcoat, he made one spring for the staircase and disappeared. I hurled after the scoundrel these vehement words of Demosthenes—

Andrew O'Phlegethon, you really make haste to fly,

and then turned to the darling of my heart, to the one-eyed! the shaggy-haired Diana. Alas! what a horrible vision affronted my eyes? *Was* that a rat I saw skulking into his hole? *Are* these the picked bones of the little angel who has been cruelly devoured by the monster? Ye gods! and what *do* I behold—*is* that the departed spirit, the shade, the ghost, of my beloved puppy, which I perceive sitting with a grace so melancholy, in the corner? Hearken! for she speaks, and heavens! it is in the German of Schiller—

"*Unt stubby duk, so stubby dun*
Duk she! duk she!"

Alas! and are not her words too true?

"*And if I died, at least I died*
For thee—for thee."

Sweet creature! she *too* has sacrificed herself in my behalf. Dogless, niggerless, headless, what *now* remains for the unhappy Signora Psyche Zenobia? Alas—*nothing!* I have done.

The Fall of the House of Usher

"The Fall of the House of Usher" is a philosophical story in that Poe stresses what mystics call "equivalences." Roderick and Madeline are twins who sense one another's feelings as twins are supposed to in folklore; the tarn reflects the house and its gloomy surroundings; the events at the close of the tale reflect the words of the book which the narrator reads to Usher; the house represents the family. Note that the narrator senses "equivalences" right at the outset. Usher, in his hereditary illness, his drugged state, and his fear, senses the unity of all things. The narrator, by the close of the tale, has come to sense it, too.

This is, then, a tale about perception, and though to perceive here is to fear, we note that, as usual in Poe, the "perceiver" envisions transcendent beauty. Roderick paints and improvises fantastic music (see note 8). Poe hints that the inspiration involved in the creative process is akin to that which will enable Usher to know that his sister is alive in her coffin.

This is also a story about death, terror, and burial alive. But before concluding that Poe is as much in the grips of fear as are Usher and the narrator, readers should examine the whimsical tale "The Premature Burial," in which Poe makes healthy fun of morbidness. They should keep in mind also Poe's obvious artistic control: "The Fall of the House of Usher" is no tale written by a madman; it is much too carefully crafted. It is philosophically consistent with related tales by Poe—see, for instance, our headnote for "Ligeia"; what is said there applies here as well. "Usher" will, indeed, "take" specialized philosophical readings, such as a careful Gnostic interpretation (St. Armand). Poe even provides a "rational" explanation for what happens: the narrator, as frightened as Usher, may be inventing details. Outer reality and states of mind are associated right at the opening of the tale, to give the reader a "margin of credibility." Poe is saying, in effect, that what "happens" and what his narrator feels may be so closely related that the reader who is unwilling to believe given parts of the action may view them as reflections of the processes of his narrator's mind. Poe allows us the possibility that this is a psychological study of the contagion of fear.

Publications in Poe's Time

Burton's Gentleman's Magazine, September 1839
Tales of the Grotesque and Arabesque, 1840
Bentley's Miscellany, London, August 1840
Bentley's Miscellany, American edition, 1840

The Boston Notion, September 5, 1840
Tales, 1845
Rufus Griswold, ed., *The Prose Writers of America,* 1847
See also note 9.

THE FALL OF THE HOUSE OF USHER

Son cœur est un luth suspendu;
Sitôt qu'on le touche il résonne.
De Béranger.[1]

During the whole of a dull, dark, and soundless day in the autumn of the year, when the clouds hung oppressively low in the heavens, I had been passing alone, on horseback, through a singularly dreary tract of country, and at length found myself, as the shades of the evening drew on, within view of the melancholy House of Usher. I know not how it was—but, with the first glimpse of the building, a sense of insufferable gloom pervaded my spirit. I say insufferable; for the feeling was unrelieved by any of that half-pleasurable, because poetic, sentiment, with which the mind usually receives even the sternest natural images of the desolate or terrible. I looked upon the scene before me—upon the mere house, and the simple landscape features of the domain—upon the bleak walls—upon the vacant eye-like windows—upon a few rank sedges—and upon a few white trunks of decayed trees—with an utter depression of soul which I can compare to no earthly sensation more properly than to the after-dream of the reveller upon opium—the bitter lapse into every-day life—the hideous dropping off of the veil. There was an iciness, a sinking, a sickening of the heart—an unredeemed dreariness of thought which no goading of the imagination could torture into aught of the sublime. What was it—I paused to think—what was it that so unnerved me in the contemplation of the House of Usher? It was a mystery all insoluble; nor could I grapple with the shadowy fancies that crowded upon me as I pondered. I was forced to fall back upon the unsatisfactory conclusion, that while, beyond doubt, there *are* combinations of very simple natural objects which have the power of thus affecting us, still the analysis of this power lies among considerations beyond our depth. It was possible, I reflected, that a mere different arrangement of the particulars of the scene, of the details of the picture, would be sufficient to modify,

---

[1] His heart is a pendant lute
Which resounds the moment touched.

Pierre-Jean de Béranger (1780–1857), among the best-known and respected poets of the period, now considered minor.

or perhaps to annihilate its capacity for sorrowful impression; and, acting upon this idea, I reined my horse to the precipitous brink of a black and lurid tarn[2] that lay in unruffled lustre by the dwelling, and gazed down—but with a shudder even more thrilling than before—upon the remodelled and inverted images of the gray sedge, and the ghastly tree-stems, and the vacant and eye-like windows.

Nevertheless, in this mansion of gloom I now proposed to myself a sojourn of some weeks. Its proprietor, Roderick Usher, had been one of my boon companions in boyhood; but many years had elapsed since our last meeting. A letter, however, had lately reached me in a distant part of the country—a letter from him—which, in its wildly importunate nature, had admitted of no other than a personal reply. The MS. gave evidence of nervous agitation. The writer spoke of acute bodily illness—of a mental disorder which oppressed him—and of an earnest desire to see me, as his best, and indeed his only personal friend, with a view of attempting, by the cheerfulness of my society, some alleviation of his malady. It was the manner in which all this, and much more, was said—it was the apparent *heart* that went with his request—which allowed me no room for hesitation; and I accordingly obeyed forthwith what I still considered a very singular summons.

Although, as boys, we had been even intimate associates, yet I really knew little of my friend. His reserve had been always excessive and habitual. I was aware, however, that his very ancient family had been noted, time out of mind, for a peculiar sensibility of temperament, displaying itself, through long ages, in many works of exalted art, and manifested, of late, in repeated deeds of munificent yet unobtrusive charity, as well as in a passionate devotion to the intricacies, perhaps even more than to the orthodox and easily recognizable beauties, of musical science. I had learned, too, the very remarkable fact, that the stem of the Usher race, all time-honored as it was, had put forth, at no period, any enduring branch; in other words, that the entire family lay in the direct line of descent, and had always, with very trifling and very temporary variation, so lain. It was this deficiency, I considered, while running over in thought the perfect keeping of the character of the premises with the accredited character of the people, and while speculating upon the possible influence which the one, in the long lapse of centuries, might have exercised upon the other—it was this deficiency, perhaps of collateral issue, and the consequent undeviating transmission, from sire to son, of the patrimony with the name, which had, at length, so identified the two as to merge the original title of the estate in the quaint and equivocal appellation of the "House of Usher"—an appellation which seemed to include, in the minds of the peasantry who used it, both the family and the family mansion.

I have said that the sole effect of my somewhat childish experiment—that of looking down within the tarn—had been to deepen the first singular impression. There can be no doubt that the consciousness of the rapid increase of my superstition—for why should I not so term it?—served mainly to accelerate the increase itself. Such, I have long known, is the paradoxical law of all sentiments having terror as a basis. And it might have been for this reason only, that, when I again uplifted my eyes to the house itself, from its image in the pool, there grew in

[2]**I know not. . . . the veil:** See our headnote. **tarn:** Mountain lake.

my mind a strange fancy—a fancy so ridiculous, indeed, that I but mention it to show the vivid force of the sensations which oppressed me. I had so worked upon my imagination as really to believe that about the whole mansion and domain there hung an atmosphere peculiar to themselves and their immediate vicinity—an atmosphere which had no affinity with the air of heaven, but which had reeked up from the decayed trees, and the gray wall, and the silent tarn—a pestilent and mystic vapor, dull, sluggish, faintly discernible, and leaden-hued.

Shaking off from my spirit what *must* have been a dream, I scanned more narrowly the real aspect of the building. Its principal feature seemed to be that of an excessive antiquity. The discoloration of ages had been great. Minute fungi overspread the whole exterior, hanging in a fine tangled web-work from the eaves. Yet all this was apart from an extraordinary dilapidation. No portion of the masonry had fallen; and there appeared to be a wild inconsistency between its still perfect adaptation of parts, and the crumbling condition of the individual stones. In this there was much that reminded me of the specious totality of old wood-work which has rotted for long years in some neglected vault, with no disturbance from the breath of the external air. Beyond this indication of extensive decay, however, the fabric gave little token of instability. Perhaps the eye of a scrutinizing observer might have discovered a barely perceptible fissure, which, extending from the roof of the building in front, made its way down the wall in a zigzag direction, until it became lost in the sullen waters of the tarn.

Noticing these things, I rode over a short causeway to the house. A servant in waiting took my horse, and I entered the Gothic archway of the hall. A valet, of stealthy step, thence conducted me, in silence, through many dark and intricate passages in my progress to the *studio* of his master. Much that I encountered on the way contributed, I know not how, to heighten the vague sentiments of which I have already spoken. While the objects around me—while the carvings of the ceilings, the sombre tapestries of the walls, the ebon[3] blackness of the floors, and the phantasmagoric armorial trophies which rattled as I strode, were but matters to which, or to such as which, I had been accustomed from my infancy—while I hesitated not to acknowledge how familiar was all this—I still wondered to find how unfamiliar were the fancies which ordinary images were stirring up. On one of the staircases, I met the physician of the family. His countenance, I thought, wore a mingled expression of low cunning and perplexity. He accosted me with

---

[3]Given the date of this story and its emphasis on gothicism and "sensations," it is likely that the word "ebon" means more than "black." Ebony, "black wood," was the code name for the proprietor of *Blackwood's Edinburgh Magazine.* See our headnote to "How to Write a Blackwood Article" and "A note of explanation" to "The Man of the Crowd" for fuller explanation. It is very characteristic of Poe to slip whimsical allusions into apparently "serious" tales. "My story," this allusion seems to say, "stands on a floor of ebony—it is based on *Blackwood's* material." The floors of the house of Usher are not *really* of ebony, of course; in the next paragraph, we learn of an oaken floor. (Some of the doors *are* of ebony; see the story's penultimate paragraph.) Poe's odd word choice might be just that—odd—for Poe liked fancy poetic language. But he loved playful allusiveness even more, and that may well be the reason for "ebon."

trepidation and passed on. The valet now threw open a door and ushered me into the presence of his master.

The room in which I found myself was very large and lofty. The windows were long, narrow, and pointed, and at so vast a distance from the black oaken floor as to be altogether inaccessible from within. Feeble gleams of encrimsoned light made their way through the trellised panes, and served to render sufficiently distinct the more prominent objects around; the eye, however, struggled in vain to reach the remoter angles of the chamber, or the recesses of the vaulted and fretted ceiling. Dark draperies hung upon the walls. The general furniture was profuse, comfortless, antique, and tattered. Many books and musical instruments lay scattered about, but failed to give any vitality to the scene. I felt that I breathed an atmosphere of sorrow. An air of stern, deep, and irredeemable gloom hung over and pervaded all.

Upon my entrance, Usher arose from a sofa on which he had been lying at full length, and greeted me with a vivacious warmth which had much in it, I at first throught, of an overdone cordiality—of the constrained effort of the *ennuyé* man of the world. A glance, however, at his countenance convinced me of his perfect sincerity. We sat down; and for some moments, while he spoke not, I gazed upon him with a feeling half of pity, half of awe. Surely, man had never before so terribly altered, in so brief a period, as had Roderick Usher! It was with difficulty that I could bring myself to admit the identity of the wan being before me with the companion of my early boyhood. Yet the character of his face had been at all times remarkable. A cadaverousness of complexion; an eye large, liquid, and luminous beyond comparison; lips somewhat thin and very pallid, but of a surpassingly beautiful curve; a nose of delicate Hebrew model, but with a breadth of nostril unusual in similar formations; a finely moulded chin, speaking, in its want of prominence, of a want of moral energy; hair of a more than web-like softness and tenuity; these features, with an inordinate expansion above the regions of the temple, made up altogether a countenance not easily to be forgotten. And now in the mere exaggeration of the prevailing character of these features, and of the expression they were wont to convey, lay so much of change that I doubted to whom I spoke. The now ghastly pallor of the skin, and the now miraculous lustre of the eye, above all things startled and even awed me. The silken hair, too, had been suffered to grow all unheeded, and as, in its wild gossamer texture, it floated rather than fell about the face, I could not, even with effort, connect its Arabesque[4] expression with any idea of simple humanity.

In the manner of my friend I was at once struck with an incoherence—an inconsistency; and I soon found this to arise from a series of feeble and futile

[4]***ennuyé:*** Bored. **Arabesque:** See "The Domain of Arnheim," note 18, for the implications of the word. Its use here is odd, and the sentence somewhat ambiguous: is it the hair or the face that is "Arabesque"? Grammatically, it is the hair, yet can hair have "expression"? A guess: among the connotations of "Arabesque" for Poe is exoticism, a quality which, along with brilliance, creativity, and mental illness, he wanted associated with Usher. The reference of the word is less important than its inclusion.

struggles to overcome an habitual trepidancy—an excessive nervous agitation. For something of this nature I had indeed been prepared, no less by his letter, than by reminiscences of certain boyish traits, and by conclusions deduced from his peculiar physical conformation and temperament. His action was alternately vivacious and sullen. His voice varied rapidly from a tremulous indecision (when the animal spirits seemed utterly in abeyance) to that species of energetic concision—that abrupt, weighty, unhurried, and hollow-sounding enunciation—that leaden, self-balanced, and perfectly modulated guttural utterance, which may be observed in the lost drunkard, or the irreclaimable eater of opium, during the periods of his most intense excitement.[5]

It was thus that he spoke of the object of my visit, of his earnest desire to see me, and of the solace he expected me to afford him. He entered, at some length, into what he conceived to be the nature of his malady. It was, he said, a constitutional and a family evil, and one for which he despaired to find a remedy—a mere nervous affection, he immediately added, which would undoubtedly soon pass off. It displayed itself in a host of unnatural sensations. Some of these, as he detailed them, interested and bewildered me; although, perhaps, the terms and the general manner of their narration had their weight. He suffered much from a morbid acuteness of the senses; the most insipid food was alone endurable; he could wear only garments of certain texture; the odors of all flowers were oppressive; his eyes were tortured by even a faint light; and there were but peculiar sounds, and these from stringed instruments, which did not inspire him with horror.

To an anomalous species of terror I found him a bounden slave. "I shall perish," said he, "I *must* perish in this deplorable folly. Thus, thus, and not otherwise, shall I be lost. I dread the events of the future, not in themselves, but in their results. I shudder at the thought of any, even the most trivial, incident, which may operate upon this intolerable agitation of soul. I have, indeed, no abhorrence of danger, except in its absolute effect—in terror. In this unnerved—in this pitiable condition—I feel that the period will sooner or later arrive when I must abandon life and reason together, in some struggle with the grim phantasm, FEAR."

I learned, moreover, at intervals, and through broken and equivocal hints, another singular feature of his mental condition. He was enchained by certain superstitious impressions in regard to the dwelling which he tenanted, and whence, for many years, he had never ventured forth—in regard to an influence whose supposititious force was conveyed in terms too shadowy here to be restated—an influence which some peculiarities in the mere form and substance of his family mansion had, by dint of long sufferance, he said, obtained over his spirit—an effect which the *physique* of the gray wall and turrets, and of the dim tarn into which they all looked down, had, at length, brought about upon the *morale* of his existence.

---

[5]Now both Usher and the narrator have been associated with drugs and with marginal states of consciousness.

He admitted, however, although with hesitation, that much of the peculiar gloom which thus afflicted him could be traced to a more natural and far more palpable origin—to the severe and long-continued illness—indeed to the evidently approaching dissolution—of a tenderly beloved sister, his sole companion for long years, his last and only relative on earth. "Her decease," he said, with a bitterness which I can never forget, "would leave him (him the hopeless and the frail) the last of the ancient race of the Ushers." While he spoke, the lady Madeline (for so was she called) passed slowly through a remote portion of the apartment, and, without having noticed my presence, disappeared. I regarded her with an utter astonishment not unmingled with dread—and yet I found it impossible to account for such feelings. A sensation of stupor oppressed me, as my eyes followed her retreating steps. When a door, at length, closed upon her, my glance sought instinctively and eagerly the countenance of the brother—but he had buried his face in his hands, and I could only perceive that a far more than ordinary wanness had overspread the emaciated fingers through which trickled many passionate tears.

The disease of the lady Madeline had long baffled the skill of her physicians. A settled apathy, a gradual wasting away of the person, and frequent although transient affections of a partially cataleptical character were the unusual diagnosis. Hitherto she had steadily borne up against the pressure of her malady, and had not betaken herself finally to bed; but on the closing in of the evening of my arrival at the house, she succumbed (as her brother told me at night with inexpressible agitation) to the prostrating power of the destroyer; and I learned that the glimpse I had obtained of her person would thus probably be the last I should obtain—that the lady, at least while living, would be seen by me no more.

For several days ensuing, her name was unmentioned by either Usher or myself: and during this period I was busied in earnest endeavors to alleviate the melancholy of my friend. We painted and read together, or I listened, as if in a dream, to the wild improvisations of his speaking guitar.[6] And thus, as a closer and still closer intimacy admitted me more unreservedly into the recesses of his spirit, the more bitterly did I perceive the futility of all attempt at cheering a mind from which darkness, as if an inherent positive quality, poured forth upon all objects of the moral and physical universe in one unceasing radiation of gloom.

I shall ever bear about me a memory of the many solemn hours I thus spent alone with the master of the House of Usher. Yet I should fail in any attempt to convey an idea of the exact character of the studies, or of the occupations, in which he involved me, or led me the way. An excited and highly distempered ideality threw a sulphureous lustre over all. His long improvised dirges will ring forever in my ears. Among other things, I hold painfully in mind a certain singular perversion and amplification of the wild air of the last waltz of Von Weber. From

---

[6]Mental illness and creativity are associated frequently in Poe, and beauty is always exotic, outré, "Arabesque." Madness, apparently, is one way to achieve contact with transcendent sources of inspiration. For an alternate route to the same kind of beauty, see "The Domain of Arnheim."

the paintings over which his elaborate fancy brooded, and which grew, touch by touch, into vagueness at which I shuddered the more thrillingly, because I shuddered knowing not why:—from these paintings (vivid as their images now are before me) I would in vain endeavor to educe more than a small portion which should lie within the compass of merely written words. By the utter simplicity, by the nakedness of his designs, he arrested and overawed attention. If ever mortal painted an idea, that mortal was Roderick Usher. For me at least—in the circumstances then surrounding me—there arose out of the pure abstractions which the hypochondriac contrived to throw upon his canvas, an intensity of intolerable awe, no shadow of which I felt ever yet in the contemplation of the certainly glowing yet too concrete reveries of Fuseli.[7]

One of the phantasmagoric conceptions of my friend, partaking not so rigidly of the spirit of abstraction, may be shadowed forth, although feebly, in words. A small picture presented the interior of an immensely long and rectangular vault or tunnel, with low walls, smooth, white, and without interruption or device. Certain accessory points of the design served well to convey the idea that this excavation lay at an exceeding depth below the surface of the earth. No outlet was observed in any portion of its vast extent, and no torch or other artificial source of light was discernible; yet a flood of intense rays rolled throughout, and bathed the whole in a ghastly and inappropriate splendor.

I have just spoken of that morbid condition of the auditory nerve which rendered all music intolerable to the sufferer, with the exception of certain effects of stringed instruments. It was, perhaps, the narrow limits to which he thus confined himself upon the guitar, which gave birth, in great measure, to the fantastic character of his performance. But the fervid *facility* of his *impromptus*[8] could not be so accounted for. They must have been, and were, in the notes, as well as in the words of his wild fantasias (for he not unfrequently accompanied himself with rhymed verbal improvisations), the result of that intense mental collectedness and concentration to which I have previously alluded as observable only in particular moments of the highest artificial excitement. The words of one of these rhapsodies I have easily remembered. I was, perhaps, the more forcibly impressed with it, as he gave it, because, in the under or mystic current of its meaning, I fancied that I perceived, and for the first time, a full consciousness on the part of Usher, of the tottering of his lofty reason upon her throne. The verses, which were entitled "The Haunted Palace," ran very nearly, if not accurately, thus:

---

[7]**Von Weber:** Carl Maria Friedrich Ernst von Weber (1786–1826), German composer. The "Last Waltz" is actually by Karl Reissiger (1798–1859). Weber copied it to use in a concert, but died suddenly, and so it was thought for a time to be his own last composition (Pollin 5). **Fuseli:** John Henry Fuseli (1741–1825), Swiss-English painter of the fantastic, who was famous in his own time.

[8]An "impromptu" is a musical work of an extemporized nature (though in point of fact there are *written* impromptus). Usher, in his high "excitement," creates beautiful and strange works. Note that the "intense . . . collectedness of concentration" is also a sign of insanity. Poe plays on the folk belief that the insane see the world of spirit.

I.

In the greenest of our valleys,
By good angels tenanted,
Once a fair and stately palace—
Radiant palace—reared its head.
In the monarch Thought's dominion—
It stood there!
Never seraph spread a pinion
Over fabric half so fair.

II.

Banners yellow, glorious, golden,
On its roof did float and flow;
(This—all this—was in the olden
Time long ago)
And every gentle air that dallied,
In that sweet day,
Along the ramparts plumed and pallid,
A winged odor went away.

III.

Wanderers in that happy valley
Through two luminous windows saw
Spirits moving musically
To a lute's well-tunéd law,
Round about a throne, where sitting
(Porphyrogene!)
In state his glory well befitting,
The ruler of the realm was seen.

IV.

And all with pearl and ruby glowing
Was the fair palace door,
Through which came flowing, flowing, flowing
And sparkling evermore,
A troop of Echoes whose sweet duty
Was but to sing,
In voices of surpassing beauty,
The wit and wisdom of their king.

V.

But evil things, in robes of sorrow,
Assailed the monarch's high estate;
(Ah, let us mourn, for never morrow
Shall dawn upon him, desolate!)
And, round about his home, the glory
That blushed and bloomed
Is but a dim-remembered story
Of the old time entombed.

VI.

And travellers now within that valley,
Through the red-litten windows see

Vast forms that move fantastically
To a discordant melody;
While, like a rapid ghastly river,
Through the pale door,
A hideous throng rush out forever,
And laugh—but smile no more.[9]

I well remember that suggestions arising from this ballad led us into a train of thought wherein there became manifest an opinion of Usher's which I mention not so much on account of its novelty (for other men[10] have thought thus,) as on account of the pertinacity with which he maintained it. This opinion, in its general form, was that of the sentience of all vegetable things. But, in his disordered fancy, the idea had assumed a more daring character, and trespassed, under certain conditions, upon the kingdom of inorganization. I lack words to express the full extent, or the earnest *abandon* of his persuasion. The belief, however, was connected (as I have previously hinted) with the gray stones of the home of his forefathers. The conditions of the sentience had been here, he imagined, fulfilled in the method of collocation of these stones—in the order of their arrangement, as well as in that of the many *fungi* which overspread them, and of the decayed trees which stood around—above all, in the long undisturbed endurance of this arrangement, and in its reduplication in the still waters of the tarn. Its evidence—the evidence of the sentience—was to be seen, he said (and I here started as he spoke), in the gradual yet certain condensation of an atmosphere of their own about the waters and the walls. The result was discoverable, he added, in that silent yet importunate and terrible influence which for centuries had moulded the destinies of his family, and which made *him* what I now saw him—what he was. Such opinions need no comment, and I will make none.

Our books—the books which, for years, had formed no small portion of the mental existence of the invalid—were, as might be supposed, in strict keeping with this character of phantasm. We pored together over such works as the Ververt et Chartreuse of Gresset; the Belphegor of Machiavelli; the Heaven and Hell of Swedenborg; the Subterranean Voyage of Nicholas Klimm by Holberg; the Chiromancy of Robert Flud, of Jean D'Indaginé, and of De la Chambre; the Journey into the Blue Distance of Tieck; and the City of the Sun of Campanella. One favorite volume was a small octavo edition of the *Directorium Inquisitorum,* by

---

[9]Poe had published this poem earlier (in the *American Museum,* April 1839). After the story was published, the poem was reprinted both as a part of "Usher" and on its own. "Law" in stanza III has the sense of patterned accompaniment, but its precise meaning is not clear to us. Poe might intend "law" in the sense of "rules" or "foundation" for the dancing spirits. According to Burton Pollin, "Porphyrogene" means "born to the royal purple."

[10]Watson, Dr. Percival, Spallanzani, and especially the Bishop of Landaff—See "Chemical Essays," vol. V [Poe's note]. Richard Watson, Bishop of Landaff (1737–1819), was an English chemist. James Gates Percival (1795–1856) was an American physician and poet. Abée Lazzaro Spallanzani (1729–99) was professor of natural history at the University of Pavia. Poe had seen Watson's work and copied out the citations from it (Mabbott 9, II, following Harry Warfel in *MLN,* February 1939).

the Dominican Eymeric de Gironne; and there were passages in Pomponius Mela, about the old African Satyrs and Ægipans, over which Usher would sit dreaming for hours. His chief delight, however, was found in the perusal of an exceedingly rare and curious book in quarto Gothic—the manual of a forgotten church—the *Vigiliæ Mortuorum secundum Chorum Ecclesiæ Maguntinæ.*[11]

I could not help thinking of the wild ritual of this work, and of its probable influence upon the hypochondriac, when, one evening, having informed me abruptly that the lady Madeline was no more, he stated his intention of preserving her corpse for a fortnight, (previously to its final interment,) in one of the numerous vaults within the main walls of the building. The worldly reason, however, assigned for this singular proceeding, was one which I did not feel at liberty to dispute. The brother had been led to his resolution (so he told me) by consideration of the unusual character of the malady of the deceased, of certain obtrusive

---

[11]Usher says he fears fear, and Poe has selected a library of dark works with which Usher can scare himself. Jean-Baptiste-Louis Gresset (1709–77), for example, wrote some works dealing with the theme of the delectation of evil. His "Vert-Vert" (1734), however, is a poem light in tone, about a parrot that lives in a convent. Carlson (2) says that *Vert-Vert* and *Ma Chartreuse* are "satirical, anti-clerical, and licentious" poems. **Niccolò Machiavelli:** The Florentine writer and political figure (1469–1527), whose name is synonymous with the amoral approach to political power. The novel to which Poe refers is a satire on marriage; the demon Belphegor, turned into a man, is henpecked by his spouse. **Emanuel Swedenborg:** Mystic, philosopher, and scientist (1688–1772), very influential on romantic authors of Poe's day. His supposed clairvoyance is relevant to Usher's. (Usher supposedly has mystical ties to his sister Madeline.) **Ludwig Holberg:** Danish dramatist, historian, and novelist (1684–1754) (Carlson 2). His *Iter Subterraneum* is about a "country inside the earth where the people are trees who walk and talk" (Mabbott 8). **Chiromancy:** The ancient pseudoscience of palmistry or palm-reading. It is, as Poe implies, an occult system in origin. **Robert Flud:** "English physician, mystic philosopher (sometimes called 'The English Rosicrucian'), scientific experimenter, and writer on pseudoscience" (1574–1637) (Carlson 2). His *Tractatus de Geomantia* is about geomancy—divination by "marking the earth with a pointed stick" (Mabbott 8). **Jean D'Indaginé:** Writer on palmistry, author of *Chiromantia* (1522) (Carlson 2). **Maria Cireau de la Chambre:** Another writer on palmistry (1594–1669) (Carlson 2), author of *Principes de la Chiromancie* (1653) (Mabbott 8). **Ludwig Tieck:** German writer and critic (1773–1853). Carlson (2) says that the book to which Poe refers deals with a journey into another world. So does "The City of the Sun" (*Civitas Solis*) by Tomasso Campanella (1568–1639), "a utopian work suggesting the ideal state in the world beyond" (Carlson 2). **Nicholas Eymeric de Gironne:** Inquisitor-general of Castille in Spain in 1356, wrote "instructions to priests examining heretics" and "a list of forbidden books." Mabbott (8 and 9, II) reports that the *Directorium Inquisitorium* was printed in 1503, long after Gironne's day. We assume that the 1503 work is the printed version of Gironne's instructions. **Pomponius Mela:** "A first-century Roman geographer, whose widely used textbook often described strange beasts" (Carlson 2). The passage which Poe has in mind is quoted in Mabbott (8). **Satyrs:** Greek woodland deities, generally human in appearance, but with goat's legs, pointed ears, small horns, and wanton ways. **Ægipans:** A name for Pan, the god of forests, flocks, and shepherds. He, too, had goat's horns and hoofs; Carlson (2) ventures the guess that Poe thought Pan a type of satyr. ***Vigiliæ Mortuorum . . . Maguntinæ:*** "'The Watches of the Dead according to the Choir of the Church of Mayence [Mainz],' printed in Basel, c. 1500" (Carlson 2).

and eager inquiries on the part of her medical men, and of the remote and exposed situation of the burial-ground of the family. I will not deny that when I called to mind the sinister countenance of the person whom I met upon the staircase, on the day of my arrival at the house, I had no desire to oppose what I regarded as at best but a harmless, and by no means an unnatural, precaution.

At the request of Usher, I personally aided him in the arrangements for the temporary entombment. The body having been encoffined, we two alone bore it to its rest. The vault in which we placed it (and which had been so long unopened that our torches, half smothered in its oppressive atmosphere, gave us little opportunity for investigation) was small, damp, and entirely without means of admission for light; lying, at great depth, immediately beneath that portion of the building in which was my own sleeping apartment. It had been used, apparently, in remote feudal times, for the worst purposes of a donjon-keep, and, in later days, as a place of deposit for powder, or some other highly combustible substance, as a portion of its floor, and the whole interior of a long archway through which we reached it, were carefully sheathed with copper. The door, of massive iron, had been, also, similarly protected. Its immense weight caused an unusually sharp grating sound, as it moved upon its hinges.

Having deposited our mournful burden upon tressels[12] within this region of horror, we partially turned aside the yet unscrewed lid of the coffin, and looked upon the face of the tenant. A striking similitude between the brother and sister now first arrested my attention; and Usher, divining, perhaps, my thoughts, murmured out some few words from which I learned that the deceased and himself had been twins, and that sympathies of a scarcely intelligible nature had always existed between them. Our glances, however, rested not long upon the dead—for we could not regard her unawed. The disease which had thus entombed the lady in the maturity of youth, had left, as usual in all maladies of a strictly cataleptical character, the mockery of a faint blush upon the bosom and the face, and that suspiciously lingering smile upon the lip which is so terrible in death. We replaced and screwed down the lid, and, having secured the door of iron, made our way, with toil, into the scarcely less gloomy apartments of the upper portion of the house.

And now, some days of bitter grief having elapsed, an observable change came over the features of the mental disorder of my friend. His ordinary manner had vanished. His ordinary occupations were neglected or forgotten. He roamed from chamber to chamber with hurried, unequal, and objectless step. The pallor of his countenance had assumed, if possible, a more ghastly hue—but the luminousness of his eye had utterly gone out. The once occasional huskiness of his tone was heard no more; and a tremulous quaver, as if of extreme terror, habitually characterized his utterance. There were times, indeed, when I thought his unceasingly agitated mind was laboring with some oppressive secret, to divulge which he struggled for the necessary courage. At times, again, I was obliged to resolve all into the mere inexplicable vagaries of madness, for I beheld him gazing upon vacancy for long hours, in an attitude of the profoundest attention, as if listening to

[12]Trestles.

some imaginary sound. It was no wonder that his condition terrified—that it infected me. I felt creeping upon me, by slow yet certain degrees, the wild influences of his own fantastic yet impressive superstitions.

It was, especially, upon retiring to bed late in the night of the seventh or eighth day after the placing of the lady Madeline within the donjon, that I experienced the full power of such feelings. Sleep came not near my couch—while the hours waned and waned away. I struggled to reason off the nervousnes which had dominion over me. I endeavored to believe that much, if not all of what I felt, was due to the bewildering influence of the gloomy furniture of the room—of the dark and tattered draperies, which, tortured into motion by the breath of a rising tempest, swayed fitfully to and fro upon the walls, and rustled uneasily about the decorations of the bed. But my efforts were fruitless. An irrepressible tremor gradually pervaded my frame; and, at length, there sat upon my very heart an incubus of utterly causeless alarm.[13] Shaking this off with a gasp and a struggle, I uplifted myself upon the pillows, and, peering earnestly within the intense darkness of the chamber, hearkened—I know not why, except that an instinctive spirit prompted me—to certain low and indefinite sounds which came, through the pauses of the storm, at long intervals, I knew not whence. Overpowered by an intense sentiment of horror, unaccountable yet unendurable, I threw on my clothes with haste (for I felt that I should sleep no more during the night), and endeavored to arouse myself from the pitiable condition into which I had fallen, by pacing rapidly to and fro through the apartment.

I had taken but few turns in this manner, when a light step on an adjoining staircase arrested my attention. I presently recognised it as that of Usher. In an instant afterward he rapped, with a gentle touch, at my door, and entered, bearing a lamp. His countenance was, as usual, cadaverously wan—but, moreover, there was a species of mad hilarity in his eyes—an evidently restrained *hysteria* in his whole demeanor. His air appalled me—but anything was preferable to the solitude which I had so long endured, and I even welcomed his presence as a relief.

"And you have not seen it?" he said abruptly, after having stared about him for some moments in silence—"you have not then seen it?—but, stay! you shall." Thus speaking, and having carefully shaded his lamp, he hurried to one of the casements, and threw it freely open to the storm.

The impetuous fury of the entering gust nearly lifted us from our feet. It was, indeed, a tempestuous yet sternly beautiful night, and one wildly singular in its terror and its beauty. A whirlwind had apparently collected its force in our vicinity; for there were frequent and violent alterations in the direction of the wind; and the exceeding density of the clouds (which hung so low as to press upon the turrets of the house) did not prevent our perceiving the life-like velocity with which they flew careering from all points against each other, without passing away into the distance. I say that even their exceeding density did not prevent our perceiving this—yet we had no glimpse of the moon or stars—nor was there any flashing forth of the lightning. But the under surfaces of the huge masses of agitated vapor, as well as all terrestrial objects immediately around us, were

---

[13]See our headnote to this story, and also the headnote to "Ligeia."

glowing in the unnatural light of a faintly luminous and distinctly visible gaseous exhalation which hung about and enshrouded the mansion.

"You must not—you shall not behold this!" said I, shuddering, to Usher, as I led him, with a gentle violence, from the window to a seat. "These appearances, which bewilder you, are merely electrical phenomena not uncommon—or it may be that they have their ghastly origin in the rank miasma[14] of the tarn. Let us close this casement;—the air is chilling and dangerous to your frame. Here is one of your favorite romances. I will read, and you shall listen;—and so we will pass away this terrible night together."

The antique volume which I had taken up was the "Mad Trist" of Sir Launcelot Canning;[15] but I had called it a favorite of Usher's more in sad jest than in earnest; for, in truth, there is little in its uncouth and unimaginative prolixity which could have had interest for the lofty and spiritual ideality of my friend. It was, however, the only book immediately at hand; and I indulged a vague hope that the excitement which now agitated the hypochondriac might find relief (for the history of mental disorder is full of similar anomalies) even in the extremeness of the folly which I should read. Could I have judged, indeed, by the wild overstrained air of vivacity with which he hearkened, or apparently hearkened, to the words of the tale, I might well have congratulated myself upon the success of my design.

I had arrived at that well-known portion of the story where Ethelred, the hero of the Trist, having sought in vain for peaceable admission into the dwelling of the hermit, proceeds to make good an entrance by force. Here, it will be remembered, the words of the narrative run thus:[16]

"And Ethelred, who was by nature of a doughty heart, and who was now mighty withal, on account of the powerfulness of the wine which he had drunken, waited no longer to hold parley with the hermit, who, in sooth, was of an obstinate and maliceful turn, but, feeling the rain upon his shoulders, and fearing the rising of the tempest, uplifted his mace outright and, with blows, made quickly room in the plankings of the door for his gauntleted hand; and now pulling therewith sturdily, he so cracked, and ripped, and tore all asunder, that the noise of the dry and hollow-sounding wood alarummed and reverberated throughout the forest."

---

[14]Unwholesome gas or atmosphere.

[15]Pollin (3) says there is no "Sir Launcelot Canning," but that Poe coined the name from a name in the works of Thomas Chatterton (1752–70), William Canynge. Chatterton undoubtedly caught Poe's imagination. A gifted youngster, he created pseudo-archaic poems, failed to achieve fame or financial rewards, and killed himself at the age of 17. There was also a well-known political leader and satiric writer, George Canning (1770–1827), whose fame might have put the name in Poe's head. Poe used the name also in his prospectus for *The Stylus,* a magazine he tried to found; on the title page of the prospectus appear three lines which he attributes to "Launcelot Canning."

[16]Poe seems to have made up the story. For a century before Poe wrote "Usher," authors had been inventing pseudoarchaic epics, tales, and ballads; by using familiar elements and characters, Poe suggests that this is either such a work or the real thing, an ancient tale. There were two real kings named Ethelred, who ruled from 866 to 871 and from 978 to 1016, respectively. A trist (tryst) is a meeting; the encounter with a hermit is a common element in tales of questing.

At the termination of this sentence, I started and, for a moment, paused; for it appeared to me (although I at once concluded that my excited fancy had deceived me)—it appeared to me that, from some very remote portion of the mansion, there came, distinctly, to my ears, what might have been, in its exact similarity of character, the echo (but a stifled and dull one certainly) of the very cracking and ripping sound which Sir Launcelot had so particularly described. It was, beyond doubt, the coincidence alone which had arrested my attention; for, amid the rattling of the sashes of the casements, and the ordinary commingled noises of the still increasing storm, the sound, in itself, had nothing, surely, which should have interested or disturbed me. I continued the story:

"But the good champion, Ethelred, now entering within the door, was sore enraged and amazed to perceive no signal of the maliceful hermit; but, in the stead thereof, a dragon of a scaly and prodigious demeanor, and of a fiery tongue, which sate in guard before a palace of gold, with a floor of silver; and upon the wall there hung a shield of shining brass with this legend enwritten—

Who entereth herein, a conqueror hath bin;
Who slayeth the dragon, the shield he shall win.

And Ethelred uplifted his mace, and struck upon the head of the dragon, which fell before him, and gave up his pesty breath, with a shriek so horrid and harsh, and withal so piercing, that Ethelred had fain to close his ears with his hands against the dreadful noise of it, the like whereof was never before heard."

Here again I paused abruptly, and now with a feeling of wild amazement—for there could be no doubt whatever that, in this instance, I did actually hear (although from what direction it proceeded I found it impossible to say) a low and apparently distant, but harsh, protracted, and most unusual screaming or grating sound—the exact counterpart of what my fancy had already conjured up for the dragon's unnatural shriek as described by the romancer.

Oppressed, as I certainly was, upon the occurrence of the second and most extraordinary coincidence, by a thousand conflicting sensations, in which wonder and extreme terror were predominant, I still retained sufficient presence of mind to avoid exciting, by any observation, the sensitive nervousness of my companion. I was by no means certain that he had noticed the sounds in question; although, assuredly, a strange alteration had, during the last few minutes, taken place in his demeanor. From a position fronting my own, he had gradually brought round his chair, so as to sit with his face to the door of the chamber; and thus I could but partially perceive his features, although I saw that his lips trembled as if he were murmuring inaudibly. His head had dropped upon his breast—yet I knew that he was not asleep, from the wide and rigid opening of the eye as I caught a glance of it in profile. The motion of his body, too, was at variance with this idea—for he rocked from side to side with a gentle yet constant and uniform sway. Having rapidly taken notice of all this, I resumed the narrative of Sir Launcelot, which thus proceeded:

"And now, the champion, having escaped from the terrible fury of the dragon, bethinking himself of the brazen shield, and of the breaking up of the enchantment which was upon it, removed the carcass from out of the way before him, and approached valorously over the silver pavement of the castle to where the shield was upon the wall; which in sooth tarried not for his full coming, but fell down at his feet upon the silver floor, with a mighty great and terrible ringing sound."

No sooner had these syllables passed my lips, than—as if a shield of brass had indeed, at the moment, fallen heavily upon a floor of silver—I became aware of a distinct, hollow metallic, and clangorous, yet apparently muffled reverberation. Completely unnerved, I leaped to my feet; but the measured rocking movement of Usher was undisturbed. I rushed to the chair in which he sat. His eyes were bent fixedly before him, and throughout his whole countenance there reigned a stony rigidity. But, as I placed my hand upon his shoulder, there came a strong shudder over his whole person; a sickly smile quivered about his lips; and I saw that he spoke in a low, hurried, and gibbering murmur, as if unconscious of my presence. Bending closely over him, I at length drank in the hideous import of his words.

"Not hear it?—yes, I hear it, and *have* heard it. Long—long—long—many minutes, many hours, many days, have I heard it—yet I dared not—oh, pity me, miserable wretch that I am!—I dared not—I *dared* not speak! *We have put her living in the tomb!* Said I not that my senses were acute? I *now* tell you that I heard her first feeble movements in the hollow coffin. I heard them—many, many days ago—yet I dared not—*I dared not speak!* And now—to-night—Ethelred—ha! ha!—the breaking of the hermit's door, and the death-cry of the dragon, and the clangor of the shield!—say, rather, the rending of her coffin, and the grating of the iron hinges of her prison, and her struggles within the coppered archway of the vault! Oh whither shall I fly? Will she not be here anon? Is she not hurrying to upbraid me for my haste? Have I not heard her footsteps on the stair? Do I not distinguish that heavy and horrible beating of her heart? *Madman!*"—here he sprang furiously to his feet, and shrieked out his syllables, as if in the effort he were giving up his soul—*"Madman! I tell you that she now stands without the door!"*

As if in the superhuman energy of his utterance there had been found the potency of a spell—the huge antique panels to which the speaker pointed, threw slowly back, upon the instant, their ponderous and ebony jaws. It was the work of the rushing gust—but then without those doors there *did* stand the lofty and enshrouded figure of the lady Madeline of Usher. There was blood upon her white robes, and the evidence of some bitter struggle upon every portion of her emaciated frame. For a moment she remained trembling and reeling to and fro upon the threshold, then, with a low moaning cry, fell heavily inward upon the person of her brother, and in her violent and now final death-agonies, bore him to the floor a corpse, and a victim to the terrors he had anticipated.

From that chamber, and from that mansion, I fled aghast. The storm was still abroad in all its wrath as I found myself crossing the old causeway. Suddenly there shot along the path a wild light, and I turned to see whence a gleam so unusual could have issued; for the vast house and its shadows were alone behind me. The radiance was that of the full, setting, and blood-red moon, which now shone vividly through that once barely discernible fissure, of which I have before spoken as extending from the roof of the building, in a zigzag direction, to the base. While

I gazed, this fissure rapidly widened—there came a fierce breath of the whirlwind—the entire orb of the satellite burst at once upon my sight—my brain reeled as I saw the mighty walls rushing asunder—there was a long tumultuous shouting sound like the voice of a thousand waters[17]—and the deep and dank tarn at my feet closed sullenly and silently over the fragments of the *"House of Usher."*

---

[17]Poe's language is probably an echo of Psalm 93. See "The Balloon-Hoax," note 9.

William Wilson

Poe's great story about conscience is unusual in several ways. Although Poe unjustly accused Hawthorne of having lifted passages from "William Wilson" for use in Hawthorne's tale "Howe's Masquerade," Poe admired Hawthorne; "William Wilson" is, indeed, his most Hawthornian story. The moral emphasis reminds one of Hawthorne, as does the manner of making a character an emblem of a spiritual trait. Poe also used Hawthorne's favorite technique for suggesting the incredible while maintaining credibility: he made the strangest occurrences in his story ambiguous. Wilson says that he could only "with difficulty shake off the belief" that he had known his double in a prior life; often the double appears when Wilson is "madly flushed" by liquor or excitement. Readers see the double as conscience and note that Wilson sometimes welcomes the interruptions. Those facts and Wilson's hereditary imaginativeness give room to interpret the events of the tale either literally or as the creations of a guilt-ridden and diseased mind.

"William Wilson" is unusual also in that it contains a very rare and uncharacteristically "realistic" description of childhood. The only other child whom Poe developed in any detail is Arthur Gordon Pym in Poe's novel. More typical of Poe is the familiar passage about how the narrator comes from an "imaginative and easily excitable race." That passage is present, too, as a prop to credibility.

Poe achieves power through accelerated rhythm as well. After the lengthy portion of the story set at Dr. Bransby's school, subsequent scenes are successively shorter. The result is almost cinematic, like the effects filmmakers can achieve through rhythmic "cutting"; the effect is to make Wilson's later adventures whiz by dizzyingly.

An interesting ambivalence is evident here and elsewhere in Poe, who can be alternately—and sometimes simultaneously—democratic and snobbish. Wilson is shown to be arrogant and aristocratic; he is, for instance, ashamed of his "common" name and regards institutions of higher learning as playgrounds for the elite. We as readers are supposed to dislike him for his snobbery. The usually antidemocratic Poe, in other words, at times reveals strong antiaristocratic biases. (Compare "The Masque of the Red Death" and "Mellonta Tauta.")

***A note of explanation:** The sources of Poe's ideas in this tale have been very thoroughly studied and make an interesting story. Details are nicely summarized in Mabbott (9, II). Poe felt so much in debt to Washington Irving's 1836 article "An Unwritten Drama by Lord Byron" that he wrote to Irving to tell him about the tie. Irving's piece outlines the idea of the double as a "spectre," "an allegorical being, the personification of conscience." It in turn involves connections from Byron to Percy Bysshe Shelley and ultimately to Calderón.*

PUBLICATIONS IN POE'S TIME

The Gift, 1840 (actually published in 1839)
Burton's Gentleman's Magazine, October 1839
Tales of the Grotesque and Arabesque, 1840
The Broadway Journal, August 30, 1845
The Spirit of the Times, Philadelphia, September 5, 6, and 8, 1845

WILLIAM WILSON

What say of it? what say [of] CONSCIENCE *grim,*
That spectre in my path?
Chamberlayne's *Pharronida*[1]

Let me call myself, for the present, William Wilson. The fair page now lying before me need not be sullied with my real appellation. This has been already too much an object for the scorn—for the horror—for the detestation of my race. To the uttermost regions of the globe have not the indignant winds bruited its unparalleled infamy? Oh, outcast of all outcasts most abandoned!—to the earth art thou not forever dead? to its honors, to its flowers, to its golden aspirations?—and a cloud, dense, dismal, and limitless, does it not hang eternally between thy hopes and heaven?

I would not, if I could, here or to-day, embody a record of my later years of unspeakable misery, and unpardonable crime. This epoch—these later years—took unto themselves a sudden elevation in turpitude, whose origin alone it is my present purpose to assign. Men usually grow base by degrees. From me, in an instant, all virtue dropped bodily as a mantle. From comparatively trivial wickedness I passed, with the stride of a giant, into more than the enormities of an Elah-Gabalus.[2] What chance—what one event brought this evil thing to pass, bear with me while I relate. Death approaches; and the shadow which foreruns him has thrown a softening influence over my spirit. I long, in passing through the dim valley, for the sympathy—I had nearly said for the pity—of my fellow men. I would fain have them believe that I have been, in some measure, the slave of

[1]William Chamberlayne's *Pharonnida* (1659) is a lengthy verse romance, but this "quotation" is not in it. A passage much like it, however, appears in Chamberlayne's *Love's Victory* (1658), which was printed with *Pharonnida* in an 1820 edition Poe probably knew. He probably scrambled them together as he did quotations in other stories (Rothwell). Poe consistently misspelled the title.

[2]Heliogabalus (204–22), Roman Emperor (218–22), whom Poe uses as an example of extreme debauchery.

circumstances beyond human control. I would wish them to seek out for me, in the details I am about to give, some little oasis of *fatality* amid a wilderness of error. I would have them allow—what they cannot refrain from allowing—that, although temptation may have erewhile existed as great, man was never *thus,* at least, tempted before—certainly, never *thus* fell. And is it therefore that he has never thus suffered? Have I not indeed been living in a dream? And am I not now dying a victim to the horror and the mystery of the wildest of all sublunary visions?

I am the descendant of a race whose imaginative and easily excitable temperament has at all times rendered them remarkable; and, in my earliest infancy, I gave evidence of having fully inherited the family character. As I advanced in years it was more strongly developed; becoming, for many reasons, a cause of serious disquietude to my friends, and of positive injury to myself. I grew self-willed, addicted to the wildest caprices, and a prey to the most ungovernable passions. Weak-minded, and beset with constitutional infirmities akin to my own, my parents could do but little to check the evil propensities which distinguished me. Some feeble and ill-directed efforts resulted in complete failure on their part, and, of course, in total triumph on mine. Thenceforward my voice was a household law; and at an age when few children have abandoned their leading-strings, I was left to the guidance of my own will, and became, in all but name, the master of my own actions.

My earliest recollections of a school-life are connected with a large, rambling, Elizabethan house, in a misty-looking village of England, where were a vast number of gigantic and gnarled trees, and where all the houses were excessively ancient. In truth, it was a dream-like and spirit-soothing place, that venerable old town. At this moment, in fancy, I feel the refreshing chilliness of its deeply-shadowed avenues, inhale the fragrance of its thousand shrubberies, and thrill anew with undefinable delight, at the deep hollow note of the church-bell, breaking, each hour, with sullen and sudden roar, upon the stillness of the dusky atmosphere in which the fretted Gothic steeple lay imbedded and asleep.

It gives me, perhaps, as much of pleasure as I can now in any manner experience, to dwell upon minute recollections of the school and its concerns. Steeped in misery as I am—misery, alas! only too real—I shall be pardoned for seeking relief, however slight and temporary, in the weakness of few rambling details. These, moreover, utterly trivial, and even ridiculous in themselves, assume, to my fancy, adventitious importance, as connected with a period and a locality when and where I recognise the first ambiguous monitions of the destiny which afterwards so fully overshadowed me. Let me then remember.

The house, I have said, was old and irregular. The grounds were extensive, and a high and solid brick wall, topped with a bed of mortar and broken glass, encompassed the whole. This prison-like rampart formed the limit of our domain; beyond it we saw but thrice a week—once every Saturday afternoon, when, attended by two ushers, we were permitted to take brief walks in a body through some of the neighboring fields—and twice during Sunday, when we were paraded in the same formal manner to the morning and evening service in the one church of the village. Of this church the principal of our school was pastor. With how deep a spirit of wonder and perplexity was I wont to regard him from our remote pew in the gallery, as, with step solemn and slow, he ascended the pulpit! This reverend man, with countenance so demurely benign, with robes so glossy and so clerically flowing, with wig so minutely powdered, so rigid and so vast,—could this be he who, of late, with sour visage, and in snuffy habiliments, administered, ferule in hand, the Draconian laws of the academy? Oh, gigantic paradox, too utterly monstrous for solution!

At an angle of the ponderous wall frowned a more ponderous gate. It was riveted and studded with iron bolts, and surmounted with jagged iron spikes. What impressions of deep awe did it inspire! It was never opened save for the three periodical egressions and ingressions already mentioned; then, in every creak of its mighty hinges, we found a plenitude of mystery—a world of matter for solemn remark, or for more solemn meditation.

The extensive enclosure was irregular in form, having many capacious recesses. Of these, three or four of the largest constituted the play-ground. It was level, and covered with fine hard gravel. I well remember it had no trees, nor benches, nor anything similar within it. Of course it was in the rear of the house. In front lay a small parterre, planted with box and other shrubs; but through this sacred division we passed only upon rare occasions indeed—such as a first advent to school or final departure thence, or perhaps, when a parent or friend having called for us, we joyfully took our way home for the Christmas or Midsummer holydays.

But the house!—how quaint an old building was this!—to me how veritably a palace of enchantment! There was really no end to its windings—to its incomprehensible subdivisions. It was difficult, at any given time, to say with certainty upon which of its two stories one happened to be. From each room to every other there were sure to be found three or four steps either in ascent or descent. Then the lateral branches were innumerable—inconceivable—and so returning in upon themselves, that our most exact ideas in regard to the whole mansion were not very far different from those with which we pondered upon infinity. During the five years of my residence here, I was never able to ascertain with precision, in what remote locality lay the little sleeping apartment assigned to myself and some eighteen or twenty other scholars.

The school-room was the largest in the house—I could not help thinking, in the world. It was very long, narrow, and dismally low, with pointed Gothic windows and a ceiling of oak. In a remote and terror-inspiring angle was a square enclosure of eight or ten feet, comprising the *sanctum,* "during hours," of our principal, the Reverend Dr. Bransby. It was a solid structure, with massy door, sooner than open which is the absence of the "Dominie," we would all have willingly perished by the *peine forte et dure.*[3] In other angles were two other similar boxes, far less reverenced, indeed, but still greatly matters of awe. One of these was the pulpit of the "classical" usher, one of the "English and mathematical." Interspersed about

---

[3]**Dr. Bransby:** A real person. Poe spent part of his childhood in England, at a school run by the Reverend John Bransby. Wilson's lengthy description of the school's complexities and windings is intended to associate it with a child's memories ("Let me then remember"). ***peine forte et dure:*** "Long and hard pain"—a medieval torture.

the room, crossing and recrossing in endless irregularity, were innumerable benches and desks, black, ancient, and time-worn, piled desperately with much-bethumbed books, and so beseamed with initial letters, names at full length, grotesque figures, and other multiplied efforts of the knife, as to have entirely lost what little of original form might have been their portion in days long departed. A huge bucket with water stood at one extremity of the room, and a clock of stupendous dimensions at the other.

Encompassed by the massy walls of this venerable academy, I passed, yet not in tedium or disgust, the years of the third lustrum of my life. The teeming brain of childhood requires no external world of incident to occupy or amuse it; and the apparently dismal monotony of a school was replete with more intense excitement than my riper youth has derived from luxury, or my full manhood from crime. Yet I must believe that my first mental development had in it much of the uncommon—even much of the *outré*. Upon mankind at large the events of very early existence rarely leave in mature age any definite impression. All is gray shadow—a weak and irregular remembrance—an indistinct regathering of feeble pleasures and phantasmagoric pains. With me this is not so. In childhood I must have felt with the energy of a man what I now find stamped upon memory in lines as vivid, as deep, and as durable as the *exergues*[4] of the Carthaginian medals.

Yet in fact—in the fact of the world's view—how little was there to remember! The morning's awakening, the nightly summons to bed; the connings, the recitations; the periodical half-holidays, and perambulations; the play-ground, with its broils, its pastimes, its intrigues;—these, by a mental sorcery long forgotten, were made to involve a wilderness of sensation, a world of rich incident, an universe of varied emotion, of excitement the most passionate and spirit-stirring. "*Oh, le bon temps, que ce siècle de fer!*"[5]

In truth, the ardor, the enthusiasm, and the imperiousness of my disposition, soon rendered me a marked character among my schoolmates, and by slow, but natural gradations, gave me an ascendancy over all not greatly older than myself;—over all with a single exception. This exception was found in the person of a scholar, who, although no relation, bore the same Christian and surname as myself;—a circumstance, in fact, little remarkable; for, notwithstanding a noble descent, mine was one of those everyday appellations which seem, by prescriptive right, to have been, time out of mind, the common property of the mob. In this narrative I have therefore designated myself as William Wilson,—a fictitious title not very dissimilar to the real. My namesake alone, of those who in school phraseology constituted "our set," presumed to compete with me in the studies of

---

[4]**lustrum:** Five-year period. Poe was at the Manor House School in Stoke Newington from 1817 to 1820, so he was younger than Wilson. ***outré:*** Strange. ***exergues:*** A numismatics term for the area on the reverse of a medal or a coin, beneath the picture or design, in which information is imprinted.

[5]**connings:** Students studied by "conning over lessons," which usually meant reading them over and over softly to themselves. **"*Oh, le bon temps, que ce siècle de fer!*":** "Oh! what a good time is this century of iron!" (in the sense of the Industrial Age). The quotation is from Voltaire's "Le Mondain" (1736), line 21, and is ironic[!]; the poet speaks sarcastically about those who refer to the good old times or the golden age.

the class—in the sports and broils of the play-ground—to refuse implicit belief in my assertions, and submission to my will—indeed, to interfere with my arbitrary dictation in any respect whatsoever. If there is on earth a supreme and unqualified despotism, it is the despotism of a master mind in boyhood over the less energetic spirits of its companions.[6]

Wilson's rebellion was to me a source of the greatest embarrassment;—the more so as, in spite of the bravado with which in public I made a point of treating him and his pretensions, I secretly felt that I feared him, and could not help thinking the equality which he maintained so easily with myself, a proof of his true superiority; since not to be overcome cost me a perpetual struggle. Yet this superiority—even this equality—was in truth acknowledged by no one but myself; our associates, by some unaccountable blindness, seemed not even to suspect it. Indeed, his competition, his resistance, and especially his impertinent and dogged interference with my purposes, were not more pointed than private. He appeared to be destitute alike of the ambition which urged, and of the passionate energy of mind which enabled me to excel. In his rivalry he might have been supposed actuated solely by a whimsical desire to thwart, astonish, or mortify myself; although there were times when I could not help observing, with a feeling made up of wonder, abasement, and pique, that he mingled with his injuries, his insults, or his contradictions, a certain most inappropriate, and assuredly most unwelcome *affectionateness* of manner. I could only conceive this singular behavior to arise from a consummate self-conceit assuming the vulgar airs of patronage and protection.

Perhaps it was this latter trait in Wilson's conduct, conjoined with our identity of name, and the mere accident of our having entered the school upon the same day, which set afloat the notion that we were brothers, among the senior classes in the academy. These do not usually inquire with much strictness into the affairs of their juniors. I have before said, or should have said, that Wilson was not, in the most remote degree, connected with my family. But assuredly if we *had* been brothers we must have been twins; for, after leaving Dr. Bransby's, I casually learned that my namesake was born on the nineteenth of January, 1813[7]—and this is a somewhat remarkable coincidence; for the day is precisely that of my own nativity.

It may seem strange that in spite of the continual anxiety occasioned me by the rivalry of Wilson, and his intolerable spirit of contradiction, I could not bring myself to hate him altogether. We had, to be sure, nearly every day a quarrel in which, yielding me publicly the palm of victory, he, in some manner, contrived to make me feel that it was he who had deserved it; yet a sense of pride on my part, and a veritable dignity on his own, kept us always upon what are called "speaking terms," while there were many points of strong congeniality in our tempers, operating to awake in me a sentiment which our position alone, perhaps, prevented from ripening into friendship. It is difficult, indeed, to define, or even to

---

[6]See our headnote.

[7]Poe was born on January 19, 1809. He did sometimes give 1813 as his birth year (Carlson 2).

describe, my real feelings towards him. They formed a motley and heterogeneous admixture;—some petulant animosity, which was not yet hatred, some esteem, more respect, much fear, with a world of uneasy curiosity. To the moralist it will be unnecessary to say, in addition, that Wilson and myself were the most inseparable of companions.

It was no doubt the anomalous state of affairs existing between us, which turned all my attacks upon him, (and they were many, either open or covert) into the channel of banter or practical joke (giving pain while assuming the aspect of mere fun) rather than into a more serious and determined hostility. But my endeavors on this head were by no means uniformly successful, even when my plans were the most wittily concocted; for my namesake had much about him, in character, of that unassuming and quiet austerity which, while enjoying the poignancy of its own jokes, has no heel of Achilles[8] in itself, and absolutely refuses to be laughed at. I could find, indeed, but one vulnerable point, and that, lying in a personal peculiarity, arising, perhaps, from constitutional disease, would have been spared by any antagonist less at his wit's end than myself;—my rival had a weakness in the faucial or guttural organs, which precluded him from raising his voice at any time *above a very low whisper.* Of this defect I did not fail to take what poor advantage lay in my power.

Wilson's retaliations in kind were many; and there was one form of his practical wit that disturbed me beyond measure. How his sagacity first discovered at all that so petty a thing would vex me, is a question I never could solve; but, having discovered, he habitually practised the annoyance. I had always felt aversion to my uncourtly patronymic, and its very common, if not plebeian prænomen. The words were venom in my ears; and when, upon the day of my arrival, a second William Wilson came also to the academy, I felt angry with him for bearing the name, and doubly disgusted with the name because a stranger bore it, who would be the cause of its twofold repetition, who would be constantly in my presence, and whose concerns, in the ordinary routine of the school business, must inevitably, on account of the detestable coincidence, be often confounded with my own.

The feeling of vexation thus engendered grew stronger with every circumstance tending to show resemblance, moral, or physical, between my rival and myself. I had not then discovered the remarkable fact that we were of the same age; but I saw that we were of the same height, and I perceived that we were even singularly alike in general contour of person and outline of feature. I was galled, too, by the rumor touching a relationship, which had grown current in the upper forms.[9] In a word, nothing could more seriously disturb me, (although I scrupulously concealed such disturbance,) than any allusion to a similarity of mind, person, or condition existing between us. But, in truth, I had no reason to believe that (with the exception of the matter of relationship, and in the case of Wilson himself,) this similarity had ever been made a subject of comment, or even observed at all by

---

[8]Achilles, the epic protagonist of Homer's *Iliad,* had according to tradition been made invulnerable except in the heel by which his mother held him when, as a baby, he was given the magical dunking which conferred godly protection.

[9]Classes.

our schoolfellows. That *he* observed it in all its bearings, and as fixedly as I, was apparent; but that he could discover in such circumstances so fruitful a field of annoyance, can only be attributed, as I said before, to his more than ordinary penetration.

His cue, which was to perfect an imitation of myself, lay both in words and in actions; and most admirably did he play his part. My dress it was an easy matter to copy; my gait and general manner were, without difficulty, appropriated; in spite of his constitutional defect, even my voice did not escape him. My louder tones were, of course, unattempted, but then the key, it was identical; *and his singular whisper, it grew the very echo of my own.*

How greatly this most exquisite portraiture harassed me, (for it could not justly be termed a caricature,) I will not now venture to describe. I had but one consolation—in the fact that the imitation, apparently, was noticed by myself alone, and that I had to endure only the knowing and strangely sarcastic smiles of my namesake himself. Satisfied with having produced in my bosom the intended effect, he seemed to chuckle in secret over the sting he had inflicted, and was characteristically disregardful of the public applause which the success of his witty endeavors might have so easily elicited. That the school, indeed, did not feel his design, perceive its accomplishment, and participate in his sneer, was, for many anxious months, a riddle I could not resolve. Perhaps the *gradation* of his copy rendered it not so readily perceptible; or, more possibly, I owed my security to the masterly air of the copyist, who, disdaining the letter, (which in a painting is all the obtuse can see,) gave but the full spirit of his original for my individual contemplation and chagrin.

I have already more than once spoken of the disgusting air of patronage which he assumed toward me, and of his frequent officious interference with my will. This interference often took the ungracious character of advice; advice not openly given, but hinted or insinuated. I received it with a repugnance which gained strength as I grew in years. Yet, at this distant day, let me do him the simple justice to acknowledge that I can recall no occasion when the suggestions of my rival were on the side of those errors or follies so usual to his immature age and seeming inexperience; that his moral sense, at least, if not his general talents and worldly wisdom, was far keener than my own; and that I might, to-day, have been a better, and thus a happier man, had I less frequently rejected the counsels embodied in those meaning whispers which I then but too cordially hated and too bitterly despised.

As it was, I at length grew restive in the extreme under his distasteful supervision, and daily resented more and more openly what I considered his intolerable arrogance. I have said that, in the first years of our connexion as schoolmates, my feelings in regard to him might have been easily ripened into friendship: but, in the latter months of my residence at the academy, although the intrusion of his ordinary manner had, beyond doubt, in some measure, abated, my sentiments, in nearly similar proportion, partook very much of positive hatred. Upon one occasion he saw this, I think, and afterwards avoided, or made a show of avoiding me.

It was about the same period, if I remember aright, that, in an altercation of violence with him, in which he was more than usually thrown off his guard, and spoke and acted with an openness of demeanor rather foreign to his nature, I discovered, or fancied I discovered, in his accent, his air, and general appearance, a something which first startled, and then deeply interested me, by bringing to mind dim visions of my earliest infancy—wild, confused and thronging memories of a time when memory herself was yet unborn. I cannot better describe the sensation which oppressed me than by saying that I could with difficulty shake off the belief of my having been acquainted with the being who stood before me, at some epoch very long ago—some point of the past even infinitely remote. The delusion, however, faded rapidly as it came; and I mention it at all but to define the day of the last conversation I there held with my singular namesake.

The huge old house, with its countless subdivisions, had several large chambers communicating with each other, where slept the greater number of the students. There were, however, (as must necessarily happen in a building so awkwardly planned,) many little nooks or recesses, the odds and ends of the structure; and these the economic ingenuity of Dr. Bransby had also fitted up as dormitories; although, being the merest closets, they were capable of accommodating but a single individual. One of these small apartments was occupied by Wilson.

One night, about the close of my fifth year at the school, and immediately after the altercation mentioned, finding every one wrapped in sleep, I arose from bed, and, lamp in hand, stole through a wilderness of narrow passages from my own bedroom to that of my rival. I had long been planning one of those ill-natured pieces of practical wit at his expense in which I had hitherto been so uniformly unsuccessful. It was my intention, now, to put my scheme in operation, and I resolved to make him feel the whole extent of the malice with which I was imbued. Having reached his closet, I noiselessly entered, leaving the lamp, with a shade over it, on the outside. I advanced a step, and listened to the sound of his tranquil breathing. Assured of his being asleep, I returned, took the light, and with it again approached the bed. Close curtains were around it, which, in the prosecution of my plan, I slowly and quietly withdrew, when the bright rays fell vividly upon the sleeper, and my eyes, at the same moment, upon his countenance. I looked;—and a numbness, an iciness of feeling instantly pervaded my frame. My breast heaved, my knees tottered, my whole spirit became possessed with an objectless yet intolerable horror. Gasping for breath, I lowered the lamp in still nearer proximity to the face. Were these—*these* the lineaments of William Wilson? I saw, indeed, that they were his, but I shook as if with a fit of the ague in fancying they were not. What *was* there about them to confound me in this manner? I gazed,—while my brain reeled with a multitude of incoherent thoughts. Not thus he appeared—assuredly not *thus*—in the vivacity of his waking hours. The same name! the same contour of person! the same day of arrival at the academy! And then his dogged and meaningless imitation of my gait, my voice, my habits, and my manner! Was it, in truth, within the bounds of human possibility, that *what I now saw* was the result, merely, of the habitual practice of this sarcastic imitation? Awe-stricken, and with a creeping shudder, I extinguished the lamp, passed silently from the chamber, and left, at once, the halls of that old academy, never to enter them again.

After a lapse of some months, spent at home in mere idleness, I found myself a student at Eton. The brief interval had been sufficient to enfeeble my remembrance of the events at Dr. Bransby's, or at least to effect a material change in the nature of the feelings with which I remembered them. The truth—the tragedy—of the drama was no more. I could now find room to doubt the evidence of my senses; and seldom called up the subject at all but with wonder at the extent of human credulity, and a smile at the vivid force of the imagination which I hereditarily possessed. Neither was this species of scepticism likely to be diminished by the character of the life I led at Eton. The vortex of thoughtless folly into which I there so immediately and so recklessly plunged, washed away all but the froth of my past hours, engulfed at once every solid or serious impression, and left to memory only the veriest levities of a former existence.

I do not wish, however, to trace the course of my miserable profligacy here—a profligacy which set at defiance the laws, while it eluded the vigilance of the institution. Three years of folly, passed without profit, had but given me rooted habits of vice, and added, in a somewhat unusual degree, to my bodily stature, when, after a week of soulless dissipation, I invited a small party of the most dissolute students to a secret carousal in my chambers. We met at a late hour of the night; for our debaucheries were to be faithfully protracted until morning. The wine flowed freely, and there were not wanting other and perhaps more dangerous seductions; so that the gray dawn had already faintly appeared in the east, while our delirious extravagance was at its height. Madly flushed with cards and intoxication, I was in the act of insisting upon a toast of more than wonted profanity, when my attention was suddenly diverted by the violent, although partial unclosing of the door of the apartment, and by the eager voice of a servant from without. He said that some person, apparently in great haste, demanded to speak with me in the hall.

Wildly excited with wine, the unexpected interruption rather delighted than surprised me. I staggered forward at once, and a few steps brought me to the vestibule of the building. In this low and small room there hung no lamp; and now no light at all was admitted, save that of the exceedingly feeble dawn which made its way through the semi-circular window. As I put my foot over the threshold, I became aware of the figure of a youth about my own height, and habited in a white kerseymere morning frock, cut in the novel fashion of the one I myself wore at the moment. This the faint light enabled me to perceive; but the features of his face I could not distinguish. Upon my entering he strode hurriedly up to me, and, seizing me by the arm with a gesture of petulant impatience, whispered the words "William Wilson!" in my ear.

I grew perfectly sober in an instant.

There was that in the manner of the stranger, and in the tremulous shake of his uplifted finger, as he held it between my eyes and the light, which filled me with unqualified amazement; but it was not this which had so violently moved me. It was the pregnancy of solemn admonition in the singular, low, hissing utterance; and, above all, it was the character, the tone, *the key,* of those few, simple, and familiar, yet *whispered* syllables, which came with a thousand thronging memories of by-gone days, and struck upon my soul with the shock of a galvanic battery. Ere I could recover the use of my senses he was gone.

Although this event failed not of a vivid effect upon my disordered imagination, yet was it evanescent as vivid. For some weeks, indeed, I busied myself in earnest inquiry, or was wrapped in an cloud of morbid speculation. I did not pretend to disguise from my perception the identity of the singular individual who thus perseveringly interfered with my affairs, and harassed me with his insinuated counsel. But who and what was this Wilson?—and whence came he?—and what were his purposes? Upon neither of these points could I be satisfied; merely ascertaining, in regard to him, that a sudden accident in his family had caused his removal from Dr. Bransby's academy on the afternoon of the day in which I myself had eloped. But in a brief period I ceased to think upon the subject; my attention being all absorbed in a contemplated departure for Oxford. Thither I soon went; the uncalculating vanity of my parents furnishing me with an outfit and annual establishment, which would enable me to indulge at will in the luxury already so dear to my heart,—to vie in profuseness of expenditure with the haughtiest heirs of the wealthiest earldoms in Great Britain.

Excited by such appliances to vice, my constitutional temperament broke forth with redoubled ardor, and I spurned even the common restraints of decency in the mad infatuation of my revels. But it were absurd to pause in the detail of my extravagance. Let it suffice, that among spendthrifts I out-Heroded Herod, and that, giving name to a multitude of novel follies, I added no brief appendix to the long catalogue of vices then usual in the most dissolute university of Europe.[10]

It could hardly be credited, however, that I had, even here, so utterly fallen from the gentlemanly estate, as to seek acquaintance with the vilest arts of the gambler by profession, and, having become an adept in his despicable science, to practise it habitually as a means of increasing my already enormous income at the expense of the weak-minded among my fellow-collegians. Such, nevertheless, was the fact. And the very enormity of this offence against all manly and honorable sentiment proved, beyond doubt, the main if not the sole reason of the impunity with which it was committed. Who, indeed, among my most abandoned associates, would not rather have disputed the clearest evidence of his senses, than have suspected of such courses, the gay, the frank, the generous William Wilson—the noblest and most liberal commoner at Oxford—him whose follies (said his parasites) were but the follies of youth and unbridled fancy—whose errors but inimitable whim—whose darkest vice but a careless and dashing extravagance?

I had been now two years successfully busied in this way, when there came to the university a young *parvenu* nobleman, Glendinning—rich, said report, as Herodes Atticus[11]—his riches, too, as easily acquired. I soon found him of weak intellect, and, of course, marked him as a fitting subject for my skill. I frequently

---

[10]Poe has pet phrases. He uses "out-Heroded Herod" in several stories. See for example "Metzengerstein," note 7, and "The Masque of the Red Death," note 7. Forrest lists Matthew 2:16 as the source of the phrase. In "Mystification," Poe says that Göttingen is the most dissolute university in Europe.

[11]***parvenu:*** A newly rich person. **Herodes Atticus:** Athenian orator and statesman (c.110–c.185), very wealthy and very famous as a large-scale benefactor of several Greek cities.

engaged him in play, and contrived, with the gambler's usual art, to let him win considerable sums, the more effectually to entangle him in my snares. At length, my schemes being ripe, I met him (with the full intention that this meeting should be final and decisive) at the chambers of a fellow-commoner, (Mr. Preston,) equally intimate with both, but who, to do him justice, entertained not even a remote suspicion of my design. To give to this a better coloring, I had contrived to have assembled a party of some eight or ten, and was solicitously careful that the introduction of cards should appear accidental, and originate in the proposal of my contemplated dupe himself. To be brief upon a vile topic, none of the low finesse was omitted, so customary upon similar occasions that it is a just matter for wonder how any are still found so besotted as to fall its victim.

We had protracted our sitting far into the night, and I had at length effected the manœuvre of getting Glendinning as my sole antagonist. The game, too, was my favorite *écarté.*[12] The rest of the company, interested in the extent of our play, had abandoned their own cards, and were standing around us as spectators. The *parvenu,* who had been induced by my artifices in the early part of the evening, to drink deeply, now shuffled, dealt, or played, with a wild nervousness of manner for which his intoxication, I thought, might partially, but could not altogether account. In a very short period he had become my debtor to a large amount, when, having taken a long draught of port, he did precisely what I had been coolly anticipating—he proposed to double our already extravagant stakes. With a well-feigned show of reluctance, and not until after my repeated refusal had seduced him into some angry words which gave a color of *pique* to my compliance, did I finally comply. The result, of course, did but prove how entirely the prey was in my toils; in less than an hour he had quadrupled his debt. For some time his countenance had been losing the florid tinge lent it by the wine; but now, to my astonishment, I perceived that it had grown to a pallor truly fearful. I say to my astonishment. Glendinning had been represented to my eager inquiries as immeasurably wealthy; and the sums which he had as yet lost, although in themselves vast, could not, I supposed, very seriously annoy, much less so violently affect him. That he was overcome by the wine just swallowed, was the idea which most readily presented itself; and, rather with a view to the preservation of my own character in the eyes of my associates, than from any less interested motive, I was about to insist, peremptorily, upon a discontinuance of the play, when some expressions at my elbow from among the company, and an ejaculation evincing utter despair on the part of Glendinning, gave me to understand that I had effected his total ruin under circumstances which, rendering him an object for the pity of all, should have protected him from the ill offices even of a fiend.

What now might have been my conduct it is difficult to say. The pitiable condition of my dupe had thrown an air of embarrassed gloom over all; and, for some moments, a profound silence was maintained, during which I could not help feeling my cheeks tingle with the many burning glances of scorn or reproach cast upon me by the less abandoned of the party. I will even own that an intolerable weight of anxiety was for a brief instant lifted from my bosom by the sudden and

[12]Card game for two people.

extraordinary interruption which ensued. The wide, heavy folding doors of the apartment were all at once thrown open, to their full extent, with a vigorous and rushing impetuosity that extinguished, as if by magic, every candle in the room. Their light, in dying, enabled us just to perceive that a stranger had entered, about my own height, and closely muffled in a cloak. The darkness, however, was now total; and we could only *feel* that he was standing in our midst. Before any one of us could recover from the extreme astonishment into which this rudeness had thrown all, we heard the voice of the intruder.

"Gentlemen," he said, in a low, distinct, and never-to-be-forgotten *whisper* which thrilled to the very marrow of my bones, "Gentlemen, I make no apology for this behavior, because in thus behaving, I am but fulfilling a duty. You are, beyond doubt, uninformed of the true character of the person who has to-night won at *écarté* a large sum of money from Lord Glendinning. I will therefore put you upon an expeditious and decisive plan of obtaining this very necessary information. Please to examine, at your leisure, the inner linings of the cuff of his left sleeve, and the several little packages which may be found in the somewhat capacious pockets of his embroidered morning wrapper."

While he spoke, so profound was the stillness that one might have heard a pin drop upon the floor. In ceasing, he departed at once, and as abruptly as he had entered. Can I—shall I describe my sensations?—must I say that I felt all the horrors of the damned? Most assuredly I had little time given for reflection. Many hands roughly seized me upon the spot, and lights were immediately reprocured. A search ensued. In the lining of my sleeve were found all the court cards essential in *écarté,* and, in the pockets of my wrapper, a number of packs, fac-similes of those used at our sittings, with the single exception that mine were of the species called, technically, *arrondées;*[13] the honors being slightly convex at the ends, the lower cards slightly convex at the sides. In this disposition, the dupe who cuts, as customary, at the length of the pack, will invariably find that he cuts his antagonist an honor; while the gambler, cutting at the breadth, will, as certainly, cut nothing for his victim which may count in the records of the game.

Any burst of indignation upon this discovery would have affected me less than the silent contempt, or the sarcastic composure, with which it was received.

"Mr. Wilson," said our host, stooping to remove from beneath his feet an exceedingly luxurious cloak of rare furs, "Mr. Wilson, this is your property." (The weather was cold; and, upon quitting my own room, I had thrown a cloak over my dressing wrapper, putting it off upon reaching the scene of play.) "I presume it is supererogatory to seek here (eyeing the folds of the garment with a bitter smile) for any farther evidence of your skill. Indeed, we have had enough. You will see the necessity, I hope, of quitting Oxford—at all events, of quitting instantly my chambers."

Abased, humbled to the dust as I then was, it is probable that I should have resented this galling language by immediate personal violence, had not my whole attention been at the moment arrested by a fact of the most startling character. The cloak which I had worn was of a rare description of fur; how rare, how extrava-

---

[13]Rounded.

gantly costly, I shall not venture to say. Its fashion, too, was of my own fantastic invention; for I was fastidious to an absurd degree of coxcombry, in matters of this frivolous nature. When, therefore, Mr. Preston reached me that which he had picked up upon the floor, and near the folding doors of the apartment, it was with an astonishment nearly bordering upon terror, that I perceived my own already hanging on my arm, (where I had no doubt unwittingly placed it,) and that the one presented me was but its exact counterpart in every, in even the minutest possible particular. The singular being who had so disastrously exposed me, had been muffled, I remembered, in a cloak; and none had been worn at all by any of the members of our party with the exception of myself. Retaining some presence of mind, I took the one offered me by Preston; placed it, unnoticed, over my own; left the apartment with a resolute scowl of defiance; and, next morning ere dawn of day, commenced a hurried journey from Oxford to the continent, in a perfect agony of horror and of shame.

I fled in vain. My evil destiny pursued me as if in exultation, and proved, indeed, that the exercise of its mysterious dominion had as yet only begun. Scarcely had I set foot in Paris ere I had fresh evidence of the detestable interest taken by this Wilson in my concerns. Years flew, while I experienced no relief. Villain!—at Rome, with how untimely, yet with how spectral an officiousness, stepped he in between me and my ambition! At Vienna, too—at Berlin—and at Moscow! Where, in truth, had I *not* bitter cause to curse him within my heart? From his inscrutable tyranny did I at length flee, panic-stricken, as from a pestilence; and to the very ends of the earth *I fled in vain.*

And again, and again, in secret communion with my own spirit, would I demand the questions "Who is he?—whence came he?—and what are his objects?" But no answer was there found. And then I scrutinized, with a minute scrutiny, the forms, and the methods, and the leading traits of his impertinent supervision. But even here there was very little upon which to base a conjecture. It was noticeable, indeed, that, in no one of the multiplied instances in which he had crossed my path, had he so crossed it except to frustrate those schemes, or to disturb those actions, which, if fully carried out, might have resulted in bitter mischief. Poor justification this, in truth, for an authority so imperiously assumed! Poor indemnity for natural rights of self-agency so pertinaciously, so insultingly denied!

I had also been forced to notice that my tormentor, for a very long period of time, (while scrupulously and with miraculous dexterity maintaining his whim of an identity of apparel with myself,) had so contrived it, in the execution of his varied interference with my will, that I saw not, at any moment, the features of his face. Be Wilson what he might, *this,* at least, was but the veriest of affectation, or of folly. Could he, for an instant, have supposed that, in my admonisher at Eton—in the destroyer of my honor at Oxford,—in him who thwarted my ambition at Rome, my revenge at Paris, my passionate love at Naples, or what he falsely termed my avarice in Egypt,—that in this, my arch-enemy and evil genius, I could fail to recognise the William Wilson of my school-boy days,—the namesake, the companion, the rival,—the hated and dreaded rival at Dr. Bransby's? Impossible!—But let me hasten to the last eventful scene of the drama.

Thus far I had succumbed supinely to this imperious domination. The sentiment of deep awe with which I habitually regarded the elevated character, the majestic wisdom, the apparent omnipresence and omnipotence of Wilson, added to a feeling of even terror, with which certain other traits in his nature and assumptions inspired me, had operated, hitherto, to impress me with an idea of my own utter weakness and helplessness, and to suggest an implicit, although bitterly reluctant submission to his arbitrary will. But, of late days, I had given myself up entirely to wine; and its maddening influence upon my hereditary temper rendered me more and more impatient of control. I began to murmur,—to hesitate,—to resist. And was it only fancy which induced me to believe that, with the increase of my own firmness, that of my tormentor underwent a proportional diminution? Be this as it may, I now began to feel the inspiration of a burning hope, and at length nurtured in my secret thoughts a stern and desperate resolution that I would submit no longer to be enslaved.

It was at Rome, during the Carnival of 18—, that I attended a masquerade in the palazzo of the Neapolitan Duke Di Broglio. I had indulged more freely than usual in the excesses of the wine-table; and now the suffocating atmosphere of the crowded rooms irritated me beyond endurance. The difficulty, too, of forcing my way through the mazes of the company contributed not a little to the ruffling of my temper; for I was anxiously seeking (let me not say with what unworthy motive) the young, the gay, the beautiful wife of the aged and doting Di Broglio. With a too unscrupulous confidence she had previously communicated to me the secret of the costume in which she would be habited, and now, having caught a glimpse of her person, I was hurrying to make my way into her presence.—At this moment I felt a light hand placed upon my shoulder, and that ever-remembered, low, damnable *whisper* within my ear.

In an absolute frenzy of wrath, I turned at once upon him who had thus interrupted me, and seized him violently by the collar. He was attired, as I had expected, in a costume altogether similar to my own; wearing a Spanish cloak of blue velvet, begirt about the waist with a crimson belt sustaining a rapier. A mask of black silk entirely covered his face.

"Scoundrel!" I said, in a voice husky with rage, while every syllable I uttered seemed as new fuel to my fury, "scoundrel! impostor! accursed villain! you shall not—you *shall not* dog me unto death! Follow me, or I stab you where you stand!"—and I broke my way from the ball-room into a small ante-chamber adjoining—dragging him unresisting with me as I went.

Upon entering, I thrust him furiously from me. He staggered against the wall, while I closed the door with an oath, and commanded him to draw. He hesitated but for an instant; then, with a slight sigh, drew in silence, and put himself upon his defence.

The contest was brief indeed. I was frantic with every species of wild excitement, and felt within my single arm the energy and power of a multitude. In a few seconds I forced him by sheer strength against the wainscoting, and thus, getting him at mercy, plunged the sword, with brute ferocity, repeatedly through and through his bosom.

At that instant some person tried the latch of the door. I hastened to prevent an intrusion, and then immediately returned to my dying antagonist. But what human language can adequately portray *that* astonishment, *that* horror which possessed me at the spectacle then presented to view? The brief moment in which I averted my eyes had been sufficient to produce, apparently, a material change in the arrangements at the upper or farther end of the room. A large mirror,—so at first it seemed to me in my confusion—now stood where none had been perceptible before; and, as I stepped up to it in extremity of terror, mine own image, but with features all pale and dabbled in blood, advanced to meet me with a feeble and tottering gait.

Thus it appeared, I say, but was not. It was my antagonist—it was Wilson, who then stood before me in the agonies of his dissolution. His mask and cloak lay, where he had thrown them, upon the floor. Not a thread in all his raiment—not a line in all the marked and singular lineaments of his face which was not, even in the most absolute identity, *mine own!*

It was Wilson; but he spoke no longer in a whisper, and I could have fancied that I myself was speaking while he said:

"You have conquered, and I yield. Yet, henceforward art thou also dead—dead to the World, to Heaven and to Hope! In me didst thou exist—and, in my death, see by this image, which is thine own, how utterly thou hast murdered thyself."

The Man of the Crowd

It is not easy to say exactly what this strange and wonderful story means: its vision of some unnamed horror in the heart of the city reminds one of the descent into New York in Melville's Pierre; *its catalogue of social classes is Whitmanesque; and its refusal to moralize is very modern—one thinks of Hemingway's "A Clean Well-Lighted Place" and other visions of urban loneliness. Although it illustrates some of Poe's least attractive attitudes, it also suggests that the artist had within him the capacity for spiritual growth. For alongside the usual condescension and racism there is in "The Man of the Crowd" an unmistakable compassion: Poe pities the poor, the prostitutes, the city's underdogs.*

The old cliché about Poe's otherworldliness crumbles before passages of almost Dickensian genre characterization, such as the long social catalogue which begins in paragraph five. Poe, we must remember, was an urban man, who, if he did not know the London in which this story is supposedly set, knew Philadelphia and New York very well. Like other Romantics, he reacted strongly to the new kind of city which modernization and the Industrial Revolution were creating.

Critics from 1847 on have noted the apparent implausibility of the events of "The Man of the Crowd"; they ignore the paragraph indicated by note 3, in which the narrator tells us that he has been ill—indeed, is still recuperating—and is in a strange and hyperacute state. This is the familiar Poe device of providing a "margin of credibility" through a peculiar state of mind: we can believe what happens, or assume that it is partially a delusion, the result of the narrator's illness.

***A note of explanation:** We feel that Poe, who had no firsthand knowledge of London (he had lived in England only briefly, as a child—see "William Wilson"), leaned very heavily on William Maginn's sketch "The Night Walker," published first in* Blackwood's Edinburgh Magazine *in November 1823. The narrator takes the reader on a tour of the busy places in London throughout the night; it begins in the theater district and moves through less respectable forms of entertainment. As in the Poe story, too, there are catalogues of trades and occupations and a telling of the hours; Maginn shows which people are seen at each hour.*

Now, Blackwood's *was an unusual magazine, witty, disputatious, satirical, brilliant. Poe loved it, and seems to have known some volumes almost by heart. Its writers had pet nicknames for one another. The code-name for the proprietor, William Blackwood, was "ebony"—black wood. We have a strong hunch that Poe's very puzzling roundabout sentence concerning Tertullian's "ebony style" has nothing to do with Tertullian (see note 8); rather, it seems to be Poe's way of tipping his hat to the wits of Edinburgh.*

Moreover, we think it possible that his colleagues across the Atlantic recognized and appreciated his gesture, for when Blackwood's *in 1847 reviewed Poe's* Tales *(1845), "The Man of the Crowd" was the tale singled out for detailed—and very favorable—discussion.*

It is likely also that Poe's story connects to Bulwer-Lytton's Pelham *(1828), one of Poe's favorite idea-mines. There is a considerable overlap of details such as the "swell pickpockets," the bogus clergyman, and the odd word "flash." See also note 1. Finally: the Dickensian tone is probably no accident; Mabbott (9, II) and others note likely connections to various works by Charles Dickens.*

PUBLICATIONS IN POE'S TIME

Gentleman's Magazine ("Burton's") and *Graham's Magazine* (formerly *The Casket*), December 1840 (The contents of the two magazines are nearly, but not quite, identical, because, with these numbers, the two were in the process of being combined. Poe shortly after became editor of *Graham's*.)
Tales, 1845

THE MAN OF THE CROWD

Ce grand malheur, de ne pouvoir être seul.
La Bruyère[1]

It was well said of a certain German book that "*es lässt sich nicht lesen*"—it does not permit itself to be read.[2] There are some secrets which do not permit themselves to be told. Men die nightly in their beds, wringing the hands of ghostly confessors, and looking them piteously in the eyes—die with despair of heart and convulsion of throat, on account of the hideousness of mysteries which will not *suffer themselves* to be revealed. Now and then, alas, the conscience of man takes up a burden so heavy in horror that it can be thrown down only into the grave. And thus the essence of all crime is undivulged.

Not long ago, about the closing in of an evening in autumn, I sat at the large bow window of the D—— Coffee-House in London. For some months I had been

[1]"This great misfortune of not being able to be alone." Poe's line is from "De L'Homme" in *Les Caractères* by Jean de la Bruyère (1645–96). The original reads, "*Tout notre mal vient de ne pouvoir être seuls. . . .*" Compare "Metzengerstein," note 3. Poe probably saw the line in Bulwer-Lytton's novel *Pelham* (1828), where it appears as the motto of Chapter 42.

[2]Poe later said this of another book. See his "Fifty Suggestions," number 46. See also note 14.

ill in health, but was now convalescent, and, with returning strength, found myself in one of those happy moods which are so precisely the converse of *ennui*—moods of the keenest appetency, when the film from the mental vision departs—the ἀχλὺς ἣ πρὶν ἐπῆεν—and the intellect, electrified, surpasses as greatly its every-day condition, as does the vivid yet candid reason of Leibnitz, the mad and flimsy rhetoric of Gorgias. Merely to breathe was enjoyment; and I derived positive pleasure even from many of the legitimate sources of pain. I felt a calm but inquisitive interest in every thing. With a cigar in my mouth and a newspaper in my lap, I had been amusing myself for the greater part of the afternoon, now in poring over advertisements, now in observing the promiscuous company in the room, and now in peering through the smoky panes into the street.[3]

This latter is one of the principal thoroughfares of the city, and had been very much crowded during the whole day. But, as the darkness came on, the throng momently increased; and, by the time the lamps were well lighted, two dense and continuous tides of population were rushing past the door. At this particular period of the evening I had never before been in a similar situation, and the tumultuous sea of human heads filled me, therefore, with a delicious novelty of emotion. I gave up, at length, all care of things within the hotel, and became absorbed in contemplation of the scene without.

At first my observations took an abstract and generalizing turn. I looked at the passengers in masses, and thought of them in their aggregate relations. Soon, however, I descended to details, and regarded with minute interest the innumerable varieties of figure, dress, air, gait, visage, and expression of countenance.

By far the greater number of those who went by had a satisfied business-like demeanor, and seemed to be thinking only of making their way through the press. Their brows were knit, and their eyes rolled quickly; when pushed against by fellow-wayfarers they evinced no symptom of impatience, but adjusted their clothes and hurried on. Others, still a numerous class, were restless in their movements, had flushed faces, and talked and gesticulated to themselves, as if feeling in solitude on account of the very denseness of the company around. When impeded in their progress, these people suddenly ceased muttering, but redoubled their gesticulations, and awaited, with an absent and overdone smile upon the lips, the course of the persons impeding them. If jostled, they bowed profusely to the jostlers, and appeared overwhelmed with confusion.—There was nothing very distinctive about these two large classes beyond what I have noted. Their habiliments belonged to that order which is pointedly termed the decent. They were undoubtedly noblemen, merchants, attorneys, tradesmen, stock-jobbers—the Eu-

[3]**ἀχλὺς ἣ πρὶν ἐπῆεν:** In Book V of the *Iliad,* Athena says to Diomedes, "Take heart in battle, for I have removed *the mist from your eyes that was there before,* so that you will be able to tell gods from men." The translation of Poe's quotation appears in italics. Editors alter the case to match the passage to its grammatical context in the English sentence. **Gottfried Wilhelm Leibniz (1646–1716); Gorgias (c.483–375 B.C.E.):** Poe contrasts the two philosophers: Leibniz, the eternal reconciler, lover of unity, order, and relationships; Gorgias, by repute so great a rhetorician that rhetoric became an end in itself, even at the expense of logic. For comments on the importance of this paragraph for the plausibility of the tale, see our headnote.

patrids[4] and the commonplaces of society—men of leisure and men actively engaged in affairs of their own—conducting business upon their own responsibility. They did not greatly excite my attention.

The tribe of clerks was an obvious one; and here I discerned two remarkable divisions. There were the junior clerks of flash houses—young gentlemen with tight coats, bright boots, well-oiled hair, and supercilious lips. Setting aside a certain dapperness of carriage, which may be termed *deskism* for want of a better word, the manner of these persons seemed to me an exact facsimile of what had been the perfection of *bon ton*[5] about twelve or eighteen months before. They wore the cast-off graces of the gentry;—and this, I believe, involves the best definition of the class.

The division of the upper clerks of staunch firms, or of the "steady old fellows," it was not possible to mistake. These were known by their coats and pantaloons of black or brown, made to sit comfortably, with white cravats and waistcoats, broad solid-looking shoes, and thick hose or gaiters.—They had all slightly bald heads, from which the right ears, long used to pen-holding, had an odd habit of standing off on end. I observed that they always removed or settled their hats with both hands, and wore watches, with short gold chains of a substantial and ancient pattern. Theirs was the affectation of respectability;—if indeed there be an affectation so honorable.

There were many individuals of dashing appearance, whom I easily understood as belonging to the race of swell pick-pockets, with which all great cities are infested. I watched these gentry with much inquisitiveness, and found it difficult to imagine how they should ever be mistaken for gentlemen by gentlemen themselves. Their voluminousness of wristband, with an air of excessive frankness, should betray them at once.

The gamblers, of whom I descried not a few, were still more easily recognisable. They wore every variety of dress, from that of the desperate thimble-rig[6] bully, with velvet waistcoat, fancy neckerchief, gilt chains, and filigreed buttons, to that of the scrupulously inornate clergyman than which nothing could be less liable to suspicion. Still all were distinguished by a certain sodden swarthiness of complexion, a filmy dimness of eye, and pallor and compression of lip. There were two other traits, moreover, by which I could always detect them;—a guarded lowness of tone in conversation, and a more than ordinary extension of the thumb in a direction at right angles with the fingers.—Very often, in company with these sharpers, I observed an order of men somewhat different in habits, but still birds of a kindred feather. They may be defined as the gentlemen who live by their wits.

---

[4]Aristocrats. Note how Poe's great catalogue of people seen from the coffee-house window is organized—it begins with the most prosperous and descends through clerks, criminals, gamblers, etc. The "dregs and lees" of society—what we would today more sympathetically call "people of the inner city"—ultimately give birth to the Man of the Crowd. Fear of him is largely fear of the city itself.

[5]**flash houses:** Firms engaged in new, showy, and speculative lines of business. ***bon ton:*** Fashionable style.

[6]The thimble-rig is the old name for the shell game—the victim is supposed to guess under which "thimble" the pea is hidden.

They seem to prey upon the public in two battalions—that of the dandies and that of the military men. Of the first grade the leading features are long locks and smiles; of the second, frogged coats and frowns.

Descending in the scale of what is termed gentility, I found darker and deeper themes for speculation. I saw Jew pedlars, with hawk eyes flashing from countenances whose every other feature wore only an expression of abject humility; sturdy professional street beggars scowling upon mendicants of a better stamp, whom despair alone had driven forth into the night for charity; feeble and ghastly invalids, upon whom death had placed a sure hand, and who sidled and tottered through the mob, looking every one beseechingly in the face, as if in search of some chance consolation, some lost hope; modest young girls returning from long and late labor to a cheerless home, and shrinking more tearfully than indignantly from the glances of ruffians, whose direct contact, even, could not be avoided; women of the town of all kinds and of all ages—the unequivocal beauty in the prime of her womanhood, putting one in mind of the statue in Lucian, with the surface of Parian marble, and the interior filled with filth—the loathsome and utterly lost leper in rags—the wrinkled, bejewelled and paint-begrimmed beldame, making a last effort at youth—the mere child of immature form, yet, from long association, an adept in the dreadful coquetries of her trade, and burning with a rabid ambition to be ranked the equal of her elders in vice; drunkards innumerable and indescribable—some in shreds and patches, reeling, inarticulate, with bruised visage and lack-lustre eyes—some in whole although filthy garments, with a slightly unsteady swagger, thick sensual lips, and hearty-looking rubicund faces—others clothed in materials which had once been good, and which even now were scrupulously well brushed—men who walked with a more than naturally firm and springy step, but whose countenances were fearfully pale, whose eyes were hideously wild and red, and who clutched with quivering fingers, as they strode through the crowd, at every object which came within their reach; beside these, pie-men, porters, coal-heavers, sweeps; organ-grinders, monkey-exhibitors and ballad-mongers, those who vended with those who sang; ragged artizans and exhausted laborers of every description, and all full of a noisy and inordinate vivacity which jarred discordantly upon the ear, and gave an aching sensation to the eye.[7]

As the night deepened, so deepened to me the interest of the scene; for not only did the general character of the crowd materially alter (its gentler features retiring in the gradual withdrawal of the more orderly portion of the people, and its harsher ones coming out into bolder relief, as the late hour brought forth every species of

[7]**statue in Lucian:** In "The Cock," the Greek satiric writer Lucian (c.125–c.200) has the cock say, speaking to himself as a ruler, "I was like those colossal statues, the work of Phidias, Myron or Praxiteles: they too look extremely well from outside: 'tis Posidon with his trident, Zeus with his thunderbolt, all ivory and gold: but take a peep inside, and what have we? One tangle of bars, bolts, nails, planks, wedges, with pitch and mortar and everything that is unsightly; not to mention a possible colony of rats or mice. There you have royalty" (Fowler translation). Poe alludes to the passage again in "Fifty Suggestions." **Parian marble:** Marble from Paros, in the Cyclades, famous in the ancient world as a fine white statuary marble. On Poe's attitudes toward the persecuted and the impoverished, see our headnote.

infamy from its den,) but the rays of the gas-lamps, feeble at first in their struggle with the dying day, had now at length gained ascendancy, and threw over every thing a fitful and garish lustre. All was dark yet splendid—as that ebony to which has been likened the style of Tertullian.[8]

The wild effects of the light enchained me to an examination of individual faces; and although the rapidity with which the world of light flitted before the window, prevented me from casting more than a glance upon each visage, still it seemed that, in my then peculiar mental state, I could frequently read, even in that brief interval of a glance, the history of long years.

With my brow to the glass, I was thus occupied in scrutinizing the mob, when suddenly there came into view a countenance (that of a decrepid old man, some sixty-five or seventy years of age,)—a countenance which at once arrested and absorbed my whole attention, on account of the absolute idiosyncrasy of its expression. Any thing even remotely resembling that expression I had never seen before. I well remember that my first thought, upon beholding it, was that Retszch,[9] had he viewed it, would have greatly preferred it to his own pictural incarnations of the fiend. As I endeavored, during the brief minute of my original survey, to form some analysis of the meaning conveyed, there arose confusedly and paradoxically within my mind, the ideas of vast mental power, of caution, of penuriousness, of avarice, of coolness, of malice, of blood-thirstiness, of triumph, of merriment, of excessive terror, of intense—of extreme despair. I felt singularly aroused, startled, fascinated. "How wild a history," I said to myself, "is written within that bosom!" Then came a craving desire to keep the man in view—to know more of him. Hurriedly putting on an overcoat, and seizing my hat and cane, I made my way into the street, and pushed through the crowd in the direction which I had seen him take; for he had already disappeared. With some little difficulty I at length came within sight of him, approached, and followed him closely, yet cautiously, so as not to attract his attention.

I had now a good opportunity of examining his person. He was short in stature, very thin, and apparently very feeble. His clothes, generally, were filthy and ragged; but as he came, now and then, within the strong glare of a lamp, I perceived that this linen, although dirty, was of beautiful texture; and my vision deceived me, or, through a rent in a closely-buttoned and evidently second-hand *roquelaire*[10] which enveloped him, I caught a glimpse both of a diamond and of a

---

[8]**ebony . . . Tertullian:** Tertullian is Quintus Septimius Florens Tertullianus (c.150–after 220), an important church writer noted for the vigor and vehemence of his denunciation of worldliness. He is said by the *Catholic Encyclopedia* to be "the most difficult of all Latin prose writers." Another source says that he wrote in "the Asianic manner," a fashionable "modern" style of his day characterized by short paratactical sentences adorned with plays on sounds and words; a style "personal, pregnant, terse and not free from obscurity," yet "powerful and passionate." But none of this really explains Poe's calling his style "ebony." See our headnote for an educated guess at what the word means.

[9]Moritz Retzsch (1779–1857), a German painter, etcher, and designer, noted for his etchings in outline to illustrate Goethe, Schiller, Shakespeare, and others.

[10]Short cloak. See "The Cask of Amontillado," note 6. Poe spelled the word "*roquelaure*" in the 1840 version.

dagger. These observations heightened my curiosity, and I resolved to follow the stranger whithersoever he should go.

It was now fully night-fall, and a thick humid fog hung over the city, soon ending in a settled and heavy rain. This change of weather had an odd effect upon the crowd, the whole of which was at once put into new commotion, and overshadowed by a world of umbrellas. The waver, the jostle, and the hum increased in a tenfold degree. For my own part I did not much regard the rain—the lurking of an old fever in my system rendering the moisture somewhat too dangerously pleasant. Tying a handkerchief about my mouth, I kept on. For half an hour the old man held his way with difficulty along the great thoroughfare; and I here walked close at his elbow through fear of losing sight of him. Never once turning his head to look back, he did not observe me. By and bye he passed into a cross street, which, although densely filled with people, was not quite so much thronged as the main one he had quitted. Here a change in his demeanor became evident. He walked more slowly and with less object than before—more hesitatingly. He crossed and re-crossed the way repeatedly without apparent aim; and the press was still so thick, that, at every such movement, I was obliged to follow him closely. The street was a narrow and long one, and his course lay within it for nearly an hour, during which the passengers had gradually diminished to about that number which is ordinarily seen at noon on Broadway near the Park—so vast a difference is there between a London populace and that of the most frequented American city.[11] A second turn brought us into a square, brilliantly lighted, and overflowing with life. The old manner of the stranger re-appeared. His chin fell upon his breast, while his eyes rolled wildly from under his knit brows, in every direction, upon those who hemmed him in. He urged his way steadily and perseveringly. I was surprised, however, to find, upon his having made the circuit of the square, that he turned and retraced his steps. Still more was I astonished to see him repeat the same walk several times—once nearly detecting me as he came round with a sudden movement.

In this excercise he spent another hour, at the end of which we met with far less interruption from passengers than at first. The rain fell fast; the air grew cool; and the people were retiring to their homes. With a gesture of impatience, the wanderer passed into a by-street comparatively deserted. Down this, some quarter of a mile long, he rushed with an activity I could not have dreamed of seeing in one so aged, and which put me to much trouble in pursuit. A few minutes brought us to a large and busy bazaar, with the localities of which the stranger appeared well

---

[11]**too dangerously pleasant:** Poe reminds us of the sickness as we approach the portion of the tale—the long "chase"—which critics consider implausible. See note 3 and our headnote. **American city:** Poe is of course right; London was enormous compared to the American cities Poe's readers knew. But he mentions the size partly to play on the traditional American fear of the large city, an agrarian bias which, urban dweller though he was, he as a Virginian may have felt. American magazines by the 1830s ran articles on problems posed by urban growth; Poe, who followed all the notable journals, certainly had read such pieces. In the 1840s, indeed, Poe himself would comment on A. J. Downing's suburban residential ideas, which grow directly out of this fear of the urban environment. See "Mellonta Tauta," note 2.

acquainted, and where his original demeanor again became apparent, as he forced his way to and fro, without aim, among the host of buyers and sellers.

During the hour and a half, or thereabouts, which we passed in this place, it required much caution on my part to keep him within reach without attracting his observation. Luckily I wore a pair of caoutchouc[12] over-shoes, and could move about in perfect silence. At no moment did he see that I watched him. He entered shop after shop, priced nothing, spoke no word, and looked at all objects with a wild and vacant stare. I was now utterly amazed at his behavior, and firmly resolved that we should not part until I had satisfied myself in some measure respecting him.

A loud-toned clock struck eleven, and the company were fast deserting the bazaar. A shop-keeper, in putting up a shutter, jostled the old man, and at the instant I saw a strong shudder come over his frame. He hurried into the street, looked anxiously around him for an instant, and then ran with incredible swiftness through many crooked and people-less lanes, until we emerged once more upon the great thoroughfare whence we had started—the street of the D—— Hotel. It no longer wore, however, the same aspect. It was still brilliant with gas; but the rain fell fiercely, and there were few persons to be seen. The stranger grew pale. He walked moodily some paces up the once populous avenue, then, with a heavy sigh, turned in the direction of the river, and, plunging through a great variety of devious ways, came out, at length, in view of one of the principal theatres. It was about being closed, and the audience were thronging from the doors. I saw the old man gasp as if for breath while he threw himself amid the crowd; but I thought that the intense agony of his countenance had, in some measure, abated. His head again fell upon his breast; he appeared as I had seen him at first. I observed that he now took the course in which had gone the greater number of the audience—but, upon the whole, I was at a loss to comprehend the waywardness of his actions.

As he proceeded, the company grew more scattered, and his old uneasiness and vacillation were resumed. For some time he followed closely a party of some ten or twelve roisterers; but from this number one by one dropped off, until three only remained together, in a narrow and gloomy lane little frequented. The stranger paused, and, for a moment, seemed lost in thought; then, with every mark of agitation, pursued rapidly a route which brought us to the verge of the city, amid regions very different from those we had hitherto traversed. It was the most noisome quarter of London, where everything wore the worst impress of the most deplorable poverty, and of the most desperate crime.[13] By the dim light of an accidental lamp, tall, antique, worm-eaten, wooden tenements were seen tottering to their fall, in directions so many and capricious that scarce the semblance of a passage was discernible between them. The paving-stones lay at random, displaced from their beds by the rankly growing grass. Horrible filth festered in the dammed-up gutters. The whole atmosphere teemed with desolation. Yet, as we proceeded, the sounds of human life revived by sure degrees, and at length large

[12]Rubber.

[13]Poe's tour of the city parallels his catalogue of its inhabitants; we move from the prosperous to the most desperate.

Hortulus anime
cum aliis q̄plurimis orationi-
bus pristine impressioni superadditis: vt tabulam in
huius calce annexam
intuenti patentissi
mum erit.

que septenis hor[is]: es ab antro ve-
cta foris: ad celi fastigia. Gaude
que nunc sublimaris: z cū christo

rie palmā: ita z nos supplices eo[rum] festa cele
brātes: participes gaudio[rum] effici mereamur.
Per dn̄m nostrū Jesum christū filiū tuū zc.
De sancto Dionysio epo z martyre. Ant.
Sancte Di-
onysi gallie
doctor z in-
clite martir
lumēq[ue] splē
didissimum
p amorē ce-
lestis exerci-
tus: q̄ fuit
comes tuo
exanimi cor-
poris: quā-
do tuū pro-
priū caput
deportasti.
Te depcor:
non despici-
as me: sed suscipias preces meas: et redime
me ex oīibus paupertatib[us] et tribulatiōibus
aīe z corporis. Rogo te sancte Dionysi: tu-
osq[ue] socios: vt suscipiatis aīam meā qn̄ p̄sen-
tata fuerit ante tribunal iudicis: z depcemi-
ni regē potentē: vt p vestra suffragia merear
liberari a tormētis ppetuis. Amen. Ora

state: me precantē defensate: a demo-
num instantia. Pia martyr Ursu-
la sponsa christi decora. Cum tuis so

Figure 5. The book that "does not permit itself to be read": Poe learned of it from Isaac Disraeli's *Curiosities of Literature,* in which an article on tasteless and obscene religious illustrations cites Grunninger's volume as especially obnoxious. (See note 14 for details; the title means "little garden of the soul," and the spelling varies from one edition to the next.) If such a book exists, two colleagues searching the British Museum collection could not find it: Grunninger and others printed many volumes of this title around 1500, but their plates are characteristic religious engravings of the age. Even the "strangest" of them, shown here, uses traditional iconography; the "odd" facial expressions are ordinary in German graphic art of the time. It may be that the book which Disraeli saw has disappeared, but pending the discovery of offensive plates, we conclude that the

bands of the most abandoned of a London populace were seen reeling to and fro. The spirits of the old man again flickered up, as a lamp which is near its death-hour. Once more he strode onward with elastic tread. Suddenly a corner was turned, a blaze of light burst upon our sight, and we stood before one of the huge suburban temples of Intemperance—one of the palaces of the fiend, Gin.

It was now nearly day-break; but a number of wretched inebriates still pressed in and out of the flaunting entrance. With a half shriek of joy the old man forced a passage within, resumed at once his original bearing, and stalked backward and forward, without apparent object, among the throng. He had not been thus long occupied, however, before a rush to the doors gave token that the host was closing them for the night. It was something even more intense than despair that I then observed upon the countenance of the singular being whom I had watched so pertinaciously. Yet he did not hesitate in his career, but, with a mad energy, retraced his steps at once, to the heart of the mighty London. Long and swiftly he fled, while I followed him in the wildest amazement, resolute not to abandon a scrutiny in which I now felt an interest all-absorbing. The sun arose while we proceeded, and, when we had once again reached that most thronged mart of the populous town, the street of D—— Hotel, it presented an appearance of human bustle and activity scarely inferior to what I had seen on the evening before. And here, long, amid the momently increasing confusion, did I persist in my pursuit of the stranger. But, as usual, he walked to and fro, and during the day did not pass from out the turmoil of that street. And, as the shades of the second evening came on, I grew wearied unto death, and, stopping fully in front of the wanderer, gazed at him steadfastly in the face. He noticed me not, but resumed his solemn walk, while I, ceasing to follow, remained absorbed in contemplation. "This old man," I said at length, "is the type and the genius of deep crime. He refuses to be alone. *He is the man of the crowd.* It will be in vain to follow; for I shall learn no more of him, nor of his deeds. The worst heart of the world is a grosser book than the 'Hortulus Animæ,'[14] and perhaps it is but one of the great mercies of God that '*es lässt sich nicht lesen.*' "

[14]Poe refers to the *Hortulus Animœ cum Oratiiunculis Aliquibus Superadditis quae in prioribus Libris non habentur* (1500) of John Grunninger (c.1455–c.1533). Poe probably learned of this work in Isaac Disraeli's *Curiosities of Literature,* a work he used frequently. Disraeli says it is exceedingly obnoxious, not so much for the text, as for the illustrations. See Figure 5. Poe began the German phrase, *er* (not *es*); most editors change it to *es* to agree with *Buch;* Mabbott (9, II) leaves it *er* to agree with *Hortulus.*

(*continued from page 128*)
skeptical humanist Disraeli, suspicious even of the "superstitious" aspects of his ancestral Judaism, was showing up—or pretending to show up—the crudities and banalities of Christianity. If he was fibbing or exaggerating, the joke is on Poe. The colophon reads, "printed at the expense of . . . Johann Koberger . . . Nuremberg . . . Frederich Peypus the printer, 1518, 12 December." Plates courtesy of the British Museum. Copyright, the British Museum.

The Murders in the Rue Morgue

Meet C. Auguste Dupin, Poe's detective hero in this "first of the modern detective stories." There are two other stories about him—"The Mystery of Marie Rogêt" and "The Purloined Letter"—in which his powers of analysis and intuition increase. Poe's "tales of ratiocination" are so popular and familiar that one is apt to miss the very considerable extent to which they exemplify his philosophy of beauty, creativity, and perception. But the usual pattern is here; to perceive the complex pattern, one must be hypersensitive, almost to the point of madness, or extraordinarily gifted. Strong hints of what is to come appear in the first paragraph of "Rue Morgue"; Dupin almost *seems able to intuit truth. See our headnote to "The Purloined Letter."*

If the secluded hideout shared by Dupin and the narrator seems familiar, it is because subsequent writers have made it so. The idea of the hero's hidden quarters has passed into popular culture; it is present in pulp and comic book material. Poe invented a great deal of the claptrap and many of the conventions of the modern commercial detective and "superhero" fiction, as A. Conan Doyle and later writers have acknowledged. Sherlock Holmes, he said, owed much to Dupin, as did the detective-heroes of other writers: "If every man who receives a cheque for a story which owes its springs to Poe were to pay tithe to a monument for the Master, he would have a pyramid as big as that of Cheops."

A note of explanation: *No one seems able to explain exactly what Poe means by "the old philosophy of the Bi-Part Soul" and the "fancy of a double Dupin . . . creative and resolvent." Numerous ancient philosophies use the concept of a dual soul: it appears, for example, in Egypt and, in different form, seems to be an underlying concept in the Homeric epics (one part or soul is associated with breath, the other with blood). But we have never found the parts called "creative and resolvent." We suspect that Poe borrowed the concept from an as-yet-unlocated passage in his reading (we have searched likely places most diligently), or that he made up the two properties out of Dupin's characteristics.*

Since Poe didn't really know Paris, we wondered where he got the texture of his Parisian setting. We are quite sure we now know: from Volume I, Chapter 23, of Bulwer-Lytton's Pelham; or Adventures of a Gentleman *(1828). Our reasons:*

1. *The references to Rousseau's* La Nouvelle Héloïse *appear in both places. Indeed, in "Loss of Breath," Poe refers to exactly the same passage cited in Bulwer-Lytton.*
2. *The references to Crébillon appear in both places.*

3. *Pelham loves the Faubourg St. Germain, and for the same reasons—its antiquity, its quaintness, its "true" feel of old France—which lead Dupin and the narrator to rent quarters for themselves there.*
4. *There is a striking matchup of mentioned place names.*

PUBLICATIONS IN POE'S TIME

Graham's Magazine, April 1841
Prose Romances, 1843
Tales, 1845
There are also three publications in French translations in 1846 and 1847.

THE MURDERS IN THE RUE MORGUE[1]

What song the Syrens sang, or what name Achilles assumed when he hid himself among women, although puzzling questions, are not beyond all *conjecture.*
Sir Thomas Browne.[2]

The mental features discoursed of as the analytical, are, in themselves, but little susceptible of analysis. We appreciate them only in their effects. We know of them, among other things, that they are always to their possessor, when inordinately possessed, a source of the liveliest enjoyment. As the strong man exults in his physical ability, delighting in such exercises as call his muscles into action, so glories the analyst in that moral activity which *disentangles.* He derives pleasure from even the most trivial occupations bringing his talents into play. He is found of enigmas, of conundrums, of hieroglyphics; exhibiting in his solutions of each a degree of *acumen* which appears to the ordinary apprehension præter-

[1]The "Rue Morgue" doesn't seem to be a real place (Carlson 2). But for a discussion of the "Morque" (*Morgue*) of Paris and the *Quartier* in which it was located see "Posthumous Letters of Charles Edwards, Esq. No. IV" in *Blackwood's* (December 1824), pp. 669–70. For other Parisian locations, see the map on pp. 136–7. To the best of anyone's knowledge, Poe had never been to France.

[2]Poe quotes *Hydriotaphia, or Urn-Burial,* a famous and beautifully written essay by Sir Thomas Browne (1605–82), English physician and essayist. Poe would have found many aspects of Browne's point of view sympathetic. The point of the quotation is that conjecture—in this story, inspired guesswork—can be helpful when pure logic fails. Browne's name was very much in the public mind when Poe's story was published, for in 1840 his coffin was opened and his skull stolen and sold. Poor Browne got his head back in 1922.

natural. His results, brought about by the very soul and essence of method, have, in truth, the whole air of intuition.

The faculty of re-solution is possibly much invigorated by mathematical study, and especially by that highest branch of it which, unjustly, and merely on account of its retrograde operations, has been called, as if *par excellence,* analysis. Yet to calculate is not in itself to analyze. A chess-player, for example, does the one without effort at the other. It follows that the game of chess, in its effects upon mental character, is greatly misunderstood. I am not now writing a treatise, but simply prefacing a somewhat peculiar narrative by observations very much at random; I will, therefore, take occasion to assert that the higher powers of the reflective intellect are more decidedly and more usefully tasked by the unostentatious game of draughts[3] than by all the elaborate frivolity of chess. In this latter, where the pieces have different and *bizarre* motions, with various and variable values, what is only complex is mistaken (a not unusual error) for what is profound. The *attention* is here called powerfully into play. If it flag for an instant, an oversight is committed, resulting in injury or defeat. The possible moves being not only manifold but involute, the chances of such oversights are multiplied; and in nine cases out of ten it is the more concentrative rather than the more acute player who conquers. In draughts, on the contrary, where the moves are *unique* and have but little variation, the probabilities of inadvertence are diminished, and the mere attention being left comparatively unemployed, what advantages are obtained by either party are obtained by superior *acumen.* To be less abstract—Let us suppose a game of draughts where the pieces are reduced to four kings, and where, of course, no oversight is to be expected. It is obvious that here the victory can be decided (the players being at all equal) only by some *recherché*[4] movement, the result of some strong exertion of the intellect. Deprived of ordinary resources, the analyst throws himself into the spirit of his opponent, identifies himself therewith, and not unfrequently sees thus, at a glance, the sole methods (sometimes indeed absurdly simple ones) by which he may seduce into error or hurry into miscalculation.

Whist has long been noted for its influence upon what is termed the calculating power; and men of the highest order of intellect have been known to take an apparently unaccountable delight in it, while eschewing chess as frivolous. Beyond doubt there is nothing of a similar nature so greatly tasking the faculty of analysis. The best chess-player in Christendom *may* be little more than the best player of chess; but proficiency in whist implies capacity for success in all these more important undertakings where mind struggles with mind. When I say proficiency, I mean that perfection in the game which includes a comprehension of *all* the sources whence legitimate advantage may be derived. These are not only manifold but multiform, and lie frequently among recesses of thought altogether inaccessible to the ordinary understanding. To observe attentively is to remember distinctly; and, so far, the concentrative chess-player will do very well at whist;

[3]Checkers.

[4]Rare, exquisite, choice.

while the rules of Hoyle[5] (themselves based upon the mere mechanism of the game) are sufficiently and generally comprehensible. Thus to have a retentive memory, and to proceed by "the book," are points commonly regarded as the sum total of good playing. But it is in matters beyond the limits of mere rule that the skill of the analyst is evinced. He makes, in silence, a host of observations and inferences. So, perhaps, do his companions; and the difference in the extent of the information obtained, lies not so much in the validity of the inference as in the quality of the observation. The necessary knowledge is that of *what* to observe. Our player confines himself not at all; nor, because the game is the object, does he reject deductions from things external to the game. He examines the countenance of his partner, comparing it carefully with that of each of his opponents. He considers the mode of assorting the cards in each hand; often counting trump by trump, and honor by honor, through the glances bestowed by their holders upon each. He notes every variation of face as the play progresses, gathering a fund of thought from the differences in the expression of certainty, of surprise, of triumph, or chagrin. From the manner of gathering up a trick he judges whether the person taking it can make another in the suit. He recognizes what is played through feint, by the air with which it is thrown upon the table. A casual or inadvertent word; the accidental dropping or turning of a card, with the accompanying anxiety or carelessness in regard to its concealment; the counting of the tricks with the order of their arrangement; embarrassment, hesitation, eagerness or trepidation—all afford, to his apparently intuitive perception, indications of the true state of affairs. The first two or three rounds having been played, he is in full possession of the contents of each hand, and thenceforward puts down his cards with as absolute a precision of purpose as if the rest of the party had turned outward the faces of their own.

The analytical power should not be confounded with simple ingenuity; for while the analyst is necessarily ingenious, the ingenious man is often remarkably incapable of analysis. The constructive or combining power, by which ingenuity is usually manifested, and to which the phrenologists (I believe erroneously) have assigned a separate organ, supposing it a primitive faculty,[6] has been so frequently seen in those whose intellect bordered otherwise upon idiocy, as to have attracted general observation among writers on morals. Between ingenuity and the analytic ability there exists a difference far greater, indeed, than that between the fancy and

---

[5]**whist:** A card game, an ancestor of the modern bridge. **Hoyle:** Sir Edmund Hoyle (1672–1769), who published in 1742 *Short Treatise on the Game of Whist* and later a number of books on other games.

[6]It was not yet clear in Poe's day that phrenology, the science of studying personality through examination of the shape of the head, was a scientific dead end. Though the field rapidly fell into the hands of quacks, the pioneers in the area had been serious scientists. Phrenology, which adapted some of the concepts of "faculty psychology," assumed that each inherent power of the mind was located in a specific portion of one's head. It was hoped that once phrenologists were sure which "faculties" were basic, they could examine subjects' crania and produce what we would perhaps call personality or aptitude profiles. The concept is not in nature different from the assumptions of 20th-century work on the physiology of the brain.

the imagination, but of a character very strictly analogous. It will be found, in fact, that the ingenious are always fanciful, and the *truly* imaginative never otherwise than analytic.

The narrative which follows will appear to the reader somewhat in the light of a commentary upon the propositions just advanced.

Residing in Paris during the spring and part of the summer of 18—, I there became acquainted with a Monsieur C. Auguste Dupin.[7] This young gentleman was of an excellent—indeed of an illustrious family, but, by a variety of untoward events, had been reduced to such poverty that the energy of his character succumbed beneath it, and he ceased to bestir himself in the world, or to care for the retrieval of his fortunes. By courtesy of his creditors, there still remained in his possession a small remnant of his patrimony; and, upon the income arising from this, he managed, by means of a rigorous economy, to procure the necessaries of life, without troubling himself about its superfluities. Books, indeed, were his sole luxuries, and in Paris these are easily obtained.

Our first meeting was at an obscure library in the Rue Montmartre, where the accident of our both being in search of the same very rare and very remarkable volume, brought us into closer communion. We saw each other again and again. I was deeply interested in the little family history which he detailed to me with all that candor which a Frenchman indulges whenever mere self is the theme. I was astonished, too, at the vast extent of his reading; and, above all, I felt my soul enkindled within me by the wild fervor, and the vivid freshness of his imagination. Seeking in Paris the objects I then sought, I felt that the society of such a man would be to me a treasure beyond price; and this feeling I frankly confided to him. It was at length arranged that we should live together during my stay in the city; and as my worldly circumstances were somewhat less embarrassed than his own, I was permitted to be at the expense of renting, and furnishing in a style which suited the rather fantastic gloom of our common temper, a time-eaten and grotesque mansion, long deserted through superstitions into which we did not inquire, and tottering to its fall in a retired and desolate portion of the Faubourg St. Germain.

Had the routine of our life at this place been known to the world, we should have been regarded as madmen—although, perhaps, as madmen of a harmless nature. Our seclusion was perfect. We admitted no visitors. Indeed the locality of our retirement had been carefully kept a secret from my own former associates; and it had been many years since Dupin had ceased to know or be known in Paris. We existed within ourselves alone.

It was a freak of fancy in my friend (for what else shall I call it?) to be enamored of the Night for her own sake; and into this *bizarrerie,* as into all his others, I quietly fell; giving myself up to his wild whims with a perfect *abandon.* The sable divinity would not herself dwell with us always; but we could counterfeit her

[7]Poe seems to have borrowed the name Dupin from a character in some articles about the French Minister of Police, François Eugene Vidocq (1775–1857), which appeared in *Burton's Gentleman's Magazine* in 1838 (A. H. Quinn). For other possibilities, see Mabbott 9, II.

presence. At the first dawn of the morning we closed all the massy shutters of our old building, lighting a couple of tapers which, strongly perfumed, threw out only the ghastliest and feeblest of rays. By the aid of these we then buried our souls in dreams—reading, writing, or conversing, until warned by the clock of the advent of the true Darkness. Then we sallied forth into the streets, arm in arm, continuing the topics of the day, or roaming far and wide until a late hour, seeking, amid the wild lights and shadows of the populous city, that infinity of mental excitement which quiet observation can afford.

At such times I could not help remarking and admiring (although from his rich ideality I had been prepared to expect it) a peculiar analytic ability in Dupin. He seemed, too, to take an eager delight in its exercise—if not exactly in its display—and did not hesitate to confess the pleasure thus derived. He boasted to me, with a low chuckling laugh, that most men, in respect to himself, wore windows in their bosoms, and was wont to follow up such assertions by direct and very startling proofs of his intimate knowledge of my own. His manner at these moments was frigid and abstract; his eyes were vacant in expression; while his voice, usually a rich tenor, rose into a treble which would have sounded petulantly but for the deliberateness and entire distinctness of the enunciation. Observing him in these moods, I often dwelt meditatively upon the old philosophy of the Bi-Part Soul, and amused myself with the fancy of a double Dupin—the creative and the resolvent.

Let it not be supposed, from what I have just said, that I am detailing any mystery, or penning any romance. What I have described in the Frenchman, was merely the result of an excited, or perhaps of a diseased intelligence.[8] But of the character of his remarks at the periods in question an example will best convey the idea.

We were strolling one night down a long dirty street, in the vicinity of the Palais Royal. Being both, apparently, occupied with thought, neither of us had spoken a syllable for fifteen minutes at least. All at once Dupin broke forth with these words:—

"He is a very little fellow, that's true, and would do better for the *Théâtre des Variétés.*"

"There can be no doubt of that," I replied unwittingly, and not at first observing (so much had I been absorbed in reflection) the extraordinary manner in which the speaker had chimed in with my meditations. In an instant afterward I recollected myself, and my astonishment was profound.

"Dupin," said I, gravely, "this is beyond my comprehension. I do not hesitate to say that I am amazed, and can scarcely credit my senses. How was it possible you should know I was thinking of——?" Here I paused, to ascertain beyond a doubt whether he really knew of whom I thought.

——"of Chantilly," said he, "why do you pause? You were remarking to yourself that his diminutive figure unfitted him for tragedy."

---

[8]A hint that Dupin ultimately has more than analytical ability, that some "faculty" unnamed by the narrator (who, like Holmes's sidekick, Dr. Watson, never *really* understands his friend) is present.

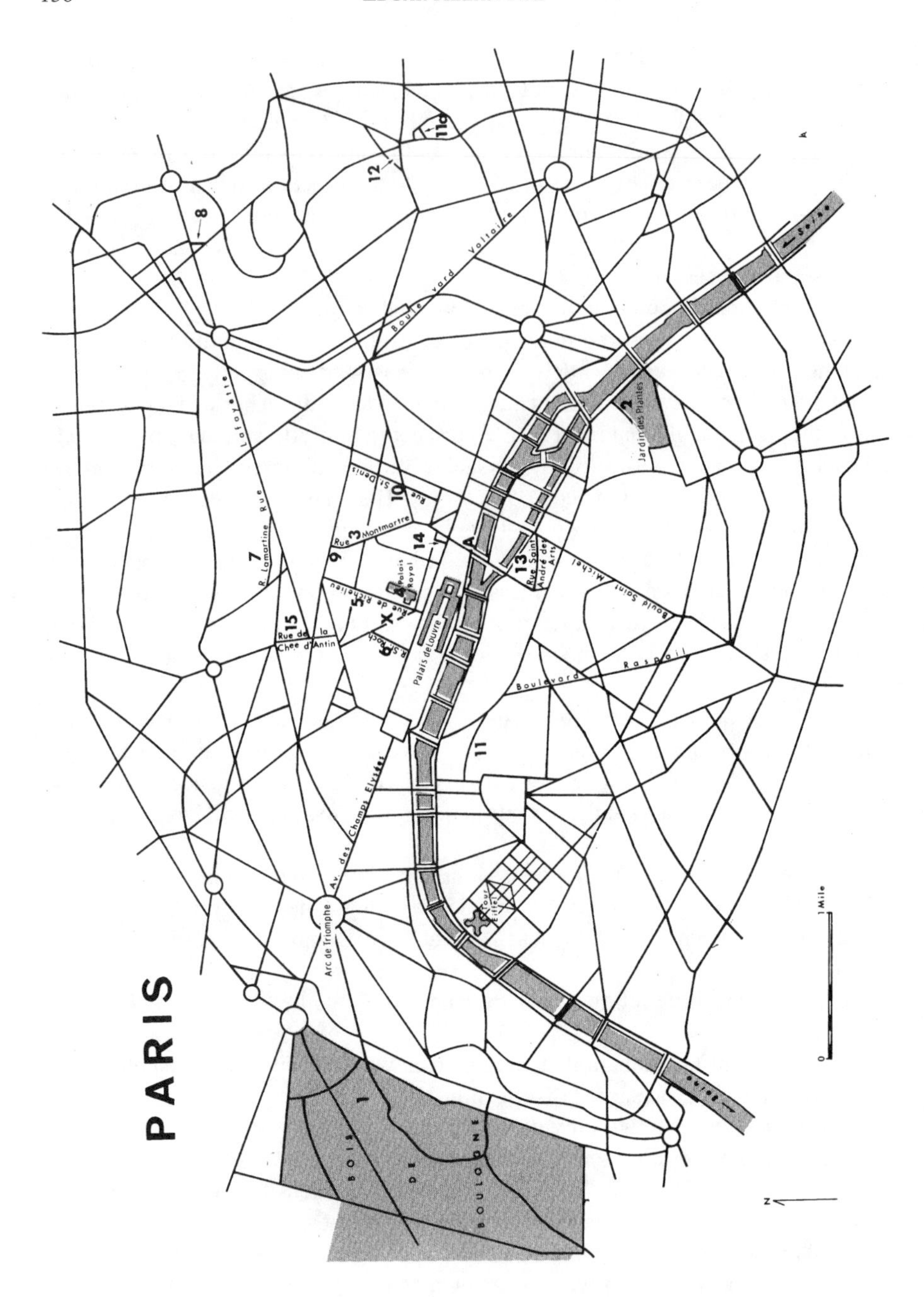

Figure 6. Poe's Paris. Places mentioned in "The Murders in the Rue Morgue" are listed first, then "The Mystery of Marie Rogêt" (not in this volume), "The Purloined Letter," and "The Duc De L'Omelette." Some modern landmarks are shown to help orient the reader. Map drawn by Lewis Armstrong.

KEY

"The Murders in the Rue Morgue"

1. Bois de Boulogne.
2. Jardin des Plantes.
3. Rue Montmartre.
4. Palais Royal.
5. Rue (de) Richelieu.
6. Rue St.-Roch.
7. Lamartine (alley): Current maps show no such alley; our map shows the narrow street, Rue Lamartine. Poe may be joking—he disliked Lamartine's work (Lombard).
8. Rue Deloraine: If this street existed in Poe's day, it is no longer on maps of Paris. Our map locates the Rue de Loraine.
9. Théâtre des Variétés.
10. Rue St.-Denis.
11. "Faubourg St.-Germain": There are three possible locations: (1) The area near St.-Germain-des-Prés on the West Bank (left of 13 on our map) is the most likely location. This is the area in which the character Pelham in Bulwer's novel *Pelham* would like to live, and Bulwer calls it "Faubourg St.-Germain." Also, Poe took much of his Parisian texture from Bulwer (see our headnote). Number 11 on the map locates the Rue Saint-Dominique where an acquaintance of Pelham lives; (2) St.-Germain-l'Auxerrois in the Arrondissement Louvre (across the street from the Louvre just above "A"); (3) near area 11 on our map, marked "11A." Since "Faubourg" means "suburb" and since the other two possibilities are in central Paris, this may be the real location. See number 12 for another reason for believing 11A is the location.
12. Rue Dubourg: We were unable to obtain a street index of pre-Haussman Paris, so we are uncertain as to whether there was a Rue Dubourg. Dupin mentions it to a sailor who does not know Paris well and, since there is a character in the story named Pauline Dubourg, it is possible that Poe made it up. Dupin, wanting a fictitious street name, could have had the name in mind. Poe, moreover, had known some people named "Dubourg" when he was in England with the Allans. Two sisters by that name kept a boarding school he attended, and their brother worked for John Allan. There is, however, a Cité Dubourg, located at number 12, which is a fairly likely site because, as Dupin says, it is "just by" his home. If "11A" above is correct, "12" probably is as well.

X. Rue Morgue: We are told no such street exists. Poe says it runs from Rue St.-Roch to the Rue (de) Richelieu. The area he had in mind, then, is near the modern Avenue de l'Opéra. "**X**" marks the spot.

"The Mystery of Marie Rogêt"

13. Rue Pavée Saint André: This is located on our map at the Rue Saint André des Arts (14).
14. Rue du Roule. Numbers 13 and 14 are opposite one another across the river Seine.

A. Approximate location of Marie's body.

"The Purloined Letter"

Rue Dunôt: Its location should be near number 11 (see explanation there), but no such street seems to exist now.

"The Duc De L'Omelette"

15. Rue de la Chaussée d'Antin.

This was precisely what had formed the subject of my reflections. Chantilly was a *quondam* cobbler of the Rue St. Denis, who, becoming stage-mad, had attempted the *rôle* of Xerxes, in Crébillon's tragedy so called, and been notoriously Pasquinaded for his pains.[9]

"Tell me, for Heaven's sake," I exclaimed, "the method—if method there is—by which you have been enabled to fathom my soul in this matter." In fact I was even more startled than I would have been willing to express.

---

[9]***quondam:*** Former. **Crébillon:** Prosper Jolyot de Crébillon (1674–1762), French dramatist who wrote a number of plays on classical subjects. The narrator is amused by the thought of the cobbler playing a heroic character based on Xerxes the Great (c.519–c.465 B.C.E.), Persian king whom the Greeks defeated at Salamis in 480 B.C.E. **Pasquinaded:** Ridiculed or lampooned.

"It was the fruiterer," replied my friend, "who brought you to the conclusion that the mender of soles was not of sufficient height for Xerxes *et id genus omne.*"[10]

"The fruiterer!—you astonish me—I know no fruiterer whomsoever."

"The man who ran up against you as we entered the street—it may have been fifteen minutes ago."

I now remember that, in fact, a fruiterer, carrying upon his head a large basket of apples, had nearly thrown me down, by accident, as we passed from the Rue C—— into the thoroughfare where we stood; but what this had to do with Chantilly I could not possibly understand.

There was not a particle of *charlatanerie* about Dupin. "I will explain," he said, "and that you may comprehend all clearly, we will first retrace the course of your meditations, from the moment in which I spoke to you until that of the *rencontre* with the fruiterer in question. The larger links of the chain run thus—Chantilly, Orion, Dr. Nichol, Epicurus, Stereotomy, the street stones, the fruiterer."

There are few persons who have not, at some period of their lives, amused themselves in retracing the steps by which particular conclusions of their own minds have been attained. The occupation is often full of interest; and he who attempts it for the first time is astonished by the apparently illimitable distance and incoherence between the starting-point and the goal. What, then, must have been my amazement when I heard the Frenchman speak what he had just spoken, and when I could not help acknowledging that he had spoken the truth. He continued:

"We had been talking of horses, if I remember aright, just before leaving the Rue C——. This was the last subject we discussed. As we crossed into this street, a fruiterer, with a large basket upon his head, brushing quickly past us, thrust you upon a pile of paving-stones collected at a spot where the causeway is undergoing repair. You stepped upon one of the loose fragments, slipped, slightly strained your ankle, appeared vexed or sulky, muttered a few words, turned to look at the pile, and then proceeded in silence. I was not particularly attentive to what you did; but observation has become with me, of late, a species of necessity.

"You kept your eyes upon the ground—glancing, with a petulant expression, at the holes and ruts in the pavement, (so that I saw you were still thinking of the stones,) until we reached the little alley called Lamartine, which has been paved, by way of experiment, with the overlapping and riveted blocks. Here your countenance brightened up, and, perceiving your lips move, I could not doubt that you murmured the word 'stereotomy,' a term very affectedly applied to this species of pavement. I knew that you could not say to yourself 'stereotomy' without being brought to think of atomies, and thus the theories of Epicurus; and since, when we discussed this subject not very long ago, I mentioned to you how singularly, yet with how little notice, the vague guesses of that noble Greek had met with confirmation in the late nebular cosmogony, I felt that you could not avoid casting your eyes upward to the great *nebula* in Orion, and I certainly expected that you would do so. You did look up; and I was now assured that I had correctly followed your steps. But in that bitter *tirade* upon Chantilly, which appeared in yesterday's

[10]And all of that sort.

'*Musée,*' the satirist, making some disgraceful allusions to the cobbler's change of name upon assuming the buskin, quoted a Latin line about which we have often conversed. I mean the line

Perdidit antiquum litera prima sonum.

I had told you that this was in reference to Orion, formerly written Urion; and, from certain pungencies connected with this explanation, I was aware that you could not have forgotten it. It was clear, therefore, that you would not fail to combine the two ideas of Orion and Chantilly.[11] That you did combine them I saw by the character of the smile which passed over your lips. You thought of the poor cobbler's immolation. So far, you had been stooping in your gait; but now I saw you draw yourself up to your full height. I was then sure that you reflected upon the diminutive figure of Chantilly. At this point I interrupted your meditations to remark that as, in fact, he *was* a very little fellow—that Chantilly—he would do better at the *Théâtre des Variétés.*"

Not long after this, we were looking over an evening edition of the "Gazette des Tribunaux," when the following paragraphs arrested our attention.

"EXTRAORDINARY MURDERS.—This morning, about three o'clock, the inhabitants of the Quartier St. Roch were aroused from sleep by a succession of terrific shrieks, issuing, apparently, from the fourth story of a house in the Rue Morgue, known to be in the sole occupancy of one Madame L'Espanaye, and her daughter, Mademoiselle Camille L'Espanaye. After some delay, occasioned by a fruitless attempt to procure admission in the usual manner, the gateway was broken in with a crowbar, and eight or ten of the neighbors entered, accompanied by two *gendarmes.* By this time the cries had ceased; but, as the party rushed up the first flight of stairs, two or more rough voices, in angry contention, were distinguished, and seemed to proceed from the upper part of the house. As the second landing was reached, these sounds, also, had ceased, and everything remained perfectly quiet. The party spread themselves, and hurried from room to room. Upon arriving at a large back chamber in the fourth story, (the door of which, being found

---

[11]**stereotomy:** The art of cutting solids, especially stones, as in masonry or, here, paving. **Epicurus (341–270 B.C.E.):** Greek philosopher who did, in fact, follow Democritus in the matter of atomism. **nebular cosmogony:** Probably a reference to Charles de Laplace's 1796 postulation of "a cosmogony of the solar system with the planets developing from rings abandoned by a rotating, contracting nebula." Poe knew of Laplace's work; interestingly, American scientific writers in Poe's day often did not. His source is likely John P. Nichol, *Views of the Architecture of the Heavens in a Series of Letters to a Lady* (1837) which Mabbott (9, II) says Poe liked. Dupin mentions Nichol three paragraphs above; Poe does not repeat the reference here, but without it, a link is missing in Dupin's chain of associations. **buskin:** A type of boot associated with actors in tragedies. ***Perdidit . . . sonum:*** May be translated, "The first letter has lost its ancient sound." **Chantilly:** The cobbler's change of name on becoming an actor and the change in spelling suggest other changes and associations: cobbler—hobbler (bad actor); Orion, a giant and a great hunter in Greek mythology and the diminutive Chantilly; and, possibly, an association in Poe's mind between cobblestone and a cobbler which could be the origin of the whole business.

locked, with the key inside, was forced open,) a spectacle presented itself which struck every one present not less with horror than with astonishment.

"The apartment was in the wildest disorder—the furniture broken and thrown about in all directions. There was only one bedstead; and from this the bed had been removed, and thrown into the middle of the floor. On a chair lay a razor, besmeared with blood. On the hearth were two or three long and thick tresses of gray human hair, also dabbled in blood, and seeming to have been pulled out by the roots. Upon the floor were found four Napoleons, an ear-ring of topaz, three large silver spoons, three smaller of *métal d'Alger,*[12] and two bags, containing nearly four thousand francs in gold. The drawers of a *bureau,* which stood in one corner, were open, and had been, apparently, rifled, although many articles still remained in them. A small iron safe was discovered under the *bed* (not under the bedstead). It was open, with the key still in the door. It had no contents beyond a few old letters, and other papers of little consequence.

"Of Madame L'Espanaye no traces were here seen; but an unusual quantity of soot being observed in the fire-place, a search was made in the chimney, and (horrible to relate!) the corpse of the daughter, head downward, was dragged therefrom; it having been forced up the narrow aperture for a considerable distance. The body was quite warm. Upon examining it, many excoriations were perceived, no doubt occasioned by the violence with which it had been thrust up and disengaged. Upon the face were many severe scratches, and, upon the throat, dark bruises, and deep indentations of finger nails, as if the deceased had been throttled to death.

"After a thorough investigation of every portion of the house, without further discovery, the party made its way into a small paved yard in the rear of the building, where lay the corpse of the old lady, with her throat so entirely cut that, upon an attempt to raise her, the head fell off. The body, as well as the head, was fearfully mutilated—the former so much so as scarcely to retain any semblance of humanity.

"To this horrible mystery there is not as yet, we believe, the slightest clew."

The next day's paper had these additional particulars.

"*The Tragedy in the Rue Morgue.* Many individuals have been examined in relation to this most extraordinary and frightful affair." [The word '*affaire*' has not yet, in France, that levity of import which it conveys with us,] "but nothing whatever has transpired to throw light upon it. We give below all the material testimony elicited.

"*Pauline Dubourg,* laundress, deposes that she has known both the deceased for three years, having washed for them during that period. The old lady and her daughter seemed on good terms—very affectionate towards each other. They were excellent pay. Could not speak in regard to their mode or means of living. Believed that Madame L. told fortunes for a living. Was reputed to have money put by. Never met any persons in the house when she called for the clothes or took them home. Was sure that they had no servant in employ. There appeared to be no furniture in any part of the building except in the fourth story.

---

[12]*Métal d'Alger* or Metal of Algiers is a combination of pewter, lead, and antimony.

"*Pierre Moreau,* tobacconist, deposes that he has been in the habit of selling small quantities of tobacco and snuff to Madame L'Espanaye for nearly four years. Was born in the neighborhood, and has always resided there. The deceased and her daughter had occupied the house in which the corpes were found, for more than six years. It was formerly occupied by a jeweller, who under-let the upper rooms to various persons. The house was the property of Madame L. She became dissatisfied with the abuse of the premises by her tenant, and moved into them herself, refusing to let any portion. The old lady was childish. Witness had seen the daughter some five or six times during the six years. The two lived an exceedingly retired life—were reputed to have money. Had heard it said among the neighbors that Madame L. told fortunes—did not believe it. Had never seen any person enter the door except the old lady and her daughter, a porter once or twice, and a physician some eight or ten times.

"Many other persons, neighbors, gave evidence to the same effect. No one was spoken of as frequenting the house. It was not known whether there were any living connexions of Madame L. and her daughter. The shutters of the front windows were seldom opened. Those in the rear were always closed, with the exception of the large back room, fourth story. The house was a good house—not very old.

"*Isidore Musèt, gendarme,* deposes that he was called to the house about three o'clock in the morning, and found some twenty or thirty persons at the gateway, endeavoring to gain admittance. Forced it open, at length, with a bayonet—not with a crowbar. Had but little difficulty in getting it open, on account of its being a double or folding gate, and bolted neither at bottom nor top. The shrieks were continued until the gate was forced—and then suddenly ceased. They seemed to be screams of some person (or persons) in great agony—were loud and drawn out, not short and quick. Witness led the way up stairs. Upon reaching the first landing, heard two voices in loud and angry contention—the one a gruff voice, the other much shriller—a very strange voice. Could distinguish some words of the former, which was that of a Frenchman. Was positive that it was not a woman's voice. Could distinguish the words '*sacré*' and '*diable.*' The shrill voice was that of a foreigner. Could not be sure whether it was the voice of a man or of a woman. Could not make out what was said, but believed the language to be Spanish. The state of the room and of the bodies was described by this witness as we described them yesterday.

"*Henri Duval,* a neighbor, and by trade a silversmith, deposes that he was one of the party who first entered the house. Corroborates the testimony of Musèt in general. As soon as they forced an entrance, they reclosed the door, to keep out the crowd, which collected very fast, notwithstanding the lateness of the hour. The shrill voice, the witness thinks, was that of an Italian. Was certain it was not French. Could not be sure that it was a man's voice. It might have been a woman's. Was not acquainted with the Italian language. Could not distinguish the words, but was convinced by the intonation that the speaker was an Italian. Knew Madame L. and her daughter. Had conversed with both frequently. Was sure that the shrill voice was not that of either of the deceased.

"——*Odenheimer, restaurateur.* This witness volunteered his testimony. Not speaking French, was examined through an interpreter. Is a native of Amsterdam. Was passing the house at the time of the shrieks. They lasted for several minutes—probably ten. They were long and loud—very awful and distressing. Was one of those who entered the building. Corroborated the previous evidence in every respect but one. Was sure that the shrill voice was that of a man—of a Frenchman. Could not distinguish the words uttered. They were loud and quick—unequal—spoken apparently in fear as well as in anger. The voice was harsh—not so much shrill as harsh. Could not call it a shrill voice. The gruff voice said repeatedly '*sacré,*' '*diable*' and once '*mon Dieu.*'[13]

"*Jules Mignaud,* banker, of the firm of Mignaud et Fils, Rue Deloraine. Is the elder Mignaud. Madame L'Espanaye had some property. Had opened an account with his banking house in the spring of the year——(eight years previously). Made frequent deposits in small sums. Had checked for nothing until the third day before her death, when she took out in person the sum of 4000 francs. This sum was paid in gold, and a clerk sent home with the money.

"*Adolphe Le Bon,* clerk to Mignaud et Fils, deposes that on the day in question, about noon, he accompanied Madame L'Espanaye to her residence with the 4000 francs, put up in two bags. Upon the door being opened, Mademoiselle L. appeared and took from his hands one of the bags, while the old lady relieved him of the other. He then bowed and departed. Did not see any person in the street at the time. It is a bye-street—very lonely.

"*William Bird,* tailor, deposes that he was one of the party who entered the house. Is an Englishman. Has lived in Paris two years. Was one of the first to ascend the stairs. Heard the voices in contention. The gruff voice was that of a Frenchman. Could make out several words, but cannot now remember all. Heard distinctly '*sacré*' and '*mon Dieu.*' There was a sound at the moment as if of several persons struggling—a scraping and scuffling sound. The shrill voice was very loud—louder than the gruff one. Is sure that it was not the voice of an Englishman. Appeared to be that of a German. Might have been a woman's voice. Does not understand German.

"Four of the above-named witnesses, being recalled, deposed that the door of the chamber in which was found the body of Mademoiselle L. was locked on the inside when the party reached it. Every thing was perfectly silent—no groans or noises of any kind. Upon forcing the door no person was seen. The windows, both of the back and front room, were down and firmly fastened from within. A door between the two rooms was closed, but not locked. The door leading from the front room into the passage was locked, with the key on the inside. A small room in the front of the house, on the fourth story, at the head of the passage, was open, the door being ajar. This room was crowded with old beds, boxes, and so forth. These were carefully removed and searched. There was not an inch of any portion of the house which was not carefully searched. Sweeps were sent up and down the chimneys. The house was a four story one, with garrets (*mansardes*). A trap-door on the roof was nailed very securely—did not appear to have been opened for

---

[13]Literally, "holy," "devil," and "my God." Poe intends for the reader to understand that the witnesses heard fragments of French expletives.

years. The time elapsing between the hearing of the voices in contention and the breaking open of the room door, was variously stated by the witnesses. Some made it as short as three minutes—some as long as five. The door was opened with difficulty.

"*Alfonzo Garcio,* undertaker, deposes that he resides in the Rue Morgue. Is a native of Spain. Was one of the party who entered the house. Did not proceed up stairs. Is nervous, and was apprehensive of the consequences of agitation. Heard the voices in contention. The gruff voice was that of a Frenchman. Could not distinguish what was said. The shrill voice was that of an Englishman—is sure of this. Does not understand the English language, but judges by the intonation.

"*Alberto Montani,* confectioner, deposes that he was among the first to ascend the stairs. Heard the voices in question. The gruff voice was that of a Frenchman. Distinguished several words. The speaker appeared to be expostulating. Could not make out the words of the shrill voice. Spoke quick and unevenly. Thinks it the voice of a Russian. Corroborates the general testimony. Is an Italian. Never conversed with a native of Russia.

"Several witnesses, recalled, here testified that the chimneys of all the rooms on the fourth story were too narrow to admit the passage of a human being. By 'sweeps' were meant cylindrical sweeping-brushes, such as are employed by those who clean chimneys. These brushes were passed up and down every flue in the house. There is no back passage by which any one could have descended while the party proceeded up stairs. The body of Mademoiselle L'Espanaye was so firmly wedged in the chimney that it could not be got down until four or five of the party united their strength.

"*Paul Dumas,* physician, deposes that he was called to view the bodies about day-break. They were both then lying on the sacking of the bedstead in the chamber where Mademoiselle L. was found. The corpse of the young lady was much bruised and excoriated. The fact that it had been thrust up the chimney would sufficiently account for these appearances. The throat was greatly chafed. There were several deep scratches just below the chin, together with a series of livid spots which were evidently the impression of fingers. The face was fearfully discolored, and the eye-balls protruded. The tongue had been partially bitten through. A large bruise was discovered upon the pit of the stomach, produced, apparently, by the pressure of a knee. In the opinion of M. Dumas, Mademoiselle L'Espanaye had been throttled to death by some person or persons unknown. The corpse of the mother was horribly mutilated. All the bones of the right leg and arm were more or less shattered. The left *tibia*[14] much splintered, as well as all the ribs of the left side. Whole body dreadfully bruised and discolored. It was not possible to say how the injuries had been inflicted. A heavy club of wood, or a broad bar of iron—a chair—any large, heavy, and obtuse weapon would have produced such results, if wielded by the hands of a very powerful man. No woman could have inflicted the blows with any weapon. The head of the deceased, when seen by the witness, was entirely separated from the body, and was also greatly shattered. The

[14]Shin bone.

throat had evidently been cut with some very sharp instrument—probably with a razor.

"*Alexandre Etienne,* surgeon, was called with M. Dumas to view the bodies. Corroborated the testimony, and the opinion of M. Dumas.

"Nothing further of importance was elicited, although several other persons were examined. A murder so mysterious, and so perplexing in all its particulars, was never before committed in Paris—if indeed a murder has been committed at all. The police are entirely at fault—an unusual occurrence in affairs of this nature. There is not, however, the shadow of a clew apparent."

The evening edition of the paper stated that the greatest excitement still continued in the Quartier St. Roch—that the premises in question had been carefully re-searched, and fresh examinations of witnesses instituted, but all to no purpose. A postscript, however, mentioned that Adolphe Le Bon had been arrested and imprisoned—although nothing appeared to criminate him, beyond the facts already detailed.

Dupin seemed singularly interested in the progress of this affair—at least so I judged from his manner, for he made no comments. It was only after the announcement that Le Bon had been imprisoned, that he asked me my opinion respecting the murders.

I could merely agree with all Paris in considering them an insoluble mystery. I saw no means by which it would be possible to trace the murderer.

"We must not judge of the means," said Dupin, "by this shell of an examination. The Parisian police, so much extolled for *acumen,* are cunning, but no more. There is no method in their proceedings, beyond the method of the moment. They make a vast parade of measures; but, not unfrequently, these are so ill adapted to the objects proposed, as to put us in the mind of Monsieur Jourdain's calling for his *robe-de-chambre—pour mieux entendre la musique.*[15] The results attained by them are not unfrequently surprising, but, for the most part, are brought about by simple diligence and activity. When these qualities are unavailing, their schemes fail. Vidocq, for example, was a good guesser, and a persevering man. But, without educated thought, he erred continually by the very intensity of his investigations. He impaired his vision by holding the object too close. He might see, perhaps, one or two points with unusual clearness, but in so doing he, necessarily, lost sight of the matter as a whole. Thus there is such a thing as being too profound. Truth is not always in a well.[16] In fact, as regards the more important knowledge, I do believe that she is invariably superficial. The truth lies not in the valleys where we seek her, but upon the mountain-tops where she is found. The modes and sources of this kind of error are well typified in the contemplation of

---

[15]A "*robe-de-chambre*" is a dressing gown. The joke, however, turns on the word "*chambre,*" chamber. In Molière's *Le Bourgeois Gentilhomme,* the nouveau riche M. Jourdain, in order to listen to chamber music better, wants his "chamber robe." He says to his servants, "*Donnez-moi ma robe pour mieux entendre. . . .*" Poe completed the sentence by adding the words "*la musique.*"

[16]**Vidocq:** See note 7. Contemporary accounts of Vidocq do not suggest that he was notable for the qualities Poe assigns to him. **Truth . . . well:** See "Ligeia," note 5.

the heavenly bodies. To look at a star by glances—to view it in a side-long way, by turning toward it the exterior portions of the *retina* (more susceptible of feeble impressions of light than the interior), is to behold the star distinctly—is to have the best appreciation of its lustre—a lustre which grows dim just in proportion as we turn our vision *fully* upon it. A greater number of rays actually fall upon the eye in the latter case, but, in the former, there is the more refined capacity for comprehension. By undue profundity we perplex and enfeeble thought; and it is possible to make even Venus herself vanish from the firmament by a scrutiny too sustained, too concentrated, or too direct.

"As for these murders, let us enter into some examinations for ourselves, before we make up an opinion respecting them. An inquiry will afford us amusement," [I thought this an odd term, so applied, but said nothing] "and, besides, Le Bon once rendered me a service for which I am not ungrateful. We will go and see the premises with our own eyes. I know G——, the Prefect of Police, and shall have no difficulty in obtaining the necessary permission."

The permission was obtained, and we proceeded at once to the Rue Morgue. This is one of those miserable thoroughfares which intervene between the Rue Richelieu and the Rue St. Roch. It was late in the afternoon when we reached it; as this quarter is at a great distance from that in which we resided. The house was readily found; for there were still many persons gazing up at the closed shutters, with an objectless curiosity, from the opposite side of the way. It was an ordinary Parisian house, with a gateway, on one side of which was a glazed watch-box, with a sliding panel in the window, indicating a *loge de concierge.*[17] Before going in we walked up the street, turned down an alley, and then, again turning, passed in the rear of the building—Dupin, meanwhile, examining the whole neighborhood, as well as the house, with a minuteness of attention for which I could see no possible object.

Retracing our steps, we came again to the front of the dwelling, rang, and, having shown our credentials, were admitted by the agents in charge. We went up stairs—into the chamber where the body of Mademoiselle L'Espanaye had been found, and where both the deceased still lay. The disorders of the room had, as usual, been suffered to exist. I saw nothing beyond what had been stated in the "Gazette des Tribunaux." Dupin scrutinized every thing—not excepting the bodies of the victims. We then went into the other rooms, and into the yard; a *gendarme* accompanying us throughout. The examination occupied us until dark, when we took our departure. On our way home my companion stopped in for a moment at the office of one of the daily papers.

I have said that the whims of my friend were manifold, and that *Je les ménageais:*[18]—for this phrase there is no English equivalent. It was his humor, now, to decline all conversation on the subject of the murder, until about noon the next day. He then asked me, suddenly, if I had observed any thing *peculiar* at the scene of the atrocity.

---

[17]A doorkeeper's apartment.

[18]I handled them tactfully.

There was something in his manner of emphasizing the word "peculiar," which caused me to shudder, without knowing why.

"No, nothing *peculiar,*" I said; "nothing more, at least, than we both saw stated in the paper."

"The 'Gazette,'" he replied, "has not entered, I fear, into the unusual horror of the thing. But dismiss the idle opinions of this print. It appears to me that this mystery is considered insoluble, for the very reason which should cause it to be regarded as easy of solution—I mean for the *outré*[19] character of its features. The police are confounded by the seeming absence of motive—not for the murder itself—but for the atrocity of the murder. They are puzzled, too, by the seeming impossibility of reconciling the voices heard in contention, with the facts that no one was discovered up stairs but the assassinated Mademoiselle L'Espanaye, and that there were no means of egress without the notice of the party ascending. The wild disorder of the room; the corpse thrust, with the head downward, up the chimney; the frightful mutilation of the body of the old lady; these considerations, with those just mentioned, and others which I need not mention, have sufficed to paralyze the powers, by putting completely at fault the boasted *acumen,* of the government agents. They have fallen into the gross but common error of confounding the unusual with the abstruse. But it is by these deviations from the plane of the ordinary, that reason feels its way, if at all, in its search for the true. In investigations such as we are now pursuing, it should not be so much asked 'what has occurred,' as 'what has occurred that has never occurred before.' In fact, the facility with which I shall arrive, or have arrived, at the solution of this mystery, is in the direct ratio of its apparent insolubility in the eyes of the police."

I stared at the speaker in mute astonishment.

"I am now awaiting," continued he, looking toward the door of our apartment—"I am now awaiting a person who, although perhaps not the perpetrator of these butcheries, must have been in some measure implicated in their perpetration. Of the worst portion of the crimes committed, it is probable that he is innocent. I hope that I am right in this supposition; for upon it I build my expectation of reading the entire riddle. I look for the man here—in this room—every moment. It is true that he may not arrive; but the probability is that he will. Should he come, it will be necessary to detain him. Here are pistols; and we both know how to use them when occasion demands their use."

I took the pistols, scarcely knowing what I did, or believing what I heard, while Dupin went on, very much as if in a soliloquy. I have already spoken of his abstract manner at such times. His discourse was addressed to myself; but his voice, although by no means loud, had that intonation which is commonly employed in speaking to some one at a great distance. His eyes, vacant in expression, regarded only the wall.

"That the voices heard in contention," he said, "by the party upon the stairs, were not the voices of the women themselves, was fully proved by the evidence. This relieves us of all doubt upon the question whether the old lady could have first destroyed the daughter, and afterward have committed suicide. I speak of this

---

[19] Strange, odd.

point chiefly for the sake of method; for the strength of Madame L'Espanaye would have been utterly unequal to the task of thrusting her daughter's corpse up the chimney as it was found; and the nature of the wounds upon her own person entirely preclude the idea of self-destruction. Murder, then, has been committed by some third party; and the voices of this third party were those heard in contention. Let me now advert—not to the whole testimony respecting these voices—but to what was *peculiar* in that testimony. Did you observe anything peculiar about it?"

I remarked that, while all witnesses agreed in supposing the gruff voice to be that of a Frenchman, there was much disagreement in regard to the shrill, or, as one individual termed it, the harsh voice.

"That was the evidence itself," said Dupin, "but it was not the peculiarity of the evidence. You have observed nothing distinctive. Yet there *was* something to be observed. The witnesses, as you remark, agreed about the gruff voice; they were here unanimous. But in regard to the shrill voice, the peculiarity is—not that they disagreed—but that, while an Italian, an Englishman, a Spaniard, a Hollander, and a Frenchman attempted to describe it, each one spoke of it as that *of a foreigner.* Each is sure that it was not the voice of one of his own countrymen. Each likens it—not to the voice of an individual of any nation with whose language he is conversant—but the converse. The Frenchman supposes it the voice of a Spaniard, and 'might have distinguished some words *had he been acquainted with the Spanish.*' The Dutchman maintains it to have been that of a Frenchman; but we find it stated that '*not understanding French this witness was examined through an interpreter.*' The Englishman thinks it the voice of a German, and '*does not understand German.*' The Spaniard 'is sure' that it was that of an Englishman, but 'judges by the intonation' altogether, '*as he has no knowledge of the English.*' The Italian believes it the voice of a Russian, but '*has never conversed with a native of Russia.*' A second Frenchman differs, moreover, with the first, and is positive that the voice was that of an Italian; but, *not being cognizant of that tongue,* is, like the Spaniard, 'convinced by the intonation.' Now, how strangely unusual must that voice have really been, about which such testimony as this *could* have been elicited!—in whose *tones,* even, denizens of the five great divisions of Europe could recognise nothing familiar! You will say that it might have been the voice of an Asiatic—of an African. Neither Asiatics nor Africans abound in Paris; but, without denying the inference, I will now merely call your attention to three points. The voice is termed by one witness 'harsh rather than shrill.' It is represented by two others to have been 'quick and *unequal.*' No words—no sounds resembling words—were by any witness mentioned as distinguishable.

"I know not," continued Dupin, "what impression I may have made, so far, upon your own understanding; but I do not hesitate to say that legitimate deductions even from this portion of the testimony—the portion respecting the gruff and shrill voices—are in themselves sufficient to engender a suspicion which should give direction to all farther progress in the investigation of the mystery. I said 'legitimate deductions'; but my meaning is not thus fully expressed. I designed to imply that the deductions are the *sole* proper ones, and that the suspicion arises *inevitably* from them as the single result. What the suspicion is, however, I will not say just yet. I merely wish you to bear in mind that, with myself, it was sufficiently forcible to give a definite form—a certain tendency—to my inquiries in the chamber.

"Let us now transport ourselves, in fancy, to this chamber. What shall we first seek here? The means of egress employed by the murderers. It is not too much to say that neither of us believe in præternatural events. Madame and Mademoiselle L'Espanaye were not destroyed by spirits. The doers of the deed were material, and escaped materially. Then how? Fortunately, there is but one mode of reasoning upon the point, and that mode *must* lead us to a definite decision.—Let us examine, each by each, the possible means of egress. It is clear that the assassins were in the room where Mademoiselle L'Espanaye was found, or at least in the room adjoining, when the party ascended the stairs. It is then only from these two apartments that we have to seek issues. The police have laid bare the floors, the ceilings, and the masonry of the walls, in every direction. No *secret* issues could have escaped their vigilance. But, not trusting to *their* eyes, I examined with my own. There were, then, *no* secret issues. Both doors leading from the rooms into the passage were securely locked, with the keys inside. Let us turn to the chimneys. These, although of ordinary width for some eight or ten feet above the hearths, will not admit, throughout their extent, the body of a large cat. The impossibility of egress, by means already stated, being thus absolute, we are reduced to the windows. Through those of the front room no one could have escaped without notice from the crowd in the street. The murderers *must* have passed, then, through those of the back room. Now, brought to this conclusion in so unequivocal a manner as we are, it is not our part, as reasoners, to reject it on account of apparent impossibilities. It is only left for us to prove that these apparent 'impossibilities' are, in reality, not such.

"There are two windows in the chamber. One of them is unobstructed by furniture, and is wholly visible. The lower portion of the other is hidden from view by the head of the unwieldy bedstead which is thrust close up against it. The former was found securely fastened from within. It resisted the utmost force of those who endeavored to raise it. A large gimlet-hole had been pierced in its frame to the left, and a very stout nail was found fitted therein, nearly to the head. Upon examining the other window, a similar nail was seen similarly fitted in it; and a vigorous attempt to raise this sash failed also. The police were now entirely satisfied that egress had not been in these directions. And, *therefore,* it was thought a matter of supererogation to withdraw the nails and open the windows.

"My own examination was somewhat more particular, and was so for the reason I have just given—because here it was, I knew, that all apparent impossibilities *must* be proved to be not such in reality.

"I proceeded to think *thus—à posteriori.*[20] The murderers *did* escape from one of these windows. This being so, they could not have re-fastened the sashes from the inside, as they were found fastened;—the consideration which put a stop, through its obviousness, to the scrutiny of the police in this quarter. Yet the sashes *were* fastened. They *must,* then, have the power of fastening themselves. There

[20] "After the fact"—that is, beginning by assuming that I was correct.

was no escape from this conclusion. I stepped to the unobstructed casement, withdrew the nail with some difficulty, and attempted to raise the sash. It resisted all my efforts, as I had anticipated. A concealed spring must, I now knew, exist; and this corroboration of my idea convinced me that my premises, at least, were correct, however mysterious still appeared the circumstances attending the nails. A careful search soon brought to light the hidden spring. I pressed it, and, satisfied with the discovery, forebore to upraise the sash.

"I now replaced the nail and regarded it attentively. A person passing out through this window might have reclosed it, and the spring would have caught—but the nail could not have been replaced. The conclusion was plain, and again narrowed in the field of my investigations. The assassins *must* have escaped through the other window. Supposing, then, the springs upon each sash to be the same, as was probable, there *must* be found a difference between the nails, or at least between the modes of their fixture. Getting upon the sacking of the bedstead, I looked over the head-board minutely at the second casement. Passing my hand behind the board, I readily discovered and pressed the spring, which was, as I had supposed, identical in character with its neighbor. I now looked at the nail. It was as stout as the other, and apparently fitted in the same manner—driven in nearly up to the head.

"You will say that I was puzzled; but, if you think so, you must have misunderstood the nature of the inductions. To use a sporting phrase, I had not been once 'at fault.' The scent had never for an instant been lost. There was no flaw in any link of the chain. I had traced the secret to its ultimate result,—and that result was *the nail.* It had, I say, in every respect, the appearance of its fellow in the other window; but this fact was an absolute nullity (conclusive as it might seem to be) when compared with the consideration that here, at this point, terminated the clew. 'There *must* be something wrong,' I said, 'about the nail.' I touched it; and the head, with about a quarter of an inch of the shank, came off in my fingers. The rest of the shank was in the gimlet-hole, where it had been broken off. The fracture was an old one (for its edges were incrusted with rust), and had apparently been accomplished by the blow of a hammer, which had partially imbedded, in the top of the bottom sash, the head portion of the nail. I now carefully replaced this head portion in the indentation whence I had taken it, and the resemblance to a perfect nail was complete—the fissure was invisible. Pressing the spring, I gently raised the sash for a few inches; the head went up with it, remaining firm in its bed. I closed the window, and the semblance of the whole nail was again perfect.

"The riddle, so far, was now unriddled. The assassin had escaped through the window which looked upon the bed. Dropping of its own accord upon his exit (or perhaps purposely closed), it had become fastened by the spring; and it was the retention of this spring which had been mistaken by the police for that of the nail,—farther inquiry being thus considered unnecessary.

"The next question is that of the mode of descent. Upon this point I had been satisfied in my walk with you around the building. About five feet and a half from the casement in question there runs a lightning-rod. From this rod it would have been impossible for any one to reach the window itself, to say nothing of entering it. I observed, however, that the shutters of the fourth story were of the peculiar kind called by Parisian carpenters *ferrades*—a kind rarely employed at the present day, but frequently seen upon very old mansions at Lyons and Bordeaux. They are in the form of an ordinary door, (a single, not a folding door) except that the upper half is latticed or worked in open trellis—thus affording an excellent hold for the hands. In the present instance these shutters are fully three feet and a half broad. When we saw them from the rear of the house, they were both about half open—that is to say, they stood off at right angles from the wall. It is probable that the police, as well as myself, examined the back of the tenement; but, if so, in looking at these *ferrades* in the line of their breadth (as they must have done), they did not perceive this great breadth itself, or, at all events, failed to take it into due consideration. In fact, having once satisfied themselves that no egress could have been made in this quarter, they would naturally bestow here a very cursory examination. It was clear to me, however, that the shutter belonging to the window at the head of the bed, would, if swung fully back to the wall, reach to within two feet of the lightning-rod. It was also evident that, by exertion of a very unusual degree of activity and courage, an entrance into the window, from the rod, might have been thus effected.—By reaching to the distance of two feet and a half (we now suppose the shutter open to its whole extent) a robber might have taken a firm grasp upon the trellis-work. Letting go, then, his hold upon the rod, placing his feet securely against the wall, and springing boldly from it, he might have swung the shutter so as to close it, and, if we imagine the window open at the time, might even have swung himself into the room.

"I wish you to bear especially in mind that I have spoken of a *very* unusual degree of activity as requisite to success in so hazardous and so difficult a feat. It is my design to show you, first, that the thing might possibly have been accomplished:—but, secondly and *chiefly,* I wish to impress upon your understanding the *very extraordinary*—the almost præternatural character of that agility which could have accomplished it.

"You will say, no doubt, using the language of the law, that 'to make out my case' I should rather undervalue, than insist upon a full estimation of the activity required in this matter. This may be the practice in law, but it is not the usage of reason. My ultimate object is only the truth. My immediate purpose is to lead you to place in juxta-position that *very unusual* activity of which I have just spoken, with that *very peculiar* shrill (or harsh) and *unequal* voice, about whose nationality no two persons could be found to agree, and in whose utterance no syllabification could be detected."

At these words a vague and half-formed conception of the meaning of Dupin flitted over my mind. I seemed to be upon the verge of comprehension, without power to comprehend—as men, at times, find themselves upon the brink of remembrance, without being able, in the end, to remember. My friend went on with his discourse.

"You will see," he said, "that I have shifted the question from the mode of egress to that of ingress. It was my design to suggest that both were effected in the same manner, at the same point. Let us now revert to the interior of the room. Let us survey the appearances here. The drawers of the bureau, it is said, had been rifled, although many articles of apparel still remained within them. The conclusion here is absurd. It is a mere guess—a very silly one—and no more. How are we to know that the articles found in the drawers were not all these drawers had originally contained? Madame L'Espanaye and her daughter lived an exceedingly retired life—saw no company—seldom went out—had little use for numerous changes of habiliment. Those found were at least of as good quality as any likely to be possessed by these ladies. If a thief had taken any, why did he not take the best—why did he not take all? In a word, why did he abandon four thousand francs in gold to encumber himself with a bundle of linen? The gold *was* abandoned. Nearly the whole sum mentioned by Monsieur Mignaud, the banker, was discovered, in bags, upon the floor. I wish you, therefore, to discard from your thoughts the blundering idea of *motive,* engendered in the brains of the police by that portion of the evidence which speaks of money delivered at the door of the house. Coincidences ten times as remarkable as this (the delivery of the money, and murder committed within three days upon the party receiving it), happen to all of us every hour of our lives, without attracting even momentary notice. Coincidences, in general, are great stumbling-blocks in the way of that class of thinkers who have been educated to know nothing of the theory of probabilities—that theory to which the most glorious objects of human research are indebted for the most glorious of illustration. In the present instance, had the gold been gone, the fact of its delivery three days before would have formed something more than a coincidence. It would have been corroborative of this idea of motive. But, under the real circumstances of the case, if we are to suppose gold the motive of this outrage, we must also imagine the perpetrator so vacillating an idiot as to have abandoned his gold and his motive together.

"Keeping now steadily in mind the points to which I have drawn your attention—that peculiar voice, that unusual agility, and that startling absence of motive in a murder so singularly atrocious as this—let us glance at the butchery itself. Here is a woman strangled to death by manual strength, and thrust up a chimney, head downward. Ordinary assassins employ no such modes of murder as this. Least of all, do they thus dispose of the murdered. In the manner of thrusting the corpse up the chimney, you will admit that there was something *excessively outré*—something altogether irreconcilable with our common notions of human action, even when we suppose the actors the most depraved of men. Think, too, how great must have been that strength which could have thrust the body *up* such an aperture so forcibly that the united vigor of several persons was found barely sufficient to drag it *down!*

"Turn, now, to other indications of the employment of a vigor most marvellous. On the hearth were thick tresses—very thick tresses—of gray human hair. These had been torn out by the roots. You are aware of the great force necessary in tearing thus from the head even twenty or thirty hairs together. You saw the locks in question as well as myself. Their roots (a hideous sight!) were clotted with fragments of the flesh of the scalp—sure token of the prodigious power which had been exerted in uprooting perhaps half a million of hairs at a time. The throat of the old lady was not merely cut, but the head absolutely severed from the body: the instrument was a mere razor. I wish you also to look at the *brutal* ferocity of these deeds. Of the bruises upon the body of Madame L'Espanaye I do not speak.

Monsieur Dumas, and his worthy coadjutor Monsieur Etienne, have pronounced that they were inflicted by some obtuse instrument; and so far these gentlemen are very correct. The obtuse instrument was clearly the stone pavement in the yard, upon which the victim had fallen from the window which looked in upon the bed. This idea, however simple it may now seem, escaped the police for the same reason that the breadth of the shutters escaped them—because, by the affair of the nails, their perceptions had been hermetically sealed against the possibility of the windows having ever been opened at all.

"If now, in addition to all these things, you have properly reflected upon the odd disorder of the chamber, we have gone so far as to combine the ideas of an agility astounding, a strength superhuman, a ferocity brutal, a butchery without motive, a *grotesquerie* in horror absolutely alien from humanity, and a voice foreign in tone to the ears of men of many nations, and devoid of all distinct or intelligible syllabification. What result, then, has ensued? What impression have I made upon your fancy?"

I felt a creeping of the flesh as Dupin asked me the question. "A madman," I said, "has done this deed—some raving maniac, escaped from a neighboring *Maison de Santé*."[21]

"In some respects," he replied, "your idea is not irrelevant. But the voices of madmen, even in their wildest paroxysms, are never found to tally with that peculiar voice heard upon the stairs. Madmen are of some nation, and their language, however incoherent in its words, has always the coherence of syllabification. Besides, the hair of a madman is not such as I now hold in my hand. I disentangled this little tuft from the rigidly clutched fingers of Madam L'Espanaye. Tell me what you can make of it."

"Dupin!" I said, completely unnerved; "this hair is most unusual—this is no *human* hair."

"I have not asserted that it is," said he; "but, before we decide this point, I wish you to glance at the little sketch I have here traced upon this paper. It is a *facsimile* drawing of what has been described in one portion of the testimony as 'dark bruises, and deep indentations of finger nails,' upon the throat of Mademoiselle L'Espanaye, and in another, (by Messrs. Dumas and Etienne,) as a 'series of livid spots, evidently the impression of fingers.'

"You will perceive," continued my friend, spreading out the paper upon the table before us, "that this drawing gives the idea of a firm and fixed hold. There is no *slipping* apparent. Each finger has retained—possibly until the death of the victim—the fearful grasp by which it originally imbedded itself. Attempt, now, to place all your fingers, at the same time, in the respective impressions as you see them."

I made the attempt in vain.

"We are possibly not giving this matter a fair trial," he said. "The paper is spread out upon a plane surface; but the human throat is cylindrical. Here is a billet of wood, the circumference of which is about that of the throat. Wrap the drawing around it, and try the experiment again."

---

[21]Insane asylum.

I did so; but the difficulty was even more obvious than before.

"This," I said, "is the mark of no human hand."

"Read now," replied Dupin, "this passage from Cuvier."[22]

It was a minute anatomical and generally descriptive account of the large fulvous Ourang-Outang of the East Indian Islands. The gigantic stature, the prodigious strength and activity, the wild ferocity, and the imitative propensities of these mammalia are sufficiently well known to all. I understood the full horrors of the murder at once.

"The description of the digits," said I, as I made an end of reading, "is in exact accordance with this drawing. I see that no animal but an Ourang-Outang, of the species here mentioned, could have impressed the identations as you have traced them. This tuft of tawny hair, too, is identical in character with that of the beast of Cuvier. But I cannot possibly comprehend the particulars of this frightful mystery. Besides, there were *two* voices heard in contention, and one of them was unquestionably the voice of a Frenchman."

"True; and you will remember an expression attributed almost unanimously, by the evidence, to this voice,—the expression, '*mon Dieu!*' This, under the circumstances, has been justly characterized by one of the witnesses (Montani, the confectioner,) as an expression of remonstrance or expostulation. Upon these two words, therefore, I have mainly built my hopes of a full solution of the riddle. A Frenchman was cognizant of the murder. It is possible—indeed it is far more than probable—that he was innocent of all participation in the bloody transactions which took place. The Ourang-Outang may have escaped from him. He may have traced it to the chamber; but, under the agitating circumstances which ensued, he could never have re-captured it. It is still at large. I will not pursue these guesses—for I have no right to call them more—since the shades of reflection upon which they are based are scarcely of sufficient depth to be appreciable by my own intellect, and since I could not pretend to make them intelligible to the understanding of another. We will call them guesses then, and speak of them as such. If the Frenchman in question is indeed, as I suppose, innocent of this atrocity, this advertisement, which I left last night, upon our return home, at the office of 'Le Monde,' (a paper devoted to the shipping interest, and much sought by sailors,) will bring him to our residence."

He handed me a paper, and I read thus:

> CAUGHT—*In the Bois de Boulogne, early in the morning of the —— inst.,* (the morning of the murder,) *a very large, tawny Ourang-Outang of the Bornese species. The owner, (who is ascertained to be a sailor, belonging to a Maltese vessel,) may have the animal again, upon identifying it satisfactorily, and paying a few charges arising from its capture and keeping. Call at No. ——, Rue ——, Faubourg St. Germain—au troisième.*

"How was it possible," I asked, "that you should know the man to be a sailor, and belonging to a Maltese vessel?"

---

[22]Baron Georges Cuvier (1769–1832), great French naturalist whose classification of animals was one of the standard guides to the subject until Darwin.

"I do *not* know it," said Dupin. "I am not *sure* of it. Here, however, is a small piece of ribbon, which from its form, and from its greasy appearance, has evidently been used in tying the hair in one of those long *queues* of which sailors are so fond. Moreover, this knot is one which few besides sailors can tie, and is peculiar to the Maltese. I picked the ribbon up at the foot of the lightning-rod. It could not have belonged to either of the deceased. Now if, after all, I am wrong in my induction from this ribbon, that the Frenchman was a sailor belonging to a Maltese vessel, still I can have done no harm in saying what I did in the advertisement. If I am in error, he will merely suppose that I have been misled by some circumstance into which he will not take the trouble to inquire. But if I am right, a great point is gained. Cognizant although innocent of the murder, the Frenchman will naturally hesitate about replying to the advertisement—about demanding the Ourang-Outang. He will reason thus:—'I am innocent; I am poor; my Ourang-Outang is of great value—to one in my circumstances a fortune of itself—why should I lose it through idle apprehensions of danger? Here it is, within my grasp. It was found in the Bois de Boulogne—at a vast distance from the scene of the butchery. How can it ever be suspected that a brute beast should have done the deed? The police are at fault—they have failed to procure the slightest clew. Should they even trace the animal, it would be impossible to prove me cognizant of the murder, or to implicate me in guilt on account of that cognizance. Above all, *I am known.* The advertiser designates me as the possessor of the beast. I am not sure to what limit his knowledge may extend. Should I avoid claiming a property of so great value, which it is known that I possess, I will render the animal, at least, liable to suspicion. It is not my policy to attract attention either to myself or to the beast. I will answer the advertisement, get the Ourang-Outang, and keep it close until this matter has blown over.' "

At this moment we heard a step upon the stairs.

"Be ready," said Dupin, "with your pistols, but neither use them nor show them until at a signal from myself."

The front of the house had been left open, and the visitor had entered, without ringing, and advanced several steps upon the staircase. Now, however, he seemed to hesitate. Presently we heard him descending. Dupin was moving quickly to the door, when we again heard him coming up. He did not turn back a second time, but stepped up with decision and rapped at the door of our chamber.

"Come in," said Dupin, in a cheerful and hearty tone.

A man entered. He was a sailor, evidently,—a tall, stout, and muscular-looking person, with a certain dare-devil expression of countenance, not altogether unprepossessing. His face, greatly sunburnt, was more than half hidden by whisker and *mustachio.* He had with him a huge oaken cudgel, but appeared to be otherwise unarmed. He bowed awkwardly, and bade us "good evening," in French accents, which although somewhat Neufchatel-ish,[23] were still sufficiently indicative of a Parisian origin.

---

[23]Neufchâtel is a town in northern France. Mabbott (9, II) suggests that "Neufchâtel-ish" implies rustic.

"Sit down, my friend," said Dupin. "I suppose you have called about the Ourang-Outang. Upon my word, I almost envy you the possession of him; a remarkably fine, and no doubt a very valuable animal. How old do you suppose him to be?"

The sailor drew a long breath, with the air of a man relieved of some intolerable burden, and then replied, in an assured tone:

"I have no way of telling—but he can't be more than four or five years old. Have you got him here?"

"Oh no; we had no conveniences for keeping him here. He is at a livery stable in the Rue Dubourg, just by. You can get him in the morning. Of course you are prepared to identify the property?"

"To be sure I am, sir."

"I shall be sorry to part with him," said Dupin.

"I don't mean that you should be at all this trouble for nothing, sir," said the man. "Couldn't expect it. Am very willing to pay a reward for the finding of the animal—that is to say, any thing in reason."

"Well," replied my friend, "that is all very fair, to be sure. Let me think!—what should I have? Oh! I will tell you. My reward shall be this. You shall give me all the information in your power about these murders in the Rue Morgue."

Dupin said the last words in a very low tone, and very quietly. Just as quietly, too, he walked toward the door, locked it, and put the key in his pocket. He then drew a pistol from his bosom and placed it, without the least flurry, upon the table.

The sailor's face flushed up as if he were struggling with suffocation. He started to his feet and grasped his cudgel; but the next moment he fell back into his seat, trembling violently, and with the countenance of death itself. He spoke not a word. I pitied him from the bottom of my heart.

"My friend," said Dupin, in a kind tone, "you are alarming yourself unnecessarily—you are indeed. We mean you no harm whatever. I pledge you the honor of a gentleman, and of a Frenchman, that we intend you no injury. I perfectly well know that you are innocent of the atrocities in the Rue Morgue. It will not do, however, to deny that you are in some measure implicated in them. From what I have already said, you must know that I have had means of information about this matter—means of which you could never have dreamed. Now the thing stands thus. You have done nothing which you could have avoided—nothing, certainly, which renders you culpable. You were not even guilty of robbery, when you might have robbed with impunity. You have nothing to conceal. You have no reason for concealment. On the other hand, you are bound by every principle of honor to confess all you know. An innocent man is now imprisoned, charged with that crime of which you can point out the perpetrator."

The sailor had recovered his presence of mind, in a great measure, while Dupin uttered these words; but his original boldness of bearing was all gone.

"So help me God," said he, after a brief pause, "I *will* tell you all I know about this affair;—but I do not expect you to believe one half I say—I would be a fool indeed if I did. Still, I *am* innocent, and I will make a clean breast if I die for it."

What he stated was, in substance, this. He had lately made a voyage to the Indian Archipelago. A party, of which he formed one, landed at Borneo, and passed into the interior on an excursion of pleasure. Himself and a companion had captured the Ourang-Outang. This companion dying, the animal fell into his own exclusive possession. After great trouble, occasioned by the intractable ferocity of his captive during the home voyage, he at length succeeded in lodging it safely at his own residence in Paris, where, not to attract toward himself the unpleasant curiosity of his neighbors, he kept it carefully secluded, until such time as it should recover from a wound in the foot, received from a splinter on board ship. His ultimate design was to sell it.

Returning home from some sailors' frolic on the night, or rather in the morning of the murder, he found the beast occupying his own bed-room, into which it had broken from a closet adjoining, where it had been, as was thought, securely confined. Razor in hand, and fully lathered, it was sitting before a looking-glass, attempting the operation of shaving, in which it had no doubt previously watched its master through the key-hole of the closet. Terrified at the sight of so dangerous a weapon in the possession of an animal so ferocious, and so well able to use it, the man, for some moments, was at a loss what to do. He had been accustomed, however, to quiet the creature, even in its fiercest moods, by the use of a whip, and to this he now resorted. Upon sight of it, the Ourang-Outang sprang at once through the door of the chamber, down the stairs, and thence, through a window, unfortunately open, into the street.

The Frenchman followed in despair; the ape, razor still in hand, occasionally stopping to look back and gesticulate at its pursuer, until the latter had nearly come up with it. It then again made off. In this manner the chase continued for a long time. The streets were profoundly quiet, as it was nearly three o'clock in the morning. In passing down an alley in the rear of the Rue Morgue, the fugitive's attention was arrested by a light gleaming from the open window of Madame L'Espanaye's chamber, in the fourth story of her house. Rushing to the building, it perceived the lightning-rod, clambered up with inconceivable agility, grasped the shutter, which was thrown fully back against the wall, and, by its means, swung itself directly upon the headboard of the bed. The whole feat did not occupy a minute. The shutter was kicked open again by the Ourang-Outang as it entered the room.

The sailor, in the meantime, was both rejoiced and perplexed. He had strong hopes of now recapturing the brute, as it could scarcely escape from the trap into which it had ventured, except by the rod, where it might be intercepted as it came down. On the other hand, there was much cause for anxiety as to what it might do in the house. This latter reflection urged the man still to follow the fugitive. A lightning-rod is ascended without difficulty, especially by a sailor; but, when he had arrived as high as the window, which lay far to his left, his career was stopped; the most that he could accomplish was to reach over so as to obtain a glimpse of the interior of the room. At this glimpse he nearly fell from his hold through excess of horror. Now it was that those hideous shrieks arose upon the night, which had startled from slumber the inmates of the Rue Morgue. Madame L'Espanaye and her daughter, habited in their night clothes, had apparently been arranging some papers in the iron chest already mentioned, which had been wheeled into the middle of the room. It was open, and its contents lay beside it on the floor. The victims must have been sitting with their backs toward the window; and, from the time elapsing between the ingress of the beast and the screams, it seems probable that it was not immediately perceived. The flapping-to of the shutter would naturally have been attributed to the wind.

As the sailor looked in, the gigantic animal had seized Madam L'Espanaye by the hair, (which was loose, as she had been combing it,) and was flourishing the razor about her face, in imitation of the motions of a barber. The daughter lay prostrate and motionless; she had swooned. The screams and struggles of the old lady (during which the hair was torn from her head) had the effect of changing the probably pacific purposes of the Ourang-Outang into those of wrath. With one determined sweep of its muscular arm it nearly severed her head from her body. The sight of blood inflamed its anger into phrenzy. Gnashing its teeth, and flashing fire from its eyes, it flew upon the body of the girl, and imbedded its fearful talons in her throat, retaining its grasp until she expired. Its wandering and wild glances fell at this moment upon the head of the bed, over which the face of its master, rigid with horror, was just discernible. The fury of the beast, who no doubt bore still in mind the dreaded whip, was instantly converted into fear. Conscious of having deserved punishment, it seemed desirous of concealing its bloody deeds, and skipped about the chamber in an agony of nervous agitation; throwing down and breaking the furniture as it moved, and dragging the bed from the bedstead. In conclusion, it seized first the corpse of the daughter, and thrust it up the chimney, as it was found; then that of the old lady, which it immediately hurled through the window headlong.

As the ape approached the casement with its mutilated burden, the sailor shrank aghast to the rod, and, rather gliding than clambering down it, hurried at once home—dreading the consequences of the butchery, and gladly abandoning, in his terror, all solicitude about the fate of the Ourang-Outang. The words heard by the party upon the staircase were the Frenchman's exclamations of horror and affright, commingled with the fiendish jabberings of the brute.

I have scarcely anything to add. The Ourang-Outang must have escaped from the chamber, by the rod, just before the breaking of the door. It must have closed the window as it passed through it. It was subsequently caught by the owner himself, who obtained for it a very large sum at the *Jardin des Plantes.* Le Bon was instantly released, upon our narration of the circumstances (with some comments from Dupin) at the *bureau* of the Prefect of Police. This functionary, however well disposed to my friend, could not altogether conceal his chagrin at the turn which affairs had taken, and was fain to indulge in a sarcasm or two, about the propriety of every person minding his own business.

"Let them talk," said Dupin, who had not thought it necessary to reply. "Let him discourse; it will ease his conscience. I am satisfied with having defeated him in his own castle. Nevertheless, that he failed in the solution of this mystery, is by no means that matter for wonder which he supposes it; for, in truth, our friend the Prefect is somewhat too cunning to be profound. In his wisdom is no *stamen.* It is all head and no body, like the pictures of the Goddess Laverna—or, at best, all head and shoulders, like a codfish. But he is a good creature after all. I like him especially for one master stroke of cant, by which he has attained his reputation for ingenuity. I mean the way he has '*de nier ce qui est, et d'expliquer ce qui n'est pas.*'"[24]

---

[24]**the Goddess Laverna:** The patroness of thieves in ancient Roman religion. ***de nier . . . n'est pas***: *Rousseau, Nouvelle Héloïse* [Poe's note]. Jean-Jacques Rousseau's *Julie ou La Nouvelle Héloïse* (1760). The French may be translated, "Of denying that which is, and of explaining that which is not."

A Descent into the Maelström

Poe's story about a Norwegian fisherman and the whirlpool suggests comparison with Coleridge's "The Rime of the Ancient Mariner"; notes 11, 14, 15, and 20 make connections with the poem which might be summarized, "The mariner's salvation is mystical and religious; the fisherman's is rational and secular." But that summary does not tell the whole story, for in the context of other tales by Poe, the fisherman's way of saving himself has mystical and quasi-religious implications, too. If, as Poe said, his aim as artist was to create the beautiful effect, and if "A Descent into the Maelström" is characteristic of that desire, then the description of the wild beauty of the interior of the Maelström on this weird and terrible night should be worth comparing with the scenes of "ideal" beauty in "The Landscape Garden." Different as this tale is, its "beautiful effect" is strangely similar. This may be simply because Poe's taste is consistent, but there seem to be other reasons, too. Mystics in all ages have taught that there are multiple paths to enlightenment and have described visions which strongly resemble these "beautiful effects" in Poe: kaleidoscopic unfoldings of complex luminosity. However we explain them, such visions are present in exceedingly dissimilar stories, and characters perceive them in very different ways. Thus, while Ellison in "The Landscape Garden" creates his beauty without difficulty, the fisherman must be frightened into the state of supersensitivity which enables him to find beauty in his strange surroundings. Apparently the more difficult the process of perceiving "beauty," the more complex the plot.

A weakness evident in several of Poe's tales shows up in "Maelström": often the language of the "simple fisherman" is not only cool, but also far too erudite to be credible. The sentences at notes 17 and 19 seem especially inappropriate. The trouble may be, as Poe says, haste (see note 12), or it may be that the repertoire of "magazinists" of his day generally did not include effective dialogue. One can read through whole volumes of the magazines in which he published without finding convincing conversations, perhaps because authors devote so much of their effort to description of the fantastic. The era of the "magazinists," as Poe called his colleagues, is a strange period in the history of literature.

Publications in Poe's Time

Graham's Magazine, May 1841
Tales, 1845
The Broadway Journal, October 1, 1845

Revue britannique, French translation, September 1846
Boston Museum, May 26, 1849
The Irving Offering (a gift-book), 1851

A DESCENT INTO THE MAELSTRÖM

The ways of God in Nature, as in Providence, are not as our ways; nor are the models that we frame any way commensurate to the vastness, profundity, and unsearchableness of His works, which have a depth in them greater than the well of Democritus.

Joseph Glanvill.[1]

We had now reached the summit of the loftiest crag. For some minutes the old man seemed too much exhausted to speak.

"Not long ago," said he at length, "and I could have guided you on this route as well as the youngest of my sons; but, about three years past, there happened to me an event such as never happened before to mortal man—or at least such as no man ever survived to tell of—and the six hours of deadly terror which I then endured have broken me up body and soul. You suppose me a *very* old man—but I am not. It took less than a single day to change these hairs from a jetty black to white, to weaken my limbs, and to unstring my nerves, so that I tremble at the least exertion, and am frightened at a shadow. Do you know I can scarcely look over this little cliff without getting giddy?"

The "little cliff," upon whose edge he had so carelessly thrown himself down to rest that the weightier portion of his body hung over it, while he was only kept from falling by the tenure of his elbow on its extreme and slippery edge—this "little cliff" arose, a sheer unobstructed precipice of black shining rock, some fifteen or sixteen hundred feet from the world of crags beneath us. Nothing would have tempted me to be within half a dozen yards of its brink. In truth so deeply

---

[1]Joseph Glanvill (1636–80) was an important English essayist. The quotation is from *Essays on Several Important Subjects in Philosophy and Religion* (1676), and Poe tinkered with his source, as he often did in such quotations. Glanvill's essay reads, "The ways of God in Nature (as in *Providence*) are not as *ours* are: Nor are the Models that we frame any way commensurate to the vastness and profundity of his Works; which have a depth in them greater than the *Well of Democritus*" (A. H. Quinn; Woodberry). Democritus was a materialist philosopher (460–360 B.C.E.) and one of the fathers of atomism ("in reality there is nothing but atoms and space") whose belief in physical causality—he held that even the "soul" is physical—Poe found sympathetic. Compare what Poe says about materialism in "The Domain of Arnheim" and in Agathos' speeches in "The Power of Words." For the "well of Democritus," see "Ligeia," note 5.

was I excited by the perilous position of my companion, that I fell at full length upon the ground, clung to the shrubs around me, and dared not even glance upward at the sky—while I struggled in vain to divest myself of the idea that the very foundations of the mountain were in danger from the fury of the winds. It was long before I could reason myself into sufficient courage to sit up and look out into the distance.

"You must get over these fancies," said the guide, "for I have brought you here that you might have the best possible view of the scene of that event I mentioned and to tell you the whole story with the spot just under your eye."

"We are now," he continued, in that particularizing manner which distinguished him—"we are now close upon the Norwegian coast—in the sixty-eighth degree of latitude—in the great province of Nordland—and in the dreary district of Lofoden.[2] The mountain upon whose top we sit is Helseggen, the Cloudy. Now raise yourself up a little higher—hold on to the grass if you feel giddy—so—and look out, beyond the belt of vapor beneath us, into the sea."

I looked dizzily, and beheld a wide expanse of ocean, whose waters wore so inky a hue as to bring at once to my mind the Nubian geographer's account of the *Mare Tenebrarum.*[3] A panorama more deplorably desolate no human imagination can conceive. To the right and left, as far as the eye could reach, there lay outstretched, like ramparts of the world, lines of horridly black and beetling cliff, whose character of gloom was but the more forcibly illustrated by the surf which reared high up against it its white and ghastly crest, howling and shrieking for ever. Just opposite the promontory upon whose apex we were placed, and at a distance of some five or six miles out at sea, there was visible a small, bleak-looking island; or, more properly, its position was discernible through the wilderness of surge in which it was enveloped. About two miles nearer the land, arose another of smaller size, hideously craggy and barren, and encompassed at various intervals by a cluster of dark rocks.

The appearance of the ocean, in the space between the more distant island and the shore, had something very unusual about it. Although, at the time, so strong a gale was blowing landward that a brig in the remote offing lay to under a double-reefed trysail, and constantly plunged her whole hull out of sight, still there was here nothing like a regular swell, but only a short, quick, angry cross dashing of

---

[2]Poe's geography is accurate. The Lofoden (Lofoten) Islands are off the northwest coast of Norway; the 68° line is just above the site on which the fisherman and narrator sit. The hamlet of Helle, a mountain of 601 meters in height, and the Lofotodden headland, a high promontory fronting the sea, are at the lower tip of Moskenes (see Figure 7).

[3]**Nubian . . . *Tenebrarum:*** Poe's source is a passage in Jacob Bryant's *A New System or, an Analysis of Ancient Mythology* (Vol. IV, 79): "By the Nubian Geographer the Atlantic is uniformly called, according to the present version, Mare Tenebrarum. Aggressi sunt mare tenebrarum quid in eo esset, exploraturi. *They ventured into the sea of darkness, in order to explore what it might contain.*" Poe uses this quotation in full in "Eleonora." See note 2 of that tale. The Nubian geographer to whom Bryant refers is al Idrisi, author of *Geographia nubiensis,* and not Ptolemy Hephæstion, as Poe says in *Eureka.* Bryant does mention Ptolemy Hephæstion, but does not call him "the Nubian geographer." Poe's error in *Eureka* may be deliberate. See "Mellonta Tauta," note 2.

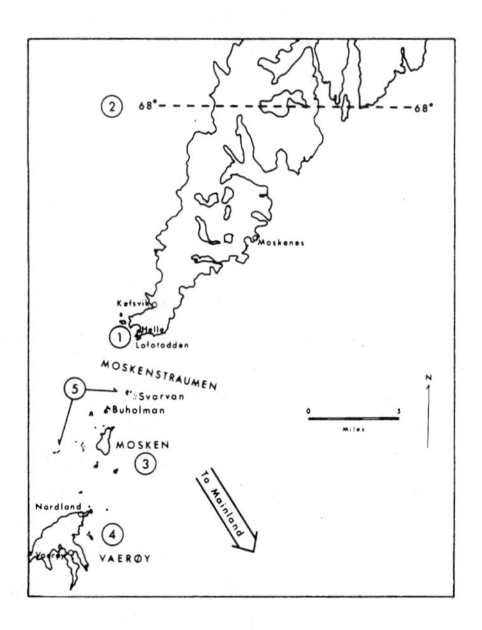

Figure 7. A map of the area in which Poe's "A Descent into the Malström" is set, showing places named in the story:

1. Lofotodden headland, the probable site of the storytelling
2. The 68° parallel
3. Mosken ("Moskoe")
4. Vaerøy ("Varrgh")
5. Tiny islands mentioned by fisherman.

Only Svarvan ("Suarven") and Buholman ("Buckholm") are named on the charts we examined. Map by Lewis Armstrong.

water in every direction—as well in the teeth of the wind as otherwise. Of foam there was little except in the immediate vicinity of the rocks.

"The island in the distance," resumed the old man, "is called by the Norwegians Vurrgh. The one midway is Moskoe. That a mile to the northward is Ambaaren. Yonder are Iflesen, Hoeyholm, Kieldholm, Suarven, and Buckholm. Further off—between Moskoe and Vurrgh—are Otterholm, Flimen, Sandflesen, and Skarholm.[4] These are the true names of the places—but why it has been thought necessary to name them at all, is more than either you or I can understand. Do you hear any thing? Do you see any change in the water?"

We had now been about ten minutes upon the top of Helseggen, to which we had ascended from the interior of Lofoden, so that we had caught no glimpse of the sea until it had burst upon us from the summit. As the old man spoke, I became aware of a loud and gradually increasing sound, like the moaning of a vast herd of buffaloes upon an American prairie;[5] and at the same moment I perceived that what seamen term the *chopping* character of the ocean beneath us, was rapidly changing into a current which set to the eastward. Even while I gazed, this current acquired a monstrous velocity. Each moment added to its speed—to its headlong

[4]Figure 7 locates the places named. Poe got all his data on whirlpools from an encyclopedia article. The story of Poe's borrowings in this tale is good fun; Poe probably would have been pleased to know that, in arguing back against an encyclopedia, he became a "source" himself for a later encyclopedia article on whirlpools (A. H. Quinn, Turner, Benson).

[5]A sound Poe had never heard, either; except for a childhood trip to England, his travels were limited, to the best knowledge of his biographers, to the eastern seaboard.

impetuosity. In five minutes the whole sea, as far as Vurrgh, was lashed into ungovernable fury; but it was between Moskoe and the coast that the main uproar held its sway.[6] Here the vast bed of the waters, seamed and scarred into a thousand conflicting channels, burst suddenly into phrensied convulsion—heaving, boiling, hissing—gyrating in gigantic and innumerable vortices, and all whirling and plunging on to the eastward with a rapidity which water never elsewhere assumes, except in precipitous descents.

In a few minutes more, there came over the scene another radical alteration. The general surface grew somewhat more smooth, and the whirlpools, one by one, disappeared, while prodigious streaks of foam became apparent where none had been seen before. These streaks, at length, spreading out to a great distance, and entering into combination, took unto themselves the gyratory motion of the subsided vortices, and seemed to form the germ of another more vast. Suddenly—very suddenly—this assumed a distinct and definite existence, in a circle of more than half a mile in diameter. The edge of the whirl was represented by a broad belt of gleaming spray; but no particle of this slipped into the mouth of the terrific funnel, whose interior, as far as the eye could fathom it, was a smooth, shining, and jet-black wall of water, inclined to the horizon at an angle of some forty-five degrees, speeding dizzily round and round with a swaying and sweltering motion, and sending forth to the winds an appalling voice, half shriek, half roar, such as not even the mighty cataract of Niagara ever lifts up in its agony to Heaven.

The mountain trembled to its very base, and the rock rocked. I threw myself upon my face, and clung to the scant herbage in an excess of nervous agitation.

"This," said I at length, to the old man—"this *can* be nothing else than the great whirlpool of the Maelström."

"So it is sometimes termed," said he. "We Norwegians call it the Moskoe-ström, from the island of Moskoe in the midway."

The ordinary account of this vortex had by no means prepared me for what I saw. That of Jonas Ramus,[7] which is perhaps the most circumstantial of any, cannot impart the faintest conception either of the magnificence, or of the horror of the scene—or of the wild bewildering sense of *the novel* which confounds the beholder. I am not sure from what point of view the writer in question surveyed it, nor at what time; but it could neither have been from the summit of Helseggen, nor during a storm. There are some passages of his description, nevertheless, which may be quoted for their details, although their effect is exceedingly feeble in conveying an impression of the spectacle.

"Between Lofoden and Moskoe," he says, "the depth of the water is between

---

[6]Accounts of where the whirlpools form conflict; some say between Mosken and Vaerøy; others say between Mosken and Lofotodden. Modern maps and Poe's narration agree, however. By "coast" Poe means the coast on which his narrator sits, near Helle.

[7]Jonas Ramus (1649–1718), author of a book theorizing that Ulysses' experience with Scylla and Charybdis really occurred in the Maelström off the Norwegian coast: *Ulysses et Otinus Unus & idem sive Disquisitio & Historica Geographica* (1702) (Benson). Poe copied Ramus's account from the *Encyclopaedia Britannica;* it, in turn, copied Erich Pontoppidan's *Natural History of Norway* (A. H. Quinn, after Woodberry).

thirty-six and forty fathoms; but on the other side, toward Ver (Vurrgh) this depth decreases so as not to afford a convenient passage for a vessel, without the risk of splitting on the rocks, which happens even in the calmest weather. When it is flood, the stream runs up the country between Lofoden and Moskoe with a boisterous rapidity; but the roar of its impetuous ebb to the sea is scarce equalled by the loudest and most dreadful cataracts; the noise being heard several leagues off, and the vortices or pits are of such an extent and depth, that if a ship comes within its attraction, it is inevitably absorbed and carried down to the bottom, and there beat to pieces against the rocks; and when the water relaxes, the fragments thereof are thrown up again. But these intervals of tranquillity are only at the turn of the ebb and flood, and in calm weather, and last but a quarter of an hour, its violence gradually returning. When the stream is most boisterous, and its fury heightened by a storm, it is dangerous to come within a Norway mile of it. Boats, yachts, and ships have been carried away by not guarding against it before they were within its reach. It likewise happens frequently, that whales come too near the stream, and are overpowered by its violence; and then it is impossible to describe their howlings and bellowings in their fruitless struggles to disengage themselves. A bear once, attempting to swim from Lofoden to Moskoe, was caught by the stream and borne down, while he roared terribly, so as to be heard on shore. Large stocks of firs and pine trees, after being absorbed by the current, rise again broken and torn to such degree as if bristles grew upon them. This plainly shows the bottom to consist of craggy rocks, among which they are whirled to and fro. This stream is regulated by the flux and reflux of the sea—it being constantly high and low water every six hours. In the year 1645, early in the morning of Sexagesima Sunday,[8] it raged with such noise and impetuosity that the very stones of the houses on the coast fell to the ground."

In regard to the depth of the water, I could not see how this could have been ascertained at all in the immediate vicinity of the vortex. The "forty fathoms" must have reference only to portions of the channel close upon the shore either of Moskoe or Lofoden. The depth in the centre of the Moskoe-ström must be unmeasurably greater; and no better proof of this fact is necessary than can be obtained from even the sidelong glance into the abyss of the whirl which may be had from the highest crag of Helseggen. Looking down from this pinnacle upon the howling Phlegethon[9] below, I could not help smiling at the simplicity with which the honest Jonas Ramus records, as a matter difficult of belief, the anecdotes of the whales and the bears, for it appeared to me, in fact, a self-evident thing, that the largest ships of the line in existence, coming within the influence of that deadly attraction could resist it as little as a feather the hurricane, and must disappear bodily and at once.

The attempts to account for the phenomenon—some of which, I remember, seemed to me sufficiently plausible in perusal—now wore a very different and unsatisfactory aspect. The idea generally received is that this, as well as three smaller vortices among the Feroe islands, "have no other cause than the collision

---

[8]Second Sunday before Lent.

[9]River of fire in Greek mythology.

of waves rising and falling, at flux and reflux, against a ridge of rocks and shelves, which confines the water so that it precipitates itself like a cataract; and thus the higher the flood rises, the deeper must the fall be, and the natural result of all is a whirlpool or vortex, the prodigious suction of which is sufficiently known by lesser experiments."—These are the words of the Encyclopædia Britannica. Kircher and others imagine that in the centre of the channel of the Maelström is an abyss penetrating the globe, and issuing in some very remote part—the Gulf of Bothnia[10] being somewhat decidedly named in one instance. This opinion, idle in itself, was the one to which, as I gazed, my imagination most readily assented; and, mentioning it to the guide, I was rather surprised to hear him say that, although it was the view almost universally entertained of the subject by the Norwegians, it nevertheless was not his own. As to the former notion he confessed his inability to comprehend it; and here I agreed with him—for, however conclusive on paper, it becomes altogether unintelligible, and even absurd, amid the thunder of the abyss.

"You have had a good look at the whirl now," said the old man, "and if you will creep round this crag, so as to get in its lee, and deaden the roar of the water, I will tell you a story that will convince you I ought to know something of the Moskoe-ström."

I placed myself as desired, and he proceeded.[11]

"Myself and my two brothers once owned a schooner-rigged smack of about seventy tons burthen, with which we were in the habit of fishing among the islands beyond Moskoe, nearly to Vurrgh. In all violent eddies at sea there is good fishing, at proper opportunities, if one has only the courage to attempt it; but among the whole of the Lofoden coastmen, we three were the only ones who made a regular business of going out to the islands, as I tell you. The usual grounds are a great way lower down to the southward. There fish can be got at all hours, without much risk, and therefore these places are preferred. The choice spots over here among the rocks, however, not only yield the finest variety, but in far greater abundance; so that we often got in a single day, what the more timid of the craft could not scrape together in a week. In fact, we made it a matter of desperate speculation—the risk of life standing instead of labor, and courage answering for capital.

"We kept the smack in a cove about five miles higher up the coast than this; and it was our practice, in fine weather, to take advantage of the fifteen minutes' slack to push across the main channel of the Moskoe-ström, far above the pool, and then drop down upon anchorage somewhere near Otterholm, or Sandflesen, where the eddies are not so violent as elsewhere. Here we used to remain until nearly time for slack-water again, when we weighed and made for home. We never set out upon this expedition without a steady side wind for going and coming—one that we felt sure would not fail us before our return—and we seldom made a

[10]**Kircher:** Athanasius Kircher (1602–80). **Gulf of Bothnia:** An outlet of the Baltic Sea, between Sweden and Finland.

[11]Compare this story to Coleridge's "The Rime of the Ancient Mariner." We are now at the end of the "frame story." Coleridge's mariner tells his tale to a wedding guest; Poe's fisherman tells his to a tourist.

miscalculation upon this point. Twice, during six years, we were forced to stay all night at anchor on account of a dead calm, which is a rare thing indeed just about here; and once we had to remain on the grounds nearly a week, starving to death, owing to a gale which blew up shortly after our arrival, and made the channel too boisterous to be thought of. Upon this occasion we should have been driven out to sea in spite of everything, (for the whirlpools threw us round and round so violently, that, at length, we fouled our anchor and dragged it) if it had not been that we drifted into one of the innumerable cross currents—here to-day and gone to-morrow—which drove us under the lee of Flimen, where, by good luck, we brought up.

"I could not tell you the twentieth part of the difficulties we encountered 'on the ground'—it is a bad spot to be in, even in good weather—but we made shift always to run the gauntlet of the Moskoe-ström itself without accident; although at times my heart has been in my mouth when we happened to be a minute or so behind or before the slack. The wind sometimes was not as strong as we thought it at starting, and then we made rather less way than we could wish, while the current rendered the smack unmanageable. My eldest brother had a son eighteen years old, and I had two stout boys of my own. These would have been a great assistance at such times, in using the sweeps, as well as afterward in fishing—but, somehow, although we ran the risk ourselves, we had not the heart to let the young ones get into the danger—for, after all is said and done, it *was* a horrible danger, and that is the truth.

"It is now within a few days of three years since what I am going to tell you occurred. It was on the tenth of July, 18—, a day which the people of this part of the world will never forget—for it was one in which blew the most terrible hurricane that ever came out of the heavens. And yet all the morning, and indeed until late in the afternoon, there was a gentle and steady breeze from the south-west, while the sun shone brightly, so that the oldest seaman among us could not have foreseen what was to follow.

"The three of us—my two brothers and myself—had crossed over to the islands about two o'clock P.M., and soon nearly loaded the smack with fish, which, we all remarked, were more plenty that day than we had ever known them. It was just seven, *by my watch,* when we weighed and started for home, so as to make the worst of the Ström at slack water, which we knew would be at eight.

"We set out with a fresh wind on our starboard quarter, and for some time spanked along at a great rate, never dreaming of danger, for indeed we saw not the slightest reason to apprehend it. All at once we were taken aback by a breeze from over Helseggen. This was most unusual—something that had never happened to us before—and I began to feel a little uneasy, without exactly knowing why. We put the boat on the wind, but could make no headway at all for the eddies, and I was upon the point of proposing to return to the anchorage, when, looking astern, we saw the whole horizon covered with a singular copper-colored cloud that rose with the most amazing velocity.

"In the meantime the breeze that had headed us off fell away and we were dead becalmed, drifting about in every direction. This state of things, however, did not last long enough to give us time to think about it. In less than a minute the storm was upon us—in less than two the sky was entirely overcast—and what with this and the driving spray, it became suddenly so dark that we could not see each other in the smack.

"Such a hurricane as then blew it is folly to attempt describing. The oldest seaman in Norway never experienced any thing like it. We had let our sails go by the run before it cleverly took us; but, at the first puff, both our masts went by the board as if they had been sawed off—the mainmast taking with it my youngest brother, who had lashed himself to it for safety.[12]

"Our boat was the lightest feather of a thing that ever sat upon water. It had a complete flush deck, with only a small hatch near the bow, and this hatch it had always been our custom to batten down when about to cross the Ström, by way of precaution against the chopping seas. But for this circumstance we should have foundered at once—for we lay entirely buried for some moments. How my elder brother escaped destruction I cannot say, for I never had an opportunity of ascertaining. For my part, as soon as I had let the foresail run, I threw myself flat on deck, with my feet against the narrow gunwale of the bow, and with my hands grasping a ring-bolt near the foot of the foremast. It was mere instinct that prompted me to do this—which was undoubtedly the very best thing I could have done—for I was too much flurried to think.

"For some moments we were completely deluged, as I say, and all this time I held my breath, and clung to the bolt. When I could stand it no longer I raised myself upon my knees, still keeping hold with my hands, and thus got my head clear. Presently our little boat gave herself a shake, just as a dog does in coming out of the water, and thus rid herself, in some measure, of the seas. I was now trying to get the better of the stupor that had come over me, and to collect my senses so as to see what was to be done, when I felt somebody grasp my arm. It was my elder brother, and my heart leaped for joy, for I had made sure that he was overboard—but the next moment all this joy was turned into horror—for he put his mouth close to my ear, and screamed out the word '*Moskoe-ström!*'

"No one ever will know what my feelings were at that moment. I shook from head to foot as if I had had the most violent fit of the ague. I knew what he meant by that one word well enough—I knew what he wished to make me understand. With the wind that now drove us on, we were bound for the whirl of the Ström, and nothing could save us!

"You perceive that in crossing the Ström *channel,* we always went a long way up above the whirl, even in the calmest weather, and then had to wait and watch carefully for the slack—but now we were driving right upon the pool itself, and in such a hurricane as this! 'To be sure,' I thought, 'we shall get there just about the slack—there is some little hope in that'—but in the next moment I cursed myself for being so great a fool as to dream of hope at all. I knew very well that we were doomed, had we been ten times a ninety-gun ship.

---

[12]Poe remarked that he had written this tale in haste, which might account for the ineffectiveness of his handling of the personal relations in it. The fisherman's language seems too cool for the situation he is describing; here, the loss of a brother is tossed off in a casual subordinate clause.

"By this time the first fury of the tempest had spent itself, or perhaps we did not feel it so much, as we scudded before it, but at all events the seas, which at first had been kept down by the wind, and lay flat and frothing, now got up into absolute mountains. A singular change, too, had come over the heavens. Around in every direction it was still as black as pitch, but nearly overhead there burst out, all at once, a circular rift of clear sky—as clear as I ever saw—and of a deep bright blue—and through it there blazed forth the full moon with a lustre that I never before knew her to wear. She lit up every thing about us with the greatest distinctness—but, oh God, what a scene it was to light up!

"I now made one or two attempts to speak to my brother—but in some manner which I could not understand, the din had so increased that I could not make him hear a single word, although I screamed at the top of my voice in his ear. Presently he shook his head, looking as pale as death, and held up one of his fingers, as if to say '*listen!*'

"At first I could not make out what he meant—but soon a hideous thought flashed upon me. I dragged my watch from its fob. It was not going. I glanced at its face by the moonlight, and then burst into tears as I flung it far away into the ocean. *It had run down at seven o'clock! We were behind the time of the slack, and the whirl of the Ström was in full fury!*

"When a boat is well built, properly trimmed, and not deep laden, the waves in a strong gale, when she is going large, seem always to slip from beneath her—which appears strange to a landsman—and this is what is called *riding,* in sea phrase.

"Well, so far we had ridden the swells very cleverly; but presently a gigantic sea happened to take us right under the counter, and bore us with it as it rose—up—up—as if into the sky. I would not have believed that any wave could rise so high. And then down we came with a sweep, a slide, and a plunge that made me feel sick and dizzy, as if I was falling from some lofty mountain-top in a dream. But while we were up I had thrown a quick glance around—and that one glance was all sufficient. I saw our exact position in an instant. The Moskoe-ström whirlpool was about a quarter of a mile dead ahead—but no more like the every-day Moskoe-ström than the whirl, as you now see it, is like a mill-race. If I had not known where we were, and what we had to expect, I should not have recognised the place at all. As it was, I involuntarily closed my eyes in horror. The lids clenched themselves together as if in a spasm.

"It could not have been more than two minutes afterwards until we suddenly felt the waves subside, and were enveloped in foam. The boat made a sharp half turn to larboard,[13] and then shot off in its new direction like a thunderbolt. At the same moment the roaring noise of the water was completely drowned in a kind of shrill shriek—such a sound as you might imagine given out by the water-pipes of many thousand steam-vessels letting off their steam all together. We were now in the belt of surf that always surrounds the whirl; and I thought, of course, that another moment would plunge us into the abyss—down which we could only see indistinctly on account of the amazing velocity with which we were borne along.

---

[13]Port, or left (as one faces the bow).

The boat did not seem to sink into the water at all, but to skim like an air-bubble upon the surface of the surge. Her starboard side was next the whirl, and on the larboard arose the world of ocean we had left. It stood like a huge writhing wall between us and the horizon.

"It may appear strange, but now, when we were in the very jaws of the gulf, I felt more composed than when we were only approaching it. Having made up my mind to hope no more, I got rid of a great deal of that terror which unmanned me at first. I suppose it was despair that strung my nerves.

"It may look like boasting—but what I tell you is truth—I began to reflect how magnificent a thing it was to die in such a manner, and how foolish it was in me to think of so paltry a consideration as my own individual life, in view of so wonderful a manifestation of God's power.[14] I do believe that I blushed with shame when this idea crossed my mind. After a little while I became possessed with the keenest curiosity about the whirl itself. I positively felt a *wish* to explore its depths, even at the sacrifice I was going to make; and my principal grief was that I should never be able to tell my old companions on shore about the mysteries I should see. These, no doubt, were singular fancies to occupy a man's mind in such extremity—and I have often thought since, that the revolutions of the boat around the pool might have rendered me a little light-headed.

"There was another circumstance which tended to restore my self-possession; and this was the cessation of the wind, which could not reach us in our present situation—for, as you saw for yourself, the belt of the surf is considerably lower than the general bed of the ocean, and this latter now towered above us, a high, black, mountainous ridge. If you have never been at sea in a heavy gale, you can form no idea of the confusion of mind occasioned by the wind and spray together. They blind, deafen, and strangle you, and take away all power of action or reflection. But we were now, in a great measure, rid of these annoyances—just as death-condemned felons in prison are allowed petty indulgences, forbidden them while their doom is yet uncertain.

"How often we made the circuit of the belt it is impossible to say. We careered round and round for perhaps an hour, flying rather than floating, getting gradually more and more into the middle of the surge, and then nearer and nearer to its horrible inner edge. All this time I had never let go of the ring-bolt. My brother was at the stern, holding on to a large empty water-cask which had been securely lashed under the coop of the counter, and was the only thing on deck that had not been swept overboard when the gale first took us. As we approached the brink of the pit he let go his hold upon this, and made for the ring, from which, in the agony of his terror, he endeavored to force my hands, as it was not large enough to afford us both a secure grasp. I never felt deeper grief than when I saw him attempt this act—although I knew he was a madman when he did it—a raving maniac through sheer fright. I did not care, however, to contest the point with him. I knew it could make no difference whether either of us held on at all; so I let him have the bolt, and went astern to the cask. This there was no great difficulty in doing; for the

[14]Compare to Coleridge's mariner, who, in a moment when he should despair, finds beauty in the creatures of the sea.

smack flew round steadily enough, and upon an even keel—only swaying to and fro with the immense sweeps and swelters of the whirl. Scarcely had I secured myself in my new position, when we gave a wild lurch to starboard, and rushed headlong into the abyss. I muttered a hurried prayer to God, and thought all was over.[15]

"As I felt the sickening sweep of the descent, I had instinctively tightened my hold upon the barrel, and closed my eyes. For some seconds I dared not open them—while I expected instant destruction, and wondered that I was not already in my death-struggles with the water. But moment after moment elapsed. I still lived. The sense of falling had ceased; and the motion of the vessel seemed much as it had been before while in the belt of foam, with the exception that she now lay more along.[16] I took courage and looked once again upon the scene.

"Never shall I forget the sensation of awe, horror, and admiration with which I gazed about me. The boat appeared to be hanging, as if by magic, midway down, upon the interior surface of a funnel vast in circumference, prodigious in depth, and whose perfectly smooth sides might have been mistaken for ebony,[17] but for the bewildering rapidity with which they spun around, and for the gleaming and ghastly radiance they shot forth, as the rays of the full moon, from that circular rift amid the clouds which I have already described, streamed in a flood of golden glory along the black walls, and far away down into the inmost recesses of the abyss.

"At first I was too much confused to observe anything accurately. The general burst of terrific grandeur was all that I beheld. When I recovered myself a little, however, my gaze fell instinctively downward. In this direction I was able to obtain an unobstructed view, from the manner in which the smack hung on the inclined surface on the pool. She was quite upon an even keel—that is to say, her deck lay in a plane parallel with that of the water—but this latter sloped at an angle of more than forty-five degrees, so that we seemed to be lying upon our beam-ends. I could not help observing, nevertheless, that I had scarcely more difficulty in maintaining my hold and footing in this situation, than if we had been upon a dead level; and this, I suppose, was owing to the speed at which we revolved.

"The rays of the moon seemed to search the very bottom of the profound gulf; but still I could make out nothing distinctly, on account of a thick mist in which everything there was enveloped, and over which there hung a magnificent rainbow, like the narrow and tottering bridge which Mussulmen[18] say is the only

---

[15]Again, compare to the behavior of Coleridge's mariner when he blesses the creatures around him.

[16]Leaned over with a side wind.

[17]**"Never . . . about me.":** See our headnote. **ebony:** There is just a chance that Poe is telling us that his story is in the tradition of those *Blackwood's Edinburgh Magazine* pieces which describes the "sensations" of narrators undergoing horrible experiences. "Ebony" is the magazinist's code word for William Blackwood, proprietor of the magazine. See "How to Write a Blackwood Article" and our headnote to it, and "The Man of the Crowd," note 8 and "A note of explanation."

[18]Moslems.

pathway between Time and Eternity. This mist, or spray, was no doubt occasioned by the clashing of the great walls of the funnel, as they all met together at the bottom—but the yell that went up to the Heavens from out of that mist I dare not attempt to describe.

"Our first slide into the abyss itself, from the belt of foam above, had carried us to a great distance down the slope; but our farther descent was by no means proportionate.[19] Round and round we swept—not with any uniform movement—but in dizzying swings and jerks, that sent us sometimes only a few hundred feet—sometimes nearly the complete circuit of the whirl. Our progress downward, at each revolution, was slow, but very perceptible.

"Looking about me upon the wide waste of liquid ebony on which we were thus borne, I perceived that our boat was not the only object in the embrace of the whirl. Both above and below us were visible fragments of vessels, large masses of building timber and trunks of trees, with many smaller articles, such as pieces of house furniture, broken boxes, barrels and staves. I have already described the unnatural[20] curiosity which had taken the place of my original terrors. It appeared to grow upon me as I drew nearer and nearer to my dreadful doom. I now began to watch, with a strange interest, the numerous things that floated in our company. I *must* have been delirious—for I even sought *amusement* in speculating upon the relative velocities of their several descents toward the foam below. 'This fir tree,' I found myself at one time saying, 'will certainly be the next thing that takes the awful plunge and disappears,'—and then I was disappointed to find that the wreck of a Dutch merchant ship overtook it and went down before. At length, after making several guesses of this nature, and being deceived in all—this fact—the fact of my invariable miscalculation, set me upon a train of reflection that made my limbs again tremble, and my heart beat heavily once more.

"It was not a new terror that thus affected me, but the dawn of a more exciting *hope.* This hope arose partly from memory, and partly from present observation. I called to mind the great variety of buoyant matter that strewed the coast of Lofoden, having been absorbed and then thrown forth by the Moskoe-ström. By far the greater number of the articles were shattered in the most extraordinary way—so chafed and roughened as to have the appearance of being stuck full of splinters—but then I distinctly recollected that there were *some* of them which were not disfigured at all. Now I could not account for this difference except by supposing that the roughened fragments were the only ones which had been *completely absorbed*—that the others had entered the whirl at so late a period of the tide, or, from some reason, had descended so slowly after entering, that they did not reach the bottom before the turn of the flood came, or of the ebb, as the case might be. I conceived it possible, in either instance, that they might thus be

---

[19]See our headnote.

[20]The key to the brilliance which the fisherman will now display: his state of mind is "unnatural." Coleridge's mariner blesses the beasts and *is* saved; Poe's hero is frightened into brilliance, becomes a kind of intuitive "poet" of natural forces, and can save himself. Compare the process by which the narrator in "The Pit and the Pendulum," in a comparable predicament, turns brilliant and so remains alive to be rescued.

whirled up again to the level of the ocean, without undergoing the fate of those which had been drawn in more early or absorbed more rapidly. I made, also, three important observations. The first was, that as a general rule, the larger the bodies were, the more rapid their descent;—the second, that, between two masses of equal extent, the one spherical, and the other *of any other shape,* the superiority in speed of descent was with the sphere;—the third, that, between two masses of equal size, the one cylindrical, and the other of any other shape, the cylinder was absorbed the more slowly. Since my escape, I have had several conversations on this subject with an old school-master of the district; and it was from him that I learned the use of the words 'cylinder' and 'sphere.' He explained to me—although I have forgotten the explanation—how what I observed was, in fact, the natural consequence of the forms of the floating fragments—and showed me how it happened that a cylinder, swimming in a vortex, offered more resistance to its suction, and was drawn in with greater difficulty than an equally bulky body, of any form whatever.[21]

"There was one startling circumstance which went a great way in enforcing these observations, and rendering me anxious to turn them to account, and this was that, at every revolution, we passed something like a barrel, or else the broken yard or the mast of a vessel, while many of these things, which had been on our level when I first opened my eyes upon the wonders of the whirlpool, were now high up above us, and seemed to have moved but little from their original station.[22]

"I no longer hesitated what to do. I resolved to lash myself securely to the water-cask upon which I now held, to cut it loose from the counter, and to throw myself with it into the water. I attracted my brother's attention by signs, pointed to the floating barrels that came near us, and did every thing in my power to make him understand what I was about to do. I thought at length that he comprehended my design—but, whether this was the case or not, he shook his head despairingly, and refused to move from his station by the ring-bolt. It was impossible to force him, the emergency admitted no delay; and so, with a bitter struggle, I resigned him to his fate, fastened myself to the cask by means of the lashings which secured it to the counter, and precipitated myself with it into the sea, without another moment's hesitation.

"The result was precisely what I had hoped it might be. As it is myself who now tell you this tale—as you see that I *did* escape—and as you are already in possession of the mode in which this escape was effected, and must therefore anticipate all that I have farther to say—I will bring my story quickly to conclusion. It might have been an hour, or thereabout, after my quitting the smack, when, having descended to a vast distance beneath me, it made three or four wild

---

[21]See Archimedes, *De Incidentibus in Fluido.*—lib. 2 [Poe's note]. Archimedes is the famous Greek mathematician, c.287–212 B.C.E. But the work in question says nothing about the behavior of such objects in water (Turner; Campbell). Moreover, Poe has its title wrong, probably because he copied an error in Isaac Disraeli's *Curiosities of Literature* (Mabbott 9, II).

[22]Is Poe right? Experiments by your editors with mixers and blenders are inconclusive.

gyrations in rapid succession, and bearing my loved brother with it, plunged headlong, at once and forever, into the chaos of foam below. The barrel to which I was attached sunk very little farther than half the distance between the bottom of the gulf and the spot at which I leaped overboard, before a great change took place in the character of the whirlpool. The slope of the sides of the vast funnel became momently less and less steep. The gyrations of the whirl grew, gradually, less and less violent. By degrees, the froth and the rainbow disappeared, and the bottom of the gulf seemed slowly to uprise. The sky was clear, the winds had gone down, and the full moon was setting radiantly in the west, when I found myself on the surface of the ocean, in full view of the shores of Lofoden, and above the spot where the pool of the Moskoe-ström *had been.* It was the hour of the slack—but the sea still heaved in mountainous waves from the effects of the hurricane. I was borne violently into the channel of the Ström, and in a few minutes, was hurried down the coast into the 'grounds' of the fishermen. A boat picked me up—exhausted from fatigue—and (now that the danger was removed) speechless from the memory of its horror. Those who drew me on board were my old mates and daily companions—but they knew me no more than they would have known a traveller from the spirit-land. My hair, which had been raven-black the day before, was as white as you see it now. They say too that the whole expression of my countenance had changed. I told them my story—they did not believe it. I now tell it to *you*—and I can scarcely expect you to put more faith in it than did the merry fishermen of Lofoden."

Eleonora

"Eleonora" should be contrasted to "Ligeia." The materials Poe used in each are similar: a beloved first wife dies and seems to be reincarnated in a second. Neither husband is a totally trustworthy narrator; readers are given the option of not believing what they are told. "The death of a beautiful woman," which Poe insisted was the most poetical of subjects, and which modern psychologists are likely to see in painfully revealing psychosexual terms, is at the heart of both tales. Each, if we believe the husbands, takes place in a magical universe, a world which is sentient and alive, which responds to and influences the characters, which, indeed, cannot really be differentiated from them. The stories are philosophically consistent with the cosmology which Poe explains in "The Power of Words."

"Ligeia," however, is a dark-hued story. It has to do with the power of the will, with the "large, old decaying city near the Rhine," where the fierce-willed, raven-haired Ligeia studied her kind of transcendentalism. It reminds us that the human will and instinct so admired by Romantic writers could turn ugly: thus Hawthorne warned in The Blithedale Romance, *where he showed a transcendental idealist transformed through excessive trust in his will into a dangerous proto-dictator. Nietzsche admired the bright Transcendentalist Emerson, but Romantic notions of will and impulse found horrible fulfillment in Hitler's perversions of Nietzsche. No accident that Hitler's cinematic propagandist called her leaden documentary "Triumph of the Will." There is the smell of sulphur about Ligeia.*

"Eleonora," in contrast, remains bright. The emphasis is less on "will" than on "impulse." The narrator-husband is to be forgiven not through any assertion of the will of a superwoman, but because, as he explains it, he could not help *loving Ermengarde. Poe sometimes mocked the Transcendentalists' bright faith in the mystical heavenly one-ness of all creation—he asked why Emerson ignored the "infernal two-ness"—but in "Eleonora" he created a sustained prose-poem to the most radiant of Romantic mystical visions. In "Eleonora," nature embodies "the glory of God"; trees do homage to the sun; Eleonora's beauty is nature's; all religions are fragmentary versions of a perennial philosophy which alone is true. Humankind, the heavens, and the earth are a whole, and the wholeness may be revealed to a visionary.*

A note of explanation: *Poe's wife was his cousin, and his mother died when he was an infant. After the marriage, the Poes did, in fact, live with Virginia's mother. Virginia Poe, his wife, died in 1847, long after the publication of "Eleonora." But the story has nevertheless often been taken as autobiographical, a kind of prose-poem to his love for his young wife who by January 1842 clearly had tuberculosis. Poe's fiancée, Sarah Helen Whitman, was in his mind by 1848. He gave her a copy of the 1845 reprinting of the story (Pollin 5).*

PUBLICATIONS IN POE'S TIME

The Gift: A Christmas and New Year's Present for 1842 (actually issued in September 1841)
The Boston Notion, September 4, 1841
Roberts Semi-Monthly Magazine for Town and Country, September 15, 1841
The New York Weekly Tribune, September 18, 1841
The New York (Daily) *Tribune,* September 20, 1841
The Literary Souvenir, November 13, 1841, and again on July 9, 1842
The Broadway Journal, May 24, 1845

ELEONORA

Sub conservatione formæ specificæ salva anima.
—Raymond Lully.[1]

I am come of a race noted for vigor of fancy and ardor of passion. Men have called me mad; but the question is not yet settled, whether madness is or is not the loftiest intelligence—whether much that is glorious—whether all that is profound—does not spring from disease of thought—from *moods* of mind exalted at the expense of the general intellect. They who dream by day are cognizant of many things which escape those who dream only by night. In their gray visions they obtain glimpses of eternity, and thrill, in awaking, to find that they have been upon the verge of the great secret. In snatches, they learn something of the wisdom which is of good, and more of the mere knowledge which is of evil. They penetrate, however rudderless and compassless, into the vast ocean of the "light ineffable" and again, like the adventurers of the Nubian geographer, "*agressi sunt mare tenebrarum, quid in eo esset exploraturi.*"[2]

We will say, then, that I am mad. I grant, at least, that there are two distinct conditions of my mental existence—the condition of a lucid reason, not to be disputed, and belonging to the memory of events forming the first epoch of my life—and a condition of shadow and doubt, appertaining to the present, and to the

[1]"In the preservation of its specific life form lies the safety of the spirit of life," from Raimon Lull (c.1235–1315), scholastic philosopher and logician (Carlson 2). Poe took the quotation from a Victor Hugo novel he was reading; Hugo got it from Henri Sauval; Sauval said he used Raimon Lull, but the passage is probably not really from Lull (Pollin 5). Poe's own (faulty) translation is: "Under the conservation/protection of specific forms the soul is safe" (Pollin 5).

[2]Nubian . . . *exploraturi:* See "A Descent into the Maelström," note 3, for identification, translation, and Poe's source.

recollection of what constitutes the second great era of my being. Therefore, what I shall tell of the earlier period, believe; and to what I may relate of the later time, give only such credit as may seem due; or doubt it altogether; or, if doubt it ye cannot, then play unto its riddle the Oedipus.[3]

She whom I loved in youth, and of whom I now pen calmly and distinctly these remembrances, was the sole daughter of the only sister of my mother long departed. Eleonora was the name of my cousin. We had always dwelled together, beneath a tropical sun, in the Valley of the Many-Colored Grass. No unguided footstep ever came upon that vale; for it lay far away up among a range of giant hills that hung beetling around about it, shutting out the sunlight from its sweetest recesses. No path was trodden in its vicinity; and, to reach our happy home, there was need of putting back, with force, the foliage of many thousands of forest trees, and of crushing to death the glories of many millions of fragrant flowers. Thus it was that we lived all alone, knowing nothing of the world without the valley,—I, and my cousin, and her mother.

From the dim regions beyond the mountains at the upper end of our encircled domain, there crept out a narrow and deep river, brighter than all save the eyes of Eleonora; and, winding stealthily about in mazy courses, it passed away, at length, through a shadowy gorge, among hills still dimmer than those whence it had issued. We called it the "River of Silence"; for there seemed to be a hushing influence in its flow. No murmur arose from its bed, and so gently it wandered along, that the pearly pebbles upon which we loved to gaze, far down within its bosom, stirred not at all, but lay in a motionless content, each in its own old station, shining on gloriously forever.

The margin of the river, and of the many dazzling rivulets that glided, through devious ways, into its channel, as well as the spaces that extended from the margins away down into the depths of the streams until they reached the bed of pebbles at the bottom,—these spots, not less than the whole surface of the valley, from the river to the mountains that girdled it in, were carpeted all by a soft green grass, thick, short, perfectly even, and vanilla-perfumed, but so besprinkled throughout with the yellow buttercup, the white daisy, the purple violet, and the ruby-red asphodel, that its exceeding beauty spoke to our hearts, in loud tones, of the love and of the glory of God.

And, here and there, in groves about this grass, like wildernesses of dreams, sprang up fantastic trees, whose tall slender stems stood not upright, but slanted gracefully towards the light that peered at noon-day into the centre of the valley. Their bark was speckled with the vivid alternate splendor of ebony and silver, and was smoother than all save the cheeks of Eleonora; so that but for the brilliant green of the huge leaves that spread from their summits in long tremulous lines, dallying with the Zephyrs, one might have fancied them giant serpents of Syria doing homage to their Sovereign the Sun.

Hand in hand about this valley, for fifteen years, roamed I with Eleonora before Love entered within our hearts. It was one evening at the close of the third lustrum

---

[3]In Greek legend, Oedipus became King of Thebes by solving the riddle of the Sphinx. Poe says, in effect, "solve it as Oedipus solved his riddle."

of her life, and of the fourth of my own, that we sat, locked in each other's embrace, beneath the serpent-like trees, and looked down within the waters of the River of Silence at our images there. We spoke no words during the rest of that sweet day; and our words even upon the morrow were tremulous and few. We had drawn the god Eros from that wave, and now we felt that he had enkindled within us the fiery souls of our forefathers. The passions which had for centuries distinguished our race came thronging with the fancies for which they had been equally noted, and together breathed a delirious bliss over the Valley of the Many-Colored Grass. A change fell upon all things. Strange brilliant flowers, star-shaped, burst out upon the trees where no flowers had been known before. The tints of the green carpet deepened; and when, one by one, the white daisies shrank away, there sprang up, in place of them, ten by ten of the ruby-red asphodel. And life arose in our paths; for the tall flamingo, hitherto unseen, with all gay glowing birds, flaunted his scarlet plumage before us. The golden and silver fish haunted the river, out of the bosom of which issued, little by little, a murmur that swelled, at length, into a lulling melody more divine than that of the harp of Æolus—sweeter than all save the voice of Eleonora. And now, too, a voluminous cloud, which we had long watched in the regions of Hesper,[4] floated out thence, all gorgeous in crimson and gold, and settling in peace above us, sank, day by day, lower and lower, until its edges rested upon the tops of the mountains, turning all their dimness into magnificence, and shutting us up, as if forever, within a magic prison-house of grandeur and of glory.

The loveliness of Eleonora was that of the Seraphim; but she[5] was a maiden artless and innocent as the brief life she had led among the flowers. No guile disguised the fervor of love which animated her heart, and she examined with me its inmost recesses as we walked together in the Valley of the Many-Colored Grass, and discoursed of the mighty changes which had lately taken place therein.

---

[4]**Eros:** The Greek god of love. In Poe's verse drama "Politian—A Tragedy," Lalage invites Politian to flee with her to America where ". . . Care shall be forgotten, and sorrow shall be no more, and Eros be all." **the harp of Æolus:** Æolus is the Greek god of the winds. An Aeolian harp plays when wind strikes it. **Hesper:** The evening star; usually refers to Venus.

[5]When Poe revised the *Gift* version of "Eleonora" for use again, he cut out an interesting passage: Poe had,

> —and here, as in all things referring to this epoch, my memory is vividly distinct. In stature she was tall, and slender even to fragility; the exceeding delicacy of her frame, as well as of the hues of her cheek, speaking painfully of the feeble tenure by which she held existence. The lilies of the valley were not more fair. With the nose, lips, and chin of the Greek Venus, she had the majestic forehead, the naturally-waving auburn hair, and the large luminous eyes of her kindred. Her beauty, nevertheless, was of that nature which leads the heart to wonder not less than to love. The grace of her motion was surely ethereal. Her fantastic step left no impress upon the asphodel—and I could not but dream as I gazed, enrapt, upon her alternate moods of melancholy and of mirth, that two separate souls were enshrined within her. So radical were the changes of countenance, that at one instant I fancied her possessed by some spirit of smiles, at another by some demon of tears. She . . .

At length, having spoken one day, in tears, of the last sad change which must befall Humanity, she thenceforward dwelt only upon this one sorrowful theme, interweaving it into all our converse, as, in the songs of the bard of Schiraz,[6] the same images are found occurring, again and again, in every impressive variation of phrase.

She had seen that the finger of Death was upon her bosom—that, like the ephemeron, she had been made perfect in loveliness only to die; but the terrors of the grave, to her, lay solely in a consideration which she revealed to me, one evening at twilight, by the banks of the River of Silence. She grieved to think that, having entombed her in the Valley of the Many-Colored Grass, I would quit forever its happy recesses, transferring the love which now was so passionately her own to some maiden of the outer and every-day world. And, then and there, I threw myself hurriedly at the feet of Eleonora, and offered up a vow, to herself and to Heaven, that I would never bind myself in marriage to any daughter of Earth—that I would in no manner prove recreant to her dear memory, or to the memory of the devout affection with which she had blessed me. And I called the Mighty Ruler of the Universe to witness the pious solemnity of my vow. And the curse which I invoked of *Him* and of her, a saint in Helusion,[7] should I prove traitorous to that promise, involved a penalty the exceeding great horror of which will not permit me to make record of it here. And the bright eyes of Eleonora grew brighter at my words; and she sighed as if a deadly burthen had been taken from her breast; and she trembled and very bitterly wept; but she made acceptance of the vow, (for what was she but a child?) and it made easy to her the bed of her death. And she said to me, not many days afterwards, tranquilly dying, that, because of what I had done for the comfort of her spirit, she would watch over me in that spirit when departed, and, if so it were permitted her, return to me visibly in the watches of the night; but, if this thing were, indeed, beyond the power of the souls in Paradise, that she would, at least, give me frequent indications of her presence; sighing upon me in the evening winds, or filling the air which I breathed with the perfume from the censers of the angels. And, with these words upon her lips, she yielded up her innocent life, putting an end to the first epoch of my own.

Thus far I have faithfully said. But as I pass the barrier in Time's path formed by the death of my beloved, and proceed with the second era of my existence, I feel that a shadow gathers over my brain, and I mistrust the perfect sanity of the record. But let me on.—Years dragged themselves along heavily, and still I dwelled within the Valley of the Many-Colored Grass;—but a second change had come upon all things. The star-shaped flowers shrank into the stems of the trees, and appeared no more. The tints of the green carpet faded; and, one by one, the ruby-red asphodels withered away; and there sprang up, in place of them, ten by ten,

---

[6]Carlson (2) says, "Probably refers to Saadi (1184?–1291?), a venerated Persian poet born in Shiraz. He wrote symbolic poetry of exceptional beauty. Shiraz was also the birthplace of Hafiz, a poet of more vehement verse (d. 1389?)."

[7]Poe's spelling of Elysium, the portion of Hades reserved, in Greek myth, for the blessed dead. See "Shadow," note 4.

dark eye-like violets that writhed uneasily and were ever encumbered with dew.[8] And Life departed from our paths; for the tall flamingo flaunted no longer his scarlet plumage before us, but flew sadly from the vale into the hills, with all the gay glowing birds that had arrived in his company. And the golden and silver fish swam down through the gorge at the lower end of our domain and bedecked the sweet river never again. And the lulling melody that had been softer than the wind-harp of Æolus and more divine than all save the voice of Eleonora, it died little by little away, in murmurs growing lower and lower, until the stream returned, at length, utterly, into the solemnity of its original silence. And then, lastly the voluminous cloud uprose, and, abandoning the tops of the mountains to the dimness of old, fell back into the regions of Hesper, and took away all its manifold golden and gorgeous glories from the Valley of the Many-Colored Grass.

Yet the promises of Eleonora were not forgotten; for I heard the sounds of the swinging of the censers of the angels; and streams of a holy perfume floated ever and ever about the valley; and at lone hours, when my heart beat heavily, the winds that bathed my brow came unto me laden with soft sighs; and indistinct murmurs filled often the night air; and once—oh, but once only! I was awakened from a slumber like the slumber of death by the pressing of spiritual lips upon my own.

But the void within my heart refused, even thus, to be filled. I longed for the love which had before filled it to overflowing. At length the valley *pained* me through its memories of Eleonora, and I left it forever for the vanities and the turbulent triumphs of the world.

* * *

I found myself within a strange city, where all things might have served to blot from recollection the sweet dreams I had dreamed so long in the Valley of the Many-Colored Grass. The pomps and pageantries of a stately court, and the mad clangor of arms, and the radiant loveliness of woman, bewildered and intoxicated my brain. But as yet my soul had proved true to its vows, and the indications of the presence of Eleonora were still given me in the silent hours of the night. Suddenly, these manifestations they ceased; and the world grew dark before mine eyes; and I stood aghast at the burning thoughts which possessed—at the terrible temptations which beset me; for there came from some far, far distant and unknown land, into the gay court of the king I served, a maiden to whose beauty my whole recreant heart yielded at once—at whose footstool I bowed down without a struggle, in the

[8]In Poe's day, "flower books" and articles, in which flowers symbolized human characteristics or even personalities, were very popular. In one, hand-colored steel engravings of a flower and a girl appear on left-hand pages, and prose sketches about Rose, Daisy, Violet, or Petunia are printed on the right-hand pages. The mood of such productions was, of course, extremely sentimental, but surprisingly tough-minded authors—notably Hawthorne—were attracted to the idea of using this insipid symbolism in their fiction, probably because of the great popularity of the "flower books." Authors could count on their readers' understanding of what they were about.

most ardent, in the most abject worship of love. What indeed was my passion for the young girl of the valley in comparison with the fervor, and the delirium, and the spirit-lifting ecstasy of adoration with which I poured out my whole soul in tears at the feet of the ethereal Ermengarde?—Oh bright was the seraph Ermengarde! and in that knowledge I had room for none other.—Oh divine was the angel Ermengarde! and as I looked down into the depths of her memorial eyes I thought only of them—and of *her.*[9]

I wedded;—nor dreaded the curse I had invoked; and its bitterness was not visited upon me. And once—but once again in the silence of the night, there came through my lattice the soft sighs which had forsaken me; and they modelled themselves into familiar and sweet voice, saying:

"Sleep in peace!—for the Spirit of Love reigneth and ruleth, and, in taking to thy passionate heart her who is Ermengarde, thou art absolved, for reasons which shall be made known to thee in Heaven, of thy vows unto Eleonora."

---

[9]Here Poe cut a passage which had appeared in the *Gift* version of the tale:

> I looked down into the blue depths of her meaning eyes, and I thought only of them, and of her. Oh, lovely was the lady Ermengarde! and in that knowledge I had room for none other. Oh, glorious was the wavy flow of her auburn tresses! and I clasped them in a transport of joy to my bosom. And I found rapture in the fantastic grace of her step—and there was a wild delirium in the love I bore her when I started to see upon her countenance the identical transition from tears to smiles that I had wondered at in the long-lost Eleonora.
>
> I forgot—I despised the horrors of the curse I had so blindly invoked, and I wedded the lady Ermengarde.

This passage and the one noted in note 5 above deal with changes in mood; Poe evidently decided that such changes were extraneous and detracted from the strong unified effect he believed was a prime aesthetic goal of short fiction. Dropping this latter passage also removed a jarring Latinate locution—"identical transition"—which certainly had hurt the earlier version.

The Masque of the Red Death

Effective, powerful, and "unified" as it is, this familiar story nevertheless reveals Poe's inconsistent social attitudes, his very consistent aesthetic stance, his close ties to American urban society, and his ever-present playfulness. We are somewhat suspicious of Poe's intentions. Since Prince Prospero and his courtiers can do nothing to combat the disease, what is so immoral in their fleeing it? Moreover, what are they doing at the abbey of which we are supposed to disapprove? They have music, ballet, wine, and "Beauty"—all of which have favorable connotations in Poe's work—and don't seem to be misbehaving. We may well ask, as Marie Bonaparte did, where are the naked women? This is supposed to be a moral parable, but the punishment which it dramatizes is for no visible crime. To feel satisfaction in the moral, we must have what is usually called a puritan sensibility—a dislike of beauty for its own sake. And that is a position against which Poe fought all his life. How can we state a "moral" for this tale? Perhaps: "Death catches all, even the mighty, in the end." More likely: "Aristocracy is in itself sinful, and will be punished." Poe, in short, plays on the antiaristocratic biases of his audience, another sign of his immersion in the spirit of his country and time, especially in view of his own predilections for both aristocracy and beauty. Resentment against aristocratic "privilege" of all kinds reached a peak in Jacksonian and post-Jacksonian America, while fascination with royalty and aristocracy, paradoxically, remained extremely strong. For all his fear of "mob" and for all his Southern-aristocratic pretensions, Poe at times revealed the same healthy democratic bias against the prerogatives of aristocrats.

Yet the aristocrat Prospero is also in a sense to be admired, for he shows all the signs of one of Poe's creators of elaborate beauty. "Some . . . would have thought him mad"; he loves the bizarre and the beautiful, and he directs the arrangements of the seven chambers of the masque himself.

Poe succeeded in "The Masque of the Red Death" in so controlling the rhythms of his sentences and the visual patterns of his decor that the story has thrilled readers into goosebumps for a century and more. But what is being said *in those sinuous sentences will often not bear close examination. It is sometimes as nonsensical as the gothic absurdities he played with in "Metzengerstein." How, exactly, can we make sure, by touching him, that Prospero is not mad? Why take fifty words to tell us that the sound of the clock is "more emphatic" when you are close to it? We would urge readers to enjoy the thrills, as Poe no doubt did himself, but also to listen closely, in those silent moments when the music stops and the ebony clock speaks in brazen tones in the velvet room, for the sound of Edgar Poe, laughing.*

A note of explanation: *Poe juxtaposed humor and horror both in the tale and in his responses to real epidemics in his time and in things he read. Poe's* *colleague Nat Willis published an account of a very large masked ball given in Paris in 1832 during a terrible cholera epidemic. "One man," Willis wrote, "immensely tall, dressed as a personification of the* Cholera *itself, with skeleton armor, bloodshot eyes, and other horrible appurtenances of a walking pestilence." Black humor, indeed; Mabbott (9, II) is sure Poe knew Willis's piece. As Mabbott also suggests, Poe certainly knew Thomas Campbell's* Life of Petrarch, *for he reviewed it, and commented on an "inappropriately humorous" sentence about a nobleman (named Barnabo) who, like Poe's Prospero, fails to lock out a plague. Poe made up the "Red Death" (see note 1), but knew about real epidemics. Humor in the face of horror is an ancient and very human reaction.*

PUBLICATIONS IN POE'S TIME

Graham's Magazine, May 1842
The Baltimore Saturday Visiter, April 30, 1842
The Literary Souvenir, June 4, 1842
The Broadway Journal, July 19, 1845

THE MASQUE OF THE RED DEATH[1]

The "Red Death" had long devastated the country. No pestilence had ever been so fatal, or so hideous. Blood was its Avatar[2] and its seal—the redness and the horror of blood. There were sharp pains, and sudden dizziness, and then profuse bleeding at the pores, with dissolution. The scarlet stains upon the body and especially upon the face of the victim, were the pest ban which shut him out from

[1]Poe's disease seems to be of his own invention; its symptoms and incubation period match those of no known plague. He defines them as he does to make possible the theatrical conclusion of his story. But Poe was familiar with major epidemics in American cities in the recent past (Philadelphia had several cholera outbreaks in the 1790s, for instance) and in his own day (Baltimore in 1831); another, apparently brought in by immigrants, appeared in the United States in 1832. Shakespeare alludes to a "red plague" in *The Tempest,* I, 2, 363, and to a "red pestilence" in *Coriolanus,* IV, 1, 13, which commentators assume is the bubonic plague. See "A note of explanation," above.

Poe also may have known of the famous case in which merchants from Genoa, pursued by Tartars in 1343, took refuge in a walled town. The Tartars besieged the town, and, when bubonic plague struck their ranks, threw the bodies of their dead over the walls. The entire town became infected, and the Genoese survivors fled to various cities, infecting them in turn.

[2]In Hindu myth, an avatar is an incarnation of a god in some earthly form.

the aid and from the sympathy of his fellow-men. And the whole seizure, progress, and termination of the disease, were the incidents of half an hour.

But the Prince Prospero was happy and dauntless and sagacious. When his dominions were half depopulated, he summoned to his presence a thousand hale and light-hearted friends from among the knights and dames of his court, and with these retired to the deep seclusion of one of his castellated abbeys. This was an extensive and magnificent structure, the creation of the prince's own eccentric yet august taste. A strong and lofty wall girdled it in. This wall had gates of iron. The courtiers, having entered, brought furnaces and massy hammers and welded the bolts. They resolved to leave means neither of ingress or egress to the sudden impulses of despair or frenzy from within. The abbey was amply provisioned. With such precautions the courtiers might bid defiance to contagion. The external world could take care of itself. In the meantime it was folly to grieve, or to think. The prince had provided all the appliances of pleasure. There were buffoons, there were improvisatori,[3] there were ballet-dancers, there were musicians, there was Beauty, there was wine. All these and security were within. Without was the "Red Death."

It was toward the close of the fifth or sixth month of his seclusion, and while the pestilence raged most furiously abroad, that the Prince Propsero entertained his thousand friends at a masked ball of the most unusual magnificence.

It was a voluptuous scene, that masquerade. But first let me tell of the rooms in which it was held. There were seven—an imperial suite. In many palaces, however, such suites form a long and straight vista, while the folding doors slide back nearly to the walls on either hand, so that the view of the whole extent is scarcely impeded. Here the case was very different; as might have been expected from the duke's love of the *bizarre.* The apartments were so irregularly disposed that the vision embraced but little more than one at a time. There was a sharp turn at every twenty or thirty yards, and at each turn a novel effect. To the right and left, in the middle of each wall, a tall and narrow Gothic window looked out upon a closed corridor which pursued the windings of the suite. These windows were of stained glass whose color varied in accordance with the prevailing hue of the decorations of the chamber into which it opened. That at the eastern extremity was hung, for example, in blue—and vividly blue were its windows. The second chamber was purple in its ornaments and tapestries, and here the panes were purple. The third was green throughout, and so were the casements. The fourth was furnished and lighted with orange—the fifth with white—the sixth with violet. The seventh apartment was closely shrouded in black velvet tapestries that hung all over the ceiling and down the walls, falling in heavy folds upon a carpet of the same material and hue. But in this chamber only, the color of the windows failed to correspond with the decorations. The panes here were scarlet—a deep blood color. Now in no one of the seven apartments was there any lamp or candelabrum, amid the profusion of golden ornaments that lay scattered to and fro or depended from the roof. There was no light of any kind emanating from lamp or candle within the suite of chambers. But in the corridors that followed the suite, there

[3]People who improvise songs.

stood, opposite to each window a heavy tripod, bearing a brazier of fire, that projected its rays through the tinted glass and so glaringly illumined the room. And thus were produced a multitude of gaudy and fantastic appearances. But in the western or black chamber the effect of the fire-light that streamed upon the dark hangings through the blood-tinted panes, was ghastly in the extreme, and produced so wild a look upon the countenances of those who entered, that there were few of the company bold enough to set foot within its precincts at all.[4]

It was in this apartment, also, that there stood against the western wall, a gigantic clock of ebony. Its pendulum swung to and fro with a dull, heavy, monotonous clang; and when the minute-hand made the circuit of the face, and the hour was to be stricken, there came from the brazen lungs of the clock a sound which was clear and loud and deep and exceedingly musical, but of so peculiar a note and emphasis that, at each lapse of an hour, the musicians of the orchestra were constrained to pause, momentarily, in their performance, to hearken to the sound; and thus the waltzers perforce ceased their evolutions; and there was a brief disconcert of the whole gay company; and, while the chimes of the clock yet rang, it was observed that the giddiest grew pale, and the more aged and sedate passed their hands over their brows as if in confused revery or meditation. But when the echoes had fully ceased, a light laughter at once pervaded the assembly; the musicians looked at each other and smiled as if at their own nervousness and folly, and made whispering vows, each to the other, that the next chiming of the clock should produce in them no similar emotion; and then, after the lapse of sixty minutes, (which embrace three thousand and six hundred seconds of the Time that flies,) there came yet another chiming of the clock, and then were the same disconcert and tremulousness and meditation as before.

But, in spite of these things, it was a gay and magnificent revel. The tastes of the duke were peculiar. He had a fine eye for colors and effects. He disregarded the *decora*[5] of mere fashion. His plans were bold and fiery, and his conceptions glowed with barbaric lustre. There are some who would have thought him mad. His followers felt that he was not. It was necessary to hear and see and touch him to be *sure* that he was not.

He had directed, in great part, the moveable embellishments of the seven chambers, upon occasion of this great *fête;* and it was his own guiding taste which had given character to the masqueraders. Be sure they were grotesque. There were much glare and glitter and piquancy and phantasm—much of what has been since seen in "Hernani."[6] There were arabesque figures with unsuited limbs and appointments. There were delirious fancies such as the madman fashions. There were much of the beautiful, much of the wanton, much of the *bizarre,* something

---

[4]These are theatrical effects, based on contemporary stagecraft. The corridor serves no function except to provide a source of artificial light which can shine through the colored windows. Prospero's name, of course, is also theatrical, from Shakespeare's *The Tempest.*
[5]Decorum in the plural; proprieties.
[6]Play (1829) by Victor Hugo which Poe knew well—another sure sign that Poe's story is an attempt to recreate in prose a stage effect which impressed him.

of the terrible, and not a little of that which might have excited disgust. To and fro in the seven chambers there stalked, in fact, a multitude of dreams. And these—the dreams—writhed in and about, taking hue from the rooms, and causing the wild music of the orchestra to seem as the echo of their steps. And, anon, there strikes the ebony clock which stands in the hall of the velvet. And then, for a moment, all is still, and all is silent save the voice of the clock. The dreams are stiff-frozen as they stand. But the echoes of the chime die away—they have endured but an instant—and a light, half-subdued laughter floats after them as they depart. And now again the music swells, and the dreams live, and writhe to and fro more merrily than ever, taking hue from the many-tinted windows through which stream the rays from the tripods. But to the chamber which lies most westwardly of the seven, there are now none of the maskers who venture; for the night is waning away; and there flows a ruddier light through the blood-colored panes; and the blackness of the sable drapery appals; and to him whose foot falls upon the sable carpet, there comes from the near clock of ebony a muffled peal more solemnly emphatic than any which reaches *their* ears who indulge in the more remote gaieties of the other apartments.

But these other apartments were densely crowded, and in them beat feverishly the heart of life. And the revel went whirlingly on, until at length there commenced the sounding of midnight upon the clock. And then the music ceased, as I have told; and the evolutions of the waltzers were quieted; and there was an uneasy cessation of all things as before. But now there were twelve strokes to be sounded by the bell of the clock; and thus it happened, perhaps, that more of thought crept, with more of time, into the meditations of the thoughtful among those who revelled. And thus, too, it happened, perhaps, that before the last echoes of the last chime had utterly sunk into silence, there were many individuals in the crowd who had found leisure to become aware of the presence of a masked figure which had arrested the attention of no single individual before. And the rumor of this new presence having spread itself whisperingly around, there arose at length from the whole company a buzz, or murmur, expressive of disapprobation and surprise—then, finally, of terror, of horror, and of disgust.

In an assembly of phantasms such as I have painted, it may well be supposed that no ordinary appearance could have excited such sensation. In truth the masquerade license of the night was nearly unlimited; but the figure in question had out-Heroded Herod,[7] and gone beyond the bounds of even the prince's indefinite decorum. There are chords in the hearts of the most reckless which cannot be touched without emotion. Even with the utterly lost, to whom life and death are equally jests, there are matters of which no jest can be made. The whole company, indeed, seemed now deeply to feel that in the costume and bearing of the stranger neither wit nor propriety existed. The figure was tall and gaunt, and shrouded from head to foot in the habiliments of the grave. The mask which concealed the visage was made so nearly to resemble the countenance of a stiffened corpse that the closest scrutiny must have had difficulty in detecting the cheat. And yet all this

[7]See "William Wilson," note 10.

might have been endured, if not approved, by the mad revellers around. But the mummer had gone so far as to assume the type of the Red Death. His vesture was dabbled in *blood*—and his broad brow, with all the features of the face, was besprinkled with the scarlet horror.

When the eyes of Prince Prospero fell upon this spectral image (which with a slow and solemn movement, as if more fully to sustain its *rôle,* stalked to and fro among the waltzers) he was seen to be convulsed, in the first moment with a strong shudder either of terror or distaste; but, in the next, his brow reddened with rage.

"Who dares?" he demanded hoarsely of the courtiers who stood near him—"who dares insult us with this blasphemous mockery?[8] Seize him and unmask him—that we may know whom we have to hang at sunrise, from the battlements!"

It was in the eastern or blue chamber in which stood the Prince Prospero as he uttered these words. They rang throughout the seven rooms loudly and clearly—for the prince was a bold and robust man, and the music had become hushed at the waving of his hand.

It was in the blue room where stood the prince, with a group of pale courtiers by his side. At first, as he spoke, there was a slight rushing movement of this group in the direction of the intruder, who at the moment was also near at hand, and now, with deliberate and stately step, made closer approach to the speaker. But from a certain nameless awe with which the mad assumptions of the mummer had inspired the whole party, there were found none who put forth hand to seize him; so that, unimpeded, he passed within a yard of the prince's person; and, while the vast assembly, as if with one impulse, shrank from the centres of the rooms to the walls, he made his way uninterruptedly, but with the same solemn and measured step which had distinguished him from the first, through the blue chamber to the purple—through the purple to the green—through the green to the orange—through this again to the white—and even thence to the violet, ere a decided movement had been made to arrest him. It was then, however, that the Prince Prospero, maddening with rage and the shame of his own momentary cowardice, rushed hurriedly through the six chambers, while none followed him on account of a deadly terror that had seized upon all. He bore aloft a drawn dagger, and had approached, in rapid impetuosity, to within three or four feet of the retreating figure, when the latter, having attained the extremity of the velvet apartment, turned suddenly and confronted his pursuer. There was a sharp cry—and the dagger dropped gleaming upon the sable carpet, upon which, instantly afterwards, fell prostrate in death the Prince Prospero. Then, summoning the wild courage of despair, a throng of the revellers at once threw themselves into the black apartment, and, seizing the mummer, whose tall figure stood erect and motionless within the shadow of the ebony clock, gasped in unutterable horror at finding the grave-cerements and corpse-like mask which they handled with so violent a rudeness, untenanted by any tangible form.

---

[8]Another sign of the essential morality of the proceedings: Prospero sees mockery of the sufferings of the afflicted as blasphemous.

And now was acknowledged the presence of the Red Death. He had come like a thief in the night. And one by one dropped the revellers in the blood-bedewed halls of their revel, and died each in the despairing posture of his fall. And the life of the ebony clock went out with that of the last of the gay. And the flames of the tripods expired. And Darkness and Decay and the Red Death held illimitable dominion over all.

The Pit and the Pendulum

Poe set this famous story not in some vague medieval era, as modern readers might suppose, but in the very recent past, the entry in 1808 of the French General Lasalle into the palace of the Inquisition in Toledo, Spain, just thirty-odd years before the tale was published. Accounts of the instruments of torture which Lasalle found appeared in a number of books and magazines which Poe knew. The Inquisition, moreover, had subsequently been reinstituted; several scholars are sure that Poe had read a detailed and bitter description of how the Catholic Church in Spain enforced orthodoxy, as recently as 1820, through slow death by sharp pendulum (Mabbott 9, II). "The Pit and the Pendulum," then, exploits recent history, political and religious attitudes, and a sensationalism which was unusually powerful because it was grounded in well-known fact.

But the story also conducts Poe's aesthetic and philosophical business. "The Pit and the Pendulum" is about the sources of insight. Its narrator must be brilliant if he is to save himself. The progression down to despair and insanity and up to insight is what makes the prisoner "brilliant." Poe is interested in the varieties of inspired creativity—hence the hint that dreams and fainting fits carry knowledge of eternity; the unconscious mind may know what will be known after death. The person just awakening, the reader is told, has dim memories of such knowledge. The narrator, in an abnormal state, tortured and frightened, has glimpses of it while awake. Thus "The Pit and the Pendulum" is a "thriller," a historical fiction, and a dramatization of a transcendental worldview.

***A note of explanation:** The narrator's transformation from torpor to inspiration determines the plot of the tale, for in Poe's fictions, the harder it is for the perceiving character to have the great vision, the more complicated is the story line. Thus we expect and get a plot rich in events in "The Pit and the Pendulum," another tale of salvation from strange surroundings. The brilliance which the narrator needs does not come as naturally as Ellison's artistic brilliance in "The Domain of Arnheim," a piece practically without dramatic events. It is more like that of the fisherman in "A Descent into the Maelström," a story which, like "The Pit . . . ," has numerous important turns of plot.*

Modern readers may wonder at the amount of space Poe devotes to describing his narrator's precise state of mind during the ordeal. The commercial reasons for such concern are clearly explained in "How to Write a Blackwood Article": "Should you ever be drowned or hung, be sure and make a note of your sensations—they will be worth to you ten guineas a sheet." Given his theory of inspiration, however, Poe also has philosophical reasons.

PUBLICATIONS IN POE'S TIME

The Gift, 1843 (published late 1842)
The Broadway Journal, May 17, 1845

THE PIT AND THE PENDULUM

Impia tortorum longos hic turba furores
Sanguinis innocui, non satiata, aluit.
Sospite nunc patriâ, fracto nunc funeris antro,
Mors urbi dira fuit vita salusque patent.
[Quatrain composed for the gates
of a market to be erected upon the site
of the Jacobin Club House at Paris.][1]

I was sick—sick unto death with that long agony; and when they at length unbound me, and I was permitted to sit, I felt that my senses were leaving me. The sentence—the dread sentence of death—was the last of distinct accentuation which reached my ears. After that, the sound of the inquisitorial[2] voices seemed merged in one dreamy indeterminate hum. It conveyed to my soul the idea of *revolution*—perhaps from its association in fancy with the burr of a mill-wheel. This only for a brief period; for presently I heard no more. Yet, for a while, I saw; but with how terrible an exaggeration! I saw the lips of the black-robed judges. They appeared to me white—whiter than the sheet upon which I trace these words—and thin even to grotesqueness; thin with the intensity of their expression of firmness—of immoveable resolution—of stern contempt of human torture. I saw that the decrees of what to me was Fate were still issuing from those lips. I saw them writhe with deadly locution. I saw them fashion the syllables of my name; and I shuddered because no sound succeeded. I saw, too, for a few moments

---

[1]Carlson (2) translates the Latin, "Here an insatiable band of torturers long wickedly nourished their lusts for innocent blood. Saved, now, our homeland; destroyed, the funereal dungeon." The Jacobins were a radical group during the French Revolution, associated with the Reign of Terror. In suggesting a similarity between the Reign of Terror and the Spanish Inquisition (the setting of "The Pit and the Pendulum") Poe associates the excesses of Catholicism with those of political radicalism. Anti-Catholic feeling ran high in Poe's America, and the French Revolution was still a controversial and lively topic, used by conservatives for scare purposes to show the results of too much democracy.

[2]The Spanish Inquisition was an independent court of the Roman Catholic Church notorious for cruelty in the prosecution of heretics and of adherents of other religions. Poe dates his story at the point in history in which the Inquisition was discontinued, the Napoleonic conquest of Spain (see note 11).

of delirious horror, the soft and nearly imperceptible waving of the sable draperies which enwrapped the walls of the apartment. And then my vision fell upon the seven tall candles upon the table. At first they wore the aspect of charity, and seemed white slender angels who would save me; but then, all at once, there came a most deadly nausea over my spirit, and I felt every fibre in my frame thrill as if I had touched the wire of a galvanic battery, while the angel forms became meaningless spectres, with heads of flame, and I saw that from them there would be no help. And then there stole into my fancy, like a rich musical note, the thought of what sweet rest there must be in the grave. The thought came gently and stealthily, and it seemed long before it attained full appreciation; but just as my spirit came at length properly to feel and entertain it, the figures of the judges vanished, as if magically, from before me; the tall candles sank into nothingness; their flames went out utterly; the blackness of darkness supervened; all sensations appeared swallowed up in a mad rushing descent as of the soul into Hades. Then silence, and stillness, and night were the universe.

I had swooned; but still will not say that all of consciousness was lost. What of it there remained I will not attempt to define, or even to describe; yet all was not lost. In the deepest slumber—no! In delirium—no! In a swoon—no! In death—no! even in the grave all *is not* lost. Else there is no immortality for man. Arousing from the most profound of slumbers, we break the gossamer web of *some* dream. Yet in a second afterward, (so frail may that web have been) we remember not that we have dreamed. In the return to life from the swoon there are two stages; first, that of the sense of mental or spiritual; secondly, that of the sense of physical, existence. It seems probable that if, upon reaching the second stage, we could recall the impressions of the first, we should find these impressions eloquent in memories of the gulf beyond. And that gulf is—what? How at least shall we distinguish its shadows from those of the tomb? But if the impressions of what I have termed the first stage, are not, at will, recalled, yet, after long interval, do they not come unbidden, while we marvel whence they come? He who has never swooned, is not he who finds strange palaces and wildly familiar faces in coals that glow; is not he who beholds floating in mid-air the sad visions that the many may not view; is not he who ponders over the perfume of some novel flower—is not he whose brain grows bewildered with the meaning of some musical cadence which has never before arrested his attention.[3]

Amid frequent and thoughtful endeavors to remember; amid earnest struggles to regather some token of the state of seeming nothingness into which my soul had lapsed, there have been moments when I have dreamed of success; there have been brief, very brief periods when I have conjured up remembrances which the lucid reason of a later epoch assures me could have had reference only to that condition of seeming unconsciousness. These shadows of memory tell, indistinctly, of tall figures that lifted and bore me in silence down—down—still down—till a hideous dizziness oppressed me at the mere idea of the interminable-

[3]This discussion of the states of sleep and of the nature of fainting "sets up" the procedure on the following pages by which the narrator gradually emerges from his madness to the brilliance which enables him to survive long enough to be rescued from his torturers.

ness of the descent. They tell also of a vague horror at my heart, on account of that heart's unnatural stillness. Then comes a sense of sudden motionlessness throughout all things; as if those who bore me (a ghastly train!) had outrun, in their descent, the limits of the limitless, and paused from the wearisomeness of their toil. After this I call to mind flatness and dampness; and then all is *madness*—the madness of a memory which busies itself among forbidden things.

Very suddenly there came back to my soul motion and sound—the tumultuous motion of the heart, and, in my ears, the sound of its beating. Then a pause in which all is blank. Then again sound, and motion, and touch—a tingling sensation pervading my frame. Then the mere consciousness of existence, without thought—a condition which lasted long. Then, very suddenly, *thought,* and shuddering terror, and earnest endeavor to comprehend my true state. Then a strong desire to lapse into insensibility. Then a rushing revival of soul and a successful effort to move. And now a full memory of the trial, of the judges, of the sable draperies, of the sentence, of the sickness, of the swoon. Then entire forgetfulness of all that followed; of all that a later day and much earnestness of endeavor have enabled me vaguely to recall.

So far, I had not opened my eyes. I felt that I lay upon my back, unbound. I reached out my hand, and it fell heavily upon something damp and hard. There I suffered it to remain for many minutes, while I strove to imagine where and *what* I could be. I longed, yet dared not, to employ my vision. I dreaded the first glance at objects around me. It was not that I feared to look upon things horrible, but that I grew aghast lest there should be *nothing* to see. At length, with a wild desperation at heart, I quickly unclosed my eyes. My worst thoughts, then, were confirmed. The blackness of eternal night encompassed me. I struggled for breath. The intensity of the darkness seemed to oppress and stifle me. The atmosphere was intolerably close. I still lay quietly, and made effort to exercise my reason. I brought to mind the inquisitorial proceedings, and attempted from that point to deduce my real condition. The sentence had passed; and it appeared to me that a very long interval of time had since elapsed. Yet not for a moment did I suppose myself actually dead. Such a supposition, notwithstanding what we read in fiction, is altogether inconsistent with real existence;—but where and in what state was I? The condemned to death, I knew, perished usually at the *autos-da-fé,* and one of these had been held on the very night of the day of my trial. Had I been remanded to my dungeon, to await the next sacrifice, which would not take place for many months? This I at once saw could not be. Victims had been in immediate demand. Moreover, my dungeon, as well as all the condemned cells at Toledo[4] had stone floors, and light was not altogether excluded.

A fearful idea now suddenly drove the blood in torrents upon my heart, and for a brief period, I once more relapsed into insensibility. Upon recovering, I at once started to my feet, trembling convulsively in every fibre. I thrust my arms wildly

---

[4]*autos-da-fé:* Public announcement and execution of sentence of the Inquisition; in common use, the execution itself, generally by burning at the stake. See our headnote. The idea of the shrinking iron cell might have come from a tale called "The Iron Shroud" in *Blackwood's Magazine* in 1830 (A. H. Quinn); Poe was a regular reader of *Blackwood's.*

above and around me in all directions. I felt nothing; yet dreaded to move a step, lest I should be impeded by the walls of a *tomb.*[5] Perspiration burst from every pore, and stood in cold big beads upon my forehead. The agony of suspense grew at length intolerable, and I cautiously moved forward, with my arms extended, and my eyes straining from their sockets in the hope of catching some faint ray of light. I proceeded for many paces; but still all was blackness and vacancy. I breathed more freely. It seemed evident that mine was not, at least, the most hideous of fates.

And now, as I still continued to step cautiously onward, there came thronging upon my recollection a thousand vague rumors of the horrors of Toledo. Of the dungeons there had been strange things narrated—fables I had always deemed them,—but yet strange, and too ghastly to repeat, save in a whisper. Was I left to perish of starvation in this subterranean world of darkness; or what fate, perhaps even more fearful, awaited me? That the result would be death, and a death of more than customary bitterness, I knew too well the character of my judges to doubt. The mode and the hour were all that occupied or distracted me.

My outstretched hands at length encountered some solid obstruction. It was a wall, seemingly of stone masonry—very smooth, slimy, and cold. I followed it up; stepping with all the careful distrust with which certain antique narratives had inspired me. This process, however, afforded me no means of ascertaining the dimensions of my dungeon, as I might make its circuit and return to the point whence I set out without being aware of the fact, so perfectly uniform seemed the wall. I therefore sought the knife which had been in my pocket, when led into the inquisitorial chamber; but it was gone; my clothes had been exchanged for a wrapper of coarse serge. I had thought of forcing the blade in some minute crevice of the masonry, so as to identify my point of departure. The difficulty, nevertheless, was but trivial; although, in the disorder of my fancy, it seemed at first insuperable. I tore a part of the hem from the robe and placed the fragment at full length, and at right angles to the wall. In groping my way around the prison, I could not fail to encounter this rag upon completing the circuit. So, at least, I thought; but I had not counted upon the extent of the dungeon, or upon my own weakness. The ground was moist and slippery. I staggered onward for some time, when I stumbled and fell. My excessive fatigue induced me to remain prostrate; and sleep soon overtook me as I lay.

Upon awaking, and stretching forth an arm, I found beside me a loaf and a pitcher with water. I was too much exhausted to reflect upon this circumstance, but ate and drank with avidity. Shortly afterward, I resumed my tour around the prison, and with much toil, came at last upon the fragment of the serge. Up to the period when I fell, I had counted fifty-two paces, and, upon resuming my walk, I had counted forty-eight more—when I arrived at the rag. There were in all, then, a hundred paces; and, admitting two paces to the yard, I presumed the dungeon to be

---

[5]The buried-alive motif is common in Poe. Some readers may take it as conclusive evidence that Poe suffered an acute psychological condition from fear of such a fate. But Poe observed that burial alive made a good commercial story topic in his day. See also "The Premature Burial," in Levine (4).

fifty yards in circuit. I had met, however, with many angles in the wall, and thus I could form no guess at the shape of the vault; for vault I could not help supposing it to be.

I had little object—certainly no hope—in these researches; but a vague curiosity prompted me to continue them. Quitting the wall, I resolved to cross the area of the enclosure. At first, I proceeded with extreme caution, for the floor, although seemingly of solid material, was treacherous with slime. At length, however, I took courage, and did not hesitate to step firmly; endeavoring to cross in as direct a line as possible. I had advanced some ten or twelve paces in this manner, when the remnant of the torn hem of my robe became entangled between my legs. I stepped on it, and fell violently on my face.

In the confusion attending my fall, I did not immediately apprehend a somewhat startling circumstance, which yet, in a few seconds afterward, and while I still lay prostrate, arrested my attention. It was this—my chin rested upon the floor of the prison, but my lips, and the upper portion of my head, although seemingly at a less elevation than the chin, touched nothing. At the same time, my forehead seemed bathed in a clammy vapor, and the peculiar smell of decayed fungus arose to my nostrils. I put forward my arm, and shuddered to find that I had fallen at the very brink of a circular pit, whose extent, of course, I had no means of ascertaining at the moment. Groping about the masonry just below the margin, I succeeded is dislodging a small fragment, and let it fall into the abyss. For many seconds I hearkened to its reverberations as it dashed against the sides of the chasm in its descent; at length there was a sullen plunge into water, succeeded by loud echoes. At the same moment, there came a sound resembling the quick opening and as rapid closing of a door overhead, while a faint gleam of light flashed suddenly through the gloom, and as suddenly faded away.

I saw clearly the doom which had been prepared for me, and congratulated myself upon the timely accident by which I had escaped. Another step before my fall, and the world had seen me no more. And the death just avoided was of that very character which I had regarded as fabulous and frivolous in the tales respecting the Inquisition. To the victims of its tyranny, there was the choice of death with its direct physical agonies, or death with its most hideous moral horrors. I had been reserved for the latter. By long suffering my nerves had been unstrung, until I trembled at the sound of my own voice, and had become in every respect a fitting subject for the species of torture which awaited me.

Shaking in every limb, I groped my way back to the wall—resolving there to perish rather than risk the terrors of the wells, of which my imagination now pictured many in various positions about the dungeon. In other conditions of mind, I might have had courage to end my misery at once, by a plunge into one of these abysses; but now I was the veriest of cowards. Neither could I forget what I had read of these pits—that the *sudden* extinction of life formed no part of their most horrible plan.

Agitation of spirit kept me awake for many long hours, but at length I again slumbered. Upon arousing, I found by my side, as before, a loaf and a pitcher of water. A burning thirst consumed me, and I emptied the vessel at a draught. It must have been drugged—for scarcely had I drunk, before I became irresistibly drowsy. A deep sleep fell upon me—a sleep like that of death. How long it lasted of course, I know not; but when, once again, I unclosed my eyes, the objects around me were visible. By a wild, sulphurous lustre, the origin of which I could not at first determine, I was enabled to see the extent and aspect of the prison.

In its size I had been greatly mistaken. The whole circuit of its walls did not exceed twenty-five yards. For some minutes this fact occasioned me a world of vain trouble; vain indeed—for what could be of less importance, under the terrible circumstances which environed me, than the mere dimensions of my dungeon? But my soul took a wild interest in trifles, and I busied myself in endeavors to account for the error I had committed in my measurement. The truth at length flashed upon me. In my first attempt at exploration I had counted fifty-two paces, up to the period when I fell: I must then have been within a pace or two of the fragment of serge; in fact, I had nearly performed the circuit of the vault. I then slept—and, upon waking, I must have returned upon my steps—thus supposing the circuit nearly double what it actually was. My confusion of mind prevented me from observing that I began my tour with the wall to the left, and ended it with the wall to the right.

I had been deceived, too, in respect to the shape of the enclosure. In feeling my way I had found many angles, and thus deduced an idea of great irregularity; so potent is the effect of total darkness upon one arousing from lethargy or sleep! The angles were simply those of a few slight depressions, or niches, at odd intervals. The general shape of the prison was square. What I had taken for masonry seemed now to be iron, or some other metal, in huge plates, whose sutures or joints occasioned the depressions. The entire surface of this metallic enclosure was rudely daubed in all the hideous and repulsive devices to which the charnel superstition of the monks has given rise.[6] The figures of fiends in aspects of menace, with skeleton forms, and other more really fearful images, overspread and disfigured the walls. I observed that the outlines of these monstrosities were sufficiently distinct, but that the colors seemed faded and blurred, as if from the effects of a damp atmosphere. I now noticed the floor, too, which was of stone. In the centre yawned the circular pit from whose jaws I had escaped; but it was the only one in the dungeon.

All this I saw indistinctly and by much effort—for my personal condition had been greatly changed during slumber. I now lay upon my back, and at full length, on a species of low framework of wood. To this I was securely bound by a long strap resembling a surcingle.[7] It passed in many convolutions about my limbs and body, leaving at liberty only my head, and my left arm to such extent that I could, by dint of much exertion, supply myself with food from an earthen dish which lay by my side on the floor. I saw, to my horror, that the pitcher had been removed. I say to my horror—for I was consumed with intolerable thirst. This thirst it appeared to be the design of my persecutors to stimulate—for the food in the dish was meat pungently seasoned.

---

[6]Writing for a Protestant audience, Poe can assume that his readers are familiar with a long tradition of stories of priestly diabolism.

[7]A strap around the body; usually, the strap which holds on a horse's saddle.

Looking upward, I surveyed the ceiling of my prison. It was some thirty or forty feet overhead, and constructed much as the side walls. In one of its panels a very singular figure riveted my whole attention. It was the painted figure of Time as he is commonly represented, save that in lieu of a scythe, he held what, at a casual glance, I supposed to be the pictured image of a huge pendulum, such as we see on antique clocks. There was something, however, in the appearance of this machine which caused me to regard it more attentively. While I gazed directly upward at it (for its position was immediately over my own) I fancied that I saw it in motion. In an instant afterward the fancy was confirmed. Its sweep was brief, and of course slow. I watched it for some minutes, somewhat in fear, but more in wonder. Wearied at length with observing its dull movement, I turned my eyes upon the other objects in the cell.

A slight noise attracted my notice, and looking to the floor, I saw several enormous rats traversing it. They had issued from the well which lay just within view to my right. Even then, while I gazed, they came up in troops, hurriedly, with ravenous eyes, allured by the scent of the meat. From this it required much effort and attention to scare them away.

It might have been half an hour, perhaps even an hour, (for I could take but imperfect note of time) before I again cast my eyes upward. What I then saw confounded and amazed me. The sweep of the pendulum had increased in extent by nearly a yard. As a natural consequence, its velocity was also much greater. But what mainly disturbed me was the idea that it had perceptibly *descended.* I now observed—with what horror it is needless to say—that its nether extremity was formed of a crescent of glittering steel, about a foot in length from horn to horn; the horns upward, and the under edge evidently as keen as that of a razor. Like a razor also, it seemed massy and heavy, tapering from the edge into a solid and broad structure above. It was appended to a weighty rod of brass, and the whole *hissed* as it swung through the air.

I could no longer doubt the doom prepared for me by monkish ingenuity in torture. My cognizance of the pit had become known to the inquisitorial agents—*the pit,* whose horrors had been destined for so bold a recusant as myself—*the pit,* typical of hell, and regarded by rumor as the Ultima Thule[8] of all their punishments. The plunge into this pit I had avoided by the merest of accidents, and I knew that surprise, or entrapment into torment, formed an important portion of all the grotesquerie of these dungeon deaths. Having failed to fall, it was no part of the demon plan to hurl me into the abyss; and thus (there being no alternative), a different and a milder destruction awaited me. Milder! I half smiled in my agony as I thought of such application of such a term.

What boots it to tell of the long, long hours of horror more than mortal, during which I counted the rushing vibrations of the steel! Inch by inch—line by line—with a descent only appreciable at intervals that seemed ages—down and still down it came! Days passed—it might have been that many days passed—ere it swept so closely over me as to fan me with its acrid breath. The odor of the sharp

---

[8]Most extreme form; literally, Farthest Thule—in ancient geography, the northernmost habitable region.

steel forced itself into my nostrils. I prayed—I wearied heaven with my prayer for its more speedy descent. I grew frantically mad, and struggled to force myself upward against the sweep of the fearful scimitar. And then I fell suddenly calm, and lay smiling at the glittering death, as a child at some rare bauble.

There was another interval of utter insensibility; it was brief; for, upon again lapsing into life, there had been no perceptible descent in the pendulum. But it might have been long; for I knew there were demons who took note of my swoon, and who could have arrested the vibration at pleasure. Upon my recovery, too, I felt very—oh, inexpressibly sick and weak, as if through long inanition. Even amid the agonies of that period, the human nature craved food. With painful effort I outstretched my left arm as far as my bonds permitted, and took possession of the small remnant which had been spared me by the rats. As I put a portion of it within my lips, there rushed to my mind a half formed thought of joy—of hope. Yet what business had *I* with hope? It was, as I say, a half formed thought—man has many such which are never completed. I felt that it was of joy—of hope; but I felt also that it had perished in its formation. In vain I struggled to perfect—to regain it. Long suffering had nearly annihilated all my ordinary powers of mind. I was an imbecile—an idiot.[9]

The vibration of the pendulum was at right angles to my length. I saw that the crescent was designed to cross the region of the heart. It would fray the serge of my robe—it would return and repeat its operations—again—and again. Notwithstanding its terrifically wide sweep (some thirty feet or more) and the hissing vigor of its descent, sufficent to sunder these very walls of iron, still the fraying of my robe would be all that, for several minutes, it would accomplish. And at this thought I paused. I dared not go further than this reflection. I dwelt upon it with a pertinacity of attention—as if, in so dwelling, I could arrest *here* the descent of the steel. I forced myself to ponder upon the sound of the crescent as it should pass across the garment—upon the peculiar thrilling sensation which the friction of cloth produces on the nerves. I pondered upon all this frivolity until my teeth were on edge.

Down—steadily down it crept. I took a frenzied pleasure in contrasting its downward with its lateral velocity. To the right—to the left—far and wide—with the shriek of a damned spirit; to my heart with the stealthy pace of the tiger! I alternately laughed and howled, as the one or the other idea grew predominant.

Down—certainly, relentlessly down! It vibrated within three inches of my bosom! I struggled violently, furiously, to free my left arm. This was free only from the elbow to the hand. I could reach the latter, from the platter beside me, to my mouth, with great effort, but no farther. Could I have broken the fastenings above the elbow, I would have seized and attempted to arrest the pendulum. I might as well have attempted to arrest an avalanche!

Down—still unceasingly—still inevitably down! I gasped and struggled at each vibration. I shrunk convulsively at its every sweep. My eyes followed its outward or upward whirls with the eagerness of the most unmeaning despair; they closed themselves spasmodically at the descent, although death would have been

---

[9]See "A note of explanation," in our headnote.

a relief, oh! how unspeakable! Still I quivered in every nerve to think how slight a sinking of the machinery would precipitate that keen, glistening axe upon my bosom. It was *hope* that prompted the nerve to quiver—the frame to shrink. It was *hope*—the hope that triumphs on the rack—that whispers to the death-condemned even in the dungeons of the Inquisition.

I saw that some ten or twelve vibrations would bring the steel in actual contact with my robe—and with this observation there suddenly came over my spirit all the keen, collected calmness of despair.[10] For the first time during many hours—or perhaps days—I *thought.* It now occurred to me, that the bandage, or surcingle, which enveloped me, was *unique.* I was tied by no separate cord. The first stroke of the razor-like crescent athwart any portion of the band would so detach it that it might be unwound from my person by means of my left hand. But how fearful, in that case, the proximity of the steel! The result of the slightest struggle, how deadly! Was it likely, moreover, that the minions of the torturer had not foreseen and provided for this possibility! Was it probable that the bandage crossed my bosom in the track of the pendulum? Dreading to find my faint, and, as it seemed, my last hope frustrated, I so far elevated my head as to obtain a distinct view of my breast. The surcingle enveloped my limbs and body close in all directions—*save in the path of the destroying crescent.*

Scarcely had I dropped my head back into its original position, when there flashed upon my mind what I cannot better describe than as the unformed half of that idea of deliverance to which I have previously alluded, and of which a moiety only floated indeterminately through my brain when I raised food to my burning lips. The whole thought was now present—feeble, scarcely sane, scarcely definite—but still entire. I proceeded at once, with the nervous energy of despair, to attempt its execution.

For many hours the immediate vicinity of the low framework upon which I lay had been literally swarming with rats. They were wild, bold, ravenous; their red eyes glaring upon me as if they waited but for motionlessness on my part to make me their prey. "To what food," I thought, "have they been accustomed in the well?"

They had devoured, in spite of all my efforts to prevent them, all but a small remnant of the contents of the dish. I had fallen into an habitual see-saw, or wave of the hand about the platter; and, at length, the unconscious uniformity of the movement deprived it of effect. In their voracity, the vermin frequently fastened their sharp fangs in my fingers. With the particles of the oily and spicy viand which now remained, I thoroughly rubbed the bandage wherever I could reach it; then, raising my hand from the floor, I lay breathlessly still.

At first, the ravenous animals were startled and terrified at the change—at the cessation of movement. They shrank alarmedly back; many sought the well. But this was only for a moment. I had not counted in vain upon their voracity. Observing that I remained without motion, one or two of the boldest leaped upon the framework, and smelt at the surcingle. This seemed the signal for a general rush. Forth from the well they hurried in fresh troops. They clung to the wood—

[10]The turning point. See "A Descent into the Maelström," note 20.

they overran it, and leaped in hundreds upon my person. The measured movement of the pendulum disturbed them not at all. Avoiding its strokes, they busied themselves with the anointed bandage. They pressed—they swarmed upon me in ever accumulating heaps. They writhed upon my throat; their cold lips sought my own; I was half stifled by their thronging pressure; disgust, for which the world has no name, swelled my bosom, and chilled, with a heavy clamminess, my heart. Yet one minute, and I felt that the struggle would be over. Plainly I perceived the loosening of the bandage. I knew that in more than one place it must be already severed. With a more than human resolution I lay *still.*

Nor had I erred in my calculations—nor had I endured in vain. I at length felt that I was *free.* The surcingle hung in ribands from my body. But the stroke of the pendulum already pressed upon my bosom. It had divided the serge of the robe. It had cut through the linen beneath. Twice again it swung, and a sharp sense of pain shot through every nerve. But the moment of escape had arrived. At a wave of my hand my deliverers hurried tumultuously away. With a steady movement—cautious, sidelong, shrinking, and slow—I slid from the embrace of the bandage and beyond the reach of the scimitar. For the moment, at least, *I was free.*

Free!—and in the grasp of the Inquisition! I had scarcely stepped from my wooden bed of horror upon the stone floor of the prison, when the motion of the hellish machine ceased, and I beheld it drawn up, by some invisible force, through the ceiling. This was a lesson which I took desperately to heart. My every motion was undoubtedly watched. Free!—I had but escaped death in one form of agony, to be delivered unto worse than death in some other. With that thought I rolled my eyes nervously around the barriers of iron that hemmed me in. Something unusual—some change which, at first, I could not appreciate distinctly—it was obvious, had taken place in the apartment. For many minutes of a dreamy and trembling abstraction, I busied myself in vain, unconnected conjecture. During this period, I became aware, for the first time, of the origin of the sulphurous light which illumined the cell. It proceeded from a fissure, about half an inch in width, extending entirely around the prison at the base of the walls, which thus appeared, and were, completely separated from the floor. I endeavored, but of course in vain, to look through the aperture.

As I arose from the attempt, the mystery of the alteration in the chamber broke at once upon my understanding. I have observed that, although the outlines of the figures upon the walls were sufficiently distinct, yet the colors seemed blurred and indefinite. These colors had now assumed, and were momentarily assuming, a startling and most intense brilliancy, that gave to the spectral and fiendish portraitures an aspect that might have thrilled even firmer nerves than my own. Demon eyes, of a wild and ghastly vivacity, glared upon me in a thousand directions, where none had been visible before, and gleamed with the lurid lustre of a fire that I could not force my imagination to regard as unreal.

Unreal!—Even while I breathed there came to my nostrils the breath of the vapor of heated iron! A suffocating odor pervaded the prison! A deeper glow settled each moment in the eyes that glared at my agonies! A richer tint of crimson diffused itself over the pictured horrors of blood. I panted! I gasped for breath! There could be no doubt of the design of my tormentors—oh! most unrelenting!

Oh! most demoniac of men! I shrank from the glowing metal to the centre of the cell. Amid the thought of the fiery destruction that impended, the idea of the coolness of the well came over my soul like balm. I rushed to its deadly brink. I threw my straining vision below. The glare from the enkindled roof illumined its inmost recesses. Yet, for a wild moment, did my spirit refuse to comprehend the meaning of what I saw. At length it forced—it wrestled its way into my soul—it burned itself in upon my shuddering reason.—Oh for a voice to speak!—oh! horror!—oh! any horror but this! With a shriek I rushed from the margin, and buried my face in my hands—weeping bitterly.

The heat rapidly increased, and once again I looked up, shuddering as with a fit of the ague. There had been a second change in the cell—and now the change was obviously in the *form.* As before, it was in vain that I at first endeavored to appreciate or understand what was taking place. But not long was I left in doubt. The Inquisitorial vengeance had been hurried by my two-fold escape, and there was to be no more dallying with the King of Terrors. The room had been square. I saw that two of its angles were now acute—two, consequently, obtuse. The fearful difference quickly increased with a low rumbling or moaning sound. In an instant the apartment had shifted its form into that of a lozenge. But the alteration stopped not here—I neither hoped nor desired it to stop. I could have clasped the red walls to my bosom as a garment of eternal peace. "Death," I said, "any death but that of the pit!" Fool! might I not have known that *into the pit* it was the object of the burning iron to urge me? Could I resist its glow? or, if even that, could I withstand its pressure? And now, flatter and flatter grew the lozenge, with a rapidity that left me no time for contemplation. Its centre, and of course, its greatest width, came just over the yawning gulf. I shrank back—but the closing walls pressed me resistlessly onward. At length for my seared and writhing body there was no longer an inch of foothold on the firm floor of the prison. I struggled no more, but the agony of my soul found vent in one loud, long, and final scream of despair. I felt that I tottered upon the brink—I averted my eyes—

There was a discordant hum of human voices! There was a loud blast as of many trumpets! There was a harsh grating as of a thousand thunders! The fiery walls rushed back! An out-stretched arm caught my own as I fell, fainting, into the abyss. It was that of General Lasalle.[11] The French army had entered Toledo. The Inquisition was in the hands of its enemies.

---

[11]Antoine Chevalier Louis Collinet, Count de Lasalle (1775–1809), Napoleonic general who fought brilliantly in Spain and entered Toledo in 1808.

THE DOMAIN OF ARNHEIM

Because it is meant to describe how artistic vision can be embodied, this piece is an excellent introduction to Poe's taste and to his aesthetic thought. Poe said that it was very important—it showed his "tastes and habits of thought." Ellison, his hero, is an inspired artist. The garden, Ellison's masterwork, is supremely beautiful, but such supernal beauty is not entirely "natural." Indeed, readers who think that Romantic aesthetics is simply a matter of "back to nature" will find "The Domain of Arnheim" surprising. Ellison's garden is downright artificial; in it one sees "scarcely a green leaf" and seems to see "rubies, sapphires, opals and golden onyxes" rolling out of the sky. Poe in fact actually uses the word "artificial." Earthly beauty as we normally find it reflects human mortality. Poe wants more than normalcy. Ellison's dreams of beauty are not tranquil or pastoral. Instead they are "fervid." They are akin to the visions, say, of the brilliant, terrified prisoner in "The Pit and the Pendulum." Ellison does not seek to restore the "original beauty of the country. The original beauty is never so great as that which may be introduced." A truly inspired artist alters nature to make it intimate the complex patterns of a seer's transcendent vision.

The result seems beautiful to the narrator, but his description of the beauty of Ellison's garden stresses complexity, strangeness, and even "funereal gloom." A key word is "arabesque." The term is important in Poe: he elaborates on it in his essay "The Philosophy of Composition" and uses it in many stories. He was familiar with theoretical writings about it, too; there are several discussions of Poe's knowledge of the Schlegels' use of "Arabesque" (Thompson 3, 4). A definition which relates arabesque design to philosophical implication is Malachi Martin's:

> *A central design extending in curved angular, straight patterns that in turn generate stars within circles, squares within stars, flowers and fruit and beads linked by fragile stems and stout columns and intertwining twigs that flow into Arabic lettering and double back to rejoin and repeat the central design. Color, rhythm and form tumble and twine in symmetries leading to the asymmetrical. Visual and tactile traceries taper into invisible tracks and then reappear in further traceries. Semicircles bud unexpectedly from the sides of squares. Curves interrupted by jagged points flow into empty spaces, to reappear beyond in aery ellipses as in epigrams of mystery.*

Philosophically as well, "The Domain of Arnheim" is central. A good entry into Poe's thought is afforded by the passage at note 7, where Poe uses the word "materialism" in a sense not familiar to many modern readers. He had the idea that inspiration, creativity, and insight were the result ultimately of physical connections which unite the entire universe. In the second paragraph he said that Ellison was lucky to believe in "the instinctive philosophy." Human intuition was capable, in Poe's scheme, of establishing contact with the force that interconnects the world. Poe shared that idea with many Romantic writers—Blake, Shelley, and Emerson, to name three very different ones—as well as with adherents of mystical and occult religions in various eras who believe that the universe is of a piece and that one is capable of merging one's consciousness with it. But unlike most other believers, Poe felt that the connection was not merely spiritual. It was based on physical, material fact, and ultimately an inspired science was likely to discover what the "force" or "carrier" was. In Eureka *he tried to spell out his theory. A very clear exemplification of it is the tale "The Power of Words," in which a character literally "speaks" a star into being.*

"The Domain of Arnheim" is interesting also for what it shows about the structure of Poe's fiction. In a great many stories, characters have visions, construct patterns, or create works of art which Poe describes with the same adjectives he uses here to describe Ellison's great landscape garden. Ellison creates his "arabesque," "Saracenic" work without apparent difficulty. He has everything—great poetic genius, enormous wealth, a lovely wife, and a fine family. He can "create beauty" under ideal conditions. Other creators in Poe are less fortunate; their visions must be induced by sickness, liquor, drugs, terror, or despair. In general, the easier it is for one of the perceptive characters in Poe to perceive, the less complex the plot of the piece in which he appears. So this is hardly a story at all: we're told who Ellison is, what he can do, and what he has. Then we're shown what he created. For comparison, see "The Fall of the House of Usher," a tale with a very complex plot. Poor Roderick Usher is also capable of contact with the sources of transcendent inspiration; he also creates works of art of Saracenic elaboration and fantastic complexity, but he must be nearly helplessly insane and frightened before the visions in his paintings and music drive him to art.

In many of Poe's stories, then, a "perceiver" has a "vision," which is usually complex, bizarre, and, to use one of Poe's pet words, "outré." The plots deal largely with what happens to the perceiving character in order to make the visionary experience possible. In tales of the sort to which "The Domain of Arnheim" belongs, nothing much happens. The creators do not have to be sick, drugged, or terrified before they can produce the complex and outré combinations which Poe calls beautiful. They are, apparently, ideal artists, able to perceive the supernal beauty of the universal order and to approximate it on earth.

A note of explanation: *This is really two stories, one overlapping the other. The shorter, older sketch, "The Landscape Garden," became, with some changes, part of the larger "The Domain of Arnheim." To make things a little more complicated: "The Landscape Garden" was published twice, and there are some small differences between the two versions (Hervey Allen thought they were identical).*

This book is not a variorum edition, but in this one case it seemed convenient and interesting to give the reader an idea of how Poe changed and expanded his own story. The changes between the two versions of the sketch are, with one exception, not important. To give a sense of Poe's tinkering, we put brackets around some passages which were in the short piece but were dropped from "The Domain of

Arnheim," and asterisks (*) before and after some of the passages which are in the later version only. The one important change is that "The Landscape Garden" ends before the explanation of how Ellison put his theory into practice, and the guided tour through the garden itself.

"The Domain of Arnheim" is generally terser and less heavily punctuated; it also uses shorter paragraphs than the earlier version. We have followed its usage.

Publications in Poe's Time

(As "The Landscape Garden")
[Snowden's] *Ladies' Companion,* October 1842
The Broadway Journal, September 20, 1845

(As "The Domain of Arnheim")
Columbian Magazine, March 1847

The Domain of Arnheim[1]

The garden like a lady fair was cut,
That lay as if she slumbered in delight,
And to the open skies her eyes did shut.
The azure fields of Heaven were 'sembled right
In a large round set with the flowers of light.
The flowers de luce and the round sparks of dew
That hung upon their azure leaves did shew
Like twinkling stars that sparkle in the evening blue.[2]

Giles Fletcher.

[No more remarkable man ever lived than my friend, the young Ellison. He was remarkable in the entire and continuous profusion of good gifts ever lavished upon him by fortune.] From his cradle to his grave a gale of prosperity bore my friend Ellison along. Nor do I use the word prosperity in its mere worldly sense. I

[1]Moore convincingly argues that the name and a part of the texture of the story were probably derived from Scott's *Anne of Geierstein,* especially chapters 11 and 21.

[2]In this excerpt from Fletcher's "Christ's Victory on Earth" Poe modernized the spelling (Harrison). Note that Poe chose a poem in which the beauty of a woman is equated with the beauty of a garden. He said, in "The Philosophy of Composition," "the death . . . of a beautiful woman is, unquestionably, the most poetical topic in the world." Fletcher's lady is asleep, not dead, but clearly Poe wants the reader to see that his sketch concerns ideal beauty. Several times he tells us that Ellison was happily married to a beautiful woman.

mean it as synonymous with happiness. The person of whom I speak seemed born for the purpose of foreshadowing the doctrines of Turgot, Price, Priestley and Condorcet[3]—of exemplifying by individual instance what has been deemed the chimera of the perfectionists. In the brief existence of Ellison I fancy that I have seen refuted the dogma, that in man's very nature lies some hidden principle, the antagonist of bliss. An anxious examination of his career has given me to understand that, in general, from the violation of a few simple laws of humanity arises the wretchedness of mankind—that as a species we have in our possession the as yet unwrought elements of content—and that, even now, in the present darkness and madness of all thought on the great question of the social condition, it is not impossible that man, the individual, under certain unusual and highly fortuitous conditions, may be happy.

With opinions such as these my young friend, too, was fully imbued; and thus it is worthy of observation that the uninterrupted enjoyment which distinguished his life was, in great measure, the result of preconcert. It is, indeed, evident that with less of the instinctive philosophy which, now and then, stands so well in the stead of experience, Mr. Ellison would have found himself precipitated, by the very extraordinary success of his life, into the common vortex of unhappiness which yawns for those of pre-eminent endowments. But it is by no means my object to pen an essay on happiness. The ideas of my friend may be summed up in a few words. He admitted but four elementary principles, or, more strictly, conditions, of bliss. That which he considered chief was (strange to say!) the simple and purely physical one of free exercise in the open air. "The health," he said, "attainable by other means is scarcely worth the name." He instanced the ecstacies of the foxhunter, and pointed to the tillers of the earth, the only people who, as a class, can be fairly considered happier than others.[4] His second condition was the love of woman. His third, *and most difficult of realization,* was the contempt of ambition. His fourth was an object of unceasing pursuit; and he held that, other things being equal, the extent of attainable happiness was in proportion to the spirituality of this object.

---

[3]**Turgot:** Anne Robert Jacques Turgot, French statesman and economist (1727–81). **Price:** Richard Price, English moral and political philosopher (1723–91). **Priestley:** Joseph Priestley, the English theologian, philosopher, and chemist (1733–1804), who fled England for the United States late in his career because of his liberal religious ideas. **Condorcet:** Marie Jean de Caritat, the French social philosopher and revolutionist (1743–94). Poe's narrator means to suggest that human perfection is indeed possible. Poe was usually contemptuous of such optimism when it was applied to people in society; he was politically conservative. But he did believe that the inspired creator, the poet (or landscape architect), could achieve transcendent inspiration and be "perfect" in that sense. Perhaps this belief accounts for his generosity to liberal theorists here. Later in this piece, indeed, we are told that Ellison himself does not believe that we can improve "the general condition of man."

[4]Poe turned this sentence around. "The Landscape Garden" reads, "He pointed to the tillers of the earth—the only people who, as a class, are proverbially more happy than others—and then he instanced . . ." etc. There are a number of changes of this sort which, henceforth, are not mentioned.

[I have said that] Ellison was remarkable in the continuous profusion of good gifts lavished upon him by fortune. In personal grace and beauty he exceeded all men. His intellect was of that order to which the acquisition of knowledge is less a labor than an intuition and a necessity. His family was one of the most illustrious of the empire. His bride was the loveliest and most devoted of women. His possessions had been always ample; but, on the attainment of his majority, it was discovered that one of those extraordinary freaks of fate had been played in his behalf which startle the whole social world amid which they occur, and seldom fail radically to alter the moral constitution of those who are their objects.

It appears that, about a hundred years before Mr. Ellison's coming of age, there had died, in a remote province, one Mr. Seabright Ellison. This gentleman had amassed a princely fortune, and, having no immediate connections, conceived the whim of suffering his wealth to accumulate for a century after his decease. Minutely and sagaciously directing the various modes of investment, he bequeathed the aggregate amount to the nearest of blood, bearing the name Ellison, who should be alive at the end of the hundred years. Many attempts had been made to set aside this singular bequest; their *ex post facto* character rendered them abortive; but the attention of a jealous government was aroused, and a legislative act finally obtained, forbidding all similar accumulations. This act, however, did not prevent young Ellison from entering into possession, on his twenty-first birthday, as the heir of his ancestor Seabright, of a fortune of *Four hundred and fifty millions of dollars.*[5]

When it had become known that such was the enormous wealth inherited, there were, of course, many speculations as to the mode of its disposal. The magnitude and the immediate availability of the sum bewildered all who thought on the topic. The possessor of any *appreciable* amount of money might have been imagined to perform any one of a thousand things. With riches merely surpassing those of any citizen, it would have been easy to suppose him engaging to supreme excess in the fashionable extravagances of his time—or busying himself with political intrigue—or aiming at ministerial power—or purchasing increase of nobility—or collecting large museums of *virtù*[6]—or playing the munificent patron of letters, of

[5]An incident, similar in outline to the one here imagined, occurred, not very long ago, in England. The name of the fortunate heir was Thelluson. I first saw an account of this matter in the "Tour" of Prince Pückler-Muskau, who makes the sum inherited *ninety millions of pounds,* and justly observes that "in the contemplation of so vast a sum, and of the services to which it might be applied, there is something even of the sublime." To suit the views of this article I have followed the Prince's statement, although a grossly exaggerated one. The germ, and, in fact, the commencement of the present paper was published many years ago—previous to the issue of the first number of Sue's admirable "*Juif errant,*" which may possibly have been suggested to him by Muskau's account [Poe's note]. Marie Joseph Sue (Eugène Sue), French novelist (1804–57). His novel, *Le Juif errant,* does concern a legacy which, invested, accrues interest over 150 years. Hermann Ludwig Heinrich Fürst Von Pückler-Muskau, German writer of books of travel (1785–1871).

[6]Rare or wonderful artifact; collector's item.

science, of art—or endowing, and bestowing his name upon, extensive institutions of charity. But for the inconceivable wealth in the actual possession of the heir, these objects and all ordinary objects were felt to afford too limited a field. Recourse was had to figures, and these but sufficed to confound. It was seen that, even at three per cent, the annual income of the inheritance amounted to no less that thirteen millions and five hundred thousand dollars; which was one million and one hundred and twenty-five thousand per month; or thirty-six thousand nine hundred and eighty-six per day; or one thousand five hundred and forty-one per hour; or six and twenty dollars for every minute that flew. Thus the usual track of supposition was thoroughly broken up. Men knew not what to imagine. There were some who even conceived that Mr. Ellison would divest himself of at least one half of his fortune, as of utterly superfluous opulence—enriching whole troops of his relatives by division of his superabundance. To the nearest of these he did, in fact, abandon the very unusual wealth which was his own before the inheritance.

I was not surprised, however, to perceive that he had long made up his mind on a point which had occasioned so much discussion to his friends. Nor was I greatly astonished at the nature of his decision. *In regard to individual charities he had satisfied his conscience. In the possibility of any improvement, properly so called, being effected by man himself in the general condition of man, he had (I am sorry to confess it) little faith. Upon the whole, whether happily or unhappily, he was thrown back, in the very great measure, upon self.*

In the widest and noblest sense he was a poet. He comprehended, moreover, the true character, the august aims, the supreme majesty and dignity of the poetic sentiment. The *fullest, if not the sole* proper satisfaction of this sentiment he instinctively felt to lie in the creation of novel forms of beauty. Some peculiarities, either in his early education, or in the nature of his intellect, had tinged with what is termed materialism all his ethical speculations; and it was this bias, perhaps, which led him to believe that the most advantageous *at least*, if not the sole legitimate field for the poetic exercise, lies in the creation of novel moods of purely *physical* loveliness. Thus it happened he became neither musician nor poet—if we use this latter term in its every-day acceptation. Or it might have been that he neglected to become either, merely in pursuance of his idea that in contempt of ambition is to be found one of the essential principles of happiness on earth. Is it not, indeed, possible that, while a high order of genius is necessarily ambitious, the highest is above that which is termed amibition? And may it not thus happen that many far greater than Milton have contentedly remained "mute and inglorious"?[7] I believe that the world has never seen—and that, unless through some series of accidents goading the noblest order of mind into

---

[7]**Materialism:** Poe means something special by "materialism." See our headnote. **"mute and inglorious":** Poe is alluding to Thomas Gray's "Elegy Written in a Country Churchyard": "Some mute inglorious Milton here may rest . . . ," which is to say, some potentially great poet who never wrote a poem.

distasteful exertion, the world will never see—that full extent of triumphant execution, in the richer domains of art, of which the human nature is absolutely capable.

Ellison became neither musician nor poet; although no man lived more profoundly enamored of music and poetry. Under other circumstances than those which invested him, it is not impossible that he would have become a painter. [The field of] sculpture, although in its nature rigorously poetical, was too limited in its extent and consequences, to have occupied, at any time, much of his attention. And I have now mentioned all the provinces in which the common understanding of the poetic sentiment has declared it capable of expatiating. But Ellison maintained that the richest, the truest and most natural, if not altogether the most extensive province, had been unaccountably neglected. No definition had spoken of the landscape-gardener as of the poet; yet it seemed to my friend that the creation of the landscape-garden offered to the proper Muse the most magnificent of opportunities. Here, indeed, was the fairest field for the display of imagination in the endless combining of forms of novel beauty; the elements to enter into combination being, by a vast superiority, the most glorious which the earth could afford. In the multiform and multicolor of the flower and the trees, he recognised the most direct and energetic efforts of Nature at physical loveliness. And in the direction or concentration of this effort—or, more properly, in its adaptation to the eyes which were to behold it on earth—he perceived that he should be employing the best means—laboring to the greatest advantage—in the fulfillment, *not only* of his *own* destiny as poet, *but of the august purposes for which the Deity had implanted the poetic sentiment in man.*

"Its adaptation to the eyes which were to behold it on earth." In his explanation of this phraseology, Mr. Ellison did much toward solving what has always seemed to me an enigma:—I mean the fact (which none but the ignorant dispute) that no such combination of scenery exists in nature as the painter of genius may produce. No such paradises are to be found in reality as have glowed on the canvas of Claude. In the most enchanting of natural landscapes there will always be found a defect or an excess—many excesses and defects. While the component parts may defy, individually, the highest skill of the artist, the arrangement of these parts will always be susceptible of improvement. In short, no position can be attained on the wide surface on the *natural* earth, from which an artistical eye, looking steadily, will not find matter of offense in what is termed the "composition" of the landscape. And yet how unintelligible is this! In all other matters we are justly instructed to regard nature as supreme. With her details we shrink from competition. Who shall presume to imitate the colors of a tulip, or to improve the proportions of the lily of the valley? The criticism which says, of sculpture or portraiture, that here nature is to be exalted or idealized rather than imitated, is in error. No pictorial or sculptural combinations of points of human loveliness do more than approach the living and breathing beauty [as it gladdens our daily path. Byron, who often erred, erred not in saying,

I've seen more living beauty, ripe and real,
Than all the nonsense of their stone ideal.][8]

In landscape alone is the principle of the critic true; and, having felt its truth here, it is but the headlong spirit of generalization which has led him to pronounce it true throughout all the domains of art. Having I say, *felt* its truth here, for the feeling is no affectation or chimera. The mathematics afford no more absolute demonstrations than the sentiment of his art yields the artist. He not only believes, but positively knows, that such and such apparently arbitrary arrangements of matter constitute and alone constitute the true beauty. His reasons, however, have not yet been matured into expression. It remains for a more profound analysis than the world has yet seen, fully to investigate and express them. Nevertheless he is confirmed in his instinctive opinions by the voice of all his brethren. Let a "composition" be defective; let an emendation be wrought in its mere arrangement of form; let this emendation be submitted to every artist in the world; by each will its necessity be admitted. And even far more than this:—in remedy of the defective composition, each insulated member of the fraternity would have suggested the identical emendation.

I repeat that in landscape arrangements alone is the physical nature susceptible of exaltation, and that, therefore, her susceptibility of improvement at this one point, was a mystery I had been unable to solve. *My own thoughts on the subject had rested in the idea that the primitive intention of nature would have so arranged the earth's surface as to have fulfilled at all points man's sense of perfection in the beautiful, the sublime, or the picturesque; but that this primitive intention had been frustrated by the known geological disturbances—disturbances of form and color-grouping, in the correction or allaying of which lies the soul of art. The force of this idea was much weakened, however, by the necessity which it involved of considering the disturbances abnormal and unadapted to any purpose. It was Ellison who suggested that they were prognostic of *death.* He thus explained:—Admit the earthly immortality of man to have been the first intention. We have then the primitive arrangement of the earth's surface adapted to his

---

[8]**Claude:** Claude Lorrain (1600–82), an important French landscape painter whose works strongly influenced many artists of Poe's day. Poe selected his example well: Claude Lorrain began with fine topographical sketches, but his final paintings are not at all literal records of the places in Italy which his sketches record. See Figure 8 (page 208). Hess argues for another painter's impact on this story; he says that Poe used both Thomas Cole's series of paintings "The Voyage of Life" and Cole's notes to his paintings (Mabbott III). **Byron . . . *ideal:*** Poe has altered lines from Canto 2, CXVIII of *Don Juan,* part of a description of Haidée, selected because Byron also compares life to sculpture:

. . . for she was one
Fit for the model of a statuary
(A race of mere imposters, when all's done—
I've seen much finer women, ripe and real,
Than all the nonsense of their stone ideal).

Figure 8. Claude Lorrain, *An Idyl* (*Pastoral Landscape*), 1640s. An especially appropriate illustration: not merely a landscape by "Claude," but one which shows an artist at work, perhaps "emending" what appears before him. See note 8. Spencer Museum of Art, the University of Kansas, Gift of the Barbara Benton Wescoe Fund.

blissful estate, as not existent but designed. The disturbances were the preparations for his subsequently conceived deathful condition.*

"Now," said my friend, "what we regard as exaltation of the landscape may be really such, as respects only the moral or human *point of view.* Each alternation of the natural scenery may possibly effect a blemish in the picture, if we can suppose this picture viewed at large—in mass—from some point distant from the earth's surface, although not beyond the limits of its atmosphere. It is easily understood that what might improve a closely scrutinized detail, may at the same time injure a general or more distantly observed effect. There *may* be a class of beings, human once, but now invisible to humanity, to whom, from afar, our disorder may seem order—our unpicturesqueness, picturesque; in a word, the earth-angels, for whose scrutiny more especially than our own, and for whose death-refined appreciation of the beautiful, may have been set in array by God the wide landscape-gardens of the hemispheres."[9]

[9]This paragraph and the one above are the most heavily rewritten in the piece. Poe apparently felt that Ellison's point about a beauty different from the kind mortal artists know was extremely important. His revisions do not change his meaning; rather, they explain it and make his point more explicit. For a fuller discussion of the idea that the design of the earth

In the course of discussion, my friend quoted some passages from a writer on landscape-gardening, who has been supposed to have well treated his theme:

> There are properly but two styles of landscape-gardening, the natural and the artificial. One seeks to recall the original beauty of the country, by adapting its means to the surrounding scenery; cultivating trees in harmony with the hills or plain of the neighboring land; detecting and bringing into practice those nice relations of size, proportion and color which, hid from the common observer, are revealed everywhere to the experienced student of nature. The result of the natural style of gardening is seen rather in the absence of all defects and incongruities—in the prevalence of a healthy harmony and order—than in the creation of any special wonders or miracles. The artificial style has as many varieties as there are diferent tastes to gratify. It has a certain general relation to the various styles of building. There are the stately avenues and retirements of Versailles[10]; Italian terraces; and a various mixed old English style, which bears some relation to the domestic Gothic or English Elizabethan architecture. Whatever may be said against the abuses of the artificial landscape-gardening, a mixture of pure art in a garden scene adds to it a great beauty. This is partly pleasing to the eye, by the show of order and design, and partly moral. A terrace, with an old moss-covered balustrade, calls up at once to the eye the fair forms that have passed there in other days. The slightest exhibition of art is an evidence of care and human interest.

"From what I have already observed," said Ellison, "you will understand that I reject the idea, here expressed, of recalling the original beauty of the country. The original beauty is never so great as that which may be introduced. Of course, everything depends on the selection of a spot with capabilities. What is said about detecting and bringing into practice nice relations of size, proportion, and color, is one of those mere vaguenesses of speech which serve to veil inaccuracy of thought. The phrase quoted may mean anything, or nothing, and guides in no degree. That the true result of the natural style of gardening is seen rather in the absence of all defects and incongruities than in the creation of any special wonders or miracles, is a proposition better suited to the grovelling apprehension of the herd than to the fervid dreams of the man of genius. The negative merit suggested appertains to that hobbling criticism which, in letters, would elevate Addison into apotheosis. In truth, while that virtue which consists in the mere avoidance of vice

---

is intended to reflect man's mortality, see his lengthy metaphysical discourse *Eureka:* "In the Original Unity of the First Thing lies the Secondary Cause of All Things, with the Germ of their Inevitable Annihilation."

[10]**healthy:** The early version has "beautiful" instead of "healthy." Most minor changes of this sort are for stylistic reasons and are not mentioned here, but this one is interesting. The garden which Ellison creates is surprisingly artificial, elaborate, un-"natural." It may be that the change here from "beautiful" to "healthy" is to make the point that the writer whom Ellison is quoting, in stressing "healthy" order, is missing the point that beauty (which we've just been told might be better perceived after death) may not be a matter of "health." Ellison says in the first sentence of the next paragraph that he rejects this writer's ideas. **Versailles:** The elaborate French palace and gardens in the city of Versailles near Paris.

appeals directly to the understanding, and can thus be circumscribed in *rule,* the loftier virtue, which flames in creation, can be apprehended in its results alone. Rule applies but to the merits of denial—to the excellencies which refrain. Beyond these, the critical art can but suggest. We may be instructed to build a "Cato," but we are in vain told *how* to conceive a Parthenon or an "Inferno."[11] The thing done, however; the wonder accomplished; and the capacity for apprehension becomes universal. The sophists of the negative school who, through inability to create, have scoffed at creation, are now found the loudest in applause. What, in its chrysalis condition of principle, affronted their demure reason, never fails, in its maturity of accomplishment, to extort admiration from their instinct of beauty.

"The author's observations on the artificial style," continued Ellison, "are less objectionable. A mixture of pure art in a garden scene adds to it a great beauty. This is just; as also is the reference to the sense of human interest. The principle expressed is incontrovertible—but there may be something beyond it. There may be an object in keeping with the principle—an object unattainable by the means ordinarily possessed by individuals, yet which, if attained, would lend a charm to the landscape-garden far surpassing that which a sense of merely human interest could bestow. A poet, having very unusual pecuniary resources, might, while retaining the necessary idea of art, or culture, or, as our author expresses it, of interest, so imbue his designs at once with extent and novelty of beauty, as to convey the sentiment of spiritual interference. It will be seen that, in bringing about such result, he secures all the advantages of interest or *design,* while relieving his work of the harshness or technicality of the worldly *art.* In the most rugged wildernesses—in the most savage of the scenes of pure nature—there is apparent the art of a creator; yet this art is apparent to reflection only; in no respect has it the obvious force of a feeling. Now let us suppose this sense of the Almighty design to

---

[11]**fervid:** Ellison comes by his creativity easily, but even his dreams are "fervid." Poe is describing the attributes of beauty, and working hard to destroy any preconceptions the reader may have about balance, symmetry, order, or serenity. **Addison:** Joseph Addison, the neoclassical essayist (1672–1719). Poe is attacking neoclassical notions of beauty by way of preparing us for the very different kind of beauty embodied in Ellison's garden. **"Cato" . . . "Inferno":** Interesting that Poe uses Addison's tragedy "Cato" (first produced in 1713) to represent the neoclassical ideals he is attacking, but groups the Parthenon, which is generally considered a triumph of classicism, with Dante's "Inferno" as an example of the more unrestrained creativity he advocated. In the earlier version of the story he used different examples:

> We may be instructed to build an Odyssey, but it is in vain that we are told *how* to conceive a "Tempest," an "Inferno," a "Prometheus Bound," a "Nightingale," such as that of Keats, or the "Sensitive Plant" of Shelley.

We guess that Poe was unsure of the examples which would illustrate works of the "negative school." Perhaps it is not entirely accurate to say that he was attacking classical ideals; his target rather was simply the idea of restraint, understood to mean a check on being "fervid" (see above). We find it hard to think of the Parthenon as "fervid." The religion which the Parthenon served, of course, was strongly occult; it might be that Poe was telling us that there is more to classicism than restraint and order: if English neoclassicism (Addison) was urbane, polished, and orderly, Greek classicism had been magical.

be *one step depressed*[12]—to be brought into something like harmony or consistency with the sense of human art—to form an intermedium between the two:*—let us imagine, for example, a landscape whose combined vastness and definitiveness—whose united beauty, magnificence, and *strangeness,* shall convey the idea of care, or culture, or superintendence, on the parts of beings superior, yet akin to humanity—then the sentiment of *interest* is preserved, while the art involved is made to assume the air of an intermediate or secondary nature—a nature which is not God, nor an emanation from God, but which still is nature in the sense of the handiwork of the angels that hover between man and God."

It was in devoting his enormous wealth to the embodiment of a vision such as this—in the free exercise in the open air ensured by the personal superintendence of his plans—in the unceasing object which these plans afforded—in the high spirituality of the object—in the contempt of ambition which it enabled him truly to feel—*in the perennial springs with which it gratified, without possibility of satiating, that one master passion of his soul, the thirst for beauty*; above all, it was in the sympathy of a woman, *not unwomanly, whose loveliness and love enveloped his existence in the purple atmosphere of Paradise,* that Ellison thought to find, *and found,* exemption from the ordinary cares of humanity, with a far greater amount of positive happiness than ever glowed in the rapt daydreams of De Staël.[13]

I despair of conveying to the reader any distinct conception of the marvels which my friend did actually accomplish. I wish to describe, but am disheartened by the difficulty of description, and hesitate between detail and generality. Perhaps the better course will be to unite the two in their extremes.

Mr. Ellison's first step regarded, of course, the choice of a locality; and scarcely had he commenced thinking on this point, when the luxuriant nature of the Pacific Islands arrested his attention. In fact, he had made up his mind for a voyage to the South Seas, when a night's reflection induced him to abandon the idea. "Were I misanthropic," he said, "such a *locale* would suit me. The thoroughness of its insulation and seclusion, and the difficulty of ingress and egress, would in such case be the charm of charms; but as yet I am not Timon.[14] I wish the composure but not the depression of solitude. There must remain with me a certain control over the extent and duration of my repose. There will be frequent hours in which I shall need, too, the sympathy of the poetic in what I have done. Let me seek, then, a spot not far from a populous city—whose vicinity, also, will best enable me to execute my plans."

---

[12]Poe tinkered extensively with the sentence structure and wording of this paragraph, mostly to increase clarity and to improve parallelism. At this point, he added a clause and changed "*harmonized*" to "*one step depressed.*"

[13]This is the end of "The Landscape Garden." The rest of "The Domain of Arnheim" is new. **Madame de Staël:** Germaine Necker (1766–1817), a French novelist and critic noted for her belief in a Romantic aesthetic. Like Poe, she contrasts clarity, order, and form with mystery, emotion, and indefiniteness, and like him, too, she prefers the latter.

[14]Timon of Athens is always used as an example of misanthropy. There are a Shakespeare play, *The Life of Timon of Athens,* a brief account of him in Plutarch's *Lives,* and a dialogue by Lucian, *Timon, or the Misanthrope.*

In search of a suitable place so situated, Ellison travelled for several years, and I was permitted to accompany him. A thousand spots with which I was enraptured he rejected without hesitation, for reasons which satisfied me, in the end, that he was right. We came at length to an elevated table-land of wonderful fertility and beauty, affording a panoramic prospect very little less in extent than that of Ætna,[15] and, in Ellison's opinion as well as my own, surpassing the far-famed view from that mountain in all the true elements of the picturesque.

"I am aware," said the traveller, as he drew a sigh of deep delight after gazing on this scene, entranced, for nearly an hour, "I know that here, in my circumstances, nine-tenths of the most fastidious of men would rest content. This panorama is indeed glorious, and I should rejoice in it but for the excess of its glory. The taste of all the architects I have ever known leads them, for the sake of 'prospect,' to put up buildings on hill-tops. The error is obvious. Grandeur in any of its moods, but especially in that of extent, startles, excites—and then fatigues, depresses. For the occasional scene nothing can be better—for the constant view nothing worse. And, in the constant view, the most objectionable phase of grandeur is that of extent; the worst phase of extent, that of distance. It is at war with the sentiment and with the sense of *seclusion*—the sentiment and sense which we seek to humor in 'retiring to the country.' In looking from the summit of a mountain we cannot help feeling *abroad* in the world. The heart-sick avoid distant prospects as a pestilence."

It was not until toward the close of the fourth year of our search that we found a locality with which Ellison professed himself satisfied. It is, of course, needless to say *where* was the locality. The late death of my friend, in causing his domain to be thrown open to certain classes of visiters, has given to *Arnheim* a species of secret and subdued if not solemn celebrity, similar in kind, although infinitely superior in degree, to that which so long distinguished Fonthill.[16]

The usual approach to Arnheim was by the river. The visiter left the city in the early morning. During the forenoon he passed between shores of a tranquil and domestic beauty, on which grazed innumerable sheep, their white fleeces spotting the vivid green of rolling meadows. By degrees the idea of cultivation subsided into that of merely pastoral care. This slowly became merged in a sense of retirement—this again in a consciousness of solitude. As the evening approached the channel grew more narrow; the banks more and more precipitous; and these latter were clothed in richer, more profuse, and more sombre foliage. The water increased in transparency. The stream took a thousand turns, so that at no moment could its gleaming surface be seen for a greater distance than a furlong. At every instant the vessel seemed imprisoned within an enchanted circle, having insuperable and impenetrable walls of foliage, a roof of ultra-marine satin, and *no* floor—the keel balancing itself with admirable nicety on that of a phantom bark which, by some accident having been turned upside down, floated in constant company

[15]Etna, the volcano in Sicily.

[16]Fonthill Abbey was an early and rather silly example of English interest in reviving Gothic architecture. When a large portion of the building collapsed, its owner is supposed to have been delighted: now he had not only his own Gothic building, but a Gothic ruin.

with the substantial one, for the purpose of sustaining it. The channel now became a *gorge*—although the term is somewhat inapplicable, and I employ it merely because the language has no word which better represents the most striking—not the most distinctive—feature of the scene. The character of gorge was maintained only in the height and parallelism of the shores; it was lost altogether in their other traits. The walls of the ravine (through which the clear water still tranquilly flowed) arose to an elevation of a hundred and occasionally of a hundred and fifty feet, and inclined so much toward each others as, in a great measure, to shut out the light of day; while the long plume-like moss which depended densely from the intertwining shrubberies overhead, gave the whole chasm an air of funereal gloom. The windings because more frequent and intricate, and seemed often as if returning in upon themselves, so that the voyager had long lost all idea of direction. He was, moreover, enwrapt in an exquisite sense of the strange.[17] The thought of nature still remained, but her character seemed to have undergone modification: there was a weird symmetry, a thrilling uniformity, a wizard propriety in these her works. Not a dead branch—not a withered leaf—not a stray pebble—not a patch of the brown earth was anywhere visible. The crystal water welled up against the clean granite, or the unblemished moss, with a sharpness of outline that delighted while it bewildered the eye.

Having threaded the mazes of this channel for some hours, the gloom deepening every moment, a sharp and unexpected turn of the vessel brought it suddenly, as if dropped from heaven, into a circular basin of very considerable extent when compared with the width of the gorge. It was about two hundred yards in diameter, and girt in at all points but one—that immediately fronting the vessel as it entered—by hills equal in general height to the walls of the chasm, although of a thoroughly different character. Their sides sloped from the water's edge at an angle of some forty-five degrees, and they were clothed from base to summit—not a perceptible point escaping—in a drapery of the most gorgeous flower-blossoms; scarcely a green leaf being visible among the sea of odorous and fluctuating color. This basin was of great depth, but so transparent was the water that the bottom, which seemed to consist of a thick mass of small round alabaster pebbles, was distinctly visible by glimpses—that is to say, whenever the eye could permit itself *not* to see, far down in the inverted Heaven, the duplicate blooming of the hills. On these latter there were no trees, nor even shrubs of any size. The impressions wrought on the observer were those of richness, warmth, color, quietude, uniformity, softness, delicacy, daintiness, voluptuousness, and a miraculous extremeness of culture that suggested dreams of a new race of fairies, laborious, tasteful, magnificent and fastidious; but as the eye traced upward the myriad-tinted slope, from its sharp junction with the water to its vague termination amid the folds of overhanging cloud, it became, indeed, difficult not to fancy a panoramic cataract of rubies, sapphires, opals and golden onyxes, rolling silently out of the sky.

---

[17]From here to the end of the tale Poe gives us a description of what to him represents ideal beauty. "Funereal gloom," intricacy, and strangeness may not match our preconceptions of the components of beauty, but the passage is important for an understanding of Poe's taste.

The visiter, shooting suddenly into this bay from out of the gloom of the ravine, is delighted but astounded by the full orb of the declining sun, which he had supposed to be already far below the horizon, but which now confronts him, and forms the sole termination of an otherwise limitless vista seen through another chasm-like rift in the hills.

But here the voyager quits the vessel which has borne him so far, and descends into a light canoe of ivory, stained with Arabesque[18] devices in vivid scarlet, both within and without. The poop and beak of this boat arise high above the water with sharp points, so that the general form is that of an irregular crescent. It lies on the surface of the bay with the proud grace of a swan. On its ermined floor reposes a single feathery paddle of satinwood; but no oarsman or attendant is to be seen. The guest is bidden to be of good cheer—that the fates will take care of him. The larger vessel disappears, and he is left alone in the canoe, which lies apparently motionless in the middle of the lake. While he considers what course to pursue, however, he becomes aware of a gentle movement in the fairy bark. It slowly swings itself around until its prow points toward the sun. It advances with a gentle but gradually accelerated velocity, while the slight ripples it creates seem to break about the ivory sides in divinest melody—seem to offer the only possible explanation of the soothing yet melancholy music for whose unseen origin the bewildered voyager looks around him in vain.

The canoe steadily proceeds, and the rocky gate of the vista is approached, so that its depths can be more distinctly seen. To the right arise a chain of lofty hills rudely and luxuriantly wooded. It is observed, however, that the trait of exquisite *cleanness* where the bank dips into the water, still prevails. There is not one token of the usual river *débris.* To the left the character of the scene is softer and more obviously artificial. Here the bank slopes upward from the stream in a very gentle ascent, forming a broad sward of grass of a texture resembling nothing so much as velvet, and of a brilliancy of green which would bear comparison with the tint of the purest emerald. This *plateau* varies in width from ten to three hundred yards; reaching from the river bank to a wall, fifty feet high, which extends, in an infinity of curves, but following the general direction of the river, until lost in the distance to the westward. This wall is of one continuous rock, and has been formed by cutting perpendicularly the once rugged precipice of the stream's southern bank; but no trace of the labor has been suffered to remain. The chiselled stone has the hue of ages and is profusely overhung and overspread with the ivy, the coral honeysuckle, the eglantine, and the clematis. The uniformity of the top and bottom lines of the wall is fully relieved by occasional trees of gigantic height, growing singly or in small groups, both along the *plateau* and in the domain behind the wall, but in close proximity to it; so that frequent limbs (of the black walnut especially) reach over and dip their pendent extremities into the water. Farther back within the domain, the vision is impeded by an impenetrable screen of foliage.

---

[18]Poe means "elaborate and intertwined, but nonrepresentational, ornamentation," as in Moorish or Arabian architecture. Much Arabesque ornamentation involves stylized representation of leaves and flowers. See our headnote.

These things are observed during the canoe's gradual approach to what I have called the gate of the vista. On drawing nearer to this, however, its chasm-like appearance vanishes; a new outlet from the bay is discovered to the left—in which direction the wall is also seen to sweep, still following the general course of the stream. Down this new opening the eye cannot penetrate very far; for the stream, accompanied by the wall, still bends to the left, until both are swallowed up by the leaves.

The boat, nevertheless, glides magically into the winding channel; and here the shore opposite the wall is found to resemble that opposite the wall in the straight vista. Lofty hills, rising occasionally into mountains, and covered with vegetation in wild luxuriance, still shut in the scene.

Floating gently onward, but with a velocity slightly augmented, the voyager, after many short turns, finds his progress apparently barred by a gigantic gate or rather door of burnished gold, elaborately carved and fretted, and reflecting the direct rays of the now fast-sinking sun with an effulgence that seems to wreath the whole surrounding forest in flames. This gate is inserted in the lofty wall; which here appears to cross the river at right angles. In a few moments, however, it is seen that the main body of the water still sweeps in a gentle and extensive curve to the left, the wall following it as before, while a stream of considerable volume, diverging from the principal one, makes its way, with a slight ripple, under the door, and is thus hidden from sight. The canoe falls into the lesser channel and approaches the gate. Its ponderous wings are slowly and musically expanded. The boat glides between them, and commences a rapid descent into a vast amphitheatre entirely begirt with purple mountains, whose bases are laved by a gleaming river throughout the full extent of their circuit. Meantime the whole Paradise of Arnheim bursts upon the view. There is a gush of entrancing melody; there is an oppressive sense of strange sweet odor;—there is a dream-like intermingling to the eye of tall slender Eastern trees—bosky shrubberies—flocks of golden and crimson birds—lily-fringed lakes—meadows of violets, tulips, poppies, hyacinths and tuberoses—long intertangled lines of silver streamlets—and, upspringing confusedly from amid all, a mass of semi-Gothic, semi-Saracenic[19] architecture, sustaining itself as if by miracle in mid-air, glittering in the red sunlight with a hundred oriels, minarets, and pinnacles; and seeming the phantom handiwork, conjointly, of the Sylphs, of the Fairies, of the Genii, and of the Gnomes.

[19] Arabian. We have now been taken, in our little boat, through a carefully programmed tour of an artificially "augmented" fairyland in which lighting effects are controlled, doors swing open as we approach, and music plays for us. The irreverent thought is irrepressible—Arnheim is Anaheim, Disneyland.

THE TELL-TALE HEART

Nathaniel Hawthorne kept notebooks in which he collected ideas to be developed into sketches and stories; some were merely news items which stirred his imagination, such as the one about the man who, on a whim, decided not to come home one night, and who did not then return to his wife for decades. "Wakefield" is the famous result. Poe's imagination responded to topics of popular interest, too. Daniel Webster, hired as a special prosecutor in a celebrated murder case, published a pamphlet account of the trial; moved by it, Poe produced "The Tell-Tale Heart," whose very language echoes Webster.

Webster wrote,

> *He has done the murder. No eye has seen him, no ear has heard him. The secret is his own, and it is safe.*
>
> . . . .
>
> *The guilty soul cannot keep its own secret. It is false to itself; or rather it feels an irresistible impulse to be true to itself. It labors under its guilty possession and knows not what to do with it. The human heart was not made for residence of such an inhabitant. . . . The secret which the murderer possesses soon comes to possess him; and like the evil spirits of which we read, it overcomes him, and leads him whithersoever it will. He feels it beating at his heart, rising to his throat and demanding disclosure. He thinks the whole world sees it in his face, reads it in his eyes, and almost hears its workings in the very silence of his thoughts. It has become his master. . . . It must be confessed, it will be confessed. (Mabbott 9, III, following Bjurman)*

As Krappe points out, there is also a Dickens tale with very similar ideas. "The Tell-Tale Heart," then, reminds us again how badly we distort Poe if we jump blithely from the horror in his prose to our pet psychological theories about his personality, for his fiction grew largely from the texture of his readings and surroundings.

PUBLICATIONS IN POE'S TIME

The Pioneer, January 1843
The Dollar Newspaper, Philadelphia, January 25, 1843
The Broadway Journal, August 23, 1845
The Spirit of the Times, Philadelphia, August 27, 1845

THE TELL-TALE HEART

True!—nervous—very, very dreadfully nervous I had been and am; but why *will* you say that I am mad? The disease had sharpened my senses—not destroyed—not dulled them. Above all was the sense of hearing acute. I heard all things in the heaven and in the earth. I heard many things in hell. How, then, am I mad? Hearken! and observe how healthily—how calmly I can tell you the whole story.[1]

It is impossible to say how first the idea entered my brain; but once conceived, it haunted me day and night. Object there was none. Passion there was none. I loved the old man. He had never wronged me. He had never given me insult. For his gold I had no desire. I think it was his eye! yes, it was this! One of his eyes resembled that of a vulture—a pale blue eye, with a film over it. Whenever it fell upon me, my blood ran cold; and so by degrees—very gradually—I made up my mind to take the life of the old man, and thus rid myself of the eye forever.

Now this is the point. You fancy me mad. Madmen know nothing. But you should have seen *me*. You should have seen how wisely I proceeded—with what caution—with what foresight—with what dissimulation I went to work! I was never kinder to the old man than during the whole week before I killed him. And every night, about midnight, I turned the latch of his door and opened it—oh so gently! And then, when I had made an opening sufficient for my head, I put in a dark lantern, all closed, closed, so that no light shone out, and then I thrust in my head. Oh, you would have laughed to see how cunningly I thrust it in! I moved it slowly—very, very slowly, so that I might not disturb the old man's sleep. It took me an hour to place my whole head within the opening so far that I could see him as he lay upon his bed. Ha!—would a madman have been so wise as this? And then, when my head was well in the room, I undid the lantern cautiously—oh, so cautiously—cautiously (for the hinges creaked)—I undid it just so much that a single thin ray fell upon the vulture eye. And this I did for seven long nights—every night just at midnight—but I found the eye always closed; and so it was impossible to do the work; for it was not the old man who vexed me, but his Evil Eye. And every morning, when the day broke, I went boldly into the chamber, and spoke courageously to him, calling him by name in a hearty tone, and inquiring how he had passed the night. So you see he would have been a very profound old man, indeed, to suspect that every night, just at twelve, I looked in upon him while he slept.

Upon the eighth night I was more than usually cautious in opening the door. A watch's minute hand moves more quickly than did mine. Never before that night, had I *felt* the extent of my own powers—of my sagacity. I could scarcely contain my feelings of triumph. To think that there I was, opening the door, little by little, and he not even to dream of my secret deeds or thoughts. I fairly chuckled at the idea; and perhaps he heard me; for he moved on the bed suddenly, as if startled.

---

[1]The narrator's "nervousness" is a version of Poe's frequently used device of establishing plausibility and tone through heightened states of consciousness.

Now you may think that I drew back—but no. His room was as black as pitch with the thick darkness, (for the shutters were close fastened, through fear of robbers,) and so I knew that he could not see the opening of the door, and I kept pushing it on steadily, steadily.

I had my head in, and was about to open the lantern, when my thumb slipped upon the tin fastening, and the old man sprang up in bed, crying out—"Who's there?"

I kept quite still and said nothing. For a whole hour I did not move a muscle, and in the meantime I did not hear him lie down. He was still sitting up in the bed listening;—just as I have done, night after night, hearkening to the death-watches in the wall.[2]

Presently I heard a slight groan, and I knew it was the groan of mortal terror. It was not a groan of pain or of grief—oh, no!—it was the low stifled sound that arises from the bottom of the soul when overcharged with awe. I knew the sound well. Many a night, just at midnight, when all the world slept, it has welled up from my own bosom, deepening, with its dreadful echo, the terrors that distracted me. I say I knew it well. I knew what the old man felt, and pitied him, although I chuckled at heart. I knew that he had been lying awake ever since the first slight noise, when he had turned in the bed. His fears had been ever since growing upon him. He had been trying to fancy them causeless, but could not. He had been saying to himself—"It is nothing but the wind in the chimney—it is only a mouse crossing the floor," or "it is merely a cricket which has made a single chirp." Yes, he had been trying to comfort himself with these suppositions: but he had found all in vain. *All in vain;* because Death, in approaching him, had stalked with his black shadow before him, and enveloped the victim. And it was the mournful influence of the unperceived shadow that caused him to feel—although he neither saw nor heard—to *feel* the presence of my head within the room.

When I had waited a long time, very patiently, without hearing him lie down, I resolved to open a little—a very, very little crevice in the lantern. So I opened it—you cannot imagine how stealthily, stealthily—until, at length a simple dim ray, like the thread of the spider, shot from out the crevice and fell full upon the vulture eye.

It was open—wide, wide open—and I grew furious as I gazed upon it. I saw it with perfect distinctness—all a dull blue, with a hideous veil over it that chilled the very marrow in my bones; but I could see nothing else of the old man's face or person: for I had directed the ray as if by instinct, precisely upon the damned spot.

And have I not told you that what you mistake for madness is but over acuteness of the senses?—now, I say, there came to my ears a low, dull, quick sound, such as a watch makes when enveloped in cotton. I knew *that* sound well, too. It was the beating of the old man's heart. It increased my fury, as the beating of a drum stimulates the soldier into courage.

But even yet I refrained and kept still. I scarcely breathed. I held the lantern

---

[2]The "death-watch" is a popular nickname for any of several kinds of insects which make a rumpus in old wood. Poe knew about them from his work on Thomas Wyatt's *Synopsis of Natural History* (Reilly, Robinson, Mabbott 9, III)

motionless. I tried how steadily I could maintain the ray upon the eye. Meantime the hellish tattoo of the heart increased. It grew quicker and quicker, and louder and louder every instant. The old man's terror *must* have been extreme! It grew louder, I say, louder every moment!—do you mark me well? I have told you that I am nervous: so I am. And now at the dead hour of the night, amid the dreadful silence of that old house, so strange a noise as this excited me to uncontrollable terror. Yet, for some minutes longer I refrained and stood still. But the beating grew louder, louder! I thought the heart must burst. And now a new anxiety seized me—the sound would be heard by a neighbor! The old man's hour had come! With a loud yell, I threw open the lantern and leaped into the room. He shrieked once—once only. In an instant I dragged him to the floor, and pulled the heavy bed over him. I then smiled gaily, to find the deed so far done. But, for many minutes, the heart beat on with a muffled sound. This, however, did not vex me; it would not be heard through the wall. At length it ceased. The old man was dead. I removed the bed and examined the corpse. Yes, he was stone, stone dead. I placed my hand upon the heart and held it there many minutes. There was no pulsation. He was stone dead. His eye would trouble me no more.

If still you think me mad, you will think so no longer when I describe the wise precautions I took for the concealment of the body. The night waned, and I worked hastily, but in silence. First of all I dismembered the corpse. I cut off the head and the arms and the legs.

I then took up three planks from the flooring of the chamber, and deposited all between the scantlings. I then replaced the boards so cleverly, so cunningly, that no human eye—not even *his*—could have detected any thing wrong. There was nothing to wash out—no stain of any kind—no blood-spot whatever. I had been too wary for that. A tub had caught all—ha! ha!

When I had made an end of these labors, it was four o'clock—still dark as midnight. As the bell sounded the hour, there came a knocking at the street door. I went down to open it with a light heart,—for what had I *now* to fear? There entered three men, who introduced themselves, with perfect suavity, as officers of the police. A shriek had been heard by a neighbor during the night; suspicion of foul play had been aroused; information had been lodged at the police office, and they (the officers) had been deputed to search the premises.

I smiled,—for *what* had I to fear? I bade the gentlemen welcome. The shriek, I said, was my own in a dream. The old man, I mentioned, was absent in the country. I took my visitors all over the house. I bade them search—search *well*. I led them, at length, to *his* chamber. I showed them his treasures, secure, undisturbed. In the enthusiasm of my confidence, I brought chairs into the room, and desired them *here* to rest from their fatigues, while I myself, in the wild audacity of my perfect triumph, placed my own seat upon the very spot beneath which reposed the corpse of the victim.

The officers were satisfied. My *manner* had convinced them. I was singularly at ease. They sat, and while I answered cheerily, they chatted of familiar things. But, ere long, I fetl myself getting pale and wished them gone. My head ached, and I fancied a ringing in my ears: but still they sat and still chatted. The ringing became more distinct:—it continued and became more distinct: I talked more freely to get rid of the feeling: but it continued and gained definiteness—until, at length, I found that the noise was *not* within my ears.

No doubt I now grew *very* pale;—but I talked more fluently, and with a heightened voice. Yet the sound increased—and what could I do? It was *a low, dull, quick sound—much a sound as a watch makes when enveloped in cotton.* I gasped for breath—and yet the officers heard it not. I talked more quickly—more vehemently; but the noise steadily increased. I arose and argued about trifles, in a high key and with violent gesticulations; but the noise steadily increased. Why *would* they not be gone? I paced the floor to and fro with heavy strides, as if excited to fury by the observations of the men—but the noise steadily increased. Oh God! what *could* I do? I foamed—I raved—I swore! I swung the chair upon which I had been sitting, and grated it upon the boards, but the noise arose over all and continually increased. It grew louder—louder—*louder!* And still the men chatted pleasantly, and smiled. Was it possible they heard not? Almighty God!—no, no! They heard!—they suspected!—they *knew!*—they were making a mockery of my horror!—this I thought, and this I think. But anything was better than this agony! Anything was more tolerable than this derision! I could bear those hypocritical smiles no longer! I felt that I must scream or die! and now—again!—hark! louder! louder! louder! *louder!*

"Villains!" I shrieked, "dissemble no more! I admit the deed!—tear up the planks! here, here!—it is the beating of his hideous heart!"

The Gold-Bug

Mr. Legrand's instability is not as serious as the narrator imagines, of course; Legrand knows what he is about. He is an impecunious scientific amateur who has been bitten by a gold-bug different from the one Jupiter imagines. Yet the hint of mental instability, the high excitement under which he operates on his quest, and the brilliance of his solution clearly indicate Poe's usual pattern—creativity is associated with madness. Note also that the relationship between the narrator and Legrand is very similar to that between the narrator and Dupin in the Parisian detective tales: the narrator is a friend who plays "straight man."

Poe's stereotype of the ex-slave Jupiter is in his usual racially offensive manner, part of the illiberal line which Kaplan feels culminates in a racist allegory at the close of Poe's novel, The Narrative of Arthur Gordon Pym. *But the treatment is at least good humored here, rather in the vein of Poe's treatment of the black character in his incomplete novel* The Journal of Julius Rodman. *Jupiter is loyal and superstitious. He also talks funny; his misunderstandings produce some bad puns. Yet he is unafraid of a skull ("somebody bin lef him head up de tree") or of climbing an enormous yellow poplar ("tulip tree").*

Some critics of Poe believe that he deliberately sustained a reputation as a kind of wizard, that the pose gave him an effective and memorable public "image." Bragging about his prowess as decipherer of codes and puzzles may have been part of Poe's pose. Magazines of the period were filled with puzzles and curiosities, and Poe exploited popular interest in them in numerous ways, among them an article in Alexander's Weekly Messenger *(December 18, 1839) in which he offered to decipher cryptograms, and a follow-up piece in* Graham's *(July 1841), in which he claimed to have solved all but one of the hundred or so submitted. His fibbing does not obscure his sure sense of reader interest; newspapers, popular magazines, and literary reviews still tantalize subscribers with puzzles of the same sort.*

Publications in Poe's Time

The Dollar Newspaper, June 21 and 28, 1843 (serially, with first part repeated on June 28)
The Dollar Newspaper, supplement, July 12, 1843
The Volunteer, Montrose, Pa., August 3, 10, and 17, 1843
Revue britannique, French translation, 1845
Tales, 1845
The Gold Bug, separate pamphlet, London, 1846–47
Boston Museum, June 22, 1848

La Democratie pacifique, French translation, May 23, 25, and 27, 1848
Le Journal du Loiret, French translation, June 17, 20, 22, and 24, 1848
Saturday Courier, July 1 and 8, 1848

THE GOLD-BUG

What ho! what ho! this fellow is dancing mad!
He hath been bitten by the Tarantula.
All in the Wrong.[1]

Many years ago, I contracted an intimacy with a Mr. William Legrand. He was of an ancient Huguenot family, and had once been wealthy; but a series of misfortunes had reduced him to want. To avoid the mortification consequent upon his disasters, he left New Orleans, the city of his forefathers, and took up his residence at Sullivan's Island, near Charleston, South Carolina.

This Island is a very singular one. It consists of little else than the sea sand, and is about three miles long. Its breadth at no point exceeds a quarter of a mile. It is separated from the main land by a scarcely perceptible creek, oozing its ways through a wilderness of reeds and slime, a favorite resort of the marsh-hen. The vegetation, as might be supposed, is scant, or at least dwarfish. No trees of any magnitude are to be seen. Near the western extremity, where Fort Moultrie stands, and where are some miserable frame buildings, tenanted, during summer, by the fugitives from Charleston dust and fever, may be found, indeed, the bristly palmetto; but the whole island, with the exception of this western point, and a line of hard, white beach on the seacoast, is covered with a dense undergrowth of the sweet myrtle, so much prized by the horticulturists of England. The shrub here often attains the height of fifteen or twenty feet, and forms an almost impenetrable coppice, burthening the air with its fragrance.

In the inmost recesses of this coppice, not far from the eastern or more remote end of the island, Legrand had built himself a small hut, which he occupied when I first, by mere accident, made his acquaintance. This soon ripened into friendship—for there was much in the recluse to excite interest and esteem. I found him well educated, with unusual powers of mind, but infected with misanthropy, and subject to perverse moods of alternate enthusiasm and melancholy. He had with him many books, but rarely employed them. His chief amusements were gunning

[1]There is a play by this name by Arthur Murphy (1730–1805), but these lines are not in it; indeed, the play is in prose (Carlson 2; Pollin 3). T. O. Mabbott (5) thinks Poe wrote the lines himself, basing them on his memories of Frederick Reynold's comedy, *The Democrat* (1789), which Poe quoted elsewhere. A tarantula bite is "supposed to cause a mania for dancing" (Carlson).

and fishing, or sauntering along the beach and through the myrtles, in quest of shells or entomological specimens;—his collection of the latter might have been envied by a Swammerdamm.[2] In these excursions he was usually accompanied by an old negro, called Jupiter, who had been manumitted before the reverses of the family, but who could be induced, neither by threats nor by promises, to abandon what he considered his right of attendance upon the footsteps of his young "Massa Will." It is not improbable that the relatives of Legrand, conceiving him to be somewhat unsettled in intellect, had contrived to instil this obstinacy into Jupiter, with a view to the supervision and guardianship of the wanderer.

The winters in the latitude of Sullivan's Island are seldom very severe, and in the fall of the year it is a rare event indeed when a fire is considered necessary. About the middle of October, 18—, there occurred, however, a day of remarkable chilliness. Just before sunset I scrambled my way through the evergreens to the hut of my friend, whom I had not visited for several weeks—my residence being, at that time, in Charleston, a distance of nine miles from the Island, while the facilities of passage and re-passage were very far behind those of the present day. Upon reaching the hut I rapped, as was my custom, and getting no reply, sought for the key where I knew it was secreted, unlocked the door and went in. A fine fire was blazing upon the hearth. It was a novelty, and by no means an ungrateful one. I threw off an overcoat, took an armchair by the crackling logs, and awaited patiently the arrival of my hosts.

Soon after dark they arrived, and gave me a most cordial welcome. Jupiter, grinning from ear to ear, bustled about to prepare some marsh-hens for supper. Legrand was in one of his fits—how else shall I term them?—of enthusiasm. He had found an unknown bivalve, forming a new genus, and, more than this, he had hunted down and secured, with Jupiter's assistance, a *scarabæus*[3] which he believed to be totally new, but in respect to which he wished to have my opinion on the morrow.

"And why not to-night?" I asked, rubbing my hands over the blaze, and wishing the whole tribe of *scarabæi* at the devil.

"Ah, if I had only known you were here!" said Legrand, "but it's so long since I saw you; and how could I foresee that you would pay me a visit this very night of all others? As I was coming home I met Lieutenant G——, from the fort,[4] and, very foolishly, I lent him the bug; so it will be impossible for you to see it until morning. Stay here to-night, and I will send Jup down for it at sunrise. It is the loveliest thing in creation!"

"What?—sunrise?"

"Nonsense! no!—the bug. It is of a brilliant gold color—about the size of a

---

[2]Jan Swammerdam (1637–80), Dutch entomologist.

[3]Beetle. A. H. Quinn says Poe's bug might be a combination of the characteristics of two insects which inhabit the area, one a large gold and green beetle, the other a common click beetle which has the spots described in the tale. The real "gold-bug," *Callichroma splendidum,* can bite, as Jupiter says, though it is not of the family scarabæus.

[4]Fort Moultrie, on the western end of the island. Poe served there in the army from late 1827 to late 1828.

large hickory-nut—with two jet black spots near one extremity of the back, and another, somewhat longer, at the other. The *antennæ* are—"

"Dey aint *no* tin in him, Massa Will, I keep a tellin on you," here interrupted Jupiter; "de bug is a goole bug, solid, ebery bit of him, inside and all, sep him wing—neber feel half so hebby a bug in my life."

"Well, suppose it is, Jup," replied Legrand, somewhat more earnestly, it seemed to me, than the case demanded, "is that any reason for your letting the birds burn? The color"—here he turned to me—"is really almost enough to warrant Jupiter's idea. You never saw a more brilliant metallic lustre than the scales emit—but of this you cannot judge till to-morrow. In the mean time I can give you some idea of the shape." Saying this, he seated himself at a small table, on which were a pen and ink, but no paper. He looked for some in a drawer, but found none.

"Never mind," said he at length, "this will answer;" and he drew from his waistcoat pocket a scrap of what I took to be very dirty foolscap, and made upon it a rough drawing with the pen. While he did this, I retained my seat by the fire, for I was still chilly. When the design was complete, he handed it to me without rising. As I received it, a loud growl was heard, succeeded by a scratching at the door. Jupiter opened it, and a large Newfoundland, belonging to Legrand, rushed in, leaped upon my shoulders, and loaded me with caresses; for I had shown him much attention during previous visits. When his gambols were over, I looked at the paper, and, to speak the truth, found myself not a little puzzled at what my friend had depicted.

"Well!" I said, after contemplating it for some minutes, "this *is* a strange *scarabaeus,* I must confess: new to me: never saw anything like it before—unless it was a skull, or a death's-head—which it more nearly resembles than anything else that has come under *my* observation."

"A death's-head!" echoed Legrand—"Oh—yes—well, it has something of that appearance upon paper, no doubt. The two upper black spots look like eyes, eh? and the longer one at the bottom like a mouth—and then the shape of the whole is oval."

"Perhaps so," said I; "but, Legrand, I fear you are no artist. I must wait until I see the beetle itself, if I am to form any idea of its personal appearance."

"Well, I don't know," said he, a little nettled, "I draw tolerably—*should* do it at least—have had good masters, and flatter myself that I am not quite a blockhead."

"But, my dear fellow, you are joking then," said I, "this is a very passable *skull*—indeed, I may say that it is a very *excellent* skull, according to the vulgar notions about such specimens of physiology—and your *scarabæus* must be the queerest *scarabæus* in the world if it resembles it. Why, we may get up a very thrilling bit of superstition upon this hint. I presume you will call the bug *scarabæus caput hominis,*[5] or something of that kind—there are many similar titles in the Natural Histories. But where are the *antennæ* you spoke of?"

"The *antennæ!*" said Legrand, who seemed to be getting unaccountably warm upon the subject; "I am sure you must see the *antennæ.* I made them as distinct as they are in the original insect, and I presume that is sufficient."

[5]"Man-head beetle."

"Well, well," I said, "perhaps you have—still I don't see them;" and I handed him the paper without additional remark, not wishing to ruffle his temper; but I was much surprised at the turn affairs had taken; his ill humor puzzled me—and, as for the drawing of the beetle, there were positively *no antennæ* visible, and the whole *did* bear a very close resemblance to the ordinary cuts of a death's-head.

He received the paper very peevishly, and was about to crumple it, apparently to throw it in the fire, when a casual glance at the design seemed suddenly to rivet his attention. In an instant his face grew violently red—in another as excessively pale. For some moments he continued to scrutinize the drawing minutely where he sat. At length, he arose, took a candle from the table, and proceeded to seat himself upon a sea-chest in the farthest corner of the room. Here again he made an anxious examination of the paper; turning it in all directions. He said nothing, however, and his conduct greatly astonished me; yet I thought it prudent not to exacerbate the growing moodiness of his temper by any comment. Presently he took from his coat pocket a wallet, placed the paper carefully in it, and deposited both in a writing-desk, which he locked. He now grew more composed in his demeanor; but his original air of enthusiasm had quite disappeared. Yet he seemed not so much sulky as abstracted. As the evening wore away he became more and more absorbed in reverie, from which no sallies of mine could arouse him. It had been my intention to pass the night at the hut, as I had frequently done before, but, seeing my host in this mood, I deemed it proper to take leave. He did not press me to remain, but, as I departed, he shook my hand with even more than his usual cordiality.

It was about a month after this (and during the interval I had seen nothing of Legrand) when I received a visit, at Charleston, from his man, Jupiter. I had never seen the good old negro look so dispirited, and I feared that some serious disaster had befallen my friend.

"Well, Jup," said I, "what is the matter now?—how is your master?"

"Why, to speak de troof, massa, him not so berry well as mought be."

"Not well! I am truly sorry to hear it. What does he complain of?"

"Dar! dat's it!—him neber plain of notin—but him berry sick for all dat."

"*Very* sick, Jupiter!—why didn't you say so at once? Is he confined to bed?"

"No, dat he aint!—he aint find nowhar—dat's just whar de shoe pinch—my mind is got to be berry hebby bout poor Massa Will."

"Jupiter, I should like to understand what it is you are talking about. You say your master is sick. Hasn't he told you what ails him?"

"Why, massa, taint worf while for to git mad bout de matter—Massa Will say noffin at all aint de matter wid him—but den what make him go about looking dis here way, wid he head down and he soldiers up, and as white as a gose? And den he keep a syphon all de time—"

"Keeps a what, Jupiter?"

"Keeps a syphon wid de figgurs on de slate—de queerest figgurs I ebber did see. Ise gittin to be skeered, I tell you. Hab for to keep mighty tight eye pon him noovers. Todder day he gib me slip fore de sun up and was gone de whole ob de blessed day. I had a big stick ready cut for to gib him d——d good beating when he did come—but Ise sich a fool dat I hadn't de heart arter all—he look so berry poorly."

"Eh?—what?—ah yes!—upon the whole I think you had better not be too severe with the poor fellow—don't flog him, Jupiter—he can't very well stand it—but can you form no idea of what has occasioned this illness, or rather this change of conduct? Has anything unpleasant happened since I saw you?"

"No, massa, dey aint bin noffin onpleasant *since* den—'t was *fore* den I'm feared—'t was de berry day you was dare."

"How? what do you mean?"

"Why, massa, I mean de bug—dare now."

"The what?"

"De bug—I'm berry sartain dat Massa Will bin bit somewhere bout de head by dat goole-bug."

"And what cause have you, Jupiter, for such a supposition?"

"Claws enuff, massa, and mouff too. I nebber did see sich a d——d bug—he kick and he bite ebery ting what cum near him. Massa Will cotch him fuss, but had for to let him go gin mighty quick, I tell you—den was de time he must ha got de bite. I didn't like de look ob de bug mouff, myself, no how, so I wouldn't take hold ob him wid my finger, but I cotch him wid a piece ob paper dat I found. I rap him up in de paper and stuff piece ob it in he mouff—dat was de way."

"And you think, then, that your master was really bitten by the beetle, and that the bite made him sick?"

"I don't tink noffin about it—I nose it. What make him dream bout de goole so much, if taint cause he bit by de goole-bug? Ise heerd bout dem goole-bugs fore dis."

"But how do you know he dreams about gold?"

"How I know? why cause he talk about it in he sleep—dat's how I nose."

"Well, Jup, perhaps you are right; but to what fortunate circumstance am I to attribute the honor of a visit from you to-day?"

"What de matter, massa?"

"Did you bring any message from Mr. Legrand?"

"No, massa, I bring dis here pissel;" and here Jupiter handed me a note which ran thus:

MY DEAR ——

Why have I not seen you for so long a time? I hope you have not been so foolish as to take offence at any little *brusquerie*[6] of mine; but no, that is improbable.

Since I saw you I have had great cause for anxiety. I have something to tell you, yet scarcely know how to tell it, or whether I should tell it at all.

I have not been quite well for some days past, and poor old Jup annoys me, almost beyond endurance, by his well-meant attentions. Would you believe it?—he had prepared a huge stick, the other day, with which to chastise me for giving him the slip, and spending the day, *solus*[7], among the hills on the main land. I verily believe that my ill looks alone saved me a flogging.

I have made no addition to my cabinet since we met.

---

[6]Brusqueness, bluntness.

[7]Alone.

If you can, in any way, make it convenient, come over with Jupiter. *Do* come. I wish to see you *to-night,* upon business of importance. I assure you that it is of the *highest* importance.

Ever yours,

William Legrand.

There was something in the tone of this note which gave me great uneasiness. Its whole style differed materially from that of Legrand. What could he be dreaming of? What new crotchet possessed his excitable brain? What "business of the highest importance" could *he* possibly have to transact? Jupiter's account of him boded no good. I dreaded lest the continued pressure of misfortune had, at length, fairly unsettled the reason of my friend. Without a moment's hesitation, therefore, I prepared to accompany the negro.

Upon reaching the wharf, I noticed a scythe and three spades, all apparently new, lying in the bottom of the boat in which we were to embark.

"What is the meaning of all this, Jup?" I inquired.

"Him syfe, massa, and spade."

"Very true; but what are they doing here?"

"Him de syfe and de spade what Massa Will sis pon my buying for him in de town, and de debbil's own lot of money I had to gib for em."

"But what, in the name of all that is mysterious, is your 'Massa Will' going to do with scythes and spades?"

"Dat's more dan *I* know, and debbil take me if I don't blieve 't is more dan he know, too. But it's all cum ob de bug."

Finding that no satisfaction was to be obtained of Jupiter, whose whole intellect seemed to be absorbed by "de bug," I now stepped into the boat and made sail. With a fair and strong breeze we soon ran into the little cove to the northward of Fort Moultrie, and a walk of some two miles brought us to the hut. It was about three in the afternoon when we arrived. Legrand had been awaiting us in eager expectation. He grasped my hand with a nervous *empressment*[8] which alarmed me and strengthened the suspicions already entertained. His countenance was pale even to ghastliness, and his deep-set eyes glared with unnatural lustre. After some inquiries respecting his health, I asked him, not knowing what better to say, if he had yet obtained the *scarabæus* from Lieutenant G——.

"Oh, yes," he replied, coloring violently, "I got it from him the next morning. Nothing should tempt me to part with that *scarabæus.* Do you know that Jupiter is quite right about it?"

"In what way?" I asked, with a sad foreboding at heart.

"In supposing it to be a bug of *real gold.*" He said this with an air of profound seriousness, and I felt inexpressibly shocked.

"This bug is to make my fortune," he continued, with a triumphant smile, "to reinstate me in my family possessions. Is it any wonder, then, that I prize it? Since Fortune has thought fit to bestow it upon me, I have only to use it properly and I shall arrive at the gold of which it is the index. Jupiter, bring me that *scarabæus!*"

---

[8]Eagerness.

"What! de bug, massa? I'd rudder not go fer trubble dat bug—you mus git him for your own self." Hereupon Legrand arose, with a grave and stately air, and brought me the beetle from a glass case in which it was enclosed. It was a beautiful *scarabæus,* and, at that time, unknown to naturalists—of course a great prize in a scientific point of view. There were two round, black spots near one extremity of the back, and a long one near the other. The scales were exceedingly hard and glossy, with all the appearance of burnished gold. The weight of the insect was very remarkable, and, taking all things into consideration, I could hardly blame Jupiter for his opinion respecting it; but what to make of Legrand's agreement with that opinion, I could not, for the life of me, tell.

"I sent for you," said he, in a grandiloquent tone, when I had completed my examination of the beetle, "I sent for you, that I might have your counsel and assistance in furthering the views of Fate and of the bug"—

"My dear Legrand," I cried, interrupting him, "you are certainly unwell, and had better use some little precautions. You shall go to bed, and I will remain with you a few days, until you get over this. You are feverish and"—

"Feel my pulse," said he.

I felt it, and, to say the truth, found not the slightest indication of fever.

"But you may be ill and yet have no fever. Allow me this once to prescribe for you. In the first place, go to bed. In the next"—

"You are mistaken," he interposed, "I am as well as I can expect to be under the excitement which I suffer. If you really wish me well, you will relieve this excitement."

"And how is this to be done?"

"Very easily. Jupiter and myself are going upon an expedition into the hills, upon the main land, and, in this expedition, we shall need the aid of some person in whom we can confide. You are the only one we can trust. Whether we succeed or fail, the excitement which you now perceive in me will be equally allayed."

"I am anxious to oblige you in any way," I replied; "but do you mean to say that this infernal beetle has any connection with your expedition into the hills?"

"It has."

"Then, Legrand, I can become a party to no such absurd proceedings."

"I am sorry—very sorry—for we shall have to try it by ourselves."

"Try it by yourselves! The man is surely mad!—but stay!—how long do you propose to be absent?"

"Probably all night. We shall start immediately, and be back, at all events, by sunrise."

"And will you promise me, upon your honor, that when this freak of yours is over, and the bug business (good God!) settled to your satisfaction, you will then return home and follow my advice implicitly, as that of your physician?"

"Yes; I promise; and now let us be off, for we have no time to lose."

With a heavy heart I accompanied my friend. We started about four o'clock—Legrand, Jupiter, the dog, and myself. Jupiter had with him the scythe and spades—the whole of which he insisted upon carrying—more through fear, it seemed to me, of trusting either of the implements within reach of his master, than from any excess of industry or complaisance. His demeanor was dogged in the extreme, and "dat d——d bug" were the sole words which escaped his lips during the journey. For my own part, I had charge of a couple of dark lanterns, while Legrand contented himself with the *scarabæus,* which he carried attached to the end of a bit of whip-cord; twirling it to and fro, with the air of a conjuror, as he went. When I observed this last, plain evidence of my friend's aberration of mind, I could scarcely refrain from tears. I thought it best, however, to humor his fancy, at least for the present, or until I could adopt some more energetic measures with a chance of success. In the mean time I endeavored, but all in vain, to sound him in regard to the object of the expedition. Having succeeded in inducing me to accompany him, he seemed unwilling to hold conversation upon any topic of minor importance, and to all my questions vouchsafed no other reply than "we shall see!"

We crossed the creek at the head of the island by means of a skiff, and, ascending the high grounds on the shore of the main land, proceeded in a north-westerly direction, through a tract of country excessively wild and desolate, where no trace of a human footstep was to be seen. Legrand led the way with decision; pausing only for an instant, here and there, to consult what appeared to be certain landmarks of his own contrivance upon a former occasion.

In this manner we journeyed for about two hours, and the sun was just setting when we entered a region infinitely more dreary than any yet seen. It was a species of table land, near the summit of an almost inaccessible hill, densely wooded from base to pinnacle, and interspersed with huge crags that appeared to lie loosely upon the soil, and in many cases were prevented from precipitating themselves into the valleys below, merely by the support of the trees against which they reclined. Deep ravines, in various directions, gave an air of still sterner solemnity to the scene.

The natural platform to which we had clambered was thickly overgrown with brambles, through which we soon discovered that it would have been impossible to force our way but for the scythe; and Jupiter, by direction of his master, proceeded to clear for us a path to the foot of an enormously tall tulip-tree, which stood, with some eight or ten oaks, upon the level, and far surpassed them all, and all other trees which I had then ever seen, in the beauty of its foliage and form, in the wide spread of its branches, and in the general majesty of its appearance. When we reached this tree, Legrand turned to Jupiter, and asked him if he thought he could climb it. The old man seemed a little staggered by the question, and for some moments made no reply. At length he approached the huge trunk, walked slowly around it, and examined it with minute attention. When he had completed his scrutiny, he merely said,

"Yes, massa, Jup climb any tree he ebber see in he life."

"Then up with you as soon as possible, for it will soon be too dark to see what we are about."

"How far mus go up, massa?" inquired Jupiter.

"Get up the main trunk first, and then I will tell you which way to go—and here—stop! take this beetle with you."

"De bug, Massa Will!—de goole bug!" cried the negro, drawing back in dismay—"what for mus tote de bug way up de tree?—d——n if I do!"

"If you are afraid, Jup, a great big negro like you, to take hold of a harmless little dead beetle, why you can carry it up by this string—but, if you do not take it up with you in some way, I shall be under the necessity of breaking your head with this shovel."

"What de matter now, massa?" said Jup, evidently shamed into compliance; "always want for to raise fuss wid old nigger. Was only funnin any how. *Me* feered de bug! what I keer for de bug?" Here he took cautiously hold of the extreme end of the string, and, maintaining the insect as far from his person as circumstances would permit, prepared to ascend the tree.

In youth, the tulip-tree, or *Liriodendron Tulipiferum,*[9] the most magnificent of American foresters, has a trunk peculiarly smooth, and often rises to a great height without lateral branches; but, in its riper age, the bark becomes gnarled and uneven, while many short limbs make their appearance on the stem. Thus the difficulty of ascension, in the present case, lay more in semblance than in reality. Embracing the huge cylinder, as closely as possible, with his arms and knees, seizing with his hands some projections, and resting his naked toes upon others, Jupiter, after one or two narrow escapes from falling, at length wriggled himself into the first great fork, and seemed to consider the whole business as virtually accomplished. The *risk* of the achievement was, in fact, now over, although the climber was some sixty or seventy feet from the ground.

"Which way mus go now, Massa Will?" he asked.

"Keep up the largest branch—the one on this side," said Legrand. The negro obeyed him promptly, and apparently with but little trouble; ascending higher and higher, until no glimpse of his squat figure could be obtained through the dense foliage which enveloped it. Presently his voice was heard in a sort of halloo.

"How much fudder is got for go?"

"How high up are you?" asked Legrand.

"Ebber so fur," replied the negro; "can see de sky fru de top ob de tree."

"Never mind the sky, but attend to what I say. Look down the trunk and count the limbs below you on this side. How many limbs have you passed?"

"One, two, tree, four, fibe—I done pass fibe big limb, massa, pon dis side."

"Then go one limb higher."

In a few minutes the voice was heard again, announcing that the seventh limb was attained.

"Now, Jup," cried Legrand, evidently much excited, "I want you to work your way out upon that limb as far as you can. If you see anything strange, let me know."

By this time what little doubt I might have entertained of my poor friend's insanity, was put finally at rest. I had no alternative but to conclude him stricken with lunacy, and I became seriously anxious about getting him home. While I was pondering upon what was best to be done, Jupiter's voice was again heard.

---

[9]*Liriodendron tulipifera,* the yellow poplar or tulip tree (Carlson 2). Poe mentions it a number of times—see "Landor's Cottage" and "Morning on the Wissahiccon" in Levine (4).

"Mos feerd for to ventur pon dis limb berry far—'tis dead limb putty much all de way."

"Did you say it was a *dead* limb, Jupiter?" cried Legrand in a quavering voice.

"Yes, massa, him dead as de door-nail—done up for sartain—done departed dis here life."

"What in the name of heaven shall I do?" asked Legrand, seemingly in the greatest distress.

"Do!" said I, glad of an opportunity to interpose a word, "why come home and go to bed. Come now!—that's a fine fellow. It's getting late, and, besides, you remember your promise."

"Jupiter," cried he, without heeding me in the least, "do you hear me?"

"Yes, Massa Will, hear you ebber so plain."

"Try the wood well, then, with your knife, and see if you think it *very* rotten."

"Him rotten, massa, sure nuff," replied the negro in a few moments, "but not so berry rotten as mought be. Mought ventur out leetle way pon de limb by myself, dat's true."

"By yourself!—what do you mean?"

"Why I mean de bug. 'Tis *berry* hebby bug. Spose I drop him down fuss, and den de limb won't break wid just de weight ob one nigger."

"You infernal scoundrel!" cried Legrand, apparently much relieved, "what do you mean by telling me such nonsense as that? As sure as you let that beetle fall!—I'll break your neck. Look here, Jupiter! do you hear me?"

"Yes, massa, needn't hollo at poor nigger dat style."

"Well, now listen!—if you will venture out on the limb as far as you think safe, and not let go the beetle, I'll make you a present of a silver dollar as soon as you get down."

"I'm gwine, Massa Will—deed I is," replied the negro very promptly—"mos out to the eend now."

"*Out to the end!*" here fairly screamed Legrand, "do you say you are out to the end of that limb?"

"Soon be to de eend, massa,—o-o-o-o-oh! Lor-gol-a-marcy! what *is* dis here pon de tree?"

"Well!" cried Legrand, highly delighted, "what is it?"

"Why taint noffin but a skull—somebody bin lef him head up de tree, and de crows done gobble ebery bit ob de meat off."

"A skull, you say!—very well!—how is it fastened to the limb?—what holds it on?"

"Sure nuff, massa; mus look. Why dis berry curous sarcumstance, pon my word—dare's a great big nail in de skull, what fastens ob it on to de tree."

"Well now, Jupiter, do exactly as I tell you—do you hear?"

"Yes, massa."

"Pay attention, then!—find the left eye of the skull."

"Hum! hoo! dat's good! why dar aint no eye lef at all."

"Curse your stupidity! do you know your right hand from your left?"

"Yes I nose dat—nose all bout dat—tis my left hand what I chops de wood wid."

"To be sure! you are left-handed; and your left eye is on the same side as your left hand. Now, I suppose, you can find the left eye of the skull, or the place where the left eye has been. Have you found it?"

Here was a long pause. At length the negro asked,

"Is de lef eye of de skull pon de same side as de lef hand of de skull, too?—cause de skull aint got not a bit ob a hand at all—nebber mind! I got de lef eye now—here the lef eye! what mus do wid it?"

"Let the beetle drop through it, as far as the string will reach—but be careful and not let go your hold of the string."

"All dat done, Massa Will; mighty easy ting for to put de bug fru de hole—look out for him dar below!"

During this colloquy no portion of Jupiter's person could be seen; but the beetle, which he had suffered to descend, was now visible at the end of the string, and glistened, like a globe of burnished gold, in the last rays of the setting sun, some of which still faintly illumined the eminence upon which we stood. The *scarabœus* hung quite clear of any branches, and, if allowed to fall, would have fallen at our feet. Legrand immediately took the scythe, and cleared with it a circular space, three or four yards in diameter, just beneath the insect, and, having accomplished this, ordered Jupiter to let go the string and come down from the tree.

Driving a peg, with great nicety, into the ground, at the precise spot where the beetle fell, my friend now produced from his pocket a tape-measure. Fastening one end of this at that point of the trunk of the tree which was nearest the peg, he unrolled it till it reached the peg, and thence farther unrolled it, in the direction already established by the two points of the tree and the peg, for the distance of fifty feet—Jupiter clearing away the brambles with the scythe. At the spot thus attained a second peg was driven, and about this, as a centre, a rude circle, about four feet in diameter, described. Taking now a spade himself, and giving one to Jupiter and one to me, Legrand begged us to set about digging as quickly as possible.

To speak the truth, I had no especial relish for such amusement at any time, and, at that particular moment, would most willingly have declined it; for the night was coming on, and I felt much fatigued with the exercise already taken; but I saw no mode of escape, and was fearful of disturbing my poor friend's equanimity by a refusal. Could I have depended, indeed, upon Jupiter's aid, I would have had no hesitation in attempting to get the lunatic home by force; but I was too well assured of the old negro's disposition, to hope that he would assist me, under any circumstances, in a personal contest with his master. I made no doubt that the latter had been infected with some of the innumerable Southern superstitions about money buried, and that his phantasy had received confirmation by the finding of the *scarabœus,* or, perhaps, by Jupiter's obstinacy in maintaining it to be "a bug of real gold." A mind disposed to lunacy would readily be led away by such suggestions—especially if chiming in with favorite preconceived ideas—and then I called to mind the poor fellow's speech about the beetle's being "the index of his fortune." Upon the whole, I was sadly vexed and puzzled, but, at length, I concluded to make a virtue of necessity—to dig with a good will, and thus the sooner to convince the visionary, by ocular demonstration, of the fallacy of the opinions he entertained.

The lanterns having been lit, we all fell to work with a zeal worthy a more rational cause; and, as the glare fell upon our persons and implements, I could not help thinking how picturesque a group we composed, and how strange and suspicious our labors must have appeared to any interloper who, by chance, might have stumbled upon our whereabouts.

We dug very steadily for two hours. Little was said; and our chief embarrassment lay in the yelpings of the dog, who took exceeding interest in our proceedings. He, at length, became so obstreperous that we grew fearful of his giving the alarm to some stragglers in the vicinity;—or, rather, this was the apprehension of Legrand;—for myself, I should have rejoiced at any interruption which might have enabled me to get the wanderer home. The noise was, at length, very effectually silenced by Jupiter, who, getting out of the hole with a dogged air of deliberation, tied the brute's mouth up with one of his suspenders, and then returned, with a grave chuckle, to his task.

When the time mentioned had expired, we had reached a depth of five feet, and yet no signs of any treasure became manifest. A general pause ensued, and I began to hope that the farce was at an end. Legrand, however, although evidently much disconcerted, wiped his brow thoughtfully and recommenced. We had excavated the entire circle of four feet diameter, and now we slightly enlarged the limit, and went to the farther depth of two feet. Still nothing appeared. The gold-seeker, whom I sincerely pitied, at length clambered from the pit, with the bitterest disappointment imprinted upon every feature, and proceeded, slowly and reluctantly, to put on his coat, which he had thrown off at the beginning of his labor. In the mean time I made no remark. Jupiter, at a signal from his master, began to gather up his tools. This done, and the dog having been unmuzzled, we turned in profound silence towards home.

We had taken, perhaps, a dozen steps in this direction, when, with a loud oath, Legrand strode up to Jupiter, and seized him by the collar. The astonished negro opened his eyes and mouth to the fullest extent, let fall the spades, and fell upon his knees.

"You scoundrel," said Legrand, hissing out the syllables from between his clenched teeth—"you infernal black villain!—speak, I tell you!—answer me this instant, without prevarication!—which—which is your left eye?"

"Oh, my golly, Massa Will! aint dis here my lef eye for sartain?" roared the terrified Jupiter, placing his hand upon his *right* organ of vision, and holding it there with a desperate pertinacity, as if in immediate dread of his master's attempt at a gouge.

"I thought so!—I knew it!—hurrah!" vociferated Legrand, letting the negro go, and executing a series of curvets and caracols,[10] much to the astonishment of his valet, who, arising from his knees, looked, mutely, from his master to myself, and then from myself to his master.

---

[10]These are terms of horsemanship; Legrand in effect kicks up his heels. The usual English spelling is "caracoles."

"Come! we must go back," said the latter, "the game's not up yet;" and he again led the way to the tulip-tree.

"Jupiter," said he, when we reached its foot, "come here! was the skull nailed to the limb with the face outward, or with the face to the limb?"

"De face was out, massa, so dat de crows could get at de eyes good, widout any trouble."

"Well, then, was it this eye or that through which you let the beetle fall?"—here Legrand touched each of Jupiter's eyes.

"'T was dis eye, massa—de lef eye—jis as you tell me," and here it was his right eye that the negro indicated.

"That will do—we must try it again."

Here my friend, about whose madness I now saw, or fancied that I saw, certain indications of method, removed the peg which marked the spot where the beetle fell, to a spot about three inches to the westward of its former position. Taking, now, the tape-measure from the nearest point of the trunk to the peg, as before, and continuing the extension in a straight line to the distance of fifty feet, a spot was indicated, removed, by several yards, from the point at which we had been digging.

Around the new position a circle, somewhat larger than in the former instance, was now described, and we again set to work the spades. I was dreadfully weary, but, scarcely understanding what had occasioned the change in my thoughts, I felt no longer any great aversion from the labor imposed. I had become most unaccountably interested—nay, even excited. Perhaps there was something, amid all the extravagant demeanor of Legrand—some air of forethought, or of deliberation, which impressed me. I dug eagerly, and now and then caught myself actually looking, with something that very much resembled expectation, for the fancied treasure, the vision of which had demented my unfortunate companion. At a period when such vagaries of thought most fully possessed me, and when we had been at work perhaps an hour and a half, we were again interrupted by the violent howlings of the dog. His uneasiness, in the first instance, had been, evidently, but the result of playfulness or caprice, but he now assumed a bitter and serious tone. Upon Jupiter's again attempting to muzzle him, he made furious resistance, and, leaping into the hole, tore up the mould frantically with his claws. In a few seconds he had uncovered a mass of human bones, forming two complete skeletons, intermingled with several buttons of metal, and what appeared to be the dust of decayed woollen. One or two strokes of a spade upturned the blade of a large Spanish knife, and, as we dug farther, three or four loose pieces of gold and silver coin came to light.

At sight of these the joy of Jupiter could scarcely be restrained, but the countenance of his master wore an air of extreme disappointment. He urged us, however, to continue our exertions, and the words were hardly uttered when I stumbled and fell forward, having caught the toe of my boot in a large ring of iron that lay half buried in the loose earth.

We now worked in earnest, and never did I pass ten minutes of more intense excitement. During this interval we had fairly unearthed an oblong chest of wood, which, from its perfect preservation, and wonderful hardness, had plainly been subjected to some mineralizing process—perhaps that of the Bi-chloride of Mercury.[11] This box was three feet and a half long, three feet broad, and two and a half feet deep. It was firmly secured by bands of wrought iron, riveted, and forming a kind of trellis-work over the whole. On each side of the chest, near the top, were three rings of iron—six in all—by means of which a firm hold could be obtained by six persons. Our utmost united endeavors served only to disturb the coffer very slightly in its bed. We at once saw the impossibility of removing so great a weight. Luckily, the sole fastenings of the lid consisted of two sliding bolts. These we drew back—trembling and panting with anxiety. In an instant, a treasure of incalculable value lay gleaming before us. As the rays of the lanterns fell within the pit, there flashed upwards, from a confused heap of gold and of jewels, a glow and a glare that absolutely dazzled our eyes.

I shall not pretend to describe the feelings with which I gazed. Amazement was, of course, predominant. Legrand appeared exhausted with excitement, and spoke very few words. Jupiter's countenance wore, for some minutes, as deadly a pallor as it is possible, in the nature of things, for any negro's visage to assume. He seemed stupified—thunder-stricken. Presently he fell upon his knees in the pit, and, burying his naked arms up to the elbows in gold, let them there remain, as if enjoying the luxury of a bath. At length, with a deep sigh, he exclaimed, as if in a soliloquy,

"And dis all cum ob de goole-bug! de putty goole-bug! de poor little goole-bug, what I boosed in dat sabage kind ob style! Aint you shamed ob yourself, nigger?—answer me dat!"

It became necessary, at last, that I should arouse both master and valet to the expediency of removing the treasure. It was growing late, and it behooved us to make exertion, that we might get every thing housed before daylight. It was difficult to say what should be done; and much time was spent in deliberation—so confused were the ideas of all. We, finally, lightened the box by removing two thirds of its contents, when we were enabled, with some trouble, to raise it from the hole. The articles taken out were deposited among the brambles, and the dog left to guard them, with strict orders from Jupiter neither, upon any pretence, to stir from the spot, nor to open his mouth until our return. We then hurriedly made for home with the chest; reaching the hut in safety, but after excessive toil, at one o'clock in the morning. Worn out as we were, it was not in human nature to do more just then. We rested until two, and had supper; starting for the hills immediately afterwards, armed with three stout sacks, which, by good luck, were upon the premises. A little before four we arrived at the pit, divided the remainder of the booty, as equally as might be, among us, and, leaving the holes unfilled, again set out for the hut, at which, for the second time, we deposited our golden burthens, just as the first streaks of the dawn gleamed from over the tree-tops in the East.

We were now thoroughly broken down; but the intense excitement of the time denied us repose. After an unquiet slumber of some three or four hours' duration, we arose, as if by preconcert, to make examination of our treasure.

The chest had been full to the brim, and we spent the whole day, and the greater

---

[11] $HgCl_2$, mercuric chloride, used to preserve museum specimens and wood.

part of the next night, in a scrutiny of its contents. There had been nothing like order or arrangement. Every thing had been heaped in promiscuously. Having assorted all with care, we found ourselves possessed of even vaster wealth than we had at first supposed. In coin there was rather more than four hundred and fifty thousand dollars—estimating the value of the pieces, as accurately as we could, by the tables of the period. There was not a particle of silver. All was gold of antique date and of great variety—French, Spanish, and German money, with a few English guineas, and some counters, of which we had never seen specimens before. There were several very large and heavy coins, so worn that we could make nothing of their inscriptions. There was no American money. The value of the jewels we found more difficulty in estimating. There were diamonds—some of them exceedingly large and fine—a hundred and ten in all, and not one of them small; eighteen rubies of remarkable brilliancy;—three hundred and ten emeralds, all very beautiful; and twenty-one sapphires, with an opal. These stones had all been broken from their settings and thrown loose in the chest. The settings themselves, which we picked out from among the other gold, appeared to have been beaten up with hammers, as if to prevent identification. Besides all this, there was a vast quantity of solid gold ornaments;—nearly two hundred massive finger and ear rings;—rich chains—thirty of these, if I remember;—eighty-three very large and heavy crucifixes;—five gold censers of great value;—a prodigious golden punch-bowl, ornamented with richly chased vine-leaves and Bacchanalian figures; with two sword-handles exquisitely embossed, and many other smaller articles which I cannot recollect. The weight of these valuables exceeded three hundred and fifty pounds avoirdupois; and in this estimate I have not included one hundred and ninety-seven superb gold watches; three of the number being worth each five hundred dollars, if one. Many of them were very old, and as time keepers valueless; the works having suffered, more or less, from corrosion—but all were richly jewelled and in cases of great worth. We estimated the entire contents of the chest, that night, at a million and a half dollars; and, upon the subsequent disposal of the trinkets and jewels (a few being retained for our own use), it was found that we had greatly undervalued the treasure.

When, at length, we had concluded our examination, and the intense excitement of the time had, in some measure, subsided, Legrand, who saw that I was dying with impatience for a solution of this most extraordinary riddle, entered into a full detail of all the circumstances connected with it.

"You remember," said he, "the night when I handed you the rough sketch I had made of the *scarabœus*. You recollect also, that I became quite vexed at you for insisting that my drawing resembled a death's-head. When you first made this assertion I thought you were jesting; but afterwards I called to mind the peculiar spots on the back of the insect, and admitted to myself that your remark had some little foundation in fact. Still, the sneer at my graphic powers irritated me—for I am considered a good artist—and, therefore, when you handed me the scrap of parchment, I was about to crumple it up and throw it angrily into the fire."

"The scrap of paper, you mean," said I.

"No; it had much of the appearance of paper, and at first I supposed it to be such, but when I came to draw upon it, I discovered it, at once, to be a piece of very thin parchment. It was quite dirty, you remember. Well, as I was in the very act of crumpling it up, my glance fell upon the sketch at which you had been looking, and you may imagine my astonishment when I perceived, in fact, the figure of a death's-head just where, it seemed to me, I had made the drawing of the beetle. For a moment I was too much amazed to think with accuracy. I knew that my design was very different in detail from this—although there was a certain similarity in general outline. Presently I took a candle, and seating myself at the other end of the room, proceeded to scrutinize the parchment more closely. Upon turning it over, I saw my own sketch upon the reverse, just as I had made it. My first idea, now, was mere surprise at the really remarkable similarity of outline—at the singular coincidence involved in the fact, that unknown to me, there should have been a skull upon the other side of the parchment, immediately beneath my figure of the *scarabœus,* and that this skull, not only in outline, but in size, should so closely resemble my drawing. I say the singularity of this coincidence absolutely stupified me for a time. This is the usual effect of such coincidences. The mind struggles to establish a connection—a sequence of cause and effect—and, being unable to do so, suffers a species of temporary paralysis. But, when I recovered from this stupor, there dawned upon me gradually a conviction which startled me even far more than the coincidence. I began distinctly, positively, to remember that there had been *no* drawing on the parchment when I made my sketch of the *scarabœus.* I became perfectly certain of this; for I recollected turning up first one side and then the other, in search of the cleanest spot. Had the skull been then there, of course I could not have failed to notice it. Here was indeed a mystery which I felt it impossible to explain; but, even at that early moment, there seemed to glimmer, faintly, within the most remote and secret chambers of my intellect, a glow-worm-like conception of that truth which last night's adventure brought to so magnificent a demonstration. I arose at once, and putting the parchment securely away, dismissed all farther reflection until I should be alone.

"When you had gone, and when Jupiter was fast asleep, I betook myself to a more methodical investigation of the affair. In the first place I considered the manner in which the parchment had come into my possession. The spot where we discovered the *scarabœus* was on the coast of the main land, about a mile eastward of the island, and but a short distance above high water mark. Upon my taking hold of it, it gave me a sharp bite, which caused me to let it drop. Jupiter, within his accustomed caution, before seizing the insect, which had flown towards him, looked about him for a leaf, or something of that nature, by which to take hold of it. It was at this moment that his eyes, and mine also, fell upon the scrap of parchment, which I then supposed to be paper. It was lying half buried in the sand, a corner sticking up. Near the spot where we found it, I observed the remnants of the hull of what appeared to have been a ship's long boat. The wreck seemed to have been there for a very great while; for the resemblance to boat timbers could scarcely be traced.

"Well, Jupiter picked up the parchment, wrapped the beetle in it, and gave it to me. Soon afterwards we turned to go home, and on the way met Lieutenant G——. I showed him the insect, and he begged me to let him take it to the fort. On my consenting, he thrust it forthwith into his waistcoat pocket, without the parchment in which it had been wrapped, and which I had continued to hold in my hand during his inspection. Perhaps he dreaded my changing my mind, and thought it best to make sure of the prize at once—you know how enthusiastic he is on all subjects connected with Natural History. At the same time, without being conscious of it, I must have deposited the parchment in my own pocket.

"You remember that when I went to the table, for the purpose of making a sketch of the beetle, I found no paper where it was usually kept. I looked in the drawer, and found none there. I searched my pockets, hoping to find an old letter—and then my hand fell upon the parchment. I thus detail the precise mode in which it came into my possession; for the circumstances impressed me with peculiar force.

"No doubt you will think me fanciful—but I had already established a kind of *connection.* I had put together two links of a great chain. There was a boat lying on a sea-coast, and not far from the boat was a parchment—*not a paper*—with a skull depicted on it. You will, of course, ask 'where is the connection?' I reply that the skull, or death's-head, is the well-known emblem of the pirate. The flag of the death's-head is hoisted in all engagements.

"I have said that the scrap was parchment, and not paper. Parchment is durable—almost imperishable. Matters of little moment are rarely consigned to parchment; since, for the mere ordinary purposes of drawing or writing, it is not nearly so well adapted as paper. This reflection suggested some meaning—some relevancy—in the death's-head. I did not fail to observe, also, the *form* of the parchment. Although one of its corners had been, by some accident, destroyed, it could be seen that the original form was oblong. It was just such a slip, indeed, as might have been chosen for a memorandum—for a record of something to be long remembered and carefully preserved."

"But," I interposed, "you say that the skull was *not* upon the parchment when you made the drawing of the beetle. How then do you trace any connection between the boat and the skull—since this latter, according to your own admission, must have been designed (God only knows how or by whom) at some period subsequent to your sketching the *scarabæus?*"

"Ah, hereupon turns the whole mystery; although the secret, at this point, I had comparatively little difficulty in solving. My steps were sure, and could afford but a single result. I reasoned, for example, thus: When I drew the *scarabæus,* there was no skull apparent on the parchment. When I had completed the drawing, I gave it to you, and observed you narrowly until you returned it. *You,* therefore, did not design the skull, and no one else was present to do it. Then it was not done by human agency. And nevertheless it was done.

"At this stage of my reflections I endeavored to remember, and *did* remember, with entire distinctness, every incident which occurred about the period in question. The weather was chilly (oh rare and happy accident!), and a fire was blazing on the hearth. I was heated with exercise and sat near the table. You, however, had drawn a chair close to the chimney. Just as I placed the parchment in your hand, and as you were in the act of inspecting it, Wolf, the Newfoundland, entered, and leaped upon your shoulders. With your left hand you caressed him and kept him off, while your right, holding the parchment, was permitted to fall listlessly between your knees, and in close proximity to the fire. At one moment I thought the blaze had caught it, and was about to caution you, but, before I could speak, you had withdrawn it, and were engaged in its examination. When I considered all these particulars, I doubted not for a moment that *heat* had been the agent in bringing to light, on the parchment, the skull which I saw designed on it. You are well aware that chemical preparations exist, and have existed time out of mind, by means of which it is possible to write on either paper or vellum, so that the characters shall become visible only when subjected to the action of fire. Zaffre, digested in *aqua regia,* and diluted with four times its weight of water, is sometimes employed; a green tint results. The regulus[12] of cobalt, dissolved in spirit of nitre, gives a red. These colors disappear at longer or shorter intervals after the material written on cools, but again become apparent upon the re-application of heat.

"I now scrutinized the death's-head with care. Its outer edges—the edges of the drawing nearest the edge of the vellum—were far more *distinct* than the others. It was clear that the action of the caloric[13] had been imperfect or unequal. I immediately kindled a fire, and subjected every portion of the parchment to a glowing heat. At first, the only effect was the strengthening of the faint lines in the skull; but, on persevering in the experiment, there became visible, at the corner of the slip, diagonally opposite to the spot in which the death's-head was delineated, the figure of what I at first supposed to be a goat. A closer scrutiny, however, satisfied me that it was intended for a kid."

"Ha! ha!" said I, "to be sure I have no right to laugh at you—a million and a half of money is too serious a matter for mirth—but you are not about to establish a third link in your chain—you will not find any especial connexion between your pirates and a goat—pirates, you know, have nothing to do with goats; they appertain to the farming interest."

"But I have just said that the figure was *not* that of a goat."

"Well, a kid then—pretty much the same thing."

"Pretty much, but not altogether," said Legrand. "You may have heard of one *Captain* Kidd. I at once looked on the figure of the animal as a kind of punning or hieroglyphical signature. I say signature; because its position on the vellum suggested this idea. The death's-head at the corner diagonally opposite, had, in the same manner, the air of a stamp, or seal. But I was sorely put out by the absence of all else—of the body to my imagined instrument—of the text for my context."

"I presume you expected to find a letter between the stamp and the signature."

"Something of that kind. The fact is, I felt irresistibly impressed with a presentiment of some vast good fortune impending. I can scarcely say why. Perhaps, after all, it was rather a desire than an actual belief;—but do you know that Jupiter's silly words, about the bug being of solid gold, had a remarkable effect on my

---

[12]**Zaffre:** Zaffer, a blue pigment made from cobalt ore. ***aqua regia:*** A mixture of nitric and hydrochloric acids, which gets its name—"royal water"—from its ability to dissolve gold. **regulus:** "Metallic mass that sinks to the bottom when ore is treated" (Carlson 2).

[13]In archaic chemical usage, caloric was a subtle fluid which produced heat.

fancy? And then the series of accidents and coincidences—these were so *very* extraordinary. Do you observe how mere an accident it was that these events should have occurred on the *sole* day of all the year in which it has been, or may be, sufficiently cool for fire, and that without the fire, or without the intervention of the dog at the precise moment in which he appeared, I should never have become aware of the death's-head, and so never the possessor of the treasure?"

"But proceed—I am all impatience."

"Well; you have heard, of course, the many stories current—the thousand vague rumors afloat about money buried, somewhere on the Atlantic coast, by Kidd and his associates. These rumors must have had some foundation in fact. And that the rumors have existed so long and so continuously could have resulted, it appeared to me, only from the circumstance of the buried treasure still *remaining* entombed. Had Kidd concealed his plunder for a time, and afterwards reclaimed it, the rumors would scarcely have reached us in their present unvarying form. You will observe that the stories told are all about money-seekers, not about money-finders. Had the pirate recovered his money, there the affair would have dropped. It seemed to me that some accident—say the loss of a memorandum indicating its locality—had deprived him of the means of recovering it, and that this accident had become known to his followers, who otherwise might never have heard that treasure had been concealed at all, and who, busying themselves in vain, because unguided attempts, to regain it, had given first birth, and then universal currency, to the reports which are now so common. Have you ever heard of any important treasure being unearthed along the coast?"

"Never."

"But that Kidd's accumulations were immense, is well known. I took it for granted, therefore, that the earth still held them; and you will scarcely be surprised when I tell you that I felt a hope, nearly amounting to certainty, that the parchment so strangely found, involved a lost record of the place of deposit."

"But how did you proceed?"

"I held the vellum again to the fire, after increasing the heat; but nothing appeared. I now thought it possible that the coating of dirt might have something to do with the failure; so I carefully rinsed the parchment by pouring warm water over it, and, having done this, I placed it in a tin pan, with the skull downwards, and put the pan upon a furnace of lighted charcoal. In a few minutes, the pan having become thoroughly heated, I removed the slip, and, to my inexpressible joy, found it spotted, in several places, with what appeared to be figures arranged in lines. Again I placed it in the pan, and suffered it to remain another minute. On taking it off, the whole was just as you see it now."

Here Legrand, having re-heated the parchment, submitted it to my inspection. The following characters were rudely traced, in a red tint, between the death's-head and the goat:

53‡‡†305))6*;4826)4‡.)4‡);806*;48†8¶60))85;]8*:‡*8†83(88)5*†;46(;88*96*
?;8)*‡(;485);5*†2:*‡(;4956*2(5*—4)8¶8*;4069285);)6†8)4‡‡;1(‡9;48081
;8:8‡1;48†85;4)485†528806*81(‡9;48;(88;4(‡?34;48)4‡;161;:188;‡?;

"But," said I, returning him the slip, "I am as much in the dark as ever. Were all the jewels of Golconda[14] awaiting me on my solution of this enigma, I am quite sure that I should be unable to earn them."

"And yet," said Legrand, "the solution is by no means so difficult as you might be led to imagine from the first hasty inspection of the characters. These characters, as any one might readily guess, form a cipher—that is to say, they convey a meaning; but then, from what is known of Kidd, I could not suppose him capable of constructing any of the more abstruse cryptographs. I made up my mind, at once, that this was a simple species—such, however, as would appear, to the crude intellect of the sailor, absolutely insoluble without the key."

"And you really solved it?"

"Readily; I have solved others of an abstruseness ten thousand times greater. Circumstances, and a certain bias of mind, have led me to take interest in such riddles, and it may well be doubted whether human ingenuity can construct an enigma of the kind which human ingenuity may not, by proper application, resolve. In fact, having once established connected and legible characters, I scarcely gave a thought to the mere difficulty of developing their import.

"In the present case—indeed in all cases of secret writing—the first question regards the *language* of the cipher; for the principles of solution, so far, especially, as the more simple ciphers are concerned, depend on, and are varied by, the genius of the particular idiom. In general, there is no alternative but experiment (directed by probabilities) of every tongue known to him who attempts the solution, until the true one be attained. But, with the cipher now before us, all difficulty is removed by the signature. The pun on the word 'Kidd' is appreciable in no other language than in English. But for this consideration I should have begun my attempts with the Spanish and French, as the tongues in which a secret of this kind would most naturally have been written by a pirate of the Spanish main. As it was, I assumed the cryptograph to be English.

"You observe there are no divisions between the words. Had there been divisions, the task would have been comparatively easy. In such case I should have commenced with a collation and analysis of the shorter words, and, had a word of a single letter occurred, as is most likely, (*a* or *I,* for example,) I should have considered the solution as assured. But, there being no division, my first step was to ascertain the predominant letters, as well as the least frequent. Counting all, I constructed a table thus:

Of the character		there are
8		33.
;	"	26.
4	"	19.
‡)	"	16.
*	"	13.
5	"	12.
6	"	11.

[14]A city in India "famous in the sixteenth century for its diamond-cutting and polishing" (Carlson 2).

†1	"	8.
0	"	6.
9 2	"	5.
: 3	"	4.
?	"	3.
¶	"	2.
—.	"	1.

"Now, in English, the letter which most frequently occurs is *e.* Afterwards, the succession runs thus: *a o i d h n r s t u y c f g l m w b k p q x z. E* however predominates so remarkably that an individual sentence of any length is rarely seen, in which it is not the prevailing character.

"Here, then, we have, in the very beginning, the groundwork for something more than a mere guess. The general use which may be made of the table is obvious—but, in this particular cipher, we shall only very partially require its aid. As our predominant character is 8, we will commence by assuming it as the *e* of the natural alphabet. To verify the supposition, let us observe if the 8 be seen often in couples—for *e* is doubled with great frequency in English—in such words, for example, as 'meet,' 'fleet,' 'speed,' 'seen,' 'been,' 'agree,' &c. In the present instance we see it doubled no less than five times, although the cryptograph is brief.

"Let us assume 8, then, as *e.* Now, of all *words* in the language, 'the' is most usual; let us see, therefore, whether there are not repetitions of any three characters, in the same order of collocation, the last of them being 8. If we discover repetitions of such letters, so arranged, they will most probably represent the word 'the.' On inspection, we find no less than seven such arrangements, the characters being ;48. We may, therefore, assume that the semicolon represents *t,* that 4 represents *h,* and that 8 represents *e*—the last being now well confirmed. Thus a great step has been taken.

"But, having established a single word, we are enabled to establish a vastly important point; that is to say, several commencements and terminations of other words. Let us refer, for example, to the last instance but one, in which the combination ;48 occurs—not far from the end of the cipher. We know that the semicolon immediately ensuing is the commencement of a word, and, of the six characters succeeding this 'the,' we are cognizant of no less than five. Let us set these characters down, thus, by the letters we know them to represent, leaving a space for the unknown—

t eeth.

"Here we are enabled, at once, to discard the '*th,*' as forming no portion of the word commencing with the first *t;* since, by experiment of the entire alphabet for a letter adapted to the vacancy we perceive no word can be formed of which this *th* can be a part. We are thus narrowed into

t ee,

and, going through the alphabet, if necessary, as before, we arrive at the word 'tree,' as the sole possible reading. We thus gain another letter, *r;* represented by (, with the words 'the tree' in juxtaposition.

"Looking beyond these words, for a short distance, we again see the combination ;48, and employ it by way of *termination* to what immediately precedes. We have thus this arrangement:

the tree ;4(‡ ?34 the,

or substituting the natural letters, where known, it reads thus:

the tree thr‡ ?3h the.

"Now, if, in place of the unknown characters, we leave blank spaces, or substitute dots, we read thus:

the tree thr . . . h the,

when the word '*through*' makes itself evident at once. But this discovery gives us three new letters, *o, u* and *g,* represented by ‡? and 3.

"Looking now, narrowly, through the cipher for combinations of known characters, we find, not very far from the beginning, this arrangement,

83(88, or egree,

which, plainly, is the conclusion of the word 'degree,' and gives us another letter, *d,* represented by †.

"Four letters beyond the word 'degree,' we perceive the combination

;46(;88*.

"Translating the known characters, and representing the unknown by dots, as before, we read thus:

th.rtee.

an arrangement immediately suggestive of the word 'thirteen,' and again furnishing us with two new characters, *i* and *n,* represented by 6 and *.

"Referring, now, to the beginning of the cryptograph, we find the combination,

53‡‡†.

"Translating, as before, we obtain

.good,

which assures us that the first letter is *A,* and that the first two words are 'A good.'

"To avoid confusion, it is now time that we arrange our key, as far as discovered, in a tabular form. It will stand thus:

5	represents	a
†	"	d
8	"	e
3	"	g
4	"	h
6	"	i
*	"	n
‡	"	o
(	"	r
;	"	t

"We have, therefore, no less than ten of the most important letters represented, and it will be unnecessary to proceed with the details of the solution. I have said enough to convince you that ciphers of this nature are readily soluble, and to give you some insight into the *rationale* of their development. But be assured that the specimen before us appertains to the very simplest species of cryptograph. It now only remains to give you the full translation of the characters upon the parchment, as unriddled. Here it is:

'*A good glass in the bishop's hostel in the devil's seat twenty-one*[15] *degrees and thirteen minutes northeast and by north main branch seventh limb east side shoot from the left eye of the death's-head a bee line from the tree through the shot fifty feet out.*'"

"But," I said, "the enigma seems still in as bad a condition as ever. How is it possible to extort a meaning from all this jargon about 'devil's seats,' 'death's-heads,' and 'bishop's hotels?'"

"I confess," replied Legrand, "that the matter still wears a serious aspect, when regarded with a casual glance. My first endeavor was to divide the sentence into the natural division intended by the cryptographist."

"You mean, to punctuate it?"

"Something of that kind."

"But how was it possible to effect this?"

"I reflected that it had been a *point* with the writer to run his words together without division, so as to increase the difficulty of solution. Now, a not over-acute man, in pursuing such an object, would be nearly certain to overdo the matter. When, in the course of his composition, he arrived at a break in his subject which

---

[15]Poe made a number of minor alterations in details of the code in the several reprintings of this tale which he supervised. In the 1845 *Tales,* he writes "forty-one" instead of "twenty-one." The cipher as presented in the other versions reads ";]8*:". Assuming that the colon is a typographical error (a semicolon was intended), that reads "twent." The next letters spell "one"—"twent one." The other version spells "fort one." Most of the variations are noted in Mabott (9) III.

would naturally require a pause, or a point, he would be exceedingly apt to run his characters, at this place, more than usually close together. If you will observe the MS., in the present instance, you will easily detect five such cases of unusual crowding. Acting on this hint, I made the division thus:

> '*A good glass in the Bishop's hostel in the Devil's seat—twenty-one degrees and thirteen minutes—northeast and by north—main branch seventh limb east side—shoot from the left eye of the death's-head—a bee-line from the tree through the shot fifty feet out.*'"

"Even this division," said I, "leaves me still in the dark."

"It left me also in the dark," replied Legrand, "for a few days; during which I made diligent inquiry, in the neighborhood of Sullivan's Island, for any building which went by the name of the 'Bishop's Hotel;' for, of course, I dropped the obsolete word 'hostel.' Gaining no information on the subject, I was on the point of extending my sphere of search, and proceeding in a more systematic manner, when, one morning, it entered into my head, quite suddenly, that this 'Bishop's Hostel' might have some reference to an old family, of the name of Bessop, which, time out of mind, had held possession of an ancient manor-house, about four miles to the northward of the Island. I accordingly went over the plantation, and re-instituted my inquiries among the older negroes of the place. At length one of the most aged of the women said that she had heard of such a place as *Bessop's Castle,* and thought that she could guide me to it, but that it was not a castle, nor a tavern, but a high rock.

"I offered to pay her well for her trouble, and, after some demur, she consented to accompany me to the spot. We found it without much difficulty, when, dismissing her, I proceeded to examine the place. The 'castle' consisted of an irregular assemblage of cliffs and rocks—one of the latter being quite remarkable for its height as well as for its insulated and artificial appearance. I clambered to its apex, and then felt much at a loss as to what should be next done.

"While I was busied in reflection, my eyes fell upon a narrow ledge in the eastern face of the rock, perhaps a yard below the summit on which I stood. This ledge projected about eighteen inches, and was not more than a foot wide, while a niche in the cliff just above it, gave it a rude resemblance to one of the hollow-backed chairs used by our ancestors. I made no doubt that here was the 'devil's-seat' alluded to in the MS., and now I seemed to grasp the full secret of the riddle.

"The 'good glass,' I knew, could have reference to nothing but a telescope; for the word 'glass' is rarely employed in any other sense by seamen. Now here, I at once saw, was a telescope to be used, and a definite point of view, *admitting no variation,* from which to use it. Nor did I hesitate to believe that the phrases, 'twenty-one degrees and thirteen minutes,' and 'northeast and by north,' were intended as directions for the levelling of the glass. Greatly excited by these discoveries, I hurried home, procured a telescope, and returned to the rock.

"I let myself down to the ledge, and found that it was impossible to retain a seat on it unless in one particular position. This fact confirmed my preconceived idea. I proceeded to use the glass. Of course, the 'twenty-one degrees and thirteen minutes' could allude to nothing but elevation above the visible horizon, since the horizontal direction was clearly indicated by the words 'northeast and by north.' This latter direction I at once established by means of a pocket-compass; then, pointing the glass as nearly at an angle of twenty-one degrees of elevation as I could do it by guess, I moved it cautiously up or down, until my attention was arrested by a circular rift or opening in the foliage of a large tree that overtopped its fellows in the distance. In the centre of this rift I perceived a white spot, but could not, at first, distinguish what it was. Adjusting the focus of the telescope, I again looked, and now made it out to be a human skull.

"On this discovery I was so sanguine as to consider the enigma solved; for the phrase 'main branch, seventh limb, east side,' could refer only to the position of the skull on the tree, while 'shoot from the left eye of the death's-head' admitted, also, of but one interpretation, in regard to a search for buried treasure. I perceived that the design was to drop a bullet from the left eye of the skull, and that a bee-line, or, in other words, a straight line, drawn from the nearest point of the trunk through 'the shot,' (or the spot where the bullet fell,) and thence extended to a distance of fifty feet, would indicate a definite point—and beneath this point I thought it at least *possible* that a deposit of value lay concealed."

"All this," I said, "is exceedingly clear, and, although ingenious, still simple and explicit. When you left the Bishop's Hotel, what then?"

"Why, having carefully taken the bearings of the tree, I turned homewards. The instant that I left 'the devil's seat,' however, the circular rift vanished; nor could I get a glimpse of it afterwards, turn as I would. What seems to me the chief ingenuity in this whole business, is the fact (for repeated experiment has convinced me it *is* a fact) that the circular opening in question is visible from no other attainable point of view than that afforded by the narrow ledge on the face of the rock.

"In this expedition to the 'Bishop's Hotel' I had been attended by Jupiter, who had, no doubt, observed, for some weeks past, the abstraction of my demeanor, and took especial care not to leave me alone. But, on the next day, getting up very early, I contrived to give him the slip, and went into the hills in search of the tree. After much toil I found it. When I came home at night my valet proposed to give me a flogging. With the rest of the adventure I believe you are as well acquainted as myself."

"I suppose," said I, "you missed the spot, in the first attempt at digging, through Jupiter's stupidity in letting the bug fall through the right instead of through the left eye of the skull."

"Precisely. This mistake made a difference of about two inches and a half in the 'shot'—that is to say, in the position of the peg nearest the tree; and had the treasure been *beneath* the 'shot,' the error would have been of little moment; but 'the shot,' together with the nearest point of the tree, were merely two points for the establishment of a line of direction; of course the error, however trivial in the beginning, increased as we proceeded with the line, and by the time we had gone fifty feet, threw us quite off the scent. But for my deep-seated convictions that treasure was here somewhere actually buried, we might have had all our labor in vain."

"I presume the fancy of *the skull,* of letting fall a bullet through the skull's eye—was suggested to Kidd by the piratical flag. No doubt he felt a kind of poetical consistency in recovering his money through this ominous insignium."

"Perhaps so; still I cannot help thinking that common-sense had quite as much to do with the matter as poetical consistency. To be visible from the devil's-seat, it was necessary that the object, if small, should be white; and there is nothing like your human skull for retaining and even increasing its whiteness under exposure to all vicissitudes of weather."

"But your grandiloquence, and your conduct in swinging the beetle—how excessively odd! I was sure you were mad. And why did you insist on letting fall the bug, instead of a bullet, from the skull?"

"Why, to be frank, I felt somewhat annoyed by your evident suspicions touching my sanity, and so resolved to punish you quietly, in my own way, by a little bit of sober mystification.[16] For this reason I swung the beetle, and for this reason I let it fall from the tree. An observation of yours about its great weight suggested the latter idea."

"Yes, I perceive; and now there is only one point which puzzles me. What are we to make of the skeletons found in the hole?"

"That is a question I am no more able to answer than yourself. There seems, however, only one plausible way of accounting for them—and yet it is dreadful to believe in such atrocity as my suggestion would imply. It is clear that Kidd—if Kidd indeed secreted this treasure, which I doubt not—it is clear that he must have had assistance in the labor. But the worst of this labor concluded, he may have thought it expedient to remove all participants in his secret. Perhaps a couple of blows with a mattock were sufficient, while his coadjutors were busy in the pit; perhaps it required a dozen—who shall tell?"

---

[16]For the exact connotations of this word in Poe, see the story "Mystification" in Levine (4). To "mystify" someone is to fool the person deliberately.

The Black Cat

Dostoyevsky thought that Poe was very "American" because, although he dealt in fantasy and terror, his visions were firmly grounded, detailed, documented. The gothic horror in "The Black Cat" is set in a tale "homely" in its texture. The narrator says that he is happily married; we know a bit about his childhood; he seems to have been a nice person. His downfall he attributes to intemperance, a most routine vice in an age when temperance propaganda was quite inescapable in American society. Even what the narrator calls "perverseness" appears really to be conscience. Guilt about his alcoholism seems to him the "perverseness" which maims and kills the first cat; guilt about those acts produces the murder of his wife—who, after all, showed him the gallows on the second cat's breast. He says, we notice, that the "incarnate Night-Mare" was "incumbent eternally upon . . . his heart.*" For all its intensity, then, the tale serves as a corrective to those readings of Poe which insist upon Poe's "unreality" and his isolation from the workaday environment around him. This tale says that the capacity for savagery is within even the nicest of us: compassionate people who like goldfish, dogs, and cats.*

In an earlier version of "The Black Cat," puss was female. That suggests the extent to which Poe based his story on the real and the everyday: Poe owned a black female cat with "not a white hair about her"; he describes her in the January 29, 1840, Alexander's Weekly Messenger, *saying that she is very intelligent, and, like all black cats, a witch.*

A note of explanation: *There is a difficult and deceptive sentence in the first paragraph. Poe has used the plural form of the French word* baroque *to make it agree with "they" (events). It reads more easily in English, where the agreement problem does not appear: " . . . less terrible than baroque."*

Publications in Poe's Time

The United States Saturday Post, August 19, 1843
Tales, 1845
The Pictorial National Library, November 1848

The Black Cat

For the most wild, yet most homely narrative which I am about to pen, I neither expect nor solicit belief. Mad indeed would I be to expect it, in a case where my very senses reject their own evidence. Yet, mad am I not—and very surely do I not dream. But to-morrow I die, and to-day I would unburthen my soul. My immediate purpose is to place before the world, plainly, succinctly, and without comment, a series of mere household events. In their consequences, these events have terrified—have tortured—have destroyed me. Yet I will not attempt to expound them. To me, they have presented little but Horror—to many they will seem less terrible than *baroques*. Hereafter, perhaps, some intellect may be found which will reduce my phantasm to the common-place—some intellect more calm, more logical, and far less excitable than my own, which will perceive, in the circumstances I detail with awe, nothing more than an ordinary succession of very natural causes and effects.

From my infancy I was noted for the docility and humanity of my disposition. My tenderness of heart was even so conspicuous as to make me the jest of my companions. I was especially fond of animals, and was indulged by my parents with a great variety of pets. With these I spent most of my time, and never was so happy as when feeding and caressing them. This peculiarity of character grew with my growth, and, in my manhood, I derived from it one of my principal sources of pleasure. To those who have cherished an affection for a faithful and sagacious dog, I need hardly be at the trouble of explaining the nature or the intensity of the gratification thus derivable. There is something in the unselfish and self-sacrificing love of a brute, which goes directly to the heart of him who has had frequent occasion to test the paltry friendship and gossamer fidelity of mere *Man*.

I married early, and was happy to find in my wife a disposition not uncongenial with my own. Observing my partiality for domestic pets, she lost no opportunity of procuring those of the most agreeable kind. We had birds, gold fish, a fine dog, rabbits, a small monkey, and *a cat*.

This latter was a remarkably large and beautiful animal, entirely black, and sagacious to an astonishing degree. In speaking of his intelligence, my wife, who at heart was not a little tinctured with superstition, made frequent allusion to the ancient popular notion, which regarded all black cats as witches in disguise. Not that she was ever *serious* upon this point—and I mention the matter at all for no better reason than that it happens, just now, to be remembered.

Pluto—this was the cat's name—was my favorite pet and playmate. I alone fed him, and he attended me wherever I went about the house. It was even with difficulty that I could prevent him from following me through the streets.

Our friendship lasted, in this manner, for several years, during which my general temperament and character—through the instrumentality of the Fiend Intemperance—had (I blush to confess it) experienced a radical alteration for the worse. I grew, day by day, more moody, more irritable, more regardless of the feelings of others. I suffered myself to use intemperate language to my wife. At length, I even offered her personal violence. My pets, of course, were made to feel the change in my disposition. I not only neglected, but ill-used them. For Pluto, however, I still retained sufficient regard to restrain me from maltreating him, as I made no scruple of maltreating the rabbits, the monkey, or even the dog, when by accident, or through affection, they came in my way. But my disease grew upon me—for what disease is like Alcohol!—and at length even Pluto, who was now becoming old, and consequently somewhat peevish—even Pluto began to experience the effects of my ill temper.

One night, returning home, much intoxicated, from one of my haunts about town, I fancied that the cat avoided my presence. I seized him; when, in fright at my violence, he inflicted a slight wound upon my hand with his teeth. The fury of a demon instantly possessed me. I knew myself no longer. My original soul seemed, at once, to take its flight from my body; and a more than fiendish malevolence, gin-nurtured, thrilled every fibre of my frame. I took from my waistcoat-pocket a pen-knife, opened it, grasped the poor beast by the throat, and deliberately cut one of its eyes from the socket! I blush, I burn, I shudder, while I pen the damnable atrocity.

When reason returned with the morning—when I had slept off the fumes of the night's debauch—I experienced a sentiment half of horror, half of remorse, for the crime of which I had been guilty; but it was, at best, a feeble and equivocal feeling, and the soul remained untouched. I again plunged into excess, and soon drowned in wine all memory of the deed.

In the meantime the cat slowly recovered. The socket of the lost eye presented, it is true, a frightful appearance, but he no longer appeared to suffer any pain. He went about the house as usual, but, as might be expected, fled in extreme terror at my approach. I had so much of my old heart left, as to be at first grieved by this evident dislike on the part of a creature which had once so loved me. But this feeling soon gave place to irritation. And then came, as if to my final and irrevocable otherthrow, the spirit of PERVERSENESS. Of this spirit philosophy takes no account. Yet I am not more sure that my soul lives, than I am that perverseness is one of the primitive impulses of the human heart—one of the indivisible primary faculties, or sentiments, which give direction to the character of Man.[1] Who has not, a hundred times, found himself committing a vile or a silly action, for no other reason than because he knows he should *not?* Have we not a perpetual inclination, in the teeth of our best judgment, to violate that which is *Law,* merely because we understand it to be such? This spirit of perverseness, I say, came to my final overthrow. It is this unfathomable longing of the soul *to vex itself*—to offer violence to its own nature—to do wrong for the wrong's sake only—that urged me to continue and finally to consummate the injury I had inflicted upon the unoffending brute. One morning, in cool blood, I slipped a noose about its neck and hung it to the limb of a tree;—hung it with the tears streaming from my eyes, and with the bitterest remorse in my heart;—hung it *because* I knew that it had loved me, and *because* I felt it had given me no reason of offence;—hung it *because* I knew that in so doing I was committing a sin—a deadly sin that would so jeopardize my immortal soul as to place it—if such a thing were possible—even beyond the reach of the infinite mercy of the Most Merciful and Most Terrible God.

On the night of the day on which this cruel deed was done, I was aroused from

---

[1]Poe borrows language and concepts from phrenology. See "A note of explanation" in our headnote to "The Imp of the Perverse" for details, and that story for a closely related passage.

sleep by the cry of fire. The curtains of my bed were in flames. The whole house was blazing. It was with great difficulty that my wife, a servant, and myself, made our escape from the conflagration. The destruction was complete. My entire worldly wealth was swallowed up, and I resigned myself thenceforward to despair.

I am above the weakness of seeking to establish a sequence of cause and effect, between the disaster and the atrocity. But I am detailing a chain of facts—and wish not to leave even a possible link imperfect. On the day succeeding the fire, I visited the ruins. The walls, with one exception, had fallen in. This exception was found in a compartment wall, not very thick, which stood about the middle of the house, and against which had rested the head of my bed. The plastering had here, in great measure, resisted the action of the fire—a fact which I attributed to its having been recently spread. About this wall a dense crowd were collected, and many persons seemed to be examining a particular portion of it with very minute and eager attention. The words "strange!" "singular!" and other similar expressions, excited my curiosity. I approached and saw, as if graven in *bas relief* upon the white surface, the figure of a gigantic *cat.* The impression was given with an accuracy truly marvellous. There was a rope about the animal's neck.

When I first beheld this apparition—for I could scarcely regard it as less—my wonder and my terror were extreme. But at length reflection came to my aid. The cat, I remembered, had been hung in a garden adjacent to the house. Upon the alarm of fire, this garden had been immediately filled by the crowd—by some one of whom the animal must have been cut from the tree and thrown, through an open window, into my chamber. This had probably been done with the view of arousing me from sleep. The falling of other walls had compressed the victim of my cruelty into the substance of the freshly-spread plaster; the lime of which, with the flames, and the *ammonia* from the carcass, had then accomplished the portraiture as I saw it.

Although I thus readily accounted to my reason, if not altogether to my conscience, for the startling fact just detailed, it did not the less fail to make a deep impression upon my fancy. For months, I could not rid myself of the phantasm of the cat; and, during this period, there came back into my spirit a half-sentiment that seemed, but was not, remorse. I went so far as to regret the loss of the animal, and to look about me, among the vile haunts which I now habitually frequented, for another pet of the same species, and of somewhat similar appearance, with which to supply its place.

One night as I sat, half stupified, in a den of more than infamy, my attention was suddenly drawn to some black object, reposing upon the head of one of the immense hogsheads of Gin, or of Rum, which constituted the chief furniture of the apartment. I had been looking steadily at the top of this hogshead for some minutes, and what now caused me surprise was the fact that I had not sooner perceived the object thereupon. I approached it, and touched it with my hand. It was a black cat—a very large one—fully as large as Pluto, and closely resembling him in every respect but one. Pluto had not a white hair upon any portion of his body; but this cat had a large, although indefinite splotch of white, covering nearly the whole region of the breast.

Upon my touching him, he immediately arose, purred loudly, rubbed against my hand, and appeared delighted with my notice. This, then, was the very creature of which I was in search. I at once offered to purchase it of the landlord; but this person made no claim to it—knew nothing of it—had never seen it before.

I continued my caresses, and, when I prepared to go home, the animal evinced a disposition to accompany me, I permitted it to do so; occasionally stooping and patting it as I proceeded. When it reached the house it domesticated itself at once, and became immediately a great favorite with my wife.

For my own part, I soon found a dislike to it arising within me. This was just the reverse of what I had anticipated; but I know not how or why it was—its evident fondness for myself rather disgusted and annoyed. By slow degrees, these feelings of disgust and annoyance rose into the bitterness of hatred. I avoided the creature; a certain sense of shame, and the remembrance of my former deed of cruelty, preventing me from physically abusing it. I did not, for some weeks, strike, or otherwise violently ill use it; but gradually—very gradually—I came to look upon it with unutterable loathing, and to flee silently from its odious presence, as from the breath of a pestilence.

What added, no doubt, to my hatred of the beast, was the discovery, on the morning after I brought it home, that, like Pluto, it also had been deprived of one of its eyes. This circumstance, however, only endeared it to my wife, who, as I have already said, possessed in a high degree, that humanity of feeling which had once been my distinguishing trait, and the source of many of my simplest and purest pleasures.

With my aversion to this cat, however, its partiality for myself seemed to increase. It followed my footsteps with a pertinacity which it would be difficult to make the reader comprehend. Whenever I sat, it would crouch beneath my chair, or spring upon my knees, covering me with its loathsome caresses. If I arose to walk it would get between my feet and thus nearly throw me down, or, fastening its long and sharp claws in my dress, clamber, in this manner, to my breast. At such times, although I longed to destroy it with a blow, I was yet withheld from so doing, partly by a memory of my former crime, but chiefly—let me confess it at once—by absolute *dread* of the beast.

This dread was not exactly a dread of physical evil—and yet I should be at a loss how otherwise to define it. I am almost ashamed to own—yes, even in this felon's cell, I am almost ashamed to own—that the terror and horror with which the animal inspired me, had been heightened by one of the merest chimæras it would be possible to conceive. My wife had called my attention, more than once, to the character of the mark of white hair, of which I have spoken, and which constituted the sole visible difference between the strange beast and the one I had destroyed. The reader will remember that this mark, although large, had been originally very indefinite; but, by slow degrees—degrees nearly imperceptible, and which for a long time my Reason struggled to reject as fanciful—it had, at length, assumed a rigorous distinctness of outline. It was now the representation of an object that I shudder to name—and for this, above all, I loathed, and dreaded, and would have rid myself of the monster *had I dared*—it was now, I say, the image of a hideous—of a ghastly thing—of the GALLOWS!—oh, mournful and terrible engine of Horror and of Crime—of Agony and of Death!

And now was I indeed wretched beyond the wretchedness of mere Humanity. And *a brute beast*—whose fellow I had contemptuously destroyed—*a brute beast* to work out for *me*—for me a man, fashioned in the image of the High God—so much of insufferable wo! Alas! neither by day nor by night knew I the blessing of Rest any more! During the former the creature left me no moment alone; and, in the latter, I started, hourly, from dreams of unutterable fear, to find the hot breath of *the thing* upon my face, and its vast weight—an incarnate Night-Mare that I had no power to shake off—incumbent eternally upon my *heart!*

Beneath the pressure of torments such as these, the feeble remnant of the good within me succumbed. Evil thoughts became my sole intimates—the darkest and most evil of thoughts. The moodiness of my usual temper increased to hatred of all things and of all mankind; while, from the sudden, frequent, and ungovernable outbursts of a fury to which I now blindly abandoned myself, my uncomplaining wife, alas! was the most usual and the most patient of sufferers.

One day she accompanied me, upon some household errand, into the cellar of the old building which our poverty compelled us to inhabit. The cat followed me down the steep stairs, and, nearly throwing me headlong, exasperated me to madness. Uplifting an axe, and forgetting, in my wrath, the childish dread which had hitherto stayed my hand, I aimed a blow at the animal which, of course, would have proved instantly fatal had it descended as I wished. But this blow was arrested by the hand of my wife. Goaded, by the interference, into a rage more than demoniacal, I withdrew my arm from her grasp and buried the axe in her brain. She fell dead upon the spot, without a groan.

This hideous murder accomplished, I set myself forthwith, and with entire deliberation, to the task of concealing the body. I knew that I could not remove it from the house, either by day or by night, without the risk of being observed by the neighbors. Many projects entered my mind. At one period I thought of cutting the corpse into minute fragments, and destroying them by fire. At another, I resolved to dig a grave for it in the floor of the cellar. Again, I deliberated about casting it in the well in the yard—about packing it in a box, as if merchandize, with the usual arrangements, and so getting a porter to take it from the house. Finally I hit upon what I considered a far better expedient than either of these. I determined to wall it up in the cellar—as the monks of the middle ages are recorded to have walled up their victims.

For a purpose such as this the cellar was well adapted. Its walls were loosely constructed, and had lately been plastered throughout with a rough plaster, which the dampness of the atmosphere had prevented from hardening. Moreover, in one of the walls was a projection, caused by a false chimney, or fireplace, that had been filled up, and made to resemble the rest of the cellar. I made no doubt that I could readily displace the bricks at this point, insert the corpse, and wall the whole up as before, so that no eye could detect anything suspicious.

And in this calculation I was not deceived. By means of a crow-bar I easily dislodged the bricks, and, having carefully deposited the body against the inner wall, I propped it in that position, while, with little trouble, I re-laid the whole structure as it originally stood. Having procured mortar, sand, and hair, with every possible precaution, I prepared a plaster which could not be distinguished from the old, and with this I very carefully went over the new brick-work. When I had finished, I felt satisfied that all was right. The wall did not present the slightest appearance of having been disturbed. The rubbish on the floor was picked up with the minutest care. I looked around triumphantly, and said to myself—"Here at least, then, my labor has not been in vain."

My next step was to look for the beast which had been the cause of so much wretchedness; for I had, at length, firmly resolved to put it to death. Had I been able to meet with it, at that moment, there could have been no doubt of its fate; but it appeared that the crafty animal had been alarmed at the violence of my previous anger, and forebore to present itself in my present mood. It is impossible to describe, or to imagine, the deep, the blissful sense of relief which the absence of the detested creature occasioned in my bosom. It did not make its appearance during the night—and thus for one night at least, I soundly and tranquilly slept; aye, *slept* even with the burden of murder upon my soul!

The second and the third day passed, and still my tormentor came not. Once again I breathed as a freeman. The monster, in terror, had fled the premises forever! I should behold it no more! My happiness was supreme! The guilt of my dark deed disturbed me but little. Some few inquiries had been made, but these had been readily answered. Even a search had been instituted—but of course nothing was to be discovered. I looked upon my future felicity as secured.

Upon the fourth day of the assassination, a party of the police came, very unexpectedly, into the house, and proceeded again to make rigorous investigation of the premises. Secure, however, in the inscrutability of my place of concealment, I felt no embarrassment whatever. The officers bade me accompany them in their search. They left no nook or corner unexplored. At length, for the third and fourth time, they descended into the cellar. I quivered not in a muscle. My heart beat calmly as that of one who slumbers in innocence. I walked the cellar from end to end. I folded my arms upon my bosom, and roamed easily to and fro. The police were thoroughly satisfied and prepared to depart. The glee at my heart was too strong to be restrained. I burned to say if but one word, by way of triumph, and to render doubly sure their assurance of my guiltlessness.

"Gentlemen," I said at last, as the party ascended the steps, "I delight to have allayed your suspicions. I wish you all health, and a little more courtesy. By the bye, gentlemen, this—this is a very well constructed house." [In the rabid desire to say something easily, I scarcely knew what I uttered at all.]—"I may say an *excellently* well constructed house. These walls—are you going, gentlemen?—these walls are solidly put together;" and here, through the mere phrenzy of bravado, I rapped heavily, with a cane which I held in my hand, upon that very portion of the brick-work behind which stood the corpse of the wife of my bosom.

But may God shield and deliver me from the fangs of the Arch-Fiend! No sooner had the reverberation of my blows sunk into silence, than I was answered by a voice from within the tomb!—by a cry, at first muffled and broken, like the sobbing of a child, and then quickly swelling into one long, loud, and continuous scream, utterly anomalous and inhuman—a howl—a wailing shriek, half of horror and half of triumph, such as might have arisen only out of hell, conjointly from the throats of the damned in their agony and of the demons that exult in the damnation.

Of my own thoughts it is folly to speak. Swooning, I staggered to the opposite wall. For one instant the party upon the stairs remained motionless, through extremity of terror and of awe. In the next, a dozen stout arms were toiling at the wall. It fell bodily. The corpse, already greatly decayed and clotted with gore, stood erect before the eyes of the spectators. Upon its head, with red extended mouth and solitary eye of fire, sat the hideous beast whose craft had seduced me into murder, and whose informing voice had consigned me to the hangman. I had walled the monster up within the tomb!

The Purloined Letter

The western world changed more drastically in Edgar Poe's lifetime than in any other brief period in human history. Instantaneous communication, engine-powered transportation, photography, and other technological miracles undreamed of before all made their appearance and their impact within Poe's short life. Industrialization and other aspects of modernized society tore apart traditional assumptions and altered the structure of families, the nature of work, and the "feel" of life itself. With the transformation came a sort of specialization which is familiar to us, but which was new to people then. Artists of Poe's time were immediately aware of the special threat to their role. In traditional societies, artists were felt to have access to power and knowledge: 19th-century artists knew that from their grounding in classical literature and from the new information being developed in the maturing fields of anthropology and archeology. Now, however, they were in danger of becoming narrowed and diminished, of being nothing more than one more kind of specialist, whose job was to produce pretties. Inconsistent, Poe sometimes argued for that specialization, as when he wrote that the business of poetry is neither truth nor duty, but only beauty. In this important tale, however, he vigorously defends the broad importance of the artistic person. The Prefect of police is a narrow specialist. His methods will never locate the purloined letter.

To learn the truth, one needs Dupin; Poe carefully emphasizes that Dupin is not only learned, but also a poet. So "The Purloined Letter" can be read as Poe's version of that argument one sees in so many Romantic authors: the world needs "inspired" artists for their power and their wisdom. The plea is there in writers as different as Ralph Waldo Emerson and Percy Bysshe Shelley; it is nowhere made more strongly than in this detective tale, which serves, among other things, as a "Defense of Poetry."

It has other important characteristics as well; no one genre *will contain it fully. Though it is famous as a detective tale, "The Purloined Letter" is also one of Poe's vengeance stories; Dupin has scores personal and political to settle with his friend the mathematician-poet-minister. The tone of the closing paragraphs of the tale is bitter, and the final allusion literally bloodthirsty. Compare this tale with other vengeance stories, such as "Hop-Frog" and "The Cask of Amontillado."*

Publications in Poe's Time

The Gift, September 1844 (dated 1845)
Chamber's Edinburgh Journal, November 30, 1844 (abridged)
Tales, 1845
Littell's Living Age, January 18, 1845
The Spirit of the Times, January 20 and 22, 1845

The New York Weekly News, January 25, 1845
The latter three used the abridged version (Mabbott 9, III).

THE PURLOINED LETTER

Nil sapientiæ odiosius acumine nimio.
Seneca[1]

At Paris, just after dark one gusty evening in the autumn of 18—, I was enjoying the twofold luxury of meditation and a meerschaum in company with my friend C. Auguste Dupin, in his little back library, or book-closet, *au troisième, No. 33, Rue Dunôt, Faubourg St. Germain.* For one hour at least we had maintained a profound silence; while each, to any casual observer, might have seemed intently and exclusively occupied with the curling eddies of smoke that oppressed the atmosphere of the chamber. For myself, however, I was mentally discussing certain topics which had formed matter for conversation between us at an earlier period of the evening; I mean the affair of the Rue Morgue, and the mystery attending the murder of Marie Rogêt. I looked upon it, therefore, as something of a coincidence,[2] when the door of our apartment was thrown open and admitted our old acquaintance, Monsieur G——, the Prefect of the Parisian police.

We gave him a hearty welcome; for there was nearly half as much of the entertaining as of the contemptible about the man, and we had not seen him for several years. We had been sitting in the dark, and Dupin now arose for the

---

[1]"Nothing is more distasteful to good sense than too much cunning" (Carlson 2). Carlson says that the quotation, in point of fact, is not from Seneca. There are any number of similar sayings: Samuel Johnson's "They who cannot be wise are almost always cunning," and Francis Bacon's "Cunning is . . . a sinister or crooked wisdom" and "Nothing doth more hurt in a state, than that cunning men pass for wise." Poe's "quotation," indeed, is so close in spirit to Bacon's essay "Of Cunning" that it could serve as its conclusion.

[2]***au troisième:*** Third (fourth) floor. For the probable location of Dupin's apartment, see the Map of Poe's Paris, p. 136–7. **Rue Morgue . . . Marie Rogêt:** Poe uses a classic device of the authors of a series of stories involving the same hero by alluding to the two earlier Dupin tales, "The Murders in the Rue Morgue" and "The Mystery of Marie Rogêt." An annotated version of the latter is in Levine (4), 153–4, 197–225, 246–7. **something of a coincidence:** So it seems to the narrator, but the hint is that our thoughts and events are really connected. Since the story is about the capacity to project oneself "poetically" into another's personality, Poe hints that the arrival of the Prefect as the narrator thinks about him is no coincidence. As Dupin says later in the story, "The material world . . . abounds with very strict analogies to the immaterial." For more on Poe's advocacy of the idea that the mind has the power to create, literally, the world around one, see "The Power of Words" and *Eureka* (Mabbott 9, III).

purpose of lighting a lamp, but sat down again, without doing so, upon G.'s saying that he had called to consult us, or rather to ask the opinion of my friend, about some official business which had occasioned a great deal of trouble.

"If it is any point requiring reflection," observed Dupin, as he forbore to enkindle the wick, "we shall examine it to better purpose in the dark."

"That is another of your odd notions," said the Prefect, who had a fashion of calling every thing "odd" that was beyond his comprehension, and thus lived amid an absolute legion of "oddities."

"Very true," said Dupin, as he supplied his visiter with a pipe, and rolled towards him a comfortable chair.

"And what is the difficulty now?" I asked. "Nothing more in the assassination way, I hope?"

"Oh no; nothing of that nature. The fact is, the business is *very* simple indeed, and I make no doubt that we can manage it sufficiently well ourselves; but then I thought Dupin would like to hear the details of it, because it is so excessively *odd.*"

"Simple and odd," said Dupin.

"Why, yes; and not exactly that either. The fact is, we have all been a good deal puzzled because the affair *is* so simple, and yet baffles us altogether."

"Perhaps it is the very simplicity of the thing which puts you at fault," said my friend.[3]

"What nonsense you *do* talk!" replied the Prefect, laughing heartily.

"Perhaps the mystery is a little *too* plain," said Dupin.

"Oh, good heavens! who ever heard of such an idea?"

"A little *too* self-evident."

"Ha! ha! ha!—ha! ha! ha!—ho! ho! ho!"—roared our visiter, profoundly amused, "oh, Dupin, you will be the death of me yet!"

"And what, after all, is the matter on hand?" I asked.

"Why, I will tell you," replied the Prefect, as he gave a long, steady, and contemplative puff, and settled himself in his chair. "I will tell you in a few words; but, before I begin, let me caution you that this is an affair demanding the greatest secrecy, and that I should most probably lose the position I now hold, were it known that I confided it to any one."

"Proceed," said I.

"Or not," said Dupin.

"Well, then; I have received personal information, from a very high quarter, that a certain document of the last importance has been purloined from the royal apartments. The individual who purloined it is known; this beyond a doubt; he was seen to take it. It is known, also, that it still remains in his possession."

"How is this known?" asked Dupin.

"It is clearly inferred," replied the Prefect, "from the nature of the document, and from the non-appearance of certain results which would at once arise from its passing *out* of the robber's possession,—that is to say, from his employing it as he must design in the end to employ it."

---

[3]Dupin's solution appears before he even knows the nature of the problem.

"Be a little more explicit," I said.

"Well, I may venture so far as to say that the paper gives its holder a certain power in a certain quarter where such power is immensely valuable." The Prefect was fond of the cant of diplomacy.

"Still I do not quite understand," said Dupin.

"No? Well; the disclosure of the document to a third person, who shall be nameless, would bring in question the honor of a personage of most exalted station; and this fact gives the holder of the document an ascendancy over the illustrious personage whose honor and peace are so jeopardized."

"But this ascendancy," I interposed, "would depend upon the robber's knowledge of the loser's knowledge of the robber. Who would dare—"

"The thief," said G., "is the Minister D——, who dares all things, those unbecoming as well as those becoming a man. The method of the theft was not less ingenious than bold. The document in question—a letter, to be frank—had been received by the personage robbed while alone in the royal *boudoir.* During its perusal she was suddenly interrupted by the entrance of the other exalted personage from whom especially it was her wish to conceal it. After a hurried and vain endeavor to thrust it in a drawer, she was forced to place it, open it was, upon a table. The address, however, was uppermost, and, the contents thus unexposed, the letter escaped notice. At this juncture enters the Minister D——. His lynx eye immediately perceives the paper, recognizes the handwriting of the address, observes the confusion of the personage addressed, and fathoms her secret. After some business transactions, hurried through in his ordinary manner, he produces a letter somewhat similar to the one in question, opens it, pretends to read it, and then places it in close juxtaposition to the other. Again he converses, for some fifteen minutes, upon the public affairs. At length, in taking leave, he takes also from the table the letter to which he had no claim. Its rightful owner saw, but, of course, dared not call attention to the act, in the presence of the third personage who stood at her elbow. The minister decamped; leaving his own letter—one of no importance—upon the table."

"Here, then," said Dupin to me, "you have precisely what you demand to make the ascendancy complete—the robber's knowledge of the loser's knowledge of the robber."

"Yes," replied the Prefect; "and the power thus attained has, for some months past, been wielded, for political purposes, to a very dangerous extent. The personage robbed is more thoroughly convinced, every day, of the necessity of reclaiming her letter. But this, of course, cannot be done openly. In fine, driven to despair, she has committed the matter to me."

"Than whom," said Dupin, amid a perfect whirlwind of smoke, "no more sagacious agent could, I suppose, be desired, or even imagined."

"You flatter me," replied the Prefect; "but it is possible that some such opinion may have been entertained."

"It is clear," said I, "as you observe, that the letter is still in the possession of the minister; since it is this possession, and not any employment of the letter, which bestows the power. With the employment the power departs."

"True," said G.; "and upon this conviction I proceeded. My first care was to make thorough search of the minister's hotel; and here my chief embarrassment lay in the necessity of searching without his knowledge. Beyond all things, I have been warned of the danger which would result from giving him reason to suspect our design."

"But," said I, "you are quite *au fait*[4] in these investigations. The Parisian police have done this thing often before."

"O yes; and for this reason I did not despair. The habits of the minister gave me, too, a great advantage. He is frequently absent from home all night. His servants are by no means numerous. They sleep at a distance from their master's apartment, and being chiefly Neapolitans, are readily made drunk. I have keys, as you know, with which I can open any chamber or cabinet in Paris. For three months a night has not passed, during the greater part of which I have not been engaged, personally, in ransacking the D—— Hôtel. My honor is interested, and, to mention a great secret, the reward is enormous. So I did not abandon the search until I had become fully satisfied that the thief is a more astute man than myself. I fancy that I have investigated every nook and corner of the premises in which it is possible that the paper can be concealed."

"But it is not possible," I suggested, "that although the letter may be in the possession of the minister, as it unquestionably is, he may have concealed it elsewhere than upon his own premises?"

"This is barely possible," said Dupin. "The present peculiar condition of affairs at court, and especially of those intrigues in which D—— is known to be involved, would render the instant availability of the document—its susceptibility of being produced at a moment's notice—a point of nearly equal importance with its possession."

"Its susceptibility of being produced?" said I.

"That is to say, of being *destroyed,*" said Dupin.

"True," I observed; "the paper is clearly then upon the premises. As for its being upon the person of the minister, we may consider that as out of the question."

"Entirely," said the Perfect. "He had been twice waylaid, as if by foot-pads, and his person rigorously searched under my own inspection."

"You might have spared yourself this trouble," said Dupin. "D——, I presume, is not altogether a fool, and, if not, must have anticipated these waylayings, as a matter of course."

"Not *altogether* a fool," said G., "but then he is a poet, which I take to be only one remove from a fool."

"True," said Dupin, after a long and thoughtful whiff from his meerschaum, "although I have been guilty of certain doggerel myself."

"Suppose you detail," said I, "the particulars of your search."

"Why the fact is, we took our time, and we searched *every where.* I have had long experience in these affairs. I took the entire building, room by room; devoting the nights of a whole week to each. We examined, first, the furniture of each apartment. We opened every possible drawer; and I presume you know that, to a properly trained police agent, such a thing as a *secret* drawer is possible. Any man

[4]Well-informed.

is a dolt who permits a 'secret' drawer to escape him in a search of this kind. The thing is *so* plain. There is a certain amount of bulk—of space—to be accounted for in every cabinet. Then we have accurate rules. The fiftieth part of a line could not escape us. After the cabinets we took the chairs. The cushions we probed with the fine long needles you have seen me employ. From the tables we removed the tops."

"Why so?"

"Sometimes the top of a table, or other similarly arranged piece of furniture, is removed by the person wishing to conceal an article; then the leg is excavated, the article deposited within the cavity, and the top replaced. The bottoms and tops of bedposts are employed in the same way."

"But could not the cavity be detected by sounding?" I asked.

"By no means, if, when the article is deposited, a sufficient wadding of cotton be placed around it. Besides, in our case, we were obliged to proceed without noise."

"But you could not have removed—you could not have taken to pieces *all* articles of furniture in which it would have been possible to make a deposit in the manner you mention. A letter may be compressed into a thin spiral roll, not differing much in shape or bulk from a large knitting-needle, and in this form it might be inserted into the rung of a chair, for example. You did not take to pieces all the chairs?"

"Certainly not; but we did better—we examined the rungs of every chair in the hotel, and indeed the jointings of every description of furniture, by the aid of a most powerful microscope. Had there been any traces of recent disturbance we should not have failed to detect it instantly. A single grain of gimlet-dust, for example, would have been as obvious as an apple. Any disorder in the glueing—any unusual gaping in the joints—would have sufficed to insure detection."

"I presume you looked to the mirrors, between the boards and the plates, and you probed the beds and the bed-clothes, as well as the curtains and carpets."

"That of course; and when we had absolutely completed every particle of the furniture in this way, then we examined the house itself. We divided its entire surface into compartments, which we numbered, so that none might be missed; then we scrutinized each individual square inch throughout the premises, including the two houses immediately adjoining, with the microscope as before."

"The two houses adjoining!" I exclaimed; "you must have had a great deal of trouble."

"We had; but the reward offered is prodigious."

"You include the *grounds* about the houses?"

"All the grounds are paved with brick. They gave us comparatively little trouble. We examined the moss between the bricks, and found it undisturbed."

"You looked among D——'s papers, of course, and into the books of the library?"

"Certainly; we opened every package and parcel; we not only opened every book, but we turned over every leaf in each volume, not contenting ourselves with a mere shake, according to the fashion of some of our police officers. We also measured the thickness of every book-*cover,* with the most accurate admeasurement, and applied to each the most jealous scrutiny of the microscope. Had any of the bindings been recently meddled with, it would have been utterly impossible that the fact should have escaped observation. Some five or six volumes, just from the hands of the binder, we carefully probed, longitudinally, with the needles."

"You explored the floors beneath the carpets?"

"Beyond doubt. We removed every carpet, and examined the boards with the microscope."

"And the paper on the walls?"

"Yes."

"You looked into the cellars?"

"We did."

"Then," I said, "you have been making a miscalculation, and the letter is *not* upon the premises as you suppose."

"I fear you are right there," said the Prefect. "And now, Dupin, what would you advise me to do?"

"To make a thorough re-search of the premises."

"That is absolutely needless," replied G——. "I am not more sure that I breathe than I am that the letter is not at the Hôtel."

"I have no better advice to give you," said Dupin. "You have, of course, an accurate description of the letter?"

"Oh, yes!"—And here the Prefect, producing a memorandum-book, proceeded to read aloud a minute account of the internal, and especially of the external, appearance of the missing document. Soon after finishing the perusal of this description, he took his departure, more entirely depressed in spirits than I had ever known the good gentleman before.

In about a month afterward he paid us another visit, and found us occupied very nearly as before. He took a pipe and a chair and entered into some ordinary conversation. At length I said;—

"Well, but G——, what of the purloined letter? I presume you have at last made up your mind that there is no such thing as overreaching the Minister?"

"Confound him, say I—yes; I made the re-examination, however, as Dupin suggested—but it was all labor lost, as I knew it would be."

"How much was the reward offered, did you say?" asked Dupin.

"Why, a very great deal—a *very* liberal reward—I don't like to say how much, precisely; but one thing I *will* say, that I wouldn't mind giving my individual check for fifty thousand francs to any one who could obtain me that letter. The fact is, it is becoming of more and more importance every day; and the reward has been lately doubled. If it were trebled, however, I could do no more than I have done."

"Why, yes," said Dupin, drawlingly, between the whiffs of his meerschaum, "I really—think, G——, you have not exerted yourself—to the utmost in this matter. You might—do a little more, I think, eh?"

"How?—in what way?"

"Why—puff, puff,—you might—puff, puff—employ counsel in the matter, eh?—puff, puff, puff. Do you remember the story they tell of Abernethy?"

"No; hang Abernethy!"

"To be sure! hang him and welcome. But, once upon a time, a certain rich miser conceived the design of spunging upon this Abernethy for a medical opinion. Getting up, for this purpose, an ordinary conversation in a private company, he insinuated his case to the physician, as that of an imaginary individual.

" 'We will suppose,' said the miser, 'that his symptoms are such and such; now, doctor, what would *you* have directed him to take?'

" 'Take!' said Abernethy, 'why, take *advice,* to be sure.' "

"But," said the Prefect, a little discomposed, "I am *perfectly* willing to take advice, and to pay for it. I would *really* give fifty thousand francs to any one who would aid me in the matter."

"In that case," replied Dupin, opening a drawer, and producing a check-book, "you may as well fill me up a check for the amount you mentioned. When you have signed it, I will hand you the letter."

I was astounded. The Prefect appeared absolutely thunder-stricken. For some minutes he remained speechless and motionless, looking incredulously at my friend with open mouth, and eyes that seemed starting from their sockets; then, apparently recovering himself in some measure, he seized a pen, and after several pauses and vacant stares, finally filled up and signed a check for fifty thousand francs, and handed it across the table to Dupin. The latter examined it carefully and deposited it in his pocket-book; then, unlocking an *escritoire,*[5] took thence a letter and gave it to the Prefect. This functionary grasped it in a perfect agony of joy, opened it with a trembling hand, cast a rapid glance at its contents, and then, scrambling and struggling to the door, rushed at length unceremoniously from the room and from the house, without having uttered a syllable since Dupin had requested him to fill up the check.

When he had gone, my friend entered into some explanations.

"The Parisian police," he said, "are exceedingly able in their way. They are persevering, ingenious, cunning, and thoroughly versed in the knowledge which their duties seem chiefly to demand. Thus, when G—— detailed to us his mode of searching the premises at the Hôtel D——, I felt entire confidence in his having made a satisfactory investigation—so far as his labors extended."

"So far as his labors extended?" said I.

"Yes," said Dupin. "The measures adopted were not only the best of their kind, but carried out to absolute perfection. Had the letter been deposited within the range of their search, these fellows would, beyond a question, have found it."

I merely laughed—but he seemed quite serious in all that he said.

"The measures, then," he continued, "were good in their kind, and well executed; their defect lay in their being inapplicable to the case, and to the man. A certain set of highly ingenious resources are, with the Prefect, a sort of Procrustean bed,[6] to which he forcibly adapts his designs. But he perpetually errs by being too deep or too shallow, for the matter in hand; and many a schoolboy is a better reasoner than he. I knew one about eight years of age, whose success at guessing

---

[5]Writing desk.

[6]In Greek mythology, the giant Procrustes tied travelers to an iron bed; he made them fit by stretching or amputating their limbs.

in the game of 'even and odd' attracted universal admiration. This game is simple, and is played with marbles. One player holds in his hand a number of these toys, and demands of another whether that number is even or odd. If the guess is right, the guesser wins one; if wrong, he loses one. The boy to whom I allude won all the marbles of the school. Of course he had some principle of guessing; and this lay in mere observation and admeasurement of the astuteness of his opponents. For example, an arrant simpleton is his opponent, and, holding up his closed hand, asks: 'Are they even or odd?' Our schoolboy replies, 'Odd,' and loses; but upon the second trial he wins, for he then says to himself, 'The simpleton had them even upon the first trial, and his amount of cunning is just sufficient to make him have them odd upon the second; I will therefore guess odd;'—he guesses odd, and wins. Now, with a simpleton a degree above the first, he would have reasoned thus: 'This fellow finds that in the first instance I guessed odd, and, in the second, he will propose to himself upon the first impulse, a simple variation from even to odd, as did the first simpleton; but then a second thought will suggest that this is too simple a variation, and finally he will decide upon putting it even as before. I will therefore guess even;'—he guesses even, and wins. Now this mode of reasoning in the schoolboy, whom his fellows termed 'lucky,'—what, in its last analysis is it?"

"It is merely," I said, "an identification of the reasoner's intellect with that of his opponent."

"It is," said Dupin, "and, upon inquiring of the boy by what means he effected the *thorough* identification in which his success consisted, I received answer as follows: 'When I wish to find out how wise, or how stupid, or how good, or how wicked is any one, or what are his thoughts at the moment, I fashion the expression on my face, as accurately as possible, in accordance with the expression of his, and then wait to see what thoughts or sentiments arise in my mind or heart, as if to match or correspond with the expression.' This response of the schoolboy lies at the bottom of all the spurious profundity which has been attributed to Rochefoucault, to La Bougive, to Machiavelli, and to Campanella."[7]

"And the identification," I said, "of the reasoner's intellect with that of his opponent, depends, if I understand you aright, upon the accuracy with which the opponent's intellect is admeasured."

"For its practical value it depends upon this," replied Dupin; "and the Prefect and his cohort fail so frequently, first, by default of this identification, and sec-

[7]Poe's list is of writers who assume all human behavior is to be understood simply in selfish terms. **Rochefoucault:** François, Duc de la Rochefoucauld (1613–80), Prince de Marsillac, celebrated French moralist and courtier, whose *Réflexions, ou Sentences et Maximes Morales* (1665) argues that self-love is the chief motive in human actions. **La Bougive:** Poe means La Bruyère (Jean de la Bruyère, 1645–96); his printer misread his handwriting (Mabbott 9, III). **Machiavelli:** Niccolò Machiavelli (1469–1527), the Italian statesman and writer whose name is synonymous with the idea of cold calculation in diplomacy. **Campanella:** Tommaso Campanella (1568–1639), Italian philosopher and Dominican monk, whose *Philosophy Demonstrated by the Senses* (1591) caused his imprisonment for heresy.

ondly, by ill-admeasurement, or rather through non-admeasurement, of the intellect with which they are engaged. They consider only their *own* ideas of ingenuity; and, in searching for anything hidden, advert only to the modes in which *they* would have hidden it. They are right in this much—that their own ingenuity is a faithful representation of that of *the mass;* but when the cunning of the individual felon is diverse in character from their own, the felon foils them, of course. This always happens when it is above their own, and very usually when it is below. They have no variation of principle in their investigations; at best, when urged by some unusual emergency—by some extraordinary reward—they extend or exaggerate their old modes of *practice,* without touching their principles. What, for example, in this case of D——, has been done to vary the principle of action? What is all this boring, and probing, and sounding, and scrutinizing with the microscope, and dividing the surface of the building into registered square inches—what is it all but an exaggeration *of the application* of the one principle or set of principles of search, which are based upon the one set of notions regarding human ingenuity, to which the Prefect, in the long routine of his duty, has been accustomed? Do you not see he has taken it for granted that *all* men proceed to conceal a letter,—not exactly in a gimlet-hole bored in a chair-leg—but, at least in *some* out-of-the-way hole or corner suggested by the same tenor of thought which would urge a man to secrete a letter in a gimlet-hole bored in a chair-leg? And do you not see also, that such *recherchés*[8] nooks for concealment are adapted only for ordinary occasion, and would be adopted only by ordinary intellects; for, in all cases of concealment, a disposal of the article concealed—a disposal of it in this *recherché* manner—is, in the very first instance, presumable and presumed; and thus its discovery depends, not at all upon the acumen, but altogether upon the mere care, patience, and determination of the seekers; and where the case is of importance—or, what amounts to the same thing in the policial eyes, when the reward is of magnitude,—the qualities in question have *never* been known to fail. You will now understand what I meant in suggesting that, had the purloined letter been hidden anywhere within the limits of the Prefect's examination—in other words, had the principle of its concealment been comprehended within the principles of the Prefect—its discovery would have been a matter altogether beyond question. This functionary, however, has been thoroughly mystified; and the remote source of his defeat lies in the supposition that the Minister is a fool, because he has acquired renown as a poet. All fools are poets; this the Prefect *feels;* and he is merely guilty of a *non distributio medii*[9] in thence inferring that all poets are fools.

---

[8]Rare, strange.

[9]"The undistributed middle" is an error in logic. The syllogism would run,

All fools are poets.
The minister is a poet.
Therefore, the minister is a fool.

The conclusion is illogical because the syllogism does not rule out the possibility that some

"But is this really the poet?" I asked. "There are two brothers, I know; and both have attained reputation in letters. The Minister I believe has written learnedly on the Differential Calculus. He is a mathematician, and no poet."

"You are mistaken; I know him well: he is both. As poet *and* mathematician, he would reason well; as mere mathematician, he could not have reasoned at all, and thus would have been at the mercy of the Prefect."

"You surprise me," I said, "by these opinions, which have been contradicted by the voice of the world. You do not mean to set at naught the well-digested idea of centuries. The mathematical reason has long been regarded as *the* reason *par excellence.*"

"'*Il y a á parier,*'" replied Dupin, quoting from Chamfort, "'*que toute idée publique, toute convention reçue, est une sottise, car elle a convenu au plus grand nombre.*'[10] The mathematicians, I grant you, have done their best to promulgate the popular error to which you allude, and which is none the less an error for its promulgation as truth. With an art worthy a better cause, for example, they have insinuated the term 'analysis' into application to algebra. The French are the originators of this particular deception; but if a term is of any importance—if words derive any value from applicability—then 'analysis' conveys 'algebra' about as much as, in Latin, '*ambitus*' implies 'ambition,' '*religio*' 'religion,' or '*homines honesti,*' a set of *honorable* men."[11]

"You have a quarrel on hand, I see," said I, "with some of the algebraists of Paris; but proceed."

"I dispute the availability, and thus the value, of that reason which is cultivated in any especial form other than the abstractly logical. I dispute, in particular, the reason educed by mathematical study. The mathematics are the science of form and quantity; mathematical reasoning is merely logic applied to observation upon form and quantity. The great error lies in supposing that even the truths of what is

---

poets aren't fools. A proper syllogism would run,

All poets are fools.
The minister is a poet.
Therefore, the minister is a fool.

Dupin cheats a little in his argument here, because the Prefect really said that poets are "only one remove" from fools. He has no way of knowing that, had the Prefect actually thought out a syllogism, even one with as dubious a premise as either of these, he would have used the incorrect version.

[10]**Chamfort:** Sebastian Roch Nicholas Chamfort (1741–94). ***'Il y a . . . nombre'***: "The odds are that every popular idea, every accepted convention, is nonsense, because it has suited itself to the majority" (Carlson 2). The quotation is from *Maximes et Pensées.*

[11]Each of the Latin words is the source of the English word, but Poe is correct; their meanings originally were quite different. ***ambitus:*** In classical times, *ambitus* referred to "going around," as in going around seeking office or going around soliciting votes (by paying for them). ***religio:*** *Religio* referred to something you were bound to do—such as religious observance or just obeying your conscience. It could apply to anything from "superstition" to "conscience." ***homines honesti:*** *Honestus,* of which *honesti* is the plural, meant just "distinguished"; it had no moral connotations.

called *pure* algebra, are abstract or general truths. And this error is so egregious that I am confounded at the universality with which it has been received. Mathematical axioms are *not* axioms of general truth. What is true of *relation*—of form and quantity—is often grossly false in regard to morals, for example. In this latter science it is very usually *un*true that the aggregated parts are equal to the whole. In chemistry also the axiom fails. In the consideration of motive it fails; for two motives, each of a given value, have not, necessarily, a value when united, equal to the sum of their values apart. There are numerous other mathematical truths which are only truths within the limits of relation. But the mathematician argues from his *finite truths,* through habit, as if they were of an absolutely general applicability—as the world indeed imagines them to be. Bryant, in his very learned 'Mythology,' mentions an analogous source of error, when he says that 'although the Pagan fables are not believed, yet we forget ourselves continually, and make inferences from them as existing realities.' With the algebraists, however, who are Pagans themselves, the 'Pagan fables' *are* believed, and the inferences are made, not so much through lapse of memory as through an unaccountable addling of the brains. In short, I never yet encountered the mere mathematician who would be trusted out of equal roots, or one who did not clandestinely hold it as a point of his faith that $x^2 + px$ was absolutely and unconditionally equal to q.[12] Say to one of these gentlemen, by way of experiment, if you please, that you believe occasions may occur where $x^2 + px$ is *not* altogether equal to q, and having made him understand what you mean, get out of his reach as speedily as convenient, for, beyond doubt, he will endeavor to knock you down.

"I mean to say," continued Dupin, while I merely laughed at his last observations, "that if the Minister had been no more than a mathematician, the Prefect would have been under no necessity of giving me this check. I knew him, however, as both mathematician and poet, and my measures were adapted to his capacity, with reference to the circumstances by which he was surrounded. I knew him as a courtier, too, and as a bold *intriguant.*[13] Such a man, I considered, could not fail to be aware of the ordinary policial modes of action. He could not have failed to anticipate—and events have proved that he did not fail to anticipate—the waylayings to which he was subjected. He must have foreseen, I reflected, the secret investigations of his premises. His frequent absences from home at night, which were hailed by the Prefect as certain aids to his success, I regarded only as *ruses,* to afford opportunity for thorough search to the police, and thus the sooner to impress them with the conviction to which G——, in fact, did finally arrive—the conviction that the letter was not upon the premises. I felt, also, that the whole train of thought, which I was at some pains in detailing to you just now,

---

[12]**Bryant:** Poe refers to Jacob Bryant (1715–1804), a learned but not always reliable English antiquarian. Poe's quotation is from his *A New System, or an Analysis of Antient Mythology* (1774–76). In the London 1807 edition, it appears in Volume II, p. 173. Poe knew Bryant's work well and used ideas from it frequently. See Levine (5 and 6). **$x^2 + px$ . . . equal to q:** Poe's formula is not a standard equation for anything; as it stands, it has no special meaning.

[13]Intriguer.

concerning the invariable principle of policial action in searches for articles concealed—I felt that this whole train of thought would necessarily pass through the mind of the Minister. It would imperatively lead him to despise all the ordinary *nooks* of concealment. *He* could not, I reflected, be so weak as not to see that the most intricate and remote recess of his hotel would be as open as his commonest closets to the eyes, to the probes, to the gimlets, and to the microscopes of the Prefect. I saw, in fine, that he would be driven, as a matter of course, to simplicity, if not deliberately induced to it as a matter of choice. You will remember, perhaps, how desperately the Prefect laughed when I suggested, upon our first interview, that it was just possible this mystery troubled him so much on account of its being so *very* self-evident."

"Yes," said I, "I remember his merriment well. I really thought he would have fallen into convulsions."

"The material world," continued Dupin, "abounds with very strict analogies to the immaterial; and thus some color of truth has been given to the rhetorical dogma, that metaphor, or simile, may be made to strengthen an argument as well as to embellish a description. The principle of the *vis inertiæ,*[14] for example, seems to be identical in physics and metaphysics. It is not more true in the former, that a large body is with more difificulty set in motion than a smaller one, and that its subsequent *momentum* is commensurate with this difficulty, than it is, in the latter, that intellects of the vaster capacity, while more forcible, more constant, and more eventful in their movements than those of inferior grade, are yet the less readily moved, and more embarrassed and full of hesitation in the first few steps of their progress. Again: have you ever noticed which of the street signs, over the shop doors, are the most attractive of attention?"

"I have never given the matter a thought," I said.

"There is a game of puzzles," he resumed, "which is played upon a map. One party playing requires another to find a given word—the name of town, river, state, or empire—any word, in short, upon the motley and perplexed surface of the chart. A novice in the game generally seeks to embarrass his opponents by giving them the most minutely lettered names; but the adept selects such words as stretch, in large characters, from one end of the chart to the other. These, like the over-largely lettered signs and placards of the street, escape observation by the dint of being excessively obvious; and here the physical oversight is precisely analogous with the moral inapprehension by which the intellect suffers to pass unnoticed those considerations which are too obtrusively and too palpably self-evident. But this is a point, it appears, somewhat above or beneath the understanding of the Prefect. He never once thought it probable, or possible, that the Minister had deposited the letter immediately beneath the nose of the whole world, by way of best preventing any portion of that world from perceiving it.

"But the more I reflected upon the daring, dashing, and discriminating ingenuity of D——; upon the fact that the document must always have been *at hand,* if he intended to use it to good purpose; and upon the decisive evidence, obtained by the Prefect, that it was not hidden within the limits of that dignitary's ordinary

[14]The power of inertia.

search—the more satisfied I became that, to conceal this letter, the Minister had resorted to the comprehensive and sagacious expedient of not attempting to conceal it at all.

"Full of these ideas, I prepared myself with a pair of green spectacles, and called one fine morning, quite by accident, at the Ministerial hotel. I found D—— at home, yawning, lounging, and dawdling, as usual, and pretending to be in the last extremity of *ennui.* He is, perhaps, the most really energetic human being now alive—but that is only when nobody sees him.

"To be even with him, I complained of my weak eyes, and lamented the necessity of the spectacles, under cover of which I cautiously and thoroughly surveyed the whole apartment, while seemingly intent only upon the conversation of my host.

"I paid especial attention to a large writing-table near which he sat, and upon which lay confusedly, some miscellaneous letters and other papers, with one or two musical instruments and a few books. Here, however, after a long and a very deliberate scrutiny, I saw nothing to excite particular suspicion.

"At length my eyes, in going the circuit of the room, fell upon a trumpery filigree card-rack of pasteboard, that hung dangling by a dirty blue ribbon, from a little brass knob just beneath the middle of the mantel-piece. In this rack, which had three or four compartments, were five or six visiting cards and a solitary letter. This last was much soiled and crumpled. It was torn nearly in two, across the middle—as if a design, in the first instance, to tear it entirely up as worthless, had been altered, or stayed, in the second. It had a large black seal, bearing the D—— cipher *very* conspicuously, and was addressed, in a diminutive female hand, to D——, the minister, himself. It was thrust carelessly, and even, as it seemed, contemptuously, into one of the upper divisions of the rack.

"No sooner had I glanced at this letter than I concluded it to be that of which I was in search. To be sure, it was, to all appearance, radically different from one of which the Prefect had read us so minute a description. Here the seal was large and black, with the D—— cipher; there it was small and red, with the ducal arms of the S—— family. Here, the address, to the Minister, was diminutive and feminine; there the superscription, to a certain royal personage, was markedly bold and decided; the size alone formed a point of correspondence. But, then, the *radicalness* of these differences, which was excessive; the dirt; the soiled and torn condition of the paper, so inconsistent with the *true* methodical habits of D——, and so suggestive of a design to delude the beholder into an idea of the worthlessness of the document; these things, together with the hyperobtrusive situation of this document, full in the view of every visiter, and thus exactly in accordance with the conclusions to which I had previously arrived; these things, I say, were strongly corroborative of suspicion, in one who came with the intention to suspect.

"I protracted my visit as long as possible, and, while I maintained a most animated discussion with the Minister, upon a topic which I knew well had never failed to interest and excite him, I kept my attention really riveted upon the letter. In this examination, I committed to memory its external appearance and arrangement in the rack; and also fell, at length, upon a discovery which set at rest whatever trivial doubt I might have entertained. In scrutinizing the edges of the paper, I observed them to be more *chafed* than seemed necessary. They presented the *broken* appearance which is manifested when a stiff paper, having been once folded and pressed with a folder, is refolded in a reversed direction, in the same creases or edges which had formed the original fold. This discovery was sufficient. It was clear to me that the letter had been turned, as a glove, inside out, re-directed, and re-sealed. I bade the Minister good morning, and took my departure at once, leaving a gold snuff-box upon the table.

"The next morning I called for the snuff-box, when we resumed, quite eagerly, the conversation of the preceding day. While thus engaged, however, a loud report, as if of a pistol, was heard immediately beneath the windows of the hotel, and was succeeded by a series of fearful screams, and the shoutings of a mob. D—— rushed to a casement, threw it open, and looked out. In the meantime I stepped to the card-rack, took the letter, put it in my pocket, and replaced it by a *fac-simile,* (so far as regards externals) which I had carefully prepared at my lodgings; imitating the D—— cipher, very readily, by means of a seal formed of bread.

"The disturbance in the street had been occasioned by the frantic behavior of a man with a musket. He had fired it among a crowd of women and children. It proved, however, to have been without ball, and the fellow was suffered to go his way as a lunatic or a drunkard. When he had gone, D—— came from the window, whither I had followed him immediately upon securing the object in view. Soon afterward I bade him farewell. The pretended lunatic was a man in my own pay."

"But what purpose had you," I asked, "in replacing the letter by a *fac-simile?* Would it not have been better, at the first visit, to have seized it openly and departed?"

"D——," replied Dupin, "is a desperate man, and a man of nerve. His hotel, too, is not without attendants devoted to his interests. Had I made the wild attempt you suggest, I might never have left the Ministerial presence alive. The good people of Paris might have heard of me no more. But I had an object apart from these considerations. You know my political prepossessions. In this matter, I act as a partisan of the lady concerned. For eighteen months the Minister has had her in his power. She has now him in hers; since, being unaware that the letter is not in his possession, he will proceed with his exactions as if it was. Thus will he inevitably commit himself, at once, to his political destruction. His downfall, too, will not be more precipitate than awkward. It is all very well to talk about the *facilis descensus Averni;* but in all kinds of climbing, as Catalani said of singing, it is far more easy to get up than to come down. In the present instance I have no sympathy—at least no pity—for him who descends. He is that *monstrum horrendum,*[15] an unprinicpled man of genius. I confess, however, that I should like very

---

[15]***facilis descensus Averni:*** When Aeneas, in Virgil's *Aeneid,* asks the Sibyl of Cumae to allow him to descend into the underworld to visit his father, she warns him, "Easy is the descent into hell [Avernus]; all night and day the gate of dark Dis stands open, but to recall thy steps and issue to upper air, this is the task, this the burden." Avernus is a smouldering crater in Italy, so foreboding in appearance it was considered an entrance to the

well to know the precise character of his thoughts, when, being defied by her whom the Prefect terms 'a certain personage,' he is reduced to opening the letter which I left for him in the card-rack."

"How? did you put any thing particular in it?"

"Why—it did not seem altogether right to leave the interior blank—that would have been insulting. D——, at Vienna once, did me an evil turn, which I told him, quite good-humoredly, that I should remember. So, as I knew he would feel some curiosity in regard to the identity of the person who had outwitted him, I thought it a pity not to give him a clue. He is well acquainted with my MS., and I just copied into the middle of the blank sheet the words—

——Un dessein si funeste,
S'il n'est digne d'Atrée, est digne de Thyeste.

They are to be found in Crébillon's 'Atrée.'"[16]

---

underworld. Carlson (2) notices that Poe has the quotation wrong: for "Averni" the original reads "Avernus." **Catalani:** Angelica Catalani (1780–1849) was a famous Italian operatic singer. For evidence of Poe's familiarity with opera, see his story "The Spectacles" in Levine (4). ***monstrum horrendum:*** Also from Virgil; the phrase means "horrible monster."

[16]"A plot so deadly, if not worthy of Atreus, is worthy of Thyestes," from *Atrée et Thyeste* by Prosper Jolyot de Crébillon (1674–1762). The play, dated 1707, is a "revenge tragedy" based on the background plot of Aeschylus' *Oresteia.* Thyestes seduces his brother's wife and plans to murder him. Atreus, his brother, kills Thyestes' three sons and makes them the main dish at a banquet for their father. Poe seems to associate Dupin with Crébillon: see "The Murders in the Rue Morgue," note 9.

The Balloon-Hoax

"The Balloon-Hoax" is strong evidence of Poe's involvement in popular interests of his day and his excellent sense of journalistically exciting topics. The media of the day were filled with related true stories; Poe used as characters in his story people who had, in fact, been involved in an extraordinary and widely reported balloon voyage; Poe disguised it as a news article in a daily paper. Moreover, a speedy brig named Moon *had made the New York–Charleston run so quickly just two months before that it had beaten the mail by three days; that made plausible the claim in* The Extra Sun *that its amazing "news" story was a scoop (for details, see notes 1 and 2). Hoax or not, the idea seems to have been exciting to Poe as well—see especially the portions of the story "by" Mr. Ainsworth. Poe probably hoped someone would take his lead and try the journey.*

A note of explanation: *Poe and his friends at the* Sun *needed all the credibility they could muster, for people remembered the paper for a famous earlier hoax. A close look at Figure 9 shows that Poe's hoax shares the front page of* The Extra Sun *with an article on Egyptology, not an unusual topic for an American paper of this period.*

Publications in Poe's Time

The New York Sun, April 13, 1844 (Brief "news" item only, promising details in an "extra" which "will positively be ready and for sale at our counter by 10 o'clock this morning." Poe said it did not actually appear until nearly noon [Mabbott 9, III].)
The New York Sun (*The Extra Sun*), April 13, 1844
New York *Sunday Times,* April 14, 1844

The Balloon-Hoax

Astounding News by Express, *via* Norfolk! The Atlantic Crossed in Three Days! Signal Triumph of Mr. Monck Mason's Flying Machine! — Arrival at Sullivan's Island, near Charleston, S.C., of Mr. Mason, Mr. Robert Holland, Mr. Henson, Mr. Harrison Ainsworth, and four others, in the Steer-

ING BALLOON, "VICTORIA," AFTER A PASSAGE OF SEVENTY-FIVE HOURS FROM LAND TO LAND! FULL PARTICULARS OF THE VOYAGE![1]

The great problem is at length solved! The air, as well as the earth and the ocean, has been subdued by science, and will become a common and convenient highway for mankind. *The Atlantic has been actually crossed in a Balloon!* and this too without difficulty—without any great apparent danger—with thorough control of the machine—and in the inconceivably brief period of seventy-five hours from shore to shore! By the energy of an agent at Charleston, S.C., we are enabled to be the first to furnish the public with a detailed account of this most extraordinary voyage, which was performed between Saturday, the 6th instant, at 11, A.M., and 2, P.M., on Tuesday, the 9th instant, by Sir Everard Bringhurst; Mr. Osborne, a nephew of Lord Bentinck's; Mr. Monck Mason and Mr. Robert Holland, the well-known æronauts; Mr. Harrison Ainsworth, author of "Jack Sheppard," &c; and Mr. Henson, the projector of the late unsuccessful flying machine—with two seamen from Woolwich—in all, eight persons. The particulars furnished below may be relied on as authentic and accurate in every respect, as, with a slight exception, they are copied *verbatim* from the joint diaries of Mr. Monck Mason and Mr. Harrison Ainsworth, to whose politeness our agent is also indebted for much verbal information respecting the balloon itself, its construction, and other matters of interest. The only alteration in the MS. received, has been made for the purpose of throwing the hurried account of our agent, Mr. Forsyth,[2] in a connected and intelligible form.

---

[1]Poe's story was a true hoax, published as an "extra" by a daily newspaper. Poe says it sold out and that scalpers sold copies at inflated prices. When it appeared, after Poe's death, in the Griswold edition, a new note by Poe had been added. It reads: The subjoined *jeu d'esprit* [joke, witticism] with the preceding heading in magnificent capitals, well interspersed with notes of admiration, was originally published, as matter of fact, in the "New York Sun," a daily newspaper, and therein fully subserved the purpose of creating indigestible aliment for the *quidnuncs* [busybodies] during the few hours intervening between a couple of the Charleston mails. The rush for the "sole paper which had the news," was something beyond even the prodigious; and, in fact, if (as some assert) the "Victoria" *did* not absolutely accomplish the voyage recorded, it will be difficult to assign a reason why she *should* not have accomplished it.

[2]**By the energy of an agent at Charleston, S.C.:** In February 1844, a ship had made a remarkably fast trip from New York to Charleston, beating the U.S. mail by three days. Poe inserts this matter to explain the *Sun*'s scoop: presumably, if there had been another fast trip, the other papers, relying on the mail service, would not yet have the story (Scudder, from Mabbott). **Sir Everard Bringhurst:** Probably a made-up name (Scudder). **Mr. Osborne, a nephew of Lord Bentinck's:** Laughton Osborn (Pollin 3) (c.1809–78), poet and dramatist. **Mr. Monck Mason:** A noted British aeronaut who had made a famous flight to Weilburg, Germany, had built a working model of a powered balloon, and had written a pamphlet, republished in America, *Account of the late Aeronautical Expedition from London to Weilburg, Accompanied by Robert Hollond, Esq., and Charles Green, Aeronaut.* The flight occurred in 1836; the U.S. printing of the pamphlet is dated 1837. Poe borrowed heavily from it. Mason is the probable author of another pamphlet, *Remarks on the Ellipsoidal Balloon, propelled by the Archimedean Screw, described as the New Aerial*

THE BALLOON.

Two very decided failures, of late—those of Mr. Henson and Sir George Cayley—had much weakened the public interest in the subject of aerial navigation. Mr. Henson's scheme (which at first was considered very feasible even by men of science,) was founded upon the principle of an inclined plane, started from an eminence by an extrinsic force, applied and continued by the revolution of impinging vanes, in form and number resembling the vanes of a windmill. But, in all the experiments made with models at the Adelaide Gallery, it was found that the operation of these fans not only did not propel the machine, but actually impeded its flight. The only propelling force it ever exhibited, was the mere *impetus* acquired from the descent of the inclined plane; and this *impetus* carried the machine farther when the vanes were at rest, than when they were in motion—a fact which sufficiently demonstrates their inutility; and in the absence of the propelling, which was also the *sustaining* power, the whole fabric would necessarily descend. This consideration led Sir George Cayley to think only of adapting a propeller to some machine having of itself an independent power of support—in a word, to a balloon; the idea, however, being novel, or original, with Sir George, only so far as regards the mode of its application to practice. He exhibited a model of his invention at the Polytechnic Institution.[3] The propelling principle, or power, was here, also, applied to interrupted surfaces, or vanes, put in revolution. These vanes were four in number, but were found entirely ineffectual in moving the balloon, or in aiding its ascending power. The whole project was thus a complete failure.

It was at this juncture that Mr. Monck Mason (whose voyage from Dover to Weilburg in the balloon, "Nassau," occasioned so much excitement in 1837,) conceived the idea of employing the principle of the Archimedean screw for the purpose of propulsion through the air—rightly attributing the failure of Mr. Henson's scheme, and of Sir George Cayley's, to the interruption of surface in the

---

Machine (London 1843), from which Poe lifted whole passages (Wilkinson). Mason died in 1889. **Mr. Robert Holland:** A spelling error: Robert Hollond, M. P., suggested the flight, paid for it, and went along. The spelling error first appears in a note to the U.S. edition of Mason's pamphlet (Scudder); it is also present in Poe's *Sun* hoax. **Mr. Harrison Ainsworth:** William Harrison Ainsworth (1805–82), a novelist. **Mr. Henson:** William Samuel Henson (Pollin 3), who had "planned a heavier-than-air machine to be driven by steam," and who had tried to get parliamentary support for his Aerial Steam Transportation Company (Scudder). **Woolwich:** A municipal borough of London, situated south of the Thames. It became an important naval station and, until 1869, a dockyard. **Mr. Forsyth:** Pollin (3) thinks Poe made up this name.

[3]**Sir George Cayley:** Scudder reports that Cayley is considered "the most important contributor to the science of aeronautics . . . during the first half of the nineteenth century." **Adelaide Gallery:** Wilkinson says that "in 1843 Monck Mason exhibited a model dirigible balloon, of his own construction, at the Royal Adelaide Gallery in London." **Polytechnic Institution:** Poe is using more information from *Remarks on the Ellipsoidal Balloon . . .* (Wilkinson).

independent vanes. He made the first public experiment at Willis's Rooms,[4] but afterwards removed his model to the Adelaide Gallery.

Like Sir George Cayley's balloon, his own was an ellipsoid. Its length was thirteen feet six inches—height, six feet eight inches. It contained about three hundred twenty cubic feet of gas, which, if pure hydrogen, would support twenty-one pounds upon its first inflation, before the gas has time to deteriorate or escape. The weight of the whole machine and apparatus was seventeen pounds—leaving about four pounds to spare. Beneath the centre of the balloon, was a frame of light wood, about ninc fcet long, and rigged on to the balloon itself with a network in the customary manner. From this framework was suspended a wicker basket or car.

The screw consists of an axis of hollow brass tube, eighteen inches in length, through which, upon a semi-spiral inclined at fifteen degrees, pass a series of steel wire radii, two feet long, and thus projecting a foot on either side. These radii are connected at the outer extremities by two bands of flattened wire—the whole in this manner forming the framework of the screw, which is completed by a covering of oiled silk cut into gores, and tightened so as to present a tolerably uniform surface. At each end of its axis this screw is supported by pillars of hollow brass tube descending from the hoop. In the lower ends of these tubes are holes in which the pivots of the axis revolve. From the end of the axis which is next the car, proceeds a shaft of steel, connecting the screw with the pinion of a piece of spring machinery fixed in the car. By the operation of this spring, the screw is made to revolve with great rapidity, communicating a progressive motion to the whole. By means of the rudder, the machine was readily turned in any direction. The spring was of great power, compared with its dimensions, being capable of raising forty-five pounds upon a barrel of four inches diameter, after the first turn, and gradually increasing as it was wound up. It weighed, altogether, eight pounds six ounces. The rudder was a light frame of cane covered with silk, shaped somewhat like a battledoor, and was about three feet long, and at the widest, one foot. Its weight was about two ounces. It could be turned *flat,* and directed upwards or downwards, as well as to the right or left; and thus enabled the æronaut to transfer the resistance of the air which in an inclined position it must generate in its passage, to any side upon which he might desire to act; thus determining the balloon in the opposite direction.

This model (which, through want of time, we have necessarily described in an imperfect manner,) was put in action at the Adelaide Gallery, where it accomplished a velocity of five miles per hour; although, strange to say, it excited very

[4]**Dover to Weilburg:** Dover is on the coast of England, very close to France. Weilburg was where Mason's crew landed. **Archimedean screw:** To Archimedes (287–212 B.C.E.) is attributed a continuous screw inside a cylinder, forming a spiral chamber. If the lower end is placed in water and the "screw" turned, water can be raised; the idea is used also in spiral conveyors and high-speed tools. Mason's device lacks the cylinder. **Willis's Rooms:** A later name of Almack's Assembly-rooms in London. From this point in Poe's tale to the words "in the opposite direction" Poe copies almost verbatim the *Ellipsoidal Balloon* pamphlet (Wilkinson).

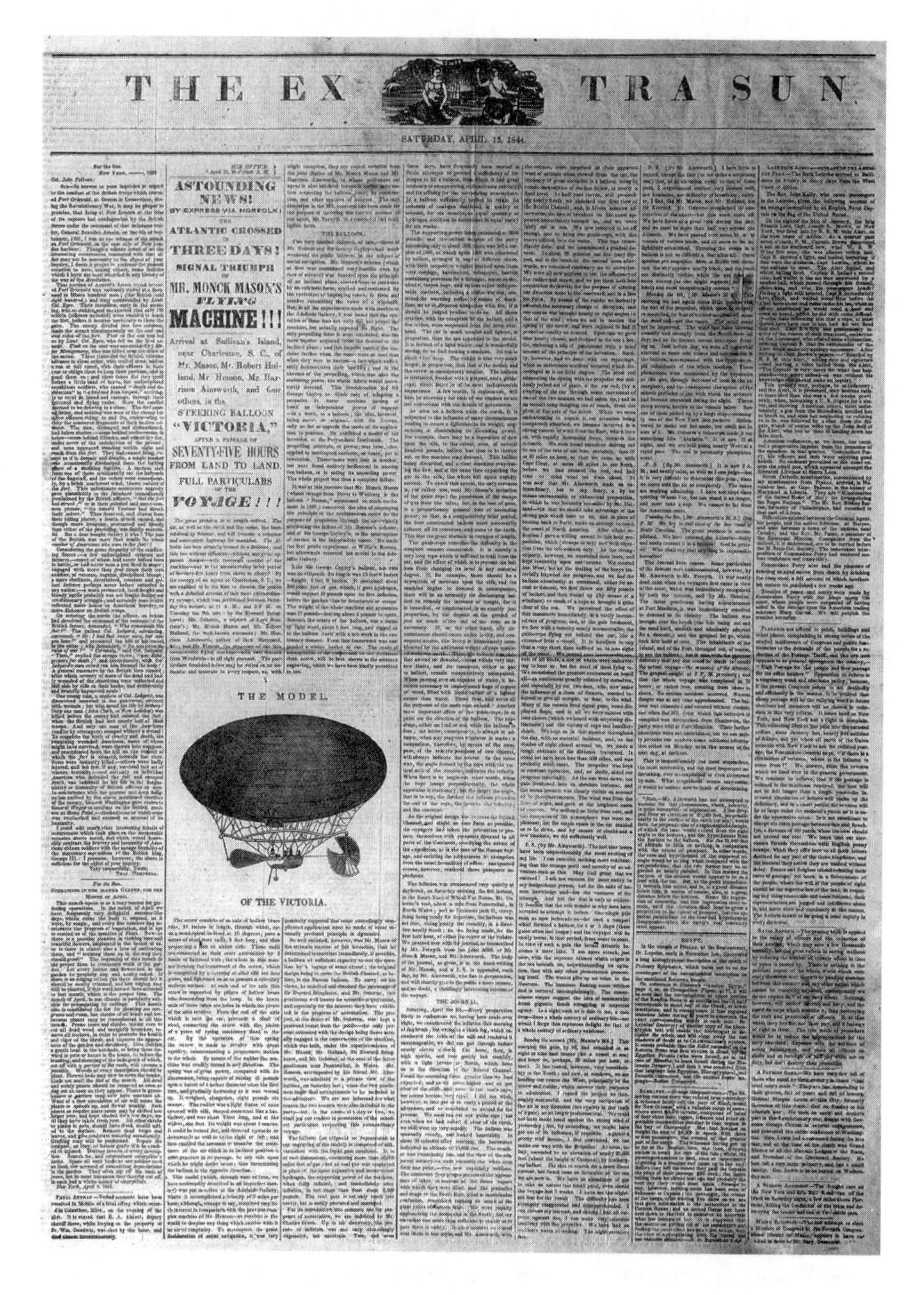

THE EXTRA SUN

SATURDAY, APRIL 13, 1844.

ASTOUNDING NEWS!

BY EXPRESS VIA NORFOLK!

THE ATLANTIC CROSSED IN THREE DAYS!

SIGNAL TRIUMPH OF MR. MONCK MASON'S FLYING MACHINE!!!

Arrival at Sullivan's Island, near Charleston, S. C., of Mr. Mason, Mr. Robert Holland, Mr. Henson, Mr. Harrison Ainsworth, and four others, in the STEERING BALLOON "VICTORIA," AFTER A PASSAGE OF SEVENTY-FIVE HOURS FROM LAND TO LAND. FULL PARTICULARS OF THE VOYAGE!!!

THE MODEL

OF THE VICTORIA.

Figure 9. *The Extra Sun,* April 13, 1844. Here is Poe's "Balloon-Hoax" as it originally appeared. The picture is a careful copy of an engraving which appears on the frontispiece of *Remarks on the Ellipsoidal Balloon,* from which many technical passages of the story are copied almost verbatim (Wilkinson). Note the article on Egyptology following the hoax. This was big news in Poe's day. See "Some Words with a Mummy" and "Mellonta Tauta." Courtesy, American Antiquarian Society.

little interest in comparison with the previous complex machine of Mr. Henson—so resolute is the world to despise anything which carries with it an air of simplicity. To accomplish the great desideratum of ærial navigation, it was very generally supposed that some exceedingly complicated application must be made of some unusually profound principle in dynamics.

So well satisfied, however, was Mr. Mason of the ultimate success of his invention, that he determined to construct immediately, if possible, a balloon of sufficient capacity to test the question by a voyage of some extent—the original design being to cross the British Channel, as before, in the Nassau balloon. To carry out his views, he solicited and obtained the patronage of Sir Everard Bringhurst and Mr. Osborne, two gentlemen well known for scientific acquirement, and especially for the interest they have exhibited in the progress of ærostation. The project, at the desire of Mr. Osborne, was kept a profound secret from the public—the only persons entrusted with the design being those actually engaged in the construction of the machine, which was built (under the superintendence of Mr. Mason, Mr. Holland, Sr. Everard Bringhurst, and Mr. Osborne,) at the seat of the latter gentleman near Penstruthal, in Wales. Mr. Henson, accompanied by his friend Mr. Ainsworth, was admitted to a private view of the balloon, on Saturday last—when the two gentlemen made final arrangements to be included in the adventure. We are not informed for what reason the two seamen were also included in the party—but, in the course of a day or two, we shall put our readers in possession of the minutest particulars respecting this extraordinary voyage.

The balloon is composed of silk, varnished with the liquid gum caoutchouc.[5] It is of vast dimensions, containing more than 40,000 cubic feet of gas; but as coal gas was employed in place of the more expensive and inconvenient hydrogen, the supporting power of the machine, when fully inflated, and immediately after inflation, is not more than about 2500 pounds. The coal gas is not only much less costly, but is easily procured and managed.

For its introduction into common use for purposes of ærostation, we are indebted to Mr. Charles Green. Up to his discovery, the process of inflation was not only exceedingly expensive, but uncertain. Two, and even three days, have frequently been wasted in futile attempts to procure a sufficiency of hydrogen to fill a balloon, from which it had great tendency to escape owing to its extreme subtlety,[6] and its affinity for the surrounding atmosphere. In a balloon sufficiently perfect to retain its contents of coal-gas unaltered, in quality or amount, for six

---

[5]**caoutchouc:** Rubber.

[6]**Mr. Charles Green:** One of Mason's crew for the Weilburg flight. See note 2, above. Green wanted to cross the Atlantic and built a model of an "Atlantic Balloon." His work was reported in the United States (Scudder). **subtlety:** In old chemistry terminology, "subtlety" was a characteristic of certain gases and "fluids." It carried implications that they were hard to detect, handle, or contain, and often that they had unusual characteristics. Phlogiston, for instance, the "stuff of fire" in which good scientists before the 1790s believed, had negative weight, which explained why some substances weighed more after combustion than before: they had given off their phlogiston. By Poe's day, although modern chemistry was securely in being, some older terms, used rather loosely, survived.

months, an equal quantity of hydrogen could not be maintained in equal purity for six weeks.

The supporting power being estimated at 2500 pounds, and the united weights of the party amounting only to about 1200, there was left a surplus of 1300, of which again 1200 was exhausted by ballast, arranged in bags of different sizes, with their respective weights marked upon them—by cordage, barometers, telescopes, barrels containing provision for a fortnight, water-casks, cloaks, carpet-bags, and various other indispensable matters, including a coffee-warmer, contrived for warming coffee by means of slacklime,[7] so as to dispense altogether with fire, if it should be judged prudent to do so. All these articles, with the exception of the ballast, and a few trifles, were suspended from the hoop over head. The car is much smaller and lighter, in proportion, than the one appended to the model. It is formed of a light wicker, and is wonderfully strong, for so frail looking a machine. Its rim is about four feet deep. The rudder is also very much larger, in proportion, than that of the model; and the screw is considerably smaller. The balloon is furnished besides, with a grapnel, and a guide-rope; which latter is of the most indispensable importance. A few words, in explanation, will here be necessary for such of our readers as are not conversant with the details of aerostation.

As soon as the balloon quits the earth, it is subjected to the influence of many circumstances tending to create a difference in its weight; augmenting or diminishing its ascending power. For example, there may be a deposition of dew upon the silk, to the extent, even, of several hundred pounds; ballast has then to be thrown out, or the machine may descend. This ballast being discarded, and a clear sunshine evaporating the dew, and at the same time expanding the gas in the silk, the whole will again rapidly ascend. To check this ascent, the only resource is, (or rather *was,* until Mr. Green's invention of the guide-rope,) the permission of the escape of gas from the valve; but, in the loss of gas, is a proportionate general loss of ascending power; so that, in a comparatively brief period, the best constructed balloon must necessarily exhaust all its resources, and come to the earth. This was the great obstacle to voyages of length.

The guide-rope remedies the difficulty in the simplest manner conceivable. It is merely a very long rope which is suffered to trail from the car, and the effect of which is to prevent the balloon from changing its level in any material degree. If, for example, there should be a deposition of moisture upon the silk, and the machine begins to descend in consequence, there will be no necessity for discharging ballast to remedy the increase of weight, for it is remedied, or counteracted, in an exactly just proportion, by the deposit on the ground of just so much of the end of the rope as is necessary. If, on the other hand, any circumstances should cause undue levity, and consequent ascent, this levity is immediately counteracted by the additional weight of rope upraised from the earth. Thus, the balloon can neither ascend or descend, except within very narrow limits, and its resources, either in gas or ballast, remain comparatively unimpaired. When passing over an expanse of water, it becomes necessary to employ small kegs of

[7]Slacked lime (calcium hydroxide), lime to which water is added.

copper or wood, filled with liquid ballast of a lighter nature than water. These float, and serve all the purposes of a mere rope on land. Another most important office of the guide-rope, is to point out the *direction* of the balloon. The rope *drags,* either on land or sea, while the balloon is free; the latter, consequently, is always in advance, when any progress whatever is made: a comparison, therefore, by means of the compass, of the relative positions of the two objects, will always indicate the *course.* In the same way, the angle formed by the rope with the vertical axis of the machine, indicates the *velocity.* When there is *no* angle—in other words, when the rope hangs perpendicularly, the whole apparatus is stationary; but the larger the angle, that is to say, the farther the balloon precedes the end of the rope, the greater the velocity; and the converse.

As the original design was to cross the British Channel, and alight as near Paris as possible, the voyagers had taken the precaution to prepare themselves with passports directed to all parts of the Continent, specifying the nature of the expedition, as in the case of the Nassau voyage, and entitling the adventurers to exemption from the usual formalities of office: unexpected events, however, rendered these passports superfluous.

The inflation was commenced very quietly at daybreak, on Saturday morning, the 6th instant, in the Court-Yard of Wheal-Vor House, Mr. Osborne's seat, about a mile from Penstruthal, in North Wales; and at 7 minutes past 11, every thing being ready for departure, the balloon was set free, rising gently but steadily, in a direction nearly South; no use being made, for the first half hour, of either the screw or the rudder. We proceed now with the journal, as transcribed by Mr. Forsyth from the joint MSS. of Mr. Monck Mason, and Mr. Ainsworth, who has in preparation, and will shortly give the public a more minute, and no doubt, a thrillingly interesting account of the voyage.

THE JOURNAL.

Saturday, April the 6th.—Every preparation likely to embarrass us, having been made over night, we commenced the inflation this morning at daybreak; but owing to a thick fog, which encumbered the folds of the silk and rendered it unmanageable, we did not get through before nearly eleven o'clock. Cut loose, then, in high spirits, and rose gently but steadily, with a light breeze at North, which bore us in the direction of the British Channel. Found the ascending force greater than we had expected; and as we arose higher and so got clear of the cliffs, and more in the sun's rays, our ascent became very rapid. I did not wish, however, to lose gas at so early a period of the adventure, and so concluded to ascend for the present. We soon ran out our guide-rope; but even when we had raised it clear of the earth, we still went up very rapidly. The balloon was unusually steady, and looked beautifully. In about ten minutes after starting, the barometer indicated an altitude of 15,000 feet. The weather was remarkably fine, and the view of the subjacent country—a most romantic one when seen from any point,—was now especially sublime. The numerous deep gorges presented the appearance of lakes, on account of the dense vapors with which they were filled, and the pinnacles and crags to the South East, piled in inextricable confusion, resembled nothing so much as the giant cities of eastern fable. We were rapidly approaching the mountains in the South; but our elevation was more than sufficient to enable us to pass them in safety. In a few minutes we soared over them in fine style; and Mr. Ainsworth, with the seamen, were surprised at their apparent want of altitude when viewed from the car, the tendency of great elevation in a balloon being to reduce inequalities of the surface below, to nearly a dead level. At half-past eleven still proceeding nearly South, we obtained our first view of the Bristol Channel; and, in fifteen minutes afterwards, the line of breakers on the coast appeared immediately beneath us, and we were fairly out at sea. We now resolved to let off enough gas to bring our guide-rope, with the buoys affixed, into the water. This was immediately done, and we commenced a gradual descent. In about twenty minutes our first buoy dipped, and at the touch of the second soon afterwards, we remained stationary as to elevation. We were all now anxious to test the efficiency of the rudder and screw, and we put them both into requisition forthwith, for the purpose of altering our direction more to the eastward, and in a line for Paris. By means of the rudder we instantly effected the necessary change of direction, and our course was brought nearly at right angles to that of the wind; when we set in motion the spring of the screw, and were rejoiced to find it propel us readily as desired. Upon this we gave nine hearty cheers, and dropped in the sea a bottle, enclosing a slip of parchment with a brief account of the principle of the invention. Hardly, however, had we done with our rejoicings, when an unforeseen accident occurred which discouraged us in no little degree. The steel rod connecting the spring with the propeller was suddenly jerked out of place, at the car end, (by a swaying of the car through some movement of one of the two seamen we had taken up,) and in an instant hung dangling out of reach, from the pivot of the axis of the screw. While we were endeavoring to regain it, our attention being completely absorbed, we became involved in a strong current of wind from the East, which bore us, with rapidly increasing force, towards the Atlantic. We soon found ourselves driving out to sea at the rate of not less, certainly, than fifty or sixty miles an hour, so that we came up with Cape Clear, at some forty miles to our North, before we had secured the rod, and had time to think what we were about. It was now that Mr. Ainsworth made an extraordinary, but to my fancy, a by no means unreasonable or chimerical proposition, in which he has instantly seconded by Mr. Holland—viz.: that we should take advantage of the strong gale which bore us on, and in place of beating back to Paris, make an attempt to reach the coast of North America. After slight reflection I gave a willing assent to this bold proposition, which (strange to say) met with objection from the two seamen only. As the stronger party, however, we overruled their fears, and kept resolutely upon our course. We steered due West; but as the trailing of the buoys materially impeded our progress, and we had the balloon abundantly at command, either for ascent or descent, we first threw out fifty pounds of ballast, and then wound up (by means of a windlass) so much of the rope as brought it quite clear of the sea. We perceived the effect of this manœuvre immediately, in a vastly increased rate of progress; and, as the gale freshened, we flew with a velocity nearly inconceivable; the guide-rope flying out behind the car, like a streamer from a vessel. It is needless to say that a very short time sufficed us to lose sight of the coast. We passed over innumerable vessels of all kinds, a few of which were endeavoring to beat up, but the most of them lying to. We occasioned the greatest excitement on board all—an excitement greatly relished by ourselves, and especially by our two men, who, now under the influence of a dram of Geneva,[8] seemed resolved to give all scruple, or fear, to the wind. Many of the vessels fired signal guns; and in all we were

[8]**beat:** Tack into the wind. **lying to:** Staying as stationary as possible, bow into the wind. **Geneva:** Gin.

saluted with loud cheers (which we heard with surprising distinctness) and the waving of caps and handkerchiefs. We kept on in this manner throughout the day, with no material incident, and, as the shades of night closed around us, we made a rough estimate of the distance traversed. It could not have been less than five hundred miles, and was probably much more. The propeller was kept in constant operation, and, no doubt, aided our progress materially. As the sun went down, the gale freshened into an absolute hurricane, and the ocean beneath was clearly visible on account of its phosphorescence. The wind was from the East all night, and gave us the brightest omen of success. We suffered no little from cold, and the dampness of the atmosphere was most unpleasant; but the ample space in the car enabled us to lie down, and by means of cloaks and a few blankets, we did sufficiently well.

P.S. (by Mr. Ainsworth). The last nine hours have been unquestionably the most exciting of my life. I can conceive nothing more sublimating than the strange peril and novelty of an adventure such as this. May God grant that we succeed! I ask not success for mere safety to my insignificant person, but for the sake of human knowledge and—for the vastness of the triumph. And yet the feat is only so evidently feasible that the sole wonder is why men have scrupled to attempt it before. One single gale such as now befriends us—let such a tempest whirl forward a balloon for four or five days (these gales often last longer) and the voyager will be easily borne, in that period, from coast to coast. In view of such a gale the broad Atlantic becomes a mere lake. I am more struck, just now, with the supreme silence which reigns in the sea beneath us, notwithstanding its agitation, than with any other phenomenon presenting itself. The waters give up no voice to the heavens.[9] The immense flaming ocean writhes and is tortured uncomplainingly. The mountainous surges suggest the idea of innumerable dumb gigantic fiends struggling in impotent agony. In a night such as is this to me, a man *lives*—lives a whole century of ordinary life—nor would I forego this rapturous delight for that of a whole century of ordinary existence.

Sunday, the seventh. [Mr. Mason's MS.] This morning the gale, by 10, had subsided to an eight or nine knot breeze, (for a vessel at sea,) and bears us, perhaps, thirty miles per hour, or more. It has veered however, very considerably to the north; and now, at sundown, we are holding our course due west, principally by the screw and rudder, which answer their purposes to admiration. I regard the project as thoroughly successful, and the easy navigation of the air in any direction (not exactly in the teeth of a gale) as no longer problematical. We could not have made head against the strong wind of yesterday; but, by ascending, we might have got out of its influence, if requisite. Against a pretty stiff breeze, I feel convinced, we can make our way with the propeller. At noon, to-day, ascended to an elevation of nearly 25,000 feet, by discharging ballast. Did this to search for a more direct current, but found none so favorable as the one we are now in.[10] We have an abundance of gas to take us across this small pond, even should the voyage last three weeks. I have not the slightest fear for the result. The difficulty has been strangely exaggerated and misapprehended. I

[9]Poe has in mind a passage from Psalm 93:

The waters lift up their voices, O Lord,
The mighty waters, breakers of the sea;
Yet above the voices of the waters
Thou, O Lord, art mighty on high.

[10]Poe's science here is sound. Wind velocities and even directions vary at different altitudes.

can choose my current, and should I find *all* currents against me, I can make very tolerable headway with the propeller. We have had no incidents worth recording. The night promises fair.

P.S. [By Mr. Ainsworth.] I have little to record, except the fact (to me quite a surprising one) that, at an elevation equal to that of Cotopaxi, I experienced neither very intense cold, nor headache, nor difficulty of breathing; neither, I find, did Mr. Mason, nor Mr. Holland, nor Sir Everard. Mr. Osborne complained of constriction of the chest—but this soon wore off. We have flown at a great rate during the day, and we must be more than half way across the Atlantic. We have passed over some twenty or thirty vessels of various kinds, and all seem to be delightfully astonished. Crossing the ocean in a balloon is not so difficult a feat after all. *Omne ignotum pro magnifico.*[11] *Mem:* at 25,000 feet elevation the sky appears nearly black, and the stars are distinctly visible; while the sea does not seem convex (as one might suppose) but absolutely and most unequivocally *concave.*[12]

Monday, the 8th [Mr. Mason's MS.] This morning we had again some little trouble with the rod of the propeller, which must be entirely remodelled, for fear of serious accident—I mean the steel rod not the vanes. The latter could not be improved. The wind has been blowing steadily and strongly from the northeast all day; and so far fortune seems bent upon favoring us. Just before day, we were all somewhat alarmed at some odd noises and concussions in the balloon, accompanied with the apparent rapid subsidence of the whole machine. These phenomena were occasioned by the expansion of the gas, through increase of heat in the atmosphere, and the consequent disruption of the minute particles of ice with which the network had become encrusted during the night. Threw down several bottles to the vessels below. Saw one of them picked up by a large ship—seemingly one of the New York line packets. Endeavored to make out her name, but could not be sure of it. Mr. Osborne's telescope made it out something like "Atalanta." It is now 12, at night, and we are still going nearly west, at a rapid pace. The sea is peculiarly phosphorescent.

P.S. [By Mr. Ainsworth.] It is now 2, A.M., and nearly calm, as well as I can judge—but it is very difficult to determine this point, since we move *with* the air so com-

---

[11]**Cotopaxi:** Volcano in Ecuador. Modern sources list its height as 19,344 feet. People in Poe's day thought that the highest peaks in the world were in South America. ***Omne ignotum pro magnifico:*** The phrase is from Tacitus, *Agricola,* XXX, and means, "What is unknown is always thought magnificent."

[12]Mr. Ainsworth has not attempted to account for this phenomenon, which, however, is quite susceptible of explanation. A line dropped from an elevation of 25,000 feet, perpendicularly to the surface of the earth (or sea), would form the perpendicular of a right-angled triangle, of which the base would extend from the right angle to the horizon, and the hypothenuse from the horizon to the balloon. But the 25,000 feet of altitude is little or nothing, in comparison with the extent of the prospect. In other words, the base and hypothenuse of the supposed triangle would be so long when compared with the perpendicular that the two former may be regarded as nearly parallel. In this manner the horizon of the æronaut would appear to be *on a level* with the car. But, as the point immediately beneath him seems, and is, at a great distance below him, it seems, of course, also, at a great distance below the horizon. Hence the impression of *concavity;* and this impression must remain, until the elevation shall bear so great a proportion to the extent of prospect, that the apparent parallelism of the base and hypothenuse disappears—when the earth's real convexity must become apparent [Poe's note].

pletely. I have not slept since quitting Wheal-Vor, but can stand it no longer, and must take a nap. We cannot be far from the American coast.

Tuesday, the 9th. [Mr. Ainsworth's MS.] *One, P.M. We are in full view of the low coast of South Carolina.* The great problem is accomplished. We have crossed the Atlantic—fairly and *easily* crossed it in a balloon! God be praised! Who shall say that anything is impossible hereafter?

The Journal here ceases. Some particulars of the descent were communicated, however, by Mr. Ainsworth to Mr. Forsyth. It was nearly dead calm when the voyagers first came in view of the coast, which was immediately recognised by both the seamen, and by Mr. Osborne. The latter gentleman having acquaintances at Fort Moultrie,[13] it was immediately resolved to descend in its vicinity. The balloon was brought over the beach (the tide being out and the sand hard, smooth, and admirably adapted for a descent,) and the grapnel let go, which took firm hold at once. The inhabitants of the island, and of the fort, thronged out, of course, to see the balloon; but it was with the greatest difficulty that any one could be made to credit the actual voyage—*the crossing of the Atlantic.* The grapnel caught at 2, P.M., precisely; and thus the whole voyage was completed in seventy-five hours; or rather less, counting from shore to shore. No serious accident occurred. No real danger was at any time apprehended. The balloon was exhausted and secured without trouble; and when the MS. from which this narrative is compiled was despatched from Charleston, the party were still at Fort Moultrie. Their farther intentions were not ascertained; but we can safely promise our readers some additional information either on Monday or in the course of the next day, at farthest.

This is unquestionably the most stupendous, the most interesting, and the most important undertaking, ever accomplished or even attempted by man. What magnificent events may ensue, it would be useless now to think of determining.

---

[13] A place Poe knew well, having served there. He used it in "The Gold-Bug." See note 4 of that story.

The Literary Life of Thingum Bob, Esq.

George Graham, like Thingum Bob, bought up and combined magazines; like Bob, he was a very *minor poet—even the indefatigable Thomas Ollive Mabbott, who devoted a lifetime of antiquarian scholarship to Poeiana, could find only one poem by Graham. But Graham was not Poe's main target in this funny, angry, affectionate piece. Poe was after the whole petty world of American magazines. The trouble is that you and I are not Americans of the 1840s; if we read the story without some help, it is not especially interesting, let alone funny. Help, however is available. We suggest reading this headnote and browsing through the notes before reading the story.*

Fiercely competitive, insecure about their own artistic worth, limited in popularity and influence, the American literary magazines of Poe's day had to create an illusion of importance in order to survive at all, and their editors were, indeed, guilty of the faults which Poe exaggerates in Thingum Bob, such as the tendency to see "the Literary History of America" in terms of their own careers. Whipple (3) has figured out one specific target of Poe's sarcasm. Lewis Gaylord Clark began in 1844 publication of the Literary Remains of the Late Willis Gaylord Clark, *his twin brother. Poe's character Thingum Bob represents Willis, but, since Willis is dead, Poe's real target is Lewis and the system of "You scratch my back and I'll scratch yours" which prevailed in magazine and book publishing circles. Note the similarity in titles. Thingum is still alive (Whipple errs here), but Poe gets the word "late" (that is, deceased) into his subtitle to make it clear to the reader that he has the Clarks'* Literary Remains *in mind. A reader of* The Broadway Journal *could hardly have missed the connection—there was a piece about Willis in the same issue in which "Thingum Bob" was published.*

The bane of the publishing world in Poe's day was "puffing": over-praising the work of friends who would then do the same for you in their *magazines. So Thingum Bob's introduction to literature involves "puffery"—his father rewards the editor-poet who praises his hair-oil. When Poe arrived in New York in 1844, he encountered all manner of puffery for Lewis Clark's edition of his brother's work.*

There is another related target: Poe's dispute with Lewis Clark stems largely from Poe's famous hostile review of Theodore Fay's Norman Leslie. *Fay fought back in a satire which, Pollin shows, was aimed at Poe: He called Poe "Bulldog," made him editor of "The Southern Literary Passenger," and said that Poe hated successful novelists because his own works were rejected by publishers. And Poe responded with this tale. Pollin (14) spells out the relationship between it and the piece by Fay:*

FAY'S "THE SUCCESSFUL NOVEL"	*POE'S ANSWER TO IT ("THINGUM BOB")*
1. Fay was a lawyer, politician, poet, and editor	*1. See text at note 5: these are the careers Thingum considers*
2. The name "Thingum"	*2. "Thingum Bob"*
3. "Capias"	*3. "Slyass"*
4. "Toadeater"	*4. "Toad"*
5. "Goosequill"	*5. "Goosetherumfoodle"*
6. "Bumble-Bee"	*6. "Gad-Fly"*
7. "Rosewater"	*7. "Oil of Bob"*

Pollin's case is strong; we can't summarize it here. Clearly Poe had Fay in mind as well as the Clark brothers, and clearly the tale is one of Poe's multiple-targeted forays against the New York literary cliques.

PUBLICATIONS IN POE'S TIME

The Southern Literary Messenger, December 1844
The Broadway Journal, July 26, 1845

THE LITERARY LIFE OF THINGUM BOB, ESQ.
Late Editor of the 'Goosetherumfoodle'[1]

BY HIMSELF

I am now growing in years, and—since I understand that Shakespeare and Mr. Emmons[2] are deceased—it is not impossible that I may even die. It has occurred to me, therefore, that I may as well retire from the field of Letters and repose upon

[1]"Thingum Bob" is an alternative spelling for "thingamabob," something you've forgotten the name of. Poe's point is that his "author" is totally unimportant. Pollin shows that Poe's choice of Bob's name and profession could have been influenced by Thomas Moore's *The Fudges in England.* In Letter Three of Moore's work, Fanny Fudge tells her cousin about "a literary man who edits 'live authors as if they were posthumous,'" and says "He was Lady Jane Thingumbob's last novel's editor" (Pollin 14). "Goosetherumfoodle" is probably nonsense. "Footle" (foodle), in fact, means "nonsense." See our headnote for the specific targets of Poe's satire and the referents of other "nonsense" words in this tale.

[2]Richard "Pop" Emmons (1788–c.1837) is a very minor writer at whom Melville also pokes fun. He was the author of "The Fredoniad," published in the *Western Monthly Review* 2:176. The point is that Thingum's literary intelligence is so low that he lumps Shakespeare and Pop Emmons together.

my laurels. But I am ambitious of signalizing my abdication of the literary sceptre by some important bequest to posterity and, perhaps, I cannot do a better thing than just pen for it an account of my earlier career. My name, indeed, has been so long and so constantly before the public eye, that I am not only willing to admit the naturalness of the interest which it has everywhere excited, but ready to satisfy the extreme curiosity which it has inspired. In fact it is no more than the duty of him who achieves greatness, to leave behind him, in his ascent, such landmarks as may guide others to be great. I propose, therefore, in the present paper, (which I had some idea of calling "Memoranda to serve for the Literary History of America,") to give a detail of those important, yet feeble and tottering first steps, by which, at length, I attained the high road to the pinnacle of human renown.

Of one's *very* remote ancestors it is superfluous to say much. My father, Thomas Bob, Esq., stood for many years at the summit of his profession, which was that of a merchant-barber, in the city of Smug. His warehouse was the resort of all the principal people of the place, and especially of the editorial corps—a body which inspires all about it with profound veneration and awe. For my own part, I regarded them as Gods, and drank in with avidity the rich wit and wisdom which continuously flowed from their august mouths during the process of what is styled "lather." My first moment of positive inspiration must be dated from that ever-memorable epoch, when the brilliant conductor of the "Gad-Fly," in the intervals of the important process just mentioned, recited aloud, before a conclave of our apprentices, an inimitable poem in honor of the "Only Genuine Oil-of-Bob," (so called from its talented inventor, my father,) and for which effusion the editor of the "Fly" was remunerated with a regal liberality, by the firm of Thomas Bob and company, merchant barbers.[3]

The genius of the stanzas to the "Oil-of-Bob" first breathed into me, I say, the divine *afflatus.*[4] I resolved at once to become a great man and to commence by becoming a great poet. That very evening I fell upon my knees at the feet of my father.

"Father," I said, "pardon me!—but I have a soul above lather. It is my firm intention to cut the shop. I would be an editor—I would be a poet—I would pen stanzas to the 'Oil-of-Bob.' Pardon me and aid me to be great!"

"My dear Thingum," replied my father, (I had been christened Thingum after a wealthy relative so surnamed,) "My dear Thingum," he said, raising me from my knees by the ears—"Thingum, my boy, you're a trump, and take after your father in having a soul. You have an immense head, too, and it must hold a great many brains. This I have long seen, and therefore had thoughts of making you a lawyer. The business, however, has grown ungenteel, and that of a politician don't pay. Upon the whole you judge wisely;—the trade of editor is best:—and if you can be a poet at the same time,—as most of the editors are, by the by,—why you will kill

---

[3]***very* remote ancestors:** That is, Bob's origins are very obscure. **effusion . . . barbers:** See our headnote.

[4]Creative spirit or inspiration.

two birds with one stone.[5] To encourage you in the beginning of things, I will allow you a garret; pen, ink and paper; a rhyming dictionary; and a copy of the 'Gad-Fly.' I suppose you would scarcely demand any more."

"I would be an ungrateful villain if I did," I replied with enthusiasm. "Your generosity is boundless. I will repay it by making you the father of a genius."

Thus ended my conference with the best of men, and immediately upon its termination, I betook myself with zeal to my poetical labors; as upon these, chiefly, I founded my hopes of ultimate elevation to the editorial chair.

In my first attempts at composition I found the stanzas to "The Oil-of-Bob" rather a draw-back than otherwise. Their splendor more dazzled than enlightened me. The contemplation of their excellence tended, naturally, to discourage me by comparison with my own abortions; so that for a long time I labored in vain. At length there came into my head one of those exquisitely original ideas which now and then *will* permeate the brain of a man of genius. It was this:—or, rather, thus was it carried into execution. From the rubbish of an old book-stall, in a very remote corner of the town, I got together several antique and altogether unknown or forgotten volumes. The bookseller sold them to me for a song. From one of these, which purported to be a translation of one Dante's "Inferno," I copied with remarkable neatness a long passage about a man named Ugolino, who had a parcel of brats. From another which contained a good many old plays by some person whose name I forget, I extracted in the same manner, and with the same care, a great number of lines about "angels" and "ministers saying grace," and "goblins damned," and more besides of that sort. From a third, which was the composition of some blind man or other, either a Greek or a Choctaw—I cannot be at the pains of remembering every trifle exactly—I took about fifty verses beginning with "Achilles' wrath," and "grease," and something else. From a fourth, which I recollect was also the work of a blind man, I selected a page or two all about "hail" and "holy light;" and although a blind man has no business to write about light, still the verses were sufficiently good in their way.[6]

---

[5]**relative so surnamed:** Willis Gaylord Clark had been named after a rich uncle (Willis Gaylord), too (Whipple 3). **two birds with one stone:** See our headnote. This list of careers identifies Thingum with Fay as well as Clark (Pollin 14).

[6]As Thingum Bob has no ancestry, so he has no education, failing to recognize Dante, Shakespeare, Homer, and Milton. **Ugolino:** Ugolino della Gherardesca is the subject of a famous passage in Dante's "Inferno"; he is consigned to the ninth circle of hell, reserved for traitors, where the memory of how he, two sons, and two grandsons were starved to death drives him in his hatred to gnaw upon the skull of Archbishop Ruggieri degli Ubaldini, leader of the rival political party which defeated Ugolino's party and murdered him. Thingum Bob is too stupid to understand Ugolino's grief over the death of his children; hence Poe's allusion to "brats." **"angels" and "ministers . . . ":** At the entrance of the ghost of his father, in *Hamlet* (I, 4, 39–40), Hamlet says,

Angels and ministers of grace defend us!
Be thou a spirit of health or goblin damn'd.

either a Greek or a Choctaw: Thingum Bob doesn't know a Creek from a Greek. The

Having made fair copies of these poems I signed every one of them "Oppodeldoc," (a fine sonorous name,) and, doing each up nicely in a separate envelope, I despatched one to each of the four principal Magazines, with a request for speedy insertion and prompt pay. The result of this well conceived plan, however, (the success of which would have saved me much trouble in after life,) served to convince me that some editors are not to be bamboozled, and gave the *coup-de-grâce* (as they say in France,) to my nascent hopes, (as they say in the city of the transcendentals.)[7]

The fact is, that each and every one of the Magazines in question, gave Mr. "Oppodeldoc" a complete using-up, in the "Monthly Notices to Correspondents." The "Hum-Drum" gave him a dressing after this fashion:

---

phrase shows racial condescension toward Native Americans, who are assumed to be stupid and ignorant savages. To confuse Homer, a "Greek" (it was not yet clear in Poe's day that a poet named Homer had not literally "written" the *Iliad*) with an Indian is as strong evidence of ignorance as Poe can devise. **"Achilles' wrath," and "grease":** The *Iliad* opens with an invocation; the goddess is asked to sing of the wrath of Achilles which brought, in the Chapman translation, "Infinite sorrowes on the Greekes." "Grease" is a bad pun on "Greece." **"Hail" and "holy light":** Book Three of Milton's *Paradise Lost* opens, "Hail, holy light! offspring of heav'n first-born." Homer is traditionally supposed to have been blind; Milton was blind.

[7]**Oppodeldoc:** Willis Clark's pen name in the *Knickerbocker* magazine was "Ollapod," a name used by Poe in "A Predicament," and similar to "Oppodeldoc" (Whipple 3). Pollin (11) points out that "Op[p]odeldoc" is the name of several very famous patent medicines based on an ages-old formula, and peddled vigorously in the United States in Poe's day. The tale contains a number of humorous turns based on that association: readers are "nauseated with a sad dose . . . " etc. Pollin (11) doubts Whipple's Ollapod-Oppodeldoc equation. Pollin (6) finds still another source for the name "Ollapod." See "How to Write a Blackwood Article," note 30. Thackeray uses Opodeldoc as the name of a horse (the medicine was recommended, in one form, as a horse linament): referring to Club Snobs, in his *The Book of Snobs* (Thackeray had written on snobs as early as 1829, but his collection published under this title appeared in 1848) he writes, "They recollect the history of that short period in which they have been ornaments of the world by the names of winning-horses. As political men talk bout 'the reform year,' 'the year the Whigs went out,' and so forth, these young sporting bucks speak of *Tarnation's* year, or *Opodeldoc's* year, or the year when *Catawampus* ran second for the Chester cup." Two other names shared by Poe in this tale and Thackeray in *The Book of Snobs* are "Daddy-Long-Legs" and "Lollipop." In Poe both are the names of journals. In Thackeray the former is another horse's name and the latter the surname of Lord Claude Lollipop, the Marquis of Sillabub's younger son. Poe's use of "Snob" as a pen name later in this tale suggests that we are correct in seeing Thackeray as a source, though we do not know whether the connection between "Thingum Bob" and *The Book of Snobs* has any special meaning. Mabbott (9, II) actually found an 1840 "Discourse on Pigs" signed "Snob" in a New York paper. **the city of the transcendentals:** Boston. Thingum Bob shows off his pretended erudition by using foreign terms whenever he can. The joke is double: first, that Transcendentalists speak a language so lofty that it's foreign; second, Thingum mixes his metaphors: the "*coup-de-grâce*" is a death-blow, inappropriate to "nascent" hopes. The idea was introduced a paragraph earlier in the wordplay about "abortions" and "labored in vain."

"'Oppodeldoc,' (whoever he is,) has sent us a long *tirade* concerning a bedlamite whom he styles whom he styles 'Ugolino,' who had a great many children that should have been all whipped and sent to bed without their suppers. The whole affair is exceedingly tame—not to say *flat.* 'Oppodeldoc,' (whoever he is,) is entirely devoid of imagination—and imagination, in our humble opinion, is not only the soul of POESY, but also its very heart. 'Oppodeldoc,' (whoever he is,) has the audacity to demand of us, for his twattle, a 'speedy insertion and prompt pay.' We neither insert nor purchase any stuff of the sort. There can be no doubt, however, that he would meet with a ready sale for all the balderdash he can scribble, at the office of either the 'Rowdy-Dow,' the 'Lollipop,' or the 'Goosetherumfoodle.'"[8]

All this, it must be acknowledged, was very severe upon "Oppodeldoc"—but the unkindest cut was putting the word POESY in small caps. In those five preeminent letters what a world of bitterness is there not involved![9]

But "Oppodeldoc" was punished with equal severity in the "Rowdy-Dow," which spoke thus:

"We have received a most singular and insolent communication from a person, (whoever he is,) signing himself 'Oppodeldoc'—thus desecrating the greatness of the illustrious Roman Emperor so named. Accompanying the letter of 'Oppodeldoc,' (whoever he is,) we find sundry lines of most disgusting and unmeaning rant about 'angels and ministers of grace'—rant such as no madman short of a Nat Lee,[10] or an 'Oppodeldoc,' could possibly perpetrate. And for this trash of trash, we are modestly requested to 'pay promptly.' No sir—no! We pay for nothing of *that* sort. Apply to the 'Hum-Drum,' the 'Lollipop,' or the 'Goosetherumfoodle.' These *periodicals* will undoubtedly accept any literary offal you may send them—and as undoubtedly *promise* to pay for it."

This was bitter indeed upon poor "Oppodeldoc;" but, in this instance, the weight of the satire falls upon the "Hum-Drum," the "Lollipop," and the "Goosetherumfoodle," who are pungently styled "*periodicals*"—in Italics, too—a thing that must have cut them to the heart.

Scarcely less savage was the "Lollipop," which thus discoursed:

"Some *individual,* who rejoices in the appellation 'Oppodeldoc' (to what low uses are the names of the illustrious dead too often applied!) has enclosed us some fifty or sixty *verses,* commencing after this fashion:

---

[8]The central gag in this series of "notices" is that the magazine editors, like Thingum Bob, are too ignorant to recognize either the sources of the stolen poems or their worth. So the "Hum-Drum" says that Dante has no imagination. Clearly, "POESY" refers to "Poe."

[9]This phrase stuck in Poe's mind. He used it in numerous variations in his (1849) poem "The Bells" (see also "How to Write a Blackwood Article," notes 27 and 28): "What a world of merriment their melody foretells!" . . . "What a world of happiness their harmony foretells!" . . . "What a gush of euphony voluminously wells!" . . . "What a tale of terror, now, their turbulency tells!" . . . "What a world of solemn thought their monody compels!"

[10]**Emperor so named:** More ignorance. There never was, of course, an emperor by this name. **Nat Lee:** Nathaniel Lee (c.1649–92) was an English tragic dramatist who spent five years (1684–89) in Bedlam.

Achilles' wrath, to Greece the direful spring
Of woes unnumbered, &c., &c., &c., &c.

"'Oppodeldoc,' (whoever he is,) is respectfully informed that there is not a printer's devil in our office who is not in the daily habit of composing better *lines.* Those of 'Oppodeldoc' will not *scan.* 'Oppodeldoc' should learn to *count.* But why he should have conceived the idea that *we,* (of all others, *we!*) would disgrace our pages with his ineffable nonsense, is utterly beyond comprehension. Why, the absurd twattle is scarcely good enough for the 'Hum-Drum,' the 'Rowdy-Dow,' the 'Goosetherumfoodle'—things that are in the practice of publishing 'Mother Goose's Melodies' as original lyrics. And 'Oppodeldoc,' (whoever he is,) has even the assurance to demand *pay* for this drivel. Does 'Oppodeldoc,' (whoever he is,) know—is he aware that we could not be paid to insert it?"[11]

As I perused this I felt myself growing gradually smaller and smaller, and when I came to the point at which the editor sneered at the poem as "*verses,*" there was little more than an ounce of me left. As for "Oppodeldoc" I began to experience *compassion* for the poor fellow. But the "Goosetherumfoodle" showed, if possible, less mercy than the "Lollipop." It was the "Goosetherumfoodle" that said:

"A wretched poetaster, who signs himself 'Oppodeldoc,' is silly enough to fancy that *we* will print and *pay for* a medley of incoherent and ungrammatical bombast which he has transmitted to us, and which commences with the following most *intelligible* line:

'Hail, Holy Light! Offspring of Heaven, first born.'

"We say, 'most *intelligible.*' 'Oppodeldoc,' (whoever he is,) will be kind enough to tell us, perhaps, how '*hail*' can be '*holy light.*' We always regarded it as *frozen rain.* Will he inform us, also, how frozen rain can be, at one and the same time, both 'holy light,' (whatever that is,) and an 'offspring?'—which latter term, (if *we* understand any thing about English,) is only employed, with propriety, in reference to small babies of about six weeks old. But it is preposterous to descant upon such absurdity—although 'Oppodeldoc,' (whoever he is,) has the unparalleled effrontery to suppose that we will not only 'insert' his ignorant ravings, but (absolutely) *pay for them!*

"Now this is fine—it is rich!—and we have half a mind to punish this young scribbler for his egotism, by really publishing his effusion, *verbatim et literatim,*[12] as he has written it. We could inflict no punishment so severe, and we *would* inflict it, but for the boredom which we should cause our readers in so doing.

"Let 'Oppodeldoc,' (whoever he is,) send any future *composition* of like character to the 'Hum-Drum,' the 'Lollipop,' or the 'Rowdy-Dow.' *They* will 'insert' it.

[11]The *Knickerbocker* had run "Jack and Jill" in May 1843, though not, of course, as "original lyrics" (Whipple 3). All of the little literary magazines were stingy of pay, hence the frequent references to payment in this tale.
[12]Verbatim and literally.

They 'insert' every month just such stuff. Send it to them. WE are not to be insulted with impunity."[13]

This made an end of me; and as for the "Hum-Drum," the "Rowdy-Dow," and the "Lollipop," I never could comprehend how they survived it. The putting *them* in the smallest possible *minion,* (*that* was the rub—thereby insinuating their lowness—their baseness,) while WE stood looking down upon them in gigantic capitals!—oh it was *too* bitter!—it was wormword—it was gall. Had I been either of these periodicals I would have spared no pains to have the "Goosetherumfoodle" prosecuted. It might have been done under the Act for the "Prevention of Cruelty to Animals." As for "Oppodeldoc," (whoever he was,) I had by this time lost all patience with the fellow, and sympathized with him no longer. He was a fool, beyond doubt, (whoever he was,) and got not a kick more than he deserved.

The result of my experiment with the old books, convinced me, in the first place, that "honesty is the best policy," and, in the second, that if I could not write better than Mr. Dante, and the two blind men, and the rest of the old set, it would, at least, be a difficult matter to write worse. I took heart, therefore, and determined to prosecute the "entirely original," (as they say on the covers of the magazines,) at whatever cost of study and pains. I again placed before my eyes as a model, the brilliant stanzas on "The Oil-of-Bob," by the editor of the "Gad-Fly," and resolved to construct an Ode on the same sublime theme, in rivalry of what had already been done.

With my first verse I had no material difficulty. It ran thus:

To pen an Ode upon the "Oil-of-Bob."

Having carefully looked out, however, all the legitimate rhymes to "Bob," I found it impossible to proceed. In this dilemma I had recourse to paternal aid; and, after some hours of mature thought, my father and myself thus constructed the poem:

To pen an Ode upon the "Oil-of-Bob"
Is all sorts of a job.
(Signed,) SNOB.

To be sure this composition was of no very great length—but I "have yet to learn" as they say in the Edinburgh Review, that the mere extent of a literary work has any thing to do with its merit. As for the Quarterly cant about "sustained effort," it is impossible to see the sense of it. Upon the whole, therefore, I was satisfied with the success of my maiden attempt, and now the only question regarded the disposal I should make of it. My father suggested that I should send it to the "Gad-Fly"—but there were two reasons which operated to prevent me from so doing. I dreaded the jealousy of the editor—and I had ascertained that he did not pay for original contributions. I therefore, after due deliberation, consigned

[13]Poe has some pet phrases which show up in both serious and satirical contexts. In "The Cask of Amontillado," we learn that Montresor's arms bear the motto, "*Nemo me impune lacessit*": "No one provokes me with impunity."

the article to the more dignified pages of the "Lollipop," and awaited the event in anxiety, but with resignation.

In the very next published number I had the proud satisfaction of seeing my poem printed at length, as the leading article, with the following significant words, prefixed in italics and between brackets:

> *["We call the attention of our readers to the subjoined admirable stanzas on 'The Oil-of-Bob.' We need say nothing of their sublimity, or of their pathos:—it is impossible to peruse them without tears. Those who have been nauseated with a sad dose on the same august topic from the goose-quill of the editor of the 'Gad-Fly,' will do well to compare the two compositions.*
>
> *P.S. We are consumed with anxiety to probe the mystery which envelops the evident pseudonym 'Snob.' May we hope for a personal interview?"]*

All this was scarcely more than justice, but it was, I confess, rather more than I had expected:—I acknowledge this, be it observed, to the everlasting disgrace of my country and of mankind. I lost no time, however, in calling upon the editor of the "Lollipop," and had the good fortune to find this gentleman at home. He saluted me with an air of profound respect, slightly blended with a fatherly and patronizing admiration, wrought in him, no doubt, by my appearance of extreme youth and inexperience. Begging me to be seated, he entered at once upon the subject of my poem;—but modestly will ever forbid me to repeat the thousand compliments which he lavished upon me. The eulogies of Mr. Crab, (such was the editor's name,) were, however, by no means fulsomely indiscriminate. He analyzed my composition with much freedom and great ability—not hesitating to point out a few trivial defects—a circumstance which elevated him highly in my esteem. The "Gad-Fly" was, of course, brought upon the *tapis,* and I hope never to be subjected to a criticism so searching, or to rebukes so withering, as were bestowed by Mr. Crab upon that unhappy effusion. I had been accustomed to regard the editor of the "Gad-Fly" as something superhuman; but Mr. Crab soon disabused me of that idea. He set the literary as well as the personal character of the Fly (so Mr. C. satirically designated the rival editor,) in its true light. He, the Fly, was very little better than he should be. He had written infamous things. He was a penny-a-liner,[14] and a buffoon. He was a villain. He had composed a tragedy which set the whole country in a guffaw, and a farce which deluged the universe in tears. Besides all this, he had the impudence to pen what he meant for a lampoon upon himself, (Mr. Crab,) and the temerity to style him "an ass." Should I at any time wish to express my opinion of Mr. Fly, the pages of the "Lollipop," Mr. Crab assured me, were at my unlimited disposal. In the meantime, as it was very certain that I would be attacked in the Fly for my attempt at composing a rival poem on the "Oil-of-Bob," he (Mr. Crab,) would take it upon himself to attend, pointedly, to my private and personal interests. If I were not made a man of at once, it should not be the fault of himself, (Mr. Crab.)

---

[14]**upon the *tapis:*** Up for consideration. **penny-a-liner:** A cheap journalist; that is, a man who works for "a penny-a-line."

Mr. Crab having now paused in his discourse, (the latter portion of which I found it impossible to comprehend,) I ventured to suggest something about the remuneration which I had been taught to expect for my poem, by an announcement on the cover of the "Lollipop," declaring that it, (the "Lollipop,") "insisted upon being permitted to pay exorbitant prices for all accepted contributions;—frequently expending more money for a single brief poem than the whole annual cost of the 'Hum-Drum,' the 'Rowdy-Dow,' and the 'Goosetherumfoodle' combined."[15]

As I mentioned the word "renumeration," Mr. Crab first opened his eyes, and then his mouth, to quite a remarkable extent; causing his personal appearance to resemble that of a highly-agitated elderly duck in the act of quacking;—and in this condition he remained, (ever and anon pressing his hands tightly to his forehead, as if in a state of desperate bewilderment) until I had nearly made an end of what I had to say.

Upon my conclusion, he sank back into his seat, as if much overcome, letting his arms fall lifelessly by his side, but keeping his mouth still rigorously open, after the fashion of the duck. While I remained in speechless astonishment at behavior so alarming, he suddenly leaped to his feet and made a rush at the bell-rope; but just as he reached this, he appeared to have altered his intention, whatever it was, for he dived under a table and immediately re-appeared with a cudgel. This he was in the act of uplifting, (for what purpose I am at a loss to imagine,) when, all at once, there came a benign smile over his features, and he sank placidly back in his chair.

"Mr. Bob," he said, (for I had sent up my card before ascending myself,) "Mr. Bob, you are a young man, I presume—*very?*"

I assented; adding that I had not yet concluded my third lustrum.[16]

"Ah!" he replied, "very good! I see how it is—say no more! Touching this matter of compensation, what you observe is very just: in fact it is excessively so. But—ah—ah—the *first* contribution—the *first,* I say—it is never the Magazine custom to pay for—you comprehend, eh? The truth is, we are usually the *recipients* in such case." [Mr. Crab smiled blandly as he emphasized the word "recipients."] "For the most part, we are *paid* for the insertion of a maiden attempt—especially in verse. In the second place, Mr. Bob, the Magazine rule is never to disburse what we term in France the *argent comptant:*[17]—I have no doubt you understand. In a quarter or two after publication of the article—or in a year or two—we make no objection to giving our note at nine months:—provided always that we can so arrange our affairs as to be quite certain of a 'burst up' in six. I really *do* hope, Mr. Bob, that you will look upon this explanation as satisfactory." Here Mr. Crab concluded, and the tears stood in his eyes.

Grieved to the soul at having been, however innocently, the cause of pain to so eminent and so sensitive a man, I hastened to apologize, and to reassure him, by

---

[15]Some magazines did, in fact, boast that they paid well for contributions, though, as Poe well knew, most paid very little, and some not at all.

[16]A lustrum is five years, so Thingum is only fourteen or so.

[17]Hard cash.

expressing my perfect coincidence with his views, as well as my entire appreciation of the delicacy of his position. Having done all this in a neat speech, I took leave.

One fine morning, very shortly afterwards, "I awoke and found myself famous." The extent of my renown will be best estimated by reference to the editorial opinions of the day. These opinions, it will be seen, were embodied in critical notices of the number of the "Lollipop" containing my poem, and are perfectly satisfactory, conclusive and clear with the exception, perhaps, of the hieroglyphical marks, "*Sep.* 15—1 *t.*"[18] appended to each of the critiques.

The "Owl," a journal of profound sagacity, and well known for the deliberate gravity of its literary decisions—the "Owl," I say, spoke as follows:

"'THE LOLLIPOP!' The October number of this delicious Magazine surpasses its predecessors, and sets competition at defiance. In the beauty of its typography and paper—in the number and excellence of its steel plates—as well as in the literary merit of its contributions—the 'Lollipop' compares with its slow-paced rivals as Hyperion with a Satyr. The 'Hum-Drum,' the 'Rowdy-Dow,' and the 'Goosetherumfoodle,' excel, it is true, in braggadocio, but, in all other points, give us the 'Lollipop!' How this celebrated journal can sustain its evidently tremendous expenses, is more than we can understand. To be sure, it has a circulation of 100,000,[19] and its subscription-list has increased one fourth during the last month: but, on the other hand, the sums it disburses constantly for contributions are inconceivable. It is reported that Mr. Slyass received no less than thirty-seven and a half cents for his inimitable paper on 'Pigs.' With Mr. Crab, as editor, and with

---

[18]"I awoke . . . famous": Thingum Bob associates himself with Byron by quoting Byron's well-known report on himself. For more of Poe's response to Byron, see "The Assignation." ***Sep.* 15—1 *t*":** Printer's code for a paid insertion—September 15, one time—of the same sort used today in many newspapers in the want ads. It means that the item is paid for, and is to run just one time. Poe implies that editors themselves write the flattering accounts of their magazines and even pay to have the "puffery" printed. He is not exaggerating very much: for a good account of what passed for professional ethics among American magazinists, see Moss (3).

[19]**excellence . . . plates:** Physical appearance sold magazines. Those which could afford plates showing exotic places, fashions, or sentimental scenes had larger circulations. Poe disliked steel plates and argued for simple and idiomatic woodcut engravings. **Hyperion . . . Satyr:** In Greek mythology, "Hyperion" can mean one of the Titans or, in later usage, Apollo, god of music and poetry. Poe probably intends the latter meaning, and contrasts Apollo with a satyr, an earthy woodland deity in more-or-less human form, with goat's legs, horns, and pointed ears, noted for energetic and wanton sexuality. **100,000:** Literary journals struggled along on tiny circulations. The figures in these "notices" are absurdly exaggerated; editors were prone to exaggerate. When Poe worked for *Graham's Magazine,* one of the most prosperous, he and the proprietor spoke of building its circulation from 5,500 to 40,000. That was enormous for a literary magazine of the day, and probably somewhat exaggerated. *Graham's,* moreover, was not really all that literary—much of its contents was closer to what we would expect to find in the American popular magazines of the early to mid 1900s. Most literary periodicals had circulations more like that of Poe's *Broadway Journal,* which had fewer than 1,000 subscribers. Even the great *Edinburgh Review* in Great Britain never had more than 14,000 paid subscribers.

such names upon the list of contributors as SNOB and Slyass, there can be no such word as 'fail' for the 'Lollipop.' Go and subscribe. *Sep.* 15—1 *t.*"

I must say that I was gratified with this high-toned notice from a paper so respectable as the "Owl." The placing my name—that is to say my *nom de guerre*[20]—in priority of station to that of the great Slyass, was a compliment as happy as I felt it to be deserved.

My attention was next arrested by these paragraphs in the "Toad"—a print highly distinguished for its uprightness, and independence—for its entire freedom from sycophancy and subservience to the givers of dinners:

"The 'Lollipop' for October is out in advance of all its contemporaries, and infinitely surpasses them, of course, in the splendor of its embellishments, as well as in the richness of its literary contents. The 'Hum-Drum,' the 'Rowdy-Dow,' and the 'Goosetherumfoodle' excel, we admit, in braggadocio, but, in all other points, give us the 'Lollipop.' How this celebrated Magazine can sustain its evidently tremendous expenses, is more than we can understand. To be sure, it has a circulation of 200,000, and its subscription list has increased one third during the last fortnight, but on the other hand, the sums it disburses, monthly, for contributions, are fearfully great. We learn that Mr. Mumblethumb received no less than fifty cents for his late 'Monody in a Mud-Puddle.'[21]

"Among the original contributors to the present number we notice, (besides the eminent editor, Mr. Crab,) such men as SNOB, Slyass, and Mumblethumb. Apart from the editorial matter, the most valuable paper, nevertheless, is, we think, a poetical gem by 'Snob,' on the 'Oil-of-Bob'—but our readers must not suppose, from the title of this incomparable *bijou,*[22] that it bears any similitude to some balderdash on the same subject by a certain contemptible individual whose name is unmentionable to ears polite. The *present* poem 'On the Oil-of-Bob,' has excited universal anxiety and curiosity in respect to the owner of the evident pseudonym, 'Snob'—a curiosity which, happily, we have it in our power to satisfy. 'Snob' is the *nom-de-plume* of Mr. Thingum Bob, of this city,—a relative of the great Mr. Thingum, (after whom he is named,) and otherwise connected with the most illustrious families of the State. His father, Thomas Bob, Esq., is an opulent merchant in Smug. *Sep.* 15—1 *t.*"

This generous approbation touched me to the heart—the more especially as it emanated from a source so avowedly—so proverbially pure as the "Toad." The words "gem" and "*bijou,*" however, used in reference to my composition, struck me as being, in some degree, feeble. They seemed to me to be deficient in force. They were not sufficient *prononcés,*[23] (as we have it in France.)

I had hardly finished reading the "Toad," when a friend placed in my hands a copy of the "Mole," a daily, enjoying high reputation for the keenness of its

---

[20]Pen name (literally, "war-name").

[21]Hardly an exaggeration. Poe wrote several articles about the poor pay for writers in his day, and there are sad letters from him to editors begging that they pay him the few dollars they promised for articles and reviews.

[22]Gem.

[23]Pronounced.

perception about matters in general, and for the open, honest, above-ground style of its editorials. The "Mole" spoke of the "Lollipop" as follows:

"We have just received the 'Lollipop' for October, and *must* say that never before have we perused any single number of any periodical which afforded us a felicity so supreme. We speak advisedly. The 'Hum-Drum,' the 'Rowdy-Dow' and the 'Goosetherumfoodle' must look well to their laurels. These prints, no doubt, surpass every thing in loudness of pretension, but, in all other points, give us the 'Lollipop!' How this celebrated Magazine can sustain its evidently tremendous expenses, is more than we can comprehend. To be sure, it has a circulation of 300,000; and its subscription-list has increased one-half within the last week, but then the sum it disburses, monthly, for contributions, is astoundingly enormous. We have it upon good authority, that Mr. Fatquack received no less than sixty-two cents and a half for his late Domestic Nouvelette, the 'Dish-Clout.'[24]

"The contributors to the number before us are Mr. Crab, (the eminent editor,) SNOB, Mumblethumb, Fatquack and others; but, after the inimitable compositions of the editor himself, we prefer a diamond-like effusion from the pen of a rising poet who writes over the signature 'Snob'—a *nom de guerre* which we predict will one day extinguish the radiance of 'Boz.'[25] 'SNOB,' we learn, is a Mr. THINGUM BOB, sole heir of a wealthy merchant of this city, Thomas Bob, Esq., and a near relative of the distinguished Mr. Thingum. The title of Mr. B's admirable poem is the 'Oil-of-Bob'—a somewhat unfortunate name, by-the-bye, as some contemptible vagabond connected with the penny press has already disgusted the town with a great deal of drivel upon the same topic. There will be no danger, however, of confounding the compositions. *Sep.* 15—1 *t.*"

The generous approbation of so clear-sighted a journal as the "Mole" penetrated my soul with delight. The only objection which occurred to me was, that the terms "contemptible vagabond" might have been better written "*odious and* contemptible, *wretch, villain* and vagabond." This would have sounded more gracefully, I think. "Diamond-like," also, was scarcely, it will be admitted, of sufficient intensity to express what the "Mole" evidently *thought* of the brilliancy of the "Oil-of-Bob."

On the same afternoon in which I saw these notices in the "Owl," the "Toad," and the "Mole," I happened to meet with a copy of the "Daddy-Long-Legs," a periodical proverbial for the extreme extent of its understanding. And it was the "Daddy-Long-Legs" which spoke thus:

"The 'Lollipop!!' This gorgeous Magazine is already before the public for October. The question of pre-eminence is forever put to rest, and hereafter it will be excessively preposterous in the 'Hum-Drum,' the 'Rowdy-Dow,' or the 'Goosetherumfoodle,' to make any farther spasmodic attempts at competition.

---

[24]Dishcloth. James Fenimore Cooper had published a very weak work called "Autobiography of a Pocket Handkerchief" in *Graham's* in 1843 (Mabbott 9, II) and had been well paid for it. That's Poe's target.

[25]"Boz" is the pen name of Charles Dickens. "This linking of Willis Clark and Dickens may have been a covert allusion to Lewis's own reference to the likeness between Martin Chuzzlewit and Willis" (Whipple 3).

These journals may excel the 'Lollipop' in outcry, but, in all other points, give us the 'Lollipop!' How this celebrated Magazine can sustain its evidently tremendous expenses, is past comprehension. To be sure it has a circulation of precisely half a million, and its subscription-list has increased seventy-five per cent. within the last couple of days; but then the sums it disburses, monthly, for contributions, are scarcely credible; we are cognizant of the fact, that Mademoiselle Cribalittle[26] received no less than eighty-seven cents and a half for her late valuable Revolutionary Tale, entitled 'The York-Town Katy-Did, and the Bunker-Hill Katy-Didn't.'

"The most able papers in the present number, are, of course, those furnished by the editor, (the eminent Mr. Crab,) but there are numerous magnificent contributions from such names as SNOB; Mademoiselle Cribalittle; Slyass; Mrs. Fibalittle; Mumblethumb; Mrs. Squibalittle; and last, though not least, Fatquack. The world may well be challenged to produce so rich a galaxy of genius.

"The poem over the signature 'SNOB' is, we find, attracting universal commendation, and, we are constrained to say, deserves, if possible, even more applause than it has received. The 'Oil-of-Bob' is the title of this masterpiece of eloquence and art. One or two of our readers *may* have a *very* faint, although sufficiently disgusting recollection of a poem (?) similarly entitled, the perpetration of a miserable penny-a-liner, mendicant, and cut-throat, connected in the capacity of scullion, we believe, with one of the indecent prints about the purlieus of the city; we beg them, for God's sake, not to confound the compositions. The author of the *the* 'Oil-of-Bob' is, we hear, THINGUM BOB, Esq., a gentleman of high genius, and a scholar. 'Snob' is merely a *nom-de-guerre. Sept.* 15—1 *t.*"

I could scarcely restrain my indignation while I perused the concluding portions of this diatribe. It was clear to me that the yea-nay manner—not to say the gentleness—the positive forbearance with which the "Daddy-Long-Legs" spoke of that pig, the editor of the "Gad-Fly"—it was evident to me, I say, that this gentleness of speech could proceed from nothing else than a partiality for the Fly—whom it was clearly the intention of the "Daddy-Long-Legs" to elevate into reputation at my expense. Any one, indeed, might perceive, with half an eye, that, had the real design of the "Daddy" been what it wished to appear, it, (the "Daddy,") might have expressed itself in terms more direct, more pungent, and altogether more to the purpose. The words "penny-a-liner," "mendicant," "scullion," and "cut-throat," were epithets so intentionally inexpressive and equivocal, as to be worse than nothing when applied to the author of the very worst stanzas ever penned by one of the human race. We all know what is meant by "damning with faint praise," and, on the other hand, who could fail seeing through the covert purpose of the "Daddy"—that of glorifying with feeble abuse?

What the "Daddy" chose to say of the Fly, however, was no business of mine. What is said of myself *was.* After the noble manner in which the "Owl," the "Toad," the "Mole," had expressed themselves in respect to my ability, it was rather too much to be coolly spoken of by a thing like the "Daddy-Long-Legs," as

---

[26]Mabbott (9, II) is quite sure this is Mrs. E. F. Ellet, a proven plagiarist "interested in stories of the American Revolution."

merely "a gentleman of high genius and a scholar." Gentleman indeed! I made up my mind, at once, either to get a written apology from the "Daddy-Long-Legs," or to call it out.

Full of this purpose, I looked about me to find a friend whom I could entrust with a message to his Daddyship, and, as the editor of the "Lollipop" had given me marked tokens of regard, I at length concluded to seek assistance upon the present occasion.

I have never yet been able to account, in a manner satisfactory to my own understanding, for the *very* peculiar countenance and demeanor with which Mr. Crab listened to me, as I unfolded to him my design. He again went through the scene of the bell-rope and cudgel, and did not omit the duck. At one period I thought he really intended to quack. His fit, nevertheless, finally subsided as before, and he began to act and speak in a rational way. He declined bearing the cartel, however, and in fact, dissuaded me from sending it at all; but was candid enough to admit that the "Daddy-Long-Legs" had been disgracefully in the wrong—more especially in what related to the epithets "gentleman and scholar."

Towards the end of this interview with Mr. Crab, who really appeared to take a paternal interest in my welfare, he suggested to me that I might turn an honest penny and, at the same time, advance my reputation, by occasionally playing Thomas Hawk for the "Lollipop."

I begged Mr. Crab to inform me who was Mr. Thomas Hawk, and how it was expected that I should play him.

Here Mr. Crab again "made great eyes," (as we say in Germany,)[27] but at length, recovering himself from a profound attack of astonishment, he assured me that he employed the words "Thomas Hawk" to avoid the colloquialism, Tommy, which was low—but that the true idea was Tommy Hawk—or tomahawk—and that by "playing tomahawk" he referred to scalping, brow-beating and otherwise using-up the herd of poor-devil authors.

I assured my patron that, if this was all, I was perfectly resigned to the task of playing Thomas Hawk. Hereupon Mr. Crab desired me to use-up the editor of the "Gad-Fly" forthwith, in the fiercest style within the scope of my ability, and as a specimen of my powers. This I did, upon the spot, in a review of the original "Oil-of-Bob," occupying thirty-six pages of the "Lollipop." I found playing Thomas Hawk, indeed, a far less onerous occupation than poetizing; for I went upon *system* altogether, and thus it was easy to do the thing thoroughly and well. My practice was this. I bought auction copies (cheap) of "Lord Brougham's Speeches," "Cobbett's Complete Works," the "New Slang-Syllabus," the "Whole Art of Snubbing," "Prentice's Billingsgate," (folio edition,) and "Lewis G. Clarke on Tongue." These works I cut up thoroughly with a curry-comb, and then, throwing the shreds into a sieve, sifted out carefully all that might be thought

[27]In a "puff" for the *Literary Remains of the Late Willis Gaylord Clark* in the July 1844 *Knickerbocker* appears the apparent source of Poe's gag: " . . . Clark was . . . as many-sided, to use an expressive German phrase, as almost any writer of whom we have knowledge" (quoted in Whipple 3).

decent, (a mere trifle): reserving the hard phrases, which I threw into a large tin pepper-castor with longitudinal holes, so that an entire sentence could get through without material injury. The mixture was then ready for use. When called upon to play Thomas Hawk, I anointed a sheet of fools-cap with the white of a gander's egg;[28] then, shredding the thing to be reviewed as I had previously shredded the books,—only with more care, so as to get every word separate—I threw the latter shreds in with the former, screwed on the lid of the castor, gave it a shake, and so dusted out the mixture upon the egg'd foolscap; where it stuck. The effect was beautiful to behold. It was captivating. Indeed the reviews I brought to pass by this simple expedient have never been approached, and were the wonder of the world. At first, through bashfulness—the result of inexperience—I was a little put out by a certain inconsistency—a certain air of the *bizarre,* (as we say in France,) worn by the composition as a whole. All the phrases did not *fit,* (as we say in the Anglo-Saxon.) Many were quite awry. Some, even, were up-side-down; and there were none of them which were not, in some measure, injured, in regard to effect, by this latter species of accident, when it occurred:—with the exception of Mr. Lewis Clark's paragraphs, which were so vigorous, and altogether stout, that they seemed not particularly disconcerted by any extreme of position, but looked equally happy and satisfactory, whether on their heads, or on their heels.

What became of the editor of the "Gad-Fly," after the publication of my criticism on his "Oil-of-Bob," it is somewhat difficult to determine. The most reasonable conclusion is, that he wept himself to death. At all events he disappeared instantaneously from the face of the earth, and no man has seen even the ghost of him since.

This matter having been properly accomplished, and the Furies appeased, I grew at once into high favor with Mr. Crab. He took me into his confidence, gave me a permanent situation as Thomas Hawk of the "Lollipop," and as, for the

---

[28]**"Lord Brougham's Speeches":** Henry Brougham (1778–1868), a most prominent editor and contributor to the *Edinburgh Review,* later Lord Chancellor. Poe would not have liked his reformist, Whig politics; his contentiousness was notorious. See "How to Write a Blackwood Article," note 4. **"Cobbett's Complete Works":** William Cobbett (1766–1835) was a radical pamphleteer and agitator who cried out against social abuses prevalent in England. Fined, jailed, forced to flee to the United States as an exile, he returned to England to continue the fight, and became a member of Parliament. Poe, who shared the Tory fear of "the mob," was not sympathetic to radicals and reformers. **"New Slang-Syllabus":** See "How to Write a Blackwood Article," note 6. **"Prentice's Billingsgate":** Pollin (3) identifies George D. Prentice as an "abusive editor"; "Billingsgate" is vulgar slang. In one of his attacks on Poe (*Knickerbocker,* 22 [October 1843] 392), Lewis Gaylord Clark quotes George Denison Prentice of the *Louisville Daily Journal* instead of writing the attack himself. Moss (2) connects this to Poe's including a reference to Prentice and Clark in his revision of "The Literary Life of Thingum Bob, Esq." for *The Broadway Journal* version. Poe intends a list of intemperate and abusive writers. **gander's egg:** There's no such thing, of course—a gander is a male goose. There is probably some slang expression involved which we've lost.

present, he could afford me no salary[29] allowed me to profit, at discretion, by his advice.

"My Dear Thingum," said he to me one day after dinner, "I respect your abilities and love you as a son. You shall be my heir. When I die I will bequeath you the 'Lollipop.' In the meantime I will make a man of you—I *will*—provided always that you follow my counsel. The first thing to do is to get rid of the old bore."

"Boar?" said I inquiringly—"pig, eh?—*aper?*[30] (as we say in Latin)—who?—where?"

"Your father," said he.

"Precisely," I replied,—"pig."

"You have your fortune to make, Thingum," resumed Mr. Crab, "and that governor of yours is a millstone about your neck. We must cut him at once." [Here I took out my knife.] "We must cut him," continued Mr. Crab, "decidedly and forever. He won't do—he *won't.* Upon second thoughts, you had better kick him, or cane him, or something of that kind."

"What do you say," I suggested modestly, "to my kicking him in the first instance, caning him afterwards, and winding up by tweaking his nose?"

Mr. Crab looked at me musingly for some moments, and then answered:

"I think, Mr. Bob, that what you propose would answer sufficiently well—indeed remarkably well—that is to say, as far as it went—but barbers are exceedingly hard to cut, and I think, upon the whole, that, having performed upon Thomas Bob the operations you suggest, it would be advisable to blacken, with your fists, both his eyes, very carefully and thoroughly, to prevent his ever seeing you again in fashionable promenades. After doing this, I really do not perceive that you can do any more. However—it might be just as well to roll him once or twice in the gutter, and then put him in charge of the police. Any time the next morning you can call at the watch-house and swear an assault."

I was much affected by the kindness of feeling towards me personally, which was evinced in this excellent advice of Mr. Crab, and I did not fail to profit by it forthwith. The result was, that I got rid of the old bore, and began to feel a little independent and gentleman-like. The want of money, however, was, for a few weeks, a source of some discomfort; but at length, by carefully putting to use my two eyes, and observing how matters went just in front of my nose, I perceived how the thing was to be brought about. I say "thing"—be it observed—for they tell me the Latin for it is *rem.* By the way, talking of Latin, can any one tell me the meaning of *quocunque*—or what is the meaning of *modo?*[31]

---

[29]More bitterness about the tightwad policies of most magazines—not only the contributors, but members of the staff, too, are underpaid.

[30]The Latin is faulty; *aper* is "wild boar." Poe is playing bilingual puns again; Mr. Crab calls Thingum Bob's father an "old bore." Poe's point is that to be a successful magazinist you have to be the sort of person who would abuse your own (kindly) father.

[31]***rem:*** This is the accusative case of the Latin word *res,* "thing." ***quocunque . . . modo:*** Apparently Poe means *quocumque modo,* "in whatever manner," or "watchemacallit" or

My plan was exceedingly simple. I bought, for a song, a sixteenth of the "Snapping-Turtle:"—that was all. The thing was *done,* and I put money in my purse. There were some trivial arrangements afterwards, to be sure; but these formed no portion of the plan. They were a consequence—a result. For example, I bought pen, ink and paper, and put them into furious activity. Having thus completed a Magazine article, I gave it, for appellation, "FOL-LOL, *by the Author of* 'the OIL-OF-BOB,'" and enveloped it to the "Goosetherumfoodle." That journal, however, having pronounced it "twattle" in the "Monthly Notices to Correspondents," I reheaded thc paper "'Hey-Diddle-Diddle' by THINGUM BOB, Esq., Author of the Ode on 'The Oil-of-Bob,' *and* Editor of the 'Snapping-Turtle.'" With this amendment, I reenclosed it to the "Goosetherumfoodle," and, while I awaited a reply, published daily, in the "Turtle," six columns of what may be termed philosophical and analytical investigation of the literary merits of the "Goosetherumfoodle," as well as of the personal character of the editor of the "Goosetherumfoodle." At the end of a week the "Goosetherumfoodle" discovered that it had, by some odd mistake, "confounded a stupid article, headed 'Hey-Diddle-Diddle' and composed by some unknown ignoramus, with a gem of resplendent lustre similarly entitled, the work of Thingum Bob, Esq., the celebrated author of 'The Oil-of-Bob.'" The "Goosetherumfoodle" deeply "regretted this very natural accident," and promised, moreover, an insertion of the *genuine* "Hey-Diddle-Diddle" in the very next number of the Magazine.

The fact is I *thought*—I *really* thought—I thought at the time—I thought *then*—and have no reason for thinking otherwise *now*—that the "Goosetherumfoodle" *did* make a mistake. With the best intentions in the world, I never knew any thing that made as many singular mistakes as the "Goosetherumfoodle." From that day I took a liking to the "Goosetherumfoodle," and the result was I soon saw into the very depths of its literary merits, and did not fail to expatiate upon them, in the "Turtle," whenever a fitting opportunity occurred. And it is to be regarded as a very peculiar coincidence—as one of those positively *remarkable* coincidences which set a man to serious thinking—that just such a total revolution of opinion—just such entire *bouleversement,*[32] (as we say in French,)—just such thorough *topsiturviness,* (if I may be permitted to employ a rather forcible term of the Choctaws,) as happened, *pro* and *con,* between myself on the one part, and the "Goosetherumfoodle" on the other, did actually again happen, in a brief period afterwards, and with precisely similar circumstances, in the case of myself and the "Rowdy-Dow," and in the case of myself and the "Hum-Drum."

Thus it was that, by a master-stroke of genius, I at length consummated my triumphs by "putting money in my purse" and thus may be said really and fairly to have commenced that brilliant and eventful career which rendered me illustrious,

---

"thingamabob." Poe is playing on the name "Thingum Bob"—Thingum doesn't recognize his own name in Latin.

[32]Thingum has now caught on to how the system works. If you want your work praised, you must be an editor with the power to praise in return. Now that he owns his own paper, his success is assured. ***bouleversement:*** Somersault.

and which now enables me to say, with Chateaubriand, "I have made history"—"*J'ai fait l'histoire.*"[33]

I have indeed "made history." From the bright epoch which I now record, my actions—my works—are the property of mankind. They are familiar to the world. It is, then, needless for me to detail how, soaring rapidly, I fell heir to the "Lollipop"—how I merged this journal in the "Hum-Drum"—how again I made purchase of the "Rowdy-Dow," thus combining the three periodicals—how, lastly, I effected a bargain for the sole remaining rival, and united all the literature of the country in one magnificent Magazine, known everywhere as the

"Rowdy-Dow, Lollipop, Hum-Drum,
and
GOOSETHERUMFOODLE."

Yes; I have made history. My fame is universal. It extends to the uttermost ends of the earth. You cannot take up a common newspaper in which you shall not see some allusion to the immortal THINGUM BOB. It is Mr. Thingum Bob said so, and Mr. Thingum Bob wrote this, and Mr. Thingum Bob did that. But I am meek and expire with an humble heart. After all, what is it?—this indescribable something which men will persist in terming "genius"? I agree with Buffon—with Hogarth[34]—it is but *diligence* after all.

Look at *me!*—how I labored—how I toiled—how I wrote! Ye Gods, did I *not* write? I knew not the word "ease." By day I adhered to my desk, and at night, a pale student, I consumed the midnight oil. You should have seen me—you *should.* I leaned to the right. I leaned to the left. I sat forward. I sat backward. I sat upon end. I sat *tête baissée,* (as they have it in the Kickapoo,) bowing my head close to the alabaster page. And, through all, I—*wrote.* Through joy and through sorrow, I—*wrote.* Through hunger and through thirst, I—*wrote.* Through good report and through ill report, I—*wrote.* Through sunshine and through moonshine, I—wrote. What I wrote it is unnecessary to say. The *style!*—that was the thing. I caught it from Fatquack—whizz!—fizz!—and I am giving you a specimen of it now.[35]

---

[33]***"J'ai fait l'histoire":*** This is from Chateaubriand's *Mémoires d'outre-tombe,* IV, Book 12.

[34]**Buffon:** Georges Louis Leclerc, Compte de Buffon (1707–88), the great French naturalist. **Hogarth:** William Hogarth (1697–1764), the British artist. What they had to say about diligence is obviously inappropriate to Thingum Bob's case: it is *not* diligence, but crafty greed. Buffon said, "Le génie, c'est la patience"; Hogarth said, "Genuis is but labor and diligence." Poe is teasing himself: James Russell Lowell wrote of him, "Mr. Poe has that indescribable something which men have argeed to call genius" (Mabbott 9, II).

[35]***tête baissée:*** Head lowered. It's French, of course, not Kickapoo. **whizz . . . now:** This breathless—and careless—style, full of dashes, cheap rhetorical tricks and slang, was, as Poe implies, typical of a great deal of magazine prose. See "How to Write a Blackwood Article" for more on magazine styles.

Some Words with a Mummy

This is a superior example of Poe's work in a journalistic mode. The foolish plot is there to provide a fictional framework in which Poe can present interesting and unusual information of the sort one used to see in Sunday supplements or the Reader's Digest. *Scientific wonders and modern technology impress the mummy not at all; things were better in ancient Egypt. "Some Words with a Mummy" suggests how very strong were Poe's ties to his time and place; it shows that he was both fascinated by the things that fascinated his readers and that he had a certain detachment from them. Like Twain, he was at once caught up in the excitement of new technology and new science, and, in another mood, skeptical that "progress" meant anything.*

Poe's frame story itself was very topical. A burst of exciting Egyptological archeology and scholarship followed Napoleon's campaigns in Egypt. Interesting new information was newsworthy for decades—to a lesser extent, it is so even today. (See, for example, Figure 9, page 276.) So Poe is playing on a topic he knows will interest his readers. "Some Words with a Mummy" is filled with local New York City jokes, references to popular subjects, and even humor based on making fun of advertisements; details are in our notes.

A note of explanation: *Poe simply lifted his technical information from handy sources; a lot of it came from the* Encyclopedia Americana *(King).*

Publications in Poe's Time

The American (Whig) Review, April 1845
The Broadway Journal, November 1, 1845

Some Words with a Mummy

The symposium of the preceding evening had been a little too much for my nerves. I had a wretched head-ache, and was desperately drowsy. Instead of going out, therefore, to spend the evening as I had proposed, it occurred to me that I could not do a wiser thing than just eat a mouthful of supper and go immediately to bed.

A *light* supper of course. I am exceedingly fond of Welsh rabbit. More than a pound at once, however, may not at all times be advisable. Still, there can be no material objection to two. And really between two and three, there is merely a single unit of difference. I ventured, perhaps, upon four. My wife will have it five;—but, clearly, she has confounded two very distinct affairs. The abstract number, five, I am willing to admit; but, concretely, it has reference to bottles of Brown Stout, without which, in the way of condiment, Welsh rabbit is to be eschewed.[1]

Having thus concluded a frugal meal, and donned my night-cap, with the serene hope of enjoying it till noon the next day, I placed my head upon the pillow, and through the aid of a capital conscience, fell into a profound slumber forthwith.

But when were the hopes of humanity fulfilled? I could not have completed my third snore when there came a furious ringing at the street-door bell, and then an impatient thumping at the knocker, which awakened me at once. In a minute afterward and while I was still rubbing my eyes, my wife thrust in my face a note from my old friend, Doctor Ponnonner.[2] It ran thus:

> Come to me by all means, my dear good friend, as soon as you receive this. Come and help us to rejoice. At last, by long persevering diplomacy, I have gained the assent of the Directors of the City Museum,[3] to my examination of the Mummy—you know the one I mean. I have permission to unswathe it and open it, if desirable. A few friends only will be present—you, of course. The Mummy is now at my house, and we shall begin to unroll it at eleven to-night. Yours ever,
>
> PONNONNER.

By the time I had reached the "Ponnonner," it struck me that I was as wide awake as a man need be. I leaped out of bed in an ecstacy, overthrowing all in my way; dressed myself with a rapidity truly marvellous; and set off, at the top of my speed, for the Doctor's.

There I found a very eager company assembled. They had been awaiting me with much impatience; the Mummy was extended upon the dining table; and the moment I entered, its examination was commenced.

It was one of a pair brought, several years previously, by Captain Arthur Sabretash, a cousin of Ponnonner's, from a tomb near Eleithias, in the Lybian Mountains, a considerable distance above Thebes on the Nile. The grottoes at this point, although less magnificent than the Theban sepulchres, are of higher interest, on account of affording more numerous illustrations of the private life of the Egyptians.[4] The chamber from which our specimen was taken, was said to be very

---

[1]Poe's device of providing a "margin of credibility" by having his narrator in an unusual state of mind even appears in humorous tales in which the credibility really isn't necessary. But the fact that it is just a device is good corrective to those who insist on seeing Poe's art as compulsive: for every narrator whose vision is induced by madness or fever, there exists one whose bad dreams are the result of too much cheese and stout.

[2]Pollin (11) suggests that Dr. Ponnonner, the one who always swears upon his honor, is "just such a character as 'Dr. Swaim' or 'Dr. Brandreth,' whose very name suggests hypocritical rascality." See note 26 below.

[3]Pollin (8) believes this is a reference to Barnum's New York Museum.

[4]**Sabretash:** Poe probably picked this name out of *Fraser's Magazine,* in which a "Captain Orlando Sabertash"—a made-up name, of course—"wrote" letters to "Oliver Yorke" (one of William Maginn's pen names). A sabretache, sabretasch[e], or sabretash is a leather satchel which a cavalry officer wears hung from long straps from the left side of his sword-belt. **Egyptians:** See our headnote.

rich in such illustrations; the walls being completely covered with fresco paintings and bas-reliefs, while statues, vases, and Mosaic work of rich patterns, indicated the vast wealth of the deceased.

The treasure had been deposited in the Museum precisely in the same condition in which Captain Sabretash had found it;—that is to say, the coffin had not been disturbed. For eight years it had thus stood, subject only externally to public inspection. We had now, therefore, the complete Mummy at our disposal; and to those who are aware how very rarely the unransacked antique[5] reaches our shores, it will be evident, at once, that we had great reason to congratulate ourselves upon our good fortune.

Approaching the table, I saw on it a large box, or case, nearly seven feet long, and perhaps three feet wide, by two feet and a half deep. It was oblong—not coffin-shaped. The material was at first supposed to be the wood of the sycamore (*platanus*), but, upon cutting into it, we found it to be pasteboard, or more properly, *papier mâché,* composed of papyrus. It was thickly ornamented with paintings, representing funeral scenes, and other mournful subjects, interspersed among which in every variety of position, were certain series of hieroglyphical characters intended, no doubt, for the name of the departed. By good luck, Mr. Gliddon formed one of our party; and he had no difficulty in translating the letters, which were simply phonetic, and represented the word, *Allamistakeo.*[6]

We had some difficulty in getting this case open without injury, but, having at length accomplished the task, we came to a second, coffin-shaped, and very considerably less in size than the exterior one, but resembling it precisely in every other respect. The interval between the two was filled with resin, which had, in some degree, defaced the colors of the interior box.

Upon opening this latter (which we did quite easily,) we arrived at a third case, also coffin-shaped, and varying from the second one in no particular, except in that of its material, which was cedar, and still emitted the peculiar and highly aromatic odor of that wood. Between the second and the third case there was no interval; the one fitting accurately within the other.

Removing the third case, we discovered and took out the body itself. We had expected to find it, as usual, enveloped in frequent rolls, or bandages, of linen, but, in place of these, we found a sort of sheath, made of papyrus, and coated with a layer of plaster, thickly gilt and painted. The paintings represented subjects connected with the various supposed duties of the soul, and its presentation to different divinities, with numerous identical human figures, intended, very

---

[5]Nineteenth-century Egyptologists often complained that sites not already plundered in the past yielded treasures which were plundered by local assistants or in transit.

[6]***platanus:*** Poe either has his trees confused or is telling us that the sarcophagus is a hoax. *Platanus* refers to the American sycamore; the Egyptian tree is *Ficus sycomorus.* **Mr. Gliddon:** A real person, George Robins Gliddon (1809–57), whom Poe had mentioned in his 1837 review of Stephens's *Arabia Petraea.* He spent much of his life in Egypt and served as U.S. Consul there, and a couple of years before Poe's story, published a work on Egypt, *Ancient Egypt* (1843). Pollin (8) points out many items in the Poe story which suggest Gliddon's *Ancient Egypt* as one probable source of story and details. **Allamistakeo:** All-a-mistake.

probably, as portraits of the person embalmed. Extending from head to foot, was a columnar, or perpendicular inscription in phonetic hieroglyphics, giving again his name and titles, and the names and titles of his relations.

Around the neck thus ensheathed, was a collar of cylindrical glass beads, diverse in color, and so arranged as to form images of deities, of the scarabæus, etc., with the winged globe.[7] Around the small of the waist was a similar collar, or belt.

Stripping off the papyrus, we found the flesh in excellent preservation, with no perceptible odor. The color was reddish. The skin was hard, smooth and glossy. The teeth and hair were in good condition. The eyes (it seemed) had been removed, and glass ones substituted, which were very beautiful and wonderfully life-like, with the exception of somewhat too determined a stare. The finger and toe nails were brilliantly gilded.

Mr. Gliddon was of opinion, from the redness of the epidermis, that the embalmment had been effected altogether by asphaltum; but, on scraping the surface with a steel instrument, and throwing into the fire some of the powder thus obtained, the flavor of camphor and other sweet-scented gums became apparent.

We searched the corpse very carefully for the usual openings through which the entrails are extracted, but, to our surprise, we could discover none. No member of the party was at that period aware that entire or unopened mummies are not unfrequently met. The brain it was customary to withdraw through the nose; the intestines through an incision in the side; the body was then shaved, washed, and salted; then laid aside for several weeks, when the operation of embalming, properly so called, began.

As no trace of an opening could be found, Doctor Ponnonner was preparing his instruments for dissection, when I observed that it was then past two o'clock. Hereupon it was agreed to postpone the internal examination until the next evening; and we were about to separate for the present, when some one suggested an experiment or two with the Voltaic pile.[8]

The application of electricity to a Mummy three or four thousand years old at the least, was an idea, if not very sage, still sufficiently original, and we all caught at it at once. About one tenth in earnest and nine tenths in jest, we arranged a battery in the Doctor's study, and conveyed thither the Egyptian.

It was only after much trouble that we succeeded in laying bare some portions of the temporal muscle which appeared of less stony rigidity than other parts of the frame, but which, as we had anticipated, of course, gave no indication of galvanic susceptibility when brought in contact with the wire. This the first trial, indeed, seemed decisive, and, with a hearty laugh at our own absurdity, we were bidding each other good night, when my eyes, happening to fall upon those of the Mummy, were there immediately riveted in amazement. My brief glance, in fact, had sufficed to assure me that the orbs which we had all supposed to be glass, and

---

[7]**Scarabæus:** A sacred beetle, symbol of resurrection to ancient Egyptians. See next item. **winged globe:** Poe means the winged disk, an Egyptian motif thought to represent the sun. Both it and the Scarabæus are in fact symbols connected with burial.

[8]A battery.

which were originally noticeable for a certain wild stare, were now so far covered by the lids that only a small portion of the *tunica albuginea*[9] remained visible.

With a shout I called attention to the fact, and it became immediately obvious to all.

I cannot say that I was *alarmed* at the phenomenon, because "alarmed" is, in my case, not exactly the word. It is possible, however, that, but for the Brown Stout, I might have been a little nervous. As for the rest of the company, they really made no attempt at concealing the downright fright which possessed them. Doctor Ponnonner was a man to be pitied. Mr. Gliddon, by some peculiar process, rendered himself invisible. Mr. Silk Buckingham,[10] I fancy, will scarcely be so bold as to deny that he made his way, upon all fours, under the table.

After the first shock of astonishment, however, we resolved, as a matter of course, upon farther examination forthwith. Our operations were now directed against the great toe of the right foot. We made an incision over the outside of the exterior *os sesamoideum pollicis pedis,* and thus got at the root of the *abductor* muscle. Re-adjusting the battery, we now applied the fluid[11] to the bisected nerves—when, with a movement of exceeding life-likeness, the Mummy first drew up its right knee so as to bring it nearly in contact with the abdomen, and then, straightening the limb with inconceivable force, bestowed a kick upon Doctor Ponnonner, which had the effect of discharging that gentleman, like an arrow from a catapult, through a window into the street below.

We rushed out *en masse* to bring in the mangled remains of the victim, but had the happiness to meet him upon the staircase, coming up in an unaccountable hurry, brimfull of the most ardent philosophy, and more than ever impressed with the necessity of prosecuting our experiments with rigor and with zeal.

It was by his advice, accordingly, that we made, upon the spot, a profound incision into the tip of the subject's nose, while the Doctor himself, laying violent hands upon it, pulled it into vehement contact with the wire.

Morally and physicially—figuratively and literally—was the effect electric. In the first place, the corpse opened its eyes and winked very rapidly for several minutes, as does Mr. Barnes[12] in the pantomime; in the second place, it sneezed; in the third, it sat upon end; in the fourth, it shook its fist in Doctor Ponnonner's face; in the fifth, turning to Messieurs Gliddon and Buckingham, it addressed them, in very capital Egyptian, thus:

---

[9]The white fibrous coat of the eye.

[10]See "Mellonta Tauta," note 5. Pollin (8) notices Poe's "scornful picture" of Buckingham whom, after an early (1837) noncommittal reference, Poe deprecates in several later references. Pollin feels that Poe's hostility may have stemmed from his notice of Buckingham's *The Slave States of America* and from his jealousy of Buckingham's success as a lecturer.

[11]***os sesamoideum pollicis pedis:*** Sesamoid bone of the big toe. ***abductor* muscle:** A muscle which draws any part of the body from its normal position, or from the median line. **the fluid:** Electricity.

[12]John Barnes (1761–1841) of the Park Theatre, New York, an extremely popular actor who had come to America in 1816 and was still on the stage in the 1830s. Noted for his "gagging," his skill at stepping out of character for laughs, he is called "one of the funniest of entertainers."

"I must say, gentlemen, that I am as much surprised as I am mortified, at your behavior. Of Doctor Ponnonner nothing better was to be expected. He is a poor little fat fool who *knows* no better. I pity and forgive him. But you, Mr. Gliddon—and you, Silk—who have travelled and resided in Egypt until one might imagine you to the manor born—you, I say, who have been so much among us that you speak Egyptian fully as well, I think, as you write your mother tongue—you, whom I have always been led to regard as the firm friend of the mummies—I really did anticipate more gentlemanly conduct from *you.* What am I to think of your standing quietly by and seeing me thus unhandsomely used? What am I to suppose by your permitting Tom, Dick and Harry to strip me of my coffins, and my clothes, in this wretchedly cold climate? In what light (to come to the point) am I to regard your aiding and abetting that miserable little villain, Doctor Ponnonner, in pulling me by the nose?"

It will be taken for granted, no doubt, that upon hearing this speech under the circumstances, we all either made for the door, or fell into violent hysterics, or went off in a general swoon. One of these three things was, I say, to be expected. Indeed each and all of these lines of conduct might have been very plausibly pursued. And, upon my word, I am at a loss to know how or why it was that we pursued neither the one or the other. But, perhaps, the true reason is to be sought in the spirit of the age, which proceeds by the rule of contraries altogether, and is now usually admitted as the solution of everything in the way of paradox and impossibility. Or, perhaps, after all, it was only the Mummy's exceedingly natural and matter-of-course air that divested his words of the terrible. However this may be, the facts are clear, and no member of our party betrayed any very particular trepidation, or seemed to consider that any thing had gone very especially wrong.

For my part I was convinced it was all right, and merely stepped aside, out of the range of the Egyptian's fist. Doctor Ponnonner thrust his hands into his breeches' pockets, looked hard at the Mummy, and grew excessively red in the face. Mr. Gliddon stroked his whiskers and drew up the collar of his shirt. Mr. Buckingham hung down his head, and put his right thumb into the left corner of his mouth.

The Egyptian regarded him with a severe countenance for some minutes, and at length, with a sneer, said:

"Why don't you speak, Mr. Buckingham? Did you hear what I asked you, or not? *Do* take your thumb out of your mouth!"

Mr. Buckingham, hereupon, gave a slight start, took his right thumb out of the left corner of his mouth, and, by way of indemnification, inserted his left thumb in the right corner of the aperture above-mentioned.

Not being able to get an answer from Mr. B., the figure turned peevishly to Mr. Gliddon, and, in a peremptory tone, demanded in general terms what we all meant.

Mr. Gliddon replied at great length, in phonetics; and but for the deficiency of American printing-offices in hieroglyphical type, it would afford me much pleasure to record here, in the original, the whole of his very excellent speech.

I may as well take this occasion to remark, that all the subsequent conversation in which the Mummy took a part, was carried on in primitive Egyptian, through the medium (so far as concerned myself and other untravelled members of the company)—through the medium, I say, of Messieurs Gliddon and Buckingham, as interpreters. These gentlemen spoke the mother-tongue of the mummy with inimitable fluency and grace; but I could not help observing that (owing, no doubt, to the introduction of images entirely modern, and, of course, entirely novel to the stranger,) the two travellers were reduced, occasionally, to the employment of sensible forms for the purpose of conveying a particular meaning. Mr. Gliddon, at one period, for example, could not make the Egyptian comprehend the term "politics," until he sketched upon the wall, with a bit of charcoal, a little carbuncle-nosed gentleman, out at elbows, standing upon a stump, with his left leg drawn back, his right arm thrown forward, with the fist shut, the eyes rolled up toward Heaven, and the mouth open at an angle of ninety degrees. Just in the same way Mr. Buckingham failed to convey the absolutely modern idea, "wig," until, (at Doctor Ponnonner's suggestion,) he grew very pale in the face, and consented to take off his own.

It will be readily understood that Mr. Gliddon's discourse turned chiefly upon the vast benefits accruing to science from the unrolling and disembowelling of mummies; apologizing, upon this score, for any disturbance that might have been occasioned *him,* in particular, the individual Mummy called Allamistakeo; and concluding with a mere hint, (for it could scarcely be considered more,) that, as these little matters were now explained, it might be as well to proceed with the investigation intended. Here Doctor Ponnonner made ready his instruments.

In regard to the latter suggestions of the orator, it appears that Allamistakeo had certain scruples of conscience, the nature of which I did not distinctly learn; but he expressed himself satisfied with the apologies tendered, and, getting down from the table, shook hands with the company all round.

When this ceremony was at an end, we immediately busied ourselves in repairing the damages which our subject had sustained from the scalpel. We sewed up the wound in his temple, bandaged his foot, and applied a square inch of black plaster to the tip of his nose.

It was now observed that the Count, (this was the title, it seems, of Allamistakeo,) had a slight fit of shivering—no doubt from the cold. The doctor immediately repaired to his wardrobe, and soon returned with a black dress coat, made in Jennings' best manner, a pair of sky-blue plaid pantaloons with straps, a pink gingham *chemise,* a flapped vest of brocade, a white sack overcoat, a walking cane with a hook, a hat with no brim, patent-leather boots, straw-colored kid gloves, an eyeglass, a pair of whiskers, and a waterfall cravat.[13] Owing to the disparity of size between the Count and the doctor, (the proportion being as two to one,) there was some little difficulty in adjusting these habiliments upon the person of the Egyptian; but when all was arranged, he might have been said to be dressed. Mr. Gliddon, therefore, gave him his arm, and led him to a comfortable

[13]**Jennings:** Another local allusion. William T. Jennings & Co. was a well-known New York clothing store, selling ready-made clothes at low prices (Mabbott 9, III). **waterfall cravat:** Waterfall neckcloth or Mail-Coach necktie, a large, usually white neckcloth with folds spreading down over the knot like a waterfall. It was common from 1818 to the 1830s.

chair by the fire, while the doctor rang the bell upon the spot and ordered a supply of cigars and wine.

The conversation soon grew animated. Much curiosity was, of course, expressed in regard to the somewhat remarkable fact of Allamistakeo's still remaining alive.

"I should have thought," observed Mr. Buckingham," that it is high time you were dead."

"Why," replied the Count, very much astonished, "I am little more than seven hundred years old! My father lived a thousand, and was by no means in his dotage when he died."

Here ensued a brisk series of questions and computations, by means of which it became evident that the antiquity of the Mummy had been grossly misjudged. It had been five thousand and fifty years, and some months, since he had been consigned to the catacombs at Eleithias.

"But my remark," resumed Mr. Buckingham, "had no reference to your age at the period of interment; (I am willing to grant, in fact, that you are still a young man,) and my allusion was to the immensity of time during which, by your own showing, you must have been done up in asphaltum."

"In what?" said the Count.

"In asphaltum," persisted Mr. B.

"Ah, yes; I have some faint notion of what you mean; it might be made to answer, no doubt,—but in my time we employed scarcely anything else than the Bichloride of Mercury."[14]

"But what we are especially at a loss to understand," said Doctor Ponnonner, "is how it happens that, having been dead and buried in Egypt five thousand years ago, you are here to-day all alive, and looking so delightfully well."

"Had I been, as you say, *dead,*" replied the Count, "it is more than probable that dead I should still be; for I perceive you are yet in the infancy of Galvanism, and cannot accomplish with it what was a common thing among us in the old days. But the fact is, I fell into catalepsy,[15] and it was considered by my best friends that I was either dead or should be; they accordingly embalmed me at once—I presume you are aware of the chief principle of the embalming process?"

"Why, not altogether."

"Ah, I perceive;—a deplorable condition of ignorance! Well, I cannot enter into details just now: but it is necessary to explain that to embalm, (properly speaking,) in Egypt, was to arrest indefinitely *all* the animal functions subjected to the process. I use the word "animal" in its widest sense, as including the physical not more than the moral and *vital* being. I repeat that the leading principle of embalm-

---

[14]See "The Gold-Bug," note 11. Poe's choice of embalming fluid is poor for reasons explained in Pollin (8).

[15]**Galvanism:** Electricity. **catalepsy:** A popular topic for writers of the day; the technical term they used is "Catochus," "a peculiar form of catalepsy, in which the patient retains the use of his various senses, while the power of motion is entirely suspended, and presents an appearance which may easily be mistaken for death." W. W. Story, "Catochus," *The Boston Miscellany of Literature and Fashion* I, vi (June 1842), 248–51.

ment consisted, with us, in the immediately arresting, and holding in perpetual *abeyance, all* the animal functions subjected to the process. To be brief, in whatever condition the individual was, at the period of embalmment, in that condition he remained. Now, as it is my good fortune to be of the blood of the Scarabæus, I was embalmed *alive,* as you see me at present."

"The blood of the Scarabæus!" exclaimed Doctor Ponnonner.

"Yes. The Scarabæus was the *insignium,* or the 'arms,' of a very distinguished and a very rare patrician family. To be 'of the blood of the Scarabæus,' is merely to be one of that family of which the Scarabæus is the *insignium.* I speak figuratively."

"But what has this to do with your being alive?"

"Why it is the general custom, in Egypt, to deprive a corpse, before embalmment, of its bowels and brains; the race of the Scarabæui alone did not coincide with the custom. Had I not been a Scarabæus, therefore, I should have been without bowels and brains; and without either it is inconvenient to live."

"I perceive that," said Mr. Buckingham, "and I presume that all the *entire* mummies that come to hand are of the race of Scarabæui."

"Beyond doubt."

"I thought," said Mr. Gliddon very meekly, "that the Scarabæus was one of the Egyptian gods."

"One of the Egyptian *what?*" exclaimed the Mummy, starting to its feet.

"Gods!" repeated the traveler.

"Mr. Gliddon I really am astonished to hear you talk in this style," said the Count, resuming his chair. "No nation upon the face of the earth has ever acknowledged more than *one god.* The Scarabæus, the Ibis, etc., were with us, (as similar creatures have been with others) the symbols, or *media,* through which we offered worship to a Creator too august to be more directly approached."

There was here a pause. At length the colloquy was renewed by Doctor Ponnonner.

"It is not improbable, then, from what you have explained," said he, "that among the catacombs near the Nile, there may exist other mummies of the Scarabæus tribe, in a condition of vitality."

"There can be no question of it," replied the Count; "all the Scarabæui embalmed accidentally while alive, are alive now. Even some of those *purposely* so embalmed, may have been overlooked by their executors, and still remain in the tombs."

"Will you be kind enough to explain," I said, "what you mean by 'purposely so embalmed?'"

"With great pleasure," answered the Mummy, after surveying me leisurely through his eye-glass—for it was the first time I had ventured to address him a direct question.

"With great pleasure," said he. "The usual duration of man's life, in my time, was about eight hundred years. Few men died, unless by most extraordinary accident, before the age of six hundred; few lived longer than a decade of centuries; but eight were considered the natural term. After the discovery of the embalming principle, as I have already described it to you, it occurred to our philosophers that a laudable curiosity might be gratified, and, at the same time, the interests of science much advanced, by living this natural term in instalments. In the case of history, indeed, experience demonstrated that something of this kind was indispensable. An historian, for example, having attained the age of five hundred, would write a book with great labor and then get himself carefully embalmed; leaving instructions to his executors *pro tem.,* that they should cause him to be revivified after the lapse of a certain period—say five or six hundred years. Resuming existence at the expiration of this time, he would invariably find his great work converted into a species of hap-hazard note-book—that is to say, into a kind of literary arena for the conflicting guesses, riddles, and personal squabbles of whole herds of exasperated commentators. These guesses, etc., which passed under the name of annotations or emendations, were found so completely to have enveloped, distorted, and overwhelmed the text, that the author had to go about with a lantern to discover his own book. When discovered, it was never worth the trouble of the search. After rewriting it throughout, it was regarded as the bounden duty of the historian to set himself to work, immediately, in correcting from his own private knowledge and experience, the traditions of the day concerning the epoch at which he had originally lived. Now this process of re-scription and personal rectification, pursued by various individual sages, from time to time, had the effect of preventing our history from degenerating into absolute fable."

"I beg your pardon," said Doctor Ponnonner at this point, laying his hand gently upon the arm of the Egyptian—"I beg your pardon, sir, but may I presume to interrupt you for one moment?"

"By all means, *sir,*" replied the Count, drawing up.

"I merely wished to ask you a question," said the Doctor. "You mentioned the historian's personal correction of *traditions* respecting his own epoch. Pray, sir, upon an average, what proportion of these Kabbala[16] were usually found to be right?"

"The Kabbala, as you properly term them, sir, were generally discovered to be precisely on a par with the facts recorded in the un-re-written histories themselves;—that is to say, not one individual iota of either, was ever known, under any circumstances, to be not totally and radically wrong."

"But since it is quite clear," resumed the Doctor, "that at least five thousand years have elapsed since your entombment, I take it for granted that your histories at that period, if not your traditions, were sufficiently explicit on that one topic of universal interest, the Creation, which took place, as I presume you are aware, only about ten centuries before."[17]

---

[16]The Cabala is a system of traditional rabbinical interpretations of the Bible. When used as a synonym for "tradition," Cabala is a singular word.

[17]Poe plays here on an extremely topical subject. Those sciences which deal with data which could reveal the age of the earth or the length of human existence upon it—geology, archeology, to some extent chemistry, etc.—underwent radical transformations in the few decades before this story was written. Estimates based on the Bible, compiled primarily by

"Sir!" said Count Allamistakeo.

The Doctor repeated his remarks, but it was only after much additional explanation, that the foreigner could be made to comprehend them. The latter at length said, hesitatingly:

"The ideas you have suggested are to me, I confess, utterly novel. During my time I never knew any one to entertain so singular a fancy as that the universe (or this world if you will have it so) ever had a beginning at all. I remember, once, and once only, hearing something remotely hinted, by a man of many speculations, concerning the origin *of the human race;* and by this individual the very word *Adam,* (or Red Earth)[18] which you make use of, was employed. He employed it, however, in a general sense, with reference to the spontaneous germination from rank soil (just as a thousand of the lower *genera* of creatures are germinated)—the spontaneous germination, I say, of five vast hordes of men, simultaneously upspringing in five distinct and nearly equal divisions of the globe."

Here, in general, the company shrugged their shoulders, and one or two of us touched our foreheads with a very significant air. Mr. Silk Buckingham, first glancing slightly at the occiput and then at the sinciput[19] of Allamistakeo, spoke as follows:

"The long duration of human life in your time, together with the occasional practice of passing it, as you have explained, in instalments, must have had, indeed, a strong tendency to the general development and conglomeration of knowledge. I presume, therefore, that we are to attribute the marked inferiority of the old Egyptians in all particulars of science, when compared with the moderns, and more especially with the Yankees, altogether to the superior solidity of the Egyptian skull."

"I confess again," replied the Count with much suavity, "that I am somewhat at a loss to comprehend you; pray, to what particulars of science to do you allude?"

Here our whole party, joining voices, detailed, at great length, the assumptions of phrenology and the marvels of animal magnetism.

Having heard us to an end, the Count proceeded to relate a few anecdotes, which rendered it evident that prototypes of Gall and Spurzheim had flourished and faded in Egypt so long ago as to have been nearly forgotten, and that the manœuvres of Mesmer were really very contemptible tricks when put in a collation with the positive miracles of the Theban *savans,*[20] who created lice and a great many other similar things.

---

adding up the "begats," suggested a "Creation" 5,000 or 6,000 years ago. The new scientific data suggested far greater age, ultimately, millions of years. The change in thinking was enormously important to people of Poe's generation, with a shock comparable to that produced by the Copernican and Galilean revolution in astronomy three centuries before.

[18]The association of "Adam" and "earth" is traditional—see I Corinthians 15:20–22, 42–58. Poe's derivation is based on the Hebrew meaning. The word appears in both Hebrew characters and corresponding heiroglyphics in Gliddon's *Ancient Egypt* (Pollin 8).

[19]**occiput:** Back part of the head. **sinciput:** Front part of the head.

[20]**Gall and Spurzheim:** Franz Joseph Gall (1758–1828) and Johann Kaspar Spurzheim (1776–1832), scientific investigators who popularized phrenology. During the period in

I here asked the Count if his people were able to calculate eclipses. He smiled rather contemptuously, and said they were.

This put me a little out, but I began to make other inquiries in regard to his astronomical knowledge, when a member of the company, who had never as yet opened his mouth, whispered in my ear that, for information on this head, I had better consult Ptolemy, (whoever Ptolemy is) as well as one Plutarch *de facie lunæ.*[21]

I then questioned the Mummy about burning-glasses and lenses, and, in general, about the manufacture of glass; but I had not made an end of my queries before the silent member again touched me quietly on the elbow, and begged me for God's sake to take a peep at Diodorus Siculus.[22] As for the Count, he merely asked me, in the way of reply, if we moderns possessed any such microscopes as would enable us to cut cameos in the style of the Egyptians. While I was thinking how I should answer this question, little Doctor Ponnonner committed himself in a very extraordinary way.

"Look at our architecture!" he exclaimed, greatly to the indignation of both the travelers, who pinched him black and blue to no purpose.

"Look," he cried with enthusiasm, "at the Bowling-Green Fountain in New York! or if this be too vast a contemplation, regard for a moment the Capitol at Washington, D.C.!"—and the good little medical man went on to detail very minutely the proportions of the fabric to which he referred. He explained that the portico alone was adorned with no less than four and twenty columns, five feet in diameter, and ten feet apart.

The Count said that he regretted not being able to remember, just at that moment, the precise dimensions of any one of the principal buildings of the city of Aznac, whose foundations were laid in the night of Time, but the ruins of which were still standing, at the epoch of his entombment, in a vast plain of sand to the westward of Thebes. He recollected, however, (talking of porticoes) that one affixed to an inferior palace in a kind of suburb called Carnac, consisted of a

---

which Poe's tale appeared, it was becoming clear that most phrenologists were quacks. But phrenology had been founded as a serious science: it seemed reasonable to assume that different portions of the human mind served different functions and that, once one knew their locations, their relative development ought to be reflected in the shape of the head. Serious studies were performed on the *crania* of men noted for various characteristics. The skulls of notable leaders, geniuses, madmen, and even criminals were often exhumed for measurement and examination, and attempts were made to apply clinically what had been learned. **Mesmer:** Friedrich (or Franz) Anton Mesmer (1733?–1815), German physician who developed the system of treatment through hypnotism called mesmerism. See our headnote to "The Facts in the Case of M. Valdemar." **Theban *savans:*** Forrest cites a biblical source—Exodus 8:16–18.

[21]**Ptolemy:** It is not clear why Poe refers to Ptolemy (fl. 127–141 or 151) here, because he lived far too late for the Count. He did, however, summarize the findings of earlier astronomy. ***de facie lunæ:*** Concerning the phases of the moon. It is doubtful that the work is Plutarch's.

[22]Historian, first century B.C.E.

hundred and forty-four columns, thirty-seven feet each in circumference, and twenty-five feet apart. The approach of this portico, from the Nile, was through an avenue two miles long, composed of sphinxes, statues and obelisks, twenty, sixty, and a hundred feet in height. The palace itself (as well as he could remember) was, in one direction, two miles long, and might have been, altogether, about seven in circuit. Its walls were richly painted all over, within and without, with hieroglyphics. He would not pretend to *assert* that even fifty or sixty of the Doctor's Capitols might have been built within these walls, but he was by no means sure that two or three hundred of them might not have been squeezed in with some trouble. That palace at Carnac was an insignificant little building after all. He, (the Count) however, could not conscientiously refuse to admit the ingenuity, magnificence, and superiority of the Fountain at the Bowling-Green, as described by the Doctor. Nothing like it, he was forced to allow, had ever been seen in Egypt or elsewhere.

I here asked the Count what he had to say to our railroads.

"Nothing," he replied, "in particular." They were rather slight, rather ill-conceived, and clumsily put together. They could not be compared, of course, with the vast, level, direct, iron-grooved causeways,[23] upon which the Egyptians conveyed entire temples and solid obelisks of a hundred and fifty feet in altitude.

I spoke of our gigantic mechanical forces.

He agreed that we knew something in that way, but inquired how I should have gone to work in getting up the imposts on the lintels of even the little palace at Carnac.

This question I concluded not to hear, and demanded if he had any idea of Artesian wells; but he simply raised his eyebrows; while Mr. Gliddon, winked at me very hard, and said, in a low tone, that one had been recently discovered by the engineers employed to bore for water in the Great Oasis.

I then mentioned our steel; but the foreigner elevated his nose, and asked me if our steel could have executed the sharp carved work seen on the obelisks, and which was wrought altogether by edge-tools of copper.

This disconcerted us so greatly that we thought it advisable to vary the attack to Metaphysics. We sent for a copy of a book called the "Dial,"[24] and read out of it a chapter or two about something which is not very clear, but which the Bostonians called the Great Movement or Progress.

The Count merely said that Great Movements were awfully common things in his day, and as for Progress it was at one time quite a nuisance, but it never progressed.

We then spoke of the great beauty and importance of Democracy, and were at

---

[23] A famous Egyptian causeway from the Nile to the site of the Giza pyramids, 60 feet wide and 5/8 mile long, is mentioned repeatedly, but we find no mention of its use of iron. Moreover, iron was practically unknown in Egypt until long after the period to which Poe refers. Mabbott (9, III) adds that Poe knew an article about how the causeway was grooved, and the grooves oiled to reduce friction. No iron is mentioned, however.

[24] The organ of the New England Transcendentalists, against whom Poe waged an unrelenting literary war.

Figure 10. The fountain at the Bowling Green. The Count admits that even Egypt has nothing to match "the ingenuity, magnificence and superiority" of this edifice. The fountain was nicknamed "the riprap fountain" after the way the irregular stones are built up "riprap style." The fire is irrelevant to Poe's tale. Repeated funny references were made to the fountain in the press; they became especially frequent in the 1850s. The plate is from a Currier Lithograph (New York, 1845) reproduced from the Eno Collection, Prints Division, courtesy of the New York Public Library, Astor, Lenox and Tilden Foundations.

much trouble in impressing the Count with a due sense of the advantages we enjoyed in living where there was suffrage *ad libitum,* and no king.

He listened with marked interest, and in fact seemed not a little amused. When we had done, he said that, a great while ago, there had occurred something of a very similar sort. Thirteen Egyptian provinces determined all at once to be free, and so set a magnificent example to the rest of mankind. They assembled their wise men, and concocted the most ingenious constitution it is possible to conceive. For a while they managed remarkably well; only their habit of bragging was prodigious. The thing ended, however, in the consolidation of the thirteen states, with some fifteen or twenty others, in the most odious and insupportable despotism that ever was heard of upon the face of the Earth.

I asked what was the name of the usurping tyrant.

As well as the Count could recollect, it was *Mob.*

Not knowing what to say to this, I raised my voice, and deplored the Egyptian ignorance of steam.

The count looked at me with much astonishment, but made no answer. The silent gentleman, however, gave me a violent nudge in the ribs with his elbows—

told me that I had sufficiently exposed myself for once—and demanded if I was really such a fool as not to know that the modern steam engine is derived from the invention of Hero, through Solomon de Caus.[25]

We were now in imminent danger of being discomfited; but, as good luck would have it, Doctor Ponnonner, having rallied, returned to our rescue, and inquired if the people of Egypt would seriously pretend to rival the moderns in the all-important particular of dress.

The Count, at this, glanced downward to the straps of his pantaloons, and then, taking hold of the end of one of his coattails, held it up close to his eyes for some minutes. Letting it fall, at last, his mouth extended itself very gradually from ear to ear; but I do not remember that he said anything in the way of reply.

Hereupon we recovered our spirits, and the Doctor, approaching the Mummy with great dignity, desired it to say candidly, upon its honor as a gentleman, if the Egyptians had comprehended, at *any* period, the manufacture of either Ponnonner's lozenges, or Brandreth's pills.[26]

We looked, with profound anxiety, for an answer;—but in vain. It was not forthcoming. The Egyptian blushed and hung down his head. Never was triumph more consummate; never was defeat borne with so ill a grace. Indeed I could not endure the spectacle of the poor Mummy's mortification. I reached my hat, bowed to him stiffly, and took leave.

Upon getting home I found it past four o'clock, and went immediately to bed. It is now ten, A.M. I have been up since seven, penning these memoranda for the benefit of my family and of mankind. The former I shall behold no more. My wife is a shrew. The truth is, I am heartily sick of this life and of the nineteenth century in general. I am convinced that everything is going wrong. Besides, I am anxious to know who will be President in 2045. As soon, therefore, as I shave and swallow a cup of coffee, I shall just step over to Ponnonner's and get embalmed for a couple of hundred years.

---

[25]**Hero:** Hero (or Heron) of Alexandria (dates unknown—probably between the third and second centuries B.C.E.) is supposed to have built a kind of steam engine. His dates are, of course, far too late for Poe's Count, who was entombed 5,050 years. **Solomon de Caus:** Norman engineer (Pollin 3) who did pioneering work on the theory of steam power (1576–1626).

[26]**Ponnonner's lozenges:** Pollin (11) feels that Ponnonner is probably based on a real name—possibly that of a patent medicine—not yet determined. He suggests a pun on "Upon my honor." See note 2 above. **Brandreth's pills:** A well-known patent laxative, and something of a popular joke. Melville says, "How to cure . . . a whale's dyspepsia it were hard to say, unless by administering three or four boat loads of Brandreth's pills, and then running out of harm's way as laborers do in blasting rocks."

The Power of Words

Carlyle's essay on "Boswell's Life of Johnson" dates from 1832, and Poe's "The Power of Words" appeared in print in 1845. The essay could well provide a motto for the tale: "Nothing dies, nothing can die. No idlest word thou speakest but is a seed cast into Time, and grows through all Eternity!" Poe knew Carlyle's work well, and this particular idea is consistent with Poe's most frequently held philosophical stance. The quasi-scriptural tone of the Carlyle passage also may have its echoes in Poe.

For the reader who wants to understand Poe's metaphysics, this is his most important story. The last two paragraphs are the center of the story and in a sense the center of the Romantic movement in literature. Modern critics generally make the mistake Oinos makes. Seeing a literary symbol, they interpret it as simile—it is "like" what it represents. Even when they interpret it as a metaphor, they assume that it merely "represents." But Romantics of Poe's sort, artists as different as Blake, Shelley, and Whitman, were attempting to restore to art its ancient properties of science, magic, and prophecy. Oinos is about to learn that the flowers are not like *"a fairy dream"; the volcanoes are not* like *"the passions of a turbulent heart." They* are *literally "unfulfilled dreams" and "passions." That Romantic authors intend such meanings is hard for us as Western rationalists to grasp, but Poe, even when in an ironic mood, is unusually consistent in the matter. There have always been important literary artists who have taken him seriously. This is the basic reason, for example, for the enthusiasm for Poe among French symbolist poets. If the idea is hard to grasp, your editors recommend John Senior's admirable book* The Way Down and Out: The Occult in Symbolist Literature *(Cornell University Press, 1959) as a reliable introduction to the field.*

Publications in Poe's Time

United States Magazine and Democratic Review, June 1845
The Broadway Journal, October 25, 1845

THE POWER OF WORDS

Oinos.—Pardon. Agathos,[1] the weakness of a spirit new-fledged with immortality!

Agathos.—You have spoken nothing, my Oinos, for which pardon is to be demanded. Not even here is knowledge a thing of intuition.[2] For wisdom ask of the angels freely, that it may be given!

Oinos.—But in this existence, I dreamed that I should be at once cognizant of all things, and thus at once be happy in being cognizant of all.

Agathos.—Ah, not in knowledge is happiness, but in the acquisition of knowledge! In for ever knowing, we are for ever blessed; but to know all, were the curse of a fiend.

Oinos.—But does not The Most High know all?

Agathos.—*That* (since he is The Most Happy) must be still the *one* thing unknown even to HIM.

Oinos.—But, since we grow hourly in knowledge, must not *at last* all things be known?

Agathos.—Look down into the abysmal distances!—attempt to force the gaze down the multitudinous vistas of the stars, as we sweep slowly through them thus—and thus—and thus! Even the spiritual vision, is it not at all points arrested by the continuous golden walls of the universe?—the walls of the myriads of the shining bodies that mere number has appeared to blend into unity?

Oinos.—I clearly perceive that the infinity of matter is no dream.

Agathos.—There are *no* dreams in Aidenn—but it is here whispered that, of this infinity of matter, the *sole* purpose is to afford infinite springs, at which the soul may allay the thirst *to know* which is for ever unquenchable within it—since to quench it, would be to extinguish the soul's self. Question me then, my Oinos, freely and without fear. Come! we will leave to the left the loud harmony of the Pleiades,[3] and swoop outward from the throne into the starry meadows beyond

---

[1]"Oinos" is the Greek word for wine but can also mean "one." "Agathos" means "good." A character named "Oinos" narrates another Poe story, "Shadow—A Parable," and identifies himself as Greek, so one assumes that Poe intended those meanings. One wonders whether Poe didn't intend a bilingual pun. "Oinos" may be pronounced *e-nos;* Enos is a Hebrew name derived from the Hebrew word for "man." "Good" and "man" (or "one") make much more sense in this tale than "good" and "wine." See our headnote to that story for more about the name "Oinos."

[2]This statement is difficult to square with Poe's general theory of inspiration and with the explicit mysticism of this story. Perhaps all Poe means by "intuition" here is guesswork, which he would feel would not lead to knowledge. He insists so many times that knowledge *does* arise from inspired intuition, from the perception of consistency via analogies, from a combination of intellection and imagination (but not from intellection alone) that some such qualification of Agathos' assertion seems necessary.

[3]**Aidenn:** From the Arabic form Aden or Adn for Eden—a paradise not precisely equivalent to the Hebrew Garden of Eden. An instance of the "Ai" spelling used by an author known to Poe is in William Maginn's poem "Cork is an Aiden for you, love and me." Poe

Orion, where, for pansies and violets, and heart's-ease, are the beds of the triplicate and triple-tinted suns.

Oinos.—And now, Agathos, as we proceed, instruct me!—speak to me in the earth's familiar tones! I understand not what you hinted to me, just now, of the modes or of the methods of what, during mortality, we were accustomed to call Creation. Do you mean to say that the Creator is not God?

Agathos.—I mean to say that the Deity does not create.

Oinos.—Explain!

Agathos.—In the beginning *only,* he created. The seeming creatures which are now, throughout the universe, so perpetually springing into being, can only be considered as the mediate or indirect, not as the direct or immediate results of the Divine creative power.

Oinos.—Among men, my Agathos, this idea would be considered heretical in the extreme.

Agathos.—Among angels, my Oinos, it is seen to be simply true.

Oinos.—I can comprehend you thus far—that certain operations of what we term Nature, or the natural laws, will, under certain conditions, give rise to that which has all the *appearance* of creation. Shortly before the final overthrow of the earth, there were, I well remember, many very successful experiments in what some philosophers were weak enough to denominate the creation of animalculæ.[4]

Agathos.—The cases of which you speak were, in fact, instances of the secondary creation—and of the *only* species of creation which has ever been, since the first word spoke into existence the first law.

Oinos.—Are not the starry worlds that, from the abyss of nonentity, burst hourly forth into the heavens—are not these stars, Agathos, the immediate handiwork of the King?

Agathos.—Let me endeavor, my Oinos, to lead you, step by step, to the conception I intend. You are well aware that, as no thought can perish, so no act is without infinite result. We moved our hands, for example, when we were dwellers on the earth, and, in so doing, we gave vibration to the atmosphere which engirdled it.

---

used the word also in "The Conversation of Eiros and Charmion" (1839). For Poe's reasons for alluding to Arabic elements, see "The Domain of Arnheim," note 18. **harmony of the Pleiades:** Poe is playing with the medieval idea of the music of the spheres (the idea that the perfect mathematics of the universe is a kind of "music") and also with the idea that after death, or in a state of heightened awareness, the "faculties" merge or are confounded, an idea he uses in several other stories (see, for example, "Mesmeric Revelation" in Levine [4], pp. 114, 139–45, and 151). Accounts by people who have used the so-called "mind-expanding" drugs often refer to similar sensations. To Poe, who seemed to believe that the consistency of the universe would be perceived in such states, this justified interest in them. Visionary perception in different stories can be induced by illness, drugs, or insanity, or may be present naturally (as in the case of Ellison in "The Domain of Arnheim"). An enlightened spirit in "Aidenn" would have it as a matter of course.

[4]A matter of considerable speculation and excitement in Poe's day. This story was first published in 1845; in 1837, Andrew Crosse performed a series of experiments which seemed to many scientists of the time to have resulted in the creation of living microorganisms, which were even classified by genus.

This vibration was indefinitely extended, till it gave impulse to every particle of the earth's air, which thence forward, *and for ever,* was actuated by the one movement of the hand. This fact the mathematicians of our globe well knew. They made the special effects, indeed, wrought in the fluid by special impulses, the subject of exact calculation—so that it became easy to determine in what precise period an impulse of given extent would engirdle the orb, and impress (for ever) every atom of the atmosphere circumambient. Retrograding, they found no difficulty, from a given effect, under given conditions, in determining the value of the original impulse. Now the mathematicians who saw that the results of any given impulse were absolutely endless—and who saw that a portion of these results were accurately traceable through the agency of algebraic analysis—who saw, too, the facility of the retrogradation—these men saw, at the same time, that this species of analysis itself, had within itself a capacity for indefinite progress—that there were no bounds conceivable to its advancement and applicability, except within the intellect of him who advanced or applied it. But at this point our mathematicians paused.

Oinos.—And why, Agathos, should they have proceeded?

Agathos.—Because there were some considerations of deep interest beyond. It was deducible from what they knew, that to a being of infinite understanding—one to whom the *perfection* of the algebraic analysis lay unfolded—there could be no difficulty in tracing every impulse given the air—and the ether through the air—to the remotest consequences at any even infinitely remote epoch of time. It is indeed demonstrable that every such impulse *given the air,* must, *in the end,* impress every individual thing that exists *within the universe;*—and the being of infinite understanding—the being whom we have imagined—might trace the remote undulations of the impulse—trace them upward and onward in their influences upon all particles of all matter—upward and onward for ever in their modifications of old forms—or, in other words, *in their creation of new*—until he found them reflected—unimpressive *at last*—back from the throne of the Godhead. And not only could such a being do this, but at any epoch, should a given result be afforded him—should one of these numberless comets, for example, be presented to his inspection—he could have no difficulty in determining, by the analytic retrogradation, to what original impulse it was due. This power of retrogradation in its absolute fulness and perfection—this faculty of referring at *all* epochs, *all* effects to *all* causes—is of course the prerogative of the Deity alone—but in every variety of degree, short of the absolute perfection, is the power itself exercised by the whole host of the Angelic intelligences.

Oinos.—But you speak merely of impulses upon the air.

Agathos.—In speaking of the air, I referred only to the earth; but the general proposition has reference to impulses upon the ether[5]—which, since it pervades, and alone pervades all space, is thus the great medium of *creation.*

---

[5]Whether or not an "ether" exists was a matter of scientific debate for centuries. The ether was understood to be the "stuff" of the universe, a perfectly elastic medium which pervades all of space. Poe needs some such stuff to make his materialistic theory work. If all thought and action has physical consequences, there has to be a "carrier." The earth's atmosphere

Oinos.—Then all motion, of whatever nature, creates?

Agathos.—It must: but a true philosophy has long taught that the source of all motion is thought—and the source of all thought is—

Oinos.—God.

Agathos.—I have spoken to you, Oinos, as to a child of the fair Earth which lately perished—of impulses upon the atmosphere of the Earth.

Oinos.—You did.

Agathos.—And while I thus spoke, did there not cross your mind some thought of the *physical power of words?* Is not every word an impulse on the air?

Oinos.—But why, Agathos, do you weep—and why—oh why do your wings droop as we hover above this fair star—which is the greenest and yet most terrible of all we have encountered in our flight? Its brilliant flowers look like a fairy dream—but its fierce volcanoes like the passions of a turbulent heart.

Agathos.—They *are!*—they *are!* This wild star—it is now three centuries since, with clasped hands, and with streaming eyes, at the feet of my beloved—I spoke it—with a few passionate sentences—into birth. Its brilliant flowers *are* the dearest of all unfulfilled dreams, and its raging volcanoes *are* the passions of the most turbulent and unhallowed of hearts.

---

will do for manual actions so far as it extends; beyond that, and for thought, he had to have another "carrier," so he used ether. His "materialism" is an attempt to ground spirituality in physical fact.

The Imp of the Perverse

This story depends for its effectiveness on the vagueness of the line which distinguished story from article in the periodicals of Poe's day. Format gave readers no clue. The story is in a way a hoax: it pretends to be a "normal" article, then turns into a story. The reader has no way of knowing that this witty and philosophical "essay" is a work of fiction until he is well into it—indeed, only in the last nine paragraphs do we discover that the narrator is a "character" and that we are to have a "plot." One has to reread the opening to see that the narrator's argument is specious. Science, he says, very reasonably, should cease trying to locate characteristics man should have, and start instead by observing characteristics which he does *have. The narrator's first point is perfectly good: phrenology can be seen as a branch of metaphysics, and metaphysicians have erred through moralistic assumptions. The trouble is that there is no such thing as the "perverseness" of which he speaks. He is not perverse; he is criminally insane.*

His examples of perversity before he begins to tell his own story show a crescendo of intensity, culminating in a passage on suicidal desire which is a miniature horror story in itself; they serve to transfer readers from the "essay" to the "story." And the narrator continues to think that his confession was perverse, not the murder itself. "The Imp of the Perverse" turns out to be conscience.

***A note of explanation:** During the period in which Poe's tale appeared, it was becoming clear that most phrenologists were quacks. But phrenology had been founded as a serious science. The idea behind it was that it seemed reasonable to assume that different portions of the human mind ("organs") served different functions and that, once one knew their locations, their relative development ought to be reflected in the shape of the head. Careful studies were done of the* crania *of men noted for various characteristics. The skulls of notable leaders, geniuses, madmen, and even criminals were often exhumed for measurement and examination, and attempts were made to apply clinically what had been learned.*

Publications in Poe's Time

Graham's Magazine, July 1845
The May Flower for 1846 (actually printed in 1845)

THE IMP OF THE PERVERSE

In the consideration of the faculties and impulses—of the *prima mobilia* of the human soul, the phrenologists have failed to make room for a propensity which, although obviously existing as a radical, primitive, irreducible sentiment, has been equally overlooked by all the moralists who have preceded them. In the pure arrogance of the reason, we have all overlooked it. We have suffered its existence to escape our senses, solely through want of belief—of faith;—whether it be faith in Revelation, or faith in the Kabbala. The idea of it has never occurred to us, simply because of its supererogation. We saw no *need* of the impulse—for the propensity. We could not perceive its necessity. We could not understand, that is to say, we could not have understood, had the notion of this *primum mobile* ever obtruded itself;—we could not have understood in what manner it might be made to further the objects of humanity, either temporal or eternal. It cannot be denied that phrenology, and in good measure, all metaphysicianism have been concocted *à priori.* The intellectual or logical man, rather than the understanding or observant man, set himself to imagine designs—to dictate purposes to God. Having thus fathomed to his satisfaction the intentions of Jehovah, out of these intentions he built his innumerable systems of mind. In the matter of phrenology, for example, we first determined, naturally enough, that it was the design of the Deity that man should eat. We then assigned to man an organ of alimentiveness, and this organ is the scourge with which the Deity compels man, will-I, nill-I, into eating. Secondly, having settled it to be God's will that man should continue his species, we discovered an organ of amativeness, forthwith. And so with combativeness, with ideality, with causality, with constructiveness,—so, in short, with every organ, whether representing a propensity, a moral sentiment, or a faculty of the pure intellect. And in these arrangements of the *principia* of human action, the Spurzheimites,[1] whether right or wrong, in part, or upon the whole, have but followed, in principle, the footsteps of their predecessors; deducing and establishing every thing from the preconceived destiny of man, and upon the ground of the objects of his Creator.

It would have been wiser, it would have been safer to classify, (if classify we must,) upon the basis of what man usually or occasionally did, and was always occasionally doing, rather than upon the basis of what we took it for granted the Deity intended him to do. If we cannot comprehend God in his visible works, how then in his inconceivable thoughts, that call the works into being! If we cannot understand him in his objective creatures, how then in his substantive moods and phases of creation?

Induction, *à posteriori,* would have brought phrenology to admit, as an innate and primitive principle of human action, a paradoxical something, which we may

---

[1]***prima mobilia:*** Prime movers, first causes. **phrenologists:** See "A note of explanation" in our headnote. ***primum mobile:*** Prime mover. ***à priori:*** The logical process of proceeding from a cause to its effect. **organ:** See "A note of explanation" in our headnote. ***principia:*** Principles. **Spurzheimites:** Johann Kaspar Spurzheim (1776–1832) was one of the popularizers of phrenology in the period when it was still taken seriously as a science.

call *perverseness,* for want of a more characteristic term. In the sense I intend, it is, in fact, a *mobile* without motive, a motive not *motivirt.*[2] Through its promptings we act without comprehensible object; or, if this shall be understood as a contradiction in terms, we may so far modify the proposition as to say, that through its promptings we act, for the reason that we should *not.* In theory, no reason can be more unreasonable; but, in fact, there is none more strong. With certain minds, under certain conditions, it becomes absolutely irresistible. I am not more certain that I breathe, than that the assurance of the wrong or error of any action is often the one unconquerable *force* which impels us, and alone impels us to its prosecution. Nor will this overwhelming tendency to do wrong for the wrong's sake, admit of analysis, or resolution into ulterior elements. It is a radical, a primitive impulse—elementary. It will be said, I am aware, that when we persist in acts because we feel we should *not* persist in them, our conduct is but a modification of that which ordinarily springs from the *combativeness* of phrenology. But a glance will show the fallacy of this idea. The phrenological combativeness has for its essence, the necessity of self-defence. It is our safeguard against injury. Its principle regards our well-being; and thus the desire to be well, is excited simultaneously with its development. It follows, that the desire to be well must be excited simultaneously with any principle which shall be merely a modification of combativeness, but in the case of that something which I term *perverseness,* the desire to be well is not only not aroused, but a strongly antagonistical sentiment exists.

An appeal to one's own heart is, after all, the best reply to the sophistry just noticed. No one who trustingly consults and thoroughly questions his own soul, will be disposed to deny the entire radicalness of the propensity in question. It is not more incomprehensible than distinctive. There lives no man who at some period has not been tormented, for example, by an earnest desire to tantalize a listener by circumlocution. The speaker is aware that he displeases; he has every intention to please; he is usually curt, precise, and clear; the most laconic and luminous language is struggling for utterance upon his tongue; it is only with difficulty that he restrains himself from giving it flow; he dreads and deprecates the anger of him whom he addresses; yet, the thought strikes him, that by certain involutions and parentheses, this anger may be engendered. That single thought is enough. The impulse increases to a wish, the wish to a desire, and desire to an uncontrollable longing, and the longing, (to the deep regret and mortification of the speaker, and in defiance of all consequences,) is indulged.[3]

We have a task before us which must be speedily performed. We know that it will be ruinous to make delay. The most important crisis of our life calls, trumpet-tongued, for immediate energy and action. We glow, we are consumed with eagerness to commence the work, with the anticipation of whose glorious result

---

[2] ***à posteriori:*** The logical opposite of *à priori* reasoning: moving from facts to principles, or from evidence to cause. ***motivirt:*** Motivated.

[3] The narrator's first example is mild; the reader still thinks he is being addressed by a witty and observant essayist. Note that the succeeding examples grow in intensity and in the seriousness of the "perverseness" displayed until the narrator steps forth to identify his own case.

our whole souls are on fire. It must, it shall be undertaken to-day, and yet we put it off until to-morrow; and why? There is no answer, except that we feel *perverse,* using the word with no comprehension of the principle. To-morrow arrives, and with it a more impatient anxiety to do our duty, but with this very increase of anxiety arrives, also, a nameless, a positively fearful, because unfathomable, craving for delay. This craving gathers strength as the moments fly. The last hour for action is at hand. We tremble with the violence of the conflict within us,—of the definite with the indefinite—of the substance with the shadow. But, if the contest have proceeded thus far, it is the shadow which prevails,—we struggle in vain. The clock strikes, and is the knell of our welfare. At the same time, it is the chanticleer-note to the ghost that has so long overawed us. It flies—it disappears—we are free. The old energy returns. We will labor *now.* Alas, it is *too late!*

We stand upon the brink of a precipice. We peer into the abyss—we grow sick and dizzy. Our first impulse is to shrink from the danger. Unaccountably we remain. By slow degrees our sickness, and dizziness, and horror, become merged in a cloud of unnameable feeling. By gradations, still more imperceptible, this cloud assumes shape, as did the vapor from the bottle out of which arose the genius[4] in the Arabian Nights. But out of this *our* cloud upon the precipice's edge, there grows into palpability, a shape, far more terrible than any genius, or any demon of a tale, and yet it is but a thought, although a fearful one, and one which chills the very marrow of our bones with the fierceness of the delight of its horror. It is merely the idea of what would be our sensations during the sweeping precipitancy of a fall from such a height. And this fall—this rushing annihilation—for the very reason that it involves that one most ghastly and loathsome of all the most ghastly and loathsome images of death and suffering which have ever presented themselves to our imagination—for this very cause do we now the most vividly desire it. And because our reason violently deters us from the brink, *therefore,* do we the more impetuously approach it. There is no passion in nature so demoniacally impatient, as that of him, who shuddering upon the edge of a precipice, thus meditates a plunge. To indulge for a moment, in any attempt at *thought,* is to be inevitably lost; for reflection but urges us to forbear, and *therefore* it is, I say, that we *cannot.* If there be no friendly arm to check us, or if we fail in a sudden effort to prostrate ourselves backward from the abyss, we plunge, and are destroyed.

Examine these and similar actions as we will, we shall find them resulting solely from the spirit of the *Perverse.* We perpetrate them merely because we feel that we should *not.* Beyond or behind this, there is no intelligible principle: and we might, indeed, deem this perverseness a direct instigation of the arch-fiend, were it not occasionally known to operate in furtherance of good.

I have said thus much, that in some measure I may answer your question—that I may explain to you why I am here—that I may assign to you something that shall have at least the faint aspect of a cause for my wearing these fetters, and for my tenanting this cell of the condemned. Had I not been thus prolix, you might either have misunderstood me altogether, or, with the rabble, have fancied me mad. As it

---

[4]Jinni, genie.

is, you will easily perceive that I am one of the many uncounted victims of the Imp of the Perverse.

It is impossible that any deed could have been wrought with a more thorough deliberation. For weeks, for months, I pondered upon the means of the murder. I rejected a thousand schemes, because their accomplishment involved a *chance* of detection. At length, in reading some French memoirs, I found an account of a nearly fatal illness that occurred to Madam Pilau,[5] through the agency of a candle accidentally poisoned. The idea struck my fancy at once. I knew my victim's habit of reading in bed. I knew, too, that his apartment was narrow and ill-ventilated. But I need not vex you with impertinent details. I need not describe the easy artifices by which I substituted, in his bedroom candle-stand, a wax-light of my own making, for the one which I there found. The next morning he was discovered dead in his bed, and the coroner's verdict was,—"Death by the visitation of God."

Having inherited his estate, all went well with me for years. The idea of detection never once entered my brain. Of the remains of the fatal taper, I had myself carefully disposed. I had left no shadow of a clue by which it would be possible to convict, or even to suspect, me of the crime. It is inconceivable how rich a sentiment of satisfaction arose in my bosom as I reflected upon my absolute security. For a very long period of time, I was accustomed to revel in this sentiment. It afforded me more real delight than all the mere worldly advantages accruing from my sin. But there arrived at length an epoch, from which the pleasurable feeling grew, by scarcely perceptible gradations, into a haunting and harassing thought. It harassed because it haunted. I could scarcely get rid of it for an instant. It is quite a common thing to be thus annoyed with the ringing in our ears, or rather in our memories, of the burthen of some ordinary song, or some unimpressive snatches from an opera. Nor will we be the less tormented if the song itself be good, or the opera air meritorious. In this manner, at last, I would perpetually catch myself pondering upon my security, and repeating, in a low under-tone, the phrase, "I am safe."

One day, while sauntering along the streets, I arrested myself in the act of murmuring, half aloud, these customary syllables. In a fit of petulance, I re-modelled them thus:—"I am safe—I am safe—yes—if I be not fool enough to make open confession!"

No sooner had I spoken these words, than I felt an icy chill creep to my heart. I had had some experience in these fits of perversity, (whose nature I have been at some trouble to explain,) and I remembered well, that in no instance, I had successfully resisted their attacks. And now my own casual self-suggestion, that I might possibly be fool enough to confess the murder of which I had been guilty confronted me, as if the very ghost of him whom I had murdered—and beckoned me on to death.

At first, I made an effort to shake off this nightmare of the soul. I walked vigorously—faster—still faster—at length I ran. I felt a maddening desire to shriek aloud. Every succeeding wave of thought overwhelmed me with new

[5]An item entitled "Madame Pilau: An Oddity of the Seventeenth Century" by C. F. Gore appeared in *The New Monthly Magazine* in 1839. It relates the incident to which Poe refers.

terror, for, alas! I well, too well, understood that to *think,* in my situation, was to be lost. I still quickened my pace. I bounded like a madman through the crowded thoroughfares. At length, the populace took the alarm, and pursued me. I felt *then* the consummation of my fate. Could I have torn out my tongue, I would have done it—but a rough voice resounded in my ears—a rougher grasp seized me by the shoulder. I turned—I gasped for breath. For a moment, I experienced all the pangs of suffocation; I became blind, and deaf, and giddy; and then, some invisible fiend, I thought, struck me with his broad palm upon the back. The long-imprisoned secret burst forth from my soul.[6]

They say that I spoke with a distinct enunciation, but with marked emphasis and passionate hurry, as if in dread of interruption before concluding the brief but pregnant sentences that consigned me to the hangman and to hell.

Having related all that was necessary for the fullest judicial conviction. I fell prostrate in a swoon.

But why shall I say more? To-day I wear these chains, and am *here!* To-morrow I shall be fetterless—*but where?*

---

[6]See our headnote. The narrator's "sanest" act, confession, seems to him "perverse."

The Facts in the Case of M. Valdemar

Poe professed to be surprised that people believed that his "article" about the strange death of M. Valdemar was true. Don't believe him; he concocted his fraud so carefully that he must have known that some readers would think it a piece of extraordinarily interesting news. This despite the fact that most of the impact of "The Facts . . ." comes from the famous horrid "effect" Poe staged at the end, and that setting up that ending is a major artistic project in the tale.

The topic of mesmerism (hypnosis) was very much in the public eye and Poe's; Mabbott (9, III) quotes factual and apparently factual pieces about an operation performed using mesmerism as an anesthetic, of a life prolonged through mesmerism, and of "spiritual" activity at the time of a death under hypnosis, accounts which Poe clearly knew. In a sense, then, "The Facts . . ." is a hoax; certainly Poe hoped that readers would consider it true or at least suspend judgment until they had read most of the story. Besides the widespread fascination with mesmerism, Poe capitalized on several other factors:

1. *The magazines in which he published contained articles as well as stories and generally did not distinguish one from the other through format. It was possible to fool the reader by pretending, as Poe did here, that a story was an article. Indeed, the terms themselves were not yet mutually exclusive; Poe often called a work of fiction an "article."*
2. *Interest in science was very high, and literary magazines ran numerous items about science, especially when they touched on issues which had to do with certain philosophical matters. In this story, for instance, the possibility that scientific proof has at last been found of the existence of life after death would have been of great interest, not merely on theological grounds, but also because Romantic artists wanted to believe that there was "something out there" with which the inspired mind was in contact. Many Romantic artists hoped that science was on the verge of discovering the force that unifies the universe, thus giving "inspiration" a physical basis (see note 1, "magnetic"). Many thought that the force would be electrical in nature. Thus one literary magazine, for instance, carried accounts of work of the French researcher Magendie on electrical stimulation of the brain, and others noted in 1837 that Andrew Crosse of the London Electrical Society seemed to have created life through the application of electricity to "silicate of potash," HCl, and iron oxide.*
3. *The line between science and pseudoscience was often ill-defined. Phrenology (reading personality and analyzing psychological problems through examination of the shape of the head) and mesmerism (hypnotism) were both taken seriously. When both "sciences" fell into the hands of*

quacks, phrenology died peacefully. Mesmerism, as hypnotism, is still very much with us as a serious field of investigation, although it is much less prominent in our popular press than it was in Poe's time.

4. *Poe makes a great show of "documentation," as in the passage at note 4. Like other magazinists, he frequently claims to be quoting from diaries, notebooks, and other sources. Poe, having pretended that he intends just to set the "facts" straight, and having "identified" Valdemar and diagnosed his symptoms, brings in not one but two doctors, two nurses, and an intern as witnesses, and then "copies" from the intern's notes.*

When the story was published in pamphlet form in England in 1846, the publishers sought to capitalize on its credibility. They changed the title to:

Mesmerism
"In Articulo Mortis"
An
Astounding and Horrifying Narrative
Shewing the Extraordinary Power of Mesmerism
in Arresting the
Progress of Death

and included an "Advertisement" which suggested that the events described were believed to be true.

As for the horror itself: the passage following note 7 is perhaps Poe's deepest penetration into what is called "gothic horror." There can be no doubt that sensationalism, the "vivid effect," and horror are his main concerns here, but note that the tale is philosophically consistent with his other fiction and with his aesthetic aims in short fiction; and that his detachment from the horrid materials he is using is very clear: he "plays games" with Valdemar's identity, fusses with storytelling devices to maintain credibility, and uses to the end a vocabulary and sentence structure more scholarly than passionate.

The last paragraph is as gruesome as anything in Poe. But before concluding that the man was mad to concern himself with such subjects, (1) Examine the contents of magazines of his day to see how common such episodes were in articles and in fiction (though Poe was far more craftsmanlike than most peddlers of the macabre); (2) Note that the tale is presented in the language of an 18th-century scientific paper; (3) Consider the care with which the mechanics of credibility and the "hoax" are handled; (4) Compare the tale to what seem to your editors to be much more deeply felt passages of horror in, say, Hawthorne and Melville—for example, the scene in The House of the Seven Gables *in which a fly walks across the open eye of a corpse, or that in Melville's* White-Jacket *in which a character pretends to relish the taste of cancer tissue.*

A note of explanation: *When Valdemar talks about the exact state of his lungs, he is bearing out mesmeric theory. Mesmeric subjects were believed to know in detail what was transpiring within their bodies. Poe knew Chauncy Hare Townsherd's book* Facts in Mesmerism *(London, 1840; Boston, 1841),* *which said, indeed, that the sick under mesmerism would even know how to prescribe medicines for themselves.*

"Valdemar," of course, is not a real person. But "P——" is meant to suggest "Poe." Mabbott (9, III) is correct in assuming that Poe meant two well-known New York physicians (one was his own doctor) by "D——" and "F——." Scholars are not sure who "L——l" might be, but Poe did have a friend who was a medical student.

PUBLICATIONS IN POE'S TIME

American (Whig) Review, December 1845, as "The Facts of M. Valdemar's Case"
The Broadway Journal, December 20, 1845
The Spirit of the Times, Philadelphia, December 23, 24, 1845
Sunday Times, London, January 4, 1846, as "Mesmerism in America: Astounding and Horrifying Narrative"
Popular Record of Modern Science, London, January 10, 1846, as "Mesmerism in America: Death of M. Valdemar of New York"
pamphlet publication, 1846 (See our headnote.)
Boston Museum, August 18, 1849

THE FACTS IN THE CASE OF M. VALDEMAR

Of course I shall not pretend to consider it any matter for wonder, that the extraordinary case of M. Valdemar has excited discussion. It would have been a miracle had it not—especially under the circumstances. Through the desire of all parties concerned, to keep the affair from the public, at least for the present, or until we had farther opportunities for investigation—through our endeavors to effect this—a garbled or exaggerated account made its way into society, and became the source of many unpleasant misrepresentations, and, very naturally, of a great deal of disbelief.

It is now rendered necessary that I give the *facts*—as far as I comprehend them myself. They are, succinctly, these:

My attention, for the last three years, had been repeatedly drawn to the subject of Mesmerism; and, about nine months ago, it occurred to me, quite suddenly, that in the series of experiments made hitherto, there had been a very remarkable and most unaccountable omission:—no person had as yet been mesmerized *in articulo mortis.* It remained to be seen, first, whether, in such condition, there existed in the patient any susceptibility to the magnetic[1] influence; secondly, whether, if any

[1]***in articulo mortis:*** In the grasp of death. **magnetic:** Hypnosis seemed to imply a "force" between subject and hypnotist, often called "magnetism" (see our headnote).

existed, it was impaired or increased by the condition; thirdly, to what extent, or for how long a period, the encroachments of Death might be arrested by the process. There were other points to be ascertained, but these most excited my curiosity—the last in especial, from the immensely important character of its consequences.

In looking around me for some subject by whose means I might test these particulars, I was brought to think of my friend, M. Ernest Valdemar, the well-known compiler of the "Bibliotheca Forensica," and author (under the *nom de plume* of Issachar Marx) of the Polish versions of "Wallenstein" and "Gargantua." M. Valdemar, who has resided principally at Harlaem, N.Y., since the year 1839, is (or was) particularly noticeable for the extreme spareness of his person—his lower limbs much resembling those of John Randolph; and, also, for the whiteness of his whiskers, in violent contrast to the blackness of his hair—the latter, in consequence, being very generally mistaken for a wig. His temperament was markedly nervous, and rendered him a good subject for mesmeric experiment. On two or three occasions I had put him to sleep with little difficulty, but was disappointed in other results which his peculiar constitution had naturally led me to anticipate. His will was at no period positively, or thoroughly, under my control, and in regard to *clairvoyance,* I could accomplish with him nothing to be relied upon. I always attributed my failure at these points to the disordered state of his health. For some months previous to my becoming acquainted with him, his physicians had declared him in a confirmed phthisis.[2] It was his custom, indeed, to speak calmly of his approaching dissolution, as of a matter neither to be avoided nor regretted.

When the ideas to which I have alluded first occurred to me, it was of course very natural that I should think of M. Valdemar. I knew the steady philosophy of the man too well to apprehend any scruples from *him;* and he had no relatives in America who would be likely to interfere. I spoke to him frankly upon the subject; and, to my surprise, his interest seemed vividly excited. I say to my surprise; for, although he had always yielded his person freely to my experiments, he had never before given me any tokens of sympathy with what I did. His disease was of that character which would admit of exact calculation in respect to the epoch of its termination in death; and it was finally arranged between us that he would send for

---

[2]**"Bibliotheca Forensica," Issachar Marx, "Wallenstein," "Gargantua":** Poe is playing games with his fictitious "well-known" character, Valdemar. Genesis 49:14 tells us that Issachar "is a strong ass crouching down between two burdens." The burdens seem to be translating Rabelais' *Gargantua* and Schiller's *Wallenstein* into Polish (Carlson 2). "Bibliotheca Forensica" would be a collection of legal works. ***nom de plume:*** Pen name. **John Randolph:** John Randolph of Roanoke (1773–1833), whose liberal political writings served as a standard point of reference for Democratic politicians. Poe is still playing games with Valdemar's identity—"You know Valdemar," he says in effect, "he's the fellow who translates books into Polish. He looks a lot like—well, his lower legs look like John Randolph's." ***clairvoyance:*** Poe's chatter about the technical aspects of mesmerism is largely intended as a prop to credibility, but he may have inserted the business about clairvoyance to excuse the fact that Valdemar is not going to report much of what he sees beyond death. **phthisis:** State of tuberculosis.

me about twenty-four hours before the period announced by his physicians as that of his decease.

It is now rather more than seven months since I received, from M. Valdemar himself, the subjoined note:

> MY DEAR P——,
>
> You may as well come *now.* D—— and F—— are agreed that I cannot hold out beyond to-morrow midnight; and I think they have hit the time very nearly.
>
> VALDEMAR.

I received this note within half an hour after it was written, and in fifteen minutes more I was in the dying man's chamber. I had not seen him for ten days, and was appalled by the fearful alteration which the brief interval had wrought in him. His face wore a leaden hue; the eyes were utterly lustreless; and the emanciation was so extreme that the skin had been broken through by the cheek-bones. His expectoration was excessive. The pulse was barely perceptible. He retained, nevertheless, in a very remarkable manner, both his mental power and a certain degree of physical strength. He spoke with distinctness—took some palliative medicines without aid—and, when I entered the room, was occupied in penciling memoranda in a pocket-book. He was propped up in the bed by pillows. Doctors D—— and F—— were in attendance.

After pressing Valdemar's hand, I took these gentlemen aside, and obtained from them a minute account of the patient's condition. The left lung had been for eighteen months in a semi-osseous or cartilaginous state, and was, of course, entirely useless for all purposes of vitality. The right, in its upper portion, was also partially, if not thoroughly, ossified, while the lower region was merely a mass of purulent tubercles, running one into another. Several extensive perforations existed; and, at one point, permanent adhesion to the ribs had taken place. These appearances in the right lobe were of comparatively recent date. The ossification had proceeded with very unusual rapidity; no sign of it had been discovered a month before, and the adhesion had only been observed during the three previous days. Independently of the phthisis, the patient was suspected of aneurism of the aorta;[3] but on this point the osseous symptoms rendered an exact diagnosis impossible. It was the opinion of both physicians that M. Valdemar would die about midnight on the morrow (Sunday). It was then seven o'clock on Saturday evening.

On quitting the invalid's bed-side to hold conversation with myself, Doctors D—— and F—— had bidden him a final farewell. It had not been their intention to return; but, at my request, they agreed to look in upon the patient about ten the next night.

When they had gone, I spoke freely with M. Valdemar on the subject of his approaching dissolution, as well as, more particularly, of the experiment proposed. He still professed himself quite willing and even anxious to have it made,

---

[3]**aneurism:** A condition marked by the dilation of the wall of an artery. A pulsating sac forms, and the victim usually suffers pain. One wonders, considering the snide fun he has in describing Valdemar, whether Poe knew that one cause of aneurism is syphilis. **aorta:** The main artery from the left ventricle of the heart.

and urged me to commence it at once. A male and a female nurse were in attendance; but I did not feel myself altogether at liberty to engage in a task of this character with no more reliable witnesses than these people, in case of sudden accident, might prove. I therefore postponed operations until about eight the next night, when the arrival of a medical student with whom I had some acquaintance, (Mr. Theodore L——l,) relieved me from farther embarrassment. It had been my design, originally, to wait for the physicians; but I was induced to proceed, first, by the urgent entreaties of M. Valdemar, and secondly, by my conviction that I had not a moment to lose, as he was evidently sinking fast.

Mr. L——l was so kind as to accede to my desire that he would take notes of all that occurred; and it is from his memoranda that what I now have to relate is, for the most part, either condensed or copied *verbatim.*[4]

It wanted about five minutes of eight when, taking the patient's hand, I begged him to state, as distinctly as he could, to Mr. L——l, whether he (M. Valdemar) was entirely willing that I should make the experiment of mesmerizing him in his then condition.

He replied feebly, yet quite audibly, "Yes, I wish to be mesmerized"—adding immediately afterwards, "I fear you have deferred it too long."

While he spoke thus, I commenced the passes which I had already found most effectual in subduing him. He was evidently influenced with the first lateral stroke of my hand aross his forehead; but although I exerted all my powers, no farther perceptible effect was induced until some minutes after ten o'clock, when Doctors D—— and F—— called, according to appointment. I explained to them, in a few words, what I designed, and as they opposed no objection, saying that the patient was already in the death agony, I proceeded without hesitation—exchanging, however, the lateral passes for downward ones, and directing my gaze entirely into the right eye of the sufferer.

By this time his pulse was imperceptible and his breathing was stertorous,[5] and at intervals of half a minute.

This condition was nearly unaltered for a quarter of an hour. At the expiration of this period, however, a natural although a very deep sigh escaped the bosom of the dying man, and the stertorous breathing ceased—that is to say, its stertorousness was no longer apparent; the intervals were undiminished. The patient's extremities were of an icy coldness.

At five minutes before eleven I perceived unequivocal signs of the mesmeric influence. The glassy roll of the eye was changed for that expression of uneasy *inward* examination which is never seen except in cases of sleep-waking, and which it is quite impossible to mistake. With a few rapid lateral passes I made the lids quiver, as in incipient sleep, and with a few more I closed them altogether. I was not satisfied, however, with this, but continued the manipulations vigorously, and with the fullest exertion of the will, until I had completely stiffened the limbs of the slumberer, after placing them in a seemingly easy position. The legs were at

[4]The credibility game again. See our headnote.

[5]He snored when he breathed.

full length; the arms were nearly so, and reposed on the bed at a moderate distance from the loins. The head was very slightly elevated.

When I had accomplished this, it was fully midnight, and I requested the gentlemen present to examine M. Valdemar's condition. After a few experiments, they admitted him to be in an unusually perfect state of mesmeric trance. The curiosity of both the physicians was greatly excited. Dr. D—— resolved at once to remain with the patient all night, while Dr. F—— took leave with a promise to return at daybreak. Mr. L——l and the nurses remained.

We left M. Valdemar entirely undisturbed until about three o'clock in the morning, when I approached him and found him in precisely the same condition as when Dr. F—— went away—that is to say, he lay in the same position; the pulse was imperceptible; the breathing was gentle (scarcely noticeable, unless through the application of a mirror to the lips); the eyes were closed naturally; and the limbs were as rigid and as cold as marble. Still, the general appearance was certainly not that of death.

As I approached M. Valdemar I made a kind of half effort to influence his right arm into pursuit of my own, as I passed the latter gently to and fro above his person. In such experiments with this patient I had never perfectly succeeded before, and assuredly I had little thought of succeeding now; but to my astonishment, his arm very readily, although feebly, followed every direction I assigned it with mine. I determined to hazard a few words of conversation.

"M. Valdemar," I said, "are you asleep?" He made no answer, but I perceived a tremor about the lips, and was thus induced to repeat the question, again and again. At its third repetition, his whole frame was agitated by a very slight shivering; the eyelids unclosed themselves so far as to display a white line of the ball; the lips moved sluggishly, and from between them, in a barely audible whisper, issued the words:

"Yes;—asleep now. Do not wake me!—let me die so!"

I here felt the limbs and found them as rigid as ever. The right arm, as before, obeyed the direction of my hand. I questioned the sleep-waker again:

"Do you still feel pain in the breast, M. Valdemar?"

The answer now was immediate, but even less audible than before:

"No pain—I am dying."

I did not think it advisable to disturb him farther just then, and nothing more was said or done until the arrival of Dr. F——, who came a little before sunrise, and expressed unbounded astonishment at finding the patient still alive. After feeling the pulse and applying a mirror to the lips, he requested me to speak to the sleep-waker again. I did so, saying:

"M. Valdemar, do you still sleep?"

As before, some minutes elapsed ere a reply was made; and during the interval the dying man seemed to be collecting his energies to speak. At my fourth repetition of the question, he said very faintly, almost inaudibly:

"Yes; still asleep—dying."

It was now the opinion, or rather the wish, of the physicians, that Mr. Valdemar should be suffered to remain undisturbed in his present apparently tranquil condition, until death should supervene—and this, it was generally agreed, must now take place within a few minutes. I concluded, however, to speak to him once more, and merely repeated my previous question.

While I spoke, there came a marked change over the countenance of the sleep-waker. The eyes rolled themselves slowly open, the pupils disappearing upwardly; the skin generally assumed a cadaverous hue, resembling not so much parchment as white paper; and the circular hectic spots which, hitherto, had been strongly defined in the centre of each cheek, *went out* at once. I use this expression, because the suddenness of their departure put me in mind of nothing so much as the extinguishment of a candle by a puff of the breath. The upper lip, at the same time, writhed itself away from the teeth, which it had previously covered completely; while the lower jaw fell with an audible jerk, leaving the mouth widely extended, and disclosing in full view the swollen and blackened tongue. I presume that no member of the party then present had been unaccustomed to death-bed horrors; but so hideous beyond conception was the appearance of M. Valdemar at this moment, that there was a general shrinking back from the region of the bed.

I now feel that I have reached a point of this narrative at which every reader will be startled into positive disbelief. It is my business, however, simply to proceed.

There was no longer the faintest sign of vitality in M. Valdemar; and concluding him to be dead, we were consigning him to the charge of the nurses, when a strong vibratory motion was observable in the tongue. This continued for perhaps a minute. At the expiration of this period, there issued from the distended and motionless jaws a voice—such as it would be madness in me to attempt describing. There are, indeed, two or three epithets which might be considered as applicable to it in part; I might say, for example, that the sound was harsh, and broken and hollow; but the hideous whole is indescribable, for the simple reason that no similar sounds have ever jarred upon the ear of humanity. There were two particulars, nevertheless, which I thought then, and still think, might fairly be stated as characteristic of the intonation—as well adapted to convey some idea of its unearthly peculiarity. In the first place, the voice seemed to reach our ears—at least mine—from a vast distance, or from some deep cavern within the earth. In the second place, it impressed me (I fear, indeed, that it will be impossible to make myself comprehended) as gelatinous or glutinous matters impress the sense of touch.

I have spoken both of "sound" and of "voice." I mean to say that the sound was one of distinct—of even wonderfully, thrillingly distinct—syllabification. M. Valdemar *spoke*—obviously in reply to the question I had propounded to him a few minutes before. I had asked him, it will be remembered, if he still slept. He now said:

"Yes;—no;—I *have been* sleeping—and now—now—*I am dead.*"

No person present even affected to deny, or attempted to repress, the unutterable, shuddering horror which these few words, thus uttered, were so well calculated to convey. Mr. L——l (the student) swooned.[6] The nurses immediately left the chamber, and could not be induced to return. My own impressions I would not pretend to render intelligible to the reader. For nearly an hour, we busied our-

[6]A squeamish lot, these interns. See our headnote.

selves, silently—without the utterance of a word—in endeavors to revive Mr. L——l. When he came to himself, we addressed ourselves again to an investigation of M. Valdemar's condition.

It remained in all respects as I have last described it, with the exception that the mirror no longer afforded evidence of respiration. An attempt to draw blood from the arm failed. I should mention, too, that this limb was no farther subject to my will. I endeavored in vain to make it follow the direction of my hand. The only real indication, indeed, of the mesmeric influence, was now found in the vibratory movement of the tongue, whenever I addressed M. Valdemar a question. He seemed to be making an effort to reply, but had no longer sufficient volition. To queries put to him by any other person than myself he seemed utterly insensible—although I endeavored to place each member of the company in mesmeric *rapport* with him. I believe that I have now related all that is necessary to an understanding of the sleep-waker's state at this epoch. Other nurses were procured; and at ten o'clock I left the house in company with the two physicians and Mr. L—-l.

In the afternoon we all called again to see the patient. His condition remained precisely the same. We had now some discussion as to the propriety and feasibility of awakening him; but we had little difficulty in agreeing that no good purpose would be served by so doing. It was evident that, so far, death (or what is usually termed death) had been arrested by the mesmeric process. It seemed clear to us all that to awaken M. Valdemar would be merely to insure his instant, or at least his speedy dissolution.

From this period until the close of last week—*an interval of nearly seven months*—we continued to make daily calls at M. Valdemar's house, accompanied, now and then, by medical and other friends. All this time the sleep-waker remained *exactly* as I have last described him. The nurses' attentions were continual.

It was on Friday last that we finally resolved to make the experiment of awakening, or attempting to awaken him; and it is the (perhaps) unfortunate result of this latter experiment which has given rise to so much discussion in private circles—to so much of what I cannot help thinking unwarranted popular feeling.

For the purpose of relieving M. Valdemar from the mesmeric trance, I made use of the customary passes. These, for a time, were unsuccessful. The first indication of revival was afforded by a partial descent of the iris. It was observed, as especially remarkable, that his lowering of the pupil was accompanied by the profuse outflowing of a yellowish ichor[7] (from beneath the lids) of a pungent and highly offensive odor.

It now was suggested that I should attempt to influence the patient's arm, as heretofore. I made the attempt and failed. Dr. F—— then intimated a desire to have me put a question. I did so, as follows:

"M. Valdemar, can you explain to us what are your feelings or wishes now?"

There was an instant return of the hectic circles on the cheeks; the tongue quivered, or rather rolled violently in the mouth (although the jaws and lips remained rigid as before;) and at length the same hideous voice which I have already described, broke forth:

---

[7]A watery, acrid fluid discharged from sores.

"For God's sake!—quick!—quick!—put me to sleep—or, quick!—waken me!—quick!—*I say to you that I am dead!*"

I was thoroughly unnerved, and for an instant remained undecided what to do. At first I made an endeavor to re-compose the patient; but, failing in this through total abeyance of the will, I retraced my steps and as earnestly struggled to awaken him. In this attempt I soon saw that I should be successful—or at least I soon fancied that my success would be complete—and I am sure that all in the room were prepared to see the patient awaken.

For what really occurred, however, it is quite impossible that any human being could have been prepared.

As I rapidly made the mesmeric passes, amid ejaculations of "dead! dead!" absolutely *bursting* from the tongue and not from the lips of the sufferer, his whole frame at once—within the pace of a single minute, or even less, shrunk—crumbled—absolutely *rotted* away beneath my hands. Upon the bed, before that whole company, there lay a nearly liquid mass of loathsome—of detestable putridity.

The Cask of Amontillado

In structure, this is among Poe's tightest tales. Montresor is as mad as any of Poe's narrators, but Poe omits the usual passage revealing that men have called him mad or that he comes from a long line of monomaniacs. The plot itself tells us.

Like many of Poe's inspired madmen, however, Montresor is akin to Poe's creative characters. Ellison created the landscape garden; Dupin solved cases by exposing baroque patterns of criminality and violence; even mad Usher painted impressively and improvised music. Montresor "creates" a horrible crime which will, paradoxically, take the adjectives Poe uses to describe the beautiful effect—strange, grotesque, outré, bizarre, complex. But there are none of the usual expository passages to explain why the narrator is mad or how he reached the state which enabled him to create the "beautiful" pattern; compare this to "Hop-Frog," a tale of vengeance which does explain these things. (Mabbott [9, III] and A. H. Quinn point out that at the time Poe wrote the tale, he was involved in an extremely bitter dispute; he certainly had "revenge" in his mind.)

Note also that our willingness to believe in this insane vengeance depends in large part on our antiaristocratic prejudices. Poe's tale is related to innumerable articles in American magazines of the period about the scandalous goings-on of continental nobility.

A note of explanation: *Because Poe almost certainly knew the Montresor family motto from childhood, and since that motto connects to the Masonic organizations which were so important in the Revolutionary era in which Poe's grandparents distinguished themselves, it is likely that a good deal of the texture of this tale grows from very personal associations. See notes 2 and 8, and Levine (8) in the Bibliography.*

Publication in Poe's Time

Godey's Lady's Book, November 1846

THE CASK OF AMONTILLADO[1]

The thousand injuries of Fortunato I had borne as I best could, but when he ventured upon insult I vowed revenge. You, who so well know the nature of my soul, will not suppose, however, that I gave utterance to a threat. *At length* I would be avenged; this was a point definitively settled—but the very definitiveness with which it was resolved precluded the idea of risk. I must not only punish but punish with impunity.[2] A wrong is unredressed when retribution overtakes its redresser. It is equally unredressed when the avenger fails to make himself felt as such to him who has done the wrong.

It must be understood that neither by word nor deed had I given Fortunato cause to doubt my good will. I continued, as was my wont, to smile in his face, and he did not perceive that my smile *now* was at the thought of his immolation.

He had a weak point—this Fortunato—although in other regards he was a man to be respected and even feared. He prided himself on his connoisseurship in wine. Few Italians have the true virtuoso spirit. For the most part their enthusiasm is adopted to suit the time and opportunity, to practise imposture upon the British and Austrian *millionaires*. In painting and gemmary, Fortunato, like his countrymen, was a quack, but in the matter of old wines he was sincere. In this respect I did not differ from him materially;—I was skilful in the Italian vintages[3] myself, and bought largely whenever I could.

It was about dusk, one evening during the supreme madness of the carnival season, that I encountered my friend. He accosted me with excessive warmth, for he had been drinking much. The man wore motley. He had on a tight-fitting parti-striped dress, and his head was surmounted by the conical cap and bells. I was so pleased to see him that I thought I should never have done wringing his hand.

I said to him—"My dear Fortunato, you are luckily met. How remarkably well you are looking to-day! But I have received a pipe[4] of what passes for Amontillado, and I have my doubts."

"How?" said he. "Amontillado? A pipe? Impossible! And in the middle of the carnival!"

"I have my doubts," I replied; "and I was willing enough to pay the full Amontillado price without consulting you in the matter. You were not to be found, and I was fearful of losing a bargain."

"Amontillado!"

"I have my doubts."

"Amontillado!"

"And I must satisfy them."

"Amontillado!"

---

[1]Amontillado is a type of Spanish sherry. It's good stuff but not, as Poe implies, really rare.

[2]**Fortunato:** The name suggests both "good fortune" and "fated" (Mabbott 6; Pollin 5). **punish with impunity:** See note 8. Poe foreshadows a passage later in the tale by having Montesor paraphrase his family motto.

[3]Poe apparently thinks that Amontillado is an Italian wine.

[4]A large cask.

"As you are engaged, I am on my way to Luchesi. If any one has a critical turn, it is he. He will tell me——"

"Luchesi cannot tell Amontillado from Sherry."[5]

"And yet some fools will have it that his taste is a match for your own."

"Come, let us go."

"Whither?"

"To your vaults."

"My friend, no; I will not impose upon your good nature. I perceive you have an engagement. Luchesi——"

"I have no engagement;—come."

"My friend, no. It is not the engagement, but the severe cold with which I perceive you are afflicted. The vaults are insufferably damp. They are encrusted with nitre."

"Let us go, nevertheless. The cold is merely nothing. Amontillado! You have been imposed upon. And as for Luchesi, he cannot distinguish Sherry from Amontillado."

Thus speaking, Fortunato possessed himself of my arm; and putting on a mask of black silk and drawing a *roquelaire*[6] closely about my person, I suffered him to hurry me to my palazzo.

There were no attendants at home; they had absconded to make merry in honor of the time. I had told them that I should not return until the morning, and had given them explicit orders not to stir from the house. These orders were sufficient, I well knew, to insure their immediate disappearance, one and all, as soon as my back was turned.

I took from their sconces two flambeaux, and giving one to Fortunato, bowed him through several suites of rooms to the archway that led into the vaults. I passed down a long and winding staircase, requesting him to be cautious as he followed. We came at length to the foot of the descent, and stood together on the damp ground of the catacombs of the Montresors.

The gait of my friend was unsteady, and the bells upon his cap jingled as he strode.

"The pipe?" said he.

"It is farther on," said I; "but observe the white web-work which gleams from these cavern walls."

He turned towards me, and looked into my eyes with two filmy orbs that distilled the rheum of intoxication.

"Nitre?" he asked, at length.

"Nitre," I replied. "How long have you had that cough?"

"Ugh! ugh! ugh!—ugh! ugh! ugh!—ugh! ugh! ugh!—ugh! ugh! ugh!—ugh! ugh! ugh!"

My poor friend found it impossible to reply for many minutes.

"It is nothing," he said, at last.

---

[5]Neither can a taste-vin, since Amontillado *is* a sherry.

[6]A short cloak. Poe's use of the word suggests that he has in mind an 18th-century setting, for that is when such cloaks were popular. See "The Man of the Crowd," note 10.

"Come," I said, with decision, "we will go back; your health is precious. You are rich, respected, admired, beloved; you are happy, as once I was. You are a man to be missed. For me it is no matter. We will go back; you will be ill, and I cannot be responsible. Besides, there is Luchesi——"

"Enough," he said; "the cough is a mere nothing; it will not kill me. I shall not die of a cough."

"True—true," I replied; "and, indeed, I had no intention of alarming you unnecessarily—but you should use all proper caution. A draught of this Medoc[7] will defend us from the damps."

Here I knocked off the neck of a bottle which I drew from a long row of its fellows that lay upon the mould.

"Drink," I said, presenting him the wine.

He raised it to his lips with a leer. He paused and nodded to me familiarly, while his bells jingled.

"I drink," he said, "to the buried that repose around us."

"And I to your long life."

He again took my arm, and we proceeded.

"These vaults," he said, "are extensive."

"The Montresors," I replied, "were a great and numerous family."

"I forget your arms."

"A huge human foot d'or, in a field azure; the foot crushes a serpent rampant whose fangs are imbedded in the heel."

"And the motto?"

"*Nemo me impune lacessit.*"[8]

"Good," he said.

The wine sparkled in his eyes and the bells jingled. My own fancy grew warm with the Medoc. We had passed through walls of piled bones, with casks and puncheons intermingling, into the inmost recesses of the catacombs. I paused again, and this time I made bold to seize Fortunato by an arm above the elbow.

"The nitre!" I said; "see, it increases. It hangs like moss upon the vaults. We are below the river's bed. The drops of moisture trickle among the bones. Come, we will go back ere it is too late. Your cough——"

"It is nothing," he said; "let us go on. But first, another draught of the Medoc."

---

[7]Médoc is a French red wine.

[8]**d'or:** Of gold. ***"Nemo me impune lacessit"*:** "No one insults me with impunity." Carlson (2) reports that this is the "motto of the Scottish royal coat of arms." In *Noctes Ambrosianæ* (see John Wilson in the Bibliography), William Hazlitt is said to have composed a verse about Christopher North (Wilson's pen name) in which he says that the thistle appears in North's crest because "*Nemo me* [is his motto] *Impune Lacesset.*" Poe knew *Noctes Ambrosianæ* well. The change in spelling from "lacessit" to "lacesset" is just a change to the future tense. Certainly all of the writers for the Edinburgh-based *Blackwood's* who produced *Noctes Ambrosianae* would have known the motto. For evidence that Poe knew it from childhood and his own family history, see Levine (8). It connects to his Revolutionary War hero ancestors, to Lafayette's triumphant tour of the U.S., to Poe's teen-age rank in a Boy Scout-like organization, to fear of a slave rebellion, and to the Masons. See also note 10.

I broke and reached him a flagon of De Grâve.[9] He emptied it at a breath. His eyes flashed with a fierce light. He laughed and threw the bottle upward with a gesticulation I did not understand.

I looked at him in surprise. He repeated the movement—a grotesque one.

"You do not comprehend?" he said.

"Not I," I replied.

"Then you are not of the brotherhood."

"How?"

"You are not of the masons."

"Yes, yes," I said; "yes, yes."

"You? Impossible! A mason?"[10]

"A mason," I replied.

"A sign," he said.

"It is this," I answered, producing a trowel from beneath the folds of my *roquelaire.*

"You jest," he exclaimed, recoiling a few paces. "But let us proceed to the Amontillado."

"Be it so," I said, replacing the tool beneath the cloak and again offering him my arm. He leaned upon it heavily. We continued our route in search of the Amontillado. We passed through a range of low arches, descended, passed on, and descending again, arrived at a deep crypt, in which the foulness of the air caused our flambeaux rather to glow than flame.

At the most remote end of the crypt there appeared another less spacious. Its walls had been lined with human remains, piled to the vault overhead, in the fashion of the great catacombs of Paris. Three sides of this interior crypt were still ornamented in this manner. From the fourth the bones had been thrown down, and lay promiscuously upon the earth, forming at one point a mound of some size. Within the wall thus exposed by the displacing of the bones, we perceived a still interior recess, in depth about four feet, in width three, in height six or seven. It seemed to have been constructed for no especial use within itself, but formed merely the interval between two of the colossal supports of the roof of the catacombs, and was backed by one of their circumscribing walls of solid granite.

It was in vain that Fortunato, uplifting his dull torch, endeavored to pry into the depth of the recess. Its termination the feeble light did not enable us to see.

"Proceed," I said; "herein is the Amontillado. As for Luchesi——"

"He is an ignoramus," interrupted my friend, as he stepped unsteadily forward, while I followed immediately at his heels. In an instant he had reached the extremity of the niche, and finding his progress arrested by the rock, stood stupidly bewildered. A moment more and I had fettered him to the granite. In its surface were two iron staples, distant from each other about two feet, horizontally. From one of these depended a short chain, from the other a padlock. Throwing the

---

[9]There is a wine called *Graves.* Poe is probably punning: Médoc (note 7) is supposed to be therapeutic, and this wine is "of the grave" (Pollin 5; Mabbott 6).

[10]A member, that is, of the secret order of Freemasons. See note 8 and "A note of explanation," in our headnote.

links about his waist, it was but the work of a few seconds to secure it. He was too much astounded to resist. Withdrawing the key I stepped back from the recess.

"Pass your hand," I said, "over the wall; you cannot help feeling the nitre. Indeed it is *very* damp. Once more let me *implore* you to return. No? Then I must positively leave you. But I must first render you all the little attentions in my power."

"The Amontillado!" ejaculated my friend, not yet recovered from his astonishment.

"True," I replied; "the Amontillado."

As I said these words I busied myself among the pile of bones of which I have before spoken. Throwing them aside, I soon uncovered a quantity of building stone and mortar. With these materials and with the aid of my trowel, I began vigorously to wall up the entrance of the niche.

I had scarcely laid the first tier of the masonry when I discovered that the intoxication of Fortunato had in a great measure worn off. The earliest indication I had of this was a low moaning cry from the depth of the recess. It was *not* the cry of a drunken man. There was then a long and obstinate silence. I laid the second tier, and the third, and the fourth; and then I heard the furious vibrations of the chain. The noise lasted for several minutes, during which, that I might hearken to it with the more satisfaction, I ceased my labors and sat down upon the bones. When at last the clanking subsided, I resumed the trowel, and finished without interruption the fifth, the sixth, and the seventh tier. The wall was now nearly upon a level with my breast. I again paused, and holding the flambeaux over the masonwork, threw a few feeble rays upon the figure within.

A succession of loud and shrill screams, bursting suddenly from the throat of the chained form, seemed to thrust me violently back. For a brief moment I hesitated, I trembled. Unsheathing my rapier, I began to grope with it about the recess; but the thought of an instant reassured me. I placed my hand upon the solid fabric of the catacombs, and felt satisfied. I reapproached the wall. I replied to the yells of him who clamored. I re-echoed, I aided, I surpassed them in volume and in strength. I did this, and the clamorer grew still.

It was now midnight, and my task was drawing to a close. I had completed the eighth, the ninth, and the tenth tier. I had finished a portion of the last and the eleventh; there remained but a single stone to be fitted and plastered in. I struggled with its weight; I placed it partially in its destined position. But now there came from out the niche a low laugh that erected the hairs upon my head. It was succeeded by a sad voice, which I had difficulty in recognizing as that of the noble Fortunato. The voice said—

"Ha! ha! ha!—he! he! he!—a very good joke, indeed—an excellent jest. We will have many a rich laugh about it at the palazzo—he! he! he!—over our wine—he! he! he!"

"The Amontillado!" I said.

"He! he! he!—he! he! he!—yes, the Amontillado. But is it not getting late? Will not they be awaiting us at the palazzo, the Lady Fortunato and the rest? Let us be gone."

"Yes," I said, "let us be gone."

"*For the love of God, Montresor!*"

"Yes," I said, "for the love of God."

But to these words I hearkened in vain for a reply. I grew impatient. I called aloud—

"Fortunato!"

No answer. I called again—

"Fortunato!"[11]

No answer still. I thrust a torch through the remaining aperture and let it fall within. There came forth in return only a jingling of the bells. My heart grew sick—on account of the dampness of the catacombs. I hastened to make an end of my labor. I forced the last stone into its position; I plastered it up. Against the new masonry I re-erected the old rampart of bones. For the half of a century no mortal has disturbed them. *In pace requiescat!*[12]

---

[11]Several critics have commented on the many repetitions in this tale: "impunity," "Amontillado," "nitre," "Luchesi"; the toasts, "A mason?" "A mason"; the blasphemous "For the love of God!"; and, finally, "Fortunato." Whether or not the tale is really a kind of Black Mass, it is strongly ritualistic in feel.

[12]**My heart grew sick . . . :** Poe teases us with the idea that Montresor's conscience is bothering him. But it's not conscience that makes his heart sick, only dampness. In *Godey's Lady's Book,* the sentence read, "My heart grew sick; it was the dampness of the catacombs that made it so." Here we follow the text from which Poe's literary executor, Rufus Griswold, worked; the changes are Poe's. ***In pace requiescat!:*** "Rest in Peace!" The last heavy irony of a heavily ironic tale. Note Montresor's constant concern for Fortunato's health, and the incongruity of clowns' bells in the cap of a man descending into dank catacombs to his death. Pollin (5) points out a further irony: an "*in pace*" was a very secure monastic prison.

Mellonta Tauta

A witty story with a number of objectives, "Mellonta Tauta" ridicules contemporary pretensions, national pride, historical accuracy, democracy, and faith in progress. In one sense, "Mellonta Tauta" is a "savage attack . . . upon contemporary civilization, especially as represented by the city and by modern democratic government" (Pollin 10). It is filled with unflattering allusions to 19th-century technology and politics, especially to American government and leaders. In another sense, it is a philosophical tale, in which Poe divides savants into two groups, those who understand the role of the intuitive imagination and those who don't. Pundita, his wacky "antiquarian" of the future, generally botches the names of those Poe doesn't like, but knows how to spell those of the "genuinely great." So in the paragraph marked by note 11, she is correct about Isaac Newton, Johannes Kepler, and Jean François Champollion.

Thus it is not accurate to say simply that Poe was hostile to science. He was hostile to grubbing for facts. The great scientists, Poe believed, were also artists and visionaries who used imagination and intuition to perceive the "consistency" of the universal order. Hence even Pundita's society remembers them accurately. In the same passage, Poe drops in a word about cryptography—the deciphering of codes—to help make his point that it takes intuition, not just mere logic, to solve difficult problems. He himself published on cryptography and even offered to decipher samples of difficult codes which readers were urged to send to him.

In a third sense, Poe attacks "progress," though he is not fully consistent. The people of 2848 are our children and share some of our faults. Although Pundita's world has learned to theorize imaginatively, building understanding on a philosophy based on the assumption that the cosmos is unified, there are things wrong with her society: Pundita is ignorant and a snob; historical knowledge remains spectacularly imperfect, and the balloon crashes into the sea.

One could also classify "Mellonta Tauta" as science fiction, for we know Poe's genuine fascination with the possibilities of contemporary technology. If these factors seem somewhat contradictory, well and good: Poe's attitudes are complex, and any system of classifying his tales is somewhat arbitrary.

A note of explanation: *Poe uses the future date and the science fiction to make his satire possible, but his interest in technology was genuine. He did not believe it would improve human nature, but it did catch his imagination; other stories involve flights across the ocean and a moon-shot. One wonders, incidentally, where Pundita and her fellow passengers are going. A month-long trip at 100 miles per hour would take one at least 72,000 miles, too far for a trip on earth, and not far enough for the space travel she mentions later.*

PUBLICATIONS IN POE'S TIME

Godey's Lady's Book, February 1849
A revised version, known as "A Remarkable Letter," appears as part of *Eureka.* Mabbott (9, III) reproduces its text.

MELLONTA TAUTA[1]

TO THE EDITORS OF THE LADY'S BOOK:—

I have the honor of sending you for your magazine, an article which I hope you will be able to comprehend rather more distinctly than I do myself. It is a translation, by my friend, Martin Van Buren Mavis, (sometimes called the "Toughkeepsie Seer,") of an odd-looking MS. which I found, about a year ago, tightly corked up in a jug floating in the *Mare Tenebrarum*—a sea well described by the Nubian geographer,[2] but seldom visited, now-a-days, except by the transcendentalists and divers for crotchets.

Truly yours,

EDGAR A. POE.

ON BOARD BALLOON "SKYLARK,"
***April* 1, 1848.**[3]

Now, my dear friend—now, for your sins, you are to suffer the infliction of a long gossiping letter. I tell you distinctly that I am going to punish you for all your

---

[1]Those things that are to be, or, as Poe translated it, "These things are in the future." Pollin (10) identifies these words as part of the reply of the messenger to Creon at the end of Sophocles' *Antigone.* They also appear as the motto added to the 1845 version of Poe's story "The Colloquy of Monos and Una."

[2]**Mavis:** Poe is playing a game with names. A well-known New York architect, Andrew Jackson Davis, was a close associate of the influential Andrew Jackson Downing, the popularizer of the idea of "cottage style" homes in the suburbs. *The Broadway Journal,* the magazine Poe actually owned for a brief period, had ridiculed Downing's ideas, so Poe would have been familiar with both men. Andrew Jackson, of course, was president before Martin Van Buren, who was to some extent his protégé, and Van Buren would have been in the public eye again when Poe wrote the story—the Free Soil Party nominated him for the presidency in 1848, and he did live near ["T"] Poughkeepsie. So Andrew Jackson Davis = Martin Van Buren Mavis. Mabbott (9, III) points out that Davis could be called a "seer" because he "practiced 'clairvoyant' healing" and other spiritualistic exercises under hypnosis. Later editors "corrected" "Toughkeepsie"; given the wordplay here, we think it possible that Poe *meant* "T," not "P." **the Nubian geographer:** One of Poe's favorite allusions. See "A Descent into the Maelström," note 3. Poe means, in effect, "never-never land."

[3]Skylark: "To engage in hilarious or boisterous frolic." Note the date of Pundita's first letter.

impertinences by being as tedious, as discursive, as incoherent, and as unsatisfactory as possible. Besides, here I am, cooped up in a dirty balloon, with some one or two hundred of the *canaille,*[4] all bound on a *pleasure* excursion (what a funny idea some people have of pleasure!) and I have no prospect of touching *terra firma* for a month at least. Nobody to talk to. Nothing to do. When one has nothing to do, then is the time to correspond with one's friends. You perceive, then, why it is that I write you this letter—it is on account of my *ennui* and your sins.

Get ready your spectacles and make up your mind to be annoyed. I mean to write at you every day during this odious voyage.

Heigho! when will any *Invention* visit the human pericranium? Are we forever to be doomed to the thousand inconveniences of the balloon? Will *nobody* contrive a more expeditious mode of progress? The jog-trot movement, to my thinking, is little less than positive torture. Upon my word, we have not made more than a hundred miles the hour since leaving home! The very birds beat us—at least some of them. I assure you that I do not exaggerate at all. Our motion, no doubt, seems slower than it actually is—this on account of our having no objects about us by which to estimate our velocity, and on account of our going *with* the wind. To be sure, whenever we meet a balloon we have a chance of perceiving our rate, and then, I admit, things do not appear so very bad. Accustomed as I am to this mode of traveling, I cannot get over a kind of giddiness whenever a balloon passes us in a current directly overhead. It always seems to me like an immense bird of prey about to pounce upon us and carry us off in its claws. One went over us this morning about sunrise, and so nearly overhead that its drag-rope actually brushed the network suspending our car, and caused us very serious apprehension. Our captain said that if the material of the bag had been the trumpery varnished "silk" of five hundred or a thousand years ago, we should inevitably have been damaged. This silk, as he explained it to me, was a fabric composed of the entrails of a species of earth-worm. The worm was carefuly fed on mulberries—a kind of fruit resembling a water-melon—and, when sufficiently fat, was crushed in a mill. The paste thus arising was called *papyrus* in its primary state, and went through a variety of processes until it finally became "silk." Singular to relate, it was once much admired as an article of *female dress!* Balloons were also very generally constructed from it. A better kind of material, it appears, was subsequently found in the down surrounding the seed-vessels of a plant vulgarly called *euphorbium,* and at that time botanically termed milk-weed. This latter kind of silk was designated as silk-buckingham, on account of its superior durability, and was usually prepared for use by being varnished with a solution of gum caoutchouc—a substance which in some respects must have resembled the *gutta percha* now in common use. This caoutchouc was occasionally called India rubber or rubber of

---

[4]The rabble or mob—literally, "dogs." The casual tossing around of the numbers of passengers is for shock value. Pundita isn't sure whether there are one or two hundred people on board, which is to say, in 2848 big balloons are common.

whist, and was no doubt one of the numerous *fungi.*[5] Never tell me again that I am not at heart an antiquarian.

Talking of drag-ropes—our own, it seems, has this moment knocked a man overboard from one of the small magnetic propellers that swarm in ocean below us—a boat of about six thousand tons, and, from all accounts, shamefully crowded. These diminutive barques should be prohibited from carrying more than a definite number of passengers. The man, of course, was not permitted to get on board again, and was soon out of sight, he and his life-preserver. I rejoice, my dear friend, that we live in an age so enlightened that no such a thing as an individual is supposed to exist. It is the mass for which the true Humanity cares. By the by, talking of Humanity, do you know that our immortal Wiggins is not so original in his views of the Social Condition and so forth, as his contemporaries are inclined to suppose? Pundit assures me that the same ideas were put, nearly in the same way, about a thousand years ago, by an Irish philosopher called Furrier, on account of his keeping a retail shop for cat-peltries and other furs. Pundit *knows,* you know; there can be no mistake about it. How very wonderfully do we see verified, every day, the profound observation of the Hindoo Aries Tottle (as quoted by Pundit)—"Thus must we say that, not once or twice, or a few times, but with almost infinite repetitions, the same opinions come round in a circle among men."[6]

April 2.—Spoke to-day the magnetic cutter in charge of the middle section of floating telegraph wires. I learn that when this species of telegraph was first put into operation by Horse, it was considered quite impossible to convey the wires over sea; but now we are at a loss to comprehend where the difficulty lay! So wags

---

[5]**"silk":** The first of Pundita's near-misses in explaining the "past." Poe is making fun of our knowledge of history by suggesting that the future will badly misunderstand the past. ***euphorbium:*** An obsolete word for Euphorbia, which can mean either a "gum resin obtained from certain . . . species of Euphorbia," or a family of plants commonly known as milkweed. Pundita's facts are straight, for a change. **silk-buckingham:** There was an author of books of travel named James Silk Buckingham; Poe makes a cheap gag of his name (Carlson 2). See "Some Words with a Mummy," note 10. **caoutchouc . . . *fungi:*** Caoutchouc is rubber, and *gutta-percha* is a rubberlike material made from the juice of Malayan trees, so Pundita is reasonable in her first guess, but of course neither is a fungus. If she is "at heart an antiquarian," she's not a very good one. "Whist" is a card game, the predecessor of bridge. Like bridge, it uses the term "rubber," hence the wordplay.

[6]**drag-ropes:** For Poe's explanation of how these work, see "The Balloon-Hoax." **I rejoice, . . . cares:** Poe's suspicions of the merits of democracy show here; he carries popular democratic thought to what he takes to be a logical conclusion, a society in which the individual does not count. **Furrier:** She means Fourier (1772–1837), a French social theorist whose schemes aroused great interest in the United States in Poe's day. Several of the socialistic communities set up in Poe's lifetime operated on modified Fourieristic principles. **Aries Tottle:** Fourier comes out Irish and Aristotle Hindu. One wonders how funny the readers of *Godey's Lady's Book* (February 1849) thought humor of this sort. For the modern reader, one suspects, the gag quickly goes stale, though undoubtedly we miss some of the topical jokes to which a reader in 1849 might have responded. **"Thus . . . men":** The lines are from Aristotle's *Meteorologica,* I, III (339b28–30).

the world. *Tempora mutantur*—excuse me for quoting the Etruscan.[7] What *would* we do without the Atalantic telegraph? (Pundit says Atlantic was the ancient adjective.) We lay to a few minutes to ask the cutter some questions, and learned, among other glorious news, that civil war is raging in Africia, while the plague is doing its good work beautifully both in Yurope and Ayesher. Is it not truly remarkable that, before the magnificent light shed upon philosophy by Humanity, the world was accustomed to regard War and Pestilence as calamities? Do you know that prayers were actually offered up in the ancient temples to the end that these *evils* (!) might not be visited upon mankind? Is it not really difficult to comprehend upon what principle of interest our forefathers acted? Were they so blind as not to perceive that the destruction of individuals is only so much positive advantage to the mass!

April 3.—It is really a very fine amusement to ascend the rope-ladder leading to the summit of the balloon-bag, and thence survey the surrounding world. From the car below you know the prospect is not so comprehensive—you can see little vertically. But seated here (where I write this) in the luxuriously-cushioned open piazza of the summit, one can see everything that is going on in all directions. Just now, there is quite a crowd of balloons in sight, and they present a very animated appearance, while the air is resonant with the hum of so many millions of human voices. I have heard it asserted that when Yellow or (Pundit *will* have it) Violet, who is supposed to have been the first æronaut, maintained the practicability of traversing the atmosphere in all directions, by merely ascending or descending until a favorable current was attained, he was scarcely hearkened to at all by his contemporaries, who looked upon him as merely an ingenious sort of madman, because the philosophers (?) of the day declared the thing impossible. Really now it does seem to me *quite* unaccountable how anything so obviously feasible could have escaped the sagacity of the ancient *savans.* But in all ages the great obstacles to advancement in Art have been opposed by the so-called men of science. To be sure, *our* men of science are not quite so bigoted as those of old:—oh, I have something *so* queer to tell you on this topic. Do you know that it is not more than a thousand years ago since the metaphysicians consented to relieve the people of the singular fancy that there existed but *two possible roads for the attainment of Truth!* Believe it if you can! It appears that long, long ago, in the night of Time, there lived a Turkish philosopher (or Hindoo possibly) called Aries Tottle. This person introduced, or at all events propagated what was termed the deductive or *à priori* mode of investigation. He started with what he maintained to be *axioms* or "self-evident truths," and thence proceeded "logically" to results. His greatest

---

[7]**Horse:** Samuel F. B. Morse (1791–1872), the painter-turned-inventor who built the first practical telegraph. **Etruscan:** It's Latin, of course—"Times change." Eric Carlson (2) thinks that by "the Etruscan" Poe means Virgil, and that Pundita's error is in attributing to Virgil a quotation from Matthias Borbonius' *Deliciae Poetarum Germanorum.* It seems likely that Poe's joke is simpler—just that Pundita doesn't know what Latin is—but either way, the point is that Pundita's facts are shaky. The phrase does, in point of fact, appear in a number of Latin writers.

disciples were one Neuclid and one Cant. Well, Aries Tottle flourished supreme until avent of one Hog, surnamed the "Ettrick Shepherd," who preached an entirely different system, which he called the *à posteriori* or *in*ductive. His plan referred altogether to Sensation. He proceeded by observing, analyzing and classifying facts—*instantiæ naturæ,* as they were affectedly called—into general laws. Aries Tottle's mode, in a word, was based on *noumena;* Hog's on *phenomena.*[8] Well, so great was the admiration excited by this latter system that, at its first introduction, Aries Tottle fell into disrepute; but finally he recovered ground, and was permitted to divide the realm of Truth with his more modern rival. The *savans* now maintained that the Aristotelian and *Baconian* roads were the sole possible avenues to knowledge. "Baconian," you must know, was an adjective invented as equivalent to Hog-ian and more euphonious and dignified.

Now, my dear friend, I do assure you, most positively, that I represent this matter fairly, on the soundest authority; and you can easily understand how a notion so absurd on its very face must have operated to retard the progress of all true knowledge—which makes its advances almost invariably by intuitive bounds. The ancient idea confined investigations to *crawling;* and for hundreds of years so great was the infatuation about Hog especially, that a virtual end was put to all thinking, properly so called. No man dared utter a truth to which he felt himself indebted to his *Soul* alone. It mattered not whether the truth was even *demonstrably* a truth, for the bullet-headed *savans* of the time regarded only *the road* by which he had attained it. They would not even *look* at the end. "Let us see the means," they cried, "the means!" If, upon investigation of the means, it was

---

[8]**Violet:** Carlson (2) thinks Poe was referring to Girond de Villette, an associate of the first man to make a balloon ascent (1783), Francois Pilatre de Rosier. Elsewhere, it has been suggested that this is a reference to Charles Green (1785–1870), English inventor and aeronaut. He was the first to use coal-gas to inflate balloons, and invented the guide-rope Pundita mentions earlier in this story. ***Savan[t]s:*** Poe consistently used the old spelling (*savans*) of this word in the *Godey's* version which we follow. Most editors modernize it to *savants.* **Neuclid . . . Cant:** She means Euclid, the Greek mathematician, and Immanuel Kant (1724–1804), the German philosopher. Poe's humor is based on the dates involved: to one writer in 2848, presumably, Greece of the third century B.C.E. and Germany of 1800 do not seem significantly far apart. **Hog:** Francis Bacon (1561–1626), British essayist and philosopher who argued for an analytical and inductive approach to knowledge and who believed that such pooled learning would in fact produce progress. Pundita makes another of her double errors here. Having called Bacon "Hog," she then confuses him with James Hogg (1770–1835), who was called "the Ettrick Shepherd," and whose name would have been familiar to magazine readers from his work in *Blackwood's Edinburgh Magazine,* his narrative poems, and his novels. ***instantiæ naturæ:*** Latinists translate this phrase as "instances of nature," and report that it does occur, starting in Medieval Latin, with the meaning Poe gives it. It seemed likely that it occurs in Bacon (see "Hog" above). We did find plentiful examples of both *instantiæ* and *naturæ,* but even our Latinist consultants could not find the two together in Bacon or in any of the Latin word lists or dictionaries of Bacon's period. ***noumena . . . phenomena:*** Pundita's contrast comes from Kant ("Cant"), who opposed *noumena,* objects understood through intellectual intuition, with *phenomena,* one's "precepts or experiences of objects in the world" about one.

found to come under neither the category Aries (that is to say Ram)[9] nor under the category Hog, why then the *savans* went no farther, but pronounced the "theorist" a fool, and would have nothing to do with him or his truth.

Now, it cannot be maintained, even, that by the crawling system the greatest amount of truth would be attained in any long series of ages, for the repression of *imagination* was an evil not to be compensated for by any superior *certainty* in the ancient modes of investigation. The error of these Jurmains, these Vrinch, these Inglitch, and these Amriccans (the latter, by the way, were our own immediate progenitors,) was an error quite analogous with that of the wiseacre who fancies that he must necessarily see an object the better the more closely he holds it to his eyes. These people blinded themselves by details. When they proceeded Hoggishly, their "facts" were by no means always facts—a matter of little consequence had it not been for assuming that they *were* facts and must be facts because they appeared to be such. When they proceeded on the path of the Ram, their course was scarcely as straight as a ram's horn, for they *never had* an axiom which was an axiom at all. They must have been very blind not to see this, even in their own day; for even in their own day many of the long "established" axioms had been rejected. For example—"*Ex nihilo, nihil fit;*" "a body cannot act where it is not;" "there cannot exist antipodes;" "darkness cannot come out of light"—all these, and a dozen other similar propositions, formerly admitted without hesitation as axioms, were, even at the period of which I speak, seen to be untenable. How absurd in these people, then, to persist in putting faith in "axioms" as immutable bases of Truth! But even out of the mouths of their soundest reasoners it is easy to demonstrate the futility, the impalpability of their axioms in general. Who *was* the soundest of their logicians? Let me see! I will go and ask Pundit and be back in a minute. . . . Ah, here we have it! Here is a book written nearly a thousand years ago and lately translated from the Inglitch—which, by the way, appears to have been the rudiment of the Amriccan. Pundit says it is decidedly the cleverest ancient work on its topic, Logic. The author (who was much thought of in his day) was one Miller, or Mill; and we find it recorded of him, as a point of some importance, that he had a mill-horse called Bentham.[10] But let us glance at the treatise!

---

[9]**true knowledge . . . bounds:** Poe means this seriously. Knowledge progresses through intuitive inspiration, not through reasoning from given premises (Aristotle) or from sorting, classifying, analyzing (Bacon). Examine the Dupin stories to see how Poe's detective reaches *his* truths, and *Eureka* for Poe's own attempt to intuit scientific truths. **Ram:** In astrology, Aries the Ram is the first sign of the Zodiac. Having called Aristotle "Aries Tottle," Poe now makes a bad pun by allowing Pundita to try her hand, inaccurately, at etymology.

[10]**Amriccans . . . progenitors:** Poe is saying that the logical outcome of American influence will be Pundita's world, long on technology, short on historical accuracy, cocky, and concerned with the masses, not the individual. Yet Pundita herself is contemptuous of "the mob" (see "A note of explanation" in our headnote) and very much a snob. Moreover, some of the things she says Poe believes are right (see note 9), so Poe's satire is not entirely consistent. ***Ex. . . fit:*** "Out of nothing comes nothing." The phrase comes from Lucretius (c.95–55 B.C.E.), whose *De rerum natura* Poe clearly knew. **Miller, or Mill:** John Stuart

Ah!—"Ability or inability to conceive," says Mr. Mill, very properly, "is in no case to be received as a criterion of axiomatic truth." What *modern* in his senses would ever think of disputing this truism? The only wonder with us must be, how it happened that Mr. Mill conceived it necessary even to hint at any thing so obvious. So far good—but let us turn over another page. What have we here?—"Contradictories cannot both be true—that is, cannot co-exist in nature." Here Mr. Mill means, for example, that a tree must be either a tree or not a tree—that it cannot be at the same time a tree and not a tree. Very well; but I ask him *why.* His reply is this—and never pretends to be any thing else than this—"Because it is impossible to conceive that contradictories can both be true." But this is no answer at all, by his own showing; for has he not just admitted as a truism that "ability or inability to conceive is *in no case* to be received as a criterion of axiomatic truth?"

Now I do not complain of these ancients so much because their logic is, by their own showing, utterly baseless, worthless and fantastic altogether, as because of their pompous and imbecile proscription of all *other* roads of Truth, of all *other* means for its attainment than the two preposterous paths—the one of creeping and the one of crawling—to which they have dared to confine the Soul that loves nothing so well as to *soar.*

By the by, my dear friend, do you not think it would have puzzled these ancient dogmaticians to have determined by *which* of their two roads it was that the most important and most sublime of *all* their truths was, in effect, attained? I mean the truth of Gravitation. Newton owed it to Kepler. Kepler admitted that his three laws were *guessed at*—these three laws of all laws which led the great Inglitch mathematician to his principle, the basis of all physical principle—to go behind which we must enter the Kingdom of Metaphysics. Kepler guessed—that is to say *imagined.* He was essentially a "theorist"—that word now of so much sanctity, formerly an epithet of contempt. Would it not have puzzled these old moles, too, to have explained by which of the two "roads" a cryptographist unriddles a cryptograph of more than usual secrecy, or by which of the two roads Champollion[11] directed mankind to those enduring and almost innumerable truths which resulted from his deciphering the Hieroglyphics?

Mill (1806–73). His *System of Logic* (1843) is an analysis of the process of inductive logic. See next item. Poe has Pundita confuse "Mill" with "Miller" to put in the reader's mind the name of Joe Miller (1684–1738), supposed author of a famous book of jokes, *Joe Miller's Jest-Book.* **Bentham:** Jeremy Bentham (1748–1832), utilitarian philosopher. Mill *was* deeply influenced by Bentham, particularly by the doctrine of the greatest happiness for the greatest number, but his independence from him is shown in his opinion of Bentham: "He was not a great philosopher but a great reformer in philosophy." The political causes for which Mill fought would not have been sympathetic to Poe: the rights of black people, women's suffrage, working class rights.

[11]**Kepler . . . Newton . . . cryptograph:** See our headnote. **Champollion:** Jean François Champollion (1790–1832), using the Rosetta Stone, learned to decipher Egyptian hieroglyphics. The stone, found in 1799, bore an inscription in two different forms of hieroglyphics and in Greek. "Solving" it was a great scholarly feat, one Poe respects for the intuition involved by spelling "Champollion" correctly.

One word more on this topic and I will be done boring you. It is not *passing* strange that, with their eternal prattling about *roads* to Truth, these bigoted people missed what we now so clearly perceive to be the great highway—that of Consistency? Does it not seem singular how they should have failed to deduce from the works of God the vital fact that a perfect consistency *must* be an absolute truth! How plain has been our progress since the late announcement of this proposition! Investigation has been taken out of the hands of the ground-moles and given, as a task, to the true and only true thinkers, the men of ardent imagination. These latter *theorize.* Can you not fancy the shout of scorn with which my words would be received by our progenitors were it possible for them to be now looking over my shoulder? These men, I say, *theorize;* and their theories are simply corrected, reduced, systematized—cleared, little by little, of their dross of inconsistency—until, finally, a perfect consistency stands apparent which even the most stolid admit, because it *is* a consistency, to be an absolute and an unquestionable *truth.*

April 4.—The new gas is doing wonders, in conjunction with the new improvement with gutta percha. How very safe, commodious, manageable, and in every respect convenient are our modern balloons! Here is an immense one approaching us at the rate of at least a hundred and fifty miles an hour. It seems to be crowded with people—perhaps there are three or four hundred passengers—and yet it soars to an elevation of nearly a mile, looking down upon poor us with sovereign contempt. Still a hundred or even two hundred miles an hour is slow traveling after all. *Do* you remember our flight on the railroad across the Kanadaw[12] continent?—*that* was traveling. Nothing to be seen, though—nothing to be done but flirt, feast and dance in the magnificent saloons. Do you remember what an odd sensation was experienced when, by chance, we caught a glimpse of external objects while the cars were in full flight? Everything seemed unique—in one mass. For my part, I cannot say but that I preferred the traveling by the slow train of a hundred miles the hour. Here we were permitted to have glass windows—even to have them open—and something like a distinct view of the country was attainable. . . . Pundit says that *the route* for the great Kanadaw railroad must have been in some measure marked out about nine hundred years ago! In fact, he goes so far as to assert that actual traces of a road are still discernible—traces referable to a period quite as remote as that mentioned. The track, it appears, was *double* only; ours, you know, has twelve paths; and three or four new ones are in preparation. The ancient rails are very slight, and placed so close together as to be, according to modern notions, quite frivolous, if not dangerous in

[12]**balloons:** Having just lectured us on consistency, Pundita is now inconsistent. She opened, we recall, by complaining that travel by balloon was a drag; now she likes it. **Kanadaw:** Canada, but Poe doesn't seem to mean the country—see the end of the paragraph. If he means the continents North and South America, and implies that they broke apart at some time between ours and Pundita's, then Pundita's talk about traveling *across* the continent is puzzling. So is his spelling of the word "Kanawdians" late in the paragraph. Perhaps he moved the "w" to keep it in the word; "Kanadians" would not have looked as odd.

the extreme. The present width of track—fifty feet—is considered, indeed, scarcely secure enough. For my part, I make no doubt that a track of some sort *must* have existed in very remote times, as Pundit asserts; for nothing can be clearer, to my mind, than that, at some period—not less than seven centuries ago, certainly—the Northern and Southern Kanadaw continents were *united;* the Kanawdians, then, would have been driven, by necessity, to a great railroad across the continent.

April 5.—I am almost devoured by *ennui.* Pundit is the only conversible person on board; and he, poor soul! can speak of nothing but antiquities. He has been occupied all the day in the attempt to convince me that the ancient Amriccans *governed themselves!*—did ever anybody hear of such an absurdity?—that they existed in a sort of every-man-for-himself confederacy, after the fashion of the "prairie dogs" that we read of in fable. He says that they started with the queerest idea conceivable, viz: that all men are born free and equal—this in the very teeth of the laws of *gradation* so visibly impressed upon all things both in the moral and physical universe. Every man "voted," as they called it—that is to say, meddled with public affairs—until, at length, it was discovered that what is everybody's business is nobody's, and that the "Republic" (so the absurd thing was called) was without a government at all. It is related, however, that the first circumstance which disturbed, very particularly, the self-complacency of the philosophers who constructed this "Republic," was the startling discovery that universal suffrage gave opportunity for fraudulent schemes, by means of which any desired number of votes might at any time be polled, without the possibility of prevention or even detection, by any party which should be merely villainous enough not to be ashamed of the fraud. A little reflection upon this discovery sufficed to render evident the consequences, which were that rascality *must* predominate—in a word, that a republican government *could* never be anything but a rascally one. While the philosophers, however, were busied in blushing at their stupidity in not having foreseen these inevitable evils, and intent upon the invention of new theories, the matter was put to an abrupt issue by a fellow of the name of *Mob,* who took every thing into his own hands and set up a despotism, in comparison with which those of the fabulous Zeros and Hellofagabaluses[13] were respectable and delectable. This Mob (a foreigner, by the by) is said to have been the most odious of all men that ever encumbered the earth. He was a giant in stature—insolent, rapacious, filthy; had the gall of a bullock with the heart of a hyena and the brains of a peacock. He died, at length, by dint of his own energies, which exhausted him. Nevertheless, he had his uses, as every thing has, however vile, and taught mankind a lesson which to this day it is in no danger of forgetting—never to run directly contrary to the natural analogies. As for Republicanism, no analogy could be found for it upon the face of the earth—unless we except the case of the "prairie dogs," an exception which seems to demonstrate, if anything, that democracy is a very admirable form of government—for dogs.

[13]The Roman emperors Nero (37–68, emperor 54–68) and Heliogabalus (204–22, emperor 218–22).

April 6.—Last night had a fine view of Alpha Lyræ, whose disk, through our captain's spy-glass, subtends an angle of half a degree, looking very much as our sun does to the naked eye on a misty day. Alpha Lyræ, although so *very* much larger than our sun, by the by, resembles him closely as regards its spots, its atmosphere, and in many other particulars. It is only within the last century, Pundit tells me, that the binary relation existing between these two orbs began even to be suspected. The evident motion of our system in the heavens was (strange to say!) referred to an orbit about a prodigious star in the centre of the galaxy. About this star, or at all events about a centre of gravity common to all the globes of the Milky Way and supposed to be near Alcyone in the Pleiades, every one of these globes was declared to be revolving, our own performing the circuit in a period of 117,000,000 of years! *We,* with our present lights, our vast telescopic improvements and so forth, of course find it difficult to comprehend *the ground* of an idea such as this. Its first propagator was one Mudler. He was led, we must presume, to this wild hypothesis by mere analogy in the first instance; but, this being the case, he should have at least adhered to analogy in its development. A great central orb[14] *was,* in fact, suggested; so far Mudler was consistent. This central orb, however, dynamically, should have been greater than all its surrounding orbs taken together. The question might then have been asked—"Why do we not see it?"—*we,* especially, who occupy the mid region of the cluster—the very locality *near* which, at least, must be situated this inconceivable central sun. The astronomer, perhaps, at this point, took refuge in the suggestion of non-luminosity; and here analogy was suddenly let fall. But even admitting the central orb non-luminous, how did he manage to explain its failure to be rendered visible by the incalculable host of glorious suns glaring in all directions about it? No doubt what he finally maintained was merely a centre of gravity common to all the revolving orbs—but here again analogy must have been let fall. Our system revolves, it is true, about a common centre of gravity, but it does this in connection with and in consequence of a material sun whose mass more than counterbalances the rest of the system. The mathematical circle is a curve composed of an infinity of straight lines; but this idea of the circle—this idea of it which, in regard to all earthly geometry, we consider as merely the mathematical, in contradistinction from the practical, idea—is, in sober fact, the *practical* conception which alone

---

[14]**binary . . . suspected:** Poe says the same thing about this star in "Ligeia." See below, "central orb." **Mudler:** Johann H. von Madler (Pollin 3), German astronomer (1794–1872). **central orb:** The idea of the rotation of stars around a common center appears in the writing of various theorists in the period; its most famous exposition, perhaps, is in Immanuel Kant (see note 8, above). The "analogy" Poe probably has in mind comes from Kant: stars move around a center as the planets move around the sun. They would have to be in motion, Kant reasoned, or gravity would draw them together and the universe would "collapse." Pundita's idea of a special relationship between Alpha Lyræ and the sun is pure stardust: all celestial bodies interact with one another, but Alpha Lyræ is too immensely distant to be in significant relationship with the sun. Carlson (2) notes, incidentally, that "there are two binary stars in the constellation of the Lyre," though this is not what Pundita claims.

we have any right to entertain in respect to those Titanic circles with which we have to deal, at least in fancy, when we suppose our system, with its fellows, revolving about a point in the centre of the galaxy. Let the most vigorous of human imaginations but attempt to take a single step toward the comprehension of a circuit so unutterable! It would scarcely be paradoxical to say that a flash of lightning itself, traveling *forever* upon the circumference of this inconceivable circle, would still *forever* be traveling in a straight line. That the path of our sun along such a circumference—that the direction of our system in such an orbit—would, to any human perception, deviate in the slightest degree from a straight line even in a million of years, is a proposition not to be entertained; and yet these ancient astronomers were absolutely cajoled, it appears, into believing that a decisive curvature had become apparent during the brief period of their astronomical history—during the mere point—during the utter nothingness of two or three thousand years! How incomprehensible, that considerations such as this did not at once indicate to them the true state of affairs—that of the binary revolution of our sun and Alpha Lyræ around a common centre of gravity!

April 7.—Continued last night our astronomical amusements. Had a fine view of the five Neptunian asteroids, and watched with much interest the putting up of a huge impost on a couple of lintels in the new temple at Daphnis in the moon.[15] It was amusing to think that creatures so diminutive as the lunarians, and bearing so little resemblance to humanity, yet evinced a mechanical ingenuity so much superior to our own. One finds it difficult, too, to conceive the vast masses which these people handle so easily, to be as light as our own reason tells us they actually are.

April 8.—Eureka! Pundit is in his glory. A balloon from Kanadaw spoke us to-day and threw on board several late papers; they contain some exceedingly curious information relative to Kanawdian or rather Amriccan antiquities. You know, I presume, that laborers have for some months been employed in preparing the ground for a new fountain at Paradise, the Emperor's principal pleasure garden. Paradise, it appears, has been, *literally* speaking, an island time out of mind—that is to say, its northern boundary was always (as far back as any record extends) a rivulet, or rather a very narrow arm of the sea. This arm was gradually widened until it attained its present breadth—a mile. The whole length of the island is nine miles; the breadth varies materially. The entire area (so Pundit says) was, about eight hundred years ago, densely packed with houses, some of them twenty stories high; land (for some most unaccountable reason) being considered as especially precious just in this vicinity. The disastrous earthquake, however, of the year 2050, so totally uprooted and overwhelmed the town (for it was almost

---

[15]In Greek mythology, Daphnis is a shepherd, the son of Hermes and the inventor of bucolic poetry. Daphnis and Chloe are the famous lovers in a Greek pastoral romance and many later works. But the moonmen, the "Neptunian asteroids," and so on are fun and games for Poe. If this nonsense is intended to mean anything, perhaps it is that, as 19th-century accomplishments are petty, as American ideas of politics are transient, so all human pride is benighted—that is, there are rational creatures superior to us in given ways.

too large to be called a village) that the most indefatigable of our antiquarians have never yet been able to obtain from the site any sufficient data (in the shape of coins, medals or inscriptions) wherewith to build up even the ghost of a theory concerning the manners, customs, &c., &c., &c., of the aboriginal inhabitants. Nearly all that we have hitherto known of them is, that they were a portion of the Knickerbocker tribe of savages infesting the continent at its first discovery by Recorder Riker, a knight of the Golden Fleece.[16] They were by no means uncivilized, however, but cultivated various arts and even sciences after a fashion of their own. It is related of them that they were acute in many respects, but were oddly afflicted with monomania for building what, in the ancient Amriccan, was denominated "churches"—a kind of pagoda instituted for worship of two idols that went by the names of Wealth and Fashion. In the end, it is said, the island became, nine-tenths of it, church. The women, too, it appears, were oddly deformed by a natural protuberance of the region just below the small of the back—although, most unaccountably, this deformity was looked upon altogether in the light of a beauty. One or two pictures of these singular women have, in fact, been miraculously preserved. They look very odd, *very*—like something between a turkey-cock and a dromedary.

Well, these few details are nearly all that have descended to us respecting the ancient Knickerbockers. It seems, however, that while digging in the centre of the Emperor's garden (which, you know, covers the whole island,) some of the workmen unearthed a cubical and evidently chiseled block of granite, weighing several hundred pounds. It was in good preservation, having received, apparently, little injury from the convulsion which entombed it. On one of its surfaces was a marble slab with (only think of it!) *an inscription—a legible inscription.* Pundit is in ecstasies. Upon detaching the slab, a cavity appeared, containing a leaden box filled with various coins, a long scroll of names, several documents which appear to resemble newspapers, with other matters of intense interest to the antiquarian! There can be no doubt that all these are genuine Amriccan relics belonging to the tribe called Knickerbocker. The papers thrown on board our balloon are filled with fac-similes of the coins, MSS., typography, &c., &c. I copy for your amusement the Knickerbocker inscription on the marble slab:—

---

[16]**Paradise:** "Paradise" turns out to be Manhattan Island. Poe's imagery comes from Coleridge's "The Pleasure Dome of Kubla Khan." For the joke about the new fountain, see "Some Words with a Mummy," Figure 10, p. 316. **Knickerbocker . . . Riker . . . Golden Fleece:** More of Pundita's scrambled history. Richard Riker (1773–1842) was Recorder of the City of New York (Pollin 3, Carlson 2), and Knickerbocker is a nickname often applied to New Yorkers (from Washington Irving's satirical *A History of New York* by "Diedrich Knickerbocker"). There is a topical joke implied in calling Riker a knight of the Golden Fleece (in Greek legend, the fleece of gold sought by Jason and the Argonauts; the "Order of the Golden Fleece was the highest decoration of the Holy Roman Empire" [Mabbott 9, III]). There had been financial scandal in the city government. "Fleece" is intended as a pun (Mabbott 9, III).

This Corner Stone of a Monument to the
Memory of
GEORGE WASHINGTON,
was laid with appropriate ceremonies on the
19TH DAY OF OCTOBER, 1847,
the anniversary of the surrender of
Lord Cornwallis
to General Washington at Yorktown,
A. D. 1781,
under the auspices of the
Washington Monument Association of the
city of New York.[17]

This, as I give it, is a verbatim translation done by Pundit himself, so there *can* be no mistake about it. From the few words thus preserved, we glean several important items of knowledge, not the least interesting of which is the fact that a thousand years ago *actual* monuments had fallen into disuse—as was all very proper—the people contenting themselves, as we do now, with a mere indication of the design to erect a monument at some future time; a corner stone being cautiously laid by itself "solitary and alone" (excuse me for quoting the great Amriccan poet Benton!) as a guarantee of the magnanimous *intention.* We ascertain, too, very distinctly, from this admirable inscription, the how, as well as the where and the what, of the great surrender in question. As to the *where,* it was Yorktown (wherever that was), and as to the *what,* it was General Cornwallis (no doubt some wealthy dealer in corn). *He* was surrendered. The inscription commemorates the surrender of—what?—why, "of Lord Cornwallis." The only question is what could the savages wish him surrendered for. But when we remember that these savages were undoubtedly cannibals, we are led to the conclusion that they intended him for sausage. As to the *how* of the surrender, no language can be more explicit. Lord Cornwallis was surrendered (for sausage) "under the auspices of the Washington Monument Association"—no doubt a charitable institution for the depositing of corner-stones.——But Heaven bless me! what is the matter? Ah, I see—the balloon has collapsed, and we shall have a tumble into the sea. I have, therefore, only time enough to add that, from a hasty inspection of the fac-similes of newspapers, etc., etc., I find that *the* great men in those days among the Amriccans, were one John, a smith, and one Zacchary, a tailor.[18]

---

[17]The Washington Monument Association of New York in 1847 held a ceremony to lay the cornerstone of a monument to be erected later. The monument was never erected, but continued to be a topic of current interest (Pollin 10).

[18]**Benton:** Pollin (10) thinks it most likely that Poe refers to Senator Thomas Hart Benton (1782–1858, senator 1821–1851). Pollin demonstrates that the expression "solitary and

Good-bye, until I see you again. Whether you ever get this letter or not is point of little importance, as I write altogether for my own amusement. I shall cork the MS. up in a bottle, however, and throw it into the sea. Yours everlastingly,

Pundita.

---

alone" was identified with Benton, an antagonist of Jackson. Pundita's calling him a poet probably reflects Poe's scorn for his optimistic and nationalistic writings on topics such as how Americans would civilize the Orient, the importance of a transcontinental road, absorbing California and Oregon, and so on. **Yorktown . . . Cornwallis. . . . sea:** Having insulted national and temporal pride as deeply as he can by showing that even the culminating military victory of the Revolutionary War is so totally forgotten in 2848 that Pundita thinks Cornwallis is a corn dealer and Americans were cannibals, Poe now tells us that even Pundita's world can't make a safe balloon. **John, a smith:** Carlson (2) thinks Poe means "John Smith, the average man." That makes sense in terms of Poe's mockery of democracy. Or he might have meant Captain John Smith (1580–1631), the Virginia colonial leader, in which case Pundita would be up to her old trick of telescoping dates to help Poe make his point about the insignificance of our history. **Zacchary, a tailor:** The president at the time the story was published, Zachary Taylor (1784–1850).

Hop-Frog

Given what we now know about Poe's dependence upon his sources for story ideas and details, it is perilous to attach strong psychological significance to his subject matter. That is especially true in this story: Poe scholars know exactly where Poe's ideas came from—see "A note of explanation," below. Moreover, "Hop-Frog" was produced at a time when he was very "commercial-minded," writing cheery notes to friends about how much material he was selling and how well he knew the market for prose.

To the critics who read Poe into Hop-Frog, Poe is rationalizing his own difficulties with alcohol by claiming, through the story, that people "force" drinks upon him. Certainly his use of one of his own failings does suggest involvement. So does the fact that the sensitive cripple is in a way an "artist," dragged from his provincial homeland (the South?) to entertain the fatheads, the men "in need of characters," who rule the land, in return for crumbs from their table. Hop-Frog's description of the "diversion" as a "country frolic" is also suggestive: it is, in fact, a tarring and feathering with flax substituted for feathers because flax burns better. Poe might be saying, "There is a well-known rural remedy for this sort of thing." Hop-Frog's strange tranquility after drinking and seeing Trippetta insulted may be another clue; it puts one in mind of another character critics have taken for a "Poe-mask," the dull-mannered, "inscrutable" aristocrat Ritzner Von Jung in the story "Mystification" (see Levine 4). There is wine-throwing in that tale, too. If his mention of liquor, in other words, suggests that Poe is feeling sorry for himself, and his presentation of the dwarf as a mistreated artist suggests a complaint about the status of the artist in society, then the dwarf's capacity for love and vengeance is an assertion of the artist's human dignity and manliness. But why, then, is the vengeance so hideous? Probably because Poe believed that every tale should create a strong effect, often bizarre, grotesque, outré.

Note the ending of the tale. Trippetta and Hop-Frog "live happily ever after." Poe seems to have a fairy-tale effect in mind. He is extremely vague about date, as though he wanted this kingdom to be some timeless never-never land. The narrator speaks of a time when jesters were still common (implying "a long time ago"), but also of "great continental 'powers,'" a relatively modern development. He says that he was present when the events of the story occurred, implying the relatively recent past, yet that orangutans were hardly known in the civilized world, implying a date at least before the age of exploration. Since Poe intends for his story to have some of the qualities of a folk tale or even a parable, this ambiguity seems deliberate. Note also the paucity of foreign phrases, quotations, or explicit literary references; Poe seems concerned more than usual with keeping things simple. The periodical in which his tale was to appear might have influenced his decision (see note 1).

***A note of explanation:** Evert A. Duyckinck wrote a piece called "Barbarities of the Theater" for* The Broadway Journal *in the month*

(February 1845) in which Poe joined its staff. In it are a young dancer and an account of how five courtiers, masquerading as hairy wild men and chained together, burned at a court party in France in 1385. Details and further sources are in Mabbott (9, III).

PUBLICATION IN POE'S TIME

The Flag of Our Union, March 17, 1849

HOP-FROG
or
The Eight Chained Ourang-Outangs[1]

I never knew any one so keenly alive to a joke as the king was. He seemed to live only for joking. To tell a good story of the joke kind, and to tell it well, was the surest road to his favor. Thus it happened that his seven ministers were all noted for their accomplishments as jokers. They all took after the king, too, in being large, corpulent, oily men, as well as inimitable jokers. Whether people grow fat by joking, or whether there is something in fat itself which predisposes to a joke, I have never been quite able to determine; but certain it is that a lean joker is a *rara avis in terris.*[2]

About the refinements, or, as he called them, the "ghosts" of wit, the king troubled himself very little. He had an especial admiration for *breadth* in a jest, and would often put up with *length,* for the sake of it. Over-niceties wearied him. He would have preferred Rabelais's "Gargantua," to the "Zadig" of Voltaire:[3] And, upon the whole, practical jokes suited his taste far better than verbal ones.

At the date of my narrative, professing jesters had not altogether gone out of fashion at court.[4] Several of the great continental "powers" still retained their "fools," who wore motley, with caps and bells, and who were expected to be

[1]Poe published this story not in a literary journal, ladies' magazine, or gift book, but in a frankly commercial "sporting magazine," saying of his decision that this was "not a *very* respectable journal, perhaps, in a literary point of view, but one that pays . . . high prices. . . ." The title given is from the first publication.

[2]Rare bird upon the earth (from Juvenal).

[3]*Gargantua* (1534) is a satirical romance about a peace-loving giant prince with a vast appetite. François Rabelais (c.1494–c.1553), French humorist and satirist, is noted for the boisterous, bawdy, and energetic nature of his work. Voltaire (François-Marie Arouet, 1694–1778), in contrast, is noted more for cleverness and wit. *Zadig, ou la destinée* (1747) is a sophisticated and bitter satire. Poe's contrast is between broad and pointed comedy.

[4]In other words, "Once upon a time." See our headnote.

always ready with sharp witticisms, at a moment's notice, in consideration of the crumbs that fell from the royal table.

Our king, as a matter of course, retained his "fool." The fact is, he *required* something in the way of folly—if only to counterbalance the heavy wisdom of the seven wise men who were his ministers—not to mention himself.

His fool, or professional jester, was not *only* a fool, however. His value was trebled in the eyes of the king, by the fact of his being also a dwarf and a cripple. Dwarfs were as common at court, in those days, as fools; and many monarchs would have found it difficult to get through their days (days are rather longer at court than elsewhere) without both a jester to laugh *with,* and a dwarf to laugh *at.* But, as I have already observed, your jesters, in ninety-nine cases out of a hundred, are fat, round and unwieldy—so that it was no small source of self-gratulation with our king that, in Hop-Frog (this was the fool's name,) he possessed a triplicate treasure in one person.

I believe the name "Hop-Frog" was *not* given to the dwarf by his sponsors at baptism, but it was conferred upon him, by general consent of the seven ministers, on account of his inability to walk as other men do. In fact, Hop-Frog could only get along by a sort of interjectional gait—something between a leap and a wriggle—a movement that afforded illimitable amusement, and of course consolation, to the king, for (notwithstanding the protuberance of his stomach and a constitutional swelling of the head) the king, by his whole court, was accounted a capital figure.

But although Hop-Frog, through the distortion of his legs, could move only with great pain and difficulty along a road or floor, the prodigious muscular power which nature seemed to have bestowed upon his arms, by way of compensation for deficiency in the lower limbs, enabled him to perform many feats of wonderful dexterity, where trees or ropes were in question, or anything else to climb. At such exercises he certainly much more resembled a squirrel, or a small monkey, than a frog.

I am not able to say, with precision, from what country Hop-Frog originally came. It was from some barbarous region, however, that no person ever heard of—a vast distance from the court of our king. Hop-Frog, and a young girl very little less dwarfish than himself (although of exquisite proportions, and a marvellous dancer,) had been forcibly carried off from their respective homes in adjoining provinces, and sent as presents to the king, by one of his ever-victorious generals.

Under these circumstances, it is not to be wondered at that a close intimacy arose between the two little captives. Indeed, they soon became sworn friends. Hop-Frog, who, although he made a great deal of sport, was by no means popular, had it not in his power to render Trippetta many services; but *she,* on account of her grace and exquisite beauty (although a dwarf,) was universally admired and petted: so she possessed much influence; and never failed to use it, whenever she could, for the benefit of Hop-Frog.

On some grand state occasion—I forget what—the king determined to have a masquerade; and whenever a masquerade, or anything of that kind, occurred at our court, then the talents both of Hop-Frog and Trippetta were sure to be called in play. Hop-Frog, in especial, was so inventive in the way of getting up pageants, suggesting novel characters, and arranging costume, for masked balls, that nothing could be done, it seems, without his assistance.

The night appointed for the *fête* had arrived. A gorgeous hall had been fitted up, under Trippetta's eye, with every kind of device which could possibly give éclat to a masquerade. The whole court was in a fever of expectation. As for costumes and characters, it might well be supposed that everybody had come to a decision on such points. Many had made up their minds (as to what *rôles* they should assume) a week, or even a month, in advance; and, in fact, there was not a particle of indecision anywhere—except in the case of the king and his seven ministers. Why *they* hesitated I never could tell, unless they did it by way of a joke. More probably, they found it difficult, on account of being so fat, to make up their minds. At all events, time flew; and, as a last resource, they sent for Trippetta and Hop-Frog.

When the two little friends obeyed the summons of the king, they found him sitting at his wine with the seven members of his cabinet council; but the monarch appeared to be in a very ill humor. He knew that Hop-Frog was not fond of wine; for it excited the poor cripple almost to madness; and madness is no comfortable feeling. But the king loved his practical jokes, and took pleasure in forcing Hop-Frog to drink and (as the king called it) "to be merry."

"Come here, Hop-Frog," said he, as the jester and his friend entered the room: "swallow this bumper to the health of your absent friends [here Hop-Frog sighed,] and then let us have the benefit of your invention. We want characters—*characters,* man—something novel—out of the way. We are wearied with this everlasting sameness. Come drink! the wine will brighten your wits."

Hop-Frog endeavored, as usual, to get up a jest in reply to these advances from the king; but the effort was too much. It happened to be the poor dwarf's birthday, and the command to drink to his "absent friends" forced the tears to his eyes. Many large, bitter drops fell into the goblet as he took it, humbly, from the hand of the tyrant.

"Ah! ha! ha! ha!" roared the latter, as the dwarf reluctantly drained the beaker. "See what a glass of good wine can do! Why, your eyes are shining already!"

Poor fellow, his large eyes *gleamed,* rather than shone; for the effect of wine on his excitable brain was not more powerful than instantaneous. He placed the goblet nervously on the table, and looked round upon the company with a half-insane stare. They all seemed highly amused at the success of the king's "*joke.*"

"And now to business," said the prime minister, a *very* fat man.

"Yes," said the king; "come, Hop-Frog, lend us your assistance. Characters, my fine fellow; we stand in need of characters—all of us—ha! ha! ha!" and as this was seriously meant for a joke, his laugh was chorused by the seven.

Hop-Frog also laughed, although feebly and somewhat vacantly.

"Come, come," said the king, impatiently, "have you nothing to suggest?"

"I am endeavoring to think of something *novel,*" replied the dwarf, abstractedly, for he was quite bewildered by the wine.

"Endeavoring!" cried the tyrant, fiercely; "what do you mean by *that?* Ah, I perceive. You are sulky, and want more wine. Here, drink this!" and he poured out another goblet full and offered it to the cripple, who merely gazed at it, gasping for breath.

"Drink, I say!" shouted the monster, "or by the fiends—"

The dwarf hesitated. The king grew purple with rage. The courtiers smirked. Trippetta, pale as a corpse, advanced to the monarch's seat, and, falling on her knees before him, implored him to spare her friend.

The tyrant regarded her, for some moments, in evident wonder at her audacity. He seemed quite at a loss what to do or say—how most becomingly to express his indignation. At last, without uttering a syllable, he pushed her violently from him, and threw the contents of the brimming goblet in her face.

The poor girl got up as best she could, and, not daring even to sigh, resumed her position at the foot of the table.

There was a dead silence for about a half a minute, during which the falling of a leaf, or of a feather, might have been heard. It was interrupted by a low, but harsh and protracted *grating* sound which seemed to come at once from every corner of the room.

"What—what—*what* are you making that noise for?" demanded the king, turning furiously to the dwarf.

The latter seemed to have recovered, in great measure from his intoxication, and looking fixedly but quietly into the tyrant's face, merely ejaculated:

"I—I? How could it have been me?"

"The sound appeared to come from without," observed one of the courtiers. "I fancy it was the parrot at the window, whetting his bill upon his cage-wires."

"True," replied the monarch, as if much relieved by the suggestion; "but, on the honor of a knight, I could have sworn that it was the gritting of the vagabond's teeth."[5]

Hereupon the dwarf laughed (the king was too confirmed a joker to object to any one's laughing), and displayed a set of large, powerful, and very repulsive teeth. Moreover, he avowed his perfect willingness to swallow as much wine as desired. The monarch was pacified; and having drained another bumper with no very perceptible ill effect, Hop-Frog entered at once, and with spirit, into the plans for the masquerade.

"I cannot tell what was the association of idea," observed he, very tranquilly, and as if he had never tasted wine in his life, "but *just after* your majesty had struck the girl and thrown the wine in her face—*just after* your majesty had done this, and while the parrot was making that odd noise outside the window, there came into my mind a capital diversion—one of my own country frolics—often enacted among us, at our masquerades: but here it will be new altogether. Unfortunately, however, it requires a company of eight persons, and—"

---

[5]Hop-Frog now creates a "brilliant" vision of revenge—complex, bizarre, and outré. For all its horror, what the dwarf creates is akin to "beauty" in Poe's aesthetics. Apparently the wine and the king's cruelty, the "madness," and the gnashing of his teeth are necessary to produce the state of "inspiration" in which Hop-Frog devises his weird plan. Compare the process to that which inspired characters undergo. See especially "The Domain of Arnheim" and "The Fall of the House of Usher."

"Here we *are!*" cried the king, laughing at his acute discovery of the coincidence; "eight to a fraction—I and my seven ministers. Come! what is the diversion?"

"We call it," replied the cripple, "the Eight Chained Ourang-Outangs, and it really is excellent sport if well enacted."

"*We* will enact it," remarked the king, drawing himself up, and lowering his eyelids.

"The beauty of the game," continued Hop-Frog, "lies in the fright it occasions among the women."

"Capital!" roared in chorus the monarch and his ministry.

"*I* will equip you as ourang-outangs," proceeded the dwarf; "leave all that to me. The resemblance shall be so striking, that the company of masqueraders will take you for real beasts—and, of course, they will be as much terrified as astonished."

"O, this is exquisite!" exclaimed the king. "Hop-Frog! I will make a man of you."

"The chains are for the purpose of increasing the confusion by their jangling. You are supposed to have escaped, *en masse,* from your keepers. Your majesty cannot conceive the *effect* produced at a masquerade, by eight chained ourang-outangs, imagined to be real ones by most of the company; and rushing in with savage cries, among the crowd of delicately and gorgeously habited men and women. The *contrast* is inimitable."

"It *must* be," said the king: and the council arose hurriedly (as it was growing late), to put in execution the scheme of Hop-Frog.

His mode of equipping the party as ourang-outangs was very simple, but effective enough for his purposes. The animals in question had, at the epoch of my story, very rarely been seen in any part of the civilized world; and as the imitations made by the dwarf were sufficiently beast-like and more than sufficiently hideous, their truthfulness to nature was thus thought to be secured.

The king and his ministers were first encased in tight-fitting stockinet[6] shirts and drawers. They were then saturated with tar. At this stage of the process, some one of the party suggested feathers; but the suggestion was at once overruled by the dwarf, who soon convinced the eight, by ocular demonstration, that the hair of such a brute as the ourang-outang was much more efficiently represented by *flax.* A thick coating of the latter was accordingly plastered upon the coating of tar. A long chain was now procured. First, it was passed about the waist of the king, *and tied;* then about another party, and also tied; then about all successively, in the same manner. When this chaining arrangement was complete, and the party stood as far apart from each other as possible, they formed a circle; and to make all things appear natural, Hop-Frog passed the residue of the chain, in two diameters, at right angles, across the circle, after the fashion adopted, at the present day, by those who capture Chimpanzees, or other large apes, in Borneo.

The grand saloon in which the masquerade was to take place, was a circular room, very lofty, and receiving the light of the sun only through a single window

[6]An elastic knitted fabric.

at top. At night (the season for which the apartment was especially designed,) it was illuminated principally by a large chandelier, depending by a chain from the centre of the sky-light, and lowered, or elevated, by means of a counter-balance as usual; but (in order not to look unsightly) this latter passed outside the cupola and over the roof.

The arrangements of the room had been left to Trippetta's superintendence; but, in some particulars, it seems, she had been guided by the calmer judgment of her friend the dwarf. At his suggestion it was that, on this occasion, the chandelier was removed. Its waxen drippings (which, in weather so warm, it was quite impossible to prevent,) would have been seriously detrimental to the rich dresses of the guests, who, on account of the crowded state of the saloon, could not *all* be expected to keep from out its centre—that is to say, from under the chandelier. Additional sconces were set in various parts of the hall, out of the way; and a flambeau, emitting sweet odor, was placed in the right hand of each of the Caryatides[7] that stood against the wall—some fifty or sixty altogether.

The eight ourang-outangs, taking Hop-Frog's advice, waited patiently until midnight (when the room was thoroughly filled with masqueraders) before making their appearance. No sooner had the clock ceased striking, however, than they rushed, or rather rolled in, all together—for the impediment of their chains caused most of the party to fall, and all to stumble as they entered.

The excitement among the masqueraders was prodigious, and filled the heart of the king with glee. As had been anticipated, there were not a few of the guests who supposed the ferocious-looking creatures to be beasts of *some* kind in reality, if not precisely ourang-outangs. Many of the women swooned with affright; and had not the king taken precaution to exclude all weapons from the saloon, his party might soon have expiated their frolic in their blood. As it was, a general rush was made for the doors; but the king had ordered them to be locked immediately upon his entrance; and, at the dwarf's suggestion, the keys had been deposited with *him.*

While the tumult was at its height, and each masquerader attentive only to his own safety—(for, in fact, there was much *real* danger from the pressure of the excited crowd,)—the chain by which the chandelier ordinarily hung, and which had been drawn up on its removal, might have been seen very gradually to descend, until its hook extremity came within three feet of the floor.

Soon after this, the king and his seven friends, having reeled about the hall in all directions, found themselves, at length, in its centre, and, of course, in immediate contact with the chain. While they were thus situated, the dwarf, who had followed closely at their heels, inciting them to keep up the commotion, took hold of their own chain at the intersection of the two portions which crossed the circle diametrically and at right angles. Here, with the rapidity of thought, he inserted the hook from which the chandelier had been wont to depend; and, in an instant, by some unseen agency, the chandelier-chain was drawn so far upward as to take the hook out of reach, and, as an inevitable consequence, to drag the ourang-outangs together in close connection, and face to face.

---

[7]Supporting columns made in the form of female figures.

The masqueraders, by this time, had recovered, in some measure, from their alarm; and beginning to regard the whole matter as a well-contrived pleasantry, set up a loud shout of laughter at the predicament of the apes.

"Leave them to *me!*" now screamed Hop-Frog, his shrill voice making itself easily heard through all the din. "Leave them to *me.* I fancy *I* can soon tell who they are."

Here, scrambling over the heads of the crowd, he managed to get to the wall; when, seizing a flambeau from one of the Caryatides, he returned, as he went, to the centre of the room—leaped, with the agility of a monkey, upon the king's head—and thence clambered a few feet up the chain—holding down the torch to examine the group of ourang-outangs, and still screaming, "*I* shall soon find out who they are!"

And now, while the whole assembly (the apes included) were convulsed with laughter, the jester suddenly uttered a shrill whistle; when the chain flew violently up for about thirty feet—dragging with it the dismayed and struggling ourang-outangs, and leaving them suspended in mid-air between the sky-light and the floor. Hop-Frog, clinging to the chain as it rose, still maintained his relative position in respect to the eight maskers, and still (as if nothing were the matter) continued to thrust his torch down towards them, as though endeavoring to discover who they were.

So thoroughly astonished were the whole company at this ascent, that a dead silence, of about a minute's duration, ensued. It was broken by just such a low harsh, *grating* sound, as had before attracted the attention of the king and his councillors, when the former threw the wine in the face of Trippetta. But, on the present occasion, there could be no question as to *whence* the sound issued. It came from the fang-like teeth of the dwarf, who ground them and gnashed them as he foamed at the mouth, and glared, with an expression of maniacal rage, into the upturned countenances of the king and his seven companions.

"Ah, ha!" said at length the infuriated jester. "Ah, ha! I begin to see who these people *are,* now!" Here, pretending to scrutinize the king more closely, he held the flambeau to the flaxen coat which enveloped him, and which instantly burst into a sheet of vivid flame. In less than half a minute the whole eight ourang-outangs were blazing fiercely, amid the shrieks of the multitude who gazed at them from below, horror-stricken, and without the power to render them the slightest assistance.

At length the flames, suddenly increasing in virulence, forced the jester to climb higher up the chain, to be out of their reach; and, as he made this movement, the crowd again sank, for a brief instant, into silence. The dwarf seized his opportunity, and once more spoke:

"I now see *distinctly,*" he said, "what manner of people these maskers are. They are a great king and his seven privy-councillors—a king who does not scruple to strike a defenceless girl, and his seven councillors who abet him in the outrage. As for myself, I am simply Hop-Frog, the jester—and *this is my last jest.*"

Owing to the high combustibility of both the flax and the tar to which it adhered, the dwarf had scarcely made an end of his brief speech before the work of vengeance was complete. The eight corpses swung in their chains, a fetid, blackened, hideous, and indistinguishable mass. The cripple hurled his torch at them, clambered leisurely to the ceiling, and disappeared through the sky-light.

It is supposed that Trippetta, stationed on the roof of the saloon, had been the accomplice of her friend in his fiery revenge, and that, together, they effected their escape to their own country: for neither was seen again.

Von Kempelen and His Discovery

Because its outrageous humor is of a sort which is popular again in our commercial media, this story suggests how modern Poe's United States was: linked together by electric communication, with a largely literate populace served by printed periodicals of all sorts, it was a society which knew and discussed the daily news. Such a place was ripe for a joker who could exploit current events. "Von Kempelen and His Discovery" is a precursor of the news-comedy we associate with The New Yorker, *television news-parody, and the political-humor "comics." Poe said that his piece was pure hoax, designed only to deceive, and that deception was his only goal in it. He wrote it early in 1849, at the height of the Gold Rush, calculating that it would create a considerable* "stir." *Yet his "exercise" (as he called it) in fooling readers is also filled with private jokes and references to people whom Poe knew—Burton Pollin (5) patiently worked them all out. Does this mean that "Von Kempelen and His Discovery" should be called a satire aimed at small targets and not a broad hoax? Our sense is that the broad joke was more important, but that in searching around for fictitious names and places, Poe naturally thought of issues and people he was concerned with or troubled by; there is even—see note 7—a private reference to the sad death of his young wife. The result is a dense web of plausible but elusive allusions and references, as well as picky quarrels about points no reader could be expected to follow because they are generated primarily out of Poe's professional experience and memory. An annotated edition should explain such references, but we do not want to give the impression that they are what the story is "about," for it remains a hoax. Lurking in it are some private jokes for those very familiar with Poe's life and works, but for almost all readers even in his own day, the story is a media gag which capitalizes on the California Gold Rush of 1849.*

Publication in Poe's Time

The Flag of Our Union, Boston, April 14, 1849

VON KEMPELEN AND HIS DISCOVERY

After the very minute and elaborate paper by Arago, to say nothing of the summary in "Silliman's Journal," with the detailed statement just published by Lieutenant Maury, it will not be supposed, of course, that in offering a few hurried remarks in reference to Von Kempelen's discovery, I have any design to look at the subject in a *scientific* point of view. My object is simply, in the first place, to say a few words of Von Kempelen[1] himself (with whom, some years ago, I had the honor of a slight personal acquaintance,) since every thing which concerns him must necessarily, at this moment, be of interest; and, in the second place, to look in a general way, and speculatively, at the *results* of the discovery.

It may be as well, however, to premise the cursory observations which I have to offer, by denying, very decidedly, what seems to be a general impression (gleaned, as usual in a case of this kind, from the newspapers,) viz.: that this discovery, astounding as it unquestionably is, is *unanticipated.*

By reference to the "Diary of Sir Humphrey Davy,"[2] (Cottle and Munroe, London, pp. 150,) it will be seen at pp. 53 and 82, that this illustrious chemist had not only conceived the idea now in question, but had actually made *no inconsiderable progress, experimentally,* in the very *identical analysis* now so triumphantly brought to an issue by Von Kempelen, who although he makes not the slightest allusion to it, is, *without doubt* (I say it unhesitatingly, and can prove it, if required,) indebted to the "Diary" for at least the first hint of his own undertaking. Although a little technical, I cannot refrain from appending two passages from the "Diary," with one of Sir Humphrey's equations. [As we have not the algebraic signs necessary, and as the "Diary" is to be found at the Athenaeum Library, we omit here a small portion of Mr. Poe's manuscript.—ED.][3]

The paragraph from the "Courier and Enquirer," which is now going the rounds of the press, and which purports to claim the invention for a Mr. Kissam, of Brunswick, Maine,[4] appears to me, I confess, a little apocryphal, for several

[1]**Arago:** François Arago (1786–1853), an important French scientist. **"Silliman's Journal":** Popular nickname for the leading American scientific periodical of the period, the *American Journal of Science and Arts,* edited by Benjamin Silliman (1779–1864). **Lieutenant Maury:** Matthew Maury (1806–73), an American scientist best known in this period for his important work in charting ocean currents and winds as an aid to navigation. **Von Kempelen:** Poe published, in 1836, an article purporting to uncover the trick which enabled an "automated" chess-playing machine to work (there was a little man inside). The machine had been invented by a Baron Von Kempelen and was a clever piece of "magic."

[2]Sir Humphry Davy (1778–1829), the great English scientist. The "Diary" is Poe's invention (Pollin 3, 5). Poe spelled his name, "Humphrey."

[3]This "editorial note" is by Poe. Pollin (5) reports that the Baltimore Athenaeum Library as of 1827 had no such volume; Mabbott (9, III) adds that there was none in the Boston Athenaeum, either.

[4]**"Courier and Enquirer":** A New York paper. Poe had sent its favorable review of *Eureka* to Eveleth (see next item). **Mr. Kissam, of Brunswick, Maine:** Pollin (5) thinks that Poe's target here is G. W. Eveleth, a medical student in Brunswick with whom Poe

reasons; although there is nothing either impossible or very improbable in the statement made. I need not go into details. My opinion of the paragraph is founded principally upon its *manner.* It does not *look* true. Persons who are narrating *facts,* are seldom so particular as Mr. Kissam seems to be, about day and date and precise location. Besides, if Mr. Kissam actually *did* come upon the discovery he says he did, at the period designated—nearly eight years ago—how happens it that he took no steps, *on the instant,* to reap the immense benefits which the merest bumpkin must have known would have resulted to him individually, if not to the world at large, from the discovery? It seems to me quite incredible that any man, of common understanding, could have discovered what Mr. Kissam says he did, and yet have subsequently acted so like a baby—so like an owl—as Mr. Kissam *admits* that he did. By-the-way, who *is* Mr. Kissam? and is not the whole paragraph in the "Courier and Enquirer" a fabrication got up to "make a talk"? It must be confessed that it has an amazingly moon-hoax-y air. Very little dependence is to be placed upon it, in my humble opinion; and if I were not well aware, from experience, how very easily men of science are *mystified,* on points out of their usual range of inquiry, I should be profoundly astonished at finding so eminent a chemist as Professor Draper,[5] discussing Mr. Kissam's (or is it Mr. Quizzem's?) pretensions to this discovery, in so serious a tone.

But to return to the "Diary" of Sir Humphrey Davy. This pamphlet was *not* designed for the public eye, even upon the decease of the writer, as any person at all conversant with authorship may satisfy himself at once by the slightest inspection of the style. At page 13, for example, near the middle, we read, in reference to his researches about the protoxide of azote: "In less than half a minute the respiration being continued, diminished gradually and *were* succeeded by analogous to gentle pressure on all the muscles."[6] That the *respiration* was not "diminished," is not only clear by the subsequent context, but by the use of the plural, "were." The sentence, no doubt, was thus intended: "In less than half a minute, the respiration [being continued, these feelings] diminished gradually, and were succeeded by [a sensation] analogous to gentle pressure on all the muscles." A hundred similar instances go to show that the MS. so inconsiderately published, was merely a *rough note-book,* meant only for the writer's own eye; but an inspection of the pamphlet will convince almost any thinking person of the truth of my suggestion. The fact is, Sir Humphrey Davy was about the last man in the world to *commit himself* on scientific topics. Not only had he a more than ordinary

---

corresponded. The reasons for Poe's grudge against Eveleth-Kissam are complicated and have to do with Eveleth's "presumption" regarding *Eureka,* and his correspondence with Professor Draper (see note 5).

[5]**moon-hoax-y air:** The "Moon-Hoax" was a celebrated journalistic hoax; for details see "The Balloon-Hoax." **Professor Draper:** John William Draper (1811–82), a New York University professor "distinguished in chemical and physical research" (Pollin 5). In 1845, he had been attacked by the New England–oriented *North American Review,* and Poe had defended him, but Pollin (5) points out that Poe came to bear a grudge against him, too.

[6]A passage very similar to this does appear in Davy (Pollin 5, Hall). Poe doctored it to produce the errors. The "protoxide of azote" is laughing gas; the source is Davy's *Researches, Chemical and Philosophical, chiefly concerning Nitrous Oxide and its Respiration* (1799).

dislike to quackery, but he was morbidly afraid of *appearing* empirical; so that, however fully he might have been convinced that he was on the right track in the matter now in question, he would never have spoken *out,* until he had everything ready for the most practical demonstration. I verily believe that his last moments would have been rendered wretched, could he have suspected that his wishes in regard to burning this "Diary" (full of crude speculations) would have been unattended to; as, it seems, they were. I say "his wishes," for that he meant to include this note-book among the miscellaneous papers directed "to be burnt," I think there can be no manner of doubt. Whether it escaped the flames by good fortune or by bad, yet remains to be seen. That the passages quoted above, with the other similar ones referred to, gave Von Kempelen *the hint,* I do not in the slightest degree question; but I repeat, it yet remains to be seen whether this momentous discovery itself (*momentous* under any circumstances,) will be of service or disservice to mankind at large. That Von Kempelen and his immediate friends will reap a rich harvest, it would be folly to doubt for a moment. They will scarcely be so weak as not to "*realize,*" in time, by large purchases of houses and land, with other property of *intrinsic* value.

In the brief account of Von Kempelen which appeared in the "Home Journal," and has since been extensively copied, several misapprehensions of the German original seem to have been made by the translator, who professes to have taken the passage from a late number of the Presburg "Schnellpost." "*Viele*" has evidently been misconceived (as it often is,) and what the translator renders by "sorrows," is probably "*leiden,*" which, in its true version, "sufferings," would give a totally different complexion to the whole account; but, of course, much of this is merely guess, on my part.[7]

Von Kempelen, however, is by no means "a misanthrope," in appearance, at least, whatever he may be in fact. My acquaintance with him was casual altogether; and I am scarcely warranted in saying that I know him at all; but to have seen and conversed with a man of so *prodigious* a notoriety as he has attained, or *will* attain in a few days, is not a small matter, as times go.

"The Literary World" speaks of him, confidently, as a *native* of Presburg (misled, perhaps, by the account in the "Home Journal,") but I am pleased in being able to state *positively,* since I have it from his own lips, that he was born in Utica,

---

[7]**"Home Journal":** Another real periodical, owned by Nathaniel Willis (see "The Duc De L'Omelette"). **"Schnellpost":** A made-up periodical. Poe got the word "Schnellpost" from the title of a German paper published in New York. Presburg, he says in "Maelzel's Chess-Player," was the home of the Von Kempelen who invented the chess-playing machine. ***Viele:*** Many. Since Poe doesn't give us the context, we can't tell how it was "misconceived." This paragraph seems irrelevant to the tale. Pollin (5) thinks it a private reference: Nathaniel Willis, during the sad days of Virginia Poe's illness and death, had printed a famous plea for help for the Poes in his *Home Journal,* and Poe's passage about misunderstanding the "German original" could refer to that. Poe had spoken often during the last year of his life (this is a very late tale) of the need to make lots of money, and it is tempting to speak of, as Pollin (5) puts it, "the transmutation of Poe into the successful gold-maker, Von Kempelen." Hence the allusions to Von Kempelen's suffering and Willis's periodical link the tale to Willis and to Virginia's death.

in the State of New York, although both his parents, I believe, are of Presburg descent. The family is connected, in some way, with Maelzel, of Automaton-chess-player memory. [If we are not mistaken, the name of the *inventor* of the chess-player was either Kempelen, Von Kempelen, or something like it.—ED.] In person, he is short and stout, with a large, *fat,* blue eyes, sandy hair and whiskers, a wide but pleasing mouth, fine teeth, and I think a Roman nose. There is some defect in one of his feet. His address is frank, and his whole manner noticeable for *bonhomie.* Altogether, he looks, speaks and acts as little like "a misanthrope" as any man I ever saw. We were fellow-sojourners for a week, about six years ago, at Earl's Hotel, in Providence, Rhode Island; and I presume that I conversed with him, at various times, for some three or four hours altogether. His principal topics were those of the day; and nothing that fell from him led me to suspect his scientific attainments. He left the hotel before me, intending to go to New York, and thence to Bremen; it was in the latter city that his great discovery was first made public; or, rather, it was there that he was first suspected of having made it. This is about all that I personally know of the now immortal Von Kempelen;[8] but I have thought that even these few details would have interest for the public.

There can be little question that most of the marvellous rumors afloat about this affair are pure inventions, entitled to about as much credit as the story of Aladdin's lamp; and yet, in a case of this kind, as in the case of the discoveries in California,[9] it is clear that the truth *may be* stranger than fiction. The following anecdote, at least, is so well authenticated, that we may receive it implicitly.

Von Kempelen had never been even tolerably well off during his residence at Bremen; and often, it was well known, he had been put to extreme shifts, in order to raise trifling sums. When the great excitement occurred about the forgery on the house of Gutsmuth & Co., suspicion was directed towards Von Kempelen, on account of his having purchased a considerable property in Gasperitch Lane, and his refusing, when questioned, to explain how he became possessed of the purchase money. He was at length arrested, but nothing decisive appearing against him, was in the end set at liberty. The police, however, kept a strict watch upon his movements, and thus discovered that he left home frequently, taking always the same road, and invariably giving his watchers the slip in the neighborhood of that labyrinth of narrow and crooked passages known by the flash-name of the "Dondergat." Finally, by dint of great perseverance, they traced him to a garret in an old house of seven stories, in an alley called Flatzplatz; and, coming upon him suddenly, found him, as they imagined, in the midst of his counterfeiting opera-

---

[8]**"The Literary World":** Poe attempted to publish this tale in *The Literary World:* it was rejected (Pollin 5). ***bonhomie:*** Good nature. **Earl's Hotel, in Providence, Rhode Island:** The site of a lecture Poe gave on December 20, 1848, and of an unfortunate alcoholic incident (A. H. Quinn) which was partially responsible for the breaking of Poe's engagement to Mrs. Helen Whitman. We think Pollin's (5) connection of those episodes with this tale is correct. **the now immortal Von Kempelen:** probably a little day-dreaming on Poe's part: "I'll be an immortal author."

[9]Poe had gold and riches on his mind; as Pollin (5) and others point out, his poem "Eldorado" is from this same period. The "discoveries" are those which set off the California Gold Rush.

tions. His agitation is represented as so excessive that the officers had not the slightest doubt of his guilt. After hand-cuffing him, they searched his room, or rather rooms; for it appears he occupied all the *mansarde.*[10]

Opening into the garret where they caught him, was a closet, ten feet by eight, fitted up with some chemical apparatus, of which the object has not yet been ascertained. In one corner of the closet was a very small furnace, with a glowing fire in it, and on the fire a kind of duplicate crucible—two crucibles connected by a tube. One of these crucibles was nearly full of *lead* in a state of fusion, but not reaching up to the aperture of the tube, which was close to the brim. The other crucible had some liquid in it, which, as the officers entered, seemed to be furiously dissipating in vapor. They relate that, on finding himself taken, Van Kempelen seized the crucibles with both hands (which were encased in gloves that afterward turned out to be asbestic), and threw the contents on the tiled floor. It was now that they hand-cuffed him; and, before proceeding to ransack the premises, they searched his person, but nothing unusual was found about him, excepting a paper parcel, in his coat pocket, containing what was afterwards ascertained to be a mixture of antimony and some *unknown substance,* in nearly, but not quite equal proportions. All attempts at analyzing the unknown substance have, so far, failed, but that it will ultimately be analyzed, is not to be doubted.[11]

Passing out of the closet with their prisoner, the officers went through a sort of ante-chamber, in which nothing material was found, to the chemist's sleeping-room. They here rummaged some drawers and boxes, but discovered only a few papers, of no importance, and some good coin, silver and gold. At length, looking under the bed, they saw *a large, common hair trunk, without hinges, hasp, or lock,* and with the top lying carelessly *across* the bottom portion.[12] Upon attempting to draw this trunk out from under the bed, they found that, with their united strength (there were three of them, all powerful men), they "could not stir it one inch." Much astonished at this, one of them crawled under the bed, and looking into the trunk, said:

---

[10]**Gutsmuth; Gasperitch:** Made-up names, but Pollin (5) has solved them: Poe had referred to Johan Christoph F. Gutsmuths (1759–1838) in a "Marginalia" item in 1845 (and left the *s* off his name there, too); Gutsmuths was a geographer who also wrote on children's education. The "Marginalia" piece also mentions, in the same list, the German statistician and geographer Adam Christian Gaspari (1752–1830), which Poe, who didn't know much German, tried to Teutonize by making it "Gasperitch." **flash-name:** Flash-language is underworld slang (Mabbott 9, III). Poe uses "flash" to signify "showy," "slang-y," or "temporary." In "The Man of the Crowd," for instance, he refers to insubstantial financial firms as "flash-houses." See "The Man of the Crowd," note 5. **Dondergat:** "Thunder-pass," roughly (Pollin 5). **Flatzplatz:** Griswold altered it to Flätplatz. Pollin (5) thinks it simply a made-up name. It seems to suggest "a place where there are flats or apartments," though Poe probably liked the comical sound of it in English. ***mansarde:*** Attic.

[11]Poe plays here on popular conceptions of the pseudoscience of alchemy, which was supposed to be the age-old attempt to "transmute" lead into gold using a mysterious stuff (Poe's "unknown substance") often called "the philosopher's stone." In point of fact, alchemy was an occult system founded on belief in the unity of all things.

[12]Compare the method of concealment in "The Purloined Letter."

"No wonder we couldn't move it—why, it's full to the brim of old bits of brass!"

Putting his feet, now, against the wall, so as to get a good purchase, and pushing with all his force, while his companions pulled with all theirs, the trunk, with much difficulty, was slid out from under the bed, and its contents examined. The supposed brass with which it was filled was all in small, smooth pieces, varying from the size of a pea to that of a dollar; but the pieces were irregular in shape, although all more or less flat—looking, upon the whole, "very much as lead looks when thrown upon the ground in a molten state, and there suffered to grow cool." Now, not one of these officers for a moment suspected this metal to be anything *but* brass. The idea of its being *gold* never entered their brains, of course; how *could* such a wild fancy have entered it? And their astonishment may be well conceived, when next day it became known, all over Bremen, that the "lot of brass" which they had carted so contemptuously to the police office, without putting themselves to the trouble of pocketing the smallest scrap, was not only gold—real gold—but gold far finer than any employed in coinage—gold, in fact, absolutely pure, virgin, without the slightest appreciable alloy!

I need not go over the details of Von Kempelen's confession (as far as it went) and release, for these are familiar to the public. That he has actually realized, in spirit and in effect, if not to the letter, the old chimera of the philosopher's stone, no sane person is at liberty to doubt. The opinions of Arago are, of course, entitled to the greatest consideration; but he is by no means infallible; and what he says of *bismuth,* in his report to the academy, must be taken *cum grano salis.*[13] The simple truth is, that up to this period, *all* analysis has failed; and until Von Kempelen chooses to let us have the key to his own published enigma, it is more than probable that the matter will remain, for years, *in statu quo.* All that yet can fairly be said to be known, is, that "*pure gold can be made at will, and very readily, from lead, in connection with certain other substances, in kind and in proportions, unknown.*"

Speculation, of course, is busy as to the immediate and ultimate results of this discovery—a discovery which few thinking persons will hesitate in referring to an increased interest in the matter of gold generally, by the late developments in California; and this reflection brings us inevitably to another—the exceeding *inopportuneness* of Von Kempelen's analysis. If many were prevented from adventuring to California, by the mere apprehension that gold would so materially diminish in value, on account of its plentifulness in the mines there, as to render the speculation of going so far in search of it a doubtful one—what impression will be wrought *now,* upon the minds of those about to emigrate, and especially upon the minds of those actually in the mineral region, by the announcement of this astounding discovery of Von Kempelen? a discovery which declares, in so many words, that beyond its intrinsic worth for manufacturing purposes, (whatever that worth may be), gold now is, or at least soon will be (for it cannot be supposed that Von Kempelen can *long* retain his secret) of no greater *value* than lead, and of far inferior value to silver. It is, indeed, exceedingly difficult to

[13]With a grain of salt. Salts of bismuth have long been used in medicine; Poe is punning.

speculate prospectively upon the consequences of the discovery; but one thing may be positively maintained—that the announcement of the discovery six months ago, would have had material influence in regard to the settlement of California.

In Europe, as yet, the most noticeable results have been a rise of two hundred per cent. in the price of lead, and nearly twenty-five per cent. in that of silver.

Bibliography

The system of citation used in the headnotes and footnotes was designed to provide full bibliographical information without being cumbersome. When we wish to express indebtedness to another scholar, we put the person's name in parentheses immediately following the information which his or her work elucidates. Such names appear again here with full citations.

To identify works of scholars who wrote more than one item on our list, we have used a numbering system. Thus "(Pollin 7)" or "(Whipple 2)" in the text refer to the seventh item listed under Burton Pollin's name or the second under William Whipple's in the Bibliography.

The pecularities of Poe's fiction are behind this system. Poe wrote about solving difficult puzzles, but his stories are the most complex puzzles he ever conceived. The tangled and interwoven lines of association which run through them, and the thousands of allusions to contemporaries, historical figures, and literary works—many of them obscure—often affect meaning. Sometimes annotation enriches a story, giving it resonance the reader would otherwise miss. Sometimes it is absolutely essential; without it the reader has no way of determining what Poe is talking about. Most of the sleuthing involved in explication requires highly specialized knowledge. Wherever we could find help in the work of other scholars, we made use of it, and strongly feel that this debt should be acknowledged. Hence our system of citations, which we hope colleagues and readers find acceptable, ethical, and useful.

Included below also are a few works which Poe used frequently as idea-mines in his stories. We include them to identify the editions we used in tracking down his sources. There is a more comprehensive separate list in Levine (4). Finally, we have added listings of good recent works on Poe published since we completed our introduction and annotations.

Those works on this list which are of general interest to the nonspecialist reader are marked with an asterisk (*). More technical items which we used in locating Poe's references, allusions, and quotations are also included.

Allen, Hervey. *Israfel: The Life and Times of Edgar Allan Poe.* 2 vols. New York, 1926. An informative older work, but read A. H. Quinn first.

*Allen, Michael. *Poe and the British Magazine Tradition.* New York, 1969. On Poe's intellectual environment.

Bandy, W. T. "Little Latin and Less French," *Poe Studies,* XIV (June 1981), 8.

Barzun, Jacques. "A Note on the Inadequacy of Poe as a Proofreader and of his Editors as French Scholars," *Romantic Review,* LXI (February 1970), 23–27.

Basler, Roy. "Byronism in Poe's 'To One in Paradise,'" *American Literature,* IX (May 1937), 232–36.

Benson, Adolph B. "Scandinavian References in the Works of Poe," *Journal of English and Germanic Philology,* XL (January 1941), 73–90.

Benton, Richard P. (1) "Is Poe's 'The Assignation' a Hoax?" *Nineteenth Century Fiction,* XVIII (September 1963), 193–97.

———. (2) "Poe's 'The System of Dr. Tarr and Prof. Fether': Dickens or Willis?" *Poe Newsletter,* I (April 1968), 7–9.

———. (3) "Poe's 'Lionizing': A Quiz on Willis and Lady Blessington," *Studies in Short Fiction,* V (Spring 1968), 239–44.

———. (4) "Reply to Professor Thompson," *Studies in Short Fiction,* VI (Fall 1968), 97.

———. (5) "Poe's Acquaintance with Chinese Literature," *Poe Newsletter,* II (April 1969), 14.

Bjurman, Gunnar. *Edgar Allan Poe.* Lund, Sweden, 1916.

Bonaparte, Marie. *The Life and Works of Edgar Allan Poe: A Psycho-Analytical Interpretation.* Translated by John Rodker. London, 1949. A translation from French of a book from the heyday of Freudian literary studies, 1933.

Broussard, Louis. *The Measure of Poe.* Norman, Okla., 1969.

Bryant, Jacob. A *New System; or, an Analysis of Ancient Mythology* (1774–1776). We refer to the third edition, London, 1807.

Bulwer, Edward, Lord Lytton. *Pelham or the Adventures of a Gentleman* (1828). A source of various literary and geographical allusions in Poe.

Campbell, Killis. "Marginalia on Longfellow, Lowell, and Poe," *Modern Language Notes,* XLII (December 1927), 516–21.

Carlson, Eric, ed. (1) *The Recognition of Edgar Allan Poe.* Ann Arbor, Mich., 1966. Reprint (paper), 1970. An anthology of criticism of Poe from 1829 to present.

*———. (2) *Introduction to Poe: A Thematic Reader,* esp. "Notes to Tales." Glenview, Ill., 1967. An edition which introduces the reader to the major genres of Poe's work.

*———, ed. (3) *A Companion to Poe Studies.* Westport, Conn., 1996. A collection of essays designed to serve as a guide in Poe studies.

Carlyle, Thomas. *Sartor Resartus: The Life and Opinions of Herr Teufelsdröckh.* Boston, 1836. First published in *Fraser's Magazine* (1833–34).

Dameron, J. Lasley, and Irby B. Cauthen, Jr. *Edgar Allan Poe: A Bibliography of Criticism: 1827–1967.* Charlottesville, Va., 1974.

Daughrity, Kenneth L. "Poe's 'Quiz on Willis.'" *American Literature,* V (March 1933), 55–62.

Disraeli, Isaac. *Curiosities of Literature.* Various editions of this work, in part or whole, have appeared since the first in 1791. We refer to the New York, 1853, edition containing *Curiosities of Literature* and *The Literary Character Illustrated* by Disraeli with *Curiosities of American Literature* by Rufus W. Griswold, and also to an 1865 edition of *Curiosities. . . .*

Engstrom, Alfred G. "Chateaubriand's *Itinéraire de Paris à Jerusalem* and Poe's 'The Assignation,'" *Modern Language Notes,* LXIX (November 1954), 506–07.

Fagin, N. Bryllion. *The Histrionic Mr. Poe.* Baltimore, 1949. Poe as a dramatist of himself.

Fisher, Benjamin F., ed. *Poe and His Times: The Artist and His Milieu.* Baltimore, 1990.

Forrest, William. *Biblical Allusions in Poe.* New York, 1928.

Glassheim, Eliot. "A Dogged Interpretation of 'Never Bet the Devil Your Head,'" *Poe Newsletter,* II (October 1969), 44–45.

Griffith, Clark. "Poe's 'Ligeia' and the English Romantics," *University of Toronto Quarterly,* XXIV (October 1954), 8–25.

Griswold, Rufus Wilmot, ed. *The Work of the Late Edgar Allan Poe, with a Memoir by Rufus Wilmot Griswold and Notices of His Life and Genius by N. P. Willis and J. R. Lowell.* New York, vols. I–III, 1850; IV, 1856.

Hall, Thomas. "Poe's Use of a Source," *Poe Newsletter,* I (October 1968), 28.

Halliburton, David. *Edgar Allan Poe: A Phenomenological View.* Princeton, N.J., 1973.

Hammond, Alexander. "A Reconstruction of Poe's 1833 Tales of the Folio Club," *Poe Studies,* V (December 1972), 25–32.

*Harrison, James A. *The Complete Works of Edgar Allan Poe.* New York, 1902. The "Virginia" and "New York" edition.

Heartman, Charles, and James Canny. *A Bibliography of First Printings of the Writings of Edgar Allan Poe.* Hattiesburg, Miss., 1940. A very valuable work even though it contains minor errors.

Hess, Jeffrey A. "Sources and Aesthetics of Poe's Landscape Fiction," *American Quarterly,* XXII (Summer 1970), 177–89.

Hirsch, David H. "Another Source for Poe's 'The Duc De L'Omelette,'" *American Literature,* XXXVIII (January 1967), 534–36.

Hungerford, Edward. "Poe and Phrenology," *American Literature,* II (November 1930), 209–31.

Hyneman, Esther. *Edgar Allan Poe: An Annotated Bibliography of Books and Articles in English 1827–1973.* Boston, 1974.

Irwin, John T. (1) *American Hieroglyphics,* Part II. New Haven, 1980, 41–235.

———. (2) *The Mystery to a Solution: Poe, Borges, and the Analytic Detective Story.* Baltimore, 1994.

Jackson, David K. "Poe Notes: 'Pinakidia' and 'Some Ancient Greek Authors,'" *American Literature,* V (November 1933), 258–67.

*Jacobs, Robert D. *Poe: Journalist and Critic.* Baton Rouge, 1969. Poe in context.

Kaplan, Sidney, ed. *The Narrative of Arthur Gordon Pym.* New York, 1960. A work containing the famous Poe-as-fundamentalist argument.

King, Lucille. "Notes on Poe's Sources," *University of Texas Studies in English,* X (July 1930), 128–34.

Krappe, Edith S. "A Possible Source for Poe's 'The Tell-Tale Heart' and 'The Black Cat,'" *American Literature,* XII (March 1940), 84–88.

Krutch, Joseph Wood. *Edgar Allan Poe: A Study in Genius.* New York, 1926. A Freudian reading, intelligent but in need of tempering in the light of more recent data on Poe.

Le Breton, Maurice. "Edgar Poe and Macaulay," *Revue Anglo-Americaine,* XXI (October 1935), 38–42.

Lease, Benjamin. *Anglo-American Encounters: England and the Rise of American Literature.* Cambridge, 1981, 69–76.

Levine, Stuart. (1) "Poe's *Julius Rodman:* Judaism, Plagiarism, and the Wild West," *Midwest Quarterly,* I (Spring 1960), 245–59.

———. (2) "Scholarly Strategy: The Poe Case," *American Quarterly,* XVII (Spring 1965), 133–44.

———. (3) *Edgar Poe: Seer and Craftsman.* Deland, Fla., 1972. A critical study of Poe's fiction: structure, philosophy, the magazine environment, the intellectual and scientific environments.

——— (4) and Susan F. Levine. *The Short Fiction of Edgar Allan Poe: An Annotated Edition.* Indianapolis, Ind., 1976; Chicago and Urbana, Ill., 1990.

——— and ———. (5) "History, Myth, Fable and Satire: Poe's Use of Jacob Bryant," *Emerson Society Quarterly,* XXI (1975), 197–214.

——— and ———. (6) "Poe's Use of Jacob Bryant in 'Metzengerstein,'" *Poe Studies,* IX (December 1976), 53.

——— and ———. (7) "Poe and Fuentes: The Reader's Prerogatives," *Comparative Literature,* XXXVI (Winter 1984), 34–53.

———. (8) "Masonry, Impunity, and Revolution," *Poe Studies,* 17, 1 (1984), 22–3.

Ljungquist, Kent. *The Grand and the Fair: Poe's Landscape Aesthetics and Pictorial Techniques.* Potomac, Md., 1984.

Mabbott, Thomas Ollive. (1) "On Poe's 'Tales of the Folio Club,'" *Sewanee Review,* XXXVI (1928), 171–76.

———. (2) "Origins of 'The Angel of the Odd,'" *Notes & Queries,* CLX (January 1931), 8.

———. (3) "Evidence That Poe Knew Greek," *Notes & Queries,* CLXXXV (July 1943), 39–40.

———. (4) "Poe and Dr. Lardner," *American Notes & Queries,* III (November 1943), 115–17.

———. (5) "The Source of Poe's Motto for the 'Gold-Bug,'" *Notes & Queries,* CXCVIII (February 1953), 68.

———. (6) "Poe's 'The Cask of Amontillado,'" *Explicator,* XXV (November 1966), Item 30.

———. (7) "Poe's 'The Man That Was Used Up,'" *Explicator,* XXV (April 1967), Item 70.

———. (8) "The Books in the House of Usher," *Books at Iowa,* 19 (November 1973).

*———, ed., (9) with Eleanor D. Kewer and Maureen C. Mabbott. *Collected Works of Edgar Allan Poe.* Vols. II and III. Cambridge, Mass., 1978.

Maginn, William. *Miscellanies: Prose and Verse.* 2 vols. Edited by R. W. Montagu. London, 1885. Stories and poems by Maginn, which appeared in a variety of literary journals during his lifetime.

Martin, Malachi. "The New Castle: Mecca," *Intellectual Digest,* IV (October 1973), 24–26.

McCarthy, Kevin M. "Another Source for 'The Raven,'" *Poe Newsletter,* I (October 1968), 29.

McClary, Ben Harris. "Poe's 'Turkish Fig-Pedler,'" *Poe Newsletter,* II (October 1969), 56.

McNeal, Thomas H. "Poe's *Zenobia:* An Early Satire on Margaret Fuller," *Modern Language Quarterly,* XI (June 1950), 205–16.

Miller, Perry. *The Raven and the Whale.* New York, 1956. A treatment of literary circles in Poe's and Melville's New York. Good in conjunction with the works by Moss and Jacobs.

Moldenhauer, Joseph J. *A Descriptive Catalog of Edgar Allan Poe Manuscripts in the Humanities Research Center Library, The University of Texas at Austin.* A Supplement to *Texas Quarterly.* Austin, 1973.

Mooney, Stephen L. "The Comic in Poe's Fiction," *American Literature,* XXXIII (January 1962), 433–41.

Moore, John Robert. "Poe's Reading of *Anne of Geierstein,*" *American Literature,* XXII (January 1951), 493–96.

Moss, Sidney P. (1) "Poe and the Norman Leslie Incident," *American Literature,* XXV (November 1953), 293–306.

———. (2) "Poe and His Nemesis—Lewis Gaylord Clark," *American Literature,* XXVIII (March 1956), 30–46.

*———. (3) *Poe's Literary Battles.* Durham, N.C., 1963. A very good book. It is difficult to understand the literary world of Poe's America without it.

———. (4) *Poe's Major Crisis.* Durham, N.C., 1970.

Norman, Emma Katherine. "Poe's Knowledge of Latin," *American Literature,* VI (March 1934), 72–77.

Ostrom, John Ward. *The Letters of Edgar Allan Poe.* 2 vols. Cambridge, Mass., 1948.

Pollin, Burton. (1) "'The Spectacles' of Poe—Sources and Significance," *American Literature* XXXVIII (May 1965), 185–90.

———. (2) "Bulwer-Lytton and 'The Tell-Tale Heart,'" *American Notes & Queries* (New Haven), IV (September 1965), 7–8.

———. (3) *Dictionary of Names and Titles in Poe's Collected Works.* New York, 1968. A useful reference tool.

———. (4) "Poe's 'Diddling': The Source of Title and Tale," *The Southern Literary Journal,* II (Fall 1969), 106–11.

*———. (5) *Discoveries in Poe.* Notre Dame, Ind., 1970. The best of the source studies: not only where Poe got ideas, but how his mind worked.

———. (6) "Poe's Dr. Ollapod," *American Literature,* XLII (March 1970), 80–82.

———. (7) "Figs, Bells, Poe, and Horace Smith," *Poe Newsletter,* III (June 1970), 8–10.

———. (8) "Poe's 'Some Words with a Mummy' Reconsidered," *Emerson Society Quarterly,* No. 60 (Fall 1970), 60–67.

———. (9) "Poe's Use of Material from Bernardin de Saint-Pierre's *Etudes,*" *Romance Notes,* XII (Summer 1971), 1–8.

———. (10) "Politics and History in Poe's 'Mellonta Tauta,'" *Studies in Short Fiction,* VIII (Fall 1971), 627–31.

———. (11) "Poe's Literary Use of 'Oppodeldoc' and Other Patent Medicines," *Poe Newsletter,* IV (December 1971), 30–32.

———. (12) "Poe's Tale of Psyche Zenobia: A Reading for Humor and Ingenious Construction." In *Papers on Poe,* ed. Richard Veler, pp. 92–103. Springfield, Ohio, 1972.

———. (13) "Poe and Thomas Moore," *Emerson Society Quarterly,* No. 63 (June 1972), 166–73.

———. (14) "Poe's 'Mystification': Its Source in Fay's *Norman Leslie,*" *Mississippi Quarterly,* XXV (Spring 1972), 111–30.

———. (15) *Poe, Creator of Words.* Bronxville, N.Y., 1980.

*———, ed. (16) *Collected Writings of Edgar Allan Poe.* 5 vols. Vol. 1, Boston, Twayne, 1981; Vols. 2–5, New York, Gordian Press, 1985–86.

*Quinn, Arthur Hobson. *Edgar Allan Poe: A Critical Biography.* New York, 1941. A work critically naive, but biographically indispensable: the book that cracked the Griswold forgery.

*Quinn, Patrick F. *The French Face of Edgar Poe.* Carbondale, Ill., 1957. Good answers to the old question, "What do the French see in Poe?"

*Rans, Geoffrey. *Edgar Allan Poe.* Edinburgh and London, 1965.

Reilly, John E. "The Lesser Death-Watch and 'The Tell-Tale Heart,'" *American Transcendental Quarterly,* II (1969), 3–9.

Rein, David. *Edgar Allan Poe: The Inner Pattern.* New York, 1960. A psychological study of Poe, similar to those of the 1920s and early 1930s, yet with some good insights.

Robbins, J. A. "The Poe 'Dictionary,'" *Poe Newsletter,* II (April 1969), 38–39. Review of Burton Pollin's *Dictionary.* . . .

Robinson, E. Arthur. "Thoreau and the Deathwatch in Poe's 'Tell-Tale Heart,'" *Poe Studies,* IV (June 1971), 14–16.

Rothwell, Kenneth. "A Source for the Motto to Poe's 'William Wilson,'" *Modern Language Notes,* LXXIV (April 1959), 297–98.

St. Armand, Barton Levi. "Usher Unveiled: Poe and the Metaphysic of Gnosticism," *Poe Studies,* V (June 1972), 1–8.

Schuster, Richard. "More on the 'Fig-Pedler,'" *Poe Newsletter,* III (June 1970), 22.

Scudder, Harold H. "Poe's 'Balloon-Hoax,'" *American Literature,* XXI (May 1949), 179–90.

Senior, John. *The Way Down and Out: The Occult in Symbolist Literature.* Ithaca, 1959.

Silverman, Kenneth, ed. *New Essays on Poe's Major Tales.* New York and Cambridge, 1993.

Stovall, Floyd, ed. (1) *Eight American Authors.* New York, 1963. Contains a forty-seven-page bibliography on Poe by Jay B. Hubbell.

———. (2) *The Poems of Edgar Allan Poe.* Charlottesville, Va., 1965. The best texts of Poe's poems.

Thomas, Dwight, and David K. Jackson. *The Poe Log: A Documentary Life of Edgar Allan Poe, 1809–1849.* Boston, 1987.

Thompson, G. R. (1) "On the Nose—Further Speculation on the Sources and Meaning of Poe's 'Lionizing,'" *Studies in Short Fiction,* VI (Fall 1968), 94–96.

———. (2) "Poe's 'Flawed' Gothic: Absurdist Techniques in 'Metzengerstein' and the *Courier* Satires," *Emerson Society Quarterly,* No. 60 (Fall 1970), 38–58.

———. (3) "Poe and 'Romantic Irony.'" In *Papers on Poe,* ed. Richard Veler, pp. 28–41. Springfield, Ohio, 1972.

*———. (4) *Poe's Fiction: Romantic Irony in the Gothic Tales.* Madison, Wis., 1973.

——— (5) and Virgil L. Lokke, eds. *Ruined Eden of the Present: Hawthorne, Melville and Poe,* West Lafayette, Ind., 1981.

Tombleson, Gary. "An Error in 'Usher,'" *Poe Studies,* XIV (June 1981), 8.

Turner, Arlin. "Sources of Poe's 'A Descent into the Maelström,'" *The Journal of English and Germanic Philology,* XLVI (July 1947), 298–301.

Varner, Cornelia. "Notes on Poe's Use of Contemporary Materials in Certain of His Stories," *The Journal of English and Germanic Philology,* XXXII (January 1933), 77–80.

Veler, Richard, ed. *Papers on Poe: Essays in Honor of John Ward Ostrom.* Springfield, Ohio, Chantry Music Press at Wittenberg University, 1972. A collection of varied articles on Poe, very useful as a survey of conflicting interpretations of Poe's fiction.

Vines, Lois, ed. *Poe Abroad: Influences and Affinities.* Iowa City, 1999. A collection of essays on Poe's international impact.

*Wagenknecht, Edward. *Edgar Allan Poe: The Man Behind the Legend.* New York, 1963. An intelligent and informed brief biography.

Walker, I. M. "The 'Legitimate Sources' of Terror in 'The Fall of the House of Usher,'" *Modern Language Review,* LXI (October 1966), 585–92.

Whipple, William. (1) "Poe's Two-Edged Satiric Tale," *Nineteenth Century Fiction,* IX (September 1954), 121–33.

———. (2) "Poe's Political Satire," *Texas University Studies in English,* XXXV (1956), 81–95.

———. (3) "Poe, Clark, and 'Thingum Bob,'" *American Literature,* XXIX (November 1957), 312–16.

Wilkinson, Ronald Sterne. "Poe's 'Balloon-Hoax' Once More," *American Literature,* XXXII (November 1960), 313–17.

Wilson, James Southall. "The Devil Was In It," *American Mercury,* XXIV (October 1931), 215–20.

Wilson, John (Christopher North), William Maginn, John Gibson Lockhart, James Hogg, and others. *Noctes Ambrosianae.* This work appeared originally as a series of articles in *Blackwood's* between 1822 and 1835. We refer to the 1863 New York edition in five volumes with "Memoirs and Notes" by R. Shelton Mackenzie.

Woodberry, George E. *The Life of Edgar Allan Poe.* 2 vols. Boston, 1909. An older study which is still useful. But check facts against A. H. Quinn or Wagenknecht.